CHILDREN OF THE BLACK

First edition. March 21, 2023.
Copyright © 2021 W J Long III.
Written by W J Long III.
Cover design by GetCovers.com

To Carolyn Ruth Scales.

Your inspiration still shines through every soul lucky enough to have loved you.

W J LONG III

CHILDREN
OF
THE
BLACK

— BOOK 1 —

Part I
Reliquary

Prologue

THE BLACK WAS TIMELESS, cold and dead. With no end, no beginning, and no true purpose, it simply existed. Life had spun into being on the countless tiny orbs floating within it, but the Black itself was nothing more than a yawning, maddening void.

And yet, for all its fearsome and unforgiving menace, fragile beings had taken to it. They had made the lifeless vacuum passable, if not pedestrian. In tiny tombs, they reached out across the dark face of oblivion and made it their own. Though it waited endlessly to consume them, they did not fear it. Instead, they respected it.

The Black demanded as much and always would.

Other forces in the universe deserved no less. Though equally fierce and unrelenting, not all were treated with the same devout reverence, and such mistakes were never forgiven.

The metallic body of Firaxis Station was being crumpled and slowly immolated for daring to challenge such a force. The station had lost its grip on the once stable orbit it took for granted.

Now Gravity sank her fangs into the long, interconnected cylinders that formed its main body and had taken a cruel joy in tearing the station apart. Most of the centrifuge rings had been ripped away, leaving only two slowly spinning arms that trailed debris like thinning foam in a blackened sea.

For all of her force and violence, Gravity savored her prey. Like a spider, she first trapped them before slowly crushing them under her inescapable power. If she had a planet nearby in her web, often she would add fire to the weapons at her disposal. Unfortunately for Firaxis, it orbited the orange gas giant, Jaiden III, and it proved to be all too willing to assist her.

The clever minds behind the research station's construction and deployment believed the ambient radiation that powered Jaiden III's endless storms would mask Firaxis' presence from enemy eyes and for a time they were right.

Chapter 1

CLAUDE DISILVA FELT the ship around him lurch as it transitioned into streamline travel. He braced himself against the narrow frame of his bunk. Breathing slowly, Claude tried to picture a universe in which he managed to keep down the artificially flavored plant gelatin that passed for lunch.

"Are you going to throw up again?" a mocking female voice inquired.

Claude didn't open his eyes or abandon any part of his ritual. He could already picture Miranda laying in his bunk with her arms crossed and an eyebrow raised to match the smirk on her full lips.

"You should be used to it by now," she continued.

Miranda was normally intense and intimidating. She didn't often fraternize with subordinates, but when reports came through saying the war might finally be at an end, she'd decided to celebrate. Now that was over.

"All hands," the ship's comms system announced. "Mission briefing in ten. I repeat, mission briefing in ten."

"The countdown continues," Miranda said, sliding from under the covers and stretching.

The Cetalon unit commander was tall and lithe, but with a hint of menace that often worked in her favor. The deep brown of her skin covered muscle as tight as a bowstring and every bit as strong.

Claude tossed her the gray sleeveless shirt beside him before slipping his pants on and providing her at least a little privacy.

This encounter seemed like a good idea when they'd both thought the missions were at an end, but Bertrand was nothing if not committed. He'd announced this "last" mission over comms just under an hour ago, which was uncharacteristically rushed for him.

"Any guesses as to what it is?" Claude asked as he focused his attention on tightening the straps along the tops of his boots.

Miranda cinched her belt. "Knowing Bertrand, it's likely to be a suicide mission to Akinos."

"We'd have been in streamline longer if that was the case," Claude sighed.

He wasn't a fan of the anomalous travel system. It involved too many concepts he couldn't wrap his head around. Streamline was like most of the more advanced technology people used. It was all inherited, and not from a trustworthy source.

Miranda strolled past him to lean on the door frame. "There's no point worrying about it now."

"Until we're off this ship, I'll always be worried about what the old man will sign us up for," Claude grouched, brushing the wrinkles from his shirt.

He'd had his fill of the war. For the last few years, the whole thing had seemed pointless to him, but that was to be expected when the fighting lasted so long.

The war had raged since well before anyone currently alive was born. In fact, the people of the Beita Systems had been killing and dying in their conflict against the Imperium of Sabien Sectors for at least a thousand years. For most, the only constant things in the universe were the war and the Black.

Claude was young when he'd joined up to fight, but now, more than twenty years later, he was ready for it to be over. As unbelievable as it was, he was beginning to hope that there was more to life than soldiering. More than that, he needed there to be more.

"Bertrand's old," Miranda said, finger-combing her short black hair as best she could. "He wants the war to be over as much as we do."

Claude chuckled in spite of himself. He met Miranda's curious gaze with a shrug. He wasn't ashamed of his reaction, even if it had been involuntary.

"You don't think so?" she asked, studying him.

Claude shook his head. "I can't imagine him doing anything but fighting this war."

Chapter 2

THE LOADING DOCK WAS a cavernous space walled with charging stations for everything from the sleek, black Lifter recon bikes to a half dozen of the bulky armored Typhoon assault vehicles. Between each of the charging stations were weapons and equipment lockers that drew most of the activity.

Almost every locker had been assigned at some point in the TaskMaster's deployment, but now nearly half of them sat empty. Several carried memorial collages. An unending parade of images and even a few short loop holo-vids showing vibrant faces that no one would ever see again.

Their last few missions had hit the crew of the TaskMaster hard. The last one, in particular, had taken a considerable physical and psychological toll.

The ship itself still carried the scars. Flak cannon rounds had nearly shredded it in their hasty withdrawal from Diegon Minor. Fortunately for the ship, it was built to withstand firepower of that caliber. The soldiers that had fallen that day were not.

Only ten days had passed since that mission fell apart, and the dull haze of loss hadn't released its grip on the soldiers who now gathered in the space. There was an evident lack of energy, but the men and women of the TaskMasters still had a job to do.

Claude was already gearing up. He'd managed to get word from a friend on the command crew that they were on approach to their target location, but that was the extent of his intel. It was something, but more info would be needed to quiet the roaring disapproval in his mind.

He'd seen the broadcast. The truce was signed. The war was over, and all ships had been officially ordered to withdraw from Sabien territory, except theirs. Evidently, some dirty deed was left to do before the smoke cleared and the task fell to them.

Claude secured his sidearm holster and stole a glance at the locker beside his. The name, "Morden, Jerek" was heat-etched neatly into the door, but no other decorations adorned the brushed, gray metal.

The memorials were reserved for the dead, or so the unwritten rule seemed to be. Jerek hadn't died, so no one had taken the initiative to decorate his locker. Claude had considered it, but that was likely to jinx the man. As far as he was aware, Jerek was still in Med sector at Eurill station, fighting for his life. The last thing he needed was for a fellow scout to stack the deck against him.

Miranda knocked on the side of Morden's locker.

"Any news?" Claude asked, retrieving his rifle.

"Not much," Miranda said, eyeing him intently. "Are we going to have a problem?"

Claude fired a glance at her as if to say, "Obviously not."

"Good, I need you sharp. You're my eyes," Miranda continued. "I hear this is a black op, and I don't like it."

Claude slung his rifle and slammed his locker door shut. "We really don't need another black op."

"You think I don't know that?" Miranda said. "Morale's low as it is. The last thing anyone needs is a glorified band of mercenaries ruining the truce by sticking their noses where they don't belong."

"If you're looking for an argument, you won't get it from me," Claude replied, sidling past her and toward the amassing crowd.

Miranda fell in step with him and lowered her voice as they neared the others.

"The pay had better be worth it. We're out of contract, and I'm not signing back up for less than triple my old rate," she whispered as they came to a stop.

Claude sighed. He hated being reminded about rates. Unlike Miranda and many of the others aboard, he wasn't actually a mercenary. His services had been secured by Bertrand in lieu of a lengthy prison sentence. While Miranda would be ending the war with a tidy sum to retire on, Claude was going to have a struggle ahead of him. It wasn't something he was excited about, but it beat having to watch people he'd served with suffer and die.

The door on the far end of the loading dock slid open as Bertrand and the rest of the command crew entered the space. The soldiers in the crowd snapped to attention as a tall, gray-bearded man stepped onto the raised platform in the center of the group.

"As you were," Bertrand barked in his deep, booming tone.

The group eased into their rest posture. The tension in the room relaxed.

Bertrand was a career soldier who had transitioned into this life to continue providing service to his people after he had maxed out his service contract. He was well known in certain circles and completely deniable in others, making the TaskMasters the go-to outfit for sensitive missions. When they had an objective that would deepen or destabilize the conflict, they called outfits like his to get it done without fear of direct retaliation.

Part of their mandate was to never implicate the Beita Systems, no matter how the mission turned out. To all outside eyes, they were as neutral as the pirates pillaging the outer territories. The arrangement worked as long as open conflict still raged. With the truce in place, Claude wasn't sure how it would function.

With the war at an end, the Sabiens would be able to focus entirely on defending their territory now. That would leave Bertrand in civilian life again, unless something changed.

"You might have heard a few things about what they've given us to do," the old soldier continued. "Intel intercepted a transmission outlining a possible target of opportunity at 07:37. After verifying, they have decided to send us to Jaiden III on retrieval."

"What are we retrieving?" a female soldier near the front asked.

Claude couldn't tell who had asked the question, but the ripple of approving noise that rang through the crowd made it clear she wasn't the only one wanting that answer.

"As we understand it, a weapons research platform in the area has gone dark. The Sabiens are sending assistance, but they shouldn't arrive until at least 13:00. That leaves us three hours to get in, grab what we can, and get back across the line to safety," Bertrand said, straightening his gray and black uniform.

Miranda cleared her throat and stepped to the front of the crowd. She locked eyes with Bertrand and held his gaze for a moment before speaking.

"I have two questions," she said, folding her arms.

"Yes, Faridan," Bertrand said with an almost inaudible growl in his voice.

"The truce is on, so this is a non-contract job," Miranda said confidently.

"That isn't a question."

Miranda looked around at the discontent faces in the crowd before continuing. "What's the rate, and why did the place go dark?"

Bertrand drew in a deep breath and straightened.

Claude could see in his face that the answer he cared about wasn't going to be a good one. Bertrand had sent them in almost blind on Diegon, and it had gone sideways immediately. This op was going to be similar, and the order likely came from the same place.

"The military is offering two million credits," Bertrand said to a chorus of disappointed groans.

"Two million, that cuts down to nothing by the time we get ours," an ebony-skinned mountain of a man complained loudly.

Claude knew the man as Stacks. It wasn't his real name, but they weren't exactly on speaking terms. Stacks had carried Morden onto the ship and gone back for three more injured soldiers during their last mission. He was a good man, but like all the others, he was doing this job for money and little else, or so he routinely stated.

"Each!" Bertrand shouted above the rising din.

The silence that fell on the crowd was as absolute as it was immediate. Claude spotted the confused glances as everyone came to realize exactly how significant a job this would actually be.

"Given the nature of the request, the pay has been raised to compensate for the risk," Bertrand boomed. "The research is classified. The reason the station went dark is unknown, and of course, we'll be risking the full brunt of Sabien retaliation if caught.

"That's why I'm only allowing a team of six volunteers to go in. It's going to be dangerous, and if the Sabiens arrive before we're done, we will have to cut bait to avoid implicating the Beita Systems," Bertrand stated and let the words hang heavy in the air.

The texture of the silence changed at the notion that they might have to leave comrades behind. No soldier took the abandonment of fellow servicemen lightly. It happened, and it had happened recently, but it was never something decent people made peace with.

"I'll leave it to you to decide if you're willing to risk your lives in there."

Without another word, Bertrand turned and led his command crew out of the room as the soldiers exploded into chatter.

"Two million?" he heard Stacks ask in disbelief.

"Yeah, but it could be some chem weapon loose in that place," a younger woman said in disapproval.

Money only went so far, and with this crowd, it went farther than most, but the unknown was hard to sell at any price. Claude didn't think it would be impossible to find six people willing to risk it all for a bigger score, but it would be difficult.

He wasn't particularly interested, but if he was honest, he didn't have anything to lose by going and nothing to gain by refusing. Sure, he would live, but with the war at an end, that prospect introduced the same number of unknowns as the mission.

He'd been a farmer's son the last time he had been free of the conflict, but that path was no longer available to him. If he was honest, he wouldn't want that life back, even if he could get it. Like every other living human in the universe, he had never lived in a time without the war.

It was an all-defining event. Every facet of both major societies existed in the context of the war. All of that would have to be torn down and rebuilt or, at best, reformed to survive in peacetime. Claude didn't know much about human nature but change seemed never to come without struggle.

He hoped that his own nature would allow it to come at all.

"You coming?" Miranda asked, forcing her way back to him.

Claude smirked at her. "That's a hell of a question.".

"On the mission," Miranda amended. "The other is likely either way."

"If we survive," Claude added.

"We?"

"I don't see why not," Claude said with a shrug. "It'll be an investment in my future."

Miranda smiled. She was beautiful in her own intense way. Claude had seen her tear enemy units to shreds with a barrage of small arms fire, and what was worse, she seemed to enjoy it. Most soldiers he knew enjoyed a good scrap, but few were as gleefully brutal in combat as she was.

He'd met her shortly after being "recruited" to the TaskMasters, and they didn't get along well at first. According to his record, he was an insubordinate, low-level grunt, and she was his unit commander, but when the missions came, he'd carried his weight. Claude liked to think that he'd done more than that, but regardless, mutual respect grew between them. That's how Claude had read it, at least. The latest development between them was a very welcome and needed surprise.

"I'm going to go grill Bertrand for as much info as I can get," Miranda said, letting the smile slip from her face.

"Let me know what you get out of him," Claude said and backed toward an enclosure stuffed with the bubbled carapaces of zero gravity suits.

Miranda gave him an enticing wink, then turned and disappeared into the crowd.

Claude sighed and shook several of the less urgent thoughts from his head. "Just focus on staying alive," he mumbled to himself.

• • • •

Bertrand eyed a holographic image of the three elongated cylinders that made up the bulk of Firaxis Station. Its simplistic design betrayed the hasty construction. Sabiens were nothing if not ornate. Almost everything they built was structured with religious reverence, like their masters before them.

He had seen more than his fair share of Sabien construction. In his early days, Bertrand had been impressed by their technological prowess, but now he saw it for what it was, dependency.

In the Beita Systems, they valued the struggles and imperfections that made them human. The work that it took for them to pull themselves up from the bondage they had endured forced them to look inward for inspiration.

There was pride found in surviving the hard times and building the better days that were to come. Bertrand believed in that. He believed that every bruise and every drop of blood he'd ever spilled was in service of that ideal.

To him, the Sabiens were little more than the houseguests of ancient monsters. They had simply outlived them and had taken ownership of their possessions. They earned nothing and deserved even less.

It was no surprise that they thought they could wander into Beita System's territory and take what wasn't theirs. Their entitled arrogance earned them the war, and it was the duty of the Beita Systems to give them their comeuppance.

It was only fitting that those bound under the yokes of the Zephiar be the ones to check their "brothers" who lived in luxury. It was more than fitting. It was justice.

The security officer's voice came through the speaker. "Sir, Major Faridan is requesting–"

"Send her in," Bertrand interrupted.

He kept his eyes on the hologram as it expanded and shifted, highlighting possible entry points.

The hull had taken a beating, and much of it was too unstable to land the ship on. The station would likely be torn apart before the Sabiens could get to it. There was a slight possibility that the damned thing would crash into the planet with them still on it, but that was why speed and efficiency were paramount.

Bertrand frowned and massaged his brow. He didn't like the mission, but he understood the need for it. Heading off every possible advantage of the enemy would keep them from being overrun when this farcical truce finally ended.

Miranda entered and snapped the standard three-fingered salute of the Beita Systems military. "Sir."

"You can leave that at the door, Faridan. We aren't military," Bertrand said, shrinking the hologram to its standard size.

He turned to face her and flashed a perfunctory smile. "You want intel, I imagine," he said, offering Miranda a seat.

"Of course, but not just that," Miranda began. "I want to pick the team."

Bertrand huffed and eased himself onto a perch on his metal desk.

"I would prefer that this be strictly a voluntary affair. It absolves you of guilt if things go sideways."

"It's hard to feel guilty if your unit gets you killed," Miranda retorted.

Bertrand looked away from her and rubbed the salt and pepper stubble on his jaw.

"Who do you want?" he asked after a long moment.

"Stacks, Octavian, Stone, Winter, and DiSilva," Miranda said immediately.

"Have you talked to them?"

"Stacks and DiSilva, yes. With them on board, the others should be easy to sell on it."

"You really want Octavian on this mission?" Bertrand asked. "He's a little–"

"He's one of the best fighters on the roster, and I trust him," she interrupted.

Bertrand looked her over for a moment, then nodded. Octavian and Miranda had joined the TaskMasters as a pair and worked well together. If this was the team she wanted, he wasn't going to fight her on it. There were no giant red flags, and he knew that Miranda was perfectly capable of pulling off what amounted to a robbery with a team that was half as capable.

"Okay, have it your way," the old man said, shifting in his undoubtedly uncomfortable spot.

"Now, about that intel," Miranda started.

"There isn't much more than what's already been said," Bertrand replied. "The orbit is decaying, so the window is tighter than just the Sabien's arrival. If you take too long, Jaiden will be your tomb."

Miranda processed the additional info and shrugged. She had worked on similar timetables before. Once they dropped out of streamline, she had no doubt the work would get done in plenty of time.

"I'm more interested in the type of research," she said in a voice that spoke to her confidence.

"That's outside my clearance level to—"

"—Spare me, sir. We both know you have more intel, don't you?"

Bertrand's eyes burned into her own, but Miranda didn't flinch or release him from the stare. It was a challenge, and she aimed to win it once again.

Bertrand and Miranda had butted heads many times in their service together, but in the end, they were damned good at their jobs. Bertrand had a knack for prying what he wanted out of his powerful friends, and Miranda knew that better than most.

He was trusted and relied upon because he got things done. To do that, he needed enough information to operate efficiently and effectively. A precious few of those in power understood that, but often, Bertrand knew exactly which people he had to pressure.

Miranda valued the lives of the soldiers under her command. It was a noble trait, but it led her into conflict with her superiors when they didn't seem to share that priority. Bertrand often felt the same, but not always. They had spit fire at each other both before and after the Diegon fiasco, and in the end, she'd been right.

The bet now was that Bertrand would blink and give Miranda what she needed, assuming he had it to begin with. He already had the blood of good soldiers on his hands, and they both knew it. The question was if he was willing to plunge his hands back into the crimson a second time. She didn't think he would, but there was always room for surprise in her line of work.

"From what I've gathered, they were working on a weapon. Something they thought would end the war and establish the Imperium as the supreme power," Bertrand admitted. "If I were to guess, I'd say they got careless or desperate, maybe both. It looks like the whole thing blew up in their faces."

"Why do we want it then?" Miranda asked.

She understood the implications of such a weapon, but she wanted Bertrand to say it out loud. She wanted him to hear himself say it.

Every one of the TaskMasters knew that Bertrand was a true believer. He was a Beita Systems hardliner that thought the Sabiens were actually pure evil. He bought the propaganda being spewed by his own government wholesale.

Miranda and the majority of the other soldiers on board didn't share that opinion. They had seen and done things that were questionable at best, and at worst, proved that there was very little difference in the way each side operated. The only significant difference was the Sabiens did their dirt in clean, white corridors while the Beita Systems tried to hide it on outdated mercenary ships.

"We want the research so we can devise a countermeasure, just in case," Bertrand said, clearly not liking the taste of the lie.

"We both know they want to build the weapon themselves," Miranda chided.

Bertrand groaned as he pushed off the desk before walking back to the hologram.

"That's your theory. I've heard nothing that confirms that," Bertrand said pointedly, keeping his back to her.

"If we're going to risk our lives for this, the least Echelon could do is tell us the truth about it," Miranda said, making her way to the door.

"Echelon knows that in wartime, the truth is subjective," Bertrand snapped.

Miranda laughed outright. She would have tried to keep it in at least a little, but Bertrand deserved her full-throated response.

"You can't believe that," she said, stealing a glance at the hologram in front of him.

"And if I do?" Bertrand challenged, firing his narrowed gaze over his shoulder.

"Then you have to concede that we are in peacetime now," Miranda said and strolled out of the room.

She was right, again. Bertrand would never tell her that, but he knew what command wanted, even if they left it unsaid.

• • • •

The sea of stars erupted in vivid purple as the streamline anomaly peeled open like flesh from a wound. At the center, the TaskMaster emerged. With a bright blue flash, its sub-light engines roared to life, pushing the modest ship through the residual barriers of the anomaly as it closed, leaving only the void.

The TaskMaster reoriented in a dance of sequenced thruster plumes and sped toward the distant, shimmering speck and the massive gas giant eager to consume it. Hundreds of miles of emptiness gave way in mere moments as the Larridon-class carrier honed in on its target.

Compared to the TaskMaster, Firaxis station was massive. Though small for a Sabien station, it easily dwarfed the incoming vessel. Structures of its kind often stretched from the size of mid-tier cities up to that of small continents. Firaxis teetered on the bottom end of that spectrum.

The TaskMaster fired several of its forward and ventral thrusters as it swooped into the gap between the station's three cylindrical body segments. The tiny ship's wings extended, firing thrusters of their own as it banked and rolled out to dodge several of the station's connecting struts and the broken support rings.

• • • •

"Sit us down over the secondary maintenance hatch," Bertrand commanded from his raised dais.

The viewport absorbed the entire front wall of the command deck. The massive window provided a fisheye view from the nose of the vessel, catching every detail of the approach.

Bertrand had spent half of his last contract rate overhauling the bridge to bring it in line with modern Beita Systems military tech. While the results were astonishing, it was nowhere near what he wanted the ship to be. He was particularly enamored with the newer command dais technology. He'd attempted to add one, but the cost deterred him. The only thing he could afford was the standardized spherical redesign for the space.

He wasn't fond of it doubling as an escape pod. It meant he no longer had the option to go down with the ship unless he was willing to let every man and woman that served beside him die as well. He would have to find a middle ground when he managed to get the upgrades he really wanted.

"Touch down in seven seconds," the newest helmsman said.

She was as green as fresh-cut grass, but she had a severe demeanor. It was one of the things that had gotten Bertrand's attention.

He'd hired on several other new crew members after Diegon Minor, but all of them had worked out well so far. It was as surprising as it was welcome, considering that none of them were still military.

Bertrand wondered how much longer he would be able to afford to run a full crew given recent developments. There were always odd jobs that needed doing, but with the war stalling out, there wouldn't be as much work, and it almost certainly wouldn't pay well enough to keep everyone on staff.

Frowning, Bertrand forced the unpleasant train of thought from his mind and felt the telltale rumble and thump as the ship touched down.

Chapter 3

CLAUDE STOOD AHEAD of his team. He was clad head to toe in gray and silver armor. The entire thing was designed for fights in the Black. It could take a beating and not break its seals. For the most part, it functioned well. Unfortunately, it was not completely resistant to barrages of high-speed projectiles, radical shifts in magnetic polarity, or hyper-focused photons, all of which were things that would be particularly useful to a scout.

Behind him stood Terra Winter, Deek Octavian, Stacks, Nina Stone, and Miranda, their unit commander. All were solid picks for the mission. Each was highly skilled in their specializations, but more importantly, they could handle themselves in a fight.

Personally, Claude would have preferred to have a medic with them, but the mission didn't allow for it. He understood the need to keep the team small and agile, but not having one seemed like it was inviting catastrophe.

Stacks shifted his weight with a loud groan.

"I hate these suits," he complained, trying to get comfortable.

"Makes sense," Winter said. "They weren't designed for people the size of buildings."

Claude smiled in spite of himself. He'd worked with every one of them before, and minus some issues with the missions themselves, he'd enjoyed it.

Winter managed to keep the mood light. She didn't take too many things seriously, but she also knew when to button up. She was a firecracker and the best marksman on the team.

Stacks was a field engineer, which always seemed odd to Claude. He was massive and evidently so was his mind. He excelled where anything tech was concerned. Given that they would likely need to bypass Sabien security locks and dig into research terminals, the big guy would be very useful.

Octavian and Stone were riflemen. Stone was similar to Claude himself. Her family had defected from the Sabiens when she was a teenager, while he had stowed away on a smuggler's ship as a child. Still, she knew more about day-to-day life in the Imperium than he did. That made her a valuable addition to each mission she'd joined.

Octavian was a strange one. He had been a captive of pirates in his younger days, and it wasn't a good experience. To hear him tell it, they'd taken turns torturing him. They even cut out his tongue, then forced him to wear it as a necklace after he'd insulted their captain in Qutongan. After that, the pirates made it a point to use Octavian for their entertainment, that is, until a Beita Systems raid set him free. Given everything he'd been through, it was no wonder he turned out to be the best fighter in the TaskMasters.

The only downsides to having him on-mission were the additional steps needed to communicate with him and his tendency to get caught up in his own head. The latter was a trait Claude could relate to.

Miranda knew Octavian best, and she trusted him fully. Together they had found a way to work around his shortcomings for the most part, but Octavian still unnerved the other unit commanders, and occasionally his teammates.

The deep blue light of the room shifted to yellow, accompanied by a slight shift in gravity. Wordlessly, each member of the team unslung their rifles and busied themselves with whatever rituals put their minds at ease.

For Claude, it was basically a long-running chant of, "Please don't let me die." He had no idea whom he was asking for that admittedly large favor, but he always asked, and so far, things had worked out.

"Ready up, TaskMasters," Miranda barked, breaking his silent chant. "We go in, we hit the research labs, we grab whatever bullshit Echelon needs and get back to the bunks."

Winters punched Claude on the shoulder, but he ignored her. News traveled fast in an enclosed biome. By the end of this mission, everyone on board would know about his liaison with Miranda.

That didn't bother him so much, but he wasn't about to feed into the gossip mill. He was better than that, or at least that's what he told himself.

The lights in the room crashed to red, and the hatch at his feet slide open with a rush of air Claude heard through his helmet.

"DiSilva," Miranda said calmly. "Lead the way."

Claude nodded, took a deep, ragged breath, and dropped into the hatch.

• • • •

The suit absorbed most of the impact from the twelve-foot drop. The rest Claude tried to nullify with a roll before getting to his feet and scanning his surroundings.

He'd landed in a service corridor lit only by a thin string of yellow emergency lights running down either side of the floor. The area was a mess. In normal conditions, a Sabien station was the picture of order and cleanliness, but chaos had visited this one. Panels from the walls, ceiling, and floors had been bent, broken, or discarded. Optical wiring had been ripped from the walls, and two bodies lay down the hall, crumpled on top of one another.

After taking a second to gather himself and ensure there were no surprises, Claude called out to his team.

"Clear!" he shouted, keeping his weapon sighted down the hall to his right.

One by one, each team member dropped into the hatch and took up their positions around him. Claude spared a glance to see if their reactions were in line with his own, and he wasn't disappointed.

"What happened here?" Stacks asked with more than a little concern in his voice.

"Looks like the Sabiens throw a hell of a party," Winter joked, but there was no humor in it.

A single line of green text drew itself across the top of Claude's face screen.

"Looks like overload damage."

The text was from Octavian, thanks to the neural interface Stacks had reverse-engineered for him. It wasn't finalized yet, but the experimental tech gave him the ability to communicate with the team.

Claude understood the need, especially in situations like these. Still, it was unsettling to have another person's thoughts inside his visor.

"Stacks, does that checkout?" Miranda asked.

The large man to Claude's right took a second, then answered.

"Maybe, overloads do crazy things, but this is on a whole new level," he said in disbelief.

A map of the hallway hovered over Stone's left palm, pulsing as it grew in intricacy and detail. She watched it intently until it stretched past the bend in the hall.

"Maps up," she stated, doing her best to ignore the intensely detailed, digital bodies. "Getting some interference, though."

Stone tapped the screen on her inner left arm, and the map blinked onto the bottom right corner of Claude's visor. With a swipe, he lowered the map's opacity, then moved down the corridor toward the bodies.

As he neared them, he could tell they were civilians. There were also no wounds aside from the odd bruise or scrape. If he had to guess, they'd fallen mid-sprint.

Toxin seemed the most likely cause of death. Stations like this were full of waste gasses. They could have been released during an overload. Without a full scope of tests, there was no way to be sure, and there wasn't time for all that. So, he chose to put the whole thing out of his mind.

Claude turned to the path ahead and left the unfortunate souls behind undisturbed. Rounding the bend in the corridor, he saw three more bodies on the floor beyond. The same mid-run drop was apparent for them as well.

"Looks clear," he called to the unit and returned his attention to the dead beside him.

Carefully, he rolled the body of the short, balding man over and found only light abrasions. The body felt like a statue. The muscles and joints were locked in a permanent running pose. The man's face was frozen in the wide-eyed terror he had felt when his life abandoned him.

"Was it a chemical or a biological agent?" Miranda asked, leading the unit toward Claude.

Claude shrugged, then remembered the bulky suit that masked the gesture.

"No idea. My rig doesn't have the sensitivity to scan for that," he said, respectfully replacing the body to its original position.

As traditions went, sparing enemy bodies undue violation wasn't exactly common. It wasn't even viewed as particularly respectful, though for Claude it was. Often there just wasn't time to give proper funeral rites in the field. In the Black, things were even worse due to the confines of ships and installations, but that was no excuse to be irreverent.

Sabiens were human too. Every soldier on both sides fought for their version of a better future. When they fell, they deserved to be left in peace, at the very least. So Claude did what he could to honor that.

"Great," Winter huffed. "Looks like we get to ride all the way home in quarantine."

"Stop complaining. You wanted to spend more time with me anyway," Stacks deadpanned.

"Keep the chatter to a minimum," Miranda said. "I want you focused."

Claude nodded, took one last look at the bodies at his feet, and moved ahead.

· · · ·

Bertrand was studying the feeds coming from the drop team as best he could. There was a massive amount of interference distorting the images and breaking up the sound. The technician next to him had managed to boost image quality on the bits coming through, but the sound was a total loss.

"Give me schematics," he barked.

"There are no schematics for this facility, sir. This is all we have," the technician said, sweat beading on his tattooed head.

Bertrand dropped his head and stuffed down his mounting frustration. Despite the money and technology that he'd put into his ship, it seemed to be failing him more and more. Sure, she still flew and kept the Black at bay, but she wasn't the fighting machine she once was.

If he was honest, she was the mate he likely deserved. Unlike the TaskMaster I, Bertrand could not be augmented back into relevance. He was old, and while that came with actionable experience, it also came with failings that he couldn't ignore.

As a younger man, he'd toyed with the idea of enhancements but had shied away from it. Nothing was more Sabien than violating the human body for the sake of easy advancement, but even they seemed to draw the line at large-scale cybernetics.

"Give me the nearest match," Bertrand said, blowing out a heavy breath and distorting his feeds even more.

"Yes, sir," the technician said, swiping an image from his data-pad to the central display.

The pale blue of a Sabien Systems space station danced into view among the distorted video feeds. Unlike them, it was solid and clear. Bertrand leaned in closer to the schematics, the white in his beard and hair glowing bright blue in their light.

"Show me the path to the main labs from the secondary maintenance hatch," he said, looking back at the technician.

"There's no labs on this—"

"Best guess, then," Bertrand growled.

The younger man swallowed hard and nodded. The tattoo on his head becoming more visible as he did so.

Bertrand recognized the symbol. It came from a liberated world renamed Reitsin. He'd fought there in the early days of his career, and it was one of the key victories that spurred him on to reenlist four times.

There were moments when Bertrand missed the thick forests and frozen fields of that world, but what he enjoyed most about Reitsin was its people. Harsh terrain and climate had given birth to a resilient people. By Bertrand's estimation, no culture in the universe loved life and celebrated it more than those on that small world. It was just a shame that the fighting had been so destructive there.

When the war reached the planet, its people were already suffering through a famine. They were poor and forgotten largely by the Crowns, rulers of the Sabien Imperium. The decadence of their distant leaders and their seeming disregard for their people had lit a fire in the Reitsiners. Angry and desperate for something new, they fought with the Beita Systems and won their independence.

The cost was high. Generations were decimated by the conflict, but their new allies were helping them rebuild and all it cost the Reitsiners was enough land for an outpost. Now the planet would be able to focus on rebuilding like everyone else.

It had always surprised Bertrand that Reitsin wasn't folded into the Beita Systems officially. As it stood, they remained an unclaimed territory as far as records went. Independence was a point of pride for Reitsiners, as was their symbol, the graystone drake breaking its chains.

Apparently, it was still a source of pride for people as young as the technician, too, since he'd elected to brand himself with it. The mark was an easy identifier and well drawn, but unnecessary. The lilting cadence of his words and odd syntax were enough to place his origin.

A red path traced itself a quarter of the way through the schematic and stopped amid a series of blinking squares. It hesitated there, then swept through each square on its way back to the thin corridors before disappearing into one of the map's many blank spaces.

"Reitsin, right?" he asked without taking his eyes from the display.

"Y-Yes, sir," the technician stammered.

"You're doing them proud," Bertrand announced. "What's your name?"

The young man rubbed the tattoo on his head and lifted his chin.

"Mattic, sir."

• • • •

Claude, Miranda, and the rest of the unit followed the newly marked path on their visors' display. It took them past countless bodies and down one ruined corridor after another until they reached the galley.

Winter whistled loudly. The sharp sound rang off the walls and disappeared into the open darkness where any Beitan would have built a ceiling.

"Would you look at this place?" she chimed, staring up into the shadows.

The map expanded rapidly to cover the size of the space. Room existed for everyone on the station to sit and eat comfortably all at once.

A pale green image showcased three tiers in the darkness above, each crisscrossed with walkways and lined with tables and benches. Six rows of the same furnishings extended along the floor, dying just before a set of serving windows that bordered this floor's massive kitchen.

"Excessive," printed across Claude's visor.

"Whatever you say, Octavian," Winter said, not taking her eyes off the upper floors. "This just screams style to me."

"You don't know what you're talking about," Stone stated coldly.

Claude pushed their chatter into the background and took point. He studied the scan, ignoring the flickers and flashes that would have otherwise frustrated him. According to the path laid out for them, they would have to move laterally through this space and out the other side, which presented a problem. The exit they were looking for was barred by a sealed bulkhead.

"Guys, we have a problem," he announced, motioning toward the barred exit.

Miranda jogged to him and followed his gaze.

"You have got to be joking," she hissed. "We don't have time for this."

"We could hit it with an explosive," Claude said, half-joking.

"I love the way you think, but the station is already a wreck," she replied, keeping her eyes on the sturdy wall of metal. "I'd prefer not to be left twisting in the Black today."

She turned to the rest of the squad and whistled to put an end to their group chat. Each member snapped their attention back to her. When she was satisfied, Miranda and Claude moved back to the group and fell into formation.

"We have a wrinkle to deal with," Miranda barked. "Hustle, mission clock's winding down."

Claude slung his rifle and marched toward the large white enameled door as the others fell into step behind him.

"Not you," Miranda said. "I need your eyes open. See if you can find us another way out of here. I doubt we're that lucky but check anyway."

"Yes, ma'am," Claude said and unslung his rifle.

He moved away as the rest of the unit examined the door and wall. It would take them a while longer to find and override the security panel.

Stacks was good, but no tech could work miracles. The likelihood was that Claude would find a viable path out before the big guy could make any headway.

The most likely place for an exit was the kitchen on the far side of the room. Food had to be transported from the docking bays to the freezers somehow, and since the galley was at the heart of this strut, that meant an access corridor had to be nearby. The areas of the strut Claude had seen suggested it was purely residential. Having so many families on a research station was odd, but given how remote it was, that checked out.

Personally, he would need a good reason to put so many innocent people at risk like this. While the entire unit had become numb to the bodies, the number of them was increasing steadily. The floors and tables here were littered with them. They were everywhere, each looking as if they would awaken at any moment.

The casualty numbers had to be outrageous. Already he was sure everyone on the station was dead, but without a clue as to what killed them, Claude found it impossible to move past the carnage. His suit's rudimentary scans showed no toxins or biological contaminants, but that didn't mean much. The others had pitched their theories, and each was more outlandish, yet just as viable as the next.

Stone had suggested a Psionic attack, but that seemed ridiculous too. At most, Psionics could only manipulate or kill two, maybe three people at a time. Even then, there were obvious signs. Blood pooled in the eyes and streamed from the noses of their victims. This looked like every person in the station was just turned off like a light.

Claude had almost lost himself in thought when movement caught his eye. A debate raged in his head as to whether he should alert the others. Given the macabre setting, he could have just been a bit jumpy.

Whatever he had seen was gone when he focused on it, and now he wasn't really sure he'd actually seen anything. Choosing to have faith in his senses and training, he elected to watch and wait for whatever it was to move again.

In the distance, at the edge of his visor's augmentation range, a plate moved. This time he was sure because he heard the scraping sound in the unnatural quiet.

There had to be a source, but Claude couldn't make it out. Even using his visor's magnification, nothing could be clearly discerned. Yet, he didn't dare move. Whatever was down there had to be as spooked as he was. If it meant to attack there'd been plenty of opportunities, so whatever it was didn't mean to harm them or it would have done so by now.

Rather than move toward the unseen thing, Claude slowly lowered himself into a crouch. Through the legs of tables, chairs, and corpses, his visor strained to make out a shape. It was small, but that was the only thing Claude could really tell about it. He got the distinct feeling that it was trying to make its own judgments about him, but without a better view, he couldn't be sure.

Usually, eyes were reflective in the visor's low light augmentation. It was an eerie side effect of the technology, but not having those tiny pinpricks of light to denote a face was all the more unsettling. Whatever Claude was looking at didn't seem to have eyes, or at least not eyes as he knew them.

There was a gap in his knowledge, and while that always made him uncomfortable on missions, this one threatened his sanity. Without knowing what exactly the Sabiens were doing on this station, he couldn't rule anything out. Claude typically made a million little judgments, all on his own. But without more information, he was left guessing. He was trying to solve a potentially deadly equation without the use of any actual figures, which led to grimmer results for himself, the team, and the mission.

"Hey Miranda, I think I found something," he called out before his head nearly exploded in intense pulsating pain.

Miranda had barely registered Claude's words before a sudden and intensifying force threatened to drive her brain out through her ear canal. The pain of it sent her crashing to the ground almost instantly. Miranda willed herself to turn and check on the rest of the team. Through unfocused eyes, she found them all writhing in pain, all except for Stone.

"It's an attack," she said coldly and unslung her rifle.

Miranda watched as Stone moved past her in swift, controlled strides. The former Sabien's movements were sharp, and unmistakably predatory. She had seen them a thousand times before, but it always made her nervous having someone on her team move the same way as the enemy.

Stone neared Claude and crouched beside him. Carefully, she sighted the shape in the shadows and fired. The flash of her rifled blinded Claude temporarily as rounds tore through the air and toward the unknown creature.

The crushing pressure disappeared immediately as the table flipped over and blocked Stone's opening salvo. Claude managed to catch a glimpse as the shape bolted toward the kitchens. Stone tracked it and squeezed off several more rounds. One of them hit the fast-moving thing in the side, causing it to give a very human yelp as blood-spattered the far wall.

Stone kept firing, but the shape dove through the open door and out of sight. She kept her gun trained as if she expected it to pop back out for her to finish it off.

"You okay? How did you do that?" Claude asked, grabbing his rifle and struggling to his feet.

Stone shook her head as if she had water in her ear. The combat rush was evening out as she backed up to him, dropping into a two-man formation.

"Implant—" she mumbled before tipping over.

Claude caught her before she hit the ground, but the suit didn't help at all. He eased her down to the floor and took aim at the kitchen door as the rest of his unit made their way to them.

"What the hell was that?" Stacks asked with naked fear in his voice.

Claude shook his head as he tried his best to find his own answer to that exact question. Every story he'd heard about Psionics painted them as soulless killers, but this one had only attacked when it was about to be exposed.

He didn't think it was overtly hostile. If it were, they would already be dead. That meant something, although he wasn't sure exactly what.

Still, it was alive, and it had to know more about the station than they did.

"I think it was a survivor," he said, looking to Miranda for a reaction.

"It's not going to be for long," Winter said, pushing past Stacks.

Octavian grabbed her by the arm. Winter spun to shove him back.

"Get off me," she hissed at him with a look that promised violence if he touched her again.

"It ran in the opposite direction of the objective. Let it go," printed across everyone's visors.

"Octavian's right," Miranda said, eyeing Stone. "We're not here for survivors."

"What do you mean, 'we're not here for survivors?'" Claude protested. "The station's going to crash."

"Exactly," Miranda said, letting him hear the steel in her voice.

"It was small. It has to be a kid or something," Claude said, motioning in the direction of the kitchens.

"It attacked us," Stacks said. "I say we either leave it or kill it. You all know what I prefer."

Stone groaned and struggled into a seated position.

"Children can't be Psionics," she said in a slightly groggy voice.

Miranda turned to Winter, "Get Stone back to the ship."

Claude watched as Winter bristled, but she did as she was commanded. Still loopy, Stone struggled to her feet with some minor assistance and nodded.

Once she was satisfied, Miranda addressed the rest of the team.

"Everyone else, with me. We get that door open, and then we get this job done," Miranda stated, leaving no room to debate.

Claude looked back and forth between Miranda and the kitchen. The blood on the wall was no higher than three and a half feet. He knew what he saw, and there was no way he could leave a child to die alone.

Stone didn't see what he'd seen. The poor kid had been startled and tried to defend itself. If the situation was reversed, any of them would have done the same. It was likely that they would have done far worse.

"Claude," Miranda said, snapping his attention back to the group.

"I can't," he said before he even realized words were leaving his mouth.

"You can't what?"

Claude sighed and squared himself against Miranda, "I can't leave a kid behind."

"We are finishing this mission with or without you," Miranda said, staring him down. "If you make us do it without you, pray you make it back before we do."

She knew him well enough to understand he had a conscience and that, from time to time, he let it rule him. It wasn't the best trait to have in their line of work, but it made him interesting to her.

She didn't exactly share his problem. Her conscience had abandoned her years prior, but there were times when she was brutally honest with herself that she wished it had stuck around. Unfortunately, this wasn't one of them.

Claude stiffened at her words. He took her meaning perfectly. If he got into trouble, he would be on his own. No rescue would be coming and that was fine. He didn't expect her to go along with him or even condone his actions, but Miranda wouldn't stop him, and that was all he needed.

"See you on the ship," he said and moved off toward the kitchens.

Miranda watched him for a moment, then lifted her chin and turned to the others. "Let's get this done."

Chapter 4

THE KITCHENS WERE SILENT. Nothing moved as Claude scanned the room from outside the door. The same lifeless calm permeated the area, and once more, it caused the hairs on the back of his neck to brush against his suit. The bodies of the cooking staff littered the floor, while unfinished meals found their way to new levels of rancidity.

Inching into the room, he stepped over the rotund body that held the door ajar. He wasn't sure where the little one was hiding. There was a slim chance that the kid had already made it to an access corridor. From where he was, Claude couldn't see one, but that didn't mean anything.

As he'd done a hundred times, Claude swept the room, paying particular attention to all the dark spaces perfect for a child to hide in. He wasn't trying to scare it, but he couldn't just leave a survivor to burn or bleed out all alone.

He'd rejected orders to do the same thing before. He'd even been court-martialed for how he'd handled it. In retrospect, there were better ways to show his disdain for the officer that forced him to leave innocent civilians to die, but a gunshot to the femur seemed to be the most fitting at the time.

And here he was again, disobeying his orders, this time to save a potential enemy. He didn't feel like it really mattered. The fact was, the war was over. That meant there was no enemy, as new as that idea was.

Claude forced that thought from his mind. Even if he wasn't on-mission, he still had a hard time limit and at least one survivor to find. Ruminating on a life he could lose if he took too long wasn't going to help.

• • • •

On the far side of the room, tiny fingers gripped the side of a mirrored Itanium stove. The small shape observed Claude cautiously. She wasn't sure what to make of him. He felt different from the woman who had hurt her, but she couldn't trust that. There wasn't much she knew about people, but the pain in her side told her that different didn't mean safe.

The man was searching for her, but why? He and his group were the first people she had seen alive since she woke up. Everyone else was cold and hollow. The new people were still warm, but they weren't like her, and she had no idea why.

The man's attention snapped to her, and she immediately collapsed into a panic. She lost control of her thoughts and bolted, disappearing down the service passage toward the only place where she still felt safe.

"Wait!" the man shouted from behind her, but the girl did no such thing.

• • • •

Miranda led her unit through the muted transit hub. With the power nonexistent, they were forced to abandon the idea of riding the lift to their destination.

The climb was brutal, and she found herself wishing that the artificial gravity would die so she could spare herself the effort. Longingly, she looked through the transparent walls at twinkling stars and the endless Black beyond.

Octavian and Stacks were right behind her, and while they seemed as uncomfortable as she was about the climb, neither complained. Miranda had dodged a bullet, having sent Winter with Stone. The amount of mindless chatter that woman spewed would likely get her shot in this circumstance.

Ordinarily, the transit platform would have been filled with people and cargo moving from one strut of the station to the others, but whatever killed the station had disrupted that routine.

There were no bodies in the space, which was a relief, but there was abandoned cargo in droves. Miranda found herself trying to fit the tiny pieces she'd seen together, but kept coming up short. Nothing matched in her experience and nothing could be ruled out. Coupling that frustration with the fact she couldn't just move past it, Miranda found her unease and desire to be done with the whole thing growing faster than her fatigue.

"If we find whoever did this, I want to be the one to shoot them," Stacks huffed, pulling himself even with Miranda.

"They are already dead," Octavian printed on their visors as he caught up.

"Doesn't mean I can't shoot them," Stacks said with a dark chuckle.

They all needed a break. The climb was killing both the team and their timetable, but Miranda obliged. As TaskMasters, they were in peak condition, but climbing over half-a-mile straight up under Akinosian gravity standards took a toll on even the best-trained bodies.

They had drilled for the "eventual" invasion of Akinos, but the planet made everything weigh one and a half times more than Beitan standards. Unfortunately for everyone, Akinos was the core world of the Sabien Imperium and thus the benchmark for all artificial gravity units in their empire.

"Looks like we have an access hatch in a few more feet," Octavian announced, pointing to a bank of dimly blinking red lights.

"Okay, Octavian, take point. I'll cover the rear," Miranda said.

She could see that Stacks wanted to protest, but he was the specialist, and they needed him to complete this mission. He had to be protected, even if he was bigger and stronger than the rest of them.

Without another word, the unit climbed to the hatch and forced it open. Compared to the transport terminal, the air inside was freezing. Miranda watched as the temperature flux warning flashed across her visor.

"Watch for breaches," she stated as Octavian slipped through the narrow entrance.

They were venturing off the path now. Miranda figured they wouldn't be fortunate enough to have a guide all the way to the labs, but the fact that it had been as correct as it had was beyond lucky.

She brought up the mission timer and sighed. The readout showed: 1h 27m. It wasn't a lot of time, but the way back would be easier than the way in. If they got really crunched for time, they could always take a walk back to the ship through the Black. It would be more direct, assuming they didn't burn up entering Jaiden III's atmosphere.

As she planned her escape, Miranda allowed herself to hope that Claude would be free and clear. She respected him, and that mattered more than anything else she may or may not have felt for him. He had been an honest and compassionate man. She hadn't known many people who not only possessed those traits but flew them like a flag. If he didn't make it out of this, she would be saddened by it. She would blame those traits she liked and even envied for his death, but she would keep moving forward. She always kept moving forward.

Before following Stacks into the access tunnel, Miranda cast one final glance at the dizzying height they had climbed. With a sigh, she slipped inside the hatch and sealed it behind her.

It was tight inside the access hatch. With the suits on, there was barely enough room for her to move. The discomfort was to be expected. The death of her map's viability wasn't.

Stone had set the team up with the survey pulse, but in here, the interference was unbearable. The image warbled with such frequency that it was all but impossible to read anything on it.

Miranda swiped it from her view and did her best to ignore the creeping dread of flying blindly into an unknowable situation.

"Exit ahead," Octavian pointed out.

Around Stacks, Miranda could barely see the blinking of orange emergency lights. She nodded to herself. They were making better time now. Hopefully, they would soon be out of this crypt with time to spare.

• • • •

Claude had been tracking the child for longer than he cared to think about. The path took him through the access corridor and out into the recreation hub of the station.

Around him were open storefronts, but all were dark. Dozens of woundless bodies littered the floor, along with merchandise of all shapes and sizes. He moved over them carefully as he scanned the tier he was on.

There were thousands of places to hide, but the blood trail the kid left drew him in the right direction. As he moved past stores that sold everything from vintage holo-vid cartridges to clothes to glittering wall-mounted orbs he'd never seen before, he found himself wondering if this was where the child had been staying.

It wasn't a terrible hideout if you didn't know the entire station was about to be molten slag. Claude could imagine a child running rampant there, without any adults to reign them in. If it weren't for the corpses, it would be the perfect playground. As it stood, the place was a graveyard.

"Come on, kid," Claude said, deciding to sling his rifle. "I'm not here to hurt you."

There was no response. Not even the filtration system that ran endlessly in other stations gave a sound. The only thing he could hear was his own breathing and the running beat of his own anxious heart.

Claude saw the blood trail turn into a broken store window. The printed images sold elaborate decor for modest dormitories. Inside, it was ransacked, and what wasn't taken was left broken on the floor. Deep shadows masked the far wall, making the store's dimensions impossible to gauge from outside.

After a moment, Claude decided not to pursue the child inside and instead wandered through the hub. He was no expert on children, but he had been chasing, and the kid had just kept running. He hoped that by letting the kid acclimate to his presence that maybe it would come to him.

There wasn't much left of the hub to explore except for the Sanctuary Hall. It was impossible to mistake it. The large entrance was marked with the imperial symbol. Five unique crowns, each set within the facets of a brilliant blue jewel.

Claude had been raised on the outskirts of the Imperium's territory. As a child, his father insisted that he learn as much about the Sabiens as he could. Not much had stuck, but he did remember the strange, almost religious zeal based around a vague yet endless progression as a people. Of course, which citizens counted as people was always a point of contention.

The Crown of Emanation ultimately decided that, and its word was respected and accepted by most, if not all, Sabiens. The Crown of Emanation was the keeper of knowledge, lineage, and the past. The populace almost deified each person that held the position. Even

Claude's father hung on his every word, calling him a gift to the Imperium. Claude just called him a propagandist, but he didn't think it mattered.

Pushing open the door on the opulent space, Claude put those thoughts aside. The interior was filled with every shade of blue crystal that could be imagined. Benches, booths, and railings were all made of the stuff, but what drew his attention was the massive hole ripped in the ceiling. The deck above him had evidently collapsed, dropping the furnishings and bodies of several rooms onto the refractive blue floor below.

Claude stared up at the damage in awe. He'd seen weapons that could do such things, but none of them could do it without scorching, melting, or exploding everything around them.

He was so caught up wondering what could cause the ceiling to rip away like the petals of a flower that he didn't notice the corpse to his right.

It shifted and lurched on the hundreds of silver spikes that held it off the ground. The movements were awkward and wrong, and by the time it struggled its way to its feet, it had gained Claude's full attention.

He stared on in disbelief as the corpse staggered toward him. Dead eyes locked not on him but on the distance beyond. In a fog of panic and confusion, Claude heard someone open fire. He felt the violent bucking of his rifle against his shoulder and realized it was him. Before he knew it, he'd dropped an entire clip into the shambling body to no avail.

Instead of being ripped apart by the rounds and returning to unmoving death, the silver spikes protruding from the dead woman began to wriggle. They wrap themselves around her, coating the discolored flesh in a shimmering, seamless armor.

Claude turned to run but slammed into the crystal railing that divided the walkway into aisles. He didn't look back at the monster haunting his steps, he didn't dare.

As a soldier, he had become accustomed to death. He had mourned those taken by it and even celebrated others he had given to it, but no one ever returned. The idea that it was even possible was the stuff of far-fetched stories and holo-vids.

He moved through the room at what seemed like a crawl. It had only taken seconds to cross beneath the hole in the ceiling, but getting back to the door was taking years.

Claude tried to call out, but nothing escaped him. Even the exhaust from his lungs was petrified. The station was as quiet as the tomb it had become, and in some distant fragment of his breaking mind, he found his own forced silence fitting.

Then he felt dead hands fall on him. Somehow, the creature had been able to keep pace. Somehow, it had caught him. Claude wasn't able to think. He was barely able to move as all the dead woman's surreal weight collapsed onto his back.

With a painful crunch, Claude fell onto his chest. Every ounce of breath in him fled. His vision blurred, and for a moment, he lost focus on everything except for the silver corpse crawling up his body. He did his best to pull himself along the faceted floor but could not find purchase. The corpse was still on him, its impossible weight pinning him to the spot.

In the crystalline reflection beneath him, Claude stared through wild streams of dirty, brown hair. The fight drained from him as the dead woman raised a fist. A new spike erupted from it, and he knew it was the end. Summoning every ounce of willpower, Claude forced himself to look away.

His eyes found the child staring from the doorway. It was a girl, a thin wisp of a girl, peering mournfully at him with solid black eyes. She was the last thing Claude saw before white-hot agony burned away his senses.

• • • •

The research strut was hit hard. Aside from the typical damage to the wall, ceiling, and floor panels, there was a decent amount of frost damage. Nearly every surface had at least been scarred by an immense cold that had since dissipated.

On top of that, it was also a utilitarian place. None of the human touches Miranda had seen in the other strut existed here. There were no posters espousing the virtues of togetherness, achievement, and communication. Small comforts like potted plants and even benches were nowhere to be found. If Miranda didn't have obvious proof to the contrary, she could have almost been convinced the place was built by machines instead of people.

"Any idea what we're looking at?" Stacks asked.

Miranda heard the unease in his voice, and she understood it. Until now, the mission had been a bloodless affair, but what faced them here was anything but. Even she assumed the station had fallen victim to some kind of poisonous influence, but this destroyed that theory.

Unlike the nearly pristine residential strut, the bodies here had obvious and gory causes of death. Many were broken and twisted in unnatural ways.

Others had their heads crushed, and all showed signs of trampling. There was no rage to it, or at least that's what Miranda felt when she looked at the carnage. What she saw was a panicked race for survival and the sad remnants of those who didn't make it.

"It was a stampede," she said.

"Poor Ban'utas," Octavian shared as he examined the nearby corpse of a gray-haired woman.

"Touch nothing," Miranda stated firmly, snapping the group's attention back to their task.

She was surprised her voice wasn't shaking. She had been part of some grisly fights, but this was not the result of aggression. The people here had been killed by their co-workers and likely their friends.

She couldn't tell what they had been running from and that put a disquieting tightness in her chest. Whatever caused this should have left its mark on the station, and while it was damaged, the cause was far from clear.

The unknown was not a realm in which Miranda liked to travel. Part of her wanted to pull up stakes and break for the ship immediately, but she wrangled it back into line. They had a job to do, she had a job to do, and she was going to see it through.

Octavian returned to his position ahead of Stacks without a second's hesitation. Whatever had happened here wasn't shaking him the way it had the rest of his team. He moved, and the others followed in a tight line.

Stacks motioned up the ruined corridor toward several transparent walls. Ice crunched underfoot as they stepped over shattered remains caught in a chemical flash freeze instead of the stampede.

A thinning white fog revealed well-furnished laboratory setups through the clear walls. The haze stood at waist height and obscured everything lower.

Miranda peered inside, searching for more corpses, and after a moment, she noticed several hands and fingers still frozen to their workstations. One body stood at a hatch along the back wall as if it were frozen in the process of trying to get someone's attention.

"The data we're looking for should be there," Stacks said, nodding to the back of the room.

"We're going to need a new entrance," Octavian sent and pointed his rifle barrel up the hall.

Falling into formation, the group followed Octavian's lead. Ahead, a frozen arm stretched through the sealed entrance to the lab. The door was ruptured from the inside, allowing a tall, emaciated man to reach through. Unlike everyone else on the station, he appeared sickly, as if he were dying before he froze. Yet, somehow, he still had the strength to tear his way to imminent freedom.

The cracked tarp of skin stretched over his visible skeleton was nearly transparent, but it was the razor-sharp metallic spikes that drew everyone's attention.

Miranda stared at the corpse for a moment, trying her best to picture what had happened. The man had been tearing through the six-inch metal door and had somehow gotten stuck there. That by itself was unbelievable, but the metal erupting from inside him was beyond her ability to comprehend. Yet it held the frozen body firmly in place.

"Octavian's right. I'm not going to be able to run a bypass with that stuck in the door," Stacks said, inching himself away from the corpse's outstretched arm.

"Fine, we'll blast our way in," Miranda said without hesitation.

She didn't want to be near the spiked body any more than Stacks, but fought not to show it. Of course, she still had concerns about what the blast might do to the station, but at this point, she'd take the risk.

The suits were designed to operate in the Black, and helmsmen of the TaskMaster had pulled off Zero-G extractions before. It was reckless, but she was ready to be done with this station.

"Fine," Stacks said as the waver in his voice lessened. "But let's go through the wall farther back. I don't want to shake that thing loose."

Without another word, the group put a healthy distance between them and the newest cadaver. Octavian got to work setting the charges with calm, practiced hands. Miranda was always impressed with his ability to keep his cool. It was one of the reasons she'd picked him for this team. He seemed to be at home anywhere, no matter how unnerving the surroundings he found himself in.

She made a mental note to talk to him once they were clear of this place. She desperately wanted to know what had put so much ice water in his veins. If he had experiences like this one bottled up inside, she wanted to know how he coped with them. Learning his secret might come in handy when sleep inevitably recalled this nightmare.

"Charges placed. We should get clear," Octavian's text read on her display.

She led Stacks and Octavian to the nearest intersection and pressed herself against the wall. The others fell in behind her and waited for the signal. With a glance and a nod, she silently gave Octavian the order to detonate.

In an instant, fire, debris, and an ear-shattering roar rolled past them. After waiting until everything was settled and stable, Miranda gave the signal to move.

The blast ripped through the transparent wall, but not enough. Miranda would be able to squeeze through unimpeded, but Stacks and Octavian would have issues. Time burned as they worked loose chunks of heavy crystal out of the wall by hand. Little by little, they managed to chip away enough of the wall for all of them fit through the gap, though not comfortably.

Miranda could feel the cold even before her visor warned of the drastic change. The blast had warmed the room some, but not enough to make it sustainable long term, even in the suits.

The cold fog still hung three feet from the ground, but the blast had shattered nearly all the lab equipment. The corpse in the door lost its lower legs but remained largely intact.

Miranda stared at it for a moment. She couldn't be sure, but she thought that the spikes had been longer and thicker before the blast. Perhaps it had broken them off, but with the fog, it was impossible to tell.

"I'm going for the drives," Stacks said, snapping Miranda out of her macabre stare.

Octavian led the way to the door, respectfully stepping around the broken piles that were once people.

Stacks disconnected the control module from his hip and went to work. His large frame looked odd hunched over such a small device, and the black plates of his suit only exaggerated the image. Miranda and Octavian turned to face the room, sweeping it slowly.

"Any minute now, Stacks," Miranda said, trying not to look at the torn blast door and the bloody handprints frozen onto it.

Stacks focused on the darkened cables behind the circular wall panel. Each line ran to a different system, and only two of the half-dozen were lit. His gut told him to keep the one on his right powered, so he ran the other line through his module and connected it to the dark line in the center.

The door groaned and shifted against the cold, then released with an audible pop.

"Got it," Stacks cheered as the door slowly eased open. "Got to love Sabien tech."

"Maybe I would if they didn't steal it from slavers," Miranda huffed.

Stacks shot her a look of mock offense, and let the conversation drop.

When there was enough of a gap, Octavian slipped past Stacks and into the room beyond. It was small and empty aside from banks and banks of silent machinery. Three protective panels sat on the floor, leaving the data ports exposed and barren.

"You've got to be joking!" Stacks shouted to no one in particular as he ran his fingers along the ports where the data drives should have been.

"What's wrong?" Miranda asked, hazarding a glance into the room.

"The drives have been removed," Octavian replied, "Somebody already took them."

Miranda spun to look into the room.

"Well, check around, maybe–"

"They're not here, Faridan," Stacks snapped. "We did all this for nothing."

Miranda forced herself to take a breath. If that was true, this mission was a failure. Failure meant the contract wouldn't be fulfilled. Going back empty-handed wasn't acceptable. If she had gotten Stone incapacitated and potentially lost Claude for nothing, she and Bertrand were going to have it out. Especially if he had more info and hadn't shared it.

That was bad enough, but she was looking forward to cracking those drives, so she could find out what the hell had happened on the station and what the team might have been exposed to.

"We need to get moving. We can't do any more here," Octavian informed them.

His words made sense, but Miranda wasn't ready yet. She was still trying to wind herself down when something fell and shattered behind her.

She spun immediately, searching for the body at the door and finding it missing. The gentle drift of fog masked any trace of where it had gone, but the crawling sensation on the back of her neck told her it was closer than she wanted it to be.

"Where did it go?" asked Stacks, readying his rifle and filing out of the hatch behind Octavian.

A slow scraping sound chilled Miranda to her core. The fog made it impossible to see the floor she was standing on, and when she tried to augment her visor, it only made things worse.

"Try thermals," Octavian offered, ushering Stacks to the hole they had created.

Miranda's vision shimmered into a kaleidoscope of blues and purples. The aftereffects of movement swirled, but the source of the disturbance remained invisible.

"Get him out of here," Miranda shouted over her shoulder, then opened fire just ahead of the motion trail.

The deep, rapid beat of rifle fire was met with the tinging and popping of her rounds ricocheting off the floor. She couldn't tell if she was hitting the damned thing, but the trail of movement didn't stop.

"Stacks is clear," Octavian reported pulling up beside her.

Miranda nodded and fell back to the exit. She turned and reached out to Stacks when she heard Octavian open fire. The face of the large man outside went slack, and then her world lit on fire.

Molten agony flowed into her at the base of her skull and coursed along every nerve in her body. Instinctively, her muscles tensed against the violent invasion. Miranda twitched on the point of an unseen silver spike like a puppet on a strung-up with razor-wire.

As she neared the far edge of her pain threshold, she felt her jaw clench so hard her molars cracked and broke apart, gagging her as the bits of bone and enamel danced their way down her throat.

The burn took her over until there was nothing left, but a scream that she wasn't even sure was hers.

Then, as suddenly as her new world of pain had begun, it ended.

Part II
Chrysalis

Chapter 5

THE NIGHTLY STORMS of Minerva Prime were something of a double-edged sword. They allowed for almost limitless power, which the citizens of that world and its government enjoyed. However, they also helped breed no end of nightmares in the minds of countless children, which Vision herself did not.

Unfortunately for her, the current nightmare was visited upon her guardian instead, and he dreamed loudly. She'd been privy to his dreams for the last few months, and they were anything but pleasant.

Vision sat up in her modest bed and threw off the weight and warmth of her covers. She wouldn't be able to sleep with Claude's nightmares reaching their odd, abstract crescendo. She'd tried before and only wound up screaming due to the confusing jumble of emotions and concepts she didn't understand.

Reluctantly, she touched her bare feet to the cold polymer flooring and winced. It wasn't quite painful, but compared to the warmth of her bed, the nip of the cool tiles seemed a little vicious.

Thunder rolled outside so loudly the walls seemed ready to crumble under its assault. Invisible, intangible bursts of ions from the storm sent disorienting static through Vision halo. The blinking crown of lights and metal never worked properly in this kind of weather, but autumn on Minerva Prime always made it worse.

The device made it possible for a little blind girl to perceive the world, though in a dull, colorless way. By emitting minute energy pulses that Vision didn't quite understand, it mapped her environment in real-time, piping that information directly into her brain.

It was a practical, if artless, solution to a problem she assumed she'd been born with. Direct neural mapping allowed her to "see" things that a pair of normal working eyes would not, but it didn't come without a list of downsides.

Light was the biggest hurdle. She simply couldn't perceive it, nor anything made from it. Without patching herself in directly, any holographic technology was invisible to her. It also blinded her to any image that wasn't sufficiently textured, forcing her to miss out on the printed pictures that were so popular at the City's Archive.

Vision forgave all of the device's faults for one important reason. Woven into its odd backward tiara design were a series of psionic inhibitors. Shortly after escaping that disintegrating nightmare, she lost the ability to control her natural psionic powers. Zhara said that her capabilities were increasing and that would come with certain drawbacks. All Vision really knew was that her abilities felt like they to want to split her head open.

The thoughts of everyone around her had a way of tearing into her mind. On the bad days, when people around her were particularly emotional, it could even cause her to black out. The inhibitors helped keep most invasive thoughts out of her head, or at least they used to. These days more seemed to leak through, and it was getting worse.

With a sigh, she stood up and made her way out of the small, spartanly furnished room. It was a short trip to the kitchen. In fact, going anywhere in the tiny apartment never seemed to take more than ten steps. There were barely four rooms in the entire space if you included the bathroom, which she found irritatingly spacious compared to hers.

She had been gifted the only bedroom immediately after moving in. Claude had taken to the ratty, peeling sofa in the main living area. He'd half lied, saying he preferred it over the bedroom because it put him directly between her and anyone that might break into the apartment. Truthfully, he just didn't feel all that comfortable sleeping in a bed with a child or forcing her to sleep on the couch.

He was a decent man most of the time, especially to her. Claude treated her with respect and compassion, but then again, he did owe her. She had saved his life by dragging him to an escape pod after his attack six years ago, and she never let him forget it.

Regardless, she knew he would always do what he could to protect her, though that often led to restrictions she'd rather not have. Mostly, that meant leaving her out of the business part of his life. She protested as often as she could, but it rarely worked and never on the interesting cases.

He tended to forget that she could read minds, or at least he ignored that fact when it made him uncomfortable. She found it either cute or annoying, depending on the context, but she knew how it made him feel. Being forced to cope with something that was so obviously uncommon would be a challenge for anyone. Luckily, he wasn't the only person looking out for her.

Over a year ago, they had stumbled across Zhara. She was too pretty and too smart for Claude, but chance had favored him for a second time. They'd bumped into each other at the Archive, and the two adults had hit it off rather well. She was a bio-mechanical engineer working on prosthetics at a major corporation, and clearly out of Claude's league. Vision was as surprised as anyone when they started actually dating, and she was even more surprised when Zhara offered to build a device that could help her navigate on her own.

It was almost too good to be true, and Claude was sure it was. It took a few months of work by both ladies in his life, but they'd been able to put most of his skepticism to rest. That only left his own doubt to contend with, and he was on his own with that problem.

Zhara was good to have around when they'd first gotten together. Now she was more than just Claude's girlfriend. To Vision, she had become a confidant and an ally. As Vision grew up, she discovered that she valued having Zhara around more and more. She'd never tell Claude, but there were often some conversations she just felt more comfortable having with another girl.

The kitchen was designed to appeal to anyone with a taste for Homeworld aesthetics. Old polymer cabinets had been stained and scarred to appear like wood, and the floors were etched in repeating patterns to seem like the tiles displayed in the Reclamation Archive.

Minerva City was filled with architecture and interior designs inspired by tiny pieces of a long forgotten planet. As Vision understood it, the same was true for much of the Beita Systems. More than anyone, Vision knew the desire to reclaim a lost past. She, too, longed for things that she had no memory of, like her family and her childhood. Without them, she was left adrift with only Claude as an anchor.

In that way, she was very much like everyone else. Sure, they had what she didn't, well most of them did, but there was still an emptiness. It was a little piece of common ground, and while she often acted like it wasn't a big deal, to her it was one of the few things that made her feel even remotely like a normal person.

Everyone carried with them a vague communal concept of a place where the human race was born. According to the histories, a species called the Zephiar had ripped humanity away from their own world and used them as a labor force. However, there was no solid information on where that planet was or what it was like. All they had were the randoms artifacts that had been harvested along with them, and even those were difficult to find.

As a species, humans had been robbed of a proper origin, and like her, they were desperately searching for it. Vision's own past had been her obsession for years, and Claude had helped her as best he could, but after six years of searching, she was beginning to lose hope.

"Water," she whispered after placing a narrow glass into the replication block. A cool stream of water flowed into the cup, stopping an inch and a half from the top.

The odd technology made Vision smile. It always did. She knew the device combined the oxygen and hydrogen molecules on command to produce the water she asked for. How the water came out so cold or stopped where it needed to, she did not know. Nor did she care.

No one really cared about the technology they used so long as it functioned properly, least of all this particular eleven-year-old. Vision was just coming out of her childish curiosity phase and believed she was finally getting a handle on the universe and how it worked. Claude was always sure to tell her how wrong she was about that, but usually, she ignored him.

In the end, she just wanted what everyone else seemed to have in abundance. She wanted some control over her life, and she needed to find a way to convince Claude to give it to her. Growing up seemed to be the best way, but she had no idea what that really meant.

Thankfully, the living space was carpeted, and Vision's tension eased immediately as her toes sank into the shaggy warmth. It wasn't the best carpet, but it was vastly better than the cold, remorseless tiles. She rounded the tired-looking old sofa and scanned the even more tired-looking man resting on it.

He was grunting and tensing in the throes of his persistent nightmare. The sensors inside Vision's halo picked up the faint lines of silver flowing under his skin. She was no doctor, but thanks to Zhara's ingenuity, she could tell that the creature he carried coated his nervous system. His "passenger," as he called it, had been forced upon him, but Claude didn't seem to be much worse off for it. In fact, it made him stronger.

Vision actually found herself a little jealous that it had come to Claude and not her, but when she really let herself think about it, she had enough to deal with. People already found her blackened eyes off-putting. If she had streams of silver on her arms and hands as well, they'd likely try to throw her into the Old City with the other monsters.

Vision carefully placed the water on the living room table and sat down between it and the sofa. She did her best to block out the steady bombardment of Claude's frenetic nightmare. Instead, she focused on the rest of the room. She could hear the slight hum of their ancient holo-projector and tapped a series of touch-sensitive lights on her halo.

She'd memorized the syncing codes of most devices so she could interface with them and not be entirely ignorant of the information others got just by glancing at the shimmering displays.

Claude had evidently fallen asleep scanning the Beita Systems' database for civilians lost in the war. He'd been attempting to match Vision's genetic profile, but that had failed again. It wasn't surprising, but the disappointment of it still stung.

The civilian casualty database was one of the few things that the Beita Systems and the Sabien Imperium had worked on together after the truce. The idea was to give people the chance to find out what happened to their loved ones amidst the chaos, and it served as a memorial to the fallen.

The Sabiens had drawn the line at allowing military casualties to be posted, or at least that was the story told in the Beita Systems. So, it left a rather large hole in the numbers for Vision's people to get lost in.

According to how the Beita Systems told the story, the Sabiens wanted to block even more but decided against it due to public backlash.

Vision doubted that. In fact, she doubted most anything from official channels that let the Beita Systems seem virtuous. She'd been living on Minerva Prime for years now, and she hadn't witnessed the shining, civilized bastion of a free society that the Beita Systems professed to be. She had seen squalor, pain, sacrifice, and suffering. Sure, there were people living well, but there were always people living well. The number of them versus those struggling to keep their families fed, clothed, and safe from the storms was tiny. And that was just on a single world. How it played out across all the systems was unimaginable to her.

Claude had told her that Minerva City never quite recovered from the Derelict plague. It forced the city to wall off a substantial portion of the industrial zone. Apparently, most of the decent-paying work had been sealed outside, and the new facilities built to replace them had massive advancements in automation. It left a great many people without homes and without work to pay for new ones; meanwhile, those with the most simply added height to their buildings, so they didn't have to see the people they felt were beneath them.

It was pure luck that Claude could scratch out a living falling back on his service in the military. He'd founded *Silver Sights Detective Agency* about a year after settling on the planet, and he'd been working sporadically ever since. Vision had come up with the name, and it fit well for what she thought the agency was going to be. She believed she would be solving cases with him, but to her disappointment, that had only happened a couple of times.

She wanted more than to just sit in a tiny apartment and be safe. She wanted to live the kind of life that people daydreamed about. She wanted to visit resort worlds and be catered to. She wanted the pulse-quickening excitement of not knowing whether the next second would bring glory or ruin. She wanted a life, but it didn't look like she would get one anytime soon.

Claude stirred behind her. She read him as the haze of sleep faded from his consciousness, and he realized where he was. She kept her presence low in his mind, but she loved that every time he woke up, she was the first thing he thought about.

When his eyes opened, the thought, *"Where's Vision?"* spilled across his mind like an all-consuming lava flow.

She couldn't help but smile. For all her complaints and gripes, Vision knew she was lucky. It was a fact that often got lost in the barrage of daily joys and frustrations, but she did honestly try not to forget it.

"What are you doing up, V?" Claude asked with a croak.

"You dream loudly," Vision said, passing the glass of water to him.

Claude took it without hesitation and gulped half of it down instantly.

"Sorry," he said, rubbing his left temple.

"The station again?" Vision asked.

She knew the dream as well as he did. She'd seen it a few dozen times since her halo started leaking, but she hadn't let Claude know.

"Yeah, it's strange, though. I keep getting other things too," Claude said. "There was a woman and a dying man. Some kind of glass blade came down between them, then just pain."

Claude slammed the rest of the water down his throat and passed the glass back to Vision.

"I brought it in here. You have to take it back," she said with a matter-of-fact tone.

"Do I now?" Claude nudged.

Vision ignored both the glass and the obvious bait.

"You think it might be your passenger's dream instead of yours?" Vision asked, genuinely curious.

She had never been able to pick up on distinct imagery during the latter parts of his dreams. To her, everything had just been a disorienting jumble of colors, shapes, and sounds that read like a kaleidoscope of pure confusion.

Claude shook his head instinctively. "If it is, I don't want to think about what it could mean."

He grunted as he rose from the couch and made his way around it.

"If it is, it might be trying to communicate," Vision offered.

"Then it picked the wrong guy," Claude said as he entered the kitchen.

"Tell me about it," Vision said under her breath.

"I heard that."

Vision scanned the list of faces streaming through her halo with a small amount of sadness. There were thousands, maybe even a million names, and that was with the age, time, and genetic filters in place. They had all been swallowed up by circumstances they couldn't control, like grain through a sieve. Sadly, Vision knew that her family hadn't dropped through some anonymous hole in the war. They had likely died on Firaxis Station.

There was no record of that place anywhere. Neither faction acknowledged its existence nor their connections to it. Claude had been very clear about everything he knew, but that didn't really help her at all. Firaxis was a black hole in all official records. Its gravity had crushed and consumed everyone who died there, never to be spoken of again.

"Still nothing?" Vision asked, feeling her shoulders slump in spite of herself.

Claude refilled his glass and leaned against the counter, ignoring both the chill in the air and the defeated tone in Vision's voice.

He'd known that finding her people would likely be impossible, and he had told her as much. Regardless, he had promised he would do everything he could to locate them. He meant it, and in the six years since, he'd devoted nearly every free moment to keeping his word.

"Nothing yet, but we have to be getting close," he responded after a careful moment.

Vision sighed heavily. She was tired of coming up empty and was nearly ready to give up on ever finding anything, even if Claude was doing the bulk of the work.

Every time a lead died, a part of her did as well. Besides, it wasn't like her life with Claude was terrible. She knew that he wouldn't leave her on the street if her people were never found, and there was a high likelihood that he wouldn't hand her over even if they were.

Still, something bothered her about the situation. A single question rolled through her mind, like the storm clouds outside. If her family wanted her back, shouldn't they be looking for her? She was reaching into the mirrored, black waters of the unknowable, but no one seemed to be reaching back.

"Why don't we just admit that we're wasting our time?" she said, disconnecting from the holographic network.

The streaming letters, numbers, and faces blinked and faded into nothingness as her environmental scanners pulled her surroundings back into prominence. The colorless echo world that she trusted expanded once again, mapping the apartment until she could perceive Claude finishing his water a second time.

Sitting with her back to him, she watched as he stretched and rubbed the last vestiges of his slumber from the corners of his eyes. He had been pushing himself hard to keep them afloat, but they were slipping into poverty, regardless.

Jobs were coming slowly, at least the completely legal ones, anyway. Vector Forge, one of the local gangs, had sent word time after time that they could use a former scout's expertise, but Claude insisted that the law was one of the few lines he wouldn't cross. He had his own valid reasons, but Vision couldn't help but feel that the day was fast approaching when 'no trespassing' wouldn't be the only rule they'd have to bend.

"Get some sleep, V," Claude said, returning to the sofa.

He eased into the soft cushions beside her and placed his hand on her shoulder. With a tiny shake, somehow, he managed to crack through the thin layer of despair growing around her.

"We have to be up early," he concluded, as he let himself slouch.

"I'm already up," Vision protested, fighting back an oncoming yawn.

"Look, I'm not trying to get distracted by you snoring on the skyway again. We almost died last time," Claude needled.

Vision huffed and let him have this debate. She would lose it anyway, not to Claude, but to her own traitorous body. She was tired, they both knew it, but she also knew Claude needed someone to talk to.

His dream had shaken him more than he let on. The last part of it was still haunting him, and he was concerned that perhaps he wasn't as in control as he thought he was.

The walking corpse that attacked him was never very far from his mind. It managed to drift to the surface every time his passenger became an obvious part of his life. It always led Claude to question how much of him was him?

Vision often picked up on his apprehension about it, but she'd never tried to broach the subject. It seemed like a deeply personal issue that only he could come to grips with. So, she waited for him to mention it. Thus far, he hadn't.

"I don't snore," Vision countered weakly and pulled herself up onto the couch.

Claude laughed out loud. It was a rolling clatter of sound that always made a room brighter, even for a girl who had issues perceiving light.

"Oh yes, you do," he said once his laugh melted into a chuckle.

"Yeah, whatever," Vision said, shoving his shoulder and rising to her feet. "Just try to keep it down out here."

Claude watched her shuffle around the couch and toward the kitchen with growing concern. She'd been complaining about her inhibitors failing, but if she was picking up his dreams in her sleep, the problem was worse than she was letting on.

He'd set up the meeting at Zhara's office to see if anything could be done. As much as he trusted Zhara, he was still more protective of Vision. He tried to keep as much of a dividing line between them as possible, but neither of them seemed to share his concerns.

There were stories about what Beita Systems researchers had done to captured psionics to "understand them better." While he didn't think that Zhara would do anything to intentionally put Vision at risk, there was always the chance someone else would.

"You just stay out of my head, and you won't have to worry about it," Claude called after the exhausted child.

"We both know your head would be empty if I wasn't in it," she said and disappeared around the corner.

Claude watched for a moment longer, then sank back into the couch. He was tired as well, but he would try not to drift off in the hours left before sunrise. With a resigned sigh, he motioned toward the hologram streaming on the table and pulled it toward him. There was still work to be done.

Chapter 6

THE OLD CITY WAS ANYTHING but inviting. It had been quiet enough for the few weeks since Dr. Rickten Eugene had found his way past the perimeter, but it wouldn't stay that way for long.

All the information he could find on the Derelicts said that they stayed more towards the centralized industrial complexes, but he wasn't a fan of testing those theories. He did, however, need a truly private and secure place to hide his work. When he'd contacted the Beita Systems' government, he was hoping to use his data drives as a way to procure a position of relative comfort. It had not worked out that way. Instead, he had been betrayed. His tattered apartment had been ransacked and bugged, but he was not an idiot.

He knew that the people he was dealing with weren't to be trusted. Any deal of value meant that at least one of the parties involved would attempt a double-cross. Eugene had honestly been willing to make the trade but the Beitan government clearly was not. Having lived his whole life as a proud Sabien, he was only slightly surprised by the fact that the Beita Systems chose to act in such a way.

The storm raged outside of the defunct hotel he now called his home. The intensely ionized air was cratering the power levels. The effect nearly blacked out both his protective field generators and the few lights he dared to use. The only thing inside the broken living space that was exceeding expectations was his paranoia.

In the near darkness, he couldn't help but shiver. It was cold in the building, but the temperature wasn't what caused the uncontrollable shudders running through him. He had the unmistakable feeling that he wasn't alone, and nothing that could have gotten inside his perimeter would be friendly to him. He didn't put it past his would-be associates to track him to this dead place just to put a round in his skull and take the research. That was assuming it was them and not the Derelicts.

The Old City's natural residents were crafty bastards. Each of them was once human, and some still possessed a significant spark of intelligence. The problem was you couldn't tell which ones. They were all dangerous, but the thinking ones truly terrified Eugene most. Each was a ghostly mutation that skewed from just off human to monstrous beyond all imagining.

The Old City had been overrun by them almost a hundred years ago. Only a last-ditch effort salvaged the energy production of the city. A massive energy field had been erected, effectively cutting the contaminated area off from the rest of the city. The glowing purple boundary stood as a protective barrier for everyone on the right side of it and a death sentence for every person, building, and business unlucky enough to be on the wrong one. And die they did, all except the Derelicts.

Their mutation had apparently made them immune to the tendrils of time. Whatever had twisted them away from being human had also made them effectively eternal. Very few things could kill them, and all of those required such an expenditure of resources that trying to became untenable.

While Derelicts were a Beita Systems problem, he had always had a fascination for them. Finding out what made them the way they were almost tempted him to defect before he'd gotten wrapped up in the Talos project. He had discussed it more than a few times with his wife, but she refused. They were Sabiens, and the Derelict infection was unique to Minerva Prime as far as anyone knew. Aside from that, no one who entered the Dead Zone seeking a specimen to study had ever returned.

The familiar creak of weight on weakened flooring stabbed through Eugene's paranoid mind. The sounds of the building swaying slightly in the storm's violent winds were nearly constant at night, but he had adjusted to them for the most part. After three weeks of fearing for his life and making his presence as small as possible, he had developed the keen senses and instincts common in other prey animals.

He had heard Derelicts move through the building before. They tended to use their massive claws to move along the walls and ceilings. Testaments of their passing marked every story of the building, but what he'd just heard was not them.

In an instant, Eugene snapped into action. He didn't have much to defend himself against soldiers, but he did have his mind. He had learned the layout of the building during the sunlit hours of his time here in the hopes that if they came for him, he could escape. He didn't anticipate that they'd risk coming at night, but he had clearly underestimated the Beita Systems' disregard for their soldier's lives.

The low-level vibrations given off by even the smallest aerial vehicles could attract Derelicts from miles around. Eugene wished he knew why. He wished many things these days.

With significant effort, Eugene shifted a fallen beam to reveal a hole ripped in the floor. It was lined with the same thin mesh his perimeter fencing was. It was a rudimentary conductor, but it served as enough of a deterrent to keep all but the most determined from interfering with it too much. With little effort, he pried open the top his makeshift cage and placed each of the three data drives in the small space.

It was a wonder to him that these tiny recording devices had been worth so much to so many people. He loathed to trade them in the first place. They had caused untold death, and if they fell into the hands of idiots who didn't see the danger they posed, a great deal more would be added to the tally.

His research had cost him everything. It had built him, then in hours, it had destroyed him. He'd been forced to learn respect for that research, and in a moment of weakness, he had given in to his own desperation.

Attempting to barter the data drives away for a chance to build something new seemed massively stupid in retrospect. The Beita Systems were no better than the Crowns and, quite possibly, a good deal worse.

They wanted to put the Talos project into full production. They wanted to mass-produce thousands as a deterrent, or so they claimed. Sitting in front of the Echelon council's faceless holograms, he was horrified by the mechanical precision of their plans. He had assumed they would be interested in the supplementary side of the project, certainly, but the Talos primary was entirely too dangerous.

He thought that specimen was lost with Firaxis station, but the soulless shades at Echelon told him the nightmarish truth. It was alive, and they were tracking it as best they could. They'd even captured and studied it for a time, before he had come forward. That had ended in disaster, but they were undeterred. Now they wanted to see if they could make more.

With disgust, Eugene placed the final drive into the mesh box and resealed it. Keying in a short code on his data-pad, he watched as a purplish glow coursed through the mesh surrounding the drives.

Once more, he contemplated eradicating them altogether. The knowledge they contained was dangerous, but the creature was already out there somewhere. Eventually, it would grow into a nearly insurmountable threat, of that Eugene had no doubt. When the time came, his research would be needed. Destroying it would damn them all. Besides, *she* wouldn't want that.

Ignoring the fresh sting assaulting his eyes, Eugene dug his feet into the stale floor and pushed. His body screamed as he wedged it against the massive metal beam. He worked the fallen column into place and granted himself a moment to breathe. The faint glow of the energized mesh was blocked out, and once again, the room fell into relative darkness.

There was only one thing left for Eugene to do, and he prayed for the only thing he held sacred to give him the strength to do it.

"Help me, Lenore," he whispered as the tears finally streamed down his cheeks.

• • • •

The mission was supposed to be simple, or as simple as any mission in the Minervan Dead Zone could be. It was a standard grab-and-go. Sneak in, snatch up some lab rat, and bounce back to extraction. Most missions of the type were done under cover of night, but unlike the others, this one introduced the possibility of the team being swarmed by man-eating monsters.

Yuri knew the mission would be a challenge, but so far, things had been quiet. The troop transport had put them down on the forty-eighth floor, and they'd slowly made their way down until they reached the level marked on his heads-up display.

So far, so good.

Yuri split the team in an attempt to cut off any escape. While he headed the Alpha team, Bravo was led by the only person he felt he could trust with the half dozen lives the mission put at risk.

The team had been handpicked specifically because Yuri knew they could each handle themselves despite this task's unpredictability. Most missions he'd undertaken as a TaskMaster were, but the prospect of coming face to face with a horde of Derelicts put him on edge.

Horror stories about them had reached nearly every corner of the known universe, but he'd always taken comfort in knowing the monsters were sequestered in some far-off corner of a world he had no interest in visiting. A world they would never escape. Now he was in that far-off place with them, and the hardened soldier Yuri had become was giving way to the frightened child he'd been when those stories first burned themselves into his memory.

"The universe is a cruel and uncaring place. It enjoys nothing more than to make monsters of men," his mother used to tell him.

It was perhaps not the best lesson to impart to a six-year-old, but he hadn't forgotten it. In his experience, his mother was right.

No one knew exactly what had made the people of this city into those creatures, so he chalked it up to the nebulous and horrifying concept of a malicious universe. There was nothing he could do against such an insurmountable opponent, so he focused on putting his efforts where they were most useful.

Shoving the small child back into his cell, Yuri carried on with the mission.

The building's central stairwell was a massive spiral column that rose the entire height of the building and terminated in a broken, stained-glass skylight so large that an entire transport could easily fit through.

The center was a hollow gap that spoke to the hotel's better days. In that bygone era, it was traversed by hovering platforms that had long since died and been claimed by the river of indiscernible sludge oozing through the first floor.

The place had the unmistakable scent of decay that Yuri could smell even through his helmet. He'd order his team to seal themselves into

Zero-G rigs just in case whatever made the Derelicts was still active. He didn't really believe it was, but why take chances?

"Lil, we're approaching position. What's your status?" he said calmly.

With a motion, he brought the other two black-suited soldiers to a stop behind him.

"We're all good, stacked up at the west stairwell," the sweet, feminine voice of a trained killer said in his ear.

"On your go," she finished through the audible clicks and buzzes of ionic interference.

Yuri took a long, shaky breath, then forced his way into the corridor beyond. They had limited time to capitalize on the surprise, speed, and numbers they possessed. With a sharp slash through the air in front of him, Yuri led his men down the ruined corridor. The soldiers behind him fanned out to cover him from behind as they sped up the hall.

Lillith and her team moved in an identical formation, closing the distance with the same speed, silence and control. There was no room for the target to blow past them on either end of the corridor.

Ideally, he would be trapped. There was still one other avenue of escape, but it was unlikely a man desperate enough to hide in the Old City would take it. Just in case, they had covered that option as well, though not as heavily.

Yuri's helmet fed him an amplified stream of light coming from a room on the right side of the hall.

"Reel it in, Lil," he said into their open comms channel and slowed as they approached.

Lillith's team reached the door a few seconds later and pressed themselves against the wall. Lillith sidled the final few feet until she rested on the opposite side of the open door. She made a crescent motion with her right hand and watched as Yuri nodded. He began a silent countdown from five, and when he reached one, the teams exploded into action.

"On the ground now!" Yuri shouted through his suit's speakers and charged into the dilapidated room.

He swept the room's corners with his rifle and slid to the side, allowing his team in after him. In the hall, the members of Lillith's team fanned out around the door to cover them.

The room was empty. There were signs that the target had been there recently, but he'd bolted. The open window on the far side of the collapsed bed made it obvious which direction he'd gone, and with him went their chances of a clean catch.

Yuri slapped a half-eaten ration pack off the warped nightstand near him in frustration before slinging his rifle.

"Target is on the scaffold. Lock him down," Yuri called to the transport hovering in the night above.

The rest of his squad filed out of the room, but Yuri hesitated. He didn't like the situation.

Dr. Eugene had been living in squalor here for weeks. He'd had the time and resources to set up a rudimentary perimeter and minor fortifications, but rather than dig in when they came for him, which he had known they would do, he ran.

Nothing in the room screamed trap, nor did anything in the hotel at all. If Eugene didn't come here to hide and he didn't set up his defenses for a fight, why come out here at all? Why not just flee off-world?

Contraband smuggling was plentiful on Minerva Prime. The doctor was a smart guy, surely that would have occurred to him. Yuri was missing something, and he didn't have the time to figure it out.

"Copy that. Moving into position," the filtered voice of the transport pilot declared.

"Remember, we need him alive," Yuri added, and closed the channel.

He had the sneaking suspicion that he needed to remind his people of that, and not because they were likely to kill him, but because the target might just do that himself.

• • • •

Eugene struggled his way up the crumbling scaffolds. He couldn't tell whether it was the storm, the height, or the threat of being shot that had his hair standing on end, but he was sure it didn't matter.

There wasn't really anywhere to go, but since the scaffolding below had long since crumbled away, that left him only one direction to travel. Over time, he'd become used to dwindling options, but he hadn't learned to like them any better.

Eugene was a man who had lived for control and comfort, but those luxuries were long gone. Such indulgences had cost him the love of his life, and now nothing held any true meaning... almost nothing.

Thunder boomed as he climbed the building's tingling, rust-addled exoskeleton. There were at least twenty stories left to climb before he reached the roof, but in the high winds, it might as well have been a hundred. It seemed like an impossible task for a younger, more fit man, and he was nowhere close to being that. Living off low-quality food and whatever pharmaceuticals he could get through the black market had taken its toll on him.

He wasn't sure he wanted this to be easy, though. While half of him still wanted the life he'd had before, the other half knew he deserved to suffer. Hubris had caused his downfall, and his fear after the fact had cost countless lives.

There were at least a dozen places where his ego had led him to make decisions that ultimately wound up shattering his reality. Pain and discomfort were his penance, no matter how much the man he used to be railed against it.

For long years, he had contemplated ending it all, but he was weak. It was his defining trait. Weakness drove him. It controlled him, and it had cost him both his wife and his soul. Because he was weak, he had demanded that Lenore be allowed to work with him on Talos. Because he was weak, he made her his assistant on the project. Because he was weak, he couldn't admit to himself that she was gone, and because he was weak, he'd fled Firaxis, leaving everyone else to die.

The hardships he had endured since were his just punishment. They were everything he deserved for all the pain he had caused, and still, something in him tried to claw back a life for which he was no longer worthy.

Lenore would be ashamed of him.

"Doctor Eugene, stop!" a filtered voice called, freezing him in place.

Eugene looked down to see one of the black-armored breather suits he remembered from the last war vids. The tinted face shield and the cascading lightning of the storm barely allowed the lower half of the soldier's face to be seen and only sporadically. It wasn't enough to read the man, so Eugene defaulted to distrust.

His first thought was to respond, but he fought that urge. There was no point in talking. He already knew what his pursuers would say. The soldier would offer him some semblance of his old life in exchange for the knowledge he had promised them. Echelon might even follow through, but he would lose everything. Everyone would.

For all his fear of death, Eugene wasn't sure he could live anymore. If he gave them what they wanted, death was the outcome anyway, whether it came from a Beita Systems firearm or by more terrifying means. The only real difference was, he might avoid yet another colossal mistake if he embraced it now.

Overhead, the deafening roar of mid-altitude engines overpowered the booming of the storm. The brilliant blue of them blinded Eugene for a moment, forcing him to look down and away.

"You called us, Doctor," the suit in the window coerced. "Let us get you out of here."

Defeat wafted over Eugene. He was not going to escape this time. They would take him and force him to share his destructive knowledge. He would relive his torturous nightmare, again and again, only so his mistakes could be repeated on a grander, more devastating scale.

He didn't want to do it. Eugene didn't know if he could do it even if he had, but he wasn't ready to let go.

"You don't know what they want from me," Eugene said, feeling the floodgates of emotion open and the sea of his sorrow rush to escape.

"No, I don't," the man in the suit said calmly. "Why don't you come back down here, and you can tell me?"

Eugene shook his head slowly.

"Listen to me. Don't let them resurrect Talos. Don't let them follow my research," he pleaded.

"That's outside my mandate, Doctor," the man said, and Eugene thought he could hear actual concern filtering through his suit's speakers.

Eugene closed his eyes and took one last ragged breath. He wasn't ready, but he wasn't sure anyone ever was. He had been ruled by weakness. Now it was time for him to finally summon his strength.

"I'm sorry," he said, hearing the fear and desperation in his own voice. "I'm sorry for everything."

Then, he let go. There was a moment of freedom and release that shook him to his core. The burden of his failures had pinned him down for so long that he welcomed the momentary sensation of weightlessness. As if it had been waiting for him to find peace, the fingers of gravity coil around Rickten Eugene and rush him into the shadows to be with his beloved Lenore.

Yuri watched helplessly as the target he was supposed to capture fell into the dark and broken streets below. He tried to make the exchange with the scientist make sense in his head, but could not.

He still didn't feel like he saw the whole picture, but that wasn't unusual. While he was used to details being withheld, this felt different. He had been accustomed to death of all sorts, but he'd never been tasked by a target to stop the people that sent him, let alone as a last wish. It was disturbing, to say the least.

Violent winds ripped him out of his contemplation and carried with it loud, agitated howls. The sounds rose from the streets below, followed by a chorus of guttural hooting cries. They spurred Yuri into action immediately. Thousands of individual voices flooded in his direction as if issuing from one pained presence and not even the walls of the building could keep them out.

There was no way of knowing how far they were from the hotel, how fast they were traveling, or how many there were. The only thing Yuri could think to do was run, and that's exactly what he did.

He ducked back inside the window and cleared out of the room as quickly as he could. Once he reunited with his team in the hall, he quickly scanned the way they'd come and decided to follow Lillith's path instead.

"We have to move, now," Yuri said, shoving two of the soldiers ahead of him.

Lillith's team followed suit as she fell in step with him.

"What happened?" she asked.

"The transport must have attracted their attention," Yuri said, forcing himself to increase his speed.

"I meant with the target," Lillith clarified, keeping pace with his full sprint.

Yuri didn't answer. He would take full responsibility for failing the mission. He didn't see a reason to saddle anyone else with the burden of it. He was the unit commander, and he would protect them as best he could. To him, that was essential.

If they made it out alive, and if he didn't get excised from the TaskMasters for this, he would consider answering her question, but that would have to wait. At the moment, there was nothing more important than getting the hell out of the Dead Zone before its residents got their claws in them.

• • • •

Yuri stood still as stone. He had been summoned to the command deck before he'd managed to get his helmet secured on its mounting bracket, and now he was waiting to receive the dressing down he'd expected since losing his target.

The command deck was immense, with pale blue running lights edging all three of its levels. Mounted into its spherical walls were concentric crescents, each serving as floors for the different ship functions managed by the command crew.

On the elevated dais in the room's center stood Bertrand and a short, almost doll-like brunette in her early thirties. She'd been onboard for several weeks, but she wasn't one of them. On a ship like the TaskMaster II, any servant of Echelon was bound to stick out like yellow battle armor.

Rumors always swirled around the clandestine organization. The latest said something big had gone down at one of their black sites. Details were sketchy, of course; they always were for the rank and file. Still, whatever happened seemed to have even the soulless bureaucrats at Echelon spooked.

As gossip went, it was interesting, but Yuri didn't put much stock in the rumor mill. He relied on what he could actually see, and it was clear that both the Executor and her superiors were desperate.

Unfortunately, Bertrand had moved his personal conversation up into the literal heart of the sphere. So, all Yuri managed to hear was the heat of the exchange without any of its substance.

While he was curious about their discussion, Yuri knew that it was above his pay grade. Typically, that would have been enough for him to put it out of his mind, but this time, he couldn't. The scientist's expression and the words he'd found so vital to share beforehand were sticking with him in a way that he couldn't shake.

He wanted to know more. The words a person chose in their final moments carried weight, though that wasn't always easy to see. His experience in the war had taught him that much. Most wanted messages imparted to loved ones or simply to be remembered. Dr. Eugene had asked for something more.

It was likely something he was incapable of doing, but he wouldn't dismiss the request before he at least understood what it was about. With no specifics, Yuri didn't even know what the scientist was supposed to do for Echelon, but he felt compelled to find out.

The voices above him quieted, and Yuri turned his eyes back to the command dais. There would be time later to debate the weight a dead man's words should carry. For now, he had to focus on the verbal assault that was surely coming his way.

• • • •

Bertrand did his best to listen to the young woman's concerns if they could be called that. He kept getting distracted by the gulf of experience between them. Marta Rais was an Executor of Echelon but not a high-ranking one. She had been tasked with overseeing the reclamation of lost assets, and she was taking her job very seriously. For all the bravado she brought to bear, she obviously didn't know that, on occasion, plans needed adjusting.

"An example must be made," she seethed. "You cannot simply ignore another failure."

The word ricocheted off the inside of Bertrand's skull, wounding his calm. The retort shot out of him before he even realized it.

"Another?"

"Yes, another," Marta shot back. "If you don't consider the debacle on Firaxis to be a failure, then you and I have conflicting definitions of the term."

Bertrand drew himself up to his full height and straightened his uniform. Firaxis was a minefield of emotions. It was a mission that had been sprung on him with almost no information, and like the Diegon Minor raid before it, he had lost people because of it.

"Eugene wasn't carrying anything when he fell," Bertrand growled. "So, the mission hasn't failed. And as for Firaxis, I would steer well clear of that if I were you."

"Would you now?" Marta needled. "If you had done as you were ordered, there would be no need for me to be here, Commander."

Bertrand could feel his lip curl into a snarl, but held his tongue. Marta had no idea what she was talking about. He had seen the mission to completion, personally handing over a member of his own team to make sure that it was done.

He would never forgive himself for betraying and abandoning those who had served him well, but he had done it to preserve what he believed to be most important. Bertrand was not naïve. He knew very well that morality and ethics were often slaughtered and that their blood paved all roads to the greater good. He'd made that sacrifice, but he doubted that Marta had ever possessed those qualities to begin with.

"If you think my team is incompetent, then I suggest you suit up and go with them," Bertrand said, managing to keep most of the venom out of his voice.

The searing glare Marta shot at him was almost worth risking everything for, and he had done just that. The Beita Systems had held up their end of the bargain after the war and built him a new ship. They had kept his outfit on as a military liaison, and paid his people well. Echelon's pet could potentially destroy all that, though it seemed unlikely. There were still needs that he and his TaskMasters fulfilled and those in power knew it.

In fact, much of what he did now was similar to the jobs before war's end. The only major difference was that instead of taking missions against the Sabiens, the TaskMasters dealt with more sensitive internal matters. It was a trade-off Bertrand was willing to make, though not without reservations. Spying and capturing civilian targets wasn't something that sat well with him, but he did his duty.

"Fine," Marta declared after taking a moment to recover herself.

Bertrand had half expected her to back down but, then again, he wasn't surprised that she didn't. Every Executor was combat trained, so Marta was theoretically capable of working within a unit. The only concern he still had was whether she and Yuri would be able to work out who was actually in control.

"I will be more than happy to provide your people the perspective and drive they lack, Commander," she continued with a smirk.

"Don't forget, they are my people. They answer to me," Bertrand said, tapping the data-pad on his sleeve and lowering the command dais. The heavy mechanical arm that held them aloft groaned as it carried Bertrand and his "guest" to the deck.

"Don't forget that if we fail, there's more than a formal reprimand coming your way," Marta threatened.

The threat wasn't subtle, but Bertrand wasn't concerned about Echelon. He had the keys needed to unlock many of their secrets, and they knew it.

What the Executor meant was more terrifying than anything her masters could send his way. A promise had been made, and he knew that since Faridan was free again, she would stop at nothing to keep it.

Chapter 7

VISION HAD BEEN DRESSED and ready to leave for twenty minutes. Her being ready before Claude was to be expected, especially when they went to see Zhara. Still, he was pushing it.

"Come on. She already knows what a slob you are," Vision chided in the condescending, sing-song tone she reserved exclusively for him.

Claude cleared his throat and debated a snarky response. She was baiting him, and when she did, there was no point in feeding into it. More often than not, she was ready for any witty comeback before he could get it out. Few things were as frustrating, but as difficult as it was to not defend himself. He avoided playing into her hands almost half the time.

"When we go out there, we represent the business," he called from the full-sized bathroom.

In one last effort to make himself look decent, Claude desperately finger combed his hair into something that looked half-way presentable. He had long ago given up any type of utensil since the perpetual static in the air played dangerously with the alien metal coating his nervous system. He used an actual comb for the first week or so, but the static buildup almost knocked him out when he touched anything metallic.

Now, it only gave him the same slight energy boost he got from the unbelievably terrible drinks that Vision liked to force on him.

With one last look at himself, Claude exited the bathroom and pulled on his dark gray jacket. It fell on him like it always did, providing both the comfort and style he was appreciated.

The jacket's cut fit him well. Its design helped accentuate his broad shoulders and chest while tapering just a hair once it reached the waist. Add the four main pockets, two of which he used exclusively to tuck his hands into, and the jacket was perfect. Best of all, it hid his holster and sidearm completely.

"It's just a ratty, old jacket, Claude. Stop falling in love with it, and let's go," Vision said, tossing his security ring at him.

Claude caught the oblong bracelet and clamped it onto his wrist. With a thought, he powered down the lights and switched the windows from transparent to opaque.

"I thought I told you about reading my mind," Claude said, moving past her to the door.

The heavy metal panel split and slid open, allowing Vision to move into the stairwell. It was dark, but since the sensors on her halo didn't require light in the same way eyes did, she didn't notice.

Claude doubted she was even aware of any difference between the now dimly lit apartment and the near-black of the upper stairwell.

"I don't have to read your mind anymore. You do the same thing every time you put it on," Vision declared as she descended.

A familiar nervousness caught Claude as he watched her take the stairs two at a time. He remembered the difficulty she'd had with them when they'd first moved into the place, but since she'd gotten her halo, she needed his help less and less.

There had been no significant stairs on Firaxis as far as he could remember. It didn't seem strange at the time, but now that he thought back on it, he wasn't sure if any Sabien structures had them. It seemed like a small thing, but it was one of perhaps a thousand slight differences between them and the Beita Systems.

Still, she'd learned to adapt, as he was doing. There were a great many things that she had found impossible when they'd first arrived but had now come to master. It was irrefutable proof that she was getting older, and he wasn't quite sure what he could or should do about it. Her growing autonomy left Claude feeling a bit more listless than he liked.

He preferred clear parameters as opposed to tasks that provided more open-ended structures. Raising a child was a job that had anything but clear parameters. No two situations ever appeared to be the same and were often nearly impossible to navigate using previous strategies. Winging it was frequently the best way forward, even if it sat at odds with the way he liked to do things.

The stairwell emptied out into the faux wood-paneled office of the Silver Sights detective agency. It was designed to feel old, even though the furnishings had only been gifted to him a little over two years ago.

A client had been obsessed with old tomes about characters who had done the same kind of work Claude did, only on the Homeworld. The man droned on and on about the stories he'd helped translate, and while Claude preferred to keep meetings with clients short and sweet, he liked getting paid, so he let the man talk... and talk.

Vision was infatuated with the man and his stories, but Claude was unimpressed.

The man was rich, and thanks to Claude's ability to prove that his future wife was still someone else's current wife on Vectra II, he had remained that way. In gratitude, he refurnished Claude's entire office on top of paying the fee.

It was the best deal he'd gotten since falling into detective work, but he did have a few bones to pick with whoever this Sam Spade guy was about interior decorating.

"So, I was thinking," Vision began, "Since I'm not in any of the databases, we should stop going that route."

Claude frowned. She'd been moving in a hopeless direction lately. Like everyone, Vision got into moods, but she'd been giving herself over to despair more and more as the years and months stretched on.

He couldn't blame her. Coming up empty so many times had damaged his optimism as well, but unlike her, Claude didn't expect results to come quickly. He knew how the higher-ups liked to try and save face.

Even Claude wasn't in the database, and given the nature of his disappearance, that didn't surprise him. Since Vision's family was on a secret research facility, it made sense that they wouldn't be in there either. He simply had no other viable leads.

"I'm not ready to give up just yet. We're only seventy-eight percent of the way through. Something might still turn up," Claude said, trying to hide his own skepticism.

Vision cast a suspicious expression at him, and this time he could almost feel her rooting around in his skull.

"If a DNA match had turned up, we'd know by now," she argued. "And there's nothing left to go by. It's not like I have a name."

"Yes, you do," Claude protested with genuine offense.

"Vision's not a name," she growled at him. "It's just another reminder of all the things I don't have."

Claude stopped beside her and did his best to smooth her static-ravaged hair. The gloom around her was almost as tangible as the tiny sparks that forced him to jerk his hand away. The discharge wasn't uncommon, but Claude wasn't really sure where it was all coming from. Sure, she had been cooped up in the office for two weeks, but so had he for the most part. Every building was supposed to be equipped with static dampeners, theirs included. If it was busted, that would cause a significant problem the next time a major storm rolled through.

"Fine, I'll just rename you, Esther," Claude said, ignoring the electrical arc that jumped from beneath her halo to his withdrawn hand.

He held a straight face well. It had helped when Claude had to bluff his way into exclusive get-togethers, and on the rare occasions he'd had to gamble to earn someone's trust. Here, the stakes were much higher.

Vision just glowered at him.

"What? Esther's a 'real' name," Claude said, regarding her with a raised eyebrow.

"You call me that, and I'll make you forget where your hands are," Vision said with almost no inflection.

"You can't do that," Claude stated with less confidence than he meant to.

"I can do all kinds of things," she warned, but couldn't keep from smiling either.

Claude sighed in relief. Levity often chipped through whatever miasma was threatening to engulf her, and for a second, he'd gotten his friend back.

The last month or so was taking a toll on them. There hadn't been any work for a while, and the bills were catching up to their modest savings. As a result, Claude had limited their travel and their food to the essentials. It was a move that neither appreciated. Still, it had to be done, though perhaps there was some wiggle room, for morale's sake. Things were getting tight, but they weren't flat broke just yet.

Vision needed a distraction. Decent food and a trip to the Archive would likely lift her spirits, but a prohibitively sized stack of credits was required to make it past the mundane stuff. Claude couldn't afford the fancy showrooms where the truly rare discoveries were displayed, but she loved the ancient relics so much he doubted that would matter.

"Let's go. We're running late," Claude said as they moved to the front door.

Vision made room for Claude at the front entrance. He'd insisted that she should never leave the building ahead of him, much to her early protestations.

She'd even tried it once, only to be accosted by a tattered hobo attempting to shake loose a few spare credits. After that, she'd understood and even appreciated the rule.

Apparently, she still remembered that encounter, even though Claude was confiden she could handle herself should another homeless man get handsy.

He'd taken that event as an opportunity to teach her a few techniques that would prove useful if he wasn't there to save the day. He'd tried to do the same for Zhara, but she had politely declined and showed him her shock ring instead.

Aside from what he'd taught her, Vision had grown formidable in her own right, which was half the reason he'd reached out to Zhara. Things hadn't been easy between them lately. They'd had some magnificent fights about where and if their relationship was progressing. They were fights Claude wasn't prepared for, and when they came to a head, he was stunned by the cold, quiet and unnerving distance left in their wake.

Still, none of that mattered where Vision was concerned. If it meant putting himself in the middle of an awkward personal situation to get her the help she needed, then that was the path he was going to walk.

"Are we grabbing food?" Vision asked as they stepped out onto the street.

The orange blast of sunlight forced Claude to guard his eyes while they adjusted. The dust levels were, thankfully, the lowest they'd been in a week, but that wouldn't hold. Usually, he would insist that Vision wear a breather, but it wasn't necessary for this trip.

With the air mostly clear, the sun's rays could clearly be seen as they stretched across the narrow strip of open air between the canyon of three and five-story buildings. In the distance, the violet glow of the ever-present energy barrier cast its light for miles in all directions, rimming the clouds overhead with purple.

The city was nothing if not unique. In all of Claude's travels, he had never seen one that adhered so closely to the images in the Archives. Minerva Prime was the beating heart of the reclamation movement, and it was reflected in every facet of society here.

Oddly enough, they had ignored the ground-based vehicles that they had discovered in favor of the convenience of the hovering technology offered on every other world. Claude appreciated that. After all, what was the benefit of stepping back in time when it would negatively impact people's lives?

Claude appreciated the historical reverence that so many in the Beita Systems had, but he didn't really share it. He preferred to live in the moment, but the past seemed to always be there, just behind him. Like some monster waiting to devour him if he ever slowed down, the past haunted his every step and dream.

"It's quiet today," Vision said as much to herself as to Claude.

"I'm not surprised," he replied, motioning toward the black, boxy sedan with wind-chipped paint that rested on the segmented street in front of them.

There weren't many hover cars docked at ground level, but a rooftop charging pad was out of Claude's price range.

"What do you have a taste for?" Claude asked.

He motioned in a wide arch, and the sedan's cab folded back to reveal its front seats.

"Eilitonian," Vision said, biting her lip.

"Really? Don't you think it's too sweet and spicy for this early?"

"Nope. Eilitonian or I'm not eating," she declared.

Claude crossed in front of the car as Vision hopped into the passenger seat. She let the harness secure itself around her shoulder and waist before Claude slid into his.

"Okay, okay, you don't have to be so dramatic," he said, sinking into his seat and motioning the sedan closed again.

With a rush of air and a deep mechanical howl, the sedan lifted effortlessly from the street. Rising clouds of loose dust swirled into the air beneath the thrusters before flowing up around the car. With a guttural growl, the sedan erupted from the newborn dust cloud and sped into the distance.

Chapter 8

FROM THE BLACK, MINERVA Prime was an unremarkable bronze ball dotted with deep gray spirals. Visually, it largely indiscernible from any of the lifeless worlds in the outlying territories. Still, its resting place in the Ireniad system made it vastly more important to the Beita Systems. The bland-looking world was the primary exporter of energy cells to their entire society, and thus it was jealously guarded.

Having such a planet at Beita System's core was a stroke of pure luck. As a result, a full battle contingent was never more than sixteen standard hours away from being deployed. That was the primary reason it represented one of the few forbidden places for miscreants like those aboard the Modus Vivendi.

The sleek, blade-like form of the repurposed Sabien assault corvette masked her age with menace. The ship's long stretched nose and razor-edged port and starboard fins were obsolete in the modern era, though no less aggressive in appearance.

The Modus Vivendi was still a beautifully designed weapon, meant to evoke its function intuitively. Every inch of the vessel looked capable of carving deep and mortal wounds into any foe her captain and crew dictated. And now she was aimed squarely at one of the Beita System's beating hearts.

• • • •

Like most of the Modus Vivendi, the command deck was outdated by modern military standards, but there was still fight left in her. She wasn't smooth or rounded where interior design was concerned. That level of comfort and complacency was better suited for the more elite ships upon which Miranda Faridan had once served.

This was a ship that still had hard edges. The Vivendi was a weapon forged in blood and battle, as was her captain. She still showed her metal instead of having it wrapped in polymer in an attempt to please the eyes of outsiders. She was purpose-built, and anything that didn't serve her primary function had been cut away and discarded.

Miranda liked that the ship wasn't afraid to show her teeth. It was a trait they had in common, though for the Vivendi, it was innate. Miranda had learned not to mask her nature through hardship and suffering. As difficult a road as Miranda had to travel, she did not envy the ship's easier path.

Without suffering, Miranda wouldn't have seen the universe as it truly was. She once believed in the same universe as so many others. She had even fought for it, but such idealism had been stripped by more concrete notions like betrayal. It was one of many things humanity's nature had forced her to accept. As difficult and painful as those lessons were, she was grateful for every nightmare and scar that still marked her re-education.

The command deck was an open space with a cold, grated floor, and a massive holographic display of Minerva Prime hovering at its center. Much of the old Sabien furnished hardware had been stripped out over the ship's lifecycle, leaving a patchwork of different technologies acquired during hundreds of raids and assaults.

The captain's chair was one of the only things on the command deck that had been left untouched by that piecemeal approach. Miranda perched in the seat, ignoring the curious and occasionally challenging glances of the command crew.

To outside eyes, she was every bit as terrifying and unpredictable as the ravenous predatory raptors shredding the skies of the countless hostile worlds. Thin strands of silver under her dark skin strayed just a few centimeters from her hairline as if it too were afraid to attract her attention. The tension of the room was mirrored on Miranda's face as she stared at the shimmering image of their destination through sharp, narrowed eyes.

She had been hunting for the better part of two years, and now she could feel her pursuit drawing to its end. Everything that was happening around her fell away as she focused the whole of her attention on solving the one problem she truly cared about.

"We have the comms buoy, Captain," announced a monotone mechanical voice in her earpiece.

Miranda shifted in her seat but didn't rise. The plan was simple, and the first step was already underway. In a civilization as large as the Beita Systems, everything began and ended with communication. It touched every home and every person regardless of how powerless or how influential and the buoys made all of that possible.

There was an elegance to the plan. It was far less direct than she preferred, but that is what gave it a better chance of success than any of Miranda's past attempts. She was no hunter, but capturing her prey required those skills. Luckily, the man standing to her left possessed the patience she lacked.

The years had treated Octavian decently, even if the events they'd brought his way had not. Regardless, he possessed the same stalwart and distant persona that Miranda had always appreciated.

Together, they had been through a great deal. It was Octavian that broken her out of captivity on Keetal. She owed him for that, but Octavian didn't seem to see it that way. He was nothing if not loyal, in his own odd way. It was a quality in short supply on a ship full of pirates.

Miranda met Octavian's eyes and simply nodded.

His vocal problems weren't something that could be resolved medically, at least not in the unaffiliated territories. Instead, technology still gave voice to his thoughts, though the means remained inelegant. A part of Miranda was tempted to see to it that he received the implant he so richly deserved, but that was a pipe dream. He would never allow her to make such a gesture.

Pirates were a cruel lot, and she could only imagine the struggles he'd faced in the years before he'd found her again. New scars on his bare arms and neck attested to that time, but she wasn't without her own. It was only the creature inside that kept the distinct signature of pain from her own skin.

Once reunited, they'd cut a bloody swath through the Black, gathering both wealth and power, which they shared with those who served beneath them. It had been intoxicating to sail the stars taking whatever they desired, but neither had forgotten their true objective.

"Make sure we get looped in on every transmission," Miranda said as she shifted in her seat. "If anyone so much as whispers the word Echelon, I want to hear about it."

Octavian nodded and moved toward the exit with the same menacing and predatory grace she had come to admire.

Miranda returned her hungry gaze to the world before her. Somewhere on that rock, her prey rested, unaware that his time was drawing to a close.

In her mind, she felt the familiar flow of the parasite shivering with anticipation. It was as excited as she was to finally tear into the person responsible for ruining their life, or so she assumed.

The creature was odd. It was clearly alive, and while it seemed sentient, Miranda couldn't fully understand it. It's motives remained hidden from her, and that lack of clarity made her skin crawl.

Since she'd awoken in the quarantine pods of the TaskMaster, it had been with her. It was with her when she was delivered to the soulless monsters on Keetal to be cut apart and harvested. And when the torment of that ordeal threatened to unmake her, it had spared her from death. Yet in all the ways that mattered, it remained a stranger to her.

She'd been tortured. "People" who wanted what had been forced on her tore her apart, and each time, the parasite undid their efforts. The lack of control still boiled her blood, and she found herself seething. She shook the past out of her head and reoriented herself. The mission was all that mattered. She wanted revenge, but as Octavian so often reminded her, there were more people to satisfy than just herself.

The crew served under her because there was always a significant reward for them. This mission would be no different. Many wealthy and weak aristocrats called Minerva Prime their home. Personally, Miranda couldn't understand it. The most popular theory on board was that the soft-bellies wanted to feel like they were living dangerously.

It was as good a reason as any, but Miranda still couldn't grasp it. There were real dangers in the universe, perhaps more than anyone realized. Early in life she'd been thrust into conflict with them, she had been molded by them, and now she wanted only one thing before walking away from those dangers forever.

These people didn't have to deal with suffering. Their paths steered well clear of dismemberment, torture, poverty, or illness, yet they wanted to flirt with such things? Nothing about that idea made sense to Miranda. These creatures were the very definition of soft-bellies, suckling at the teat of a society that nurtured and protected them. If they only knew.

A wolf's smile curled her lips.

If living dangerously is what they desired, she would grant them their secret wish in abundance.

She'd promised her crew the chance to pillage the elites of the inner systems and all the wealth and infamy that came along with such an act. It was a bold proposition. Pirates did not sack the inner worlds. The Beita Systems would drop the hammer on them as hard as they could, assuming the message reached them.

That was the second benefit to hijacking the comms buoy. Apart from scanning for any missives from Miranda's personal target, she would also have access to all other communications in and out of Minerva City. That included distress calls. It was as solid a plan as she'd worked with in months, and she really did have to thank Octavian for it.

• • • •

Octavian watched through the safety shielding as the buoy was hauled into the cargo bay. The device was enormous, nearly filling more than half of the cavernous space. Its partially mirrored surface reflected the hexagon-paneled walls, grated floors, and the sealed room where he stood. Scoring marked from its dances in and out of the planet's atmosphere, giving the whole thing the look of a tiny world all its own.

Once the hangar doors thumped closed, Octavian waited with the techs for the room to pressurize and flood with a breathable atmosphere. They seemed on edge, but Octavian was not. He wasn't innately skilled with technology, at least technology not designed to kill or destroy, but he had learned to trust and oversee those who possessed knowledge he lacked.

It was one of the things that made him a decent second. He knew when to take the lead on a task and when to delegate for the best results. The part where others stumbled most often was in knowing which people could be trusted to see the job done properly. Octavian had taken the time to learn the crew, especially the heads of the disciplines essential in keeping the ship functional. The tech workshops were where he'd been forced to spend significant time lately, but due to circumstances outside of his control, they were still a bit of an unknown variable.

Beside him, Ashe fiddled with an earpiece. She looked uncomfortable with its feel, but that didn't seem to stop her from stealing glances at him when she thought he wasn't looking.

Octavian had given Ashe the earpiece as a means of communicating with the team. She was usually below the line of people that he'd bother dealing with officially, but the ship was missing a lead technician, and she was the obvious choice to fill the position.

He promised both her and himself that it had nothing to do with their occasional dalliances. Those encounters, while enjoyable, had been fleeting and constituted no real emotion from either party, so far as he could tell.

Her promotion remained unofficial since only the captain had final say, but he was confident Miranda would agree. She often approved of his assessments, and while she knew of the potential complications, Octavian felt sure they would not be a problem.

Even though he knew Ashe had the expertise required to do the job, he still had a few misgivings. He didn't trust many people aside from Miranda, but Ashe was a unique case. She'd been a crew member since before the takeover, and she'd elected to serve under the new regime. Her reasoning remained unknown, and that raised his suspicions. Her nebulous motivations were only compounded by the fact that she'd been a friend to one of the chief dissenters.

Those issues had put her on his radar in the first place. He conducted a thorough investigation, and when Ashe had come up clean, he allowed things to... progress.

Months had passed since then, and while she had done nothing to maintain his suspicions, Octavian didn't believe that time could wash away doubt. So, he kept an eye on her, ever ready for the inevitability of betrayal. So far, it hadn't come.

"So, we're blocking outgoing distress signals and monitoring high-level communications?" Ashe asked in the scratchy voice of someone barely awake.

He eyed her for a moment before nodding.

She could have almost passed for innocent with her large blue eyes and girlish features. Only the slash of vibrant blue hair braided down the center of her otherwise shaved head hinted that she wasn't. Like most of the crew and pirates in general, Ashe stood out. They all cultivated and ruthlessly protected an enhanced sense of individualism that people in both "civilized" societies often didn't feel the need to.

Each pirate was their own brand. Like most freelancers, they marketed themselves to potential crews on skill, determination, and dependability, but if all those categories came up even, an appealing persona could help tip the scales.

"Rumors say she talks to herself," Ashe said, choosing her words very carefully.

Octavian did not respond. It was his job to keep order on the ship and see to it that Miranda's commands were carried out. He knew for a fact that whispers persisted and that many of them were true, but until Miranda believed they should be addressed, he did nothing.

"Personally, I don't care. Chell't, I chat myself up pretty often, but it's got a lot of the crew concerned about her sanity," Ashe continued, biting back a grin when Octavian shifted his stance after hearing her curse.

She'd been trying her best to get a response out of him, any response. In the short time, they'd stood near each other, she had closed the distance between them considerably to gauge his reaction. Subtlety wasn't her strong suit, but a little Qutongan profanity had gotten the rise she wanted and confirmed a theory she had about the world he'd come from.

Octavian let his stance ease once more and chose to ignore Ashe's breach of decorum. Obviously, she was unfamiliar with the etiquette that was second nature to him. That wasn't something he could fault her for. Ashe was a pirate, from blood to bone. He was not, yet he served aboard a pirate ship. Allowances had to be made, no matter how uncomfortable the idea might make him.

"You can tell her that if she needs someone to talk to, I'd be happy to volunteer," Ashe said, and Octavian could tell she was serious.

He knew Ashe wasn't one to take hints, though Octavian's silence was a poor hint to give. Most of the crew had never received a message from him, nor would they be capable without the earpieces.

The lack of speech was difficult to overcome while he had served during the war, but it was harder still in the wild and unpredictable hellscape of piracy.

What he had managed to accomplish while being mute was impressive to Miranda, but it wasn't enough for him. Octavian thought that, as second, his disability held him back. The crew was unnerved by him, which was fine, but the fact that so many did not understand him was not.

With incremental upgrades, he had gone from speaking only through text on compatible devices to translating his thoughts into a computerized voice via specially made earpieces.

Ashe pulled the earpiece out and rubbed her aching ear. She inspected it for a moment, then frowned.

"Do you mind if I take this thing apart after we're done here?" she asked, then placed the earpiece back to hear Octavian's response.

"Why?" the mechanical voice said in its usual flat tone.

"I think I can figure out a way to make it so that the ship's broadcast system can do what this does," she responded with a sheepish grin.

Octavian was gripped by his usual suspicions but being able to make ship-wide announcements himself instead of roping in another crewman to do it was intriguing. He couldn't tell what angle she was playing with the offer, but he felt capable of avoiding any trap she could spring on him.

"Is that all you can do with it?" he asked with a raised eyebrow.

Ashe's grin widened, and this time it touched her eyes and colored her cheeks.

"I won't know until I get some alone time with it," she said, lowering her voice to a purr.

Octavian smirked and rolled the idea over in his head. He had other things on his agenda, but there might be a few worthwhile benefits at the minimal cost of an hour or two.

"We will talk more when your current task is complete," Octavian sent to her earpiece, clearly selecting the most neutral wording possible.

Chapter 9

THE CITY'S TRAFFIC flow finally began to resemble its daily rhythm by the time Claude's sedan reached the main skyway. Only a few dozen hover cars dotted the thoroughfare, which felt as strange as it did lucky. Normally just accessing the busy traffic lanes before they devolved into an infuriating mess of angry, ego-driven commuters and the deadly missiles they piloted.

After stopping for a late first meal, he and Vision began the long trek to their destination. Luckily, Minerva City had been designed in a spiral pattern instead of another, more traditional municipal layout. Swaths of the planet's natural rocky surface rested between the city's layers. The negative space made ground-based travel was a nightmare. Fortunately for most citizens, hover technology ruled supreme here, as it did most places.

Claude and Vision lived on the outermost edge of the spiral with their backs to the wall, almost literally. Their District, aptly named Violet, was forever stained by the purple hue of the energy field separating it from what off-worlders called the Dead Zone.

Violet had become home to many of the displaced citizens when the Old City fell. Over ninety years had passed since then, but the promised reintegration had yet to materialize. A new industrial district was spun up outside the city but, by the time it did, advances in automation had done what they always did. People were left to rot, and the corporations they used to work for were more than happy to allow it.

It was a sad, broken-down place full of sad, beaten-down people, but it still had its soul. Other districts weren't so lucky. Claude had chosen to live in Violet because it put him at ease somehow. They were largely ignored, and the building was cheap by Minerva Prime standards, but those were only part of his reasoning.

Having grown up in the dirt of an outlier farm, Claude had always been accustomed to struggle. His family made a decent living, but that money went back into the soil for the next harvest. As a child, he resented it, but over time he'd come to see it differently. Now he viewed it as a key component in the unique mix of events, people, and places that made him who he was. In the end, it was his desire to instill the importance of frugality, resourcefulness, and, above all, patience in Vision that tipped the scales.

None of those things seemed particularly important to him when he was a child, but he understood and respected those traits now. He had no doubt the same would be the case for Vision. He'd seen what happened to people when those attributes didn't take root, and he was unwilling to watch her erode in the same way others had.

Beside him, Vision had somehow managed to roll onto her side while still in her harness. She was doing the typical purring/snoring hybrid that always declared she was solidly asleep. Vision needed the rest. He'd listened to her toss and turn for the rest of the night, but, luckily, his nightmare hadn't grafted itself onto her as they sometimes did. A restless night was better than a torturous one, and unfortunately, Vision had suffered through more than she deserved.

She took it in stride, but the chaos her abilities caused her unnerved him, though Claude tried not to show it. When they had first settled here, she was in constant torment. Merciless swarms of thought forced their way through her mind. He wasn't quite sure what was going on with her then, but in time, her penchant for answering his thoughts, as opposed to his actual questions, clued him in.

Now he did everything he could to help her quiet her mind when the flare-ups got particularly bad, but in the end, there wasn't much that could be done.

Psionic resonance wasn't a thing that he understood in any practical way. Unfortunately, neither did most people in the Beita Systems. That lack of knowledge had cost lives during the war. Now that same ignorance led to a child's pain, and somehow, to Claude, that was even more unbearable.

Sunlight splashed across the car's right side, and the sedan's polarization adjusted accordingly. The Cascade district stretched out in front of Claude, shimmering in all its meticulously manufactured glamor. The climb in both the quality and elevation of the buildings was unmistakable. Clean, expensive vehicles flanked him on all sides, each costing more than two standard months of Claude's income.

He had visited the area on business several times, but it always made him feel insignificant. People had a way of not seeing, or at least not acknowledging him on the ground, and in the skies, it was worse.

Upper society people tended to let their cars do the driving, often with predictably terrible results. These glorified passenger drones lacked the snap decision-making and natural pathfinding abilities human beings possessed and usually managed to create chaos when the skyways were too crowded.

That was one of the reasons he'd agreed to meet with Zhara at her job instead of stopping by her new apartment. There were other more prominent reasons, of course, but he shoved them back into the corners of his mind where they could do less damage. With another glance at the sleeping girl beside him, Claude eased into his seat and turned on the broadcast system, making sure to keep the volume low.

"Aloo Minerva City," a crooning male voice said through hidden speakers. "Truce week. Don't you all love it?"

Claude groaned. He did appreciate the war being over, but the yearly celebration seemed a little tasteless. People had died the week and even the day before the truce was signed. An annual party wasn't the most respectful way to honor their sacrifice. It was fine for people to want to mark the ending of an era, but there had to be better ways.

"If you're anything like me, you're working out your plans for what kind of trouble you want to get into but be careful out there," the man on the radio continued. "PlanSec is on the prowl, and they're hungry this year. So, keep those speeds down and those credits close."

The voice went on, but Claude let his mind drift.

The sedan passed through the border from Cascade and over the dry, cracked, natural surface of the planet. The spacers were designed to give the storms room to pick up the charged particles needed to generate the power Minerva Prime was known for. They could have been used to build much-needed housing, but harvesting was the city's priority.

To Claude, it seemed like a waste of open space, but he wasn't a scientist, nor was he an urbanist. He liked to believe he was more practical than anyone in those positions. They didn't even seem to be aware that many citizens in his district were living in squalor. Putting buildings in those empty spaces could save lives and restore dignity to those in the sewer communes.

Vision stirred beside him and yawned herself back into consciousness.

"Is it Truce Week already?" she asked, stretching.

"I thought you were supposed to go back to sleep last night," Claude said, ignoring her question.

She raised her seat back into line with his own and rubbed the corners of her eyes.

A slight static pop triggered in the car, scrambling several non-essential systems. The speakers went silent for a second before slowly returning to their previous volumes. In the last few weeks, static interference had become a common occurrence when Vision fell asleep in the car.

She never seemed to notice the effect, but it always made Claude's silver passenger tingle in disquieting ways. It wasn't exactly painful, but it wasn't comfortable either. The feeling reminded him of endlessly colliding and merging ripples, like when rain fell on water. It was a distracting sensation, to say the least, but thankfully, it always passed quickly.

"I tried," she offered, adjusting her halo and yawning one last time.

"We're getting close," Claude said, succumbing to the contagious yawn Vision had given him.

"We'd be there already if you would just go to—" Vision began.

"Not another word," Claude said, taking his eyes off the sky and fixing Vision with a fiery glare.

Vision shrugged. "I'm just saying."

"And I'm telling you to stop," Claude said through his teeth. "I made the call. It's done."

With a heavy sigh, he twisted the steering yoke to the left, lowering the car from the inter-district lane.

Minerva Prime's skyway appeared complicated at first glance. Thousands of hovering vehicles with countless destinations all weaved their way through and around each other. They danced that way at all hours, but rarely did they collide. It was no less than a miracle of engineering and social programming.

The skyway was divided not only by inbound and outbound lanes that followed the ground-level streets' layout but also split into lanes via elevation. No hover vehicle was allowed to traverse above two thousand feet. Just below that existed the inter-district routes, which moved at speeds made impossible at any of the lower altitudes. Below that were the District lanes, and from there on down, traffic was divided by region, quarters, and finally by individual streets.

Claude was sure he'd kill himself trying to navigate the city when he'd first arrived, but the system was surprisingly easy to learn. Now he was as adept at it as those who were born on Minerva, maybe even more so.

The car slid into the corporate district of Fauldwin. More modern design elements marked the central district as the most upscale region of the city. Of course, it still shared some of the reclaimed aesthetics that existed everywhere in the Beita Systems, but the companies that called this place home were unafraid to embrace newer technologies as well.

Most skyscrapers were built to accommodate skyway traffic. Large holes were carved into their bodies at the regional, quarter, and street traffic heights to minimize congestion and confusion.

The Artemis Industries building was no different. Instead of the typical square or rectangular pass-throughs, whoever had designed the Artemis building intended to impress with a diamond cutout. And it was indeed impressive. Flying into it always gave Claude the sense of being inside a finely crafted jewel. Offices and labs were on display in each facet of the diamond, though those working within never seemed to notice the wide-eyed stares cast their way.

Upper and lower brackets were responsible for docking inbound and outbound hover cars. Each was comprised of a broad, flat platform with mechanical docking arms that gripped and stored the vehicles beneath the main walkway. Both brackets could hold more than twenty cars while allowing a massive open space for foot traffic to pass unimpeded.

The entire building shared a similar upscale, or as Claude saw it, pretentious air. It reminded him of how different the same world could be for different people. The rings of the spiraled city catered to the distinct realities of their inhabitants, and not all of them were ideal.

That was the allure, though. In the Beita Systems, you could be whatever you had the will to become, or at least that was the marketing line. In reality, many of the systems in place, though initially well-meaning, had grown twisted and distorted over time.

Like moving from district to district in Minerva City, changing your circumstances in the Beita Systems was almost impossible. But the fact that it was only "almost impossible" meant that if the stars aligned just right and you were in a position to capitalize, the promise wasn't a complete fabrication. Such open progress for individuals was one of the primary differences between them and the Sabiens. Here there was no Crown of Orchestration to dictate your place, just money and the opportunities it purchased.

Claude had lived in both dominant societies, and he didn't see much of a meaningful difference for the people on the ground. The Sabiens did provide for the most basic needs of its people, which was only mildly better than the Beita Systems. Sadly, that mild concern for the lives of every citizen came with a heavy reliance on an ancient and harsh caste system.

There were trade-offs to both social structures, but only in the details. The majority of people didn't see or care about such minute variations. Instead, they just kept their heads down and tried their best to hold on to the meager amount of prosperity they managed to attain. The only real upside for them was that the tiny variables between the two rival societies didn't seem worth killing each other over anymore.

Claude guided the sedan down to the lower bracket and allowed the docking arms to latch onto the chassis. The automated system only took a moment to slide the car out of the way and release the cab's in-flight locks. Vision exploded out of her harness like a pre-teen missile and bounced onto the walkway with boundless excitement. The display of raw youth made Claude immediately feel ancient and exhausted.

"Calm down, it's not like we haven't been here a dozen times," Claude groaned, stepping out of the open cab.

"But it's so nice here," she said, marveling at the busy platform.

Claude didn't respond. Instead, he took the time to scan the area, putting his years of training to use.

The bracket wasn't exactly crowded, but the people moving on it were compelled by the rapid, momentum typical of Fauldwin. Many of them were scientists or executives eager to return to work or enjoy a break somewhere else. Still, they were just ordinary people to Claude.

The majority of employees wandering towards the entrances seemed to have just woken up, making Claude feel as close to comfortable as he ever got in Fauldwin. Aside from a few curious glances in their direction, nothing seemed out of place.

He was used to stares and whispered comments due to the silver visible under his skin. Most often, people just moved on without issue, but on the rare occasions where he'd been confronted about it, he just told them it was a body modification he'd gotten during a wild vacation off-world.

With Vision, it was slightly more complex. Her halo was uniquely designed, but sensory units weren't entirely outside of common knowledge. Blindness wasn't a widespread deficiency, but people knew about it, and sensory units were often used to help to correct it. Typically, they were little more than a few connected patches worn on the brow, so the idea that hers was of a different construction usually didn't need a deeper explanation.

Luckily, Vision never really seemed to notice the strange looks, and Claude never drew her attention to them. There were too many things that threatened to steal her childhood away. If he could keep the judgments of strangers from being added to the list, he'd do so gladly. She deserved that much. Every child did.

Once he was satisfied that they were safe, Claude dipped back into the car to grab the small, wrapped package. It wasn't until he slipped back out again that he noticed the signature green and light brown of a Planetary Security cruiser on the bracket above.

It wasn't altogether uncommon to see PlanSec camped out at the Artemis building. They policed the entirety of the planet after all. Still, it seemed almost spiteful how well patrolled Fauldwin was given the blatant animosity the corporations had for PlanSec's officers.

Regardless, it made sense to for PlanSec coordinate with corporate security to better protect the district, and their reputations, but Claude viewed everything from a soldier's perspective. Those running the corporations on Minerva tended not to see it the same way. To them, it was more of an inconvenience, if not outright interference with their businesses.

They were clashing pillars of Minerva City's structure, but nothing could be done about it. PlanSec wasn't going to suddenly ignore Fauldwin, and the executives weren't going to accept the persistent distraction local law enforcement presented.

"Imagine if we lived here," Vision said pointedly.

Her words snapped Claude out of his thoughts and back to the task at hand.

The sedan sealed itself before the automated docking rig carried the car under the walkway and out of sight.

"You could. I'm sure they have plenty of spare cages for lab animals," Claude said flatly, reaching out toward her.

Vision took his hand and matched his pace, her shorter legs working to compensate for his longer strides. Without another word, the two made their way across the platform to the building's entrance.

Chapter 10

ZHARA'S OFFICE WAS as cozy a place as it could be, given the dozens of regulations limiting personal effects and decorations issued by people on the top floors. With its ten-foot ceiling, trendy furnishings, and transparent walls, it was much more opulent than she needed it to be.

Sunlight poured in and bounced off the white polymer floor, bathing the room in both light and warmth. The expansive city stretched for miles behind beyond the wall behind her desk, and if you knew just where to look, you could see a few inches of the large dome under which rested the Minervan Archive.

The view was spectacular, but Zhara's pride and joy was something much less grand and elegant. At the corner of her desk, in a resin mug with tiny holes punched out near its bottom, grew a single green stalk. She treasured the tiny living thing and had cast away a great many frustrations just watching it grow.

In fairness, it hadn't grown that much. The fact that it grew at all on an electrified rock like Minerva Prime was a miracle all its own. Zhara wasn't used to green things. Most of the worlds she'd visited had been barren aside from the manufactured settlements placed on them. Still, she'd always wondered about the more exotic biomes of the universe.

Hearing stories about the liquid crystal sea of Akinos and the wild carnivorous jungles of Eiliton had motivated her to expand her knowledge and further her education. In the end, she'd settled on the narrow field of biomechanics and was snapped up by Artemis Industries straight out of the academy.

Now she worked to counteract the adverse effects of unshielded streamline exposure when she wasn't being asked to consult on the projects of her fellow employees. It was slow-going work and only just inside her area of expertise, but it kept the days interesting.

If she was perfectly honest with herself, she preferred tinkering with the more mechanical side of things. Working with the biochemists on enzymes that could reverse the loss of bone rigidity was interesting, but it wasn't where she felt she was best suited.

Zhara liked working with her hands. It was something that she had learned about herself in her younger days, and even though she had traveled a long way from the mining colony where she was born, it was still a part of her.

Looping her shoulder-length black hair behind her ear, Zhara tore her attention away from the little miracle plant. In front of her was a report on the last measures they had taken to relieve subject B-37's symptoms. The enzyme cocktail she and her team had devised wasn't as successful as she would have preferred, though the man was no longer confined to his bed. She tried to take comfort in the fact that their theories were sound, but she had hoped to crack it this time.

"Got time to eat?" a familiar voice asked with a decidedly unfamiliar lack of confidence.

Zhara looked up and fixed her bright bluish-gray eyes on a man in his late thirties and then on the little girl peeking around him.

Without a second thought, she closed her report and smiled at them both.

"Depends on what you've got," she said, moving around the desk and motioning for Vision to come to her.

Claude released Vision's hand before she ripped his off in her hurry to get to Zhara.

"Vision wanted Eilitonian," Claude said, inching into the room and hovering near the door.

Zhara noticed his awkwardness but didn't address it. She felt similar, but she figured that was normal considering the way they'd left things.

"Zee, I was hoping we could visit your new place," Vision said, clinging onto the older woman's side. "I can't believe it came with a piano."

Zhara turned to Claude with a confused look on her face. He simply shrugged and gave a smile that said, "I tried to tell you."

Zhara walked Vision over to the fold-out loveseat near the door and sat down with her. She took a moment to look the girl over, paying particular attention to the device she wore.

It was a crown of lights, circuitry, and tiny disc like inhibitors housed inside a flexible latticework frame. Zhara had designed and built it based on what usable information she could find about old defense schematics used during the war. It functioned, but it wasn't something Zhara was proud of. There was just too little information to build something better. In the war, the Beita Systems had only designed things meant to keep Psionics out of the minds of their soldiers.

What Zhara had attempted to construct served the exact opposite function. She did her best to reverse engineer those older devices to keep Vision's abilities contained, but it was a miracle she'd managed as well as she had.

Upon inspection, Zhara found all of the individual inhibitors flashing nominally, as well as the short-range sensors. If there was an issue with the apparatus, it wasn't immediately apparent, which dashed another of Zhara's hopes.

"Tell me about the piano," She said, lifting her arm so Vision could rest against her.

"It's your piano," Vision said with a hint of suspicion in her voice.

"I know, but–" Zhara began before Vision interrupted.

"Oh, you want to know how bad the leakage is," Vision said, straightening herself back up.

Zhara nodded despite herself. She had dealt with the sightless before, but Vision was different. Aside from the sensors feeding her complete three-dimensional representations of her environment in real-time, she could also read minds. That ability made her brain operate differently than others with her condition.

In the early days, Zhara had determined that Vision simply wasn't wired for sight. Her optic nerve was deadened completely, and her occipital lobe had to be trained to receive signals instead of doing so naturally. The cause wasn't trauma-induced and didn't seem to be the product of any defect on record. Vision's brain was perfectly healthy, but like a plant that couldn't produce flowers, it simply couldn't produce sight. What it could produce was psionic energy, in abundance. Claude had theorized that she was altered by whatever had fried the research station where he'd found her. Zhara couldn't argue against that, though she didn't quite buy into it fully.

Every document Zhara could find said the Sabiens had produced Psionics through extensive experimentation. It was difficult to imagine such a thing being achieved by accident.

"Normally, I just get people's really strong thoughts, but if I push, I can get more," Vision said sheepishly.

Zhara furrowed her brow as she tried to make Vision's words fit her admittedly narrow perception. Often, she didn't completely understand when Vision talked about her abilities. Without a frame of reference for what "strong thoughts" meant, she was left to make assumptions, as uncomfortable as that made her.

"Can you try it now?" Zhara asked politely.

Vision allowed a sigh to escape her, then closed her eyes. Tension reddened her face as she forced more of herself through the intangible barrier of her inhibitors.

"There's a girl upstairs that hopes you like her report enough to add her to your team," Vision began in a strained voice. "And Claude wants to put your food on your desk, but he's scared to move."

Vision drew in a sharp breath and gave her head a slight shake. Her eyelids fluttered as she pulled herself back inside the inhibitors. "Sorry, I didn't mean to scare you."

Zhara fought to quiet her initial anxiety. The last thing she needed to do was let that take hold. Vision wasn't at fault for what was happening. Her mind worked the way it worked, and she needed the people close to her to be understanding, not fearful.

"Do you fight the inhibitors often?" Zhara asked, nodding for Claude to do as he wanted with the food he was still holding.

Still nervous, but doing his best to hide it, Claude crossed the room as quietly as he could, taking only a moment to meet Zhara's eyes.

"Only sometimes," Vision said sheepishly. "I try not to, but I just get curious, so..."

Zhara frowned at the dozens of scenarios racing through her head.

Vision's mind produced an energy similar to the bio-electricity all nerve cells used, only vastly amplified. All Psionics did, but not on the same level. With practice, they could all use it to sync with the brainwaves of others. Some could even manipulate them; a skill that, so far, Vision had not showcased.

Zhara had redesigned the inhibitors to feed off that charge, reinforcing a deadening field around the wearer. Vision was somehow overfilling that system and apparently shutting parts of it down at will.

Claude leaned on the desk and stroked his chin as he took in the girls' conversation. "Is it possible she could have outgrown the halo? I mean, if her abilities are like a muscle, maybe she's gotten too strong for the inhibitors," he suggested.

Zhara considered his take for a moment. No one outside of the government had been able to study the few Psionics captured during the war. After encountering Vision, Zhara had hunted down every piece of information she had the proper clearance for. It wasn't much, but there was nothing to indicate that Psionics could grow their powers through use. In theory, they might be able to sharpen their skill, but whether that could lead to an increase in overall power was questionable. If that were the case, holding any Psionic against their will would eventually lead to catastrophe.

"That doesn't seem possible," Zhara countered. "But, I don't know enough to rule it out completely."

When she'd built the device, Zhara had used the best inhibitors she could acquire. There were better models, but Artemis didn't make them and ordering items with such a limited purpose could raise questions.

"Maybe it's just broken," Vision snapped, tiring of the adults talking around her.

Zhara turned her attention back to Vision and took hold of her hands. "How long has it been giving you problems?"

She was considering it from the outside perspective. If the problem wasn't with the inhibitors, then they would just have to live with things as they were.

"She first mentioned it to me a little over two weeks ago," Claude interjected, sensing Vision's hesitation.

"And you're just bringing her in now?" Zhara said through her teeth.

"I didn't think it was a good time," Claude replied, wincing at how the words sounded.

"You could have stopped after the first three words," Zhara huffed before turning her attention back to Vision.

Claude took a deep breath and let it wash out all of the rebuttals swirling in his head. He wanted to defend his decision, to tell her that she wasn't answering his calls. He wanted to say that he wasn't ready to re-litigate their last argument. He could have said that Vision told him everything was fine, but none of that would make a difference. In the end, Claude knew he should have put his feelings aside and done what was required. Vision deserved that.

"So, V, tell me, exactly what's been going on," Zhara said, returning to an even, calming tone.

Vision sighed and let her posture slump a bit. She didn't want to put herself between Claude and Zhara. No one would benefit from that.

"Come on. I can't help if I don't know what you need me to do," Zhara prodded, positioning herself to face Vision head-on.

After a long quiet moment, Vision pressed her lips into a flat line, then straightened and resigned herself to answer.

"I just want to be able to keep people out again. I don't want to feel their emotions anymore," Vision said, glancing in Claude's direction guiltily.

Claude mouthed, "It's okay," back to her with a wink and a fragile smile.

"Sometimes it still works like normal, but other times...," Vision trailed off, trying to hide her face from Zhara's gaze.

Vision and Zhara had grown close in the last few months, but the adult's blowup made everything strange. Vision had not reached out to Zhara, though Claude would certainly have allowed it. She chose to hold herself back because she knew she would to try fixing things between them.

She read both of them often, but this situation was different. There were emotions involved that she couldn't begin to understand. If she tried to soothe the storm between Claude and Zhara, it could make things much worse.

Eventually, the moment would come when they realized she'd been picking up on their thoughts and feelings. So far, it hadn't happened, but Vision still dreaded it.

Adult relationships were beyond her understanding, and she really wished that she could block out the tempest of their raw, unrestrained emotions.

"The biggest problems I get are from Claude and now from you," Vision admitted, wincing as her words sank in.

Zhara's mind folded in the new information. Vision could feel her sampling and measuring it but avoiding any immediate reaction. It had to be difficult, which made her appreciate Zhara all the more. Vision feared the reaction, but as the milliseconds rolled by, she allowed herself to relax. Instead of reading the telltale heat of betrayal and anger, she found sympathy and a little bit of sadness stained with regret.

Zhara forced herself to smile and focused on the work ahead rather than the burdens Vision carried.

"Okay, I need to run a full system diagnostic, which means−"

"I'm going to have to take my halo off," Vision interrupted with a sigh.

"Are you sure about that?" Claude asked, rising from the desk and moving toward Vision protectively. "When that thing comes off, it's torture for her."

Vision touched Claude's arm and felt the contact cool his agitation.

Claude took a deep breath and did everything in his power to resign himself to Vision's choice. He wasn't quite sure what to expect when the device came off this time. It had been months since the last time, and he could still hear Vision's wailing as if she was still suffering from it.

"It's a halo," Vision declared, as though the name was common knowledge. "It's not just a *thing*, or an *inhibitor*, at least not to me."

"Okay, I'll need your halo, then," Zhara replied playfully, then stuck her tongue out at the girl.

The "halo" was designed to be a permanent fixture with a waterproof structure to allow for bathing and even swimming, should Vision find herself on a world where the latter was possible. Zhara had thought the design through and had crafted something that Claude had to admit was genuinely remarkable.

Given its fragile look, He had doubted it would function at all, but he'd obviously been wrong. While he was expecting something more solid, what Zhara had delivered was more akin to a web comprised of lightweight metals with dozens of lights and sensors interlaced within it.

Vision didn't seem to mind it, but Claude was still a little displeased with the look, though he hid it as well as he was able. With a deep frown and a deeper discomfort, Claude looked from Vision to Zhara. They seemed to be set on this course, so he put his reservations to the side and steeled himself for whatever was to come.

"Make it quick," he said in a low voice and kneeled in front of Vision.

"I'll do what I can," Zhara said, rising from her seat and moving to her desk to gather her tools.

Claude took both of Vision's delicate hands in his own calloused palms and massaged them with his thumbs. They seemed fragile and cold to him, but he ignored those thoughts and focused instead on the wavering black eyes painting a mural of concern and dread.

"If you don't want to do this..." Claude said, knowing she'd read the rest already.

Vision didn't say anything. She just closed her eyes and took several deep breaths. As Zhara moved back across the room, Claude felt Vision's hands tense in his own.

"I'm going to have to test all of the inhibitors separately. It's going to take a few minutes," Zhara said, trying to put it as gently as she could.

Vision nodded, but still said nothing. Silence wasn't something she embraced often, but when she did, it was usually because her thoughts were too fast and too numerous to capture with words.

Claude fired a glare at Zhara that wasn't so much a complaint as it was a plea, though he wasn't sure which way she'd take it. At the moment, he wasn't sure he cared so long as Zhara minimized the pain she was about to inflict.

Zhara did her best to avoid Claude's eyes, failed, then focused on pulling on her dampening gloves. She wasn't as comfortable with taking off the halo as she let on. The amount of energy the inhibitors could successfully abate was significant. Removing them could open the floodgates on a force she didn't fully understand.

Zhara assumed there would be a psionic pulse and did her best to prepare for it. She guessed that Claude, having been around Vision without the device before, had some idea of what was about to happen as well, but there was no telling how far Vision's powers had grown since then.

Vision, however, was about to face a problem that neither she nor Claude was equipped to aid her with. There was very little data on how Psionic's abilities worked, and more importantly, felt from the user's perspective. They were all sailing headlong into murky waters, and Zhara's shaking hands were the only ones on the helm. She hoped that what rested between them and their destination was a peaceful sea, but her gut screamed otherwise.

With her gaudy, insulated gloves secured, Zhara placed a hand on either side of Vision's halo and hesitated. The frame gave under the pressure of her fingers, then stiffened as the webbed design compressed. She felt nothing through the gloves, but the readout on her wrist told her that she'd be getting a moderate shock if she'd attempted this without them.

"Alright, this is it, V," Zhara said with a quiver in her voice.

"I'm ready," Vision said after a long, tense moment.

Zhara and Claude shared the first truly unified thought since the fight. It had only been weeks, but at that moment, it felt like years. Being on the same wavelength again felt good, but the circumstances did little to help her cherish the sensation.

Zhara eyed Claude with inquisitive and desperate eyes, and he nodded for her to continue.

With a slightly off-balance tug, the halo lifted from Vision's head and set her free.

The grayscale textures in Vision's mind disappeared, leaving only a screaming, expanding, and impenetrable darkness.

A wave of pressure crashed down on her as the halo she'd become so accustomed to abandoned her. She fought it, but every ounce of effort she put into trying to push the invisible weight off her doubled the sensation.

"It's too much," she heard herself say as she began to buckle under the strain.

In the deafening nothing around her, she began to hear voices, hundreds at a time. They crashed onto her mind like waves on some alien shore. The constant skull-cracking pressure gave way to an intense and continuous rhythm made not of sound but of thought.

She could make out nothing explicitly, but there, on the boundary between her mind and a sea of others, she began to perceive the "voices" and the variable levels of intent, urgency, and emotion they carried.

The power held at bay by the device tore free with the ferocity of a once caged beast. The invisible pulse nearly knocked Claude unconscious. Everything in the room that wasn't firmly secured to its spot shifted at least two inches as the ripple effect crashed into it. Only the loveseat, shelving, and desk were spared.

If Claude hadn't been dangling on the fraying strand of awareness, he would have been both impressed and terrified. He had been expecting something, but he'd thought Vision would catch the worst of it. Maybe he was right, but it didn't look that way. She sat still and rigid as a statue. The expression she wore transitioned from anguished to focused.

Her hands trembled in his, though. Tiny sparks that he felt but couldn't see, dug into his palms like needles. Claude did his best to ignore the pain and to focus on the lost little girl.

With a grunt, he said, "I'm here, Vision. Focus on me."

Vision's face twitched for a second before her pitch-black eyes shot open.

Claude's voice echoed across the surface of the waves. It was distorted and twisted, but for the first time since the darkness had overtaken her, she perceived actual words.

She wasn't exactly sure how to do what he'd told her, but the words came through the crashing waves like a physical object, and attached to them were two light and fragile strands. Vision reached out and seized on the ghostly tethers and followed them into the crashing waves.

With Claude's emotion and intent firmly in hand, she let the sea of thoughts wash over her. Again, she felt the pressure of all those minds, but this time she let them pass through her as she submerged, ignoring the echoing clatter of voices and emotions.

Vision had assumed being at the mercy of the waves would break her, but she was wrong. Like a fish in its native waters, Vision discovered that here, under the waves, she was agile, graceful, and resilient. She felt capable of navigating this boundless sea, but as strong as that feeling was, she wasn't sure if she could trust it.

Instead of releasing Claude's tethers and exploring these new depths, she used her grace and speed to power her way toward their source. She tightened her grip on Claude's intent until it cut into her. The slight discomfort melted away, birthing vivid hues. Vision perceived Claude as an intense, vibrant silver. His tethers glowed so intensely that she could feel their heat and understand their meaning.

The tethers she held to were representations his concern for her. The color of Claude's emotion cast away the darkness of the waters around her.

"I can see you," she said with absolute wonder in her voice.

"Good..." she both felt and heard him say in that order. "... stay with me."

The tethers glowed brighter but shifted color slightly. Now, instead of a searing white-hot silver, it had cooled to a slight blue as fear and concern were doused with relief.

As Claude's tension eased, so did Vision's. Her grip on his mind eased, and she began to better survey the thoughts surrounding her. Still drifting closer to what she thought was Claude's core, she noticed other streams of light and color. It was impossible to count them all. Each possessed their own set of emotions and intentions. All had fully developed minds and tethers that Vision could reach out and latch on to.

With the halo on, she could perceive the thoughts of others, but they were more like scents on the breeze. Without it, her world was entirely alien to the one that others knew. In this place, there were no boundaries, no limitations to what she could do.

Endless possibilities ran through her mind. She began wondering if she was just a passive observer in this place. Could she redirect these thought currents in new directions? Could she erase them or perhaps even edit them? Could she do more than that?

Without thinking, Vision reached out for a vibrant red line and grabbed onto it. The tooth-grinding reverberation of conflicting emotions and thoughts from both Claude and the other mind burned its way into her. She felt herself frying like an overloaded circuit until she forced herself to let go.

Clinging only to Claude's tether, she felt her essence return to normal, cooled by Claude's steady, comforting, rhythmic thoughts.

One at a time, she thought to herself, *Lesson learned*.

• • • •

The silver under Claude's skin bled to the surface, doing what it could to absorb the stream tiny shocks jumping from Vision's hands into his own. He could feel the immediate relief but also the growing vibration running through his entire body. He focused through his own ordeal and watched the little girl's face as it shifted and changed. He had no clue what was going on inside her head, but he hoped that being there with her did some good.

At the far end of the loveseat, Zhara worked swiftly while fighting off the dizzying effects of Vision's pulse. Claude could tell by her slight lean and occasional overcorrections that Zhara was recovering slower than he was.

The pulse was strong, but Claude couldn't tell if it was powerful enough to affect anything outside the office. If it had, there was no telling how the others in the building would react, but it was a safe bet they wouldn't be calm and rational.

"Zhara, how much longer?" he asked.

"I'm on the last one now," Zhara said, blinking and giving her head a slight shake.

Her voice was tight and sharp like it always was when she was plagued with stress headaches.

As she worked on the halo's last inhibitor disc, Claude found himself missing her. She had the corner of her lip firmly between her teeth and her eyebrow raised like she did when she found herself fully engaged in a task. He knew that for her, the rest of the world had fallen into the background. Being so close to her, Claude cursed himself for jeopardizing his chance with her, even if it had to be done.

Since their blowup, he hadn't allowed himself much time to think about her, fearing that he would buckle and give in. Now he wanted to do just that, but that would be reckless. Claude needed to stand his ground. What she'd proposed was dangerous, and he wasn't entirely sure she'd thought it through.

He had, and certain boundaries needed to be maintained for her own safety. There was nothing he wanted more than to take their relationship to the next level. It just wasn't safe. He and Vision weren't ordinary people. They came with the sort of baggage others didn't. Zhara knew that, but Claude didn't believe she understood what it meant, not entirely.

If he could get her to accept it, there wasn't any reason why they couldn't still be together. As far as he knew, that was still something they both wanted. He just didn't know if he could rectify the situation in a way that would make that outcome possible.

If he gave Zhara what she wanted, and if he was honest, what he wanted too, Claude would knowingly endanger her life even more than he already had. If he held the line, he risked letting her walk away entirely, and she would eventually. It was simply a matter of time. Either way, the next move was squarely in his shaking, terrified hands. Before he chose a path, Claude needed to find a middle ground, something that allowed them to progress and remain safe at the same time, as impossible a task as that seemed.

"Talk to her," Vision said in an almost ethereal tone.

Claude snapped his attention back to her, but she didn't seem to be any more present than she had been a moment ago. What was worse, Zhara acted like she hadn't heard Vision say anything.

"Did you hear what she said?" Claude asked.

"Who? Vision? She hasn't said anything since I removed the inhibi...halo," Zhara said with a curious and fleeting glance in his direction. She took an impossibly deep breath and moved closer to Vision. With trembling arms, she raised the halo over the girl's head and hesitated.

"Okay, when this goes on, the pulse will stop," she said with a noticeable slur in her words.

Claude nodded. Was the pulse ongoing? For him, things normalized shortly after the initial pulse, but Zhara's reaction said otherwise. When she'd looked at him, her eyes had been wide and her pupils swam instead of remaining fixed. It had to be a result of the pulse emanating from Vision, yet somehow Zhara had been able to work through it.

"We might lose consciousness for a while," she continued. "Be ready."

Claude was used to being assaulted by things he didn't understand, but he didn't expect so many to come from Zhara. He knew he had been talking to Vision, and she had been speaking to him. They were well within earshot, yet Zhara had only heard him. Now she was telling him that whatever had happened when Vision's halo had been removed was still in effect even though he couldn't feel it.

Something more had to be going on. He simply didn't understand it. Zhara wouldn't outright lie to him, not over something like this. Was it his passenger? Could it be affecting him, blocking the pulse's effects?

Claude shut down his wandering thoughts as Zhara began to gently slide the inhibitor back into place. Wild wisps of floating blonde hair were ensnared by the flexible, metallic cage as it lowered onto Vision's crown. What slammed into Claude felt unmistakably like a concussion grenade going off directly in front of him. His sight, hearing and balance all frayed at, once sending the room around him into a violent tilt. The world shifted and moved in slow motion seconds before he felt the dull impact of his head hitting the floor. Before unconsciousness claimed him fully, Claude saw Vision's wide eyes blink once again.

• • • •

Worry started to creep its way into Vision. The shock of being snapped back into Zhara's office from the ethereal world she'd been adrift in took some getting used to, but when she did, both Claude and Zhara weren't moving. She checked and found them both to be asleep, but no matter how hard she tried, she couldn't wake them.

Instead of panicking and bringing an outsider into the situation, she'd elected to wait. That strategy led to nearly half an hour with no changes. Now she considered throwing open the door to the panic she'd so successfully managed to shut out.

A groan issued from the man on the floor beside her, and Vision's heart lurched at the sound. The explosion of relief triggered a very nervous, very shaken laugh.

"Claude, are you okay?" she asked, curling her hands to her chest.

A part of her wanted to hug him, but she didn't know if she'd just make things worse.

"No," he said, struggling to sit up. "What about you?"

"You know me," Vision said nervously, steadying him to keep his arms from giving out. "Just wondering when you were going to stop being lazy and get us back home."

Claude groaned again and raised his eyebrow at the clear juxtaposition of her words and actions.

"What about Zhara?" he croaked while tousling Vision's hair.

He could see that she was still unconscious, but unlike him, she'd had the good sense to find a soft seat before her sudden nap.

"Same as you," Vision said, popping up to her feet and helping Claude to his.

She guided him to the loveseat, then ushered him down beside Zhara.

"There's been a lot of noise and yelling in the hall," Vision informed him.

Claude looked over at Zhara. She was beautiful when she slept, and he kept coming back to how much he'd missed being around her. It was distracting, and he needed to focus.

"We should probably get her out of here," Claude said, tearing his gaze away.

She seemed peaceful, but he wasn't willing to let the appearance fool him. Vision's psionic pulse had scrambled her brain in a way he didn't understand. He hoped it was just a very temporary, very harmless thing, but he had no way of knowing. In fact, the only person who might know was snoring lightly beside him.

"How? We didn't even sign in today," Vision inquired, gesturing toward the sleeping woman. "They're not going to let us just carry her out of here."

Claude massaged his forehead with his thumb and middle finger and sighed. A growing headache was gnawing at his brain, his girlfriend was unconscious, and Vision's anxious energy wasn't really helping. She was right to be scared, but that was only making his grasp on the scenario more tenuous. He needed distance to see the situation more clearly, so he closed his eyes and attempted to give himself just that.

The rest of the building was likely going through the same thing they were, only with less knowledge and preparation. The people out there were just waking up. They were terrified and confused. Security would be on high alert, and the building would likely be in lockdown soon, if it wasn't already.

He didn't foresee a scenario where he and Vision could safely carry a sleeping Zhara to his car without being detained, questioned, and, worst of all, documented. He was drawing a blank on a workable plan that called for anything besides hiding behind Zhara's desk and being very quiet.

"Why, in all the mysteries of the Homeworld, did I do that?" Zhara groaned beside him.

Claude let himself collapse against the back cushions of his seat, relief taking all the tension and rigidity out of his spine for a moment. Despite the developing situation outside the office, Claude chose to take time and enjoy the brief, much-needed luck that had floated their way.

"Zhara!" Vision exclaimed and fell on the lounging woman with a smothering hug.

Claude just smiled. Vision needed her own moment of catharsis and while there was a slight sting in her reaction to Zhara's return, he would survive.

"I think we might be in trouble," Vision said as Zhara fought to get herself upright.

"There's a panic in the building, apparently," Claude added with a shrug.

Zhara cleared her throat and tried to blink the lingering confusion away. She could hear a commotion coming from the corridor, but thankfully, she'd set the wall to opaque for privacy's sake. That, combined with the fact that all the office walls were nearly soundproof, blocked them from getting anything useful from the hall without stepping into it.

"Okay, I need to get you two out of here," she said, pushing herself up to her feet.

She seemed stable for all of three seconds before she collapsed back down to the loveseat.

"You won't be getting us anywhere in your condition," Claude said.

"I hate to say it, but Claude's right," Vision conceded.

She could feel Claude's ego puff up at the words and ignored the nearly half dozen haughty responses he was mulling over. Thankfully, he chose to keep them to himself.

"Fine, but we need to get our story straight at the very least," Zhara said, collapsing beside Claude.

· · · ·

Zhara had just gotten her legs under her when she, Claude, and Vision had left the office. By the time they made it down the corridor and into the lift, she was almost stable. When they reached the newly formed security checkpoint, only her thoughts remained unbalanced.

She had read about the effects of a psionic assault, but they were woefully understated. Merely reading the word disorienting on a holo-feed didn't do justice to the experience.

"Okay, two more, and we're up," Claude said softly.

Zhara was boxed in on all sides. She was flanked by the very concerned faces of Claude and Vision. To her rear, there was a line of other coworkers down the corridor. Every one of them as eager to leave the building as she was, though obviously for different reasons.

"Did we really have to leave the salad?" Vision complained for the fifth time.

"It'll be fine. It's just food," Claude said firmly.

"It's not just food," Vision said with a pout. "It's an Eilitonian Citric Salad with the works."

Zhara thought about chiming in, but it seemed like Claude had the issue handled. Instead, she focused on the two men in differing uniforms, studying each worker's identification.

The first guard was Tarence Wilks, a man she'd exchanged small talk with for the past seven years. She'd even shared a few cups of tea with him in the commissary on occasion. She knew him to be a decent person but a devoted security officer. She could possibly get him to clear their exit if it weren't for the other man.

He wore the tan and green street-level uniform of a Planetary Security officer, as well as the trademark scowl they carried. Zhara couldn't pick up much more about the man aside from his mop of oily brown hair and crooked nose.

"PlanSec?" Zhara mumbled in Claude's general direction.

"Great," he said in a low growl of a voice.

Vision narrowed her eyes as though she was staring through the men blocking their passage before she was racked with an intense shiver.

"It's Phalen," she said, grimacing as if the name tasted horrible.

Claude's hand found his forehead again as he did his best to massage the throbbing pain away.

"*The* Phalen?" Zhara managed to ask.

"Yeah," Vision said with a thick layer of disdain.

"What else did you get?" Claude asked.

"He thinks this whole mess is a waste of his time," Vision relayed, "and he's rating all the female employees on a would–"

"Okay," Claude said, interrupting her. "Forget you ever read that."

"Wish I could," she groaned, shaking the foreign thoughts from her head.

"Next!" Tarence said in an authoritative voice that boomed through the building's cavernous lobby.

The disinterested look on Phalen's round and sparsely bearded face dissolved immediately once he spotted Claude. A glint flashed in his eye and he straightened himself as if it would make him more threatening.

"Well, you're a long way from home, DiSilva," he stated venomously.

"Yeah, I was bringing lunch to my girlfriend," Claude replied in as neutral a voice as he could.

Zhara observed the unmasked animosity between the two men and wondered what it was about. For the most part, Claude kept his work life guarded, especially where clients were concerned. He'd mentioned Phalen in much the same way someone might mention a household pest. So, she treated him much the same way.

"Claude and his daughter brought me Eilitonian," she told Tarence, taking a light conversational tone.

Tarence looked up from his data-pad and flashed Zhara a generous smile. "My husband loves, Eilitonian."

"Then, he has great taste," Vision told the aging guard with a bright smile of her own.

Tarence almost did a double-take at the sight of Vision. His mind scrolled through the typical responses to her appearance. First was discomfort, then curiosity, and finally, uneasy acceptance.

"I like to think he does," Tarence said once he reached the end of his mental process.

"Did you ever get him to agree to that thing you were telling me about?" Zhara asked with faux innocence.

A wide grin stretched the older man's face as he said, "He wants final approval, but if I can find someone that fits the criteria..."

He let the words trail off, but Zhara understood. She was about to wish him luck before the PlanSec officer's leering caught her attention again. Phalen made almost as big a spectacle of eyeballing her from head to toe as he did of ignoring the little girl standing directly in front of him.

Claude clenched his fist and felt the silver flow in, reinforcing his knuckles for the punch he pictured himself throwing. "Something to say, Phalen?"

"Nah, just admiring the view," the PlanSec officer said as he dragged his eyes back to Claude. "And remembering."

Phalen had been a nuisance for the past two years, but since he was PlanSec, there was no good way to get him to back off. Claude first crossed paths with him while working a divorce case for the man's wife and things had only gotten worse since then. Luckily, the Ban'uta wasn't that great an officer, so he mostly got the patrols and assignments that others didn't want. That meant that unless Claude was particularly unlucky, he didn't have to deal with him.

Sensing the outcome of Claude and Phalen's muted confrontation, Vision retched in a loud, disgusting outburst that erased every ounce of tension from all four adults. Everyone within earshot reacted viscerally to the sound of impending vomit, with Phalen lurching backward in an attempt to save his shoes and pants from the expected splash.

Claude was by Vision's side instantly. He swept her hair back gently and did everything in his power to sell the act to anyone who cared to look.

"You okay?" he asked, loud enough for the Artemis guard to hear.

"I don't feel good," Vision said, playing up her role to the fullest.

Zhara stepped closer to Tarence and did her best to mask the guilt she felt for manipulating him.

"All this has really affected the little one," she began. "We need to get her out of here and see if that helps."

Zhara didn't really have to put on much of the famous Riggs charm, and she doubted it would have worked on Tarence, regardless. He was a good man, and she had the feeling that he wanted to trust her. He just needed a slight nudge.

After seven years of working diligently, keeping her head down, and being a personable coworker, she had found that most people she had any contact with either liked her outright or at least trusted her to do her job. She'd often told Claude that it was her ace in the hole. She'd even tried to get him to do the same, but that idea was as likely to stick as snow would be on molten stone.

After a long moment, Tarence nodded.

"Okay, Ms. Riggs, I've got you marked down. You can go ahead," he said, letting his eyes drop back down to Vision.

Zhara smiled and waved her thanks, then moved over to Claude and Vision.

"Hey guys, we're holding up the line," she let herself be heard saying.

Phalen fumed, but he said nothing. Instead, he marked several places on his own data-pad and angled it at the group in front of him.

"Hey DiSilva!" he shouted.

Claude reflexively spun toward Phalen, ready for anything the man could throw his way except an image capture. He could feel the silver flowing near the surface and knew it would appear on the stolen image.

"Thanks," Phalen said with a smile made entirely of spite.

Claude glowered at the low-rent PlanSec officer for another second, then elected to ignore him. Scooping Vision up in his arms, he did his best to calm the silver back to its normal posture inside him.

. . . .

"So, you're saying I'm the problem," Vision said with a pout.

She stood mere feet from the most beautiful thing she'd ever been in the presence of. While she couldn't tell that the piano was actually black, she could and did admire every inch of its handcrafted surface.

"That's not what I said at all," Zhara protested. "I'm telling you that the inhibitors are working as intended."

Claude watched as Vision reached out to the glossy black instrument but stopped herself just before she actually touched it. He hadn't seen her so apprehensive in a long time. Vision wasn't really known to have a light-touch, but he could see on her face that, for her, this was an almost religious experience.

He envied her a bit. She was at least reaching out for what she wanted. Claude was standing on broken glass, or at least that's how he felt.

The marbled, black floor tiles were anything but uncomfortable; however, he couldn't shake the feeling that he didn't have the right to be there. Claude's own apprehension stabbed and sliced deeper into him with each passing second.

"So how do we fix this?" he asked, forcing his own inner conflict into the periphery.

Zhara crossed from the open kitchen to the living space and eased herself onto the cloud-like white cushion beside him. She took a moment to enjoy a long sip of her purple smoothie before she attempted an answer.

"I'm not so sure this is actually a problem. The inhibitor readings say her activity has spiked significantly. It corresponds with what you told me earlier," she explained.

Zhara pulled up a hovering display of the information she gathered in the office. She sorted through it with deft movements and wide, fascinated eyes, but Claude didn't understand what she meant. How could the halo's leakage not be a problem?

If it was an issue, that would give him something to resolve. He was good at that sort of thing. When there was an objective to achieve, he did just that. Any obstacles he encountered were either destroyed, removed, or otherwise circumvented on his way to said goal. The vague statement Zhara had presented wasn't at all what he was hoping for.

"I think we're just looking at growth," Zhara concluded with another slow sip of her drink.

"So, I just have to live with it?" Vision said, still regarding the piano as she circled it for what had to be the tenth time.

She was like a talon fish closing in on her prey. She wanted so badly to make contact, but she was also afraid that it might break if she did. The instrument seemed sturdy according to the scanners, but she couldn't shake her own misgivings.

She'd never seen something so large, intricate, and so lovingly designed based on Homeworld records. Scanners told her it was constructed from the same versatile polymer that made up nearly everything, but it was painstakingly crafted to mimic the tiny textured lines of wood.

Ordinarily, Vision's scanners worked on a wide three-hundred-and-sixty degree band to map her full environment, but she'd narrowed her field to study the piano in granular detail. The information streaming directly into her brain made her almost forget the frightening ideas the adults were discussing.

Once more, she reached out toward the instrument's exposed keys. Her nimble fingers creeping to within centimeters of them before she pulled back again.

"Go ahead. You can play some," Zhara said with a casual motion toward the piano.

Vision spun around so fast that the intensely detailed feed from her halo was dizzying. Her near swoon forced her onto grab the piano's frame for stability.

Claude smiled, then lowered his head. When he'd taken Vision on as his long-term client, he hadn't expected to like her so much. Nothing in his history made him think that time around a child would be anything more than a burden, but that turned out to not be the case.

Often, she was a challenge, but most of the time, she was a joy to be around. Moments like this reminded him that no matter how capable she was or uncannily wise she could be at times, Vision was still a little girl experiencing much of the universe for the first time.

"Are you sure?" Vision asked once she'd readjusted her halo.

Her face was contorted in a smile so broad that it looked like it might be painful.

"Sure. You can't play any worse than I do," Zhara said, sharing in the child's explosive joy.

Without hesitation, Vision slid onto the bench and attacked the keys with relentless fervor.

Claude and Zhara both winced, then burst into laughter at the auditory chaos attacking their ears.

"You might live to regret that," Claude said when his laughter died down.

"I think I already do," Zhara said without fear of Vision hearing. "I should show you the view."

Claude quirked an eyebrow at the lovely scientist, but said nothing. He was confident she didn't mean what he pictured, but silence was often a better option than putting his foot in his mouth. It certainly tasted better.

Zhara narrowed her eyes at him.

"From the balcony," she said and motioned to the transparent wall that faced out over the city."

Without another word, she stood and moved across the living space and into the open air. Claude followed, stopping only to squeeze Vision's shoulder.

The would-be musician gave him another incandescent smile and turned her attention back to the noisemaker in front of her.

"I've told you before that I don't know much about Psionics," Zhara began. "We could try to find stronger inhibitors, but that would take time and attract attention. Neither of us wants that.

"Besides, even if I could get my hands on newer hardware, who knows if it would work? Psionic energy is finicky despite it being nearly identical to the normal bio-electrical impulses our muscles use. Vision just produces so much of it that it can alter her brainwave patterns."

"That's not very reassuring," Claude replied, looking down to the ornately manicured courtyard below.

Zhara followed his gaze to a couple moving briskly between the high-rise buildings. "Then focus on what we do know. She's a child, and children are always changing," she stated, and hoped she was right.

Claude took a moment to drink in the skyline of Minerva City. It was losing the light rapidly, leaving only a dark stain overhead where the sky had been.

The weakening sun cast the last burnt orange light of day sidelong across the buildings before him. It would have been a beautiful sight if the telltale strikes of lightning weren't already visible on the horizon's edge. Even then, the view wasn't half bad.

"So, you think she's just growing up?" Claude asked, hoping for a simple yes.

Zhara sighed and turned to lean back on the balcony railing, her glass still held gently by her slender, undecorated fingers. She looked like an oasis in the long desert of Claude's own creation, and he wanted nothing more than to sweep the last few weeks away.

He almost did, but it was hardly the time to talk about what he wanted. That conversation would happen, and if he had his way, they would have it before it was too late.

"I definitely think that's part of it," Zhara said, letting herself really look at him for the first time since he'd appeared in her office.

He was older than she was and much more worn down by the worlds he'd visited, but there was a spark of energy in his eyes that still burned rather brightly.

Zhara wasn't really sure why or how she had become so smitten with him. Usually, she danced on the intellectual floors of the dating scene, but somehow, Claude's simple, rustic nature had made an impact. In the end, she supposed he reminded her of home. He was a worker at the end of the day. Like the people of her home colony, Claude made his own tomorrows with labor, planning, and the willingness, if not zeal, to get his hands dirty with tasks that others would seek to delegate. The more she thought about it, the more it was likely she had been attracted to him initially because she missed that simpler life.

"And the other part?" Claude prompted.

Zhara gave her head a tiny shake and threw him a lidded smile that made Claude move up the timetable on that overdue conversation.

"I can't even begin to guess. As far as I've seen, there are no mentions of children with psionic potential, and I have seen quite a few stolen Sabien documents," Zhara finally continued.

With another sip of her drink and an offer of it to Claude, which he denied, she went on.

"There's no metric by which to judge what growing up means to for a Psionic. There's no way of knowing where her abilities are supposed to be at this age.

"I can't even tell where she'll to end up. As it stands, she has, at most, another year before the inhibitor is just a gaudy headdress," she concluded with a large gulp to finish her drink.

Claude exhaled a breath he didn't know he'd been holding. Zhara's words were disappointing but rational, and he found himself rubbing his forehead as he processed them. His record with the unknown wasn't ideal. If it was all the same, he'd just as soon avoid run-ins with it all together, but that wasn't going to be an option here. As discomforting as this news was for him, he could only imagine what it would be like for Vision.

She was under the impression that things were going to get back to normal. Unfortunately, that was a long wait for a ship that wasn't coming, if Zhara was right.

"So, what do we tell her?" Claude asked, hazarding a glance back at Vision.

"Honestly, I'd start with the truth and see how it goes," Zhara said.

The truth had many impressive powers, but granting reassurance was rarely one of them. Obviously, it was the right course, but it would cause more pain and confusion in the short term. Vision would appreciate having open access to knowledge over having the information hidden from her... eventually. But how long would it be between then and now?

"Okay. I'll tell her on the ride home," Claude said, tearing his eyes away from the raucous concert going on inside the apartment.

"Are you heading back tonight?" Zhara asked tentatively.

Again, Claude's rogue eyebrow betrayed him.

"I mean, that car of yours isn't exactly new, and the storms can really do a number on the older models," Zhara said, allowing an almost predatory smirk to curl her lips.

"She's a tough one," Claude said, electing to play the situation out.

"Still," Zhara purred as she eased herself closer to him, "I imagine she could probably use a little downtime."

Claude smiled as he watched Zhara's eyes trail from his own down to his lips.

"Now that you mention it, why take the risk?" Claude said and leaned in to complete the kiss.

Chapter 11

SINCE LEAVING SABIEN hands, the Modus Vivendi had survived a great deal, but the night storms of Minerva Prime proved too much for her. Ions ruthlessly bombarded her atmospheric shielding, tearing through it and forcing her to touch down on the planet's broken surface or risk being forced into it more violently.

The ship had taken refuge amidst a series of carved canyons, and there she stayed. The lights of Minerva City glowed dimly in the distance but too far away for the purposes of the captain and crew. That had been hours ago, and while the crew was at work repairing the damage, the Minervan dust crept in on their captain along with both boredom and anticipation.

Miranda sat at the foot of the loading dock's gangplank watching the dusty soil of Minerva Prime drift over her boots. She'd been on better worlds and a few that were worse. Her preference was for planets with lush green vegetation and an abundance of cool, clear water. This rock had none of those things, at least not naturally.

The tech team was busy carving through thousands of planetary transmissions. That took time, as did deciphering which ones would be of interest to their captain. In the meantime, Miranda had been left with two hours of downtime and counting. The deep, unsettling quiet of the ship, mixed with the lack of engine vibrations, left Miranda with an unfamiliar need to put her feet on the ground and listen to the wind.

She was a child of the Black, born in the cold void instead of on a stable world. That weightless expanse was more of a home to her than any planet could ever be. In fact, the defense platform where she'd come screaming into this universe was only two streamline transitions away from where she now sat. Still, here she was, breathing in the warm air of a planet she cared nothing for.

Since her earliest days, it seemed she was destined to serve the Beita Systems as both her parents, her uncle, two aunts, and grandmother had. Being a soldier had been a point of pride for her, but Firaxis had wasted all that. She'd served with distinction and gave the Beita Systems her all, only to be betrayed, mutilated, and now hunted by them.

Returning from Firaxis, she had expected and even understood the lengthy quarantine she and her team had been subjected to. She even cooperated, but when they had been released, and she had not everything changed.

Initially, the other members of her team visited her, but after a week in isolation, only Octavian maintained a steady schedule.

She didn't know what had happened to her, but she did know that something slumbered under her skin. It was apparent to anyone who cared to look at her. The web of silver that pulsed and flowed through her nervous system presented a stark contrast beneath her brown skin.

She expected others to be interested in her and in removing the organism. What she didn't expect was that Echelon would treat her as a disposable container. They had done just that, only to find out she was not so easily discarded.

Miranda clenched her fists and watched as the silver flowed up to coat them. It shimmered in the weak light of the loading dock in a way that was oddly calming to her.

Often it did this when she thought back on the events between her last official mission and her rescue. The silver seemed to whisper to her, though she knew that it must have been her imagination. The creature was alive, but it did not speak. It was just a low-level parasite, one the Sabiens had somehow weaponized, and yet, in the quietest moments, she could almost convince herself that she heard it.

"It won't be long now," she said to the rippling mass coating her hands. "Just have to wait."

The intel was good. Her contact wouldn't dare betray her. He knew full well what she was capable of. Risking his life to send her into the core systems, hoping that she would die, was a flawed calculation for anyone with even an ounce of intelligence.

Miranda had slipped the noose more than a dozen times. If this mission went sideways, she would undoubtedly do so again. Death wasn't ready to take her yet. Honestly, she was starting to believe she would have to choose death's frozen touch to ever feel it. It would never be forced upon her.

She had watched as masked "monsters" flayed her open for science. She had been unable to do anything but scream in world-rending pain as her body knit itself back together with the aid of the thing living within her.

Once again, her fists clenched, only this time several hardened spikes erupted around her digits. They gleamed like the polished fangs of some ancient predator. Miranda caught her own sneering face in their imperfect reflection and found herself admiring how fearsome she appeared.

She was a new thing now, and when she found the man who had sold her to Echelon, she was going to show him all the horrors a new thing could visit upon an old one. The mere thought of being face to face with the villain of her story was almost intoxicating.

Sacrifices had been made to get her even this close. Miranda had deigned to lower herself to the point of consorting with and even leading pirates, but she never saw herself as one of them. They were base creatures that served a purpose, and they would never be anything more than that.

They lived for their own bloodlust and enrichment, and while she saw to it that those desires were fed, she never relished in them. Unlike those who now served under her, the guiding star she pursued was vengeance.

When she escaped the well-worn hell of the Echelon labs, she had only one task on her mind, and now, three years later, she was nearing the close of it. She could feel the push toward rash action, and for the first time in as long as she could remember, she wasn't able to silence it, not entirely.

The echo of boots on the grated metal gangplank snapped Miranda back to the present. She didn't turn, instead electing to wait until whoever was seeking her decided to make their presence known.

"Ma'am, we have something you might find interesting," one of the younger pirates said nervously.

Miranda turned to see what she would casually call a boy standing well outside of arm's reach. She would have been surprised if his lungs had tasted twenty years of oxygen yet, but that didn't matter on a ship like this.

Since pirates replenished their numbers from those aboard ships they raided, it was not uncommon to find the very young among their ranks. Those who were press-ganged into service had more value as members of the crew than the number of credits they could be sold for. Someone had made such a call where this youth was concerned, though Miranda wouldn't have.

"Is that all?" Miranda said, noticing the boy's brown eyes were locked on the silver spikes growing from her hands.

"Miss Ashe made it sound urgent," the boy said, bowing as Miranda got to her feet.

With a slight groan, Miranda stretched and pushed away the cold. She did her best to hide the slight shiver the silver sent through her body as it receded.

"Then take me to her, urgently," she said, gesturing for the youth to take the lead.

• • • •

The comms room was always cramped. With a complete monitoring team, there was barely enough room for Miranda to squeeze around the aging equipment and the nervous pirates operating it. Putting aside her discomfort, Miranda worked her way toward the woman with the blue braided mohawk at the holographic display toward the back. She vaguely remembered the woman's face, but the woman's blue hair jogged her memory.

Octavian had recommended Miranda make her the head of the tech discipline. It hadn't been a priority, though perhaps it should have been. The hunt for Bertrand would begin in this narrow alcove and the person in charge would be instrumental in achieving the proper outcome.

"You have something?" Miranda asked by way of greeting.

Ashe spun to face Miranda and stiffened. "I believe so, Captain."

Miranda narrowed her eyes at the woman. Something hid just below her girlish features and her stiff, perfunctory bow. Miranda didn't sense anything openly aggressive, but among pirates, that meant little.

With a single gesture from the woman across from her, an explosion of small, pale green holographic boxes filled the space between them. Miranda blinked away the tiny sting the new images inflicted and scanned each casually.

"There was a disturbance at Artemis Industries today," Ashe stated, expanding one of the boxes to show an elevated PlanSec drone presence around an ornate glass tower deep within the city.

"At first, it didn't seem like anything important, but reports were sent off-world. So, I dug in and found that twenty-two employees lost consciousness simultaneously," she continued, looking for any sign of interest from Miranda.

"What happened?" Miranda asked, studying the looping footage.

This information wasn't quite what she was looking for, but it was alluring. For as good as she believed her intel to be, there was still a gap in her knowledge. Miranda didn't know why her target had come to this world, and she couldn't afford to dismiss anything out of hand. He could be involved, considering the tasks that he'd been known to undertake.

"PlanSec filed a report on it, listing persons of interest," Ashe stated, shrinking the holo-vid. "However, they don't seem to know the actual cause."

New boxes sprang to life. Several of them contained the text of the PlanSec report, with keywords and phrases highlighted in shimmering gold. Several images of the upscale central district cycled at regular intervals, as if to accent Ashe's words.

"Artemis declined a full PlanSec investigation, but I thought you might be interested in this guy," Ashe said.

She sped through the images, eventually stopping on one that froze Miranda in place.

"Ban'gaio," Ashe said with a flourish.

Hovering just inches away was a face Miranda knew perhaps too well. The hologram perfectly captured the man's strong jawline, tanned skin, and piercing, dark brown eyes. He was practically unchanged from when Miranda had last seen him all those years ago. Age had touched him, certainly, but it had been kind.

For a dead man, he looked as strong and healthy as he had when they'd parted ways. Miranda studied the floating image, drinking in each detail. Her eyes fell upon the thin strands of silver at his neck, hands, and around his hairline, and without realizing it, Miranda smiled.

"That bastard," she said without malice. "How?"

Ashe blinked in confusion.

"Isn't this the guy you're looking for?" she asked.

Miranda kept her eyes locked on the floating image. "No, but get on the network. Find out where he works, where he sleeps, and who he knows. I want to know everything."

"That will be difficult from here. We're too far from the city nodes to access personal networks," Ashe stated, furrowing her brow.

"Can't you use the comms relay? Maybe... boost our signal?" Miranda asked, letting the heat of her annoyance creep into the words.

"I can, but it will be noticeable. Isn't discretion key to our operation here?" Ashe protested.

Miranda groaned audibly. The technician was right. Claude was, at best, a distraction. The objective had to come first.

Still, Miranda found herself torn. Something pushed her, and now that she knew he was alive, she felt a desperate need to see him again.

DiSilva carried the same creature she did, which meant he might know something more about it. Until now, Miranda believed she was the only one with a passenger of this type, but that notion was now dead. A new reality had dawned in its place, and for reasons she didn't fully understand, she was instantly drawn to explore it.

In the end, it was another powerful urge toward rash action; one that Miranda couldn't afford to give in to. So, she fought it and discovered that she couldn't fully silence this one either. It occurred to her that moving the Modus Vivendi closer to the city would put them in sensor range. On the other hand, boosting their signal through the relay would add their signature to its transmissions. Either action could lose her the element of surprise, squandering yet another opportunity.

"You're right," Miranda started, hating the taste of the words. "Keep an eye on this, but Echelon is the priority."

"Aye, captain," Ashe said, crossing her fists in a crisp pirate's salute.

Miranda nodded and took her leave. She flowed out of the oppressive space and into the corridor beyond. Curious glances from the crew cut her way, but she was too consumed in thought to notice.

Her mind plowed through all viable options. Already she could see a few that would achieve her new goal without jeopardizing the broader mission. Her quarry would no doubt be just as interested in DiSilva. He would want the same answers she did, if not more. Echelon would be curious about how Claude had returned to the realm of the living, and they wanted the creature.

There was a very real possibility that this new variable would draw her prey out of his hole. If true, all she needed to do was wait and listen. Monitoring technology had its uses, but having a few pairs of eyes on the streets would be preferable. There would be no shortage of crew members eager to enter the city and do a little reconnaissance. She just needed the right ones.

Octavian would know which she could rely on. She would delegate that task to him. After all, direct interaction with the crew was his responsibility.

Miranda forced herself into a calm, moderate pace as she plotted the course for her quarters. She could feel herself getting antsy, though she wasn't exactly sure why. She was as close to ending her long game as she'd ever been, but that knowledge seemed to be providing little comfort.

As she rounded the next bend in the corridor, she clamped down on the sensation.

"We're hunting, not chasing," she said so softly that only the silver could hear it.

Chapter 12

THE ORANGE GLOW OF Minerva's sun beat back the long shadows of Zhara's bedroom, not caring that its assault was being witnessed. The early light started innocently enough, but it grew more brazen and boorish as time marched forward, until its presence could no longer go unnoticed.

Claude had watched day strangle night for hours now. He had tried to rest in the soft, smooth microfiber covers but found himself unable to. The bed was too soft for his tastes, but that wasn't the real problem.

He had wanted to slow things down, to talk, but there wasn't room for that last night. While he wasn't about to complain, a part of him was concerned that staying the night with Zhara might have done additional damage to their strained relationship.

Zhara had opened her life to both him and Vision. She'd offered them a home with her in the same apartment that they'd stayed the night in. Claude had vehemently refused. And so began the conflict.

Vision's growth, as he now understood it, had forced them back together, and need, or more aptly, desire had done so again. Claude wasn't sure their coupling was as helpful to their long-term situation as it was enjoyable, but here he was.

It occurred to him that maybe he was overthinking it, but he couldn't help himself. Zhara had become an essential pillar of his life, and he needed her to be both safe and happy, in that order. It was the reason he had declined to move in with her so definitively. That, and an old-fashioned belief that he should provide a place for them instead.

Still, he had somehow managed to mess things up. He believed that Zhara would be pulled deeper into the mess that was his life without properly understanding what that meant. He knew he was protecting her, but when the fight broke out, he learned that doing so might have destroyed their chance to be happy together.

Now he was naked in her lavender sheets, wondering if he should sneak away before the sun finished its daily abuse. He wanted to stay, but he couldn't shake the feeling that the longer he did, the bigger their problems would become. Still, there wasn't much good to be gained from bailing without a word. He knew that much from experience.

Zhara watched Claude silently. He was so lost in thought that he hadn't noticed her eyes on him. She'd been awake for at least twenty minutes just studying him and the passenger he carried.

The creature in his body had grown more defined. Where there had only been hints of it at his hands, feet, and spine in their early days together, now Zhara could easily trace it through the bulk of his body. It was still more apparent in the extremities, but now it was traceable across nearly every nerve if you looked hard enough.

"You awake?" she moaned, pretending as though she had just stirred.

Claude spun to face her with wide eyes and an honest smile on his lips.

"Yeah, this bed of yours is a little too soft on my back," he said, shifting in the covers to face her.

It was a half-truth, she knew. If she had to guess, he had been contemplating an exit. It's what she would have done if they'd ended up at his place, so she didn't hold it against him. Instead, she just reached out and trailed her fingertips across his bare chest, following the lines of silver that splintered and branched out across his body.

"Your passenger is fascinating," she said.

"Just him?" Claude replied, fishing for a compliment.

"Him, huh?" Zhara asked snidely.

She rested her head on her hand and locked eyes with him. The warmth that spread through her mind when he held her gaze was something she had missed since their falling out.

He was with her, completely locked in the moment, and if the steady stare he focused on her meant anything, it was the only place he wanted to be.

"Of course, it's a Him," Claude said with a playful inflection. "If it was female, I doubt it would put up with me."

Zhara felt her cheeks redden until she couldn't hold back a smile. She felt that perhaps a corner had been turned. She didn't know if he'd changed his position on the living together question, but at least they were proving the relationship still had road left to travel.

In the end, that was what the fight was about. Zhara was fully invested in him, and she wasn't sure if he felt the same. So, when she offered to move them in, and he refused, it seemed like a confirmation of her fears and insecurities. It wasn't pretty, and as a rational woman, she knew exactly what was happening, she was just powerless to stop it. Once the rending was done, pride held it in place.

Time caused the wound to ache until the needs of a psionic child forced them back together. If Zhara hadn't witnessed the truth firsthand, she could have believed it was the little girl's plan all along.

"I'm not sure 'he' is entirely compatible with you either," Zhara said, shifting into her scientist mentality for a moment.

Claude sat up nervously, pulling away from her touch. "Why do you think that?"

The action was purely reflexive, she knew, but that knowledge didn't take any of the sting or the suddenness out of his reaction.

"Consider what we know," Zhara straightened, ignoring his glances at her uncovered form. "Whatever the creature is, it feeds off the electrical impulses generated by your nervous system, but it's also highly conductive. It skims power off you each time you move."

"Is that a problem?" he asked and didn't like having to.

"Yes. It causes your body to generate a larger amount of energy for every function," Zhara explained, as she lost herself in the science of him. "What you get in return are heightened reflexes, agility, and strength due to the creature's conduction speed and its ability to reinforce you as a means of protection."

"But I don't feel any worse," Claude said, suddenly feeling cold and a little uncomfortable.

"Not yet, but your body isn't made to produce that much energy. It's like you're using a standard car charge box to power a starfighter. It'll work for a while, but eventually, the power cells will give out. The more power you use, the faster that happens," Zhara concluded.

"I'm being careful. I don't use what I don't need," Claude said defensively.

"I believe you, but there has been a big change in the... passenger, since the last time we..." Zhara said, letting her words trail off. "Growth requires energy, Claude."

Claude knew that she meant well, but no one wanted to be told that they were being eaten alive. Aside from the obvious, he wasn't sure what was making him so upset. The basic facts he had already known. Only the creature's growth in relation to its energy consumption was actually news to him, and even then, it was only a minor reveal.

He felt fine physically, but the cold hadn't released him. There was no way the temperature had dropped. If anything, it had to have risen. The fact that the sun was now touching his skin meant that he should have actually felt warmer, yet nothing changed.

While the cold was off-putting, it was the extreme mental discomfort that bothered him most. It didn't feel like a natural emotion. Bad news always had a way of finding him, but he never took it badly. This barely qualified under his definition, and yet he found himself shaking.

Zhara reached out and took his hands gently.

"We'll figure something out, Claude. I won't give up on you," she said with a cheeky smile. "Any of you."

Claude felt some of the alien discomforts melt away as the temperature returned to something he would call normal. He let out a pent-up breath and leaned in to kiss Zhara's forehead. Zhara moved to catch his lips on hers and rolled on top of him. She pinned his wrists and looked down at him with a wicked grin.

"Since it would be inconsiderate of me to force you to do the work, you just take it easy," she said with a low, hungry growl.

Claude let himself ease into the mattress and felt the corners of his lips curl into a grin. Zhara's hair tickled his face as she kissed down to his collarbone, but he ignored it.

He was just beginning to relax when his data-pad chimed.

Zhara groaned in frustration but didn't roll off him until the second ring. They both recognized the distinct tone Claude selected for his work communications.

"I thought you said business was slow," she said as her breathing returned to normal.

Sloppily, Claude rolled over and fumbled through his discarded clothes for the data-pad.

"It is," he said, struggling to fish the flat, card-like device from its holster on his shirt sleeve.

With a loud grunt, he lifted the pad and pulled his upper body back onto the mattress.

"You alright there?" Zhara asked mockingly.

Claude huffed in her general direction and lost his grip on the smooth comms device. Reflexes took over as he snatched it from the air again. Instead of gripping it harmlessly around the outer edge, the maneuver placed Claude's finger on the blinking word "answer."

The strong bearded jaw, silver hair, and immaculate posture of TaskMaster Commander, Kerrid Bertrand, erupted into existence above him.

Intense holographic eyes scanned both Claude and Zhara for a split second before they both shouted, "Cut video!"

• • • •

Claude and Vision made good time back to their home district, but neither had much to say. Vision was still cranky after being awakened by shouting and then being hurried into the car. Claude was lost in thought about what his former commander's reappearance could mean for them. He'd barely managed to keep the sedan under the travel speed guidelines while he let his mind wander. Often, he found himself well over the posted limit and speeding past other hovercars without realizing it.

Vision huffed in her seat and curled her body to face the passenger window. Claude watched her for a moment, then turned his attention back to the skyway ahead.

The sedan was almost through the barren strip that separated Cascade from the lower-class Violet district. He would have to start negotiating their descent soon. He'd done it maybe a thousand times since they'd settled on Minerva Prime and he wasn't concerned with something as trivial as being cut off by an early morning asshole.

Bertrand was coming. If Claude had to guess, he'd say that his former commander was already there, or at least his scouts were. Either way, Claude was walking himself and Vision into a potentially unstable situation.

If he'd been thinking straight, he would have arranged a meet in a very neutral and very public place, but he did no such thing. They were going to meet at his office like almost all of his clients did.

Zhara was due at work only two hours after they'd left, and he wasn't about to leave Vision on her own. She could probably handle it, but something about the idea didn't sit well with him. So he'd taken her back with him, and she wasn't pleased with that decision.

Neither choice was particularly good, but he decided she'd be better protected if she was with him. Vision didn't see it that way, but she'd just have to deal with it.

Claude sank the sedan into the rising canyon of blocky buildings for the rest of the trip. The view screen adjusted to compensate for the clouds of dust that so often plagued Violet. With no other sound in the cab, the whir of the filtration system was almost deafening as the vehicle did its best to keep the air inside clean enough to breathe.

"When we get there, I need you to–" Claude said before Vision cut him off.

"Hide upstairs. I know," she huffed, still refusing to look at him.

"Look, Bertrand was my former commander. The man is crafty, he–"

"Can't be trusted. Yeah, I know. You don't need to say it twice," Vision snapped, turning to glare at him.

"Are you even trying to–" Claude tried to ask before he was answered.

"No, it just happens sometimes. The more worried you get, the more your brain shouts at me," Vision declared, turning her focus back to the world outside of the conversation.

Claude let it drop. He was walking her into a situation that she had no bearings for, and he wasn't even sure if it was the right move.

Bertrand had said that he wanted to meet to discuss a proposition but hadn't let any details slip. Claude assumed that it was because Bertrand knew there were other ears in the vicinity. The old man had always been sparse with the information he chose to impart, so it didn't immediately trigger a red flag.

Still, Claude's skin crawled with the timing. Less than twenty hours after the events at Artemis, Bertrand contacts him directly. It wasn't a coincidence. Bertrand had to have been on Minerva already, but why?

Streamline travel was fast, but there was no way he would hold a post deep in the core systems. Even with the war over, Claude couldn't imagine Bertrand staying so far away from what had been his home territory for decades. There had to be something Claude wasn't seeing. If Bertrand was there for him, why not just wait for him to return home unawares and make a move then. Instead, he'd spun him up. Why?

"Maybe he wants you to focus on him, so you don't notice something else," Vision offered with a yawn.

"Like a shell game?" Claude asked the girl rooting through his thoughts.

"Like a distraction," Vision offered, rolling over to him and fixing him with a curious look.

Her eyes were wide and sightless, but he had the distinct impression that she was staring into him regardless. It wasn't a new sensation, and it hadn't been for many years, but given everything he had learned about her capabilities recently, he could feel the shadow of unease beginning to stir.

With a conscious effort, he stomped the feeling out, but not before he noticed the slight flicker of a frown darken Vision's face.

"Okay, so I have to find out what he's trying to distract me from," Claude said, as though declaring such a thing was an everyday occurrence.

"I could help," Vision said.

Claude gave her another evaluating look. She was the picture of innocence, with her hands curled under her chin. Her eyes blinked slowly as she fought the final tendrils of sleep, and Claude admitted to himself that she could be a trustworthy ally if he gave her the chance.

The fight over whether or not Vision should have a place in his work was a war of attrition. Morally, Claude had long since taken the stance that it was wrong. However, as she grew older and pushed him harder, even ignoring his wishes and offering insights she'd taken from clients on her own, he had felt the absolute righteousness of his position begin to slip.

It was a slope that he still wasn't comfortable sliding down, but against such an unknown as Bertrand, he couldn't afford to dismiss her offer out of hand. It would be wise to allow Vision the opportunity to help him. After all, she would be contributing to her own protection, in theory. On the other hand, exploiting a child, and no matter the reasoning, still remained unsavory.

"Stop treating me like a kid," Vision said, inserting herself into the debate in his mind. "I'm not a kid anymore. I'm your partner."

Claude couldn't stop himself from laughing.

"You're not my partner," he said and immediately felt a little bad about it.

· · · ·

Claude was careful to schedule the meeting so he would have at least an hour before Bertrand was supposed to arrive, accounting for the worst traffic imaginable. The skyways proved oddly cooperative, and that left them with a little under two hours to wait.

In that time, they had washed, changed clothes, caught up on the news of the day, brewed some Merloct tea, and gotten unbelievably bored.

Vision was on her third cup of the warm, milky green beverage as she sat behind his desk with her feet up. She made little humming noises with each sip she took, and Claude couldn't decide if it was annoying or endearing.

He paced, as he always did before a client arrived. Only this time, he was slicing his usual ellipse at nearly double speed. He was doing his best to keep his mind on what he knew, but that wasn't an easy thing to do. He wanted to believe that he had chosen to meet at his office instead of neutral territory because it was highly likely Bertrand already knew where he lived. In reality, he simply panicked and resorted to his default meeting place.

That didn't change the situation, though. The old man believed in the value of reconnaissance, and he likely had eyes on them even now. It was one of the things that Claude had come to respect about him when he served as a TaskMaster. It also made keeping the element of surprise a challenge. The fact that Bertrand had contacted him on his professional line meant that he'd spent time digging up all the details available on Claude.

The only thing he might not know was that Vision was a Psionic. With any luck, his former commander would believe that she was just born blind. It was a lie he often told, and there would be little reason for Bertrand to doubt it.

"Will you stop?" Vision finally asked after a large slurp of her tea.

Claude fixed her with a scowl that bounced off her like a foam dart. She knew him well, and what she hadn't learned in her time with him, she could easily read.

Claude was an open book, and apparently, it was even easier for her to flip through his pages this morning.

"You're going to make my sensors overheat," Vision scolded.

Claude made a conscious effort to place himself in one of the chairs on the client-side of the desk.

"I can't help it. There's too much I don't know," he said, sounding almost like a spoiled child.

"Join the club," Vision said, nursing her cup in both hands.

Claude ignored her and stroked the stubble on his jaw. He fell back into his own mind only to find Vision focusing on him intently.

"No," Claude grumbled at her.

"You don't even know what I'm going to ask."

"The answer's still no," Claude stated firmly.

Vision huffed and made it all of twenty seconds before blurting out, "We need more work."

"We?" Claude asked.

Vision spawned a sinister-looking smile and slid her empty mug onto the empty desk.

"Yes, we. My name is on the door too," she stated, motioning to the partitioned wall behind Claude that separated the office from the rest of the first floor.

"Silver Sights is no one's name, Vision," Claude sighed. "Besides, you're a kid. You are supposed to be doing kid stuff."

Vision rolled her eyes. The motion lost nearly all of its impact, considering there was no difference between the color of her pupils, irises, and scolera. Only the exaggerated motion of her head came close to selling the gesture.

"Like reading minds or doing couples' therapy?" Vision asked, with naked sarcasm dripping from her words. "The Valdez job was months ago, Claude. That money is drying up. We need a new payday, and you need my help."

"Look, something will come along. Something always does," Claude said, turning away from the obvious bait.

"You sent the last four potential clients away," Vision whined. "How can 'something come along' if you keep rejecting jobs?"

"I have rules, V. We can't afford to get caught up on the wrong side of PlanSec," Claude declared, hearing his voice raise without intending it.

"And what good has that done us?" Vision asked, slamming her hands on the desk.

Claude fixed her with a razor-edged stare. She was getting dangerously close to the line with her attitude, even if her argument was sound. As much as he hated to admit it, she was right, though they would have to work on how she made her points in the future.

For all of his rising frustration, Claude could understand her position. He had signed them up for a struggle that was clearly not paying off, and none of that was Vision's fault.

When Silver Sights was formed, he made only one hard rule. He would not take on a job that put them at risk of discovery. It had kept them safe for a while, but Claude was good at getting things done. Word spread and his reputation grew. Normally that would be a good thing, but in Violet, not every potential client that sought him out was on the up and up.

Smugglers, drug dealers, prostitutes, and thieves were prevalent in the district. Often they came to him with one task or another. The money offered was usually substantial, but so was the risk. Wading into the muck of Violet district wasn't a thing to be taken lightly, and with Vision in tow, Claude simply refused.

So, he had sacrificed golden opportunities. Many of those offers would have bettered their position on this world, but it had to be done. He already had one PlanSec officer sniffing around him. Getting involved with criminals would only make that worse.

In the end, it didn't seem to make much difference, and Vision was right to point it out. Taking the high road had led to the same outcome and with, perhaps, fewer resources to deal with it. Bertrand's imminent arrival was proof that he had signed them up for a more challenging life for no reason.

"As long as the bills get paid, and you don't go hungry, we're good. I will meet with Bertrand and see what he wants. Then, when he's gone, I'll figure out what comes next," Claude said, attempting to relax and failing miserably.

"And what if they try to take us?" Vision asked.

"Then you distract them with that sparkling personality of yours while I think of something," Claude said with a surprisingly natural smile.

Vision chewed on the grin, fighting its way to the surface but eventually gave in.

"You have no idea what you're doing, do you?" Vision asked, trying to hide her face.

"Does anybody?" Claude replied, taking a sip of his cold tea and grimacing.

• • • •

The sun blazed down from high overhead when Bertrand stepped out of the hovercar he'd rented only a standard hour earlier. Dust hung thick in the air. Growlett Pass was filled with the drone of filtration rigs, slaving away to save their masters' lungs from the same particulates that clung to Bertrand's ill-fitting civilian garb.

He'd never set foot on Minerva Prime before, though he had seen it from orbit more than once. And as he adjusted his hooded coat and checked his breather, he realized he hadn't been missing much.

As environmental gear went, breathers were the worst. The damned things were the bane of Bertrand's existence when he'd been a grunt, and it appeared that all these years and technological advancements later, nothing about them had really changed. Discontented with the quality of air he was receiving, Bertrand ratcheted up his pace as he searched the surrounding buildings for Evelion VII.

Despite the poor conditions, the street was far from empty of pedestrians. Those milling around seemed unconcerned with newcomers, but Bertrand kept a sharp eye on them, regardless. He'd done his research, and Violet wasn't the best place to be caught unawares. Precautions had been taken, and he'd chosen both his clothes and hovercar wisely. Neither should have invited envious eyes, but human nature was a hurricane of unseen variables, especially in places like this.

Like all low-class districts, this one was littered with both perks and drawbacks. The greatest of which was, typically, anonymity. That was why Bertrand believed his former scout had settled here. Such relative invisibility would prove valuable for him as well. Avoiding curious, roaming eyes was always a benefit, especially in these last few years.

Bertrand was a marked man, no matter how well regarded he was by those in power. Since the destruction of the black site on Keetal, he'd taken every precaution he could. So far, he remained alive and ahead of the specter stalking him, but the stress alone threatened to kill him.

Some had said that being hunted made them feel alive, but it hadn't done much for Bertrand besides turn his salt and pepper hair wholly white and maroon him on his new ship. He had never been one to submit to paranoia, but ever since he'd learned what his pursuer was capable of, he had allowed himself a heavy dose of it.

It was for that reason Bertrand almost never left his ship. He had half a mind to turn around and flee back to it even now, but he was no coward, and the endless game he was playing with his own personal reaper was getting tiresome.

Still, Bertrand was no fool. Before setting foot on the street, he'd stationed scouts and snipers around the block shortly before making the call to DiSilva. His people had maintained constant contact with him, feeding him intel on what he could expect. Nothing dangerous had been reported so far, which is why he had decided to keep the appointment in light of everything.

Bertrand's swift, confident strides brought him to a dust-caked metal door with the words Silver Sights Detective Agency etched into it. With a deep breath and a hand on the sidearm holstered inside the lining of his coat, he knocked three times and waited.

"Still reading all clear, sir," Yuri's familiar voice declared in Bertrand's earpiece.

"Keep your eyes sharp," he responded. "If our intel is right, Faridan's people will blend perfectly in a place like this."

"Aye, sir," Yuri's filtered voice said, giving Bertrand the mental image of the young man snapping a salute.

The audio in his earpiece cut out as the door slid to the side. A sturdy, world-worn man of medium height stood in front of Bertrand and met his eyes with an uncertain yet unwavering stare.

The man was shorter than Bertrand by about three inches and in desperate need of a shave. He still had his military bearing and was clearly in fighting shape, but something in his eyes had changed.

"DiSilva," Bertrand offered by way of greeting.

"Commander," Claude replied flatly.

The barest curl of a smile crossed Bertrand's lips.

"I can't believe you're alive," he said, letting his professional veneer crack.

"I can't believe I am either," Claude said, stepping to the side and gesturing for Bertrand to enter.

Before the door finished sealing itself, Bertrand was removing his breather and coat. He gave the place a once-over, drinking in the lobby's high ceiling and faux hardwood floors.

"How did you afford all this?" Bertrand asked.

The frosted glass door to the office stood open, and Claude led Bertrand inside.

"The building, I rent. The furnishings and remodel were a gift," Claude said, walking around the desk and easing into his seat.

Bertrand draped his effects over the back of one seat and took the other in a move calculated to inspire confidence in the other man.

"Before we get started, sir, I'm going to ask that you put the sidearm on the desk," Claude said matter-of-factly. "I'd like to keep things in the open, if you don't mind."

Bertrand removed his pistol and placed it on the desk without much hesitation. He figured that DiSilva would spot it quickly. The gun wasn't meant for him and given all he knew about the particular affliction Claude suffered from, it likely wouldn't do much if things took a turn for the worse.

"I see you've kept yourself sharp," Bertrand said. "I've seen many lose their edge in civilian life."

"My work demands it. Besides, you've seen Violet," Claude replied, keeping Bertrand fixed with a wary stare.

"I'm afraid I can't spend much time catching up, DiSilva—"

"Claude, please."

Bertrand nodded and removed his earpiece before continuing. With a tiny, audible click, he deactivated the two-way device and turned his attention back to Claude.

"With respect to the last mission you undertook for me, I'm going to give you as much information as I can," Bertrand said, looking at the earpiece disdainfully.

"I appreciate that," Claude said, letting his eyes drift from Bertrand to the earpiece and back again.

"We've lost a scientist," Bertrand began with a heavy sigh. "Dr. Rickten Eugene, a Sabien defector who fled here after the war. He was in possession of data drives I thought we lost on..."

"Firaxis," Claude stated in disbelief.

"Yes," Bertrand said, swallowing his distaste for the interruption. "We had struck a deal with him, but Eugene bolted, and then got himself killed."

Flickers of shame and disappointment flashed over Bertrand's weary face as his mask of absolute self-assurance cracked. It was a subtle shift, one that lasted only a fraction of a second. If Claude hadn't been through as many of the old man's briefings as he had, he might have missed it altogether.

"And you think he hid them somewhere?" Claude inquired.

"Yes," Bertrand cleared his throat, then drew an impossibly long breath before continuing. "We would attempt a second retrieval ourselves, but that would take time. Besides, a military operation of that size on a central world would be too obvious. I could use an inside man on this, someone I can trust to keep things quiet, and someone who won't shine a light on our involvement here."

Claude leaned back in his seat and folded his hands together. Bertrand had dropped a considerable amount of information on him, and he needed to unpack it.

The TaskMasters were more than capable of handling this job themselves. He'd been involved in dozens of missions just like this while he had worked for them. Maybe Bertrand's well-practiced dissertation was the truth, but it wasn't the whole truth. There was a catch here, and it was huge. It was up to Claude to find it, and Bertrand was too experienced to be tricked into giving it up.

"Where did your man die?" Claude asked, studying Bertrand's every move.

Bertrand flashed a tight and uncomfortable smile.

"In the Old City," Bertrand said and almost seemed to choke on the words.

Claude's mirage of calm slipped. "You can't be serious?"

"Unfortunately, I am, and if it were up to me, I would let the damned things rot out there, but Echelon is involved, and I need this done," Bertrand declared, fixing Claude with a pleading stare.

Claude rubbed the skin of his forehead so roughly that it began to feel like it might start a friction fire. This was exactly the type of situation he both needed and had been afraid of.

With Firaxis, Echelon, and Bertrand all floating around in the same stew, it made for a seriously disturbing recipe. However, if he played it right, there might be a way to find some much-needed answers about his situation, and hopefully, Vision's family.

"What do they have on you?" Claude asked with genuine curiosity.

"Nothing salacious, but they've been keeping me on a tight leash since one of their research bases was destroyed three years ago," Bertrand said, tossing his hands in the air in frustration.

"Did you have anything to do with it?"

Bertrand's face drew into a horrendous scowl as the words sunk into his mind.

"Of course not!" he growled. "You know me better than that."

Claude shrugged but didn't break eye contact with the older man. "It's been a long time. Things change."

"Not everything," Bertrand said, allowing his temper to cool.

"So, you want me to get these drives and hand them over to you?" Claude asked, moving the conversation along.

"And I'd like you to keep it as quiet as possible," Bertrand added, regaining his sly smile.

"I'd be lying if I said I didn't have an interest in those drives for my own reasons," Claude admitted, leaning forward to press his elbows into the desk.

This was where the game would be played. Claude was putting his cards on the table in an attempt to force a move from the old man. If things worked out as he expected, Bertrand would forbid any attempt to read the drives. If there were some hidden motives, Claude expected his former commander to lie and say he didn't care one way or the other.

The truth was, Echelon didn't share secrets, especially with someone like him, and Bertrand wouldn't cross them so that Claude DiSilva could study up on the thing living under his skin. Either way, if he decided to take this job, he would find out what was on those drives. The only question was whether the risk outweighed the reward.

For better or worse, he suspected there was a little mind upstairs trying to fish out every detail of Bertrand's plans, despite his protests. He knew her far better than he knew Bertrand, and there was no way she could resist. Still, he wasn't about to depend on Vision to gather the information he needed, especially considering the potential pitfalls.

The problem was, when he eventually asked her for whatever insight she'd gleaned, Vision would extract a heavy price. Claude wasn't looking forward to that, but considering they might have to deal with both Derelicts and Echelon, he was going to have to eat crow and make some sort of temporary arrangement for both her help and her protection.

"I don't care, DiSilva, just keep it to yourself. Echelon are the secret keepers. You and I are just the means they use to gather them," Commander Kerrid Bertrand said, right on cue.

It was everything Claude was afraid of. Yet having the double-cross in the open made it seem less scary. A part of Claude wanted to trust his former comrade but knowing he couldn't made plotting against him that much easier.

He'd take the job, even the money if he could, but the minute Bertrand's ulterior motive showed itself, he'd be ready. He only hoped he would be quick and clever enough to find himself free when the jaws of the trap snapped shut.

'Find something we can use, V,' he thought as "loud" as he could manage and hoped he was right about her, too.

"Great," Claude said, using his best mask to hide both his disappointment and relief.

"I'm guessing this is the part where we haggle over price," Bertrand said, leaning forward as best he could in the well-padded chair.

"Oh no. We aren't haggling," Claude said with a slight chuckle. "You have Echelon on deck for this one. I'm going to tell you my price, and you're going to pay it, or we shake hands and part ways."

• • • •

The room fell silent aside from the slight creaking of the building, leaving Bertrand to think, and as he stared across at DiSilva's haughty expression, his lips pressed into a line and his eyes narrowed. He'd played his hand, and now it was time to ante up for the next round. Claude was no fool, and he was worth every single credit he was sure to demand, but the higher the price, the more problems Bertrand would have to contend with.

He already had an Executor on his ship, corrupting his ground team. That was half the reason he'd come to DiSilva in the first place.

When Bertrand discovered that Claude was alive, he'd insisted on getting him to do the job for him. It was an efficient way to sidestep Marta and keep control of the situation. He'd even gone so far as to hide the fact that DiSilva possessed the same creature that Faridan had.

If he got his way, the drives would be acquired quickly and quietly. He'd hand them over to Marta and be off-world with no one knowing the exact details of this deal except the accountants on Myridorn. Unfortunately, he wasn't likely to get his way. A plan had been drawn up for that too, though Bertrand would prefer to avoid that route if he could.

DiSilva was a good man, and he had served both Bertrand and the Beita Systems well in the past. One of Bertrand's greatest regrets was the way Firaxis had turned out, and it would be regrettable if he had to betray the man's trust now on top of that.

Sadly, war called for sacrifice, and Bertrand wasn't exempt from that call. He heard it louder than many others, and he had answered it more times than he cared to think about. If the siren's song beckoned him once again, Bertrand would do as commanded, no matter how much it turned his stomach.

What he wanted for himself had never really mattered all that much when measured against what was needed from him, and the universe kept finding ways to ensure that he knew it.

• • • •

Vision did her best to follow the conversation, but it wasn't easy. She had started the meeting upstairs like she was told, but had only been able to read Claude from up there. The new guy was significantly quieter with his thoughts, so she decided to get a little closer.

That took her to the stairs, but it wasn't until she was over halfway down them that she was able to pick up anything at all from the stranger. So, she crept farther down, dodging the creaky stair near the bottom, and making her way to the first floor.

Once she was sure she would be out of their sightline, Vision tried again and finally got something. It wasn't a thought so much as it was a feeling of dread and shame. It wasn't uncommon that people asking for Claude's help felt those emotions, but something told her to keep digging.

Choosing to trust her instincts, Vision sat with her back against the wall and faced the stairs. She hugged her knees and put all of her concentration into Claude's old boss.

At first, it was like trying to carve through a mountain with just her fingernails, but once she was able to chip away at the surface, she found the walls around his mind were more fragile than they seemed. She could tell that Bertrand was proud and that he was genuinely pleased to see Claude alive. She could also feel his inner conflict over being here and that he was even sad that decades of his efforts had collapsed down to having to basically beg for Claude's help.

Vision shifted away from the man's surface level emotions with a slight head shake and tried to dig into his recent memories. There was less resistance along that path, as if she were swimming with the current.

Usually, time flattened a memory's detail and left large gaps. Each sight, sound, and smell became almost spectral, eventually fading away entirely as it aged, but this memory was still largely intact.

Vision gave herself to it, drifting alongside the incorporeal version of Bertrand as he moved through the well-maintained corridors of a large ship. A feeling of pride swelled in him as Bertrand strode into his quarters, only to be confronted by a woman.

Vision immediately tensed, feeling Bertrand's revulsion as if it were her own. The feeling was odd, and it hadn't happened to her quite like this before. While she often felt what other people did while reading them, normally there was a boundary, a point where they ended and she began. This was different, and she could have definitely lived without it.

The woman was Echelon, and she was Bertrand's overseer, a fact he deeply resented. In the memory, Bertrand discarded an errant thought about shoving the woman into an airlock, followed by many other mental images that drove Vision to look elsewhere.

She needed something useful and combing through all of a senior's memories would take too long. He was military, and if his mind worked like Claude's, there would be a place for missions.

From everything Claude had told her, Vision got the idea Bertrand took pride in his service. She didn't exactly see why, but she was willing to bet that Bertrand held his own achievements in high regard. So, she started there.

With a destination set, Vision surged through Bertrand's mind as quickly as she could. Any memories or thoughts that didn't correspond to her new parameters parted as she moved through them.

As the immense wave of thoughts surged past her, Vision could detect hundreds if not thousands of notions pertaining to missions Bertrand had been involved with. Most of them were bright, vibrant spots in his life. They shined like stars, but Vision wasn't looking for missions that he felt good about, so she rejected the brightest ones.

Those left over were compromised missions with less than stellar outcomes. Vision dove deeper, finding Firaxis, something called Operation Fullbright, and the raid on Diegon Minor among them. They were almost cloaked in a fog of shame and regret, making them a quagmire to move through.

It reminded Vision of an old story Claude had read her, where a young boy was forced to watch his animal friend sink into a swamp made of sadness and die because it chose to just give up.

Vision felt the sting of tears prick her eyes as she experienced the sorrow Bertrand associated with these failures. She wanted to dig further into them, Firaxis in particular, but what she was looking for wasn't a failure. It was simply incomplete.

With substantial effort and a sniffle that she hoped no one else would hear, Vision shoved the failed missions to the side and focused on a dim, flickering orb floating alone in the cavern of Bertrand's mind.

Her pulse quickened as she heard Bertrand's raised voice, followed by Claude's loud but even one. If she knew Claude at all, this was a price negotiation, which meant she was running out of time. With a deep breath, she redoubled her efforts, and approached her target. However, when she tried to touch it, flickering light flitted out of reach.

Confused and a little frustrated, Vision tried again, and again the memory dodged her.

Vision gritted her teeth and launched herself at the dim little light, but it countered her speeds, angles, and intentions with every attempt.

"Fine," she said under an angry breath. "Let's play then."

Fast, nimble fingers made angry jabs at several lights on Vision's halo, decreasing the inhibitors' ability to hold her true power at bay. She was smart enough not to turn them completely off. All she needed was enough room to flex more of her mental muscles.

With a slight smirk, she dove back into Bertrand's mind, past his current thoughts, through his military triumphs, and into the gulf of his guarded secrets. She sniffed out the most recent mission, and like a sea-borne predator, she circled it.

Part of her wanted to launch a full assault, but she had a feeling that wouldn't work. Bertrand's mental defenses here were sharp. They would detect and compensate for such a maneuver.

Since a direct approach was doomed to failure, Vision settled on a more deceptive angle. She had picked stories from the minds of clients that vacationed on tropical worlds. The one that seemed relevant said that if a fish is too wily for the spear, the wise fisherman should use the net instead. The finer details of that lesson were lost on her at the time, but here it seemed to make sense.

She imagined the depths of Bertrand's mind as a clear ocean and his guarded secret as the wily fish. She didn't know if she had a net, but the uninteresting sediment of Bertrand's mind was a tool all its own. By digging sloppily into the other thoughts and feelings around her, she was able to stir up that silt.

Her usual surgical precision was abandoned in favor of smashing open as many of Bertrand's neatly organized memories as possible. She muddied the waters around her true target, and when she was confident that she could reach out and take a triumphant bite of the forbidden, she struck.

Vision expected a big, juicy, delicious secret that she could use to barter her way into Claude's job and maybe get a little bit of adventure for once. What she got was like a mind full of electric spines that lit her up with white-hot agony and seared several small images into her mind.

Again, she saw the ship and the woman, Marta. She saw a holo-vid of a man that felt somehow familiar falling over a railing and into the howling darkness. There was a vat of acid deep inside the inner workings of a giant machine she had no reference for and the ravenous, rage-filled face of a woman with brown skin shouting words she couldn't hear from the thick transparent monitoring window of a small cell.

Vision tried to hold on to the thoughts, but the harder she held, the worse the pain got. Soon, she had no choice but to retreat. The stream of memories, emotions, and images raced back past her, and the burning pain she felt in her skull cooled until, at last, she was back in her own mind again.

She fumbled at her halo, desperately trying to return it to full power. The rush of thoughts and voices that she'd quieted with her single-minded focus crashed down on her now, and she was too weak to keep them out. Her trembling fingers did all they could to resolve the problem, but they lacked the effortless speed and grace they'd had just moments earlier.

Claude had told her some of the military's higher-ups had undergone training to guard their minds against Psionic assault, but like most things Claude said, she didn't completely believe it. She assumed that he was exaggerating and disregarded the information, only to have it proven so painfully true.

He hadn't been exaggerating. In fact, if anything, he had downplayed the severity of those defenses, and Vision had gotten a lesson she didn't expect to learn.

As she finally managed to punch in the correct code, the inhibitors bled out all the voices that didn't belong. Exhausted, out of breath, and nursing a pulsing pain behind her eyes, Vision sat motionless in the cool shadow of the stairwell.

She tried to focus, slow her breathing, and root herself in the physical world once more.

"Lesson learned," she whispered lazily to herself and lost her tenuous grip on consciousness.

. . . .

Tiny trickles of red drew Claude's attention. He did his best not to let his eyes widen as blood stained much of Bertrand's white mustache. The older man seemed unaware as it dripped to the floor, but for Claude it was impossible to ignore.

He had noticed a level of confusion and a slurred speech earlier, but had dismissed it. That could have been chalked up to Bertrand's age or the indignation he felt at Claude's astronomical asking price. Now, it was clear the old man had been fighting a war on two fronts, and odds were he didn't even know it.

Bertrand was still pleading his case aggressively, but Claude had already drowned him out. The only thing on his mind was whether Vision was safe.

Bertrand looked and sounded as if a bomb had gone off between his ears, and something very near to that had likely happened. While the old man was still standing and pontificating as if nothing was wrong, Vision might not have been so fortunate.

She'd read the minds of clients before, but there'd been no signs. This time, something had gone seriously wrong, and Claude needed to find out what.

Despite his claim, Claude fully expected to negotiate at least a little, but the situation had clearly changed. He needed Bertrand out, and he needed him out immediately.

"... asking is impossible," Bertrand concluded as another drop of blood fell from his mustache and onto Claude's desk.

"I don't really have any more time to debate this, Commander. If you want my help, that's the price," Claude said, rushing from his side of the desk and around toward the office door.

Bertrand took the hint but let fury and disapproval twist his face into the kind of scowl that would have been disconcerting if Claude wasn't already on the verge of panic for more significant reasons. Clearly, he saw Claude's actions as a negotiation tactic, and he wasn't going to cave.

Bertrand pushed past the younger man with his jaw set and his chin high. He likely expected Claude to reconsider at the door, but he'd be disappointed. If the door closed without a solid deal in place, someone would have to re-establish contact, and that person would lose their negotiating position.

Claude had been receptive to his plight, and Bertrand was confident that coming to terms on price would be a relatively straightforward process, but that wasn't the case.

Bertrand knew Claude could use the credits, and Echelon had the finances to pay it without much of an effort. His concern was the number. If it was too large, he wouldn't be able to keep the deal a secret, which was paramount. Three hundred thousand credits was simply too much for Myridorn to ignore.

They would ask for confirmation from their lackey, and she would demand to be let in on the details. Endless debates would spark about where the money was going and why Claude deserved so much when others would surely take the job for less.

Nervous sweat beaded on Claude's forehead as he ushered Bertrand to the door. He grabbed the man's coat and spread it wide to force Bertrand into turning away from the unconscious little girl lying in the stairwell. The maneuver worked, and once the coat was on Bertrand's shoulders, Claude positioned himself to keep Vision blocked from sight.

Bertrand turned to Claude and fixed him with a narrow, penetrating scowl designed to re-establish the old Commander/Subordinate dynamic from years prior.

It was the last card he had to play, and he prayed it would work. If Claude refused to budge, Bertrand would have to negotiate from the least stable and desirable position he could think of, though not immediately.

"Disappointing," Bertrand growled and turned his back on Claude before stepping back into the street.

The old man did not look back and strode confidently, but not quickly, to his vehicle. Claude watched until the door slid shut with the audible *thunk* that denoted it was sealed and locked, then sprinted across the room.

He leaped over the chairs and sofa designed for waiting patrons and slid to a stop at the foot of the stairs. Vision lay slumped partially against the wall with her neck bent at an angle that made Claude think twice about moving her. He forced himself to calm down and use his field training.

It took him only a second to focus and realize that she was all right. Her chest rose and fell normally, and she was warm to the touch, but it wasn't until he tickled the inside of her elbow and she moved her arm that he knew it was safe to take her upstairs.

Claude spat out a sigh of relief, scooped her limp form off the floor, and carried her up to the apartment. She was heavier than he remembered, though it had been at least a year since she'd tried to get him to carry her.

She'd grown out of things like that as she'd gotten older, and Claude found himself lamenting it. He used to fly her around like the "S-man" from the old archive drawings that captured his imagination, and he'd given many thousands of rides through the apartment while crawling on all fours. But as the years rolled by, those times had apparently faded into obscurity.

Vision was growing up, and somewhere deep inside, he always knew that she would. He realized that fact, just as he knew that one day she would leave him behind entirely, either as an adult or when he found her people.

Both outcomes were real, but somehow still abstract in his mind. He never really let himself focus on what they would be like. Even now, he was shaking the ideas free from their moorings. Secretly, he hoped they would float toward some distant place where he wouldn't have to deal with them, or at least no time soon.

He had been right when he told her that she wasn't his partner, but it left him questioning what she actually was to him. While Claude didn't like to think of her as his charge or obligation, he couldn't conjure up a term that truly fit their relationship.

She was Vision, and by the time he reached the well-worn sofa that doubled as his bed, he had settled himself into the idea that Vision was the only thing she needed to be.

Chapter 13

ASHE WAS EXHAUSTED. Her time with the executive officer had been productive, but it didn't come without a price. As a favor to the friends who had covered for her, Ashe had agreed to pull a double shift and she was hating herself for it.

She bit back a yawn and wiped tired tears from her eyes as she stared at two transmission signatures that she'd singled out only moments before. The comms room was only lightly populated given the early hour, but there were enough souls present to help her begin the work of decrypting them.

She'd only given herself three hours after Octavian left to sleep and be back on duty. It was nowhere near enough. Now, a fog clouded her mind, slowing her down, and again she cursed herself. If only she'd allowed herself more time, she might have been in better shape this morning.

Not everything she'd done the previous night had been frivolous. Though a fair amount of her night had been recreational, she did manage to tamper with the earpiece she'd inherited and set the ship's comms array to receive similar signals.

She would be lying if she said it was the most exciting part of her time away, and even though Ashe prided herself on being a pirate, she strived to keep herself at least somewhat honest.

The sun had spent several hours beating down on the hull and turning the ship's interior into an oven by the time Ashe had picked up pings both to and from Echelon. She'd been so tired and thirsty she had almost missed the damned things. If it hadn't been for the organization's penchant for repeating orders, their message might have gone entirely unnoticed.

Ashe never understood why they did that, but given how formidable their encryption was, she figured it was simply hubris. Echelon's code was brutal, and breaking it was a time-consuming chore to pull off. For Ashe and her team, all that the task required was a lot of skill and a little patience. This transmission was using a slight variation on Echelon's standard encryption, but Ashe was confident she could crack it. The algorithms she used were versatile and effective, but like their current adversary, they were getting a little old. Regardless, the job would still get done, though Ashe was unlikely to return to her bunk before nightfall.

"What's our progress?" Ashe asked the two other technicians plugging the few characters they'd deciphered into a plausible position.

"I wouldn't risk a guess," a man more than twice Ashe's age replied over his shoulder.

He went by Nazier, but this was Ashe's first time working with him directly. He was older than much of the crew, with thinning hair and minimal experience in comms, though his dedication made up for what he lacked in relevant knowledge. He had lost a leg sometime before she'd arrived on the Vivendi and, to hear him say it, he'd been bounced from discipline to discipline trying to find a place he could still serve when he should have been seeking to retire.

Ashe didn't let his age, or any factor aside from his willingness to work and learn, taint her view of the man, nor was she taking it easy on him. A warm body that couldn't do the job didn't serve a purpose. She had pointed that out to him when he'd arrived. To which he simply stated that he could pull his weight. So far, he was holding up fairly well.

"Keep at it. I'd love to have at least two words that rub together before taking this to the captain," Ashe said and turned back to the floating mosaic of dancing orange code.

She knew she was technically in violation of the captain's order. She'd sent a message to Octavian the minute she'd found the ping, but she hadn't heard back from him. That made the decision hers. If they didn't like the fact that she preferred to deliver an actual message instead of wasting everyone's time, he and his master could come down here and take it up with her.

With another yawn and a stretch, Ashe rose from her seat and went to check Nazier's work. She nodded approvingly after watching for a moment, then decided to excuse herself. The door slid open, almost blinding her before she strode through it and into the corridor beyond.

The running lights along the walkway had given way to the more powerful overhead panels. The cycle was a holdover from when the

Sabiens still owned the ship, and no one had seen fit to change it. Ashe preferred the darker aesthetic, but that was part of her nature, she supposed. The ship she'd been born on was a dimly lit place, and when the Vivendi was in the night portion of its cycle, she could almost believe she was home again.

The smell of the mess hall seemed to almost summon her. Ashe had ignored the protests of her stomach for the last four hours. Work had gotten done, but now the tendrils of a headache were stretching through her skull. Between that and the smell of what passed for food on the ship, Ashe was helpless to stop herself.

Almost every soul she passed seemed to be just as off-kilter as she felt. Some were still adjusting to the additional gravity of the planet, but the majority were barely functional due to the early hours.

Mornings were typically rough aboard vessels like this since conduct codes tended to be lax, but things were different on the Modus Vivendi.

Captain Faridan wasn't a typical pirate captain. She was a soldier, and she ran the ship like one, much to the dissatisfaction of her crew. For the most part, the Modus Vivendi was a military vessel or as close to one as possible. The captain and her second did occasionally grant some leeway for the crew to be pirates, but only when mutiny would become the obvious alternative.

Early on, insubordination had been much more of a problem for everyone. A mutiny had been planned, but the leaders of that movement were dispatched by the captain herself. Rumors still persisted about the grisly affair, but Ashe didn't put much stock in the whispers of secret killing rooms. It was fearmongering nonsense... unless it turned out to be true.

The mutiny and the people who planned it had been real things, and so were their executions. All had been forced to attend as the mutineers were committed to the Black, followed by their heads. It was a strong and clear message to all who might attempt such a thing. Most of the crew had gotten that message, but whispers persisted.

Ashe, personally, had mixed feelings about the whole situation. Since she owed her newly elevated station to those executions, she didn't feel she had the right to do much complaining. Still, she had lost a mentor to get to where she was.

Jergen had been killed as much by his own ego and recklessness as he had by the "silver butcher." She knew that, but Ashe couldn't completely accept it. She harbored both a sense of respect and animosity for Faridan that she couldn't reconcile no matter how hard she tried.

Her emotions toward her captain were every bit as tangled and distressing as her feelings about things like fire and the Black. Each force was monstrous and brutal but also powerful, beautiful and sure. While the other two were steady and unchanging, the captain was not. Faridan could easily become an ally or an enemy, and as much as Ashe wanted a definitive answer as to which she was, she was too afraid to seek one out.

As Ashe neared the mess hall, she did her best to shove her bubbling dilemma down deep and focus on finding something that seemed remotely edible.

The mess hall often lived up to its name. It was nothing to find some unlucky soul scrubbing food from the deck. Ashe stepped past the man, cleaning protein paste out of the metal grating, making a conscious effort not to meet his pleading eyes.

Like much of the ship, the grates were obsolete in the modern age. Still, they allowed the corvette's sensor cross-section to stay small, making it almost impossible to detect at any decent speed.

Ashe approved of the overall effect, though she would have preferred the newer ships' maintenance crawlspaces. Perhaps, if the captain kept her word and they took the Beita Systems ship they'd tracked here, she might actually get her wish.

Thinking about the privacy and quiet she could steal in places like those gave her goosebumps. As it stood, she was forced to share her quarters like most aboard the ship, and the idea of being able to steal a quiet, uninterrupted nap at will was better than shore leave to her.

Ashe cleared the rows of tables and benches that made up the bulk of the room. Ignoring a dozen loud, groggy, and dissatisfied sailors, she made her way to the so-called "slop trough." Real food was rare onboard, and since they had put down on a mostly barren rock instead of a lush agro-colony, that wasn't likely to change.

Ashe grabbed a thick metal tray with a suspiciously head-shaped dent in the center and made her way down the line of processed grain, protein chips, and vitamin pastes until she had a tray full of "food" that she could almost trick herself into believing she liked. She figured the quality of food in the mess hall was poor on purpose. Ashe tended to enjoy long conversations over a good meal if there was someone even passably interesting nearby, and she imagined that kind of thing was what captains all over the spectrum were desperate to avoid.

The warped metal table where she sat was empty except for two weapon technicians at the far end. She was their boss now, but she tended to leave the gun jockeys alone.

Ship maintenance and comms were her areas of expertise. Much of the knowledge needed to do their jobs eluded her, and the last thing anyone wanted was to be in a firefight and have the tech you just pissed off hand you a rifle primed to blow up in your face.

"Ayo, Ashana," a loud, melodic male voice almost sang from across the room,

The beaming smile and gangly raised arm of a man Ashe knew as Dogura caught her eye. He was impossibly tall compared to her and lacked any sense of grace or elegance in his movements. She found herself wondering for the millionth time how he managed not to break his front teeth, tripping over his feet when he walked.

She watched warily as the overly excited helmsman crossed the room toward her. They had come aboard together at Veralles and bonded in those early days. She had done her best to move past that, but Dogura hadn't. He seemed to still view her as an older sister of sorts, which was just as annoying as it was, secretly, charming.

"Congrats on the big leg up," he said softly with an over-the-top wiggle of his eyebrows, then sat across from her.

"News travels fast," Ashe said, stirring her red vitamin paste with a broken sliver of chip.

"Small ship, Mama," he said with a wicked smile. "The vents sing."

"So do my knuckles," Ashe said, watching as Dogura waved off her threat.

"I not in your business, Ashana. I have news," he said, leaning in conspiratorially.

Ashe didn't believe him. Dogura fancied himself an information broker, but he was really more of a gossip. When it came to actual news about the ship or upcoming missions, there were very few reliable channels, and he wasn't among them.

"I told you to stop calling me that," Ashe said, refusing to take his bait.

Dogura's smile widened immensely, and he gave her a wink.

"Why? Ashana, beautiful name," he said as he watched her fume with twinkling blue eyes.

"That's exactly why," Ashe growled through her teeth.

Ashe always bristled at her given name. She'd dropped it after the flotilla she had called home was raided by Beita Systems forces. Ashana was the fun-loving girl that had watched through a bulkhead viewport as her family and friends melted apart in an oxygen fire. That girl had died with them, and when the smoke cleared only Ashe remained.

Dogura had befriended her, and in one of her weaker moments, she told him her story. Ever since then, he called her nothing but Ashana, though only when no one else would notice.

"Ashe, she a mask," Dogura said, rubbing the tattoo of the dragon and the broken chain on his shoulder. "Ashana underneath. When she returns, I be here."

Ashe shook off the haze of conflicting feelings his words often inflicted on her. She liked him, but there was something weird about Dogura, aside from his Reitsini dialect. His oddly casual demeanor reminded her too much of everything she had tried so hard to leave behind.

"We'll see," she said, finally stuffing the chip in her mouth. "You said you had news?"

Dogura rubbed his hands together greedily and fixed her with a look coursing with childish excitement.

"You gonna love this, Mama," he began as a tingle ran through his fingers.

Despite her misgivings, Ashe felt herself lean in to catch every detail about to be thrown her way.

"Harlow and Berns got orders. Spin up the old Lifters and double-check the weapons, they say. Harlow tells me scouts went out yesterday, but all secret-like. Very hush-hush," Dogura said, as if spinning an epic tale.

"Why keep it a secret?" Ashe asked, letting genuine curiosity take her. "It doesn't make sense."

"Ah, unless they not scouting what they supposed to be scouting," Dogura said, tapping his temple.

Ashe let out an exasperated sigh. Dogura's news was anything but informative. Standards dictated that, whenever possible, scouts were sent to gather what intel they could, so raiding parties didn't go in blind. Everyone knew that, so keeping that a secret just seemed strange. Still, Ashe wasn't ready to believe Dogura's take on the situation, but she couldn't outright dismiss him either.

Trusting Faridan wasn't something she was about to do blindly, but she was a solid captain. There was little reason to assume that she would actively work against the interests of her own crew. It was universally unwise to do so, but then again, not everyone had access to living metal that did their bidding.

Ashe fixed Dogura with a withering glare and choked down another chip, "I don't buy it."

Dogura waved off her skepticism, snatching a chip from Ashe's tray despite her scowl. "You gotta believe what you do, Ashana," he said playfully. "I just tell you only what I hear."

• • • •

Miranda sat curled up on the coarse sheets of her bunk. She hugged her knees tightly, but found no comfort. Cold sweat covered her skin, chilling her almost to the bone.

With the Modus Vivendi grounded, the hours crawl by. The ship's walls seemed to close in around her inch by inch. It was impossible.

Her mind was playing tricks on her, and yet, as the seconds ticked away, Miranda didn't know how much more she could take.

Like the ship around her, Miranda was a predator. She needed to move, to hunt and all this waiting ran counter to her instincts. She needed to act, but without a direction to travel, she could only waste energy and resources. So, she sat and waited with nothing else to do but dive deeper into the troubling waters of her own mind. But a monster slithered beneath that glassy surface.

Shaking away the intense dread she felt at the concept of self-reflection, Miranda focused on the feelers she'd sent out into Minerva City. They were the best scouts and infiltrators available, but aside from a single sighting in the city's low rent district, there was no news on Bertrand. He had slipped his tail and disappeared again, leaving her no closer to finding his ship than she had been before.

Her emotions had been growing more erratic for some time, but when the news of Bertrand's evasion reached her, she had to isolate herself. By the time she made it to her quarters, Miranda was ready to slash out the heart of the nearest person she saw. She'd caught herself before the impulse took over and took steps to protect herself and her plans from her own unpredictable responses to the stress and disappointment of the situation.

The intensity of these rogue emotions made little sense to her, especially when she knew her former commander was no fool. No one climbed as far up the chain as Bertrand had without the ability to slip the noose, but that didn't seem to matter. She never assumed that he would be anything other than a worthy opponent, but being so close made the wait for actionable information unbearable.

What made things worse was that the silver that lived inside her was as restless as she was. It swam through her body and pooled on her skin, almost in tune with her own anxiety and eagerness. It had truly become an extension of her as the years stretched on, but she couldn't shake the creeping thought that it was more than she had first assumed.

When Keetal fell, her use of the creature was limited. Now it did whatever she could imagine. From time to time, she had even managed to produce varying amounts of electrical energy with it, though the exhaustion and nausea that resulted made that trick useful only as a last resort.

The silver was now a part of her, no different from her own arms or legs. It coursed over her body in an embrace that brought no warmth and little consolation. She was accustomed to it being there to augment her when she needed it. It was her fifth limb, and she worked with it the same way she stretched and trained the rest of her body. Miranda wielded it proudly, but wisdom decreed that she only expose her true self in secret.

Octavian had advised against using the silver in the presence of the crew. His concern was valid, and managing them could quickly become a problem should their captain become inhuman in their eyes. To a point, she even agreed with him. The crew kept the ship running and made it possible for her to continue the hunt. But Miranda was beginning to tire of hiding from them. Binding herself to safeguard the mindsets of lesser creatures had grated on her nerves since the beginning, and she was so very far beyond that now.

Their job was to serve, and hers was to lead. Miranda had little patience for coddling frightened children. Not one of them had the foresight or fortitude to command even one of the missions they had profited from since she'd taken the reigns. They owed her, not the other way around.

In the past weeks, Miranda had come to see the crew as an even more burdensome tool than usual. One that she needed, but also one she resented. Every step she wished to take needed justification from the perspective of the crew. Everything had to be good for them as well. Balancing her desires and their needs had become more trouble than she thought it to be worth, and that feeling was only growing in intensity the longer she sat with nothing to distract her.

Eventually, there would be a point of no return. Miranda would stand on one side of the widening rift, and the crew would stand on the other. The only reason it hadn't happened yet was because of the allegiance, dedication, and wisdom of the one man who straddled the gap.

Her respect for Octavian and what he'd sacrificed to win her freedom kept her loyal to him. It was his job to mediate, and she did not envy his position. So, when she could, she attempted to make his task more manageable. Miranda had no doubt that were he to ever disappear and leave her alone with the crew, the ship would be awash in their blood within a week.

The silence of the room melted away as the proximity chime sounded from above the door.

"Speak," Miranda croaked, realizing just how long it had been since she'd moved from her spot.

The mechanical voice she had come to know as Octavian's sounded through her room speakers, surprising her.

"Ashe has detected an Echelon transmission. Most of it has been decoded already," Octavian said through the wall.

"Enter," she called out.

The bolts at the door's top and bottom slid back into their housings with a heavy metallic thump, allowing it to retract into the wall. Without a moment's hesitation, Octavian stepped inside and did his best to ignore the scent of stale sweat that accosted him.

Miranda craned her neck slowly and fixed him with a nearly lifeless stare.

"What does it say?" Miranda asked, finally getting her voice to produce the proper sound.

"There seems to be a rift between Bertrand and the Echelon Executor he's working with. There's a power struggle aboard their ship," Octavian reported doing his best not to look at his captain.

"That would be useful if we knew where their ship was," Miranda said, willing the silver to retract into her fingers so she could release her knees and stretch.

"I was under the impression that you wanted any news," Octavian said as he turned away from her respectfully.

"I want news of Bertrand's objectives and location," Miranda said, finishing her stretch and willing all silver back under her skin.

"He is a careful man, and if he already has enemies on his ship, he would seek allies elsewhere," Octavian said.

Three silver insect-like legs grew from Miranda's back and found purchase on the wall behind her. Effortlessly, they lifted her body from the mattress and carried her across the ceiling to her clothing locker.

Octavian stole a glance at his captain's dangling form as she hung from the ceiling like the body of a spider and sorted through her clothes. Looking at her in what had become her natural state filled him with unease, but he was too smart to indicate it in any way.

He knew all too well how she would take his innate reaction. They were allies and maybe even still friends, but all that could change quickly if he caught her in the wrong mood.

He was aware of just how much Miranda had changed in the last three years. She had been capable and even devious before, but now she seemed to have turned a corner. He wasn't sure what she would be like once they finally put an end to Bertrand, but he hoped it would send her back toward something that resembled her normal self.

"You think that's why he was alone when the scouts saw him?" Miranda asked, sliding into her uniform as though it were a new skin.

"It would cut the Executor out of whatever he has planned," Octavian replied with a deep relaxing breath. "Which is exactly what I would do."

"Maybe," Miranda said under her breath and finished buttoning her uniform bottoms before dropping to the floor and retracting the silver back into her.

She turned to Octavian but barely saw him. With nothing else to focus on besides the wait, Miranda was tearing through the new information. She didn't know Bertrand's mind, but she understood what Echelon valued even more than the word of one of their executors.

"He's after DiSilva," Miranda announced with a predatory grin.

"I thought so too," Octavian agreed.

"Maybe we should pay him a visit," Miranda said, feeling her mood brighten to something akin to normal.

Octavian stiffened. He had to disagree, but he wasn't sure how she would take it. Putting Miranda in the city proper would create several potential issues.

"Captain," he began, "I'm not sure that you stepping into sensor range is the best thing."

"It's been three years, Octavian. They must have forgotten about me by now," Miranda said, straightening her uniform jacket and inspecting it in a mirrored panel built into the locker.

"Unlikely," Octavian countered. "The creature you carry is rare. They will want it back. Stepping into the city will put both the hunt and the raid at risk."

Miranda felt the flash of searing heat rise from the base of her skull and burn its way through her brain.

Octavian was right. She had to concede, but doing nothing ate her up inside. She needed to get out of the ship. Yet, once again, she had to deny herself for the sake of the crew.

The second she crossed a networked lens, her face would be transmitted to Echelon. Ships would launch into Streamline and arrive in orbit within a standard day.

The Modus Vivendi was a formidable weapon, but against top-tier Echelon ships, she would implode almost instantly. Everyone would die, maybe even Miranda herself, and worse, Bertrand would get away. If she didn't die with her ship, Miranda would once again face a fate much worse, only this time there would be no loyal friend to save her.

"Fine," she snapped. "I want our people to keep their eyes open not just for Bertrand but DiSilva too."

Octavian nodded. It wouldn't be too difficult to make that happen. He was reasonably sure they had nailed down where DiSilva was staying, so tagging and tracking him wouldn't take too much effort.

"Anything else, Captain?" he asked as Miranda finished dressing and checked her appearance in the mirror.

"Give Ashe and her team my thanks," she said as the heat in her head abated.

Octavian gave Miranda the three-fingered Beita Systems salute without thinking about it, and she returned the gesture. He noticed the hint of a smile on her face as they both realized what they'd done.

"And give yourself some downtime," Miranda said, motioning him toward the door. "You clearly need it."

Chapter 14

VISION WOKE TO A SERIES or rhythmic explosions behind her eyes. Each burst of pressure and pain made her wish she'd kept to herself. What little information she'd gleaned was in no way worth the intense throbbing torment promising to crack her skull apart.

Lying on the sofa doing her best to wish the pain away, Vision sorted through what she'd found. The dark-skinned woman she'd seen before in Claude's dreams/memories, but clearly, Bertrand viewed her differently.

What she'd witnessed in his mind was the personification of rage and death, or as close to it as a human being could get.

The other two images meant nothing to her. While the falling man felt familiar, she couldn't place him, nor the location with the vats. When her head stopped hurting, she'd tell Claude about them and see if they made more sense to him, though she had a feeling they wouldn't.

That was one of the many downsides to reading minds. Context always mattered. People weren't books. Their thoughts and feelings weren't even organized for the most part. Memories didn't come complete with a full index of connected events, references, and relationship details.

More often than not, Vision needed to search for that context, though she rarely had the time or the inclination to do so. In the case of Bertrand, she simply lacked both the will and the skill, and thus she had failed to glean anything that might help her prove she could pull her weight.

Light scraping and knocking came from the area behind the couch. At first it took Vision a moment to place the sounds, but her sensors stripped away the mystery. Claude was in the kitchen doing something that could technically be called cooking, though the odds were low that he'd actually managed to produce something edible.

He had many skills, but preparing food suitable for human consumption was not one of them. This time, however, whatever he'd cobbled together actually smelled good, and Vision found her mouth watered in spite of herself.

Claude had carried her up to the apartment and kept an eye on her, something she made a mental note to thank him for. Since leaving Zhara's place, she hadn't been particularly kind to him, and among the day's other regrets, that one felt the worst.

"Claude," she called out. "Do we have anything for a headache?"

The halo fed her a fuzzy, imprecise outline of Claude through the back of the sofa. He nearly jumped at the sound of her voice, which brought a thin smile to her lips.

"We have the regular stuff, but I doubt it would help," Claude said as he rounded the sofa and looked down on her.

"Great," she snarked and tried to sit up before a new flare of agony forced her to give up on the idea.

"Psionic headaches aren't exactly common on Minerva, V," Claude said, tapping her legs.

Vision shifted on the sofa and allowed Claude the space to sit beside her.

"Zhara said you might have a headache when you came to," he continued without looking at her. "She thought food might help."

"Maybe," Vision said, wincing at a new pulse of pain running through her head. "She does know her stuff."

Claude simply nodded. Miraculously, things were finding their way back on track where he and Zhara were concerned, though they were still far from where they had been before. They'd have to take it slow, and maybe, with enough time and patience, they could put this whole mess behind them.

"I didn't want you involved," Claude said, rubbing his brow.

"I know," Vision said sheepishly. "I just wanted to help."

"I get that, but next time wait for me to ask at least," Claude said with a heavy breath.

"I did," Vision said, letting a smile slip.

"If you don't hear my voice, I didn't ask."

Vision pulled her legs from behind him and struggled to sit up once more. This time, she was able to bear the thumping in her skull long enough to pull it off properly.

"Technically..." she said.

"If you have to use 'technically,' you've already lost your point. Just accept it," Claude said, steadying her as she tipped in his direction. "Besides, we both know you were in his head well before that."

Vision just shrugged rather than give Claude the satisfaction of being right.

"Did you take the job?" she asked, switching gears.

"I was going to, but negotiations got cut a little short," Claude said, leaving the rest hanging.

"Are you going to talk to him again?"

"In a while. I want to wait for Bertrand to stew a little bit. We could use the money, but going into the Old City isn't something I'm eager to do," Claude admitted.

Vision relaxed into him and felt the pulsing pain begin to ease as he put his arm around her shoulders.

"You scared of a few Derelicts?" Vision said in a teasing tone.

"Hell yes," Claude said sharply. "The only reason you aren't is because you've never seen one."

Vision took comfort in Claude's warmth and familiarity. Things were changing for her, and the fact that he hadn't decided to distance himself was something she was just now realizing she was grateful for.

The only fundamental constant that she could count on was him. Since they'd found each other, they had somehow become inseparable, though there were times she had wished otherwise. Claude had done everything he had promised he would. She needed for nothing, and when he could afford to provide her with the things she wanted, he did, within reason.

Most importantly, he was content just to be there when she needed him most. She had peered into his mind and knew what he really thought of her, and, unlike most people, he saw her as little more frightening than a child.

"What does he want you to do out there?" she asked, willing herself to just enjoy the moment.

"He thinks someone stashed data drives out there," Claude said dismissively.

Vision could feel the apprehension in him as he spoke. There was more to it, but she had gotten her fill of prying. For now, she was content to let him tell her what he wanted her to know. There was little doubt he would give her the rest when he felt comfortable. Claude rarely tried to keep secrets from her long-term. It was yet another thing that gave her solace.

"So, call him. You know you want to," Vision said, aiming her gentle prod so as to avoid too strong a push back.

"I don't know if I can trust him," Claude replied, falling back into the cushions of the sofa and bringing Vision with him.

"You used to."

Claude sighed heavily.

"Things are very different now. If he's changed anywhere near as much as I have, there's no telling where his loyalties are," Claude stated apprehensively.

Vision didn't know what to say to that. She'd had little experience dealing with people in any normal sense. What she had learned about building and honoring trust in the usual way was extremely limited. Most of the time, she could just have a look to see if someone was worth trusting, and even then, that changed from situation to situation. She didn't really have any friends, and her family was a giant question mark, so that left only Claude and Zhara.

When she thought about it, there should have been a large hole in the center of her life, but she didn't feel it. Normal children had social interactions with others around their age, or at least they were supposed to.

Vision never had that, and she didn't feel like she was missing all that much. What could she possibly have in common with others who shared only her age? Interacting with adults was difficult enough. Trying to interface with incomplete versions seemed like a hassle she'd just as soon avoid.

Even with adults, there were things she didn't quite grasp. She was still learning the difference between what people thought about doing and what they intended to do. Others had to wait and see which manifested. Vision did not. She'd always had full access to the snack container, figuratively. So why should she have to wait until someone handed her something when she could get whatever she wanted for herself?

The answer was trust.

While peering into the minds of others had been opportune in the early days, she was fast learning that it wasn't something she could or should keep doing if she ever wanted to integrate into anything resembling a normal life.

"So, what are we going to do for the rest of the day?" Vision inquired with an exaggerated sigh.

Claude took a moment to survey the vast tracts of nothing he had planned. He was just realizing how dull the day would be when the apartment sensors' shrill voice interrupted his thoughts.

"Combustion alert! Combustion alert!" erupted from every room and launched Claude to his feet.

He leaped over the couch and was hauling the octagonal dish out of the oven with silver-covered hands before Vision managed to fight herself into a decent sitting position. He stuffed the molten concoction into the washbasin and slammed the lid, letting the chemical bath do the heavy lifting.

Vision's halo fed her the steady stream of nearly panicked movements as she focused her attention on Claude and his ruined lunch plans. She couldn't help but laugh at him, but she did try to keep it to a respectful volume. No matter how hard he tried, the simple things just kept eluding him, and if she was honest, she loved him for it.

"Hey," Vision said, getting Claude's attention. "What do you say we stop by Hogan's?"

• • • •

Bertrand had taken it upon himself to check through the communications log and find out what had transpired in his absence. Marta was keen on working around him to achieve her ends, but she didn't seem to understand he possessed the crew's loyalty. Most of it anyway.

There was little activity, though his attention had been called to a transmission Marta had erased from the ship's correspondence records. If it hadn't been for his communications officer feeding him the relay points on the correct comms buoy, Bertrand would have been none the wiser.

Unfortunate for her, Marta shared Echelon's persistent folly. They only ever saw people as tools to be used and discarded, not valuable commodities to be nurtured, cultivated, and treasured. Bertrand had served with enough men and women to understand that their worth was more than what you could squeeze out of them. In his long years, he had discovered that what people elected to do for you far outstripped what you could make them do.

Mattic was a prime example. The Executor had forced him to delete her message, but he had chosen to provide his captain with all the information needed to undermine her order, and for that Bertrand was grateful.

The comms buoys held complete records of every transmission that bounced off them, and if you had the proper clearance codes, you could access them all. Bertrand did, and in a matter of minutes, he would have the entire message and its reply in front of him.

While he waited, he considered his meeting with Claude. Most of it had gone according to plan, but he'd discovered a nosebleed once he made it to the hovercar. He put that together with Claude's urgent ending to their meeting, but there was still a slight gap in his understanding. It was possible that the environment had caused the bleed, but that didn't explain Claude's reaction.

Anyway, he needed Claude to close the deal and find the drives for him. If he was forced to send in his people a second time, he had no doubt there would be casualties.

Derelicts had migrated toward the hotel Eugene had chosen as a hideout, and there was no way a transport could land there without drawing their attention. To give his people a fighting chance, he would need to send a full contingent to secure the building, and the deaths of such an incursion would be untenable. It was a situation Bertrand would avoid at all costs.

No one deserved to die at the hands of monsters, least of all loyal soldiers, but Marta and her masters wouldn't see it that way. Echelon had sent countless men to their deaths in attempts to reclaim the Old City after it first fell. They managed to achieve nothing except adding half a mile's worth of names to the Beita Systems' Memorial Wall on Myridorn.

Thankfully, Bertrand wasn't in the service then, but many were not so fortunate. The bones of family rested somewhere beneath the filth-coated streets of the Minervan Dead Zone, and he would be damned if he would send those under his command to share that fate.

"Transmission decrypted," a soft female voice called without an ounce of true humanity.

Bertrand spun his seat to face the screen over his desk that now displayed clearly readable text. Electing to bypass Marta's outgoing message, Bertrand settled himself into his chair and decided to dig into the return message from Myridorn.

He knew much of what Marta would say. She'd said it to his face already, but he was most concerned with what the desk jockeys at her secretive organization would do about her complaints. It turned out that he didn't need to worry, not yet at least. For all intents and purposes, the anonymous reply was a flat-out refusal to act, which left Bertrand with a feeling of not just relief but near elation.

Apparently, Myridorn wanted to maintain the status quo for the time being. Short of taking over field operations, Marta was still ordered to support Bertrand in his acquisitions.

That word made Bertrand's blood freeze in his veins. As far as anyone knew, they were only supposed to collect the data drives, one acquisition. If he was supposed to bring in multiple targets, that was news to him, though not unexpected news.

Reading on, he found that the last few lines of the message were not addressed to Marta, but to him directly.

The lines read:

Commander Bertrand, Kerrid C, it has been discovered that an Omen-level organism resides on Minerva Prime. Mission F-44-10A has been amended to include the capture and delivery of said organism to Laidlaw Station. Full compliance is expected.

It was concise and clear. Echelon had gotten the same PlanSec report he had, and they'd come to the conclusion he dreaded. Bertrand had gone to DiSilva for two reasons. He hoped that a scout with local expertise would be able to succeed where his team had failed. He also wanted to see whether DiSilva had the same parasite that had infested Faridan.

Now Echelon knew what he did, and they wanted Bertrand to bring them another specimen for their experiments.

"Damn them," Bertrand said, slamming his fist onto his desk hard enough to disrupt the screen projected above it.

The last thing he wanted to do was betray yet another soldier to the soulless puppeteers pulling his strings. He'd done that once, and the repercussions still haunted him. Faridan still stalked him, both in his mind and somewhere out in the Black. He carried that anxiety and guilt with him every second of every day, and now he had to add on to it.

Bertrand did his best to push back his disdain for the new orders and focus on what needed to be done next. If he could get the drives and failed to acquire DiSilva, that would at least be a partial success. Maybe he could make that work and buy DiSilva time enough to disappear.

It was a weak plan, but it was still better than putting an innocent man's neck on the block for the "crime" of surviving. If he'd been smarter, he would have done something similar years ago, but what was done could not be undone.

"Open a direct line to Mattic," Bertrand said as the throb in his fist died down.

A cycling series of notes rang through the room's broadcast system for a moment before a voice, sporting a Reitsini accent, took its place.

"This Mattic, sir," a chipper young man's voice called.

"I need you to get me in touch with someone immediately and keep it quiet."

Chapter 15

THE INTERIOR OF PHALEN'S cruiser was a mess of discarded wrappers, cups, and carry-out containers. He kept it the same way he kept everything else in his life, with the exception of his uniform, which was always in superb condition.

The job was something he was very precious about. It was what had given him solace after his family took off and left him with little else in the way of a purpose. After that, he'd poured himself into the job, but not because he believed in what he was doing or that he thought it might make Minerva City a better place. Instead, he did it because it was something to do. It was a form of structure in an otherwise meaningless life. It was an escape pod amid the ravenous Black, and he did everything he could to keep it viable.

That meant early mornings and late nights stalking the streets of the city. Phalen maliciously enforced the laws of the world on any who caught his attention. No offense was too minor. In fact, the smaller ones brought him the most satisfaction and the least amount of work.

If headquarters was displeased with his actions, he was blissfully unaware of it. He had received no complaints about his behavior, though he had been given a citation about the condition of his cruiser, which he had promptly added to its interior landscape.

Violet district was of particular interest to Phalen. He was given patrols in the area mainly because others didn't like the unsavory neighborhoods and rampant disrespect that they faced from the citizens forced to call the district home.

Phalen didn't see that as a problem. He thrived here. His numbers were substantial, and there was never really any issue finding perpetrators to run through the system. His eagerness to harass and arrest those he caught bending the law gave him a certain level of respect when his cruiser was seen.

More prominent criminals found it easier to cut Phalen in on some of their activities as a way of insurance against his direct interference. It seemed to make them feel good, but he didn't really care. Big collars would only draw attention from the higher-ups, which he would just as soon avoid.

Phalen was a bottom feeder, and he knew it. He knew a little about ecosystems, and someone had to pick clean the corpses left behind by the larger and more dynamic predators. He was happy to be just that. His belly was always full, and when the eyes of said predators turned his way, it was easy to find cover until the heat was off.

He'd been sitting above Growlet Pass for the last three hours. It was a dusty, ruined street that seemed to imagine it was something more. Hogan's Deli made it something of a destination, especially since the old fool refused to raise his prices regardless of how popular his establishment became.

Phalen had taken full advantage of the man's ignorance many times, but he always took his sandwiches to go. If he had his way, he would never mingle with the refuse that wandered the streets of any district, let alone Violet.

While Hogan's drew most of the attention, Phalen was most interested in a small office/apartment hybrid a quarter mile up the street. The address was familiar to him. He'd seen it in messages his ex-wife had thought she'd deleted.

Phalen ground his molars just thinking about what the bastard inside that office had cost him. So what if he'd been paid to look the other way by one of the local pimps? It was his business, not his wife's, and most definitely not Claude DiSilva's.

He lost the ability to see his son all because he elected to borrow a whore who hadn't even been that good at her job. DiSilva had tailed him like he was some criminal and exposed him to his family. It was humiliating.

He had dedicated a large amount of his time since then to stalking DiSilva, watching and waiting for him to make a mistake so that he could return the favor. Claude had a business and a freak that he raised as a daughter. Phalen would see those things stripped away from him, and then, when the man was at his lowest, maybe he'd finish him off.

He hadn't gotten anywhere near that far in his plans, though. DiSilva had remained frustratingly clean, or at least clean enough that Phalen couldn't run him in without bringing himself under scrutiny. So he waited, and he watched, but these days he'd actually been paid to do what he'd gladly done for free these last two years.

The deep growl of a late model Lifter bike pricked up Phalen's ears before he could even see the damned thing. He wasn't expecting to see the hoodlum that rode it so early, but surprises happened all the time in Violet. The black raptor-shaped body of the hoverbike drifted into his cruiser's sensor range as it stirred up a cloud of dust to mark its path. A dreadlocked man straddled the monstrous thing. Even though his face was hidden behind the breather he wore, Phalen knew his scarred features all too well.

He was unmistakably a pirate or something of the sort. Phalen had noticed both the way he almost never stepped off the bike and the way his limbs shook in their attempt to hold him up against the gravity of the planet. Those things would have only identified him as a Child of the Black, but when added to the ominous and unique flair he possessed, it screamed pirate.

Phalen had thought about running him in, but when the man mentioned an interest in DiSilva by name, all thoughts of arresting the pirate died. They'd struck a deal, and Phalen did what he always did. He watched and waited, only now he fed that information to the pirate whose name he had never seen fit to ask. There was little doubt in his mind that eventually, it would lead to DiSilva's ruin, and he was more than happy to assist in that, especially in such an innocuous and deniable way.

The pirate skidded to a stop less than three feet from Phalen's cruiser and killed his engine. He stared into the driver's side portal through the tinted visor of his mask as the dust cone overtook him.

Phalen made a point of finishing his tea and staring right back at the man. He figured it was an intimidation tactic that he wasn't about to play into. It took a moment for the dust to settle and for the pirate to motion for Phalen to open his onboard comms.

Phalen instead elected to step out of the car and lean against the door. The last thing he needed was PlanSec listening in on his conversations, even if it was highly unlikely they would do so. His ex-wife had been kind enough to keep their divorce away from his job, and for whatever reason, DiSilva had done the same. There was no way he'd jeopardize that for this chat.

"Still in there?" the pirate inquired.

The filtration on the mask trapped the sound of his natural voice but used a speaker to play a mechanical approximation in its place. It was easy to understand but devoid of that certain something that told Phalen he was actually speaking to a person.

"They got some delivery, but no movement from DiSilva since the old man left yesterday," Phalen said casually.

The pirate tossed Phalen a pouch that jingled when he caught it. It was heavier than it looked, but Phalen assumed that was just what wealth felt like.

They'd negotiated payment in deritrium tokens to keep everything untraceable. Most financial transactions and records were done via data transfer, but data was immaterial. No matter how advanced technology got, there was always a use for physical currency. This was one of them.

Deritrium was valued everywhere. As a semi-rare metal, it was used mostly for currency and decoration. It's worth was such that small square tokens forged from the stuff were the universal currency of nearly all illegal dealings both in the Beita Systems and the Neutral Territories beyond.

Phalen had accepted them because there were several ways to transfer them into credits without drawing suspicion. He'd done so several times before, and none of those previous transactions had ever come back to bite him.

"Do I need to count these?" Phalen asked, locking his gaze to where he imagined the pirate's eyes were.

"If you want to waste your time," the pirate snapped as something down the street caught his eye.

Phalen tossed the pouch into the car before he spotted Claude and his little girl heading to their beat-up old car.

He was curious where they could possibly be going so early in the morning, but not curious enough to follow them. He'd been awake for a solid eighteen hours, and now that his pay had arrived, he was more than excited to find his way to bed before the tea left his system, and he crashed.

The pirate shot him an unreadable glance as DiSilva's hovercar took to the air, then revved his bike and took off in pursuit. Both the sedan and the bike curved toward the energy field before dropping out of sight.

Phalen slipped back into his cruiser and decided to count the tokens after all. He had no reason to believe the pirate would stiff him on his pay, but then again, he was certain no one became a pirate because of their high moral fiber.

• • • •

The call had come in yesterday, but Claude elected to wait until morning before making his move. The skyway heading toward the violet energy field was barren most of the time, but doubly so in the early hours.

"I wonder what it's like out there?" Vision chirped beside him.

Claude glanced over to see a bright and all-encompassing smile firing back at him. He couldn't help but give her one of his own, despite knowing that visiting the Old City would be anything but a good time.

"I'd prepare myself for anything if I were you," he replied, unwilling to shatter her hopes entirely.

From what Claude remembered, there was an abandoned, eroding beauty to the Dead Zone, so long as you stayed high enough to avoid the smell.

As the tip of the spiral, the Old City was part of the original colony, founded shortly after the fall of the Zephiar. The settlement began modestly, but eventually grew into the massive, unwieldy form of Minerva City proper.

Its broken streets and collapsing buildings held a tremendous amount of history, which he knew would be of interest to Vision. She was fascinated with the idea of the past and all that humanity had lost to it. Claude did his best to feed that interest as much as possible, but regular trips to the Archive weren't exactly cheap. New artifacts were constantly being discovered and displayed, which kept admission prices high while credits were harder to come by.

Vision's halo strobed so fast that its lights forced Claude to look away. She'd maxed out the range and refresh speed of her sensors in an attempt to absorb every detail she could. Claude didn't really have the heart to tell her that there was nothing in the Dead Zone worth getting excited about. Instead, he'd tried his best to temper her expectations. But, like a grain of sand in an ion storm, his words were swept away by her gale-force optimism.

"I need you to understand that it's dangerous out there," Claude said, guiding the sedan off the main thoroughfare and into the caverns of empty buildings that bordered the violet barrier.

Vision grunted and grabbed onto her halo as they passed into the radiant glow of the massive intangible wall.

"Hold on," Claude said, opening a panel in the sedan's center console to reveal a set of tactile buttons.

Punching in the sequence he'd memorized more than a year ago, Claude activated the sedan's onboard shielding unit and synced it with the energy field ahead.

Traditionally, anyone with business in the Old City stopped at the checkpoints and presented the PlanSec officers there with identification and the proper permits. For Claude and anyone else seeking to keep their passage off the record, that was far from ideal.

A year ago, he'd taken a mission to retrieve the remains of a client's family matriarch. He'd needed to modify his car to do it, but the pay was worth it. Though why anyone wanted a set of broken and gnawed bones was beyond him. Luckily, understanding client reasoning was rarely part of the job.

"Better?" Claude asked, watching Vision's pained expression fade.

"Why didn't you do that before?" she asked incredulously.

Claude eased the sedan into the energy barrier and ignored the slight shudder that jarred the vehicle as it disappeared into the wall.

"The frequency isn't exactly made for hover cars," he replied. "If I leave it on for too long, we'll lose power and fall out of the sky."

Vision frowned at him. "Then you need a new car," she said, turning her attention back to the world outside the vehicle.

The barrier was still affecting her halo, but not to such a painful degree. Static frayed every detail her sensors captured, and it worsened as they moved farther and farther into the energy field. As they passed into the center of the half-mile barrier, the interference consumed her halo's feed, effectively blinding her.

"Still with me?" Vision heard Claude ask.

"How long is it going to be like this?" she asked impatiently.

Claude checked the sedan's Global Position readout only to see that the holo-feed was dark.

"No idea, but it shouldn't be that much longer," he said.

"Can you speed us up?"

"The faster we move, the faster the shield burns our battery," Claude said, leaning back and guiding the control yoke with one hand.

He wasn't exactly happy with the quality or the service he'd gotten where the shielding unit was concerned, but since he was a motivated buyer and the rig was very illegal, Claude wasn't left with much room to shop around.

He had considered getting a newer hovercar, but his sedan was one of the last models produced before onboard tracking systems became mandatory. There was no way he could allow any corporation to know exactly where he was and what he was doing with his vehicle.

Luckily, he wasn't the only person who felt that way. The entire scenario had opened a keg of brille that still hadn't completely died down. A few dozen lawsuits were filed alleging breaches of privacy and the like, but nothing had changed, of course. Nothing ever did when it came to battles between ordinary people and massive companies.

The holo screens blinked back into existence as the decaying husk of the Old City lost the warbling purple filter.

"Finally!" Vision said, blinking rapidly.

Claude always wondered why she blinked so much when her sensors were having issues, though he'd never actually asked her. He assumed it was like closing your eyes when you sneezed. It was just one of those things Vision did. She had a set of quirks that were easier to just accept than to question.

"I thought you said this place was terrible," Vision said with a look of awe on her face.

Claude hadn't quite had the same reaction when he'd first seen the Old City, but he understood how she could. Aside from its decaying state, the Old City was one of the few places where the underground rivers of Minerva Prime had managed to tear their way through to the surface. Sinkholes had developed. Massive parts of the city had collapsed into the waters below, damming them and making immense stagnant pools.

Vision had never really been in contact with large bodies of water before, at least not to his knowledge. She had only ever been on the research station, a few ships and finally Minerva City. None of those environments possessed an abundance of water, or trees, or even animals, for that matter. To her, the Old City must have been like visiting a new world, and Claude prayed silently that she would have a better experience than he'd had last time.

"What happened to this place?" Vision asked as she leaned against the door panel.

Claude took a second to make sure that the door's locks were still active before deciding how to answer her question.

"They say a mining crew broke into a pocket of old Zephiar remains, and that's what caused the mutations," Claude said.

Vision wrinkled her nose. The Zephiar were largely a mystery to her and every other person in the Beita Systems. They'd all died out four millennia ago, and the people who had lived during that time were more than happy to forget them altogether. Still, Claude's story didn't add up.

"I thought the Zephiar didn't have physical bodies, and that's why they needed us," Vision said, doing her best not to make it sound like she was outright challenging his answer.

Claude shrugged and checked their location against the destination he'd been given. They were half an hour out, and Vision was already asking questions beyond his ability to answer.

"I don't really believe it either, V," Claude said. "That's just what people say. No one really cared about what made the Derelicts, they were all just trying to survive."

"Yeah, I guess so," she said with a clear note of disappointment in her voice.

"On the bright side, Derelicts are supposed to be almost immortal, so maybe they know what happened," Claude said jokingly.

"Really?" Vision asked and Claude instantly saw the mistake he'd made.

"Hey, that was a joke. You are absolutely not going to try and get in the head of one of those things," Claude declared and hoped that she would actually listen this time.

Vision ignored him. She wasn't willing to go out of her way to try and find answers, but if the chance presented itself, how could she let it go to waste?

Curiosity often drove her to take risks, but she never felt the dangers were particularly unreasonable. Claude tended to see it differently.

"So exactly what's on these drives, anyway?" Vision asked once the initial awe had worn off.

"Honestly, I have no idea. We're just here to find them and collect our quarter-million credits," Claude said, hoping the number would distract the little girl from how vague he was being.

"Why can't your old boss do it himself?" Vision inquired, with a raised eyebrow.

Claude sighed. He was beginning to regret several of his recent decisions. Vision's questions were punching holes in the thin veneer of control that he had painted over the entire job. In truth, he didn't know much more than she did, and that bothered him.

Claude was never one for going in blind, yet here he was again, working in dangerous conditions with very little information of value, and this time he'd brought a child along for the ride.

Vision wasn't exactly a normal child and she could be an asset to the kind of jobs he did. She told him so frequently, but he still saw her as a little girl. No matter how capable she was, there were still glasses in the top cabinets she couldn't reach. The meanings of some fairly common words still eluded her, and when she woke from her nightmares, she still came and curled up with him on the sofa.

On the other hand, she had incapacitated thirty-two people in the Artemis building, or that was the latest tally Zhara had given him. She'd even managed to overpower some of Bertrand's mental defenses, though it had taken a toll on both of them.

Few things bothered him, like the idea of Vision in peril. Claude had grown undeniably attached to her, and that was a very real problem. Their arrangement was for him to find her family and get her back to them. He had been searching diligently, but with every lead that died, Claude found himself more conflicted.

He wasn't sure exactly what they were to each other, and he was unwilling to try and put a name on it, but whatever they were felt right to him. Having that ripped away, either because he had to let her go or because he was putting her in danger, was unbearable to consider.

Unfortunately, Bertrand knew where he lived, and Claude couldn't trust the man not to raid the place. Ordinarily, he would have left Vision at home, but that too was a massive risk. Pawning her off on Zhara seemed wrong as well.

Things between him and Zhara seemed to be back on a good track, but Claude wasn't ready to strain their connection if he could manage it. It was possible Zhara wouldn't have had an issue taking Vision with her to work. It was even possible that Claude was overreacting, but he had set boundaries and he needed to respect them.

That left him with only one play. It was risky, and probably stupid. Claude could admit that. Still, it felt like the best way forward. If he had her with him, he could keep Vision safe from any move Bertrand might make. Plus, it would give him and Zhara the time they needed to strengthen their relationship. Besides, he was sure he could keep her safe... mostly sure, anyway.

"Bertrand works in secret. It's been that way since the war. I'd bet he doesn't want to draw attention to his activities on-world," Claude said, uncomfortable with how weak the answer was.

"It's the Old City. Does he think PlanSec runs patrols out here?" Vision parsed out as she did her best not to laugh at the idea.

"I have no clue, but that's what he told me," Claude said while dodging a leaning skyscraper.

The tall castle-like design of the Derita Hotel loomed ahead, shimmering in the brilliant orange sun. Much of the exterior was scarred by wind and time, but even with all the years that had passed, the Derita was still impressive. Claude could see the four corner towers and the central domed skylight of the building in the distance. A sinkhole had claimed much of the structure's western side, rendering it far less stable than the eastern half.

Bertrand had been vague about the condition of the building or what to expect once inside, no doubt because he hadn't actually set foot inside the building himself; that and the fact he was hiding something substantial.

Claude half-expected Derelicts to be crawling all over the place, and he'd planned his approach accordingly. Daylight wasn't the mutants' best friend, though no one knew exactly why. It didn't appear to hurt them in anyway. They just avoided it whenever possible.

By arriving when the sun was high overhead, Claude hoped to catch them sleeping. If he had his way, it would be a simple matter of staying quiet, snatching the drives, and sneaking back up to the car again.

"When we get there, I need you with me. No wandering off. No exploring. Got it?" Claude said, taking a moment to watch Vision's response.

She nodded and pursed her lips, but didn't turn to face him.

"I'm serious, V. We need to do this as quickly and quietly as possible," he stated as he slowed the sedan for the final descent.

The hotel was massive. It could easily have been the central attraction in Violet, but here it was just one among the hundreds of once impressive structures being reclaimed by Minerva Prime's ravenous appetite.

The sedan slowly and gently touched down on the sunbaked rooftop until, with a soft scrape, it settled its full weight on the building.

The sun was blazingly bright above the shadeless skyline. At midday, it was possible to see for a hundred miles if you were high enough above the consistently swirling dust that choked the lower levels of their home district.

In the Old City, rampant sinkholes turned most of that dust into mud, keeping the air almost completely clear. As a result, the rocky canyons and the serpent-like structures that wove their way through and around them were as clear as Claude had ever seen them.

Stepping out of the sedan and toward the sturdier edge of the roof, Claude found himself wandering across the roof toward the ancient structures and marveling that they still stood. But it wasn't until Vision caught up to him that he realized just how lost he'd been staring at the handiwork of his long-dead ancestors and wondering how exactly they had managed to build such things without modern technology.

"What are you staring at?" Vision asked, doing her best to hide her sensitive skin from the blistering sun.

For all the marvels her sensors allowed, distance was their one true weakness. The structures were frozen in a dance at the horizon's distant edge, and there was no way her halo could reach out that far. Zhara had constructed an impressive device, one that could pull images and thermal readouts through most walls, ceilings, and floors. At a glance, it could read half a dozen micro-textures and material compositions, but it could never relay the simple beauty of a sunrise, nor glimpse the wonders of a shooting star.

After taking another long moment to drink in the world stretched out before him and process a fraction of the complex feelings it invoked, Claude said, "The slave fields."

Minerva Prime was one of many planets where humanity had worked and lived as slave labor for a long dead alien race. Evidence of that past was strewn all throughout the known universe, yet Claude had seen little of it.

As a result, he rarely took the time to think about what the Zephiar had taken, and what they had given to his people. No one he'd ever known had been enslaved, at least not by any race other than humans. Millennia had passed since the Zephiar had died out, leaving humanity to its own devices, and yet some still carried that bit of painful history with them like an open wound.

For Claude, those events were unfathomable. The only thing he could understand was how it might motivate people to advance, to grow, and to ensure that such things could never happen again. Still, as he looked at the mysterious writhing forms in the distance, it occurred to him that, as a species, humanity may not have come that far after all.

Why the Old City had been built in view of the slave fields when there was no end of land elsewhere was anyone's guess. Perhaps the original settlers had chosen the site as a reminder of the hardships they'd endured, but Claude thought it had to be simpler than that. He imagined water had been the reason.

Just like the newer districts of Minerva City, this place had been built with the intention of capitalizing on the rivers and various minerals that ran beneath the planet's surface.

"Jump in and take a look," Claude said, tapping his temple.

He didn't turn away from the horizon and instead did his best to feel Vision as she entered his mind. He felt nothing, as usual, but he still liked to try whenever he was aware it was happening.

When she was younger, the process had been clumsy, and Claude had suffered massive headaches whenever Vision tried to access any part of his mind that he was actively focusing on, but she had gotten better at it. Now he felt equal parts pride and unease when he failed to detect her.

Even now, he had no way of knowing if she was looking through his eyes, so he continued marveling at the fields in the distance until she told him not to.

"They're beautiful," she said and took his hand.

Tears brimmed in her wide, dark eyes, but she wiped them away on her sleeve instead of allowing them to fall.

"Not sure that's the word I'd pick," Claude said, hugging her to his side. He waited a long moment, just feeling her beside him.

He straightened and said, "Daylight's burning. We should probably get on with it."

With a nod and a sniffle, Vision pushed away from him and hid her face.

"Yeah, let's go," she said and cleared her throat.

• • • •

The Derita hotel was once a monument to the craft and artistry of the people who had once called the Old City their home. Its immense spiral staircases wound down from the roof to what used to be a lobby, and it had seen better days. The broad white stone stairs once coursed with veins of shimmering deritrium. Many had long since been lost to time and gravity, while those that remained were so coated in grime that the vibrant shock of the emerald metal within was effectively invisible.

The elegant spiraling guard rails had crumbled to dust, leaving behind needle-like rods that reminded Claude of exposed ribs. On the lobby's west side, much of the lower floors had been eaten away by the planet itself, leaving what looked like a ragged, sneering, man-made upper jaw to match a natural lower one carved from weathered rock.

According to Bertrand, they were looking for the twenty-sixth floor, which should have been below their current position. Claude wasn't sure exactly how he and Vision were supposed to get there. The ruins of the staircase didn't provide many options for traversal. If he still had access to his old scout gear, the light thrusters could have aided them in jumping past the next twenty or so missing stairs. Unfortunately, he was a civilian now, or as close to one as he would ever be.

Something low and quiet in the back of his mind gave him the impression that he could make that jump, but even if that were true, Vision would never be able to. Leaving her behind was a laughably bad idea, considering all the muddy handprints he could see trailing way up the walls. At least he hoped they were muddy.

The odors hanging in the building's stale air strongly suggested otherwise, but he threw that thought as far into the back of his mind as possible.

"You weren't lying about the smell," Vision said, gagging slightly.

She was having a tough time with it since they'd found the access hatch on the roof. The trapped air had all but knocked her over and made Claude happy that he'd vetoed Vision's demand for a pre-work meal.

"Get a few deep breaths in. It will make it easier to ignore," Claude said, keeping his voice just above a whisper.

Behind him, he could hear Vision taking his advice. She'd asked to be a partner, and while he still didn't consider her as one, she was definitely going to get a clearer picture of exactly how "glamorous" the job actually was.

"Ugh, it's not working," she complained and buried her nose in the crook of her elbow again.

Claude couldn't keep himself from smiling as he turned around and moved back up to the last door they'd passed.

"Well, it was worth a shot," he said as he moved back past her.

"It's not funny, Claude," Vision snapped, her voice losing much of its intended bite while muffled by her sleeve.

"Come on, we have to see if there's another way down," he said, and pressed himself against the wall beside the door. Vision followed his lead, making sure to keep her nose covered.

Claude looked back at her and shook his head in the direction of the door. Vision narrowed her eyes for a few seconds, then nodded. Tortured metallic groans echoed through the open lobby as Claude slid the door along its rusty track. He winced and waited for any sign of movement or life within the ruined hotel. When none came, both he and Vision shared a sigh, then moved into the hall beyond.

Claude did his best to adjust his balance to the slight upward slant of the building and scanned the hall. It was a mess of crumbling walls, cracked ceilings, and filth-coated floors. Much of the damage seemed ancient, but there were holes ripped in the walls that seemed like newer additions.

Slashes of dim orange sunlight carved their way through the otherwise darkened hallway, illuminating tiny glittering particles of dust in a sad and silent waltz. What looked like moss grew in damp shadows cast along walls the sun refused to touch. Dark spatters of hundred-year-old blood stained the area forming a macabre testament to a massacre Claude was glad to have missed.

Once he was sure that there weren't any immediate threats, he backed to the door and motioned for Vision to follow.

"Do you–"

Claude spun and pressed a finger to her lips before she could finish her sentence.

"They've been here," he whispered in a voice so soft he wasn't sure she'd be able to hear him.

She did, and his words seemed to freeze the blood in her veins instantly. Her question died as she desperately pored over every ounce of data that her halo streamed into her brain.

Claude had only seen one of the creatures, but that had been enough. Physically, it was unassuming, and he was grateful for that. Still, something about the ghostly white creature made him believe every story he'd ever been told. It looked like a juvenile, if a Derelict could be such a thing. In reality, it was probably four times as old as he was, but it still had the baseline body of a boy younger than Vision.

There were subtle hints of its mutation. Its musculature was too pronounced for a child of its size, but the eyes were what Claude remembered most. Those hauntingly iridescent turquoise irises that searched the darkness for him. They told him that whoever the kid had been before the change was long gone. Whatever process he'd gone through was unimaginable and thorough. The boy had become something completely inhuman; they all had.

Claude drew his sidearm and took Vision by the hand. He watched as she thawed to his touch and came back to herself.

"I've got you," he said, taking the time to focus entirely on her.

It wasn't much of a reassurance, but it was all he could give, and he meant it. There was no way he would let them get to her if he had so much as a breath left to him, and he hoped she could feel that.

Claude and Vision crept up the hall, with Claude taking the time to sweep each room as they passed. He didn't see any of the mutants as they made their way to the western stairwell, but he couldn't shake the feeling they were being watched.

The heavy metal doors at the hallway's end stood ajar. Taking a moment for his eyes to adjust to the pure darkness beyond, Claude caught himself hoping it was Bertrand's people who had opened this path.

"Maybe I should have stayed in the car," Vision said and winced as her voice echoed off every wall on its way the stairwell.

Unlike the lobby, this staircase had no skylight. It was a shaft of total blackness. If Derelicts chose to ambush them inside it, there would be no room to maneuver, but it wasn't all bad. Without exposure to the elements, there would be less damage to the stairs and railings.

"That's not true," Vision said, rebutting his thoughts. "Some of the stairs are rotten, or whatever. They won't be able to hold our weight."

Claude nodded his thanks but said nothing. Activating the light under the barrel of his gun, he began his descent into the darkness below. With every step, he scanned the path ahead before advancing. He expected there to be teeth and claws just waiting to leap out of the darkness, but the stairwell appeared to be as empty as it was quiet.

Still, if they were going to get themselves into trouble, it would be in an environment like this. The suffocating, humid darkness was almost alien. Minerva Prime was an arid world for the most part, but the open water in the Old City challenged that idea.

Here, the air was thick and oppressive when combined with the midday heat. The enclosed staircase seemed to compound that muggy quality, even though Claude had expected the opposite. This was more like a bog than the dry heat he'd become accustomed to.

Vision had never been in any environment like this as far as she could remember, and she wasn't enjoying it. She'd imagined what it would be like to explore other worlds, but she hadn't thought that one existed just on the other side of the barrier. Now she wished she was back in the climate-controlled apartment, bored and safe.

It occurred to her that she had lived a very sheltered life and that it might not have been such a bad thing. She liked knowing that when she went somewhere, there wasn't going to be some kind of monster waiting to tear her apart. She imagined that Claude did too, but still, he had lived a more adventurous life. But sometimes, in quiet moments, she could catch him wishing for something a little more like this than the mundanity she was used to.

Adventure had its lures, and while Vision wasn't ready to swear it off entirely just because she was choking on whatever it was that stank so badly, she now understood why some people were more than happy to avoid it.

Claude turned back to her and held up three fingers, which she interpreted as three floors to go. She wasn't sure how far down they'd come since leaving the car, and the walls of the staircase were so thick she wasn't able to peer through them to make a guess like she had in the hall.

The only thing she could do was follow Claude and occasionally warn him about a stair or two that would likely drop him to his death.

"Not that one," Vision said suddenly.

Claude skipped the stair Vision was pointing at and nodded to her.

"Keep the advice coming," he said as he waited for her to catch up to him.

"Would the fall really kill you?" Vision asked.

Claude shrugged. "I'd rather not find out."

Chapter 16

AN HOUR HAD PASSED since word reached Miranda about DiSilva crossing into the Dead Zone. She almost sprinted through the ship to get to the hoverbikes but managed to restrain herself. The stillness and lack of news had been driving her stir-crazy, so this was precisely the kind of action she needed to get back to herself.

She had forgone a breather mask. Unlike the rest of her squad, she didn't require it. Having her lungs coated in rock dust wasn't a thing that could harm her, at least not permanently. If being a "guest" of Echelon had taught her anything, it was that she was nearly indestructible. Of course, there were things she had not been tested against, but it was DiSilva who concerned her now. She had no idea what his silver could do or if she'd be able to counter it should they come to blows, and that made her feel more alive than she had in years.

Octavian had taken volunteers for the ride into Derelict territory, and luckily, each of them were every bit as eager to breathe new air as she was. No one became a pirate to sit in the sand, yet only these four had elected to join her expedition.

Miranda didn't know any of them personally, but they seemed capable enough. Though the skinny one called Dogura didn't seem particularly up to the task, but she trusted Octavian's instincts. It could not be said of Captain Miranda Faridan that she did not provide opportunities for her crew to prove themselves.

They had all covered themselves against the stinging dust particles and the static buildup to the point where they were all but indistinguishable from one another. Yet Miranda didn't care. She'd drilled them on their number designations before they left the gangplank. They would do their jobs, and she would come away with a better understanding of Bertrand's purpose on Minerva, if not a new ally against him.

Barren rock walls gave way to crude shelters carved from stone in ages past. As they sped past, Miranda felt a swell of satisfaction rise up from inside her. She wasn't one to marvel at her environment but here in the canyon, under the baking sun and surrounded by the stonework huts humanity was once bound to, Miranda felt truly free.

It wasn't true, and on some level, she still knew that. However, the wind whipping through her hair, coupled with the static discharge dancing along her silver-coated skin and nerves, allowed her to forget her bonds. For a moment, she allowed the vendetta she had sworn to wash away. Her commitments to her station and her crew were lost in the wake of her Lifter bike, but there was one thing she could not simply choose to leave behind.

Inside her, the creature whispered, drowning out the roar of the wind, and it made Miranda's sweat cool rapidly along her spine. The soft call was more sensation than sound. It was the thing crawling in her head, burrowing deeper, like a worm tunneling through fertile soil.

For perhaps the first time, it was letting Miranda know it was really there. She had seen the silver moving on and under her skin countless times. In private moments, she had even wondered whether it was infecting her with its own thoughts and feelings, but never had she sensed it so clearly.

The silver wanted something from her. It coaxed her forward rather than pushing or commanding. Its way was subtle and far more seductive. There, in the blinding light of the desert, Miranda felt it breach the surface of her own thoughts for just a moment before fading beneath the waves of her subconscious, where it forever dwelled.

For the first time since she awoke with silver strands under the brown of her skin, she felt afraid of the thing living inside her. After all these years, she still knew almost nothing about it, and in all honesty, she didn't want to.

The spike of innate panic stood like the worm-like spires that towered over the shallowing canyon. It was undeniable, but just like those structures, it was crumbling as the moment passed. Each new thought reminded Miranda of all that the silver provided. She remembered the nearly insurmountable tasks they had seen completed together, and the final challenge that lay ahead.

"Bertrand," she said through gritted teeth.

What was once a towering spire of fear and doubt blew away in the searing gale of Miranda's hate. Killing Bertrand was her guiding star. It lit her way in the darkness, but as she grew closer to that objective it also threatened to burn her alive.

With a strong pull on the bike's control yoke, Miranda increased her altitude and saw that her crew followed her lead. The outermost lip of the Old City raced beneath them as the loose formation of bikes cleared the rooftops of the first colony structures and tore through the sky toward the city proper.

Clouds of dust fell away, leaving Miranda with an impressive view of Minerva City's modest beginnings. The first seeds of what had eventually grown monstrous were pleasantly mundane and not very different from the slave huts that walled the canyons behind her.

In the distance, beyond the purple wall of light, the shining towers of Fauldwin were only barely visible. They provided both an impressive and sickening contrast to the more grounded lifestyles the early settlers once lived.

That simpler city had been consumed by monsters that needed no sustenance yet feasted all the same. Viewing both the city's inception and its conclusion, Miranda couldn't find much difference between the Derelicts and the humans that feared them so much.

In her mind, the Derelicts were slightly better. They didn't attempt to mask their monstrosity behind the desire to do good or better themselves. They just consumed, and when they couldn't, they slept. Humans never slept, nor did they ever have enough. When there was nothing else to consume in all the universe, they began consuming each other, and when that had almost killed them all, they then elected to consume themselves.

In the back of her mind, she knew that she was one of them, but unlike the wretches that wandered blindly in the dust of a thousand worlds, she was now elevated. She was more.

Her Lifter bike skimmed its way up and over the buildings of the Dead Zone as she set the instruments to search for traversal signatures. The cityscape was massive. The Old City could have easily housed millions of people in its prime. Now it housed only a handful.

Miranda's scout had stopped short of tracking DiSilva across the barrier. That left her very little to work with aside from the knowledge that her old subordinate was nearby. She hoped that she had arrived quickly enough to snag the aftereffects of his engine wash and track him that way, but so far, that hadn't worked out.

"Fan out," she said, uncertain if the bike's onboard recorder would pick up her voice in the wind.

"Trackers on," came the response as the pirates behind her followed her order and spread across the rooftops.

• • • •

Claude did his best to ignore Vision's panting as they descended deeper into the bowels of the hotel. The trip down was relatively uneventful, and yet it was still one of the most harrowing experiences of his life. Aside from the exhaustion, Vision seemed to be handling it well since she'd adjusted to the situation. Several times, Vision had saved him from a disastrous step, and he was sure each and every one of her life-saving warnings would come up the next time she decided to push him on the whole "partners" thing.

It wasn't until they reached the thirtieth floor that things started to get truly uncomfortable. Vibrations under his skin spiked Claude's anxiety despite there being no danger in sight, but when rhythmic breathing echoed up from the darkness below, he came to appreciate it.

Looking back at Vision, he noticed that she was as pale as moonlight, with a look of abject horror that mirrored one he'd worn only once on the floor of Firaxis' crystal sanctuary. Claude pulled her close, placing her between himself and the wall. Together, they took the last few steps as slowly and as quietly as humanly possible.

The stairway thrummed with the gentle snoring of unseen monsters. As the sounds grew clearer, Claude doused his light and forced himself to trust exclusively in Vision's sensors for guidance.

Vision's breathing came in shallow, hitched gasps as they descended into the heart of the stairwell. The stench of decay grew exponentially with each step, as did the unmistakable sense of living movement in the dark.

Claude did his best to hide the dread pulsing through him even as it welled up at the base of his skull. Something told him, in a not-so-subtle way, that he had gone as far as he should, and nearly every fiber of his being agreed. Unfortunately, the last few doors had been welded shut, and doubling back would make the risks they'd taken so far pointless.

Vision tugged on his jacket, stopping him from taking the next step. She was shaking violently and teetering on the edge of hyperventilation.

"I-I can see them," she whispered so faintly that Claude had to think twice about whether he'd even heard her.

"The next door," Claude told her and kissed her hair. "It's not far now."

He ignored the jolt of static that stung his lips and forced himself to hold her for a moment longer than he would have otherwise. The vibrations of Claude's passenger had grown deafening to him, and if a trained soldier was nearing the point of panic, he couldn't imagine how it was affecting an eleven-year-old.

He felt Vision nod and released her. When they moved again, they stepped as one unified force against the ravenous, slavering abyss surrounding them. Claude felt his way along the wall, searching for the door, but kept his eyes on the darkness around him.

He wished, for perhaps the first time, that he had better night vision. He knew that Vision's sensors didn't need the bounce of light to make out their surroundings, but since he was the only one that was armed, that wouldn't do them much good if a fight came their way. Technically, neither would his pistol, but he actively chose to ignore that fact.

Cool metal brushed Claude's fingertips as he caught the door's frame, and his heart lurched in his chest. It was all he could do to keep himself from frantically searching for anything that would allow him to force the doors apart. He blindly explored the dense metal, wincing at the echoed scrapes his skin made as it slid over the loose rust clinging to the doors.

Like everything else in the hotel, the once-ornate doors were old and worn. Rusted, fragile flakes fell away from the double doors at Claude's touch. Each rained down onto the stairs in soft ticks that sounded like tiny explosions to him as he struggled to keep his calm. A guttural snort rebounded off the walls of the stairway below their feet. At the sound, tiny pinpricks of light danced through the blackness as Claude's blood pressure spiked. He froze, but small, warm hands took his own and guided them to the seam he had so desperately been searching for.

"Hurry," Vision whispered as she shivered against him.

Her sensors painted an image of bodies suspended along the far wall of the stairwell. They had wedged themselves awkwardly beneath the stairs above and were no doubt resting in similar positions below them as well. Some twitched and shifted in their sleep, but a great many more simply hung there, still as the skeletons lining the streets outside.

In her colorless world, the Derelicts looked like men and women with thick, cracked, almost stone-like skin and misshapen limbs. Most had at least one elongated arm with a massive, clawed hand that had to be the size of her torso.

She couldn't make out their faces due to the wild, inky hair that clung to them like loose cloth. Above her, a large one shifted and sniffled the way Vision did when she fought to stay in bed longer than she ought to. With a shudder, she pressed herself closer to Claude and prayed that monsters had greater willpower than she usually did.

Claude couldn't get his fingers into the crease. It was simply too thin a divide. He needed a tool of some kind. If he had a gordric divider or even a pry bar, he could have wrenched the doors apart with little effort, but he'd brought nothing of the sort.

As if in answer to his needs, the silver inside him surged through his body, down his arms, and out through his fingertips. The semi-liquid creature oozed its way through the crease and hardened almost instantly. Without a second thought, Claude pulled the doors open, forcing the rusted metal to creak and squeal as it was forced to function for the first time in generations.

Light streamed into the stairwell and threatened to stab all the sight out of Claude's eyes. The bright sting was at once excruciating and blissful as he stretched the sliver of light into a wide beam. The violent blade of sun slashed its way across half a dozen sleeping Derelicts exposing them to the orange light of Minervan day.

Claude heard the stairwell come alive with pain, surprise, and finally movement, but ignored it. He used his leg to shove Vision into the hallway beyond before slipping through himself.

The doors slammed shut behind him with a clang so loud that it shook the dust off every wall for ten feet. The cries of confused and newly awakened Derelicts reverberated through the entire hotel, forcing Vision to cover her ears as they backed away from the thick metal door.

Claude blinked against the daylight and moved swiftly toward Vision.

"Do you think it'll hold?" Vision asked, falling into step ahead of Claude.

"Nope," Claude replied through clenched teeth.

His eyes were still locked on the rusted metal as the angry shouts of countless Derelicts gave way to one deep, rolling bellow. Claude turned from the door and scanned the corridor for any immediate threats.

"So, what do we do now?" Vision said, turning to him with a slack expression of shock on her face.

"We run," Claude said.

He knelt just long enough for Vision to jump onto his back.

"Hold on," he said over his shoulder and launched down the hall at a brisk jog.

He wasn't sure if the Derelicts would come out into the sunlit halls of the hotel after them. He didn't even know if they could recognize the difference between the light from a door opening or some natural occurrence, like a wall crumbling away, but he took no chances.

The area they were looking for was below them, and without any real knowledge of the building's condition, Claude wasn't sure how to get there without heading all the way back to the central stairwell. He had no clue if the stairs would be intact enough to take them where they needed to go, and even if they were, the drives could be hidden anywhere on that floor.

The information Claude had was only Bertrand's best guess. There wasn't going to be time for a thorough search of the hotel if the old man turned out to be wrong, especially not now.

"Did your passenger just open that door?" Vision asked once she'd gotten used to the jostling ride.

Claude looked at the metallic creature still covering his hands and took a second to think about what had happened for the first time. It had done what he needed it to do, and it had done it on its own.

He knew his passenger was alive, of course, but it had never acted in such an overt way before. For all the discomfort he had about a sentient creature living inside him, he couldn't deny that it could be a valuable tool in certain situations. Claude only hoped that there wouldn't be very many of them.

'*Friend. Ally. Comrade.*'

Vision stiffened at the odd series of thoughts.

"Did you..." Vision began.

"We don't have time right now. We'll figure it out later," Claude said and picked up speed as a new round of banging rang through the hall.

Vision scanned the area. Near the entrance, the large corridor split into two parallel halls. Smaller walkways connected them, reminding Vision of a ladder as it stretched into the distance. Capping the hall was another set of double doors, much like the ones she and Claude had come through. Rooms lined both outer walls, but the rooms in the center drew Vision's attention. Like little islands, they were locked between the two branches of the hall and narrow walkways that connected them. To her, they seemed lonely and sad. With no windows, the rooms seemed more like well-designed cells than anything she would want to spend credits on.

Shaking away the thought, Vision turned her attention to the floor below. The materials used in the floors and ceilings agreed with her sensor pings more than the hotel's stairway walls. Vision smiled and refocused her halo's sensor range for the task at hand.

The first thing that jumped out at her was the low-level repulsor current running along a block of rooms. Crudely assembled barricades sectioned them off, but they had largely been dismantled some time earlier. Still, the current carved its way through the rooms and concentrated in a small box at the center of the least damaged room Vision had scanned since she'd entered the hotel.

"I think I found what we're looking for," Vision said and pointed down.

"Bertrand already told me what floor," Claude said.

"Yeah, but I know what room," she said and gave Claude a smug grin.

Claude sat Vision down as they neared the far doors before prying them apart. As soon as the gap was wide enough, he urged her through, then followed.

Vision scanned the central column, paying particular attention to the stairs below. They were solid enough so long as they didn't need to jump for any reason, and the door was already wide open.

"Are we clear?" Claude asked, eyeing the stairs and platform beyond the door suspiciously.

"It looks okay, but be careful," she replied and followed him onto the stairs.

Claude heard the guttural rumble of approaching vehicles before Vision and forced his attention to the skylight above.

"Company's coming," Vision said absently.

"Great," Claude said and frowned down at her, "More company."

• • • •

Dogura looked out over the Old City with mild appreciation. It certainly lived up to its name with its decaying square buildings and precisely gridded streets. Nothing about the dilapidated skyline shocked him. How could it?

Back on Reitsin, he'd spent years scratching out a living for himself and his sisters in a settlement that looked very similar. The only difference was no flesh-eating monsters had caused the destruction there, just regular people fighting over what the planet and its populace could do for them.

What had happened here was an unpredictable and hopefully unrepeatable tragedy. What had happened on Reitsin was likely to happen again countless times until the universe stopped spinning.

"There's the car," a voice called through his bike's broadcast system.

Dogura scanned the rooftops until he found the unmistakable glint of relatively new metal against the rundown surfaces. With a thrill of excitement for the action to come, he pulled his bike around and moved toward the Derita Hotel's domed skylight.

The other four bikes all converged on the same half-collapsed building. All eyes were on Captain Faridan as she contemplated their next move.

"Kill the car," she said, and swung her bike around to hover directly over the skylight.

Two of the riders cocked the control yokes of their Lifter bikes and began their weapons' charging cycle with a thin mechanical whine.

Dogura watched eagerly as the sound of their front-mounted cannons spooled up and out of his hearing range. The plasma bolts shimmered a brilliant blue as they bit into the dark metal of the lifeless sedan.

The car began melting immediately, its metal bubbling and popping as it returned to the slag from which it was born. If the plasma had stopped there, the vehicle would have simply been a useless chunk of metal, but the long cooling time of plasma meant that it was just the beginning.

Every rider eased their bikes back another twenty feet, anticipating the pop. Dogura had never been so close to a power cell explosion, and he was eager to see if it was everything he had imagined.

The plasma ate its way through the cab and into the ventral engines of the sedan in seconds. Metal scraped against metal as the cooling system tried to keep the power cells from succumbing to the heat. It wasn't until the plasma had made its way into the engine itself that the scraping stopped, and the power cell erupted.

The explosion tore a hole in the roof twice the sedan's size and knocked the dust and glass out of nearly every building in a half-mile radius. Vivid arcs of once captive ions escaped into the air and along surrounding surfaces, making Dogura's eyes sting and every hair on his body stand on end.

He glanced over to see the captain tense against the energy that was oddly attracted to her. Arcs coursed through and around her body until slowly, she absorbed them with a shout that was equal parts pain and ecstasy.

At the moment, Dogura took the shout as her battle cry, though somehow, it echoed in what seemed like a dozen voices. He shook the thought from his head as his captain forced her bike forward and into the hole left by the explosion.

"Find him!" she demanded, and every rider followed her lead with excited shouts of their own.

Chapter 17

THE HOTEL SHOOK VIOLENTLY, raining down dust and broken shards of skylight, but Claude and Vision were too focused on reaching the twenty-sixth floor to care. Claude slid to a stop, causing Vision to slam into his back. Each of the last five stairs to their destination cracked and broke away from their moorings, leaving a clear and nauseating view of the sludge-filled river below.

"So, I guess they're not friendly," Vision said.

A renewed chorus of screams and hoots rose up around them as every nearby Derelict was forced out of its daylight slumber.

"Of course," Claude complained, "the pay is too good for anything else."

He kneeled and motioned for Vision to climb on his back. She did so and locked her ankles around him as he stood once more.

"I'm not sure anything down there will hold both of us at the same time," Vision declared over the growing engine noise.

She gave the floors above a scan, hoping for some alternative.

"We'll have to chance it, V," Claude said, his voice in a higher octave than she had ever heard it before.

He stared into the abyss below. In the dim light, Claude could see a sea of misshapen bodies and reflective, turquoise eyes surging upward. The swarm of bodies coursed around the river, pouring over each other and gathering speed as they grew closer.

"Whatever you're planning better work," she said, bracing herself.

"Well, if it doesn't, the fall will likely kill us before the mutants do," Claude said and put every ounce of strength he had into the jump.

Part of him suspected that the fall wouldn't be fatal, at least not for him, but he put that out of his mind as they sailed through the air.

Normally, the fifteen-foot gap to the next stair might have been possible if he'd made the jump alone. With Vision's added weight, it should have been impossible. Claude had expected to have to grab the closest stair with his fingertips, but instead he overshot all of them. His stomach fluttered as he realized where his jump arc was leading him.

Without any real way of controlling himself in the air, Claude did his best to land on the nearside of the door, but he sailed past the entire platform.

His feet touched down six stairs on the opposite side of the door he'd intended to enter and the grime covered stone disintegrated on contact. In the split second of weightless panic, Claude heard Vision scream then felt gravity threaten to drag him into the filth-ridden hellscape below.

His shout mixed with Vision's as he did the only thing he could think of. It shouldn't have worked. Tiny ridges in the sheer wall should have torn the flesh from his fingertips as he clawed at it, but his fall slowed, then stopped altogether. A strained grunt escaped him and stars exploded before his eyes. Vision's grip tightened around his throat, nearly causing him to black out, but the pain kept him conscious.

Claude didn't need a doctor to tell him what had happened. The searing sensation was all too familiar. Gravity's excited pull had been defeated, but it came at a price, the dislocation of his shoulder.

Dangling above the climbing mass of twisted bodies, he felt the silver flow into the joint and slide his arm back into alignment. His passenger stayed to reinforce the muscles and neutralize the pain.

"Uh, Claude," Vision said as she fought to believe what her sensors were telling her.

Claude swung himself around and watched as liquid silver flowed over his free hand. It stretched from his fingertips and hardened into a set of short, serrated claws. Confused and uncertain, Claude sank his new talons into the wall. They sliced through the stone effortlessly, then thickened to grant him a better purchase.

His passenger was aiding him. Somehow, it knew what he needed and had responded for a second time. That proved that the silver was a thinking creature, and that knowledge did nothing to put Claude's mind at ease. A sentient creature living inside him meant....

"Claude!" Vision shouted, pulling him back to the moment at hand.

Shaking his newest dread away, he moved. It only took him a few seconds to make his way back up to the door and swing around inside it. During the climb, he barely noticed his own weight or that of the child on his back.

"Down there!" a filtered voice boomed out above them.

Claude stole a glance upward and saw a squad of five hoverbikes descending the column toward them. He took in their appearance and formation in the split second before he disappeared through the door.

"Who are they?" Vision asked, holding on to him as they moved at a full sprint through the debris-strewn hall.

"Pirates, I think," Claude said, only half aware of his environment.

It moved past him so quickly, he barely had time to register the obstacles in his way before he flowed over and around them with unfamiliar ease and precision.

"How are you doing this?" Vision asked, taking note of the speed at which they were moving.

"I don't know," Claude answered honestly.

He had suspicions, but he had spent so much time doing everything in his power to ignore his passenger's existence that he couldn't be entirely sure what was happening. He had no idea what it was capable of and finding out in a situation like this was not the way he would've chosen.

"Take a left," Vision said, pointing to the right instead.

"A left's left, or a Vision left?" Claude asked, sliding to a stop.

Vision thought for a moment, then said, "A Vision left."

"So, a right?" Claude said with a smirk.

"Just go," Vision said, rolling her black eyes.

The hall behind them exploded in a wave of heat and dust. Claude smelled the sting of plasma before the cloud of smoke and molten debris cleared. He glanced back to see the squad of pirates guiding their hoverbikes through what used to be the entrance to the hall. They each guided their mounts slowly, taking care to avoid the reddened edges of their handiwork as they drifted into the corridor.

The bikes were big, but the hotel hallways seemed to accommodate them easily, though maneuvering in such a tight space would clearly be a weakness. Normally, Lifter bikes were stable and agile due to their longer "tails" and unique internal gimbals. Those traits made them the perfect vehicles for recon missions, but they were designed for open spaces. The halls around them were only about twice as wide as the bikes themselves.

That didn't leave much room for them to drift and maneuver as intended. On top of that, formation riding would be entirely impossible.

Claude had some experience with Lifters as a TaskMaster. He'd taken every opportunity he could to ride one. It was going to be a shame to destroy these, especially since he was pretty sure that the explosion that he'd heard earlier had been his car.

"*Maybe I'll save one for the escape,*" he thought and ducked around the corner as the bikes moved down the hall.

Once he was out of sight, he kneeled and sat Vision down. The world warped in that distinct way that only came with the approach of peak exhaustion.

"Are you all right?" Vision asked, concern written plainly across her face.

Claude waved the question away and chose to take a few deep breaths instead of answering.

"Do you think you can get the drives?" Claude said once he was sure his voice wouldn't falter.

Vision shook her head slowly even as she answered, "I guess."

She was confused and scared, plus Claude wasn't feeling his best, despite everything he had just shown himself capable of. Her worry was more for him than for herself.

Vision wasn't sure that she could handle a group of pirates. The best she could hope for was to read them before they had a chance to get too close, but with Claude's strength fading fast, that wouldn't be of much use. If she understood what had happened at Artemis, she might be able to repeat it here, but that would incapacitate Claude as well.

"I need you to get to the drives," he said, then squeezed her shoulder. "Grab them and wait for me, okay?"

Vision's face melted into a frown as she did her best to read him. On the surface, she found a mirror of her own concern. His thoughts were for her, not himself, but she took heart in his determination to see her safely back to Violet, no matter what he had to do to make it happen. And it was enough for her.

Vision let out a breath she hadn't realized she'd been holding and nodded to him.

"Make sure you come back for me," Vision said seriously.

Claude ruffled her hair and forced himself to stand. His legs held him, despite feeling like gelatin. He ignored the mounting fatigue and focused on what came next. The nascent plan he'd tried to hide from Vision was weak, but all of his plans tended to be. Claude was never one for elaborate machinations when a level head and healthy dose of improvisation would do.

For now, he needed her as far out of the way as he could get her. Experience told him a fight was coming his way, and it was best if she didn't see what he was about to do.

Looking into Vision's concerned eyes, Claude said, "Always," and he meant it.

A flicker of doubt played across her features, then disappeared behind a wall of determination.

"*Save. Protect. Defend.*"

Vision blinked at the odd series of thoughts that jumped out at her. She searched Claude's face but found no hint that they were his. Evidently, they were meant for her and her alone. A million questions flooded forward, and she hoped there would be time to indulge her curiosity later.

"Go," Claude said and consciously forced himself to release her shoulder.

He waited for Vision to turn away and run down the opposite hall from the hoverbikes before turning his attention to the dangers approaching.

• • • •

Miranda hovered at the ruined entrance to the twenty-sixth floor. Her men were in pursuit of the two people she'd seen during her descent, but something didn't feel right. With her attention split between the clambering bodies of Derelicts working their way up the hotel walls and the pirates carrying out her orders, she didn't have time to figure out exactly what it was.

Despite the oncoming horde, there was still time for them to get the job done, but it would be close. Of that, she had no doubt. The Derelicts were an unpredictable element, but she was still confident her men could capture two people on foot with minimal losses. At this point, ending the mission wouldn't do much to make the situation any better for them, and worse, it would leave her without any of the answers she so desperately desired.

She wondered if Bertrand had decided to utilize DiSilva because he had similar capabilities to herself or if it was just a matter of his innate skill at whatever the job was. If she had been in Bertrand's position, she would have tasked DiSilva with keeping her safe instead of sending him into the Dead Zone. Then again, she was likely more aware of the situation than the old man was.

It seemed like a waste, but from the messages they'd intercepted, perhaps he wasn't willing to share his new asset with Echelon just yet. Bertand's motivations were his own, and to be honest, Miranda really didn't care what they might be. In a few minutes, she would have DiSilva in hand, and another one of Bertrand's pieces would be off the board.

"He's going for the western stairwell," a voice shouted through filtered speakers, and it spurred Miranda into action.

With practiced grace, she angled her bike toward the floor above, cocked the plasma cannon, and fired. The wall melted away, and Miranda maneuvered her bike through the smoldering gap. The hall beyond was largely empty aside from several free-standing emitters. Miranda wasn't sure what purpose they were meant to serve, but it was clear they had lost power some time ago.

Ignoring them, she angled her bike down the hall and propelled it forward. She poured on more speed as she moved in an attempt to beat DiSilva to the stairwell on the far side.

• • • •

The pirates were getting comfortable in the confined space, which was less than ideal. With each step, Claude lost more and more ground. He found himself missing the speed he'd had just moments before, then banished the thought.

He didn't really have much of a plan aside from leading the bikes away from Vision and maybe doubling back if he could manage it. A part of him hoped that the Derelicts he'd stirred up earlier would be waiting to tear into his pursuers, but his luck was seldom that good.

The door was less than a hundred yards away as the first bike rolled up on him. He could feel the aura of heat behind him just before he jumped. With more than a little surprise, Claude stared in disbelief as he cleared both the nose of the bike and the rider to land on the seat behind him.

"Hey!" the pirate shouted lamely, before Claude shoved him off the bike.

The pirate landed with an audible crunch but attempted to get back up on an obviously broken leg. Claude hadn't been trying to kill the man, but he wouldn't have lost any sleep over it if he had. There were only two people in the entire Old City he cared about, and pirates weren't on that list.

A new wave of fatigue rushed to overtake him, but Claude fought it back. Shaking the blurriness from his vision, he jerked the control yoke of the bike and urged it forward. With a tap of the brake, he slowed to a stop and waited for the plasma cannon to reach full charge. Stealing a glance behind him, Claude registered three more bikes closing on him, each with a single rider plus the downed pirate limping after them.

He could have sworn he'd counted five bikes in the lobby, but there wasn't time to figure out where the last one had gone. Instead, Claude returned his focus to the metallic door ahead and launched the blue ball of plasma into it. The force of the impact shook the hall and bathed Claude in enough heat that he worried his hair might be on fire. When the retina-searing flash died down, he patted his head and let out a sigh of relief.

Most of the wall that adjoined the stairwell was gone. Sunlight crept in through the far side, but the amount of plasma that had made its way there had to have been minuscule, given the tiny hole it left.

The bikes behind Claude didn't slow, which was good. He needed them distracted if he had any chance of making this work. With a quick eyeball measurement, he guessed there might just be enough room to whip the bike around to face his attackers. Doing so meant turning his back to the hooting beasts clawing their way up the hole behind him. Hopefully, he wouldn't wind up as strips of meat between a Derelict's teeth for doing so.

Claude drew in a deep breath and pulled the bike around, ignoring both the irritating scrape its tail made on the walls and the symphony his passenger was performing up and down his spine.

"Let's go," he said, mostly to himself, and revved the bike into motion.

He heard himself yelling and thought he was maybe an octave or two higher than where he needed to be for it to sound truly intimidating. Letting that bit of self-criticism go, Claude pulled the bike up and to his left before he kicked off it. The bike groaned in protest from the sudden shift in orientation and weight, then rolled its way down the hall. The sleek vehicle sped away from Claude, careening toward the oncoming pirates in a cascade of sparks and debris.

The pirates tried their best to adjust course, but Claude's bike took up too much of the hall. Only the rider farthest away managed to escape it. His brake flaps flared wide as he drifted around the nearest corner and into the parallel hall, narrowly avoiding a head-on collision with the rolling metal speeding his way.

The two bikes closest to Claude took the hit hard after their riders did the only thing they could. Both pulled their Lifters up, putting the chassis of their bikes between them and the impact, though only one rider bailed beforehand.

The other didn't get the angle quite right. The wreckage pinned his foot with a wet crunch and a scream that nearly drowned out the reverberating engine noise. There was nothing he could do as he tumbled end over end with the bikes landing on top of him. When his body came to rest ten feet away from the impact, the broken pirate gurgled behind his mask, then went still.

Claude did his best to ignore the dying man and focused his attention on the two that were left standing. The uninjured pirate was the one nearest to him and thus, the greater threat. The other was limping his way up to join his friend, but he wasn't exactly moving at top speed.

"Ayo!" the nearest pirate shouted, pulling his sidearm from its holster.

The lanky pirate ripped off his mask, exposing a hateful sneer. He was just a kid, or at least he looked like one to Claude. He couldn't have been more than twenty years old, but the anger on his face did a good deal to remove the idea that he was to be taken lightly.

"We supposed to take you alive," the pirate said in a lilting cadence that instantly marked him as Reitsini.

"And now?" Claude asked, extending his arms.

"And now you killed Deran, so you die!" the pirate shouted and fired at Claude.

Claude bolted as super-heated metal streaked his way. Without cover to move between, closing on the pirate directly was suicide, so he did the next best thing and sprinted for one of the rooms to his left.

The kid was young and Claude prayed that rage would ruin his aim, but everyone on Reitsin knew their way around a weapon. It was a required survival trait.

Again, he was left with only his normal running speed, so it was no surprise when the first round hit him three steps from relative safety. It hit him in the ribs, then the kid landed two more, one in Claude's left calf and the other in his right shoulder.

None of the shots hurt, but they destroyed Claude's balance. His momentum was enough to get him through the door, but he knew that would be of little consequence. Any experienced gunman was guaranteed to follow him and put at least one round through his eye socket.

Claude hurtled toward a wall-mounted chest of drawers just inside the room, shattering it into splinters of dry polymer on his way to the floor. Before his breath returned to him, he took a second to look down at the severity of his wounds, but found none. There was no odor of singed flesh; there wasn't even a drop of blood. What he did find were holes in his shirt, pants and, most importantly, his jacket. Beneath them, the skin where the shots connected was coated in silver that slowly receded back into his body.

Claude closed his eyes and offered a wordless thanks to his passenger for another massive assist before drawing his pistol. Claude sucked in a deep breath and held it until his hands steadied.

He waited for his attacker to burst through the door, but it didn't happen. Instead of the footsteps he expected, Claude heard the deep rumble of the final hoverbike coming down the hall.

"Zacka!" the Reitsini called.

"Yeah?" a filtered voice responded.

"He in there. Slag it," the kid commanded with a decidedly sinister chuckle.

Claude rolled to his feet and scanned the dilapidated cage he'd trapped himself in. It was a basic hotel room. Aside from the age, disrepair, and the threat of monsters, it might have even been a nice place to bring Zhara on vacation, but the lack of a second exit was a dealbreaker.

For a moment, he thought maybe the silver could help him tear his way through the walls, but they were thick and made of the same reinforced earthen material the stairwell had been. His passenger could slice into it but carving away large enough chunks to get out seemed unlikely.

That left him one way out of his predicament, and it would take everything he had to pull it off. Closing his eyes tight and calming his nerves, Claude prepared himself for the worst.

• • • •

Dogura's pulse pounded in his ears. Deran had been a good friend. He'd kept him in line and on task even when he was less than cordial about it. He still owed Dogura thirty-two deritrium tokens, and he was going to be missed, but first, he would be avenged. The Ban'uta that killed him was going to burn, and then Deran would receive the send-off he deserved. Dogura would see to that.

Zacka spun the bike to face the room, then turned to his friend. Dogura nodded and the masked pirate cocked the steering yoke with a bit more flair than was necessary. The whine of the plasma cannon spooled up, marking the countdown to the stranger's fiery death. It wouldn't be long.

Dogura would take the heat for disobeying the captain himself. He was more than willing to face her if it meant that his friend got to take the last journey in peace. He'd seen enough people be left to rot back home, he'd even been forced to leave family behind in the ruins, but those days were over.

He stared at the open door intently, willing the cannon to charge faster so he could hear Deran's murderer scream his way into oblivion. What he got instead was a streak launching itself out of the room a split second before the plasma bolt turned the space to molten rock.

Claude tucked, hit the floor, and rolled to his feet. He thought he'd be able to take a moment to survey the situation, but a pistol round caught him in the shoulder, and spun him halfway around with the impact. He stumbled as three more shots found their marks, tearing through his jacket but bouncing off the coating on his skin.

The room he'd just escaped moaned as plasma melted through the floor and into the room below. The hallway was awash in a heat so intense Claude could almost feel the sweat on his skin turn to steam. Rounds kept flying his way. The Reitsini kid continued firing even as he began to understand how useless it was.

Claude was tired of it. He had lost his patience for pirates playing at revenge and decided to give him one final warning.

"If you shoot me one more time, I'm going to put a round in each lung and let you drown in your own blood," Claude growled.

Dogura stopped firing, but not because of the threat. He was having a difficult time processing what he was seeing. He was no marksman, but he knew he'd landed at least five shots. The stranger should have been a corpse, but instead, he was merely pissed off.

If he were a little closer, Dogura might have recognized the telltale strands of silver under Claude's skin. Unfortunately, he wasn't. If he were less distracted by the man's outright refusal to die, he might have recognized that he was being maneuvered into a position that put his back to the stairwell, but again, he wasn't. Instead, he was trying to decide whether he was a good enough with his sidearm to put a round in the man's eye, and sadly, he knew he wasn't.

Claude watched as the kid circled with him and saw the newly formed trap taking shape. If he kept going, eventually, the kid would have him in the perfect position to get shot in the back by his friend, assuming enough time had passed to properly recharge the plasma cannon.

It was clever and a lot like his own plan. The kid had a spark of intelligence and resourcefulness, even if he wasn't as attentive as he should have been. The pirate was so singularly focused on Claude that he didn't hear the shuffling and scratching coming from the destroyed wall behind him.

The rider behind Claude saw the creature first, but was apparently unable to warn his friend, so Claude did it for him. He pointed a single finger to the ceiling behind the kid and waited for him to slowly turn around.

It took Dogura a second to understand what he was looking at. A slick, naked form clung to the ceiling above him. Loose skin hung from the corners of its mouth and dripped with thick translucent saliva. The creature's head twisted around backward, and it stared down at him with curious and hungry turquoise eyes. It looked almost human, which was the thing that froze the pirate in place. His mind tried to process what exactly was wrong with it, but it would never get the chance to finish.

The Derelict dropped onto him and smashed him to the floor. It untwisted its emaciated alabaster form and leaned back. Loose jowls shivered as its lips parted to display flat, crooked human teeth.

Dogura screamed. He tried to fight the monster off, but his body was paralyzed. He could only watch as that mouth opened wider and wider until it clamped its jaw down on his skull. Finally, his hands answered his commands, flailing and shooting in all directions. He couldn't remember taking a breath, but he must have, because for what seemed like an eternity, he never stopped screaming.

The creature ground its teeth, tearing its way through the flesh of the pirate's scalp and face. It swiveled its head and neck, trying to find a better angle, all the while tasting the soft wetness of the pirate's eyeball inside its mouth.

Dogura's voice went hoarse as the creature's jaws finally crunched into his skull. With an excited flourish, the Derelict ripped its prize free, crunching the bone between its molars as it chewed with an open mouth. Dribbles of blood and brain fell to the ruined carpet as it swallowed and released an echoing series of hoots.

The open stairwell erupted with twisted white forms, all responding to the call of their Alpha and desperate for meals of their own.

Claude turned and sprinted away from the ravenous horde. He sped past the mounted pirate who had found his voice but not his motor functions.

"Go!" Claude shouted as he passed him.

He wasn't a big fan of pirates, let alone those who would try to melt him down to primordial goop, but no one deserved what was coming. The shout was a common courtesy, since stopping was out of the question. He hoped the pirate would snap out of it and get clear, but if he wasn't smart enough to run, he would at least slow down a few of the mutants.

The limping pirate was already heading in the right direction, but he had very little chance of escaping. Claude felt bad for him as he passed by and did his best not to look the panicked pirate in the eye.

He was directly responsible for the horrible death coming the man's way, but he hadn't known they intended to take him alive. If they had announced their intentions earlier, things might have gone a little differently.

"V, where are you!" Claude shouted as he put his pang of guilt to the side and poured on the speed.

Ten doors up the hall to his left, a door opened, and Vision leaned out. Her face blanched immediately, and Claude assumed she had gotten a good scan of what was following him.

The mounted pirate blasted past Claude and ignored Vision completely as he made his way up the hall. Claude found himself wishing that he'd taken the time to steal the bike from him when he had the chance.

All the running was starting to wear on him, but he didn't dare entertain the idea of slowing down. What he'd witnessed had all but scrambled his brain. He'd heard stories, everyone had. He had even seen a Derelict in the wild, but this was different. With the swarm of monsters speeding toward him, Claude didn't think he could will his legs to stop churning, even if he wanted to.

He glanced over his shoulder to see how much space was between him and the monsters and saw the limping man nearly bisected by a clawed hand half as wide as his shoulder span. The creatures swarmed over his corpse, tearing him apart in a spray of crimson and a wave of bloodthirsty cries.

Claude turned away just in time for the world to dissolve into a blinding azure light. He dove forward instinctively, blinking the bright spots from his vision. Behind him, a female pirate rode through the molten crater and toward the mass of naked forms gaining on him.

He leapt back to his feet. Ignoring the conflict raging behind him, Claude sprinted the last few yards to the open door before urging Vision back into the room.

"Did you see that?" Vision asked in awe.

"I dodged that," Claude replied, forcing the sliding doors closed with some help from his passenger. "Where are the drives?"

Vision walked over to a fallen beam in the middle of the room and kicked it.

"Under this," she said and kicked the beam again.

Claude crossed to the beam and politely shooed Vision out of the way.

"Don't do that. You'll break your foot, and trust me, you're going to need it," Claude said and slid the beam to the side with little effort.

"I wasn't kicking it that hard," she pouted.

Claude ignored her protest and kneeled down to study the three black shapes through the mesh box embedded in the floor. He was half expecting the damned things to be torn to shreds, but the elongated triangles were in pristine condition. He stared into their mirrored black finish. People had died for the knowledge contained in these drives. He almost had, and here he was again. Part of him wanted to destroy them outright, but where was the sense in that? So much had been sacrificed already. Plus, the answers they might contain presented a lure that was too great to simply ignore.

"We need to start thinking about how we're going to get out of here," Claude said, gathering up the drives and passing them to Vision.

She slid the drives into the interior pockets of her jacket and frowned at the added weight.

"Can we make it back to the car?" Vision asked honestly.

Claude shook his head, "I'm pretty sure that explosion was the car."

"Chell't," Vision said, then immediately covered her mouth.

"Exactly, and never say that again," Claude said and crossed to the window.

"What about the other guys? Can we catch a ride with them?" she asked, rubbing her chin.

"There are only two left and no spare bikes," Claude said, leaning out the window into the sunlight.

Vision's brow furrowed as she leaned on her abilities. She expected to be forced to pick through countless Derelict thoughts, but she didn't find even a single mind in her inhibited range.

"I think they stopped," she said in disbelief.

"Impossible."

Chapter 18

THE BRIGHT, BLUE HEAT of concentrated plasma splashed across the ghostly skin of half a dozen Derelicts, causing them to scream in pain and turn away from the hoverbike.

Miranda was only mildly surprised that the plasma didn't kill them immediately, but pain was a good consolation prize. Silver segmented "legs" extended from her back and slashed at any creatures that dared to advance on her while the cannon recharged.

It wasn't a perfect solution. It wasn't even working since the Derelicts were regenerating from their wounds before her eyes. But it did hold them back for the moment. As much as Miranda hated to admit it, she would need help when the horde decided to make a concerted push. Luckily, they weren't willing to be slashed and burned just to take her down... yet.

She was pretty sure they wouldn't be able to kill her, but that was just a guess. The creature inside her had pieced her back together from otherwise fatal injuries before, but there was no way of knowing if it could out-heal the damage hundreds of teeth and claws would do to her. Finding out wasn't part of her plan, so she was prepared to beat a tactical retreat if things changed. With the full team, she might have been able to push the monsters back, but she'd only seen one of her men alive. Given the bloody maws on some of the mutants, it was obvious the others had likely met grisly ends.

DiSilva was faster than she expected and had slipped past her, but Miranda had more significant issues at the moment. She'd broken through the floor in an attempt to corner him, but instead slammed headlong into the stuff of nightmares.

"Captain," a filtered voice called as another bike approached her from behind.

Miranda nodded as the masked rider fell in line with her and fired another plasma bolt into the retreating mass of bodies.

"Stay sharp and alternate your shots," she ordered.

215

The other rider nodded, but she could feel his eyes on the silver extending from her. His gaze made her skin crawl, and she hated the sensation.

When Octavian told her about the crew's reaction to her creature, she had dismissed it without a second thought. Now she knew hiding this part of herself was the practical choice. This was the first time she had openly relied on the silver since executing the would-be mutineers, and it was evident that at least this crewman saw her as something only slightly better than the monsters they were facing.

If anyone had asked her about it, she would have told them that the opinions of others didn't matter, but somewhere deep inside, she knew that was a lie. In an even darker and more secluded place, she shared their fears.

The whine of her cannon's charge spooled up and out of her hearing range, but before she could fire again, a large, bloodied creature lumbered forward. It carried the body of one of her people, or what was left of him, anyway. Standing a towering eight feet tall, its disproportionate right arm dragged the ground when it walked. Each claw on its oversized hand was the size of a meat cleaver and every bit as sharp. The massive creature let out a long bellow, and the others parted as it lumbered to the front of the mob.

Miranda fired without hesitation, but the creature calmly planted its large hand on the floor, lifted its entire body off the ground and twisted to take the plasma hit along its back. The nauseating stench of searing flesh and hair wafted up the hallway. Miranda gagged at the smell but watched as the once white skin of the creature turned red hot before cooling back to its natural state.

"We have a problem," Miranda said as she stared in disbelief.

The Alpha turned and sneered at her, its jowls vibrating with the deep, chittering sound of mounting rage. The mass of Derelicts began to echo their leader, chittering loud enough to hurt Miranda's ears. Every one of them turned their piercing blue eyes in her direction as their noises fell into an alien harmony.

Miranda and Zacka turned and launched themselves up the hall. They had barely reached a quarter of their top speed when the broken, half-eaten corpse of Dogura cleaved Zacka off his bike. Miranda looked back to see the Alpha creature roar its celebration before launching off its right arm and onto the ceiling.

Zacka's riderless bike sped off ahead of her but was stopped cold by a sturdy-looking man that had to have been DiSilva. He ushered a child onto the seat before mounting it himself and sharing a weighted look with her as she passed.

"Well, well," Miranda said and took another glance back at him.

• • • •

Claude revved the bike and forced it into motion as the Derelicts closed in.

They snapped and scratched at the bike's tail, attempting to spin him out, but he fishtailed as best he could to compensate. The maneuver kept the bike from flipping over, but it lost speed in the process.

"This is not good," Claude said, kicking a particularly swift Derelict in the face as it lurched closer to the bike.

He looked back to see the Alpha gaining on them. The thing was fast and agile, given its size. Using its outsized limb, it launched its body along the ceiling effortlessly, then, before gravity pulled it too low, it caught itself and repeated the process with the same elongated arm.

Claude found himself wondering what could have turned a human being into a creature like that, but when the Alpha swiveled its head a hundred and eighty degrees to lock him in its cold, turquoise stare, he filed the thought away for another time.

• • • •

Vision took a deep breath and pushed her fears into the smallest corner of her mind. Claude was doing his best to save their lives, but he needed help. It was obvious that if they were going to make it out of this hotel, she was going to have to do something drastic.

Vision wasn't sure what would happen if she took her halo off here, but she hoped for something similar to what had happened at the Artemis building. Though, if she could avoid knocking Claude out while he was driving a speeding hoverbike, that would be ideal. With another sharp inhalation, she snatched the device from her head and crashed into a sea of simplistic, agitated minds.

She took a split second to wheel around and get her bearings, noting Claude's silvery ribbon and another fainter but almost identical one. She ignored them both and turned her attention to the plethora of foreign, green threads that could only belong to the Derelicts.

There were hundreds of them, all thinking as if they were connected somehow. Vision could see the individual strands, but each one spiraled loosely around a single, more prominent mind.

Against everything her instincts screamed at her, Vision grabbed hold of the central strand and squeezed.

• • • •

Claude felt a rippling coolness in his mind and knew exactly what was happening. The feeling was similar to the last time Vision had removed the halo, but this time it didn't come with the disorientation. This time, he could feel the pulse's persistent rhythm. It just wasn't affecting him as much. It seemed muted, and given the situation, he was more than pleased with that.

"*Come on, come on. Please let us get out of here,*" Claude thought to no one in particular, but when Vision answered him in his head, her "voice" was clear as crystal.

"*I'm working on it,*" she responded.

Claude tried to blink away the shock of having a voice in his head that very clearly was not his own. He poured everything he had into trying to carve as perfect a line as he could through the hall.

The Derelicts had either slowed, or the bike had gained enough speed to outpace them, but he couldn't tell which. The instruments had shattered when he caught the bike, leaving him all but blind in that regard.

He'd crumpled the front end to such a degree that he was amazed he could even steer the thing. Still, as long as the engine worked, that was all he needed from it.

"Move right," Vision's voice shouted in his head. *"Real right."*

Claude winced as Vision's "voice" shot a spike of pure agony through his skull, but somehow, he still managed to pull the bike to the right. Above them, the Alpha shrieked, clutched its head, and crashed to the floor with enough force it made Claude's teeth chatter.

Vision slammed the halo back on and collapsed against him. She had done it, but both the physical and mental exhaustion had robbed her victory of any joy. The Alpha was down, but the cost was likely to be high. Images of pain, confusion and soul shattering loss were now forever etched into her being. She touched a mind that had lived in torment for nearly a century and there would be years of nightmares ahead. But she would be alive to cope with them.

"That was you?" Claude asked, risking a chance to grip the arm she had wrapped around him. "You took that thing down?"

"Roddic," she said weakly, "his name was Roddic."

Claude gave a barely perceptible nod to the creature that was once a man and the little girl that had just saved his life by stopping it.

"Don't crash out on me yet, V. We still have to get out of here."

• • • •

The thick stone wall blasted outward, and Miranda sailed into the relatively open air of the Derita Hotel's central column once more. She maneuvered her bike into the middle of the space and eyed the hundreds of bodies clambering up the sheer sides of the column.

By her estimation, DiSilva had five minutes before the second wave of Derelicts cut off his escape and she was content to wait here and see if he made it out. She was in no immediate danger, but she gave herself a bit more altitude all the same.

If DiSilva survived, she had a great many questions, but she doubted she'd be able to escort him back to her ship. The DiSilva she had known would be mistrusting, especially after all this, and she didn't know if she could force him considering what they had in common. Even if she could, there were other issues to consider.

Octavian's objections were already ringing in her ears. "It is unwise to bring him back alive when so many of our own are dead," she knew he would say, and he would be right. Even when he was just an echo in her head, he was right. Still, a growing part of her didn't seem to care. She just wasn't ready to give in to it yet. She still needed the crew. They served a purpose, and as long as they did, she had to do right by them. That meant listening to Octavian.

There would be no bodies to commit to the Black, and that more than anything would drive the crew to demand blood if she brought Claude back. He would fight, they would die, she would have to intervene, and nothing she wanted to get out of this mission would happen.

Miranda blew out a heavy sigh and brushed her hair out of her face seconds before a second Lifter exploded from the newly formed exit. DiSilva maneuvered it the same way she had, climbing to match her altitude.

He hadn't changed much from that last goodbye. He was still in good shape, though there were a few gray whiskers on his chin that hadn't been there before. Part of her felt as if she could brush the distance and time that had separated them away, and she might have tried if he had been alone on the bike.

A little girl peered around him and fixed Miranda with chilling black eyes. The color wasn't uncommon, but something about the little girl made her uneasy. She couldn't put her finger on it, but it was there like an itch in her throat, and she couldn't just ignore it.

"It's been a long time, Miranda," Claude said pointedly and with no warmth in his tone.

Miranda forced a smile to her lips and nodded slightly. "That it has."

"One of your men said you wanted me alive," Claude said flatly.

It wasn't a question, and Claude wasn't feeling up to niceties at the moment. She was almost convinced that if the plasma cannon on his bike was functional, he would have simply blasted her out of the sky and made his way home with his conscience clear.

"It's true. I'm after your client, not you," Miranda said, cutting to the heart of the matter. "Tell me where he is, and we can all get out of this place."

Miranda set her jaw and swallowed her disappointment. This wasn't how she wanted the conversation to happen, but if Claude wasn't going to tell her, no amount of sweet-talking would change that. In the past, he had always favored the direct. It was likely he would respond better to straight talk.

"I have no idea where he is," Claude stated truthfully.

He kept his bike pointed squarely at the nose of Miranda's as they slowly circled each other. There was no way he would give her an easy shot at them or directly expose Vision to plasma fire. Besides, he doubted she could tell the plasma cannon on his bike wasn't working.

Hopefully, this standoff wouldn't get any more hostile than it already was. Claude didn't have it in him to fight her, not after all that running.

"Then tell me what you do know, and I will tell you what you don't," Miranda said, putting a soft purr into her voice.

She watched as Claude mulled it over. He had nothing to lose by sharing information with her, and she knew that. He was simply angry at how things had turned out, but so was she. He would likely pout about it for a while, but in the end he would do the practical thing. The only wildcard was the child. Children tended to make people irrational.

Claude took a deep, labored breath, then blew it out disdainfully.

"Fine," he said. "We'll talk, but somewhere miles from here. I've had enough of this place."

Miranda nodded and maneuvered her bike up toward the broken skylight.

• • • •

Vision sat in what little shade the hoverbike offered. The sun battered rooftop was scorching in most places, but the shadow of the bike had cooled it just enough for her to sit on.

The hotel was out of even her widest sensor range, but to her, it wouldn't be far enough away until she was safely back in Violet.

Claude had chosen this particular rooftop due to its distance from the hotel and its height. Unlike other buildings nearby, this one was short enough to catch the hint of a breeze off the nearest sinkhole. While it felt good, the tiny spray of moisture came with smells that Vision was content never to experience again.

He'd been curious about Miranda, saying that he thought she might have "useable intel."

Vision was skeptical.

Claude had downplayed his encounter with the pirates, but Vision knew him pretty well. He was wary of the woman, but for some reason, he couldn't just refuse to hear her out. Vision had no such qualms. She didn't know the woman and she didn't want to. Everything about her just seemed wrong somehow. That's why Vision had chosen to keep her distance. Well, that, and the fireball in the sky that threatened to melt the skin right off her bones.

From this distance, she couldn't hear the adults' conversation, and after latching onto Roddic's mind and seeing the horrors nesting in what was left of his psyche, she was reluctant to attempt a read on them. Instead, she simply studied their body language.

Claude was well out of the woman's reach with his arms folded and resting his weight on his back foot while the stranger was adamantly pleading her case. She was using her hands to talk, a trait Vision found endlessly amusing, and leaning forward while still straddling her Lifter.

Somehow neither of them were melting in the uncharacteristically hot weather and she envied that. Truce Week always landed in the early part of what passed for autumn on Minerva Prime. Usually, that meant cooler days that rolled into colder nights, but this year the temperature had been a great deal hotter.

Vision didn't know why, nor did she really care. She simply wanted the adults to wrap up their little chat so that she could get back to a climate-controlled location as soon as possible.

• • • •

"You don't owe him anything," Miranda said with a little more heat in her voice than she had intended.

"I don't owe you anything either," Claude replied coolly.

Miranda threw her hands into the air and sighed out her frustrations.

"I wouldn't be coming to you with this, but I'm too close to let him slip away," Miranda said sharply. "He deserves everything I've got planned for him, and none of it will come close to what he allowed them to do to me."

Claude felt a pang of sympathy. He had known Miranda before, and what he saw in front of him was a distant variation on that woman. The Miranda he served with would never have fallen in with pirates. She would have never killed and robbed the innocent, and she would never plot the execution of her former commanding officer. Just about the only things this woman shared with the Miranda he knew was a face and an overwhelming compulsion to survive.

"Look, I can't be part of killing him," Claude began. "I don't have the animosity you do, but I understand your position."

Miranda fixed him with a suspicious glare but did not interrupt him.

"But I need you to understand mine. We still have business with Bertrand, and we need those credits. I can't let anything happen to him until after I drop off these drives and get paid," he continued, keeping his voice calm but firm.

The last thing he needed was to have risked his life for nothing. The money was one of the primary reasons he'd elected to take the job in the first place.

Vision had been right about their situation, though he wasn't about to admit that to her. Bertrand had presented a very tempting offer on all fronts, and when he'd called back to continue the negotiation, Claude accepted the first reasonable counteroffer.

Now, he knew a little more about why Bertrand had come to him in the first place. The Derelicts were the main obstacle, but there were others as well. He believed the Echelon part, but there had been something else under the surface. Meeting Miranda at the hotel made him wonder if she wasn't the part his former commander was trying to hide.

Miranda flashed a glance to the miserable-looking child hunched in the shrinking shadow of Claude's battered bike.

"Did he tell you what's on them?" she asked absently.

Claude watched her as the gears of her mind whirred toward some unknown purpose.

"No idea. All he told me was that Echelon had tracked a defector out here and that he had some information I needed to retrieve," Claude said, deciding not to share any part that would attract undue attention.

Miranda visibly sneered at that. It was an oddly animalistic reaction, Claude thought, but it was likely she felt the same way he did about the vagueness of the mission.

"That checks out. We intercepted transmissions from someone in Bertrand's ranks and Myridorn. They talked about retrievals," Miranda said, leaning back from the control yoke of the bike.

"Plural?" Claude asked.

Miranda nodded. "I'd watch my back if I were in your place. If Bertrand knows about you, Echelon knows about you."

The thought had crossed Claude's mind, but he didn't want to believe Bertrand would throw him to the wolves. Talking to Miranda had severely damaged that notion, but it still wasn't completely gone. He suspected Bertrand might try to stiff him on the credits, but an outright abduction seemed extreme.

"I doubt that," Claude declared. "I've seen no signs of Echelon's hand anywhere near my part in this."

"They're snakes, Claude. They sidle up close, and when you're not paying attention, they strike," Miranda hissed. "You know this, just like you know Bertrand is in their pocket."

She was right about Bertrand being bonded to Echelon, but she didn't know everything. Miranda seemed to be either unaware or simply didn't believe that there was a rift between the two. Claude had looked into the man's eyes while he spoke of it, and there was no lie in them. Still, she had provided him with enough to doubt his own certainty.

He wasn't going to give Bertrand up if he had other options, but Miranda being on-world added another variable to an already complicated equation. If he managed to balance it just right, there was a possibility everything would come out in his favor, however unlikely that was.

"I'll take my chances," Claude said coldly.

"I don't doubt you will, but we have so much more to talk about," Miranda said, trying to find the old charm that had worked on DiSilva in the past. "Come back to my ship. We'll get out of this heat and compare notes on our silver friends."

Claude thought about it for a moment. He couldn't deny that he had more questions. It was possible Miranda knew things about his passenger he didn't, but going with her invited too much risk.

Something told him Miranda was not to be trusted. She had an angle, and she was playing it well. Unfortunately for her, Claude's experience, the warnings the silver was hammering out on his nerves, and the fact that he had Vision in tow meant there was no way he was ever going to set foot on a ship full of pirates.

"I'm going to have to decline, but I'm guessing you have my contact code," Claude said.

Miranda's face darkened as she processed his refusal. Claude really wished Vision was there to tell him what emotions she was actually feeling in that moment, then reprimanded himself for the thought.

"I'm sure I can find it," Miranda said, suppressing the indignation she felt at his refusal.

Miranda did everything she could to keep her emotions off her face, but she could tell by the sharpness in DiSilva's eyes that her mask had slipped. Her illusion had failed her, and he'd seen her naked reaction. There was no point in hiding herself away from him now.

After all, why should she hide? Who was he compared to her? He was nothing. He was as weak and soft as the thing cowering under the bike's shadow. She wanted to kill them both at that moment, but stayed her hand. She needed DiSilva to bring Bertrand out of hiding, and as long as she did, that meant he was off-limits, even to her.

"One last word of advice," Miranda said, revving her bike's engine back to life and lifting it into the air.

Claude blocked the initial gust of warm air from his eyes with his forearm.

"I'm all ears," he shouted over the growl of the engine.

Miranda smirked down at him, but the expression was drained of any sense of amusement.

"When you meet with Bertrand, make sure it's somewhere public! That way, maybe someone else will see the knife before he buries it in your back," Miranda chided, then disappeared over the ledge of the roof.

Claude watched as the bike sped out across the broken rooftops of the Old City, and part of him honestly wished he'd been able to see the real Miranda Faridan one last time.

Chapter 19

ONLY TWO MILES OF DESOLATE cityscape and a towering wall of violet energy separated Claude and Vision from the rest of Minerva City, and the latter grew closer with each passing second. Thanks to Claude's diligence, their bike hadn't dipped below the rooftops for most of the tiring and uncomfortable return trip, but that would have to change. If they were going to get back into city proper without the benefit of Claude's sedan, he and Vision would need to descend to ground level.

Vision was still clung to him, but her mind was somewhere else entirely. He had no idea what she had seen in the big mutant's head, but trying to dig into that now seemed like a mistake. She needed some downtime and a comfortable spot where she would be safe. Clearly, that wouldn't be the apartment.

Bertrand knew where they lived, and apparently, so did Miranda's people. Between the unpredictable actions of a band of pirates and Echelon, that place would never be truly safe again.

When he got back into the city, Claude would have to call Zhara and beg her to let them crash at her place until he could sort everything out. After that, he would do what he could to pick up the pieces and move on. He hoped that Zhara would agree to help, but it was by no means a forgone conclusion. He'd rejected her offer to do exactly what he was about to ask her for, and it would only be right for her to say no.

"How are we getting back?" Vision asked.

Her voice still lacked its usual energetic nature, but it was good that she was actually speaking again.

"I'm going to see if I can barter with Gorman," Claude replied over his shoulder.

"You're joking," Vision said, perking up a bit. "You know how that'll go, right?"

Claude sighed. The last thing he wanted to do was enter the sewers. He'd been in those tunnels before and it wasn't pleasant. People lived down there, of course. The streets weren't exactly safe for the homeless when the storms rolled in, but just because people could live down there, didn't mean it was anywhere near ideal.

A number of settlements had been built in and around those dark, moist corridors and the people who lived in them had managed to cobble together whatever they needed from spare parts. Often, said parts were scavenged from the ruins closest to the wall. Everything else they stole from the people of Violet district.

The place Claude was aiming for was called Divide. It was aptly named. They had managed to piggyback the emitters and run their entire power grid off the wall above. It was an ingenious solution to a potentially suffocating problem, and since no one was going to debate pouring more resources into the barrier, Divide had all the power it would ever need.

It was run by a man named Gorman, who was as mean as he was greedy. Luckily, he was always willing to make a deal. The only catch was that the deals he was particularly keen to accept had to benefit either himself or the rest of his Vector Forge compatriots.

Claude wasn't a fan of dealing with gangs, but he had to get back across the border. Divide's scavengers made regular excursions into the Old City and back. Like it or not, that path was the best way back into Minerva City without drawing PlanSec's attention.

"We could always hit the checkpoint without a pass and see how long it takes Phalen to catch up to us," he said with a smirk.

He could feel Vision cringe at the thought of being around that man. Phalen was perhaps her least favorite human being. He had called her a parasite to her face when she was six and she had not taken it well. The last time he'd acknowledged her existence, he had referred to her as a thing instead of a person, and that had earned him an inexplicable headache. Claude did his best to get her to ignore him, but she fixated on those encounters. Now her distaste for the PlanSec officer grew exponentially every time he crossed their path.

"Fine, the sewers it is," Vision conceded with a heavy exhalation.

Claude angled the bike downward and ignored the vibrations under his skin. The rippling purple wall cast an intense glow on everything, but instead of the eery, stretched shadows causing additional anxiety, it did the opposite. As they passed closer, the barrier seemed to banish the ever-present threat of another Derelict ambush. The energy field was expensive and draining to maintain, but it was one of the few things anyone had discovered that actually deterred Derelicts.

Claude could only imagine the sight of massive hordes swarming into it and crumpling under the persistent downward force. What a victory that must have been. According to the histories, the field was originally generated by hundreds of ships projecting wide violet beams down onto the city in a massive, coordinated effort.

It was the kind of thing that was all but impossible in the modern era. Luckily, it was no longer necessary. The Dolvan emitters stood as a testament to the hard work and ingenuity of the Beitans as a whole, though they were named for the general who had commissioned the project. Each of the frail-looking towers had been erected by the best minds and hands in the Beita Systems when they could be spared from the war effort, of course.

It was meant as a deterrent, but no one expected it to work quite so well. When the Derelicts stopped attacking the barrier in less than a standard week, everyone celebrated. When they began the same roving patterns, they still followed almost a century later, the party was over and the Sabiens became the priority once again.

Some people still wondered why the creatures had never tried to assault the barrier again, but Claude figured there was still some part of them that remembered what the wall was capable of and chose to avoid it.

The thought of them remembering and altering their collective behavior based on that ran a chill down his spine. If they could remember the wall and its effects, what else could they remember? So far, there was only one person in the whole galaxy that might have the answer, and she was unlikely to share it anytime soon.

The bike sank between a canyon of crumbling buildings to skim the wind-worn streets of the Old City. The rumble of the Lifter's engines echoed off every cracked surface, destroying the silence of those long dead. Weather-beaten stone walkways and demolished storefronts painted a picture of a place that was as curious as it was tragic.

"I can't even imagine what it would have been like to live here," Vision said as she marveled at the composite buildings and ruined six-wheeled rover-like vehicles.

"Maybe it was like living in Violet," Claude said. "You live as best you can, put food on the table, and try to find whatever moments you can to keep yourself going."

"That doesn't sound like much of a life," Vision said dreamily.

"You'd be surprised," Claude replied and throttled up.

Despite the lifelessness of his surroundings, Claude managed to spot several signs that the area had been picked clean. The unmistakable damage and disrespect of scavengers was clearly visible on several of the vehicles. Roughly hewn handholds on the sides of multiple buildings desecrated what were the final resting places of untold thousands.

"We're getting close," Claude warned. "The interference is going to be bad from here on out."

He felt Vision's grip on him tighten as she braced herself and felt bad for her. So many parts of this world had an adverse effect on her, but settling here had still been the right call. Minerva had been good to them, in her way. She had provided a livelihood, decent people, for the most part, and best of all, concealment.

Minerva City was a place to disappear. Hundreds, if not thousands, of people lived there without any record of them having existed at all. It had been that way for so long that no census method ever devised could resolve the issue.

When the Old City fell, refugees just slipped through the cracks and everyone else was more than happy to let them. Time had advanced and Violet became an ideal hideaway. Now anyone who wanted to vanish had very little trouble doing so.

Claude had elected to make more ripples than he otherwise would have when they'd arrived. The path of least resistance would have put them underground, but he didn't think the sewer settlements were any place for a child to live. In his uninformed opinion, children needed open sky, sunshine, and air as fresh and clean as could be managed.

Minerva Prime was no Abarix, not by any stretch of the imagination. There were no lush fields of hallock, no dense marshlands, and no rainy magenta sunsets. Minerva offered only harsh rock scarred by lightning, wind, and dust. Yet, it was more of a home than the farming world he'd been raised on. Here, Vision had someone who cared about her, someone who would put everything on the line to protect her, which was more than Abarix had offered in the end.

There wasn't much that Claude understood about raising a kid, but he knew what he needed and did his best to provide that for Vision. So far, it seemed to be working.

A crude symbol etched into the wall to his right caught Claude's attention, bringing him back to himself. He instantly recognized Divide's strangely simplistic crest. Its two circles with a horizontal line carved between them marked the corner of a nearby building, along with an arrow pointing the way.

"You okay?" Claude asked, drifting the bike around the corner and spotting a second marker.

"I can't wait to get underground," Vision said through gritted teeth.

The interference was bad. Her sensors were completely useless, but luckily the wall had no effect on her inhibitors. Aside from whatever leaked through them, she was effectively blind, if one could be blinded by sensory overload.

"We're almost there," Claude said and guided the bike along a large crater and into the ruptured metal tube beneath it.

The vibrant purple of the wall did almost nothing to illuminate the darkness inside. With the front end of the bike crumpled, its light was ruined. That left them at the mercy of his pistol's narrow beam and Vision's sensors, assuming they would function underground.

Creeping slowly through the thick shadows, Claude asked, "V, can you—"

"It's clear," she said, cutting him off with a heavy exhalation.

The dense metal walls of the sewer tunnel did a great deal to block the interference from the energy barrier above. Vision's sensors were able to scan twenty yards ahead with only an occasional hitch in the feed.

Claude unholstered his sidearm and activated the under-barrel light. It was every bit as effective as trying to stab a hole in a bulkhead door with a stiletto, but it was better than nothing. After disconnecting the light from the pistol, he held it between his teeth, put his sidearm away and pushed the Lifter bike forward more confidently that before.

Vision snickered. "You look ridiculous right now."

Her chuckles echoed off the round metal tube before the growl of the Lifter's engine drowned them out for good. A list of witty comebacks flashed through Claude's mind, but holding the flashlight was more important than holding his own against an eleven-year-old. So, he let her have her laugh and guided the bike around a curve in the tunnel in silence.

The intensity of the Lifter's growling engine was lessened greatly by keeping its speed painfully slow, but even then, it was far from quiet. The sound announced their arrival to anyone with a set of working ears.

Every instinct Claude had told him to ditch the bike and proceed with Vision on foot. As a scout, that would have been the right call, but as a man in need of passage, he had more leverage with the bike than without it.

"Three people are waiting around the next curve," Vision whispered.

Claude closed his eyes and thanked whatever force guided the universe that he had chosen to take Vision with him for this job. She had proven to be invaluable, and he wasn't sure how he was going to say no when she inevitably demanded to go on jobs with him in the future.

"You're not," she whispered with a smile Claude could hear in her voice.

Claude huffed and pulled the bike to a stop, waiting for the strangers to present themselves. The idling engine's sound still rang off the walls, but he wasn't going to move another inch until whoever was waiting for them made the first move.

It wasn't likely they would attack, but just in case, he drew his sidearm and reattached the light. The pistol was only moderately powerful, but people in the sewer settlements didn't exactly have the best body armor or training. Hopefully, he wouldn't have to fight his way through them. Yet, in his experience, it was always best to be prepared.

"Who's there?" a throaty male voice called from the darkness.

"Someone looking for passage to Violet," Claude shouted and immediately regretted the volume he'd used. "Tell Gorman I've got a gently used Lifter bike to trade for it."

Silence stretched on for a long moment and Claude assumed the man was checking with his boss. Although, he couldn't be entirely sure. Taking a deep breath, he arched his back until he felt a much-needed pop. After spending nearly an hour leaning over the bike, he had never missed the temperature-adjusting bucket seats of his sedan more.

"Licensed?" the man finally asked with genuine curiosity.

"Nope, it's clean," Claude replied.

"Sure, tell me another one," the man chuckled then yelled, "Lights."

The tunnel around the curve lit up as dozens of mounted strips blinked to life. Claude groaned as his eyes took the time they needed to adjust to the sudden brightness.

"Bring it here, nice and slow," the man said, and Claude obliged.

He eased the bike around the corner with one hand, his sidearm in the other. A portly man with sweat stains on a dirty yellow shirt stood opposite him, brandishing an improvised personal flak cannon that seemed to be made from old hovercar parts.

"Gently used, my ass," the man said, eyeing the bike.

"It's better than the one he's got now," Claude said and watched as the fat man quirked his lips and shrugged.

"The guns go away now," he said and slung his weapon onto his back.

Claude holstered his pistol and breathed a sigh of relief. He noticed eight apparently handmade repulse emitters mounted on the rounded metal walls. They still cast a hint of violet that decorated the tunnel as he eased the bike past them. He assumed they'd been deactivated to give their people the element of surprise, but he wasn't sure if that was wise.

"You could have just left the energy field on," Claude said.

The portly man fell into step with the bike and shrugged again. "It would have been easier, but that way I don't get to shoot people."

Claude let that uncomfortable nugget of information float past. Clearly, he wasn't dealing with someone that had a great deal of respect for the locals. The man stubbed his fingers on his data-pad and the purple energy field flashed back into place behind them.

Vision winced, causing their escort focus his attention squarely on her for the first time. His eyes latched onto her halo, completely ignoring the girl wearing it.

"You trading that too?" he asked hungrily.

"No," Claude said in a tone that left no room for interpretation.

"Hmph," the man snorted and knelt down to pull open a hatch cut into the bottom of the tunnel.

Claude powered the bike down and stepped off it. He wasn't comfortable leaving it unguarded, but the hatch was too small to ride it down into the settlement. It was his only bargaining chip down here and while he was reasonably sure he could fight his way out if he had to, he preferred a more peaceful solution.

"I don't like this, Claude," Vision said softly. "I'm not getting good vibes from that guy."

"Vibes?" Claude asked with a smirk.

She narrowed her eyes at him and lifted her arms so he could help her off the inclined back of the Lifter bike. She felt lighter than normal. In fact, she seemed to weigh even less than she had at the hotel.

As her feet touched the slick metal surface, Claude shook the idea away. It was just another strange thing to add to the list. After all he had experienced in the last day and a half, what was one more? He was learning to take them in stride, whether he wanted to or not.

As a scout, he'd learned to hold onto his expectations with a loose grip. Missions rarely went according to plan, though nothing in the war could have completely prepared him for what he was dealing with now. Vision's abilities and the creature living inside him were unknowables. Bertrand and Miranda were a little more predictable as variables went but putting all of them in the same equation made it impossible to guess the overall outcome.

"Just focus on getting us out of here," Vision said.

Claude nodded his acknowledgment and for maybe the first time he saw something in her that registered as more than just a child, more than just his charge. The girl that looked back at him seemed more like a...

"The word you're looking for is partner," Vision said, answering his thoughts once again.

"I thought I told you to stay out of my head," Claude said and offered her his hand.

Vision gripped it tightly, and the two made their way into the hatch.

• • • •

Second meal had come early, but Gorman wasn't complaining. It had been a slow day, for once, and he wasn't above taking a little time to enjoy it. Before he'd gotten the call about someone at the barrier, the only meeting he had on the books was an early trip home to surprise his wives. Now he had the opportunity to get something that would take his crews months to reverse engineer, but once they'd done it...

He let the grin spread across his face unrestrained and marveled at how good it felt. Gorman only had a moment to bask in his good fortune before a knock on the door brought back his game face. He waited until the knock came again before he truly allowed himself to accept that it was time to get to work.

"Enter," Gorman said in his raspy croak of a voice.

The stocky, short-haired man and the little blonde girl that entered his domain were filthy, haggard, and windblown, but that was to be expected, considering where they'd come from. He noticed the holes in the man's clothes and thanked the Homeworld that he had the good sense not to bleed on his office floor.

"DiSilva, I hear you brought me a new toy," Gorman said, rising from his seat at the crude metal-work table.

"If we can come to a deal," Claude said and let the door close behind him.

Vision stood just behind his right arm and did her best to get a read on the balding man at the other end of the room. He was guarded and untrustworthy, but he wasn't quite rotten all the way to the core. She picked up on genuine interest in the trade, though he was as likely to try and steal from them as he was to honor any agreement.

"So, you want me to grant you passage, but that seems like a big ask when I could just keep the bike and give you nothing," Gorman said with a wide smile that was anything but friendly.

Claude made a show of rolling out his shoulders before he strode across the room to a row of seats on the left wall. He had met with Gorman before, but he knew him better by reputation. He was shrewd and dangerous, but he could be reasoned with, unlike most of Vector Forge's other bosses. Gorman was less likely to take things to a physical place if he didn't have to, so Claude had to make sure to establish the fact he could get to him before of his guards could intervene.

"How is that a big ask?" Claude inquired as he watched Vision make her way over to him.

"It exposes me and my good nature. My associates don't really value compassion and generosity," Gorman said sinking back into his seat.

"I believe the bike covers that angle," Claude snorted.

He fixed the greedy man with a glare but got nothing but a placid stare in return. It was clear Gorman was willing to make a push everyone would regret.

"But it's only one bike and as I understand it, it's not in the best of conditions."

"We both know you aren't going to ride the damned thing," Claude snapped, letting his frustrations get the better of him.

A light hand touched his arm, quietly reminding him what was on the line. Gorman was the only member of the Vector Forge gang that he had even passable ties with, and he was the exclusive holder to the gateway back to civilization.

"Careful, DiSilva. You don't want to find yourself back out the way you came," Gorman threatened. "I like you, but it seems to me that you have a whiff of desperation about you. It would be bad business not to capitalize on it."

"What do you want?" Claude asked with an exasperated sigh.

"I want to know what you were doing out there, where you got the bike, and more importantly, how you survived," the bald man said, sitting back down to his meal.

"You know how it is. A client sent me out there on a hunch. We came up empty-handed but the bastard's coughing up my fee regardless," Claude lied.

He couldn't afford to mention the data drives or the person that sent him out there. The gangs were paranoid. They always thought that everyone was trying to take them down. Somehow, they believed they'd managed to make it onto the government's priority list when nothing could be farther from the truth. Even PlanSec was barely concerned with their activities, so long as they didn't extend their reach outside of Violet. But paranoia was rarely rooted in reality.

"And am I supposed to believe that the bike you brought me is fast enough to outrun the Derelict hordes?" Gorman asked, slurping on a strand of pasta that made Claude's stomach growl.

"Show him," Vision said coldly.

Claude glared at her, but Vision only nodded. Her expression asked for his trust, and while he wasn't comfortable putting his secret in the open for someone like Gorman, he didn't have a better idea.

Resigning himself to the fight he knew would be coming, Claude stepped toward Gorman's table and placed his hand on it. He sighed heavily, spreading his fingers across the wavy metal surface.

"If I told you how I managed it, you wouldn't believe me," he said, locking eyes with the feasting man. "You're just going to have to see it for yourself."

With a silent plea to the good nature of his passenger, he did his best to will the silver to the surface of his skin. It took a second, which oddly registered as a protest in Claude's mind, but the living liquid eventually flowed up through his pores to coat his hand. His passenger trailed from his fingers, creating little tendrils with hooks on the ends.

"Well, that's new," Vision said under her breath as her sensors fed her every flowing motion of the creature.

Gorman backed out of his chair, causing his carefully prepared meal to rain down around him like Jurillian hail. His utensil danced noisily on the patchwork metal of the table as the tendrils slashed and slithered their way toward him.

"What the hell is that thing?" he demanded, putting as much distance between himself and Claude as the room would allow.

"This is my passenger," Claude said and marveled at how freeing it felt to actually discuss it openly. "It's how we survived the Derelicts and it's why you're going to play nice. Take the bike and let us pass."

Gorman had lost his words even though he was still moving his mouth. His wide eyes stayed locked on the silver as it continued its measured advance. Beads of cold sweat streamed down Gorman's face for another long moment before finally he caved. Still, he couldn't bring himself to form the words, so with great effort and urgency, he put every ounce of willpower he still possessed into nodding his agreement.

Claude nodded in return but let a small, respectful smile cross his lips. He closed his fist, and the silver retreated back into him. It retracted three times faster than it had slithered forth and gave him an uncomfortably cold, stinging sensation as it did. It wasn't quite painful, but Claude had to stop himself from shaking the sting out of his fingers to save the illusion.

"*Objectify. Degrade. Humiliate.*"

Vision raised an eyebrow at the thoughts that jumped out at her. On the ride over, she had realized these untamed thoughts were separate from Claude's. It had just been a working theory, but now she knew she was right.

She'd told Claude before that it might've been trying to communicate, but she thought it was trying to do so with him. Apparently, it wanted to talk to her instead, though she wasn't sure why. It really didn't matter. The fact that Claude's passenger could share its thoughts was a helpful development. It meant there was someone else looking out for the jerk. That made three of them, and between their combined efforts, he might just live long enough to get old... well, older.

"*I understand*," she tried to send back, but got no response.

As far as she knew, she could only read thoughts, not project them. Still, she tried. There was no reason not to. Who could say what she was capable of now? Things were changing so rapidly there was no telling what would work and what wouldn't.

It had once been a fairly harmless thing to read a mind, but now each time she thought about doing it there was a kernel of hesitation there. She found herself concerned about what she might find and how it would affect her. Zhara would probably call that growth, but she called it terrifying. Her abilities had been causing her much more pain than she wanted lately. The only safe place to go outside of her own head seemed to be Claude's, but even his mind had its risks.

If he was an ocean, Vision tended to stay near the surface. In earlier days, she would test herself by seeing how deep she could dive into him. Then she'd crossed into his war experiences and it put an end to her exploring. Now she respected his privacy, for the most part. She was still curious how he felt about or saw certain situations, and that curiosity had a way of getting the better of her, but she did try and that seemed to be enough for Claude.

"G-get out! Get out of my city," Gorman said, at last.

His tanned skin had lost most of its color and rivulets of sweat still streamed down his face and neck.

Claude nodded at the man and turned calmly toward the exit. He could feel Gorman's wide, frightened eyes still locked on him, but that didn't matter anymore. Vision tried to emulate Claude's stride but couldn't resist throwing the horrified man a snide wink.

Gorman pressed his back against the window overlooking the cavern settlement stretched out below. He was undoubtedly in full view of anyone willing to look up to his office, but primal fear had a way of melting the pride and self-respect away from lesser men.

When the doors closed behind them, Vision asked, "I know seeing your passenger can be a little unsettling, but what was his problem?"

Claude took a moment to think on her question as they descended the set of dingy gray stairs toward the cavern below.

"He's never seen an alien before," Claude said with a shrug. "Derelicts are one thing, they used to be human, but he has no frame of reference for something completely foreign."

Vision frowned at that. For all she knew, the Zephiar were the only intelligent alien race that humans had known, and there was plenty of evidence to back that up, but the silver never occurred to her as an alien.

What was alien and what wasn't meant very little when your race was spread across hundreds of worlds. Eilitonians, Reitsinis, and even an eleven-year-old Firaxian could all be considered aliens to a person who had never left Minerva Prime and yet they were all just human to most people.

"But why would that scare someone so much? He has to know that aliens exist out there somewhere," Vision continued and noticed for the first time how her voice echoed off the natural stone walls. "I mean the Zephiar took us from our Homeworld, after all."

"Yes, but it's Truce Week, Vision," Claude replied, as if it should explain everything.

Vision's brow furrowed as she tried to make sense of the words. She knew what Truce Week was, but...

"What does that have to do with aliens?"

Claude stopped on the landing and leaned against the cold and damp cavern wall. He took a second to find the easiest way to express his idea to her before he said, "What do you think? He's maybe forty-three standard years old, right?"

"At least," she said, ignoring the deep drumbeats rising from the settlement below.

"That means he's seen a lot of celebrations and every Truce Week. He probably has a routine at this point. Maybe he gets an early dinner, maybe he sleeps in, whatever, but today he saw an actual alien with his own two eyes. After what he saw, it's no longer the second day of Truce Week, it's the day he saw an alien. Tomorrow will be the day after he saw an alien. Every Truce Week will mark the anniversary of when he first saw an alien.

"His life, his whole inner world, is different now, and he has no way of going back. He lost control of his reality, that's why he was so afraid," Claude explained and pushed off the wall.

"Do you think he'll be all right?" Vision asked with a newfound concern.

"Don't know," Claude said, beginning his final descent into the bustling cavern settlement of Divide. "It's best not to dwell on it. I know for a fact he's done worse to better people."

"That doesn't make it okay," Vision said under her breath and followed Claude into the crowd.

Truce Week celebrations were already in full swing for Divide. Families laughed as they danced around dozens of painted stalagmites. Stalls crowded with people looking to buy colorful headdresses and wondrous smelling foods littered the main thoroughfare. Live music and loud conversation filled the space and somehow didn't dissolve into the same chaotic soundscape Vision experienced in the tunnels.

Her sensors nearly overloaded with all the moving bodies, hanging needlework banners, and streams of glittering tassels in the air, each swaying with the music. She had been to the Archive celebration the previous year, but it was nowhere near as lively and festive as this underground celebration.

"Can we get something to eat?" she shouted to Claude over the noise.

"Sure, if we can find anything that seems edible," Claude yelled back and reached out.

Vision took his hand and pulled him into the beating heart of Divide.

• • • •

"So, you've known the drives were from Firaxis this whole time and didn't tell me?" Vision asked, ignoring the curious looks strangers directed at her.

Claude met several stares head-on and waited for the other patrons to turn back to their own tables. Then, he turned his attention to back to Vision.

"I was going to tell you when I knew what was on them," he said with his mouth still partially full. "Clearly, I should have stuck to that plan."

"Why?" Vision hissed at him.

"Because I didn't want this," he said, motioning at her. "I didn't want you getting all spun up about the possibilities. There was no point in getting your hopes up if it was just going to lead to another letdown."

Vision visibly cooled. His reasoning was sound, but she was still upset he'd intentionally kept something so important from her. She was his partner, after all. If the drives had information relevant to her, she knew he would have shared it eventually, but that didn't make her feel any better. She deserved to know what they were risking their lives for. The only thing it would have changed was her level of investment in seeing the job completed.

"You didn't do this for the client, did you?" Vision finally asked.

Claude shook his head. "I did it for us. I couldn't care less about Bertrand getting the information."

Vision leaned back into her seat and admired the restaurant. It was a cozy little place, radiating with the warmth of the crowd filling its relatively small space.

The corrugated metal walls were welded together from half a dozen different source materials, but they had been decorated in such a way that it reminded her of the place where she and Claude first met. Each segment on the walls showed the same image but from slightly different angles, like the faceted edges of a gem. It was a similar to Firaxis' crystal sanctuary, only far more rudimentary and lived in. The whole aesthetic of the restaurant made Vision wonder if the owner was Sabien, since the crystalline design wasn't exactly popular in the Beita Systems.

While it was an interesting place to look at, the best thing about it was the intoxicating smell of food. Everything had the will-shattering aroma that only came from a grill and an open flame.

Vision loved it. Every time the old woman in the kitchen sent a dish out to be delivered, a new delicious scent was added to the elaborate tapestry wafting through the air. Each mouth-watering aroma made a promise of exotic culinary joys that were faithfully honored.

Vision wasn't exactly sure what was in the food here, but then she didn't know what the food topside was made of either. What she did know was that whenever a meal was made to order, it tasted amazing. She had settled on a Deep Root Stew while Claude had gone with a Runner's Wrap. He seemed to be enjoying his meal even more than she was, since he was nearly done and she still had over half of hers to go.

"So, what do we do now?" Vision asked, stirring her stew and deciding that she might not have enough space left to finish it.

"We can't stay at the apartment," Claude said, purposefully avoiding her eyes.

"I figured. The pirates had to have known where we were. Them showing up was no accident," Vision deduced.

"Not just that, I'm sure Bertrand has been keeping an eye on the place as well," Claude said and pushed the tail end of his wrap toward the center of the table.

"Do you think she's right about him?" Vision asked.

Claude knew these people well enough, but she wasn't comfortable using their names just yet.

"Miranda has her own motives, but that doesn't make her our enemy," Claude began. "Her people were supposed to take me alive, after all."

"So, what happened?" Vision asked, leaning on her palm.

"Nobody told me that the pirates running me down weren't trying to kill me, so I reacted, then they reacted, then the Derelicts came," Claude said, rubbing his forehead.

"But do you think Bertrand will sell you out like she said?" Vision asked, though she could guess the answer.

"There's a real possibility, but on the upside, I don't think he knows about you," he said.

"So that makes me your secret weapon then, right?" Vision said excitedly.

That idea knocked a grunt loose from Claude. She was so eager to put herself in harm's way to help him, but he was more than certain it was because underneath all the impressive powers and her sharp mind, she was still just a child.

"Wrong," he said sternly. "You're sitting the rest of this job out at Zhara's, if I can get her to agree."

Vision crossed her arms. She read his seriousness, so arguing was unlikely to change his mind. But that didn't mean she wasn't going to give it a shot.

"You need me, Claude. This isn't just another job and you know it. Both sides know you and how you think. You're going to need a wildcard if you're going to throw them off," Vision protested.

"That's a good point, but I'm not taking you back out there. I promised I would protect you and I will. That means leaving you out of this," he stated forcefully.

"What if I don't let you?" Vision seethed. "What if I erase this conversation from your mind and make you take me?"

Claude glared at her. He wasn't sure if she could actually do what she was threatening, but that didn't change anything. The idea she was flirting with was betrayal on the highest level, and while he didn't think she would actually do it, he had to shake her off this path for good, because one day she might actually be able to.

"Do you know what happened to the Psionics?" Claude asked sharply.

Vision shook her head in silent defiance.

"The Sabiens made them. They took volunteers and experimented on them until they figured out how to turn them into human weapons, and then they sent them out to fight. For a while, they decimated us. We lost planet after planet to Sabien control, then suddenly we stopped seeing them in the field. No one on our side had any idea why until several imprisoned Psionics were discovered locked in inhibitor cages at an abandoned outpost.

"Grunts weren't given much information, but what we managed to piece together painted a desperate picture. Long story short, the Psionics at that outpost lost the ability to separate the thoughts of their fellow soldiers from their intentions. Basically, they became like the rest of us, except we can't read every stray thought that pops into another person's head. They could."

Vision looked down at the cooling stew and did her best not to be interested in the story, but failed. She stirred the few chunks of vegetables she had left and sighed before facing Claude once more.

Claude leaned forward. Gently, he took the spoon from Vision and placed it neatly beside her bowl before continuing.

"You see, they saw no difference between what a person thought about doing, what they wished they could do, and what they would do. People naturally distrust others and the more different they are, the more aggressive that distrust becomes. The regular soldiers fell victim to that part of their nature and the Psionics must have picked up on it. They saw no difference between the people fighting beside them and the people fighting against them, especially when both thought heavily about how to kill them," Claude explained pointedly.

Vision shifted uncomfortably in her seat. She fought hard to hold on to her defiant posture, even though her heart was no longer in it.

"No one knows exactly what the Sabiens did to the rest of the Psionics after that, but we do know there don't seem to be many around anymore."

"So, what the point?" she mumbled.

"The point is, V, the universe is a complicated and confusing place for everyone. That will go double for you, because, unlike the rest of us, you will be subjected to the raw, irrational, and untempered thoughts of everyone around you. Don't lose yourself and don't forget who your friends are. You're going to need them," Claude concluded and stood up from the table.

He freed his ruined jacket from the back of his seat and slipped into it with a smooth, well-practiced flourish before turning back to the little girl wearing a deep frown.

"Come on, we need to get moving," he said, and let the subject drop.

Vision didn't need to be badgered about what she'd done. She had lashed out in anger and disappointment, but in the years that Claude had been with her, he'd discovered that returning those actions with negative feedback almost always escalated things. His objective was always to defuse the situation and get her to see what she'd done from outside her own personal bubble. Usually, she corrected herself after that. It was a strategy that had worked well several times over, and Claude had determined it to the best way to teach her, without stomping out the flame that made her so unique.

Vision rose from her seat with a pout that infected her whole body, then bent over to steal one last bite of stew before rounding the table. She had made a point of walking around him and leading the way to the exit.

Claude watched and suppressed a smile. She was in a mood, but she would have to get over it. At some point, she had to accept that she was the child, and he was the adult. There was only one way to get around that fact and it would take her seven years to reach it, minimum.

Chapter 20

BERTRAND WAS BEGINNING to regret not demanding a firmer timeline. DiSilva had agreed to the job and sent word he would head to the old hotel in the morning. Morning had come and gone, as well as much of the day, but there had been no message from him.

Odds were high that he wouldn't make it out alive, but the scout Bertrand had known was likely to find a way. That was something the older man had a great deal of faith in. Still, the silence was deafening all the same. Hanging in limbo like this was torment.

Mattic had been monitoring PlanSec communications on Bertrand's orders, but again he was met with nothing of value. The kid had grown into his role well, but even the best comms officer couldn't make intel appear when there was none.

The TaskMaster II hovered over the southern boundary of the Cascade District. With her being a fair amount larger than his original ship, she required more care in her maneuvering and placement. Holding position at the edge of Violet made it less likely a rogue drone or drunken civilian would veer off course and smear themselves across the invisible belly of the ship.

Advancements in the intervening years meant that few things short of military-grade weaponry could pierce the ship's hull, but they had their costs. The most obvious was a drastically different form factor, even if its function remained largely the same. Where the first ship had all the grace of a bird in flight, the TaskMaster II was much less elegant in design.

She now bore the image of the weapon she had become. Her bulkier body tapered toward a forward section that always reminded Bertrand of an ax head if it were made to stab instead of cleave. He wasn't altogether pleased with the new ship's look, but since he'd installed the cloaking engine, that complaint had been rendered moot.

Like the TaskMaster I, this one was also a silent runner, making it easy for her to get into and out of areas that would otherwise be impassible by a Beita Systems ship. In this case, the mission called for a good deal of discretion where the general populace was concerned. The TaskMaster II was ideally constructed for such an endeavor.

The paranoia of Echelon was legendary but warranted here. Minerva Prime was mostly a corporate world, and the bevy of executives tended to share that trait. Many had power and influence in the government, and they would want a piece of whatever research was recovered on their turf. And since Echelon was always opposed to sharing any and everything except accountability, Bertrand had been called.

He'd also made the decision to moor the ship on-world instead of in orbit since planetary travel was common but normal transportation was restricted to twenty-two hundred feet. The TaskMaster II was holding an altitude more than five times that, which made detection all but impossible.

Echelon had granted him clearance to block aerial sensor readings, allowing him to remain undetected by the planet's satellite coverage. To top it all off, Bertrand had access to the full comms network of the planet as well, which was as useful as it was bothersome.

The executor Echelon had sent was savvy and mistrustful. She was more than eager to second guess him and had already attempted to rip his command away from him. If he wasn't so well connected with the people at the top, it might have worked. Instead, what Bertrand had now was a house divided. A number of the newer soldiers were easily swayed by the executor, while those that had served with him longer remained loyal.

Blame for this new friction laid squarely at the feet of Marta Rai. She was an actual agent of Echelon, while Bertrand was technically just hired help. It was easy to see how less experienced troops could get twisted and confused by the dynamics at play, and he didn't hold it against them. Once he finished the mission and removed Marta's influence from his ship, things would return to normal, or so he hoped. In the meantime, he had been dodging her and doing his best to keep tabs on what she was up to. So far, she had managed to discover his deal with DiSilva, but since he was an external variable, she had no control over him.

Like Bertrand, she was stuck waiting until word came back about the state of the mission. That left nothing but time. Time, he had reluctantly decided to use to attempt to mend the rift between himself and the troublemaking interloper on his ship. A very large part of him wanted nothing more than to make her disappear, but that would be wasteful. If he could get her closer to his side, it would make whatever came next much easier.

With that in mind, he had issued a request to parley with her. For Bertrand, there was no greater asset than a unified team, clear in its purpose and confident in its abilities. Many a task had been mastered by such teams, and he liked to think that he fostered them.

In his years as an officer, he had seen countless men and women forge themselves into something more than soldiers. He hoped that by coming to terms with Marta, he could take the thorn from his side and wield it as a sword, but it wasn't entirely up to him.

His door's proximity chime rang through the room, shattering his silent worry. With a sigh and a crossing of his arm, Bertrand barked, "Come in."

The metal door slid open to reveal the tightly controlled curls and unhampered scowl that belonged to the newest bane of his existence.

"Captain," Marta hissed as she stepped into his quarters.

Bertrand pushed himself back from the desk but made no effort to ease the tension of the situation.

"Executor," Bertrand said and motioned at the seat across the desk from him. "I called you here to help clear up some of the issues between us."

Marta eyed him warily. Something in her gaze reminded him of a feral creature that was unsure if the morsel being offered to it was a free meal or bait. Cautious intellect shone through her stare, but there was no hint of a true reaction.

"We have to put whatever this is behind us before it sours the mission. Too much is at stake," Bertrand said, this time doing nothing to hide his own discomfort with the situation. "Don't you agree?"

Marta cocked her head to the side slightly, which only intensified Bertrand's initial impression, then reluctantly moved further into the space. Her shoulders relaxed as she reached some unstated conclusion, but still, she refused to sit. Instead, she dug her fingers into the back of the chair and continued to fix him with her distrustful glare.

Bertrand decided to do nothing further except to project an aura of openness. He really did believe that the unification of the disparate sides would be to everyone's benefit. If DiSilva succeeded, he was going to need every facet of this operation working at its fullest to see the plan through to a favorable end. Having the deck stacked against them would only lead to ruin.

His ability to freeze her out was weak, but so was hers. They were at an impasse, and Bertrand, like all military men, was well-versed in the costs of a destructive, long-running stalemate.

"I know you have questions about–" Bertrand managed to say before Marta's words trampled his own.

"Why did you see fit to put our entire mission in the hands of an outsider?" she seethed, finally making her way to his desk.

Bertrand stared daggers at her, but she gave no sense of concern about his mood.

"I didn't," Bertrand said and swept his open palm over his desk.

Holo screens activated, bringing up several files from Claude's military record to life in layers of shimmering light. With a spin of his wrist, Bertrand righted the text so that Marta could read it.

She scanned the hologram for a moment then cleared her throat. She could admit when she was wrong, but it wasn't as simple as that. The man's record was riddled with monstrous contradictions and red flags that screamed out from the cool, bluish-green text.

"So, he's unreliable," Marta stated disapprovingly.

"You don't know what you're talking about," Bertrand growled, then caught himself.

"His record indicates his own morality is his guiding star. On top of that, he's insubordinate and dangerous. None of that works for this mission," Marta replied.

Bertrand squeezed his eyes shut tight enough to see starbursts behind his eyelids, then said, "DiSilva has come through for me in the past... but I'd be lying if I said he was a sure thing."

The captain's admission took Marta by surprise. She expected he would fight her and guard his plan against any complaint she could levy at it. What she hadn't expected was to be lured into an honest conversation about the asset he had chosen to get them involved with.

"But I believe he will work just fine. He's a straight shooter, Rai, and he has a personal stake in this," Bertrand explained. "To motivate a man like DiSilva, you have to be honest with him."

Marta seemed to almost cringe at the concept. Maintaining the compartmentalization of information was rule one for those who lived and breathed Echelon. They were a different breed, trained to always come at things sideways. So it didn't surprise Bertrand at all to see her lack of faith in his methods.

"Coming from Myridorn, I don't expect that to make much sense to you, but out here, people want to be respected. If you want them to do things for you, you have to give them that," Bertrand said, unintentionally sounding much like a teacher in his own ears.

Marta's face twisted again as though she'd caught a sniff of something she didn't like. "What you call respect, I call inefficiency. You've left too much slack in the line, and it's likely to snap," she countered.

"We'll see," Bertrand said with an honest smile. "I know the man. I know how he thinks, but more importantly, I know what he carries."

Bertrand pushed his hand over his desk again, and the PlanSec image of Claude absorbed the text of his record. The man in the picture leered at them with loosely held disdain, but what grabbed Marta's attention were the thin but distinct lines of silver around his face.

"Is that..."

"Yes," Bertrand said.

"You are a clever bastard, aren't you?" Marta asked with a smirk.

"I like to think so."

"No wonder my bosses trust you. Deep down, you're the same," Marta said with a laugh that sounded like rain falling on bells but felt like acid in Bertrand's ears.

"Does that mean you're going to stop fighting me at every step?" Bertrand asked, trying to keep the irritation out of his voice.

"No, it doesn't," Marta said coldly. "It means that you are going to loop me into your plans from now on, and as long as I agree with the steps you're taking, you will have my support."

Bertrand grimaced. It was progress, but not to the extent he needed. Marta would still cause problems for him, but maybe if he gave her a little knowledge, he could keep her interference from becoming truly problematic.

Suppressing a sigh of both disappointment and resignation, Bertrand said, "Go to Mattic in Comms. Have him link you in on conversations from DiSilva. Tell him I said so."

The executor watched him blankly for a few seconds, then nodded slightly before turning to leave the room. As she exited, Bertrand felt himself relax and sink further into the padding of the chair.

He had to accept that he'd done the best he could, but his peace offering hadn't been fully accepted. Marta was going to remain an uncontrollable variable. Still, if she elected to link her comms, at least Bertrand would have begun the process of building a level of trust between them.

Admittedly, anything he could do to lessen the chances of her shooting him in the spine was a victory, no matter how small it seemed.

· · · ·

Marta had been on several Trion class light frigates in her time but the TaskMaster II was by far the most advanced. Typically, the military didn't overhaul their ships with the latest technology and instead chose to build new ones. The old Trion classes had been retired shortly after the truce went into effect, making way for the smaller, faster Jirelon class frigates.

Bertrand was not military, at least not directly, and the fortune he'd made off contracts with his former superiors made it possible for him to outfit the older ship with many state-of-the-art features afforded to newer and better models. As a result, the layout of several decks had been greatly modified. Those modifications made navigation difficult for someone who hadn't been particularly knowledgeable about them to begin with.

Marta had been on her way to operations when she was summoned to the captain's suite for a thoroughly unexpected chat. Now, she was more confused about the man than before. Given her actions and his own up to this point, she was expecting to fight him tooth and nail for the entirety of the mission, but instead, he had surprised her.

War was deception, but Marta got the feeling the man wasn't lying to her. He had even shared a few choice details with her that her higher-ups had held back. The fact that DiSilva carried the same parasite as Faridan was valuable information, information Myridorn had shared with him and not with her. For reasons she didn't understand fully, Echelon seemed to trust that Bertrand had their best interests at heart, but Marta could feel that something wasn't quite right. The denial she'd gotten to her request to assume command had been less than ideal, but the orders given to Bertrand directly were a complete slap in the face. That only stung more when it was the mercenary captain who shared them with her instead of the organization she had given her life to.

In her bid to take full control of this mission, she had made sure to place the death of Dr. Eugene at the top of her report. For reasons unknown, it hadn't garnered the desired response. If she were issuing the orders, such a failure would be cause for Bertrand to be stripped of all contracts and considerations. But as an executor, she had to abide by the ruling as it was handed down, even if it was shortsighted and obviously incorrect.

By the time she reached the comms room, Marta could feel her pulse raging. Her presence was unexpected, as all of the technicians' surprised looks attested. After basking in their initial shock, she focused on the one with the Reitsini crest on his scalp.

"You," she said, singling out the young man.

The man pointed to himself nervously, and Marta nodded. The two technicians near him moved away swiftly and did their best to avoid eye contact with him.

"You're Mattic, right?" she asked him but watched the room for reactions.

Several heads nodded, but none of them belonged to the technician Marta had asked.

"You ran a civilian call through Bertrand's quarters, did you not?" she asked heatedly.

The young man cleared his throat and managed to somehow find his courage. He was six inches taller than the executor but seemed to possess a timid demeanor she was more than willing to exploit if he let her.

"Yes," he said, straightening. "He still the captain. Why you care?"

Marta inhaled sharply and clenched her jaw to keep from unleashing on the man. If anyone knew about her attempt to supplant Bertrand, the comms techs would. It wasn't a well-guarded secret among the crew that she had issues with the captain and he with her. Yet, now that the word was out, she had found more and more open defiance coming from the crew. Whenever possible, they had started to make her time aboard the ship difficult, to say the least.

"He has given me access to comms between himself and DiSilva. I want all records of those calls, and I want them immediately," Marta seethed.

The man looked at her curiously. Much of the initial concern he'd had was melting away in front of her eyes, and that was going to make things harder than they needed to be.

"Captain has private comms privileges," he said, meeting her frigid gaze.

Marta let a slight grin curl her lips. "Call him then. He'll authorize it."

She knew full well that it was possible he might not, but there was little to gain from that except a spiteful jab at an adversary who wouldn't really care. She had believed Bertrand to be smarter than that. He hadn't survived in these treacherous waters this long by stooping to petty revenge.

The man who must have been Mattic ran through his comms protocol and connected to the captain. He was smart and chose to block open-air access to both audio and visual signals, routing it through his earpiece instead.

To Marta, the tension was delicious. She often found that she enjoyed the tiny little limbo moments before her personal universe settled on a path. Those moments allowed infinite possibilities to exist until reality snuffed out all but one. Before she had joined Echelon, her life was made entirely of these moments, or so she seemed to remember. Then, when she was drowning in them, she had found no joy in the unknown, but now they had all but disappeared from her life. So, she had come to cherish the little ones that she did receive. They were small, sweet joys, and like all such things, this one too melted away in seconds.

"I approved your request," Mattic said with obvious dissatisfaction on his face.

Marta fired him a beaming smile of pure spite, but inside, she was still confused. It hadn't been an act, or maybe it still was, and she didn't know the stakes. Either way, she had gotten a seat at the table. She wasn't about to become Bertrand's subordinate, but he had offered her more than she would have been able to take from him by force.

She turned without another word and strode out into the corridor, her curiosity now piqued. Who was this man that Bertrand had so much faith in, and was he really worthy of so much trust? There was only one way to know. She would have to look into him directly.

Moving swiftly and weaving around those that didn't share her sense of immediacy, Marta Rai set her mind to the task. Claude DiSilva was an unknown to her, and in order to solve that problem, she was going to have to pour all of her attention into him. He was going to need a personal touch, and that couldn't be given from so high above the Minervan surface.

With a groan, Marta began forming a plan that would require a talent she hadn't used since her early days at the Myridorn Academy.

• • • •

Ashe was out of sorts. The sweltering corridors of the Modus Vivendi all blurred into a dull gray haze as she made her way through them. No destination presented itself as she moved. For an hour, she had burned her way through the ship ignoring confused, judgmental, and sympathetic expressions alike. Word of the captain's return had come hours ago, but she had arrived alone. Ashe had tried to wait. She tried to convince herself that the others would return as well. Perhaps they had gotten separated. Ashe wanted to believe that maybe *he* had gone on into the city proper to assist in reconnaissance, but she knew it wasn't true.

When that knowledge had crushed every ounce of hope she could rally against it, she'd begun to move, and in an hour and fifty-three minutes, she hadn't found a place to stop. Some time ago, a ship-wide broadcast had stated the obvious. All the usual platitudes were made. The announcement had used all the words expected, but it rang hollow. The voice she had given Octavian spoke of how bravely and fiercely they had given their lives. It declared that they would never be forgotten, but as well-crafted as the speech had been, it still missed its mark. Instead of inspiring, the speech had infuriated.

Ashe blinked sweat from her eyes and finally willed her feet to still themselves. The sting provided a momentary distraction from the unending storm shredding her from the inside. When she looked around, she noticed a weight on those moving around her.

Caught up in her own anger, she had missed the change in the atmosphere. She was far from the only one aboard upset by the news. Many didn't seem to understand why they had left the ship in the first place. The captain had returned with nothing but her bike, blood-stained clothes, and a sour disposition. The fact that it was her second who addressed the crew and that he didn't even do it in person only stirred the simmering discontent shared among them.

Ashe had felt it growing in every darkened corner. Whispers had grown louder. Nervous glances had steeled themselves, becoming indignant stares, but she had convinced herself that nothing would come of it. Now she knew that was a lie.

Deep down, Ashe could feel her own dissatisfaction twisting, mutating into a form that frightened her. If her emotions were mirrored in others, there was no telling what it could do. Their rage was unpredictable and violent, but so was Faridan.

While others might direct their gathering fury toward their captain, Ashe had a better place to put hers, should her courage carry her all the way to his door.

. . . .

"Octavian!" Ashe shouted, slamming her fist against the rough metal repeatedly.

In her head, she knew there was no need to bang on it. Proximity sensors and projection devices would do more to alert him of her presence than her fist ever could, but it just felt better to hit something.

She had not been the best friend to Dogura in the past months, but she did care about him. That much never changed. He was a fearless idiot and as likely to get himself killed while playing shadow broker as he was on the mission he volunteered for, but he deserved more than a few syrupy words spat by a man who had been miles away and in safety when he died.

Ashe wasn't sure what she meant to accomplish by confronting a superior like this, but it was the only place she felt she could direct her pain. They had shared more time than either of them had expected to since arriving on Minerva, and while that didn't mean much, it did mean that he was going to listen to her now.

The door slid open to reveal a dark room. The soft cool breath of the space touched her skin, and for just a moment, she felt calm threaten to return.

"Enter," the room itself said to her.

Ashe took a second to reconnect with the bubbling lava flow that was her motivation and stepped inside.

"What the hell happened out there?" Ashe demanded as she stormed into the room.

She ignored everything but the man staring into the mirrored panel across from her.

Octavian was still dressed in his uniform even though he had been off duty for hours. He stood in front of his own reflection, studying it, judging it, and finding himself displeased with the man he saw there.

His sharp, green eyes fixed on Ashe's own through the reflection, and he pointed to the ceiling while remaining silent.

It took Ashe a moment to kick her brain out of its boiling fury and into a state that let her understand what he meant. When he spun to face her, he did so with such speed that it almost startled her. In his outstretched hand, he held one of his earpieces. With a deep breath, she took the device from him and fit it as snuggly into her ear as she could manage.

Octavian powered down the room's broadcast system and disconnected it from the ship's main network via an open panel behind his locker. He felt Ashe's attempts to stare a hole through him while he did so but chose to ignore the sensation. When he was finished and felt secure enough in their privacy, he once again turned his attention to the blue-haired pirate.

"The mission went sideways. Men died. No one ever wants it to happen, but it does," the mechanical voice droned into her ear.

"She killed him, Octavian," Ashe seethed. "She killed them all. Dogura was a helmsman. Zacka worked the kitchens. Those men were not fighters. They had no business out there. She knew that, and she took him anyway, knowing they would die."

Octavian let out a long, exasperated breath. He knew how she felt, how most of the crew felt. He and Miranda had come to the ship as outsiders and maneuvered their way into command. They weren't pirates in the same way the others were, and as a result, they always carried with them a thin film of otherness that led to distrust and suspicion. He had done as much as he could to try and alleviate that, but Miranda had been moving farther and farther in the opposite direction. She chose to embrace the discomfort her presence created rather than minimize it.

For that reason, Octavian had taken it upon himself to be the screen between her and the crew. He had spent months attempting to build a rapport with them, but the captain had been making it increasingly difficult. The mission into the Old City had been only the latest example of that.

"The captain did not select the team. They volunteered, and I allowed them to go," Octavian said through Ashe's earpiece. "No one was meant to die. What happened to your friend..." Octavian attempted to assure her.

"Dogura," Ashe growled. "His name was Dogura Metzan."

She could feel her whole body begin to shake as his name spilled across her lips. Dogura had been energetic, excitable, and more than a little annoying, but he was a good person underneath it all. He had taken to the ship like an amphibian to water, and he'd helped her do the same. But for all that he'd done, Ashe had shrugged him off. She had avoided him in the corridors and ignored his comms. When she'd last seen him, he had been trying to tell her something, and she had dismissed it, dismissed him.

Now, her friend was gone without so much as a body to commit to the stars and not just him. Deran, Virgil, and Zacka had died out there as well. All four men were no more than a feast for monsters now, and no pirate deserved that fate. No human deserved it either, yet their captain had left them to it. It was unforgivable.

Deep inside, a part of Ashe realized there wasn't any way Faridan could have reclaimed their bodies, but she didn't care. Dogura's corpse was just the last added to the pile at that woman's feet, and it was too much for her to reconcile.

"No one who leaves their crew to be eaten alive should hold the rank of captain," she spat out before her brain had the chance to catch up to her.

Octavian froze as Ashe's words rang off his barren walls. She had put into words what was dancing around in at least half the minds on the Vivendi. He had seen it. The sentiment was in the eyes of the helmsmen on the Command Deck and the cooks in the Mess Hall. It had even been in the gaze of his own reflection, much to his own dismay.

"Never say that again," the emotionless voice whispered into her ear. "She is our Captain."

Ashe wanted to let her rage explode, and a part of her wished for the fire of it to consume him and his master, but the heat of her glower met actual concern in his eyes. Those disparate components collided in the cool air of the Octavian's quarters and merged into something Ashe had not been expecting.

"However, it is obvious she has changed," he continued. "Miranda has always been driven, but now she cares about nothing except her target."

"Then you should do your job," Ashe commanded through gritted teeth.

She turned to leave, but the surprisingly warm hand of a man she often thought of as all but mechanical closed around her wrist. She spun on him, but instead of the severe outsider she had come to shout her feelings at, she was confronted by someone she wasn't so eager to put a label on.

"I am, but removing Miranda from her position isn't part of it."

"It is if she's unfit," Ashe snapped.

"We don't know what happened out there. She may have tried to save them," Octavian stated.

For the first time, he was glad that the machine speaking his words stripped all the emotion from them.

"Do you actually believe that?" Ashe asked, fixing him with her icy stare.

Octavian didn't answer. He didn't need to. His face said everything she was willing to hear.

"That's what I thought."

"Don't go out there angry, Ashana. It leads to mistakes," the earpiece told her.

Ashe wanted to pull away, to scream that he didn't have the right to use that name. A part of her needed to punch him with every ounce of strength she had, but for some reason, she did not. She didn't do anything. In the quiet of the room, Ashe found herself just standing there, feeling the rhythmic rise and fall of each breath.

"I will listen if you need to talk," the dispassionate voice said, and somehow, the truth of those words overcame the limitations of the machine's tiny audio processor.

As the other emotions caught up to her anger, she let herself give in to the crushing fluid pressure of them. For all of the toughness of her self-made facade, the tickle of a few small drops of saline was all it took to break her apart.

Octavian gave her a small tug, and Ashe provided no resistance. He sat her down on his bunk, then settled himself on the floor in front of her. He waited, and when she was ready to speak, he did exactly what he said he would. He listened.

Chapter 21

ZHARA HAD BEEN TO VIOLET only a handful of times since she began her life on Minerva Prime. It was a place that made her sad whenever she actually took the time to think about it. What had happened to the district wasn't the fault of anyone now living there. They had simply been caught in the midst of forces that they had no control over.

She had seen hard-working people get crushed under the weight of the universe so often that she wished she could get used to it the way so many others had. Unfortunately, Zhara was born on the Dagger, and that tiny colony had instilled a strong sensitivity toward people who were typically viewed as insignificant.

Personally, she still saw herself as the daughter of miners, but that wasn't what the world chose to see. They tended to see a successful corporate engineer and researcher who had a big apartment in Cascade and an easy, if not sheltered, life. Both views were valid, but neither of them showed the full picture. As always, individual perceptions never told the whole story.

She guided her white hovercar down toward the district traversal lanes, gathering judgmental glances from the drivers around her. Zhara chose to think it was because she drove a Regent, and the people of Violet weren't accustomed to seeing them.

Traffic was heavy but not overly so, which made her mergers challenging instead of impossible. The true headaches wouldn't start until tomorrow when traversing the districts would be like flying in an ion storm. The city tended to explode into one big party on the night of the truce's actual signing. It was a government-mandated holiday, as was the rest of the week, except for essential workers like PlanSec and the Traversal Bureaus.

Granting nearly everyone that downtime was a much needed and appreciated move. Especially, since her corporate overlords had stripped the celebration down to only the signing day before Myridorn's decree forced their hand.

For the most part, the city was just a bit more lively during Truce Week, but problems always sprang up. Tensions didn't just disappear because there was a party going on, and when intoxicants were introduced, things could get out of hand quickly.

PlanSec had adopted drone systems to help offset their limited manpower two years ago, but they were rarely used in force. There were always times when additional backup was required, but it wasn't until holidays like Truce Week and the Solstice celebrations that they really became familiar sights. Even then, she rarely saw the bulbous machines in Cascade.

Violet tended to get the most attention since it got a little rowdy, but it was always a little rough there. The reasons why were understandable and tragic, but for all the talk of revitalizing the district, she'd never heard a decent solution. It was just a bad situation made worse by poorer-than-average living conditions.

Most worlds in the Beita Systems had worked out a relative equilibrium with the working-class population, but Minerva Prime seemed to maintain an archaic disdain for them. Zhara could never really understand it, but then again, she wasn't that far away from being "lower-class" in the first place.

Claude had asked to meet her at Hogan's, so she slid her vehicle into the second northbound lane and settled in. Hogan's was a restaurant near Silver Sights and a pretty good one at that. Claude had taken her there early in the nervous dating phase of their relationship. She remembered liking the food, but she wasn't sure if it was the restaurant's quality or the company that colored her memory of it. With a shrug, she decided that if she had the time, she'd grab a sandwich and put that inner debate to bed.

The dust-filled streets stretched out beneath her car as she hit the heart of the district. Traffic had slowed to such a crawl that many people had decided to park and walk to their destinations. Floating columns of cars did a solid job blocking out the afternoon sun while kicking up a dust storm for the pedestrians below.

Zhara had another hour at least under these conditions, so she set the Regent to auto-drive and leaned her seat back. When she'd initially planned out her Truce Week vacation, she had intended to spend most of her time lounging around her apartment but laying out in the cab of her hovercar would have to do.

"Check messages," she said with a stretch and watched as the face of her mother hovered over her.

The older woman had the same blue-gray eyes, slight freckles, and full lips as her daughter, but the rest Zhara had gotten from her late father. Her mother had lived a demanding but ultimately good life, even if she did love to complain about it.

"Hey Bird, I was just missing you and thought I would give you a call. Everything is okay here, but the metal is selling a little slow. You know, the miners could still use a good doctor, and so could I," the hologram of Zhara's mother said.

Ruth was terrible at leaving messages, and that seemed to be something that would never change. Everything had a way of turning into bullet points, but that was when she decided not to disconnect outright. Still, the fact she was using last year's origin gift was comforting. It had been a nightmare trying to talk her through setting up the holo-recorder, but here she was using like a professional.

People on the Dagger had lived on the colony for generations, and they knew how the old tech worked, so anything new usually took years' time to catch on.

"Anyway, that's enough about us. I want to know about you. Last time we talked, you said you were working on fake arms for soldiers. Is that really what you left here to do? I'm not judging. I just want to know because it doesn't sound all that exciting," her mother continued.

Zhara felt a slight smile escape her as her mother did her best to implement a patented Ruth Riggs interrogation asymmetrically. She had been so busy in the city that she hadn't taken time to get in touch, and despite the rapid barrage coming from her mother, Zhara could only feel grateful that she'd taken the time to reach out.

Her mother's call blinked away abruptly, replaced by an image of the Artemis security chief Tarence Wilks. His deep-set dark eyes, brown skin, and short-cropped gray hair contrasted sharply on the ghostly hologram.

"I hate to bother you, Miss Riggs, but there's a PlanSec officer here. She says she needs to talk to you about the man you were with the other day," Tarence said with more than a few nervous glances to his right.

She liked Tarence, but in their dealings, she'd managed to gather that he was a company man. Like many people she worked with, he had a genuine distrust for the government. Everything she knew about him said he wouldn't have contacted her if he'd had any choice in the matter. This PlanSec officer must have been forcing his hand, and that immediately raised her suspicions.

Zhara gave him a smile that was anything but genuine and replied, "It's going to be a while before I can make it back to the office, Tarence. I was on my way out of town."

Tarence nodded with a tight, thin smile and once again looked at what was no doubt the PlanSec officer outside of her view.

"I'm sure you can clear this up when you get here, Miss Riggs," he said and killed the link.

Zhara sighed, wondering exactly what PlanSec wanted with Claude. He'd had his run-ins with Phalen, but those were largely personal affairs. For all his faults, Claude was always smart enough to keep his nose clean where the law was concerned, so this struck her as odd.

She put her curiosity to rest and settled back into her seat. In her head, she adjusted her mental checklist. Talking to PlanSec wasn't a priority of hers, though it would have to happen sooner or later. So, she elected to make it later. Getting back home before the storms blew in was already going to be enough of a challenge.

Zhara stretched again and asked the onboard computer, "How much longer?"

"Estimated arrival, thirty-seven standard minutes," the polite female voice she'd selected for her onboard computer almost sang.

Zhara closed her eyes and willed herself to make the absolute least of the next half hour.

• • • •

Claude wasn't concerned about the amount of time it took for Zhara to reach them, but Vision was beginning to panic just a little. He'd made the mistake of explaining that the apartment was likely under surveillance, and instead of simply cluing her in, the information had terrified her.

He could understand, considering the day's events, but it wasn't what he'd hoped for. A scared Vision was tricky to deal with. Platitudes didn't work on her since she could just pluck the truth from his mind like ripe fruit. Instead, all he could do was avoid adding to her fear and let her ride it out.

"Are you sure this place is safe? I mean, it's not that far away," Vision sputtered with wide, wild eyes.

"I think we're okay. Miranda could have tried to kill us in the Old City, and Bertrand will want the drives before he makes a move," Claude said in as calm and understanding a voice as he could muster.

"What's taking Zhara so long?" Vision asked.

Claude put his arm around her shoulders and pulled her closer to him. He could almost convince himself that he felt the nervous energy crackling off her but did his best to ignore it.

"You know how traffic is in the city," he said. "If you add Truce Week to that..."

Vision sighed, and he felt her relax a bit.

"Can we at least order drinks?" she asked, sounding more like the bottomless blackhole Claude knew so well.

He failed to catch a laugh before it escaped and waved over the nearest server drone.

The small hovering bot buzzed its way toward them like some mechanical insect. The dark orb at its center turned to focus squarely on Claude. It was a soulless thing but not without its own unique charms.

"I'll have a large Winterine Black and..."

"And a Howling Red Blitzer!" Vision shouted before Claude could order something more conservative.

The drone chirped, adjusted its tiny thrusters, and flew away in a moderate hurry. Claude made a show of furrowing his brow at Vision but was met with her own blazing smile.

"The last thing you need is a fructose buzz," he said, shaking his head.

"I think it's exactly what I need," Vision countered. "I need something to take my mind off all the nightmares I'm going to have later."

Claude shifted in the booth seat to face her. The worn, thinly padded benches and wide table didn't leave much room for maneuvering, but he did his best.

"You know you can tell me about anything, right?" Claude said.

Vision decided to test that statement the most thorough and blunt way she could imagine.

"I think you're being stupid," she said firmly.

The words hit Claude like a slap but somehow he managed to clamp his lips shut before a roiling flood of replies escaped them. It took everything he had to master himself and let her words wash over him. The heat in his face died down as he did his best to understand what point she was trying to get across.

"How?" he finally managed to say when he thought he could trust himself again.

"You should have said yes," Vision said.

She didn't need to be more specific. Claude knew what she meant, and the scans she read of his face made it obvious.

"It would have been irresponsible," Claude replied, mastering his indignation. "Look at the life we have. Look at the kinds of people that show up on our doorstep. Zhara isn't a part of that, and it would be wrong to drop that on her."

Vision shook her head. "What if she doesn't care?"

Claude rubbed his forehead and drew in a deep frustrated breath. He'd opened this door, and now he had gotten his hand caught in it. Vision had a point, but it didn't invalidate the risks he was trying to mitigate.

"Look, I'll talk to Zhara about it when I get a chance, okay?" he conceded and watched Vision's features soften as she realized he was telling her the truth.

"Your turn," Vision said. "Hit me with it."

Claude took a moment to organize his thoughts then realized it wouldn't really matter.

"I think you have been talking to me in my head," he said against his better judgment.

A look of intense confusion flashed across Vision's face for a moment before fading into casual skepticism.

"Are you sure?" she asked.

"Not really, but nothing else makes sense," he admitted.

"Maybe it's the silver. I've been getting weird broken messages that I think are coming from it. You could be getting that too," Vision said as evenly as if she were telling him the time.

"What did it say?" Claude asked with equal amounts of dread and interest.

Vision shrugged instinctively.

"Nothing much. The impression I got makes me think it's looking out for you," she said distractedly. "It hasn't tried to hurt you, has it?"

"Not that I can tell," Claude said quietly. "It actually saved me in the hotel."

"See, it's friendly, like I told you," Vision boasted.

"Can you talk to it now?" Claude inquired.

If Vision believed his passenger was on their side, that was convincing enough for Claude. Now, he wanted to learn as much about what was going on with him as he could. That was a small part of why he'd chosen to take this job.

The creature was still a mystery. All he'd known until a moment ago was that it was burning up his nervous system. Whether or not it was actively trying to kill him didn't actually change the end result, but maybe it wasn't that simple.

Claude couldn't deny his own desire to know more. He felt that if he could understand it, if he could learn its intentions, its limitations, or even its weaknesses, he might be able to at least lower his anxiety where it was concerned. With enough information, it might even be possible to remove it altogether.

Claude took a moment to watch Vision's focused expression and did his best to quiet his own mind. If she was able to read the creature, his own thoughts might only get in the way.

Vision frowned and shook her head sharply.

"It's not really interested in talking to me, I guess," she said dejectedly. "It's not the most social alien in the universe, that's for sure. Maybe that's why it picked you."

"Ha. Ha," Claude said, pouring as much sarcasm as he could into the two tiny sounds.

A gentle buzzing swelled, announcing the arrival of their drinks. Vision spun to track the nimble little drone and the bubbling red confection it carried on its back.

"Finally," she said excitedly.

And just like that, the open conversation that Claude had sparked was over. Talking to an eleven-year-old had its benefits, but longevity was almost never one of them.

He had been able to speak to her more before she started to read his mind regularly. Since then, it was faster and easier for her to just skip the talking part altogether. More often than not, she chose to answer his thoughts aloud and cut through the actual listening part too. It was every bit as frustrating as it was understandable.

It occurred to him that the way he thought of communication was archaic, especially where a Psionic was concerned. He had no idea how they communicated with each other. Vision was the only friendly Psionic he'd ever heard of, and the Sabiens weren't sharing information with anyone on this side of the neutral territories.

If there were any detailed records of Psionic behaviors, it was secure somewhere under the crystal waves of Akinos. Claude wanted to know what they were like, and more importantly, he wanted Vision to know. She needed a sense of belonging that he didn't feel he could give her. His failings had left her stranded without a background, and somewhere in his mind, it occurred to him that if she could discover more about people with her talents, it might lessen that burden for both of them.

Vision bounced in her seat as the drone lowered its spindly little legs onto the table and chirped at them. Eager fingers loosened the harness for the drinks and snatched the Blitzer off the drone's back.

Claude let the little machine scan his data-pad and removed his drink as well. He sipped the room temperature drink and let the rich, savory flavor wash over his tongue. He loved the taste of a good

Winterine Black, but he didn't usually order it. As far as drinks went, it was expensive and often prepared wrong by more inexperienced hands.

Zhara had told him that the drink could help offset some of his passenger's short-term effects, but he was already a fan before then. He had shared a pitcher of Winterine as a way to help wash away the sting of defeat after Diegon Minor, and to him, it was the best tasting version of the brew he'd ever had, but Hogan seemed to have a decent recipe as well.

"How's your liquid candy?" Claude asked, leaving a hint of judgment in his tone.

"It's amazing," she sang and took another massive gulp of the fizzy mess.

Claude roughed her hair when she finally lowered the cup from her lips. She grunted her disapproval and slapped his hand away.

"You don't always have to go for the hair," she protested and tried her best to make it her version of presentable.

"Yeah, but it's the only thing that gets this kind of response," Claude said with a sly grin.

Vision stuck her bright red tongue out at him and turned her full attention back to her Blitzer.

A white, luxury hovercar caught the corner of Claude's eye through the transparent panel facing the dust-filled street. He watched Zhara step out of the vehicle and cough before slipping her admittedly fetching breather over her face. She didn't see him watching her, but that wasn't uncommon. As a scientist, she hadn't really honed her sense of awareness. She was often oblivious to things going on around her, but then again, not everyone functioned like a scout.

She strode nervously into the deli and scanned the room. It took her a second to spot them, but Claude could see the moment of recognition even through the opaque, plastic mask.

Claude took another sip of his drink then stood as Zhara approached.

"I didn't want to bother you, but I need someone I can trust," Claude said cautiously.

"You didn't bother me, Claude, but I would like to know what's going on," Zhara said, waving away his apology and sliding into the booth opposite him and Vision.

"First, you have to taste this," Vision said energetically as she slid what was left of her drink across the table.

A shadow of confusion flickered across Zhara's features before she banished it.

"Um, what exactly is it?" she asked, eyeing the vivid red liquid.

"Perfection," Vision answered immediately.

Zhara cast a wary glance to Claude, who mouthed only one word, "No."

"I appreciate it, V, but I think I'm going to have to pass," Zhara said diplomatically.

She passed the cup back across to Vision, who took it without a hint of hesitation.

"Your loss," she said and took another large gulp.

Zhara turned to Claude and searched his complicated expression for a moment before asking, "So what's going on?"

"In short, everything," he began. "I've told you a little about my time with the TaskMasters. Well, let's just say that part of my past has come back to haunt me."

Zhara nodded as she took the information in. She could clearly see Claude was uncomfortable, but she couldn't quite tell if that was because he was sharing this with her or sharing it in general.

"Anyway, my old CO sent me on a job to retrieve data drives from Firaxis," Claude relayed as he struggled to find the right words.

"What?" Zhara asked, managing to keep her voice low. "You told me the station crashed into the planet. How could there be data drives that still function, and how are they here?"

Claude shook his head and tossed his hands into the air, "Apparently, one of the scientists took off with them before the place got torn apart. Bertrand was sent here to retrieve them, but he tasked me with it instead."

"And?" Zhara asked.

She could feel her curiosity transforming into excitement. For as long as she had known Claude, she'd been working and theorizing in the dark where his passenger was concerned. If she had access to the Sabiens' information, she might finally be able to understand what she was dealing with.

"And we got the job done," Vision bragged, patting her hand against something hard inside the lining of her oversized jacket.

"We were hoping you might know of a way to crack Sabien security coding. If so, maybe we could get a look at exactly what I'm being asked to hand over," Claude said while actively avoiding Zhara's gaze.

"Is it encrypted?" Zhara asked.

Claude shrugged. "I assume so. I'd secure it, wouldn't you?"

Zhara thought about it for a moment. It definitely could be, but she knew they didn't secure storage drives at Artemis unless there was a valid reason. Why would the Sabiens be any different? They were still people, after all.

"I can take a look, but I'd be more concerned about translating the storage codices," Zhara offered.

"Storage what now?" Vision asked.

"The Sabiens don't use the same computing language we do," Zhara began. "For us, the biggest issues are the different ways they store and compress data."

Zhara turned her attention from the confused little girl sitting across from her to the more confused man whose eyes were as wide as saucers.

"Don't worry, I've been able to open Sabien files before, but it takes a while," Zhara said and motioned for another drone. "If I can't do it alone, I'll just have to go back to the office, which could turn out to be a little tricky."

"Why? What's going on there?" Claude asked.

He was reasonably sure Artemis were investigating the mass mental blackouts but, that shouldn't complicate matters for Zhara. They had been to see Zhara at work more than a few times before, so he didn't think he and Vision's presence would have drawn unnecessary attention to her.

"There's a PlanSec officer asking around. I'll have to deal with them if I go digging for translation programs," Zhara said nonchalantly.

"Why would PlanSec be there?" Vision asked, scraping the bottom of her cup on the table accidentally. "Don't they have better things to do?"

"Rarely," Zhara said. "Things stay pretty quiet in the central districts."

Zhara turned back to Claude and searched his drawn features again. Over time, she had learned to read him almost as well a Vision, and there was more bothering him than what he had told her.

"What else?" she asked, unwilling to let Claude off the hook.

"We don't have a place to stay," Vision blurted. "Claude thinks our place is being watched."

Claude gave Zhara a tight smile, "I just need a place for Vision until things resolve themselves."

"Hey..." Vision began, but the intense mix of emotion radiating off Claude stopped her short.

Zhara leaned toward the little drone and whispered something before returning her attention to Claude. When the little machine was far enough away, and there was no risk it would overhear them, she said, "My place is open to you, you know that, but if they have your place under surveillance, they'll figure out where you've gone."

"Hopefully, this will be over before then," Claude said softly. "I won't let you get caught up in this any more than you already are."

Zhara smiled, but there was a fair amount of disappointment in it.

"I've been caught up in this since I met you," she admitted. "So, stop trying to freeze me out."

Claude didn't respond. By asking her to come here, he had already put her at risk, but he had no other alternatives. None of the choices left to him were ideal, but there was little he could do about them. Still, he would protect her as best he could, given the circumstances.

Zhara was a good woman and a better friend. She deserved more than to get pulled into his antics, as did Vision, but neither seemed to agree.

"Can we go now?" Vision said, mourning the empty cup where her drink used to be.

"Soon," Zhara said. "I just ordered a Velic and cheese wrap."

• • • •

The sugar rush hit Vision with all the force of a capital ship falling out of Streamline. She had barely made it through half of the holo-vid they'd put on before dreams took her. Claude carried her to the guest room when it was over, but she was so far gone by then he doubted she'd notice her new surroundings until morning.

Once that was done, he and Zhara disappeared into the bedroom with the data drives. Neither of them wanted to try and crack them with Vision over their shoulders. There was no telling what they had on them. Given the data came from a weapons research facility, the odds it contained something an eleven-year-old shouldn't be exposed to were reasonably high.

Zhara found compatible hook-ups for the drives while Claude removed the wall panels and any connections that might link the apartment to the wider planetary network.

When the drives were connected, Zhara's holo screen erupted in a multicolored cross current of Sabien glyphs that flowed in what seemed to her like random directions.

"Yep, it's what I thought," Zhara said with an exasperated sigh.

"You can't do it?" Claude asked nervously.

Zhara shook her head, "No, it's doable. I'm just looking at a long night."

"Sorry," Claude said stupidly.

He didn't know what else to say. Computers of this nature weren't part of his daily life, and even when he did use them, it was always to do something relatively simple. He still recorded his accounting books manually when and where possible. This wall of swimming symbols was beyond him, and for the second time in as many days, he was forced to acknowledge how lucky he was that Zhara knew so many things he didn't.

"So, this PlanSec officer, what do you know about him?" Claude asked, changing the subject to something closer to his comfort zone.

Zhara swiped two green glyphs into positions where they locked in and turned gold while Claude looked on with a furrowed brow.

"Tarence said he thinks the officer is actually looking for you," she replied without turning away from the code.

"Is it Phalen?" Claude asked.

"No. It's a woman," Zhara said and turned to watch Claude's reaction closely. "Any ideas what this could be about?"

Claude's face scrunched in concentration as he tried to imagine a female PlanSec officer that he might know. It didn't take long for him to come up empty. His work meant that he'd encountered a few PlanSec people, but aside from Phalen, none of them had ever been particularly interested in him.

Bertrand's call had come after the Artemis incident, so there was no way this officer could be connected to any of his current problems. That only left Phalen, but the last thing he would do was draw another officer into his plotting.

"I've got nothing," Claude said, scratching the stubble on his cheek.

"So, tell me about your day," Zhara said and swiveled her seat back around to face the coded cascade that was eating up half of her bedroom wall. "Feel free to give me as many details as you can. I imagine they'll be useful."

"There's not much in the way of good news to tell. This job is a disaster. I'm pretty sure the whole thing is going to go up in flames and take me with it," Claude said, putting his suspicions into words. "My former commanders showed back up, and they're at war with each other. Miranda has a serious vendetta against Bertrand, and now that she knows I'm here, she wants me to put myself in the middle of it."

"Miranda? That's your ex, right?" Zhara said, hoping she sounded appropriately neutral.

Claude couldn't see her face, but the slight strain in her voice told him there was at least a little concern there.

"That's not how I'd phrase it," he said. "We had a moment a long time ago, but the woman I met in the Dead Zone is not the same person. Honestly, I'd prefer to avoid her altogether if I can manage it."

"Didn't she leave you to die, on Firaxis? Why in the Homeworld would she think you'd help her now?" Zhara asked, continuing her almost mechanical tone as she tried to manipulate the code.

"I don't put that on her," Claude said in a strained voice. "She was the unit commander. I went off-mission, and she made the right call. She knows that as well as I do."

Zhara spun on him. She fixed him with a look that made it plain she didn't see it the same way he did.

"I will never understand you military types. In the real world, leaving someone to burn to death is never the right call," Zhara declared, leaving very little room for Claude to argue.

"I hope the universe lets you keep that mindset, Zee. I really do."

Zhara huffed and launched out of her seat and moved across the room to sit beside Claude.

"So, what does she want from you?"

"She asked me where Bertrand was," Claude said flatly.

"And you don't know?" Zhara asked, seeking out his eyes.

Claude sighed heavily, "Maybe, I can run a trace if I contact him again, but I tried that when he called last night and got nothing."

"Would you be willing to give him up if you did know?" Zhara asked.

Claude let himself fall back onto the bed and stared up at the ceiling. He'd spent much of the ride back to Violet asking himself that exact question, but somewhere deep down, the idea didn't sit right. Putting himself in the middle of whatever had happened between Bertrand and Miranda was unavoidable, unfortunately. Taking the job put him squarely in the crossfire, and he didn't see a way to get clear aside from finishing the job as quickly as he could.

"Not if I don't have to," Claude finally answered. "But if it comes down to keeping you and Vision safe, I will do whatever I need to."

"I know that, but what do you want to do?" Zhara asked, slipping off her shoes.

"It's not a matter of want, Zee."

"But what if it was?" she prodded.

Claude grunted his disapproval at the question but let himself think on it anyway. The first and most important thing he wanted was to keep Vision and Zhara safe. After that, he wanted to know what the drives contained, but that's where all sense of clarity ended. His two primary goals appeared, for all the world, to be in his grasp. The drives were being translated, and the ladies in his life were safe, but how long would that last?

As the situation developed, the drives were pushing him into one uncontrollable scenario after another. Going to the Old City, meeting Miranda, even coming here to Zhara's, were all things he didn't feel that he had much choice in. A part of him felt like they were a weight pulling him and those he cared about down into the crushing depths of the unknown. It was that same part that wanted desperately to offload them immediately.

But when he took time to quiet his emotions and think about it, handing the drives over to Bertrand, and subsequently Echelon, without knowing what was on them, seemed risky as well. The fact they wanted them badly enough to hunt a defector all the way into the Old City told him that whatever the drives contained was significant.

Echelon wanted the information on them for a reason, as did he. The difference was Claude wouldn't use it for nefarious ends. This was Echelon's second attempt to secure the drives, and it was going about as well as it had six years ago. Blindly handing them over when Myridorn was clearly desperate for what they contained would be irresponsible.

When he'd been sent with the TaskMasters all those years ago, Echelon wanted the research data for one logical reason, to win the war. He saw no reason that objective would change. The problem was, everything else had. In all this time, the universe had only just begun to release the collective breath that it was holding. Peace was being accepted by most, if not by all, as a viable way forward. The truce had lasted and would likely remain if neither side did anything categorically stupid.

Claude wholeheartedly believed that the only reason the war hadn't been rekindled was because it would just lead to another stalemate. If there was a significant spike in technology or weaponry on either side, it would lead both sides back into conflict, or so common logic dictated.

Bertrand had said the drives contained research files. There was no reason to doubt him, especially after what he had experienced on Firaxis. If the drives contained detailed records about whatever had taken down that station, they could eventually lead the universe back into blood. If he was right, and Claude suspected he was, handing them over would make him directly responsible for every life the new war snuffed out. He had seen what a conflict like that could do. He'd seen how it ground men, women, children, and entire worlds into little more than powder, and he couldn't be responsible for unleashing that beast a second time.

Unfortunately, taking such a stance placed his feet firmly on a hard road. That winding and brutal path was inlaid with jagged questions that would exact their toll on him. Each one would draw blood, and they would all require sacrifices he'd rather not make. Claude could already see the questions, and he'd barely moved along that twisted trail.

What was he willing to do to prevent renewed conflict? Was he ready to fight for it? Was he prepared to die for it? Could he accept a path where he might be asked to exchange the lives of those that he loved for the futures of strangers he might never meet? Somewhere deep down, Claude knew the answers, and he resented with them. There were men who could have accepted what he knew to be the truth, but he could not?

Instead of resigning himself to the mission laid out before him, like the soldier he had once been, Claude racked his brain, trying to find a new scenario. There had to be a way to stave off the beast while avoiding the sacrifices he knew would come. Sadly, the only idea that came to him was wholly disappointing.

He had to stall. He had to take the pressure, but worst of all so did Vision and Zhara. They would take it with him willingly, even if it threatened to cripple them. Claude knew that, but it didn't make it any easier to watch them suffer.

Someone had leaped into the depths on his behalf in the past, and when he'd been old enough and brave enough to go back for him, there was nothing left of him to find. This was different, but it felt almost the same. Either way, his hands were tied. The girls weren't exactly going to sit it out. That was abundantly clear. The question was, should he give them a choice?

Claude chose to put that decision off for at least a while longer. It wasn't like he could read the drives at the moment anyway. He was going to have to wait for access, and if he used the extra time wisely, he might just be able to figure a way out of the likely double-cross heading his way.

The major downside was that the longer he held the drives, the more time he remained in this current fire.

"What I want is impossible," Claude finally answered.

Zhara flopped down on the bed beside him and rested her hands behind her head.

"Nothing's impossible," she said, and Claude could tell she truly believed that.

"Time travel is," Claude said with a cheeky grin.

Zhara elbowed him in the ribs and had the audacity to laugh at his pained reaction. In truth, he deserved the elbow, but he'd caught himself thinking about the concept more than once recently. If he could, he would go back and stop himself from ever letting Bertrand into his office in the first place. It was the only way things could ever be normal again, as far as he could tell.

"Well, the good news is, we aren't in danger now. No one knows you're here, and if you keep your head down, we'll have time to figure this all out," Zhara said when her chuckles finally died down.

She wasn't able to piece together the full picture in quite the same way Claude had, but she was intuitive enough to understand his concern. Zhara handled stress differently than he did. She shared. Claude internalized. It led to more than a few tense moments in their relationship, but she had gotten him to share some of the thoughts stirring around in his skull. She took it as a small victory.

"So, what's the next step?" she asked, rubbing some of the tension out of her neck and shoulder.

The tightness in her muscles fought against her touch, but reluctantly gave way to her intent massaging until she eventually felt something akin to normal. The mixture of relaxation and pain managed to block out the tiny whistles of breath coming from her left.

"Do you think Bertrand can be trusted not to cheat you?" she asked but again got no response.

She turned swiftly, prepared to berate Claude for ignoring her when she realized he'd fallen asleep. For a moment, she considered waking him up to finish their conversation but thought better of it.

Long days took heavy tolls and considering what he'd told her on the ride back about his passenger's activities, it was clear he needed the rest. Zhara wished she could curl up with him, but she had work to do. With great effort, she pried herself away from the temptations of her mattress and planted herself in the chair.

Turning her back on the man wheezing gently, Zhara focused on the swirling symbols that seemed determined to lock away the knowledge she sought. There wasn't a person under her roof that didn't want to know what was on those drives. The hours it would take to get to it were going to be a headache, but the end result was guaranteed to be worth it, or so she assumed.

For years a number of questions had plagued her. What exactly lived inside her boyfriend? Where did it come from? What were the Sabiens planning to use it for? Those answers had always eluded her. She had been told that the only place they existed had crashed into a planet light-years out of reach. Now she had them encased in tiny metal devices resting defiantly on her desk.

Even though her body kept sending telltale signals of exhaustion, her mind was anything but ready for sleep. It moved as if it had fallen into Streamline. Thoughts and patterns blazed through her mind faster than she could fully process. Her fingers were woefully incapable of matching such reckless speeds, so she forced herself to slow down.

Her excitement was almost more than she could handle, but the idea of what could happen if she made an error in the translation was sobering. Zhara wasn't sure exactly what those consequences might turn out to be, but she did know it wouldn't be good. Translation errors could have a million different effects, from displaying text and images inverted or jumbled characters, even full data degradation. What she feared most was corrupting the data. It was a possibility, and while remote, she knew how lucky she had felt lately. Claude and Vision would forgive her if she lost the data but forgiving herself would be an impossibility, assuming the data wasn't already ruined.

Aside from her own substantial curiosity, Claude and Vision needed that information, either to find a family in Vision's case or to understand what had bonded itself to him in Claude's.

He put on a good show, but Zhara could see in his eyes how much the encounter in the Old City had shaken him. She hadn't pressed too hard for the details, but what he'd told her about his passenger acting on its own would have been enough to scare anyone. She admired the strength it must have taken to keep his composure in front of Vision, but she wished he could open up to her a little more. Claude wasn't superhuman, and she didn't need him to be, but so far, she hadn't been able to convince him of that.

Something halfway between a sigh and a yawn escaped her mouth as she streamed another few glyphs into place. Every symbol flowing counterclockwise had been locked down, and that helped Zhara decide which part of the code to tackle next.

More than that, the more sporadic motion she stopped, the easier it became to identify the remaining symbols and plug them into their correct spots. Sabien code was odd because it was built on Zephiari syntax. Both they and the Beitans used it as a base for their written languages, but unlike what was used in the Beita Systems, Sabiens kept the multi-axis layering that made the text almost impossible to interpret without years of study.

The Beita Systems language was built in secret from pieces of mostly forgotten human languages and large chunks of Zephiari, but since they were the lesser slaves, they weren't taught how to read and write it. As a result, they fit it into a new language with its own formulations and rules. After a few thousand years evolution, the two languages were now about as different in the written form as anything could be.

Zhara had been taught a bit of both while she lived in the neutral territories, but it wasn't until she landed at the academy that she mastered what people called Beitan. It was simpler than Sabien to read and write. Yet, the varying rules on tenses, conjugation, and just which words to use in formal and informal contexts made it the more difficult of the two in common use, even if it only moved in one direction.

Zhara's eyes watered as she slid the code into position at a quickening pace. She had plenty left to decode, but she couldn't stop herself from imagining what she might find. It had occurred to her some time ago that the silver coating Claude's nervous system might actually be alien in origin. Claude had broached the topic, and she was coming around to that idea as well.

The word alien was debatable since the Zephiar were a known and familiar influence on every established society. Aside from that long-dead race, humans were the only intelligent life anyone knew of in the universe. Common knowledge dictated that the Black had to be teeming with other intelligent races but finding them was unlikely considering its size and scope.

If the Sabiens had found a world with actual aliens on it, that was the find of the millennium. It would change the way both societies saw the universe in fundamental and potentially dangerous ways.

While Zhara wanted to know for academic reasons, others would have different motivations. If the silver passenger was from a new intelligent race, the Sabiens had already attempted to study and likely weaponize them. Echelon was no doubt eager to follow suit, which wasn't an ideal way to begin a relationship with a new race.

Zhara wasn't surprised. She knew the darker pits of human nature, though those places weren't unique to mankind.

The Zephiar had ripped humanity from their Homeworld for the purposes of slavery, possession, and, if some old stories were to be believed, reproductive experimentation. Those stories were widely dismissed but given that the Zephiar had died out because of their inability to hold physical forms, such experiments made a lot of sense.

It was a cold, soulless course of action, but she doubted humans would be any different if faced with a very real extinction timeline. In fact, she was confident that they would do worse. In the time that they had been in control of their own fates, human beings had attempted no shortage of atrocities on one another. They were lifeforms addicted to conflict, and even though there was relative peace Zhara had her doubts about how long that would last.

She hadn't spoken with anyone who thought the truce was a permanent fixture. Everyone seemed to be waiting for the wheel to finish its rotation so everything could go back to normal, as sad an idea as it was. Zhara felt the same way from time to time, although she was loathed to admit it.

Everyone knew that war was the natural state of their universe. While the pause in bloodshed was refreshing and novel, no one in authority believed it was the new future. The notion was just too radical to be taken seriously. She wished it weren't the case, but if she were placed in control of the government, there was a chance she would act in the exact same way.

With a heavy breath, Zhara locked the last of the clockwise rotating glyphs into place and collapsed against the padded back of her seat. Her spine ached, and her eyes were sore, but her budding sense of accomplishment did a great deal to numb the pain. Only the vertical axis remained, and it was pretty basic from what she could tell. If she had to guess, there was less than an hour's worth of work left to be done, and then the drives would be open to her.

She checked her data-pad and blinked at the readout. It had been three hours since she started the translation process, but it didn't feel like it. Her body was more than willing to attest to the passage of time, but still, it seemed wrong.

Either way, the job was nearly finished, and her inquisitive nature wasn't about to let her give up the pursuit just to sleep. So, she rubbed the fatigue from her eyes and buckled down for the last stretch.

The glyphs were falling into place with regular frequency, and she thanked whatever minds had seen fit to keep the Sabien code to simple characters as opposed to the more complicated glyphs that she'd seen in their "religious" texts.

Zhara's father had insisted that she learn to read his copy of the Compendium of Ages. Like all children, she protested but was made to read it anyway. He'd told her it was important that she recognize her heritage, that she needed to know the stories of her people. At the time, she had no understanding of the tome's importance, either to him or to the society he had left behind.

Those contentious days had come in handy as she'd moved through life. There was no way her father could have predicted when or how they would aid her, but he'd been right to insist. Hindsight proved that. He'd been an invaluable part of her foundation growing up, and she missed him. Most of her less orthodox views of the universe had either come from or were encouraged by him.

Her father was possessed of some strange notions where human nature, politics, and the war were concerned. She remembered how convinced he was that if the two sides could ever sit down, they would find commonality and come to their senses. It turned out he was at least partially right, but he never got to see it. He'd died a little more than a year before she set off for the academy. He had been sick for years but refused to leave the colony for fear it would bring unwanted attention to it. Instead of getting the care he needed, he elected to waste away, and no one could convince him differently.

It was an irrational fear, but it was his all the same. He had survived the destruction of a flotilla trying to escape to the neutral territories, and it was there that he'd lost his first family. It wasn't until years later that she learned how his experiences there fueled his paranoia. Her father's death was preventable, and it drove Zhara into the medical field. Yet, when she achieved her goal of becoming a physician, she couldn't bring herself to return to that place, no matter how much her mother pleaded with her to do so.

The sting of exhaustion was replaced with that of sadness and pain as Zhara became aware of the tears staining her cheeks. Unresolved trauma still hid under the surface, and she knew she'd have to deal with it one day, but that day had yet to come.

She dropped the last glyph into place and watched as the file coding translated itself into Beitan before her burning eyes. It took her readout a second to reconfigure and present the data stored on the drives into different columns that hovered where the coding interface had once been.

"Video chronicles," she said to herself, marveling at the shoddy translation.

The word "chronicle" was technically correct, although there wasn't a term in Beitan that matched the glyph perfectly. She shook the critique from her mind and opened the group listing.

A stream of images filled her view. Each of them showed the same man in varying stages along the road to total disarray. Each picture she scrolled past had him looking more and more broken until she elected to skip all the way to the end. The man was almost wild in the last image. His tunic was stained, his hair was unkempt, and his eyes were difficult to look at. He was clearly gripping the tattered edges and trying to hold himself together, but what drained the color from Zhara's face was the blurry form behind him.

"It can't be," she heard herself say.

Chapter 22

THE MODUS VIVENDI'S officer briefing room was seldom used, so when Miranda received Octavian's message, her interest was immediately piqued. She had used the space only once and had ordered it sealed immediately after. No one on the ship could access it aside from Octavian and herself, and since he regularly took information directly to her quarters, the request caught her unawares.

Located just beneath the command deck and connected via a stairwell adjacent to the main lift, the briefing room was designed for the captain and her crew to discuss upcoming courses of action, but it had never been put to that use. It was a convenient and private place if one happened to be on the command deck, but Miranda had been in her quarters.

She would have been happy to remain in her civvies, but because she had to set foot on the command deck to get to her destination, that meant following her own rules and dressing appropriately.

It only took her a few minutes to get herself adequately attired and to the lift. That time had allowed her wary mind time to paint all manner of unpleasant scenarios. She was aware her return had started a new round of buzzing throughout the ship. Word of secret talks in the ship's narrow passages had reached her, although no conspirators had been named.

Octavian's advice was the same as it had always been. He'd urged her to keep her ears open and to do nothing for the time being. His "suggestions" had gotten predictable lately, but they often proved to be prudent courses of action, though she wasn't always inclined to follow them.

In this case, there wasn't anything she could do about the whispers. Rumors were often like smoke, but it was impossible to efficiently stifle them until a fire could be located.

The lift's soft hum did little to put her at ease. If she was honest with herself, Miranda had been on edge since before her trip to the Old City, and after returning, her skin seemed to crawl constantly.

The conversation with DiSilva had yielded almost nothing of value aside from the most minor of details. She thought about accosting him and dragging him back to the ship by force, but he had the same advantage that she did. His silver would undoubtedly share the regeneration capabilities of hers unless there were actual variances between them.

She didn't know if that was possible but starting a fight without such knowledge seemed foolish. Miranda wasn't one to rush into conflict, even if she felt the increasing desire to do so. Keeping DiSilva on her good side was still the right move, especially since he was the only person who had actually seen Bertrand face to face. Persuading him to give up the old man was still a possibility, though a hefty price would be needed. DiSilva didn't seem to be living all that well, and children tended to be expensive little beasts, or so she'd heard.

Her memory of the child sent a fresh shiver along every nerve in her body. The black eyes of the thing had burrowed in into her. Its empty sightless stare jarred Miranda in a way that few things ever had. Something about the thing seemed to both thrill and terrify her simultaneously, but she couldn't figure out why; then, there was its vague familiarity. All she knew was the idea of bringing it aboard her ship had helped motivate her to part ways with DiSilva on that roof.

With a thin whine, the doors of the lift slid open, revealing the short corridor that led to the command deck. The crew on duty had very little to do aside from monitoring incoming sensor sweeps and keeping the ship primed for its eventual liftoff.

To her right, the red strip of light that normally denoted the briefing room as lock now shone a cool green. Miranda straightened at the sight and took a second to quiet the swirling tempest inside her mind before stepping inside.

Octavian and a man she didn't recognize turned to her as she entered. Her old friend seemed slightly pleased, but the other man was visibly nervous. He didn't meet her eyes and seemed more preoccupied with the deep slashes carved into the walls.

"Captain, this is Luudo, one of our infiltrators in Cascade," Octavian announced through the room's broadcast speakers.

Miranda regarded the man a second time and took in his pedestrian appearance. He had none of the flair typical of others in her crew, but since he was an infiltrator, that made sense. Most of the souls onboard would stand out among the soft-bellies of an upscale district like Cascade.

"Is there news?" Miranda said, unwilling to let herself imagine what he might say.

Luudo stroked his blonde goatee and cleared his throat before speaking. "I believe we have an opportunity, Captain. Tomorrow is the biggest day of the Truce Week celebrations, and according to the information we have gathered, PlanSec will be spread thin throughout the city. They will be focused heavily on the Violet district, leaving Cascade virtually undefended."

Even for Miranda, the thought of a successful raid on so rich a target was seductive, but such an act presented new problems. The crew needed the motivation, and a move like this would strengthen her hold on them, especially amidst the brewing dissent. Sadly, a raid of that size required would leave no room for anonymity.

Every Beitan ship for three systems would be alerted almost as soon as their attack began, and the Vivendi would be no match for them. The only chance they would have for survival would be to flee before they arrived, losing her yet another chance of finishing her business with Bertrand.

"Truce Week continues for two more days at least," she said definitively. "We will wait."

The look on Octavian's face screamed his disapproval louder than any voice ever could, but she ignored him. He was not captain, and while she valued his opinion, she did not need it.

"Captain, with respect, there won't be a better time. The distraction will fade, and we will lose our best chance," Luudo managed to say.

"Credits are the least of my concerns," Miranda said as she fixed her eyes on him. "They are easy to come by and meaningless. I came to this planet for a bigger prize, and exposing ourselves prematurely will jeopardize it."

Luudo shot his glance to Octavian, then back to Miranda as though he expected the XO to back him up. When that didn't happen, he had to bite back a response fueled by all the rumors and gossip he'd heard about the captain.

"We are pirates," he began once he was sure he had control of himself. "We fight for currency. It's why every man and woman serves on this ship. Credits are the only reason you have a crew in the first place."

Miranda felt the rippling heat of the silver traveling up her nervous system and tried to push it away. A growing part of her wanted to rip the man to shreds, and she could do it with ease, but that wouldn't be the best move. Wave after wave of heat crashed against her resolve as the infiltrator cast more insolence her way. The meat standing before her had forgotten its place and needed reminding. They all needed reminding. They existed in the presence of something they could never fully understand, and an example needed to be made.

The urge to act was intoxicating, but Miranda did all she could to strangle it. Before, she had been able to master herself with minimal difficulty but now found herself struggling. For only the second time in her life, she felt a divide in her own mind. Her rational self was at odds with the intense emotional beast that was clawing for release.

She was not a strategist, but even she could see that killing this man for speaking his mind in such a way was not a wise move. Tensions on the ship were high, and another death among the crew would do nothing to relieve them. If anything, it would all but ensure a revolt that she would then be forced to put down.

That fight would put her farther from her end goal than ever. It was a wholly unacceptable outcome, but still, she felt the heat and rage boiling her all the same. It bubbled its way into her chest and continued to climb unabated.

Panic reached out and dug its talons into her then. Miranda squeezed her eyes shut and did everything in her power to calm herself, to put reason ahead of fury, but still, the heat ripped its way up the back of her neck and into her skull.

"At least let me put together a plan. I'm confident I can–" Luudo's voice cut off with a sick wet gurgle.

Warm blood slashed its way across Miranda, Octavian, and the rest of the room. Miranda's mind struggled to grasp the situation around her as she wiped scarlet warmth from her face.

The face she had been looking into had somehow been replaced with a pair of gore-coated boots. They dangled on the ends of twitching legs that beckoned for her to look up. Craning her neck, Miranda found Luudo pinned to the ceiling by a silver insect-like limb that she didn't remember summoning.

His still warm body was slashed open from pelvis to gullet, leaving him to hang by the crook of his lower jaw like a gutted fish. Weakening arterial spray arched, spattering first the walls, then the conference table, and finally just himself.

"Why?" was the only word Octavian could force through his naked shock.

He was barely able to process what had just happened due to the speed, brutality, and suddenness of the act. He'd seen Miranda kill before but never with such a gruesome flourish. His eyes fell from what was once a loyal crewman to what was once his harsh but fair captain. She neither moved, turned, nor spoke. Like a figure carved from stone, she just stood there, her face etched with all the surprise and horror he felt.

Streaming crimson and stunned silence embraced Miranda. As quickly as it appeared, the silver limb retracted back into her body, dropping Luudo's corpse to the floor like the carcass of a butchered animal. She flinched instinctively at the crunching sound it sent into the weighted stillness. The motion was as involuntary as the ragged, broken breaths that she took. The only parts of her body she could will into motion were the muscles in her eyes and neck as she stared down at what had been a man just seconds ago.

"Why did you kill him?" Octavian demanded once he found himself.

His words blasted their way through the haze that encompassed Miranda. Her legs felt soft and unstable as she staggered away from the dead man and fixed her terrified eyes on Octavian.

"D-did I...," she stammered before she snapped her mouth shut against both her own unraveling thoughts and the taste of fresh blood.

The symphony of emotions conducted by Octavian's facial muscles neared its crescendo when Miranda finally regained control of herself. She could hear the thrum of her pulse slowing its relentless rhythm and felt the silver settle inside her once again.

"Tell no one about this," she growled at Octavian. "This room stays sealed until we leave this rock. Understood?"

"This needs to be cleaned up, Captain," Octavian challenged, and for a second, Miranda imagined she could hear anger in his mechanical speech.

His face still told Miranda that he despised her recent actions as much as she did, only he knew better than to say so. She was grateful for his self-restraint, especially since she wasn't sure she had the strength to match it anymore. She had wanted to lash out at the infiltrator, but she didn't think she had actually done it.

Every other time Miranda used the silver, she had consciously decided on an action, then executed it. This time it was like the creature read her mind and attacked proactively. It was terrifying, and she couldn't be sure it wouldn't happen again if Octavian pressed her.

One thought screamed through the tattered neurons of Miranda's mind. She had to get away from him. She had to isolate herself until she could understand what had just happened, but more importantly, she had to get out of this room.

"No one else on the ship can be trusted," Miranda snapped. "If it bothers you, then clean it yourself. But no one else enters this room."

Octavian said nothing. He had watched men die. He had killed more than a few himself, but he'd never reveled in it. He'd never mutilated them, nor had he ever seen Miranda do so. When she took a life, she was focused and determined, maybe even a little relieved but never surprised. What he saw in her eyes was unmistakable. She was as shocked as he was, and no matter how much she attempted to hide it, it was obvious, and it scared him.

"Am I understood?" Miranda barked, staring her old friend down.

Octavian nodded with a labored breath. The hard edge in Miranda's eyes softened at his gesture, but he thought he could see something else moving in them.

"Good," Miranda grunted and broke eye contact with him.

Without another word, she stormed out of the room in a near run, leaving both Octavian and Luudo's corpse behind without a second look.

Octavian stared after her as the doors sealed themselves and remembered his visit with Ashe. Ever since then, he had forced himself to look at matters on the ship from the angry and fearful perspective of the crew. Now, for the first time, it took no effort.

Miranda was Octavian's oldest friend, but the woman who had disappeared through those doors was as close to a stranger as she'd ever been. Her actions, her words didn't fit with the woman he'd known so well. He wondered if some event in the Dead Zone could have caused this imbalance. If so, it was possible that after some time, perhaps after they found Bertrand, she would find her way back to normal.

He needed to believe that, and so he chose to.

With a silent prayer for Luudo's soul, Octavian wiped the blood off as best he could. He prayed silently for the infiltrator to find his way through the cold cruelty of the Black and into the paradise of his choosing and for his time in that place to be more fulfilling than it had been here.

Chapter 23

ZHARA WOKE WITH A START. Her nightmares had cast her into a world much less pristine than the one she awakened to, yet she was only slightly relieved. The two weren't so different in her estimation. They seemed to be the larval and adult stages of the same beast, and she couldn't quite shake the feeling that the world she was inhabiting now careened toward the tipping point.

With a dizzying groan, she sat up and let her legs hang to the floor. The large area rug saved her feet from the chill of the tile beneath, but it was only a small comfort. The cool, pre-dawn air was the more threatening assault on her.

In an act of sheer determination, Zhara had taken it upon herself to coax the drives into spilling their contents. She'd dived in hoping to find some morsel that would sate her curiosity, and what she had found did so much more than that.

The Sabiens must have been driven truly mad by the state of the war because only that could explain the drastic and unethical decisions required to form what they called the Talos project. In its purest form, it was a weapons research initiative, but that was a chaste assessment. If they had been sane, they would have taken a decade to properly understand what they were working with before making any attempts at weaponizing it. As it stood, that did not happen, and the end results were as predictable as they were catastrophic.

It was no wonder Echelon was interested in the research gathered. It was exactly the kind of destructive chaos they would believe they could control, and just like the Sabiens, they would be dead wrong.

Zhara couldn't shake the dread and anger she felt when she thought about it. Claude had been clear when he told her about the state of Firaxis station, but without the proper context, it was impossible to understand. She had that context now, or at least as much as she ever wanted, and now Zhara found herself forced into a situation she didn't want to face.

She eased off the bed and onto her feet, being careful not to disturb Claude as he snored lightly behind her. It was best if she didn't bring him into what she had planned. For all his strengths, there were some things he was better left out of.

Eventually, she'd tell him, but there was no need to wake him for that. Her newfound knowledge was a burden she could bear alone for a while longer. It wouldn't be easy, but it was necessary, and Claude, of all people, had no right to hold that against her.

Zhara moved swiftly and quietly to the closet and sifted through her inventory of outfits. There wasn't much there that was notably different or eye-catching, and that was no accident. She was on Minerva Prime to work, and she didn't need high-end designer clothes to do that. She'd made the most out of the clothes that were handed down to her as a child, and now that she was an adult, she was more than happy to wear practical clothing as opposed to flashier outfits.

The Beita Systems, as a whole, were much more pragmatic in the way they viewed the universe, so appearances tended to be more stripped-back and comfort-based than anything else. It was a proclivity but not a rule.

The young people of Cascade were more likely to stomp on that idea with gaudily designed boots, but it would be there for them when they got older. The counterculture of youth was far more interested in living their lives for individuality, but such moments never lasted.

Zhara didn't blame them. Minerva wasn't the kind of place a young person with no real struggles would appreciate. They needed battles to fight as everyone did, theirs were just superfluous, and one day they would have to realize that.

For her, a simple off-white top, deep blue layered leggings, and her casual, comforting footwear were enough for the day. It wasn't much different from what she would wear if she were working, but it was her style. Zhara had no real need to change it unless there was a fancy dinner in her future, and a quick glance at the dozing man wrapped in her covers made that possibility unlikely for the time being.

• • • •

Morning couldn't come soon enough for Vision. She had dreamed the memories of a monster, and though they weren't really as terrifying as she had assumed, they were emotionally draining. She'd awoken just as tired as she had been when she had fallen asleep in the first place. Now she was caught in the seemingly eternal loop of wanting to roll back over into quiet oblivion and desiring never to sleep again.

There was no clock in her room, and if there had been, she wouldn't have been able to read its holographic readout anyway. The best part about being blind to holograms was she never had to worry about being late since she had a built-in excuse, but in times like these, it meant Vision had no idea how long she had to wait for the adults to begin first meal preparations. Just the thought of it made her stomach rumble enough to get her up.

Groggy and aimless, Vision slid out of bed. She found a new appreciation for her halo. It fed the same images to her mind regardless of how tired she was, which made sleep a challenge but made being awake a breeze.

She knew that other people had to blink, and she did too. The difference was they missed things when their eyes closed, and she did not. She had a full three-hundred-and-sixty-degree view of the world in her immediate vicinity whenever she wanted it. It made navigating the apartment easy, even in absolute darkness.

The temperature was still too cool for the sun to be up, so it was unlikely anyone else would be awake. There would be no first meal, but there would be an unrestrained raid of Zhara's upscale food storage unit, and that put a broad smile on Vision's face. It was still there when she rounded to the corner to the living room and noticed Zhara perched at the counter dividing the common area from the kitchen. Her grin crumbled instantly.

"What are you doing up?" Vision asked incredulously.

Zhara shushed her and motioned for Vision to come closer.

She was fully dressed, and her hair was pinned back as though she'd been awake for some time.

"Are you leaving?" Vision asked in a lowered voice.

Zhara nodded slowly and offered Vision the stool beside her. Reluctantly, Vision moved across the cool tile floor and eased herself onto the seat.

"Why?" she asked softly.

Zhara offered Vision some of her smoothie, which the little girl refused and sighed.

"I have something at the office I need to take care of," Zhara stated. "I was hoping to be back before either of you woke up."

"What kind of something is it?" Vision asked, her curiosity piqued by Zhara's intentionally vague wording.

"It's better if you don't know," Zhara said.

"Does Claude know?" Vision inquired.

She already knew the truth. It radiated off Zhara almost like a scent. To Vision, it felt like guilt, but only a minor version of it. Zhara wasn't entirely sure about what she was going to do, but Vision could tell that she felt compelled to do something.

Without pressing into Zhara's mind, Vision wouldn't be able to glean any further details, but some secrets weren't worth such effort. She just hoped that this was one of them.

"No. He doesn't, but I'll tell him later. I need to get this done as early as I can, and I don't have time to argue about it," Zhara offered by way of explanation.

Vision took a deep breath and nodded, choosing to trust Zhara's judgment. She'd earned it a dozen times over in the past, and if she said this was important, it had to be.

Zhara was a friend, and while Vision had stolen peeks at her inner thoughts before, how she felt about doing so was evolving. With Claude, she was able to push a little farther before she began to feel like an invader, but with Zhara, she preferred not to. She deserved some distance, and Vision had set personal boundaries for what she was and wasn't willing to do. They were fast and loose rules, and she wasn't responsible for what bled through, but in terms of actively plucking secrets from the woman's head, Vision was generally against it.

"I'll let you off the hook, but I'm going to need full access to the snacks," Vision said playfully.

"Will you now?" Zhara asked and slid off her stool.

Sluggishly, she scooped her data-pad from the counter and finished her smoothie. She kissed Vision on the crown of her head and was startled by a pop of static electricity.

"Sorry," Vision said nervously. "I can't control it."

Zhara rubbed her nose and squeezed Vision's arm.

"Not a problem," she said with a smile. "I needed the help staying awake anyway."

Vision watched as Zhara moved through the sliding door of the apartment, and when she disappeared from her sensors, a weight fell onto her shoulders. It wasn't too heavy, but it was there all the same. Vision knew a secret now, and keeping such things from Claude never seemed to go as planned. He couldn't read minds, but he knew her well enough to divine information whenever she tried to hide it. She only hoped that Zhara would manage to return before Claude even noticed she was gone.

Vision swiveled on the stool and leaned on the cool metal countertop. Being involved in the affairs of adults was tiring, especially when she was already exhausted. They seemed to get themselves in all sorts of unnecessary trouble for reasons she really didn't understand, and yet she often found herself in the mix. If they only knew how much she'd already done to help them out.

For all the added pressure she'd received just for wanting a tiny snack, there was one good thing about it...

"She didn't say no," Vision said to herself and let a mischievous grin spread across her face once more.

• • • •

Marta had visited many worlds in her career. She'd been given missions throughout the Beita Systems, but this was different. Minerva Prime was one of the few batteries that powered her civilization, and as a result, it was tightly controlled.

She'd been assigned to quell a brewing uprising as a favor to the numerous corporations that ran the world, but she had never actually set foot in the planet's capital. The city wasn't the largest on the desert rock, but it was the first, and as a result, it was naturally chosen as the seat of local government. It had all the features such cities were known for, though it was all funded and micro-managed by large, self-interested companies like Artemis Industries.

The Artemis building was a tremendous, expensive eyesore jabbed into the corporate district at the city's center. It was an ostentatious reminder that Artemis Vaal had gotten rich off the back of Echelon contracts and used that money to wedge himself into the heart of the Beitan society.

Ritzy elitist types had always rubbed her the wrong way with their sensitivities and oddly specific rules of engagement. They played games while everyone else fought and died to protect their right to avoid living in the real universe.

Though it was odd for her, she found herself doubting her current course of action as she strode across one of the arrival platforms. The sun beat down on her, making the commandeered PlanSec uniform hot as well as itchy and generally uncomfortable.

Since Bertrand had given her access to DiSilva's records, Marta had been tempted to simply wait and roll with him to the pick-up, and when the call came in, she would. As it stood, there had been no contact, and that left plenty of time for her to find beneficial ways to keep herself busy.

One of the many lessons she had learned in her service was that the more you knew about a person, the easier it was to predict their responses. Sadly, DiSilva's files only gave her a vague idea of who he had been before his disappearance. They said nothing about the man as he existed now. Luckily, a few questions to the slovenly officer who responded to the Artemis incident pointed her directly to someone capable of fixing that.

Apparently, DiSilva had visited with a woman who worked in the building, and Marta had identified her as Zhara Riggs. This Zhara was initially trained as a physician but was hired by Artemis and "developed," as they called it, into a biomechanical engineer. Marta would have found that impressive, but the company Riggs kept proved that she wasn't as brilliant as she seemed.

For the second day in a row, Marta strode through the ornate reception area and cut a line directly to the security booth. This time she had arrived just as the morning sun began its assault of the lobby, bringing light and, regrettably, heat.

Across the lobby, in the security booth, sat a familiar yet not altogether welcoming face. The dark, barrel-chested man stood to greet her, his eyes simultaneously bright but tired-looking. As she approached, he gave a small respectful bow and stretched out his large hand.

"Officer," the older man said.

Marta took it and faked a cheerful smile. "Chief Wilks, we meet again. Do you ever get time off?"

"Couldn't get any of the kids here to cover the holiday, and please call me Tarence," he said as a sly grin added new creases to his face.

Marta had little doubt the man saw right through her false flirting, but it could not be helped. Older security personnel had a way of sniffing out untruths, she knew. The best way to fool them was to present something fairly innocuous to mask the true deception. It seemed to work on Tarence, and he was more than willing to play the part of a flattered, older gentleman. His eyes gave away his suspicions, though, and they told Marta that she needed to keep her gloves up, so to speak.

"Tarence it is," Marta said and leaned on the wall of the booth. "Have you seen her yet?"

Tarence shook his head and swiped through two different holo-screens. He locked his gaze back on the false officer and watched her intently as he spoke.

"Not yet, but she should be in sometime today. She never lets business wait for long," Tarence said, studying the carefully crafted look of disappointment Marta wore. "If I know her, she's likely on her way right now."

Marta let herself be heard sighing before she asked the one question she cared most about. "Is there any way I could just wait for her in her office this time? I swear I won't touch anything."

The wary, experienced gaze of the security chief scanned Marta's facade for weaknesses but found none. To him, she seemed to be one of those young women who thought every man wanted to feel desired by every woman, but that was a fallacy of youthful thinking. It wasn't the kind of dishonesty that presented a red flag.

"Okay, but make sure you don't," Tarence said firmly. "I'll be keeping an eye on you up there."

"Promise?" Marta said with what she hoped was the right amount of honey on the word.

Tarence just cleared his throat and waved in the direction of the lifts down the corridor. He watched as the shapely officer made her way out of sight and caught himself thinking that perhaps it wasn't just the young that liked getting a little attention now and then.

All the offices Marta passed were sparse, drab affairs. They were honestly more akin to cells than workspaces, but they did have excellent views.

The city was an almost mythical beast stretching out to the horizon. It was cloaked in what seemed like a mist, but she knew to be dust caught in high, heated winds. If she had to judge the city by its skyline, Marta would be willing to live here, but Minerva City wasn't an ideal place, no matter how picturesque the image was. No city ever was. No planet was, for that matter.

She had seen the ugly side of the beautiful so often she could no longer be fooled by it the way most people were. Marta knew what the universe was really like, and no amount of hoping, wishing, working, or praying would ever change it. The best anyone could do was simply ride its bloody, brutal waves and do their best not to become one of the bodies that littered its immeasurable depths.

As if by counterpoint, Marta noticed the weak, little stalk standing on the desk defiantly. Almost in spite of herself, Marta found herself giving the little plant a snide smile.

"Oh, you think you're different, do you?" Marta asked, her voice full of snark. "You, just wait."

The little thing was on the wrong world for such rugged perseverance. Minerva was not the place for standing out. It was the place for being beaten down and carved into something as course and lifeless as the planet itself. The tiny thing would have much better chances elsewhere, but such was the way of things. Rarely did one get the proper conditions required to reach their true potential.

Marta grunted to herself as she spotted the most likely spots for surveillance along the smooth panels of the ceiling. She had no doubt that the guard would be doing exactly what he said he would. The problem was she needed to do all the snooping she could before Zhara arrived.

Luckily, Artemis Vaal was one of those hypocritical peace lovers who was all about presenting himself as a true socialist to the people while simultaneously maintaining the best security systems that credits could buy. Apparently, his belief in the innate good of people didn't extend to actually trusting them.

It was fine that he wanted to protect his considerable investments. Marta thought it would be idiotic not to. What she didn't respect was the public-facing lie that Vaal liked to perpetrate. He believed in the classic "mine-not-thine" mantra that most citizens of his standing lived by. He just didn't want to be seen doing it. That level of asinine hypocrisy should come with a prison term, but Marta didn't make the laws. She simply broke them when she needed to.

Laws passed for the protection of private property weren't high priorities where Echelon was concerned. Often, they were shattered into a million useless pieces and blown out into the Black, where no one would ever know. In other cases, they were simply bent beyond all recognition.

The Detron refractor that Marta carried with her was a device designed to aid in circumventing such laws. Since all patents for new inventions had to be filed with the Myridorn's civil bureau, that meant particularly curious or paranoid agencies had access to the design specifications for each and every one of them. Private security specs were of great interest to Echelon, as were devices used to circumnavigate such systems.

The refractor captured and displayed a high-quality hologram that could fool most top-of-the-line surveillance systems. Marta had used the device upon entering the office to record herself and her environment for several minutes, and now that she was reasonably sure where Wilks' invasive eyes would be spying from, she could set the projection.

The flash of the device blinking to life happened so quickly that Marta almost didn't see it. The only hint that it was working at all was the telltale stinging sensation in her eyes, but once that momentary discomfort was gone, there was no way to tell a hologram was in place inches from the ceiling.

Marta immediately took a seat behind the desk and pulled up the holo-screen. She found nothing of particular interest for the first few minutes. Almost everything fit with Zhara Riggs' expertise. The executor was beginning to think snooping was a waste of her time when she spotted six data transfer requests for secure files on Psionic research.

It was by no means a great find, but it was curious. None of Riggs' assigned work had anything to do with Psionics, and each request had, of course, been almost immediately denied, but it begged a significant question.

"What are you up to?" Marta said to herself.

• • • •

Claude watched a hovercar similar in build to Zhara's shrink into the distance from the open-air balcony of her apartment. He did his best to estimate how far the Artemis building was from the apartment and why Zhara hadn't made it back yet.

She'd apparently left early, and he hadn't even noticed. He'd been exhausted from the events of the previous day, but that was no excuse. What kind of scout couldn't detect a woman slipping out of bed beside him and creeping out of the room?

"She's going to be fine," Vision said from the doorway behind him.

"I know," he said without conviction as the shimmering white vehicle disappeared from view.

"You need to relax, Claude. Not everyone needs your personal brand of overprotection," Vision chided.

She leaned on the railing beside him. Her sensors made her almost blind at the height they were standing. The apartment was easily sixty-seven stories above the ground, and besides the two sister towers across the sizable communal courtyard suspended between them, there weren't many things for her sensors to ping.

"Can I use your eyes?" Vision asked weakly.

Claude reached over and gently squeezed her hand.

"What are you going to do when I'm not around for you to mooch off?" he asked jokingly.

Vision sighed, "Hopefully, I'll have a better halo by then."

Claude smiled and looked back out over the city. It was morning, and the ion harvesters were nearing the end of their retraction cycles. What looked like wiry metal trees on the roofs of all the buildings in sight were folding in on themselves for protection against the planet's common barrages of high winds. They were the lifeblood of this world, but they were also frail enough to snap off at a moment's notice, and often they did just that.

The harvesters each cost somewhere near three and a half million credits, and while they needed to be extended during the nightly storms. Any other risks to them were to be strictly avoided. They justified their cost since a single week's worth of collecting could power an entire region for a month, but then they were too costly to have to keep replacing.

The excess charge was stored and converted into power cells used in everything from air filtration units to starships. While the corporations conducted a large amount of research on Minerva Prime, it was the harvesting of energy that justified nearly all of the interest in the planet.

Without the abundant ion storms, Minerva Prime was just an inhospitable bronze stone, no matter how hauntingly beautiful it could be at times.

The orange sun danced its way over the horizon, spraying its harsh, brilliant radiance across the skyline. The beams of morning light bounced endlessly off the reflective walls of towering structures throughout Cascade, giving much of the district at least a taste of what the upper floors were bathed in.

Morning here was different from Violet in many ways. Unlike Claude's home district, there was never an end or even a slowing of traffic in Cascade. People were apparently willing to pay exorbitant prices for their homes but seemed to never want to be in them. They were always out for one reason or another, be it a meal, exercise, or even prayers.

Staying busy was the end goal, or so Claude assumed. To him, it made sense that a group of people removed from the fight for survival needed to remain active unless they wanted to waste away to nothing.

Personally, he didn't understand it, but like most things in the universe, he didn't need to. Things were the way they were, and the sooner a person could wrap his mind around that fact, the easier he could coexist with it. Rarely was there anything that didn't serve one purpose or another, whether Claude could fathom it or not.

Like the residents he found himself judging, he was eager to start his day, but there was little he could do until Zhara cracked the drives. He needed to set up a meet with Bertrand before his former commander decided to hunt him down, but the prudence of waiting hadn't waned just because the sun was now rising.

That meant the only thing he could do was sit uncomfortably in the luxuriously furnished apartment he had elected not to live in and wait for the return of a beautiful woman who was far more intelligent than he was. It was yet another thing he had to accept.

"Stop overthinking it," Vision said, plucking his thoughts out of his skull yet again. "You need her help and mine. There's nothing wrong with that. You want us to come to you when we need you, so it's okay for you to do the same."

Claude sighed but didn't respond. He didn't need to. Vision was right, of course, and judging by the widening smile on her face, she had likely pillaged that nugget from his mind as well.

For as wise as the eleven-year-old's words were, he was still a scout at heart. Most of his former life was about being self-sufficient and coming through for the sake of his entire squad. Letting others do for him disagreed with both his training and his personality. He was used to being the first one in. He was used to acting with immediacy, but after retrieving the drives, there wasn't anything more for him to do.

Claude let himself think about the situation he'd leaped into for the first time since the Old City, and he wasn't at all pleased with it. He'd let his emotions get in the way of his decision-making and didn't even ask if Vision could have stayed with Zhara.

Instead, he took her into the most dangerous and unpredictable environment on the entire planet. They'd almost been killed, and all because he was scared of facing the consequences of rejecting Zhara's offer.

If Miranda had not been in a talkative mood, things could have gone poorly, and he would have been nearly powerless to change that. Now he was playing another dangerous game. By holding the drives, he was escalating tensions for the same woman he had pushed away, and now Zhara was putting herself in Echelon's path to back his play. It was irresponsible of him, and if he didn't know what kind of carnage Sabien weapons research could cause, he would just shove the damned things into a dropbox somewhere and have Bertrand retrieve them. He couldn't, though. That would have been an even more irresponsible thing to do.

Claude sighed heavily and hoped Vision was so distracted by the dazzling view that she wouldn't dig into him any deeper. He was knowingly and willingly putting her at risk, and for that was tearing him up inside. But the universe was bigger than he was, and there was more at stake than just the people he cared for. Claude would just have to find a way to make peace with the trade and hope he didn't end up regretting it.

The war had touched every inch of the known universe, from Minerva Prime to Akinos, to Myridorn, and even Veralles, as lawless a place as it was. Every world had bled into the Black for nearly a thousand years. But against all odds, the conflict had abated in his time.

He owed it to the friends he had watched die, to the family he had lost, and the child standing beside him to do all he could to prevent such a thing from happening again.

Vision pressed into his side tightly but didn't look away from the city. "What are you going to do?" she asked somberly.

"I'm not sure," Claude said, sounding more defeated than he would have liked. "If the drives could restart the war, they have to be destroyed. If not, I'm going to have to hand them over. Either way, being around me won't be safe for either of you."

He intentionally chose not to focus on the outcomes he foresaw, hoping that Vision wouldn't be able to see them as clearly in his mind. It was a small hope, but Vision's abilities always surprised him with their strengths as well as their limitations.

"What if we don't want to be safe?" Vision asked. "Are we supposed to wait until you decide it's okay to come back? Are we supposed to just let you disappear out there somewhere?"

She made an effort to look at him even though she only saw herself. Though it was disorienting, she watched the heat of his glare focus on her and held it, rather than releasing the use of his eyes.

"You're supposed to live," Claude said, letting his voice boom at her. "I don't want to go, V. I want this to go away so we can go back to the way things were, but that's not going to happen."

"Then we leave," Vision decided. "We get on a transport and go to the farthest rock from here and start over, You, me, and Zhara."

Claude felt himself shaking his head before he had fully decided on a response. Echelon would hunt him now that they knew what he was carrying. Miranda had told him that much. What they had done to her they would do to him if they caught him, and Echelon wasn't at all shy about making innocent people disappear to keep their activities a secret.

"They would find us," Claude said with a somber hitch in his voice.

The eleven-year-old turned to face him fully, planted her hands on her hips, and leaned toward him like a woman five times her age.

"You made a promise to me," Vision stated fearlessly. "You don't get to just walk away from that."

"I'm not walking away! People will be hunting me. No matter how this plays out, the Beita Systems will come for me," Claude said forcefully. "If you get killed, I can't exactly keep my promise, can I?"

Vision threw her hands up and grunted in frustration.

"Then you need to find another way because we're partners, and you don't get to just leave me behind," she lectured. "We are supposed to be in this together."

"Why do I have to keep telling you this?" Claude growled. "We are not partners."

The words escaped his lips before he had a chance to fully process them and their effect was immediate.

Whatever hope Vision had been holding on to shattered, and he could see it in her face. Her wide, shocked eyes welled with tears, but she disappeared into the apartment before they had a chance to fall.

Claude tried to massage the growing tension from his forehead but failed utterly. He had meant what he said. They weren't partners. He was her guardian, her protector, but the only thing he didn't seem capable of protecting her from was himself.

He did his best to ignore the sound of her crying and focus on the spot on the skyline where he thought Zhara would be. She would be a better parent than he could ever hope to be. She would be able to provide a safe and stable life for Vision, and whether she wanted it or not, that's what every child needed.

Claude was a vehicle of destruction. He always had been. His father would always keep him away from the crops when he was Vision's age for that exact reason, and even when he joined the military, he was sent to target and eliminate obstacles. There wasn't a point in his life where he actually built or repaired anything. He demolished things, and the longer he spun his wheels in the same place, the more he tore into the foundations beneath him.

He didn't want to have another blow-up with Vision. She was right in some regard. He was being selfish, but not in the way she assumed. He wanted to keep her and Zhara safe, and he was unwilling to give them much of a say in that process. Maybe it wasn't the best thing to do from a moral standpoint, but morals didn't matter to corpses. His mission was to keep them alive, even if he had to break them to do it.

They would lean into each other when he was gone. Zhara wouldn't abandon Vision. She would be cared for, and if things went wrong for him, then time would do what it always did. They would move on, and he could make peace with that, no matter what happened to him in the meantime.

Claude dropped his head and wished for the hundredth time that he'd simply ignored Bertrand's call and spent the day doing anything except putting himself in the crosshairs of his old commander.

Claude froze. The seed of an idea fell into the fertile soil of his concerns and grew rapidly into what might eventually be a workable plan. What he had been trying to do was akin to crossing a mile of open terrain while calm and comfortable snipers took careful aim at him. He had been assuming that taking the hit was inevitable, but what if it wasn't?

He hadn't factored in all the aspects of his hypothetical environment. In fact, he'd been trying to run away from it. In this scenario, he couldn't change the terrain. It was fixed, but if he played his cards just right, he could cross during the gathering storm. All he had to do was make sure that he put himself and the snipers squarely amid the tempest that was Miranda.

The silver under his skin rippled as the thickening roots of his plan took hold. Claude could somehow tell that the creature wasn't pleased, but if the plan worked out the way he wanted, the damned thing could protest in safety for decades to come. That was a big *if*, but considering the odds of successfully evading Echelon for the rest of his life, it was the best option he had.

• • • •

In her mind, Zhara felt she was doing a solid job of selling a casual and unhurried pace, but in reality, she failed miserably. The few employees and vendors still in the lobby greeted her with curious and confused expressions as she sped past. Her focus rested on the kind face at the security booth, so the multitudes of sidelong glances and raised eyebrows did nothing to banish her delusion.

Tarence spotted her halfway through the doors, gave her a smile, then returned his attention to his lower holo-screen. It wasn't uncommon for him to be distracted with other security concerns, but something about this struck her as odd considering the relaxed atmosphere of the day.

Stopping at the counter, Zhara flashed her bracelet ID pointedly. It only took a second for Tarence to confirm it before his eyes drifted back to the holo-screen once more.

"Is everything okay?" she asked, doing her best to sneak a peek at the guard's feed.

"I sent that PlanSec officer up to your office, but the feed seems weird somehow," he said, only sparing her a brief glance.

"She's here already?" Zhara asked. "Eager, isn't she?"

Tarence gave a chortle that came out more like a snort. "She's after something. I'd handle this one with care."

Zhara nodded subconsciously as she sipped on the older man's words. It seemed that she wasn't the only one suspicious of Planetary Security's sudden interest. She wondered if the surveillance footage hadn't given away something in the investigation, but if it had, the person waiting in her office would have been from the upper floors, not PlanSec.

"Enjoy what you can of your holiday, Mr. Wilks," Zhara said as the man waved her through.

"It's Tarence, Miss Riggs," he said with an honest smile.

"It'll be Tarence when you start calling me Zhara," she said and trotted out of earshot.

Faint yellow light to Zhara's left announced that the roomy communal lifts were all deactivated due to low traffic. She let out a grunt of frustration at being forced to take one of the comparatively narrow private lifts. They were interesting honeycomb-shaped contraptions built entirely of the same transparent metal that comprised most of the building's exterior.

The design was meant to alleviate the claustrophobic nature of more traditional lifts, but it only managed to trade one deep-seeded fear for another. Neither tight spaces, nor heights really bothered Zhara, but she still preferred the communal lifts. Usually, the more open space provided people for her to talk to instead of the long, silent ascent awaiting her. Today, that silence was filled with a pint of uncertainty and just a sprinkling of dread. It was a mixture she wasn't fond of, so she kept her focus on the task at hand and ignored the toxic brew bubbling in the recesses of her mind.

Clearing her throat, Zhara did her best to run through all of the steps required to copy the files she needed and exit the building. There were quite a few. Provided the arrival of PlanSec didn't lead to a massive derailment, she was confident she could accomplish them all with no real repercussions.

The program she'd come for wasn't something she was supposed to have access to, but friends had looped her in when the project's clearances were assigned. The team working on this particular bit of code was prone to tunnel vision, and they knew it. Zhara had been gifted clearance because she possessed outside eyes and had a half-decent understanding of Sabien coding protocols. They had needed more people than had been assigned to get their program working, but after war's end, the board was less motivated to see the project to completion.

Regardless, it became an obsession that the team just couldn't let die. Often the team could be found late at night perfecting their invention when there was little chance of being discovered by their supervisors, or when their higher priority work stalled out.

Officially, the Kill Code, as it was affectionately dubbed, was a bust. For all the executives knew, it was just another resource drain that had gone nowhere, but unofficially, it was perfectly functional, if inefficient. It took hours for the damned thing to do its job, but given the proper time, it would work. Zhara just had to get the PlanSec officer out of her workspace so she could copy it and get back to her apartment.

The lift slowed, then eventually came to a stop as a pleasant male voice announced, "Destination reached. Have a productive day."

Zhara rolled her eyes at the automated message and stepped into the corridor. It was quiet and barren of all life. As she moved past one nearly identical workspace after another, the faux wooden walls giving way to transparent panels and the offices beyond.

The building had been impressive when she'd first been hired, and it continued to be until she realized the ornate design didn't stretch beyond the places visitors were allowed to go. The flashy, futuristic facade was just a showy mask for an utterly mundane core structure. The corporation was nothing if not image-conscious, and while transparent offices were pretty to look at, they were really just another way to ensure no one took unauthorized breaks.

Zhara didn't hate her job, but like most people, she had simply moved past the honeymoon phase with it. She was still able to do the kind of work that mattered to her. For all its faults, Artemis Industries provided her a chance to make people's lives better. That wasn't the case with many employers. It wasn't even the case with most of her coworkers.

Dozens of inspirational projects were canceled every year. Those workers were placed elsewhere with little in the way of concern for whether their new tasks suited them or not. Zhara was lucky, her work for the disabled was both financially viable and well received by the general public. If it weren't for those two all-important factors, it was likely she would have shared the same fate long ago.

Zhara put her musings to the side as she neared her office. Through the transparent wall, she noticed a rather small, anxious-looking woman perched on her loveseat. She wore the standard deep green of the PlanSec patrol uniform and seemed at home in it, even if it was a little tight in the hips.

It took the woman a moment to notice Zhara approaching, but when she did, she almost leaped from the couch and blasted out a radiant smile.

Oh great, a morning person, Zhara thought, then instinctively flinched away from such an unguarded judgment.

Her time with Vision had altered how she conducted her thoughts, which she felt was interesting in and of itself.

Any other time Zhara would have let that train of thought spin her off into an involved contemplation about consistent internal censorship and what it could do to a person or even a society over a long enough period of time. Fortunately, she caught herself and filed those thoughts away. There would be time to explore the long-lasting psychological effects of endlessly policing one's own mind later. At the moment, she needed to focus on getting this woman to leave without arousing any undue suspicions.

She gave the woman a terse nod as she entered her workspace.

"Hello, Miss Riggs," the PlanSec officer said brightly. "I'm Officer Dawes. Forgive the intrusion, but headquarters assigned me to follow-up with several employees regarding the incident a few days ago."

Zhara didn't stop her forward movement, though she kept her eyes on the woman. She didn't have much experience with PlanSec personally, but the stories she had gotten from others didn't inspire trust in the organization.

"How can I help you?" Zhara asked as politely as she did pointedly.

The woman's smile dropped as she switched mental gears.

Dawes was not much taller than five feet, Zhara guessed, yet somehow, she still possessed an intimidating demeanor. It wasn't enough to make Zhara outright uncomfortable, but she felt it all the same. Fortunately, she was buoyed by being in her element, though it wasn't impossible to imagine the petite officer as quite a threat under the right circumstances.

"The focus of our investigation has shifted to include guests and visitors present during the incident," the officer began. "Our report says there were two with you that day, but they weren't signed in."

In her head, Zhara cursed Claude just a little. He was notorious for dodging the sign-in process. That particular quirk of his had caused minor issues for her in the past. They had spoken about it at length and she'd come away thinking the problem was solved. Apparently, it didn't stick.

"My boyfriend and his daughter. They visit me from time to time," Zhara said curtly and made a mental note to address the situation with Claude when she made it home.

"And were they affected by the incident?" the petite woman asked, making short jabbing motions at her data-pad.

"We all woke up at about the same time, so yes," Zhara lied.

The woman across the desk didn't seem overly convinced, but Zhara assumed interrogations didn't work very well if the officer believed the first thing a person said. Luckily, there appeared to be no way to prove she had lied. If there were, she'd likely be having this conversation in bindings.

"I'm going to have to follow up with them directly. That won't be a problem, will it?" Dawes said, making the question more of a statement.

Zhara stared into intense, confident eyes and saw the woman for what might as well have been the first time. There was a fire in the deep brown of them and it told her in no uncertain terms, that "no" wasn't a valid response. She would have to give the officer something, but what?

Zhara allowed herself to sink into the seat behind her desk and opened her holo-screen. She couldn't give her true task the full attention it demanded, but she could at least attempt to use her time wisely. Plus, it would give her a reason to seem distracted, even if it was a lie.

It was possible to pull the file from the Artemis network remotely, but that required linking Zhara's home to her work in a permanent and potentially intrusive way. She'd avoided working from home for years to prevent just such a parasitic connection. So instead, she had disconnected every piece of networking hardware in her apartment in the hopes of translating the drives in as isolated and secure an environment as possible.

"Do I need to ask again?" the officer asked with a bit of a glower on her face.

Zhara ripped her eyes away from her screen and focused on the small woman. "Let's save time here, Officer. What are you asking for, specifically?"

The officer's face twisted in thought for a moment before she said, "I need to talk to him."

Zhara latched on to the last word. It stood out so starkly that she had to make a conscious effort not to show her surprise. Up until now, officer Dawes had been vague about her real interest. In fact, the entire visit had seemed innocuous. Everything she'd asked could have been done over comms, but it was all a ruse just to get to this point.

Her true motive wasn't a surprise, however. Tarence had given Zhara a heads-up, and she had come into the office knowing the woman's ultimate goal was Claude. What Zhara didn't know was why.

Officer Dawes, if that was her actual name, wasn't going to let that answer slip. In fact, there was little point in playing the game any further except to potentially lead her astray.

"I don't know," Zhara said, leaning back in her chair. "The last time I saw him was the night of the incident. It's kind of our thing, I think. Ships passing in the Black, you know?"

Officer Dawes didn't seem surprised by that statement, nor did she seem to buy it.

"So, he brings his daughter to see you, but you aren't that serious?" the officer asked, with acidic skepticism dripping from her every word.

Zhara gave as casual a shrug as she could manage. She figured if she was going to play a part, it might as well be one she had seen a million times.

Her coworker, Fione, tended to overshare relationship details, particularly the reckless rush toward the physical. Though she always wound up complaining about the compromises made to reach that destination. Unlike Fione, Zhara wasn't the type of person to share her private life, but she had no issue pretending to be if that ended this conversation sooner.

"I wonder about that too sometimes, but it's his call," Zhara said with a flick of her wrist. "If he wants to bring her along, and it doesn't affect my experience, I say let him."

Officer Dawes seemed to dismiss that line of questioning in pure disgust, which relieved Zhara. The words felt wrong in her mouth, but somehow, she kept the image intact.

"Is there a place he's likely to be?" Dawes asked flatly, swiping up on her data-pad. "Some place you've met him before? A bar, or his home, perhaps?"

Zhara pretended to think about that for a moment before she finally answered.

"He has an apartment," Zhara said absently. "He spends a lot of time out, but it's a place to start, I guess."

"And where is that?"

"Growlett Pass in Violet. Evelion VII, I think. We mostly meet in Cascade or here, so I might be a little off, but it's around there," Zhara replied, doing everything she could to appear disinterested.

The image of a bio-mechanical engineer who was unable to remember the address of her lover would seem odd to some people, but Zhara knew very well that the sharper a mind was in one facet, the dimmer it could be in others. Many of the people working in her own building struggled with life outside of their offices. She could think of a few offhand who didn't even know how to fix a clogged thruster on their cars, let alone how to manage an interpersonal relationship. She tried to stop herself short of wondering whether she was just as bad, but couldn't shake it off before the question hit home.

The small woman nodded and let a tight smile crack her newly stern features. It took a second before the gears shifted back into place, and the amiable morning person returned fully.

In a smooth, practiced motion, she slipped her data-pad into her breast pocket, then reached out to shake Zhara's hand. Without so much as a hint of hesitation, she swept the refractor off the edge of the desk with her free hand and dropped it into a pouch at her belt.

The move was timed perfectly. The hologram's death flash fell in the middle of Zhara's blink, though its effect wasn't masked entirely. Her eyes still stung, and her tear ducts still drowned her eyes in saline, but no question was asked, and no answer was offered.

"I think that gives me a decent place to start," the officer said in her previous pleasant demeanor. "I'll be in touch if I need you for anything else."

Zhara stood and shook the woman's hand before asking, "Do you think he was responsible for what happened?"

Dawes' face wrinkled for a moment, then her smile returned, "I can't say."

Dawes withdrew her hand and nodded a final time before exiting.

Zhara watched the woman move out of sight and then fell back into her chair. She was, at once, relieved and newly anxious now that the conversation was over.

Drawing in a deep, calming breath and exhaling as much of her anxiety as she could manage, she turned her full attention to the holo-screen and the task at hand.

• • • •

Marta let the mask of Officer Dawes crumble away as she made her way down the corridor. The scientist was clever, but she wasn't much of an actress. In the end, she had verified several key points that would prove helpful.

As much as she distrusted Bertrand, he had provided her with accurate information about DiSilva. The address matched the one he'd given her, and the greasy louse at PlanSec was spot on about him caring for a child.

The scientist had tried to play opposites with Marta, but that was easy enough to see through. She and DiSilva were close, and it was likely they had discussed the possibility of such a conversation in advance.

It didn't really matter. Marta expected any scout to be wary, especially one Bertrand thought so highly of. Her mission was less about cornering DiSilva than learning as much as she could about what he was capable of.

To that end, this meeting had been a moderate success. She hadn't gotten a current location for the man himself, but she did get a perfect opportunity to head him off. The fact Bertrand really had opened his operation to her added to her peace of mind.

The jury was still out on whether she would allow herself to trust him fully, but she was at least confident he wouldn't have his people shoot her in the heart and leave her to rot. It was something she might consider herself if their roles were somehow reversed. Luckily, it seemed lifelong military devotees didn't think like their Echelon counterparts.

Marta breezed past the security desk and ignored the old fool who attempted to wish her a nice day. She was done with this place and everyone in it, including Officer Dawes. If she needed to confront Riggs again, she'd drop by her home but not as a friendly PlanSec officer. For now, her next objective was clear. She only had a few hours left before her presence would be missed back on the ship and local traffic would eat up the bulk of that time. Fortunately, she had other more viable options than a rushed trip to the slums.

She hit the lobby door and let the orange sun splash across her. Marta took a moment to think before she freed the data-pad from her pocket and tapped it several times.

"Go for Yuri," the voice said on the other end.

"Get your team ready. I have a mission for you," Marta purred.

Chapter 24

ALMOST FIVE HOURS HAD passed since Claude woke up in bed alone. He'd heard nothing from Zhara in that time, and all the worst scenarios he could imagine were beginning to tear through his calm.

It didn't help that there was very little for him to do in Zhara's apartment. She had only moved into it a month or so prior, and while the place was solidly furnished, she hadn't gotten around to stocking it with much in the way of entertainment.

The only upside to the entire situation was that it gave him time to smooth things over with Vision. She didn't talk to him for two hours following their argument, but after a while, she came around. He'd been harsh with her. He was more than willing to admit that, but it was also important that she acknowledge who was the adult and who was the child. Vision's opinion wasn't invalid, but the way she had presented left much to be desired. Eventually, she was able to reluctantly concede that point.

After that, Vision resumed her quest to take a detailed inventory of the apartment. She surveyed everything that was of any interest to her. The piano lost its luster quickly, which was a good thing, but that led to her spending most of her time scouring the house for anything remotely exciting. It was all Claude could do to keep her out of Zhara's bedroom. He figured that was a courtesy to both of them, but the rest of the house was pretty much a lost cause. Zhara had let her roam before, so who was he to step in? As he saw it, his job was to keep Vision from breaking anything he couldn't afford to replace.

After some time, she came up with a game called Dysen, but the chips it used as its false currency were color-coded, so that was a bust. Then she raided the food storage unit, but there wasn't much left in it meant for a child, especially not one with such unhealthy tastes.

At the moment, she was borrowing Claude's eyes to read one of her quarterly lessons, and neither was enjoying it very much.

"Please stop moving your eyes so fast," Vision seethed.

"Then read faster," Claude grumbled.

"I would be done with this by now if mine actually worked," she retorted, leaning away from him with crossed arms.

"We would both be done if you would just sync up instead of hijacking my brain," Claude said mockingly.

Vision groaned loudly and disentangled herself from Claude's mind.

"Fine," she said and stretched her hand out for the data-pad.

Claude handed the device over and rose to his feet. He stretched the muscles in his lower back and winced when a loud, painful pop almost forced him to crash back down on the sofa.

"You okay, old man?" Vision asked with a smirk.

Claude frowned at her, but his heart wasn't in it. He was still feeling a little guilty about the blow-up on the balcony, and he was glad that she'd bounced back so quickly.

He knew he had been a little unreasonable, but he still believed he was right. Vision was too young to understand, but one day she would. Until then, she was just going to have to accept his judgment. There was no way he could be sure that was something she would do, but he just had to believe it. Otherwise, he couldn't move forward. He had to know she would be safely away from him if his plan was to work. If Vision was at risk, it would compromise his ability to pull it off, and he couldn't have that.

Of course, he'd have to discuss the finer points of his plan with Zhara when she returned, and he was dreading that conversation. If he knew her as well as he thought he did, she would have pretty much the same reaction Vision had. Claude just had to have faith she would see his logic, even if she didn't want to.

"Are you going to be okay?" Claude asked.

Vision shrugged and dialed the correct sync code into her halo. The persistent scans of the room died a slow death, giving over to the floating greenish readout of her lesson on Streamline measurements.

She sighed heavily before responding, "I guess, but can you tell me why they want kids to know the correct unit of distance for travel in Streamline?"

A smile curled Claude's lip.

"It's a Dueral. They represent distance traveled over a standard minute in the anomaly," he said, taking a moment to show off.

Vision groaned again. "I'm never going Streamline," she said definitively.

"Then you'll be bone dust fifteen times over before you get out of the system," Claude offered by way of contradiction.

Vision stuck her tongue out in the general direction Claude's voice had come from.

"I'll be on the balcony," Claude said, then moved away from the sofa.

"Yeah, yeah."

Since their trip to the Artemis building, they had been neglecting her lessons, but it couldn't be helped. Vision wasn't a normal kid, and she didn't adhere to the typical standards of the Beita Systems' Education Commission.

There wasn't another Psionic student under the jurisdiction of the BSEC, though as far as they knew, she was just as normal as the next kid... maybe a bit smarter.

Claude didn't know if it was because she spent so much time picking up the thoughts of adults or if she was just naturally gifted, but she processed, retained, and understood new information at a level that couldn't be normal. He certainly didn't remember being as sharp when he was her age. Zhara believed Vision was in the upper percentile of her age group. She was a bit biased, but the results for last quarter's assessment backed her up.

The warm air of the balcony smelled of the same heat and indiscernible minerals that he'd become accustomed to, but at the apartment's height, it was much less oppressive. Judging by the sun's position and the truncated day-night cycle of the planet, the day would be winding down soon. It would be dark in another six hours, and the air would cool significantly.

Claude was grateful for that. The colder nights hinted at the rainy season to come and a much-needed reprieve from the constantly swirling dust in the streets.

Violet was not a pretty sight in the rainy season since the people in the sewer settlements had to move up to the surface. The entire district became a miserable, soggy, overcrowded mess, but at least you didn't have lightly ionized particles trying to coat your lungs.

Vision liked the rainy season because the ion storms were less powerful, but the rains only came once every two standard years. She complained that the world would be perfect if the seasons were reversed, but Claude always pointed out how lucky she was Minerva didn't have a typical winter. She'd never lived through one, and while she was curious, she was not a fan of the cold. What he considered a cool night made her shiver uncontrollably, which was odd because children of the Black were usually more accustomed to lower temperatures.

Like so many others, Vision had been born among the stars, or so he assumed. She was so young on Firaxis, he imagined she had been born on the station. He could have been wrong, of course, but most Sabien children weren't allowed to leave the safety of their birth planet until they were at least seven. He knew that edict very well since it had saved him from conscription by the Sabien military when the war came to Abarix.

Claude shook the painful memory away and focused on the city instead. He tried to allow himself to just look at it, but his mind wouldn't let go. He saw the High Ordinae escorting his brother away from their home. He saw his father looking on without lifting a finger to stop it.

Claude felt himself burning with an old, familiar fury at the thought of the men he still held responsible for tearing his family apart, and tried once again to suppress it. He'd let that anger drive him to dark and haunting places in the past. It took him many years to see his rage as the useless fetter it was, and in that time he had let it drag him far from the planet he was fated to live and die upon.

Eventually, he defected to the Beita Systems against the demands of his feckless father. The man who had stood idly by and let the faceless, soulless gears of the Sabien war machine consume his oldest son. As a child, Claude found it unforgivable. As an adult, he had come to understand the dynamics of the situation and often wondered what he would have done if he were in his father's place.

Finding Vision had ended that debate. He was a different man than his father, and Vision was a very different child from Levine, but the answer was still clear. However, in those years between leaving his old home and finding his new one, nothing had been.

Ignorance drove him forward in hopes of finding and killing the Ordinae who had taken his brother and led him to his death, but all he had done was fed more blood to a ravenous monster.

It didn't take long for him to become lost in it. He ate and slept, fought, and breathed the war as did so many, and while others died for it as well, miraculously, he did not. Soon, there was no other reason to live. Claude's life became nothing more than a string of missions. He did his best to block out that time, but he would never forget the pursuit of victories that would never come and the perpetual chase of relief he would never feel.

It wasn't until he had been faced with his own impossible choice that he snapped out of the stupor he'd worked himself into. It was another rash and, at the time, stupid decision, but it put him on a path that had led him here. Claude was so lost in his past that he almost didn't hear Vision moving behind him. She pressed against his side but didn't speak. They just stood there together, the man lamenting his broken past and the girl awash in emotions she could not quantify.

With a deep breath, Claude blinked away his regrets and painted on an utterly unconvincing smile.

"I thought you were doing your lesson?" he asked in as normal a voice as he could.

Vision's dark eyes seemed to look through him for a moment as she did nothing to hide the concern she felt.

Claude read the question on her face and the internal battle over whether or not to ask it. He let her inner fight play out. For a myriad of reasons, he had kept much of his past to himself. Claude hadn't quite squared with it, and it was unfair to hoist such a burden onto others.

Of course, he'd talked about his life on Abarix with Zhara, but there was still a great deal he'd held back. Zhara hadn't pried, and he hadn't offered more. So far, that arrangement seemed to be working just fine, but he did intend to tell the girls about Levine at some point. He just wasn't able to do it yet.

"Zee's on her way up," Vision said finally. "She sent a message."

She handed Claude his data-pad back and gave him a sympathetic smile before heading back into the apartment.

Claude let out a heavy breath and put his emotions back in order before following her.

· · · ·

It took Zhara less than fifteen minutes to copy the code into her system, although she decided not to introduce it to the drives yet. There would be time for that later. For all the stress acquiring the Kill Code had caused, she didn't want to implement her plan without first showing Claude why she had come up with it in the first place.

"What was that?" Claude asked from the doorway.

"Come in and close the door, please," Zhara said with a grave tone in her voice.

Claude did as she asked, biting down on the obvious questions threatening to break free.

Once the door was closed, Zhara took a long moment to look into his wide, confused eyes before she spoke again.

"Last night, I managed to translate the drives," she said slowly.

"Good," Claude said. "Let's see them."

Zhara sighed and gave an almost imperceptible shake of her head.

"We will, but I need you to listen first," she stated, and felt the pressure of the words to come. "I went to the office to get what we call a Kill Code."

Claude found the seriousness of her expression unnerving somewhere deep down near his core, but he fought to keep it off his face.

"What did you find?" he asked, matching her tone.

Zhara didn't answer. Instead, she swiveled her seat to face the hovering code and swiped in a circular motion. The swirl swept away the code and replaced it with the neatly organized groupings she'd uncovered the night before.

"The drives are divided by text, audio records, and video logs," Zhara declared. "There's more information here than we could get through in a standard year, but it seems like the biggest moments of the project were documented in the video logs."

"Is there any mention of Vision?" Claude asked.

For as much as he wanted to know what his passenger was and what it was doing to him, Vision's concerns came before his own.

"We'll get to that," Zhara said as she navigated to the video grouping.

"You're making this sound bad, Zee," Claude said, hearing the nervousness in his own voice.

Again, Zhara didn't respond. She didn't know how he would take what she'd discovered or what she'd decided to do about it.

In silence, she selected the first video log and gave him the chair, choosing instead to sit on the bed with her legs folded.

Claude took the offered seat and glanced back at Zhara, who wore an inscrutable expression on her face as the video began.

"This is project day forty-three, and I'm Talos project lead Rickten Eugene," a middle-aged man with thin, but well-defined features said.

The man was clearly in a lab, though much of its technology was indiscernible to Claude. The room matched what he could remember of the architecture on Firaxis station, but in his memory, it was far less pristine.

"Word came down from the Crowns that we are to split the project base down the center. I will be directly overseeing the Talos 1 specimen research, but Kailen Saulk will be brought on to develop the control protocols," Eugene said through clenched teeth.

The cords of muscle in his jaw flexed between his words, displaying his displeasure with the idea. His pale skin reddened as he talked.

"Lenore says I shouldn't get emotional about this, but it's an insult, and I don't really care if it gets back to operations that I said so," Eugene seethed. "This was supposed to be my opportunity. I fought hard for it, and when Greyvor finally saw reason, he put me in charge because I was the man for the job. Now, I admit that there have been setbacks, but I refuse..."

The video cut off abruptly, and Claude was left more confused than he thought he would be.

"What just happened?" he asked no one in particular.

"There are a few defects in the videos. I'm not sure if they were on the drives before you got them or if it's a translation mistake I made," Zhara offered.

She motioned across several video files and picked another one.

The familiar face of Eugene popped up in front of Claude again, forcing him to slide the chair away from the hologram to regain any sense of personal space.

"Day sixty-two, Rickten Eugene, here," the man said in an exhausted manner.

The lab around him was the same, except the lights had been dimmed. Several lab assistants moved behind him, carrying equipment of various sizes.

"The specimen is interesting, although it is primordial in structure. It seems to react positively to electrical stimuli, but it still doesn't seem capable of forming itself into a solid state," Eugene explained. "We've done hundreds of stimulation tests on it, and we have gotten very little in the way of usable responses.

"We've discovered that it consumes energy, however. It doesn't eat much if that's even the right term, but the amount is measurable. Also, several technicians have said that they've seen the specimen moving on its own while they were completing their assigned tasks, which I'm not sure I believe."

Claude felt a prickle at the back of his neck and scratched at it. He knew all this already, but something about hearing this man say it put him on edge. Apparently, his passenger wasn't any more comfortable than he was, since it shivered inside him every time it was mentioned in the video.

"Can we move on?" he asked Zhara.

She shushed him and made no effort to answer his question. Instead, she just scrolled the video back to cover what he'd missed.

After a short moment, the video began once again.

"However, if it's true, that would mean it is at least capable of more than we have assumed. It would also mean that the specimen is displaying behaviors that require a certain level of self-awareness."

A loud bang tore through the relative quiet of the lab.

"Sorry. That was my fault," a young man's voice called from somewhere the hologram didn't show.

Eugene looked away from the capture device abruptly. "It's okay, Lian," he said, then shrugged, and turned his attention back to the recording.

"We'll be leaving the specimen unattended for the next few days to see if we can capture these movements. Personally, I believe this is a waste of time, but Lenore says it can't hurt, and I could use a few days to rest and refresh," he said before the video cut out again.

Claude rubbed his forehead. He was unsure what he was expecting out of the drives, but this wasn't it. The face of a single individual reporting progress on a project he didn't understand was all but useless to him.

"Stick with it," Vision's voice called from the door.

Both Zhara and Claude snapped their attention to her so fast it made her consider running out of the room.

"I'm not sure this is good for you to–" Claude began, but Vision cut him off.

"This is what we almost died for, right?" Vision asked. "I risked my life too, so I should be here."

Logically, her point was sound, but that changed little for Claude. There were a dozen good reasons why she shouldn't be directly involved with the discovery process. He wasn't having the best time sorting through them all, but he did know that exposing Vision to the kinds of things people did during the war was a bad idea.

"I don't think you want to be in here for this, V," Zhara said, giving a weak smile. "I pored through a lot of these files last night, and it's pretty boring."

"We'll dig through this, then we'll get you in here for the good parts," Claude said, trying to make it seem like less of an exclusion.

Vision's eyes narrowed instinctively as she scanned the faltering expressions on both adults' faces. They were hiding something from her. That much was clear. She could even tell that they thought it was for her own good, though she didn't buy it.

Claude was nothing if not annoyingly protective. Usually, Zhara took her side, and together they whittled him down, but that strategy was off the table. As a united front, Claude and Zhara could be scary. Vision imagined that was what parents were like, and a secret part of her hurt just a bit more at that realization.

"Okay, fine," Vision sighed and slipped out of the room to close the door behind her.

Zhara and Claude exchanged a look that weighed as heavy with suspicion as it did with disbelief.

"I don't like how easy that was," Zhara said.

"Yeah, she'll be in our heads any second now," Claude replied with a scowl.

Zhara smiled and wiggled her finger for him to approach.

"Now?" Claude asked, although he was already following her unspoken command.

"I have an idea," Zhara said with a wicked grin.

As soon as Claude was within range, Zhara launched herself at him and pulled him into a hungry kiss that was so sudden Claude's eyes shot wide before he let himself enjoy it.

"Oh, come on!" Vision shouted through the wall at maximum volume.

Zhara pulled away from Claude and shook violently with suppressed laughter.

Claude wasn't sure how he felt about being used in such a way, but he figured he'd allow it. He was being pulled in several directions already, but at least Zhara understood the value of giving him an obvious upside.

"That should buy you some time," Zhara declared and swiped for the next video to begin.

Claude looked between Zhara and the sheets before putting his optimism to bed and turning back to the hologram. There would be time later. For now, he needed to learn what had Echelon so desperate.

"Right," he said to himself. "Work, then play."

Chapter 25

FIRAXIS STATION WAS a marvel of modern Sabien engineering. Assembled and deployed in less than half a standard year, the research facility was a testament to the ingenuity and efficiency of a people dedicated to progress. She was a beautiful blend of form and function, designed specifically to house and facilitate the exact kinds of scientific advancements that Eugene had spent his life dreaming of.

Yet, in the past weeks, he had lost perspective. He'd allowed the infantile meddling of the Crowns to get to him. Their floundering and infighting had clouded his vision, and he was ashamed of that. A few days of rest had helped him to reorient himself in a way that he knew would make him more productive.

Lenore had left earlier. She'd insisted he ease himself back into his normal routine, and he listened. She was right about a great many things, and while he didn't always see or even acknowledge that fact, in his bones, he still knew it.

The lift whirred softly as it carried him and two dozen other scientists and technicians from their homes on the residential strut to the isolated research labs. It was a relatively long distance to travel, but at least the ride was safe, spacious, and peaceful.

Eugene watched as the massive orb that was Jaiden III gave way to the light of its distant blue sun.

"The Black is cold and deadly, but it's damned beautiful," he thought as the light spilled across the billowing cloud cover of the planet.

The expanse of twinkling white fixtures beyond was what truly interested him, though. The unknown had a way of calling to curious souls, and Eugene counted himself among them.

When he'd heard the reports coming from the Vertoos' crew, it was as if the unknown had reached directly for him. Eugene had done everything he could to speak with the survivors of the doomed ship, and that hard work proved worthwhile.

What they had encountered, what they had lived through, was incredible and promising. Armed with those reports and the last known return signals from the Vertoos itself, Dr. Rickten Eugene battered down the walls of ignorant absurdity surrounding the Crown of Operations until Greyvor himself granted him permission to retrace the ship's path. It took over a year to find the unnamed world and even longer to find the creature described by the survivors. Now that part of the job was complete, and his work had begun in earnest.

The lift slowed and locked into place with an echoed clang. Eugene followed the masses as they made their exodus. He traded the cavernous space of the lift for the comparatively narrow corridors that led to the labs.

The chattering mob of intellectuals walking with him splintered off to their various projects, but his destination was beyond them. Their work was important, but to him, it seemed to only be background decoration. Nothing else on the station compared to his research.

If it worked, Talos would signal the end of the war. Better than that, it would secure a Sabien victory, and it would work. Eugene would see to that.

The concept was remarkable, although not without its share of problems to solve. Weaponizing an alien entity required a significant amount of study and understanding, but it was possible. The psionics program proved the original purpose of a creature could be changed if the wills and minds involved were dedicated enough to see it through. However, that program had only manipulated humans and not an unclassified organism, as he was attempting to do. Still, it gave him hope.

The first step was to truly understand the specimen, and that was time-consuming. At first, Eugene assumed he could reformat its structure into a malleable drone of sorts, but that idea had fallen away. The creature was incapable of such independent tasks. What it was better suited to was more controversial among his team, although no less appealing to him.

Talos 1 was the label he'd given the specimen, and he was very insistent that everyone who worked on the project used it at all times. Eugene was very protective of the creature. It was the only one of its kind as far as he knew, and it had been discovered entirely by accident.

The survivor reports were hyperbolic, to say the least. They described an all-consuming monster that stalked the remaining crew of the Vertoos from within, but the specimen he'd found was anything but that.

To his eye, it looked like a viscous silver mass that was essentially inert. It possessed several fascinating and potentially unnerving properties, but he saw no sign of the villain the reports detailed.

There had been some scattered rumors that the specimen displayed more autonomous properties when it wasn't being watched closely, however.

Eugene was never one to dismiss rumors wholesale, but these he found hard to place any stock in. The data simply didn't support them, at least not yet. If they turned out to be right, what he and his team were working on was unprecedented in all of Sabien history. No one had ever been able to fully document a new form of intelligent life in detail, and there was always glory in being first.

There was still the matter of the data, however. Proving Talos 1 was actually intelligent would be a feat. So, Eugene was unwilling to let himself be wholly convinced just yet, but he was inclined to believe at least a portion of the story the survivors told.

After all, they had found the creature nestled inside the decomposed remains of one of their crewmen. So, it was difficult to simply deny their claims outright. The more outlandish assertions still didn't match the information he'd found in his time with the creature. Regardless of his misgivings, Eugene had sent a formal request to allow volunteers to interface directly with Talos 1. So far, Crown Greyvor hadn't responded.

The crowd thinned as Eugene moved closer to his labs. He'd set up a buffer between his project and the other work done on the strut. It was a generally good idea to keep prying eyes away from the lab, especially since he had been directed to keep his team and their work quiet.

Crown Greyvor wanted Talos to produce weapons, and Eugene wasn't against working toward that end. Most of his contemporaries would have bristled under such expectations, but Eugene was more pragmatic. He knew that without the war, Operations would kill almost every project on Firaxis. He owed the ongoing conflict for making such risky ventures possible, and he would do as he was asked. Eugene had committed himself to do so, and he would not fail in his task, even if it was short-sighted.

How he would get from research to weapon production, he still didn't know, and that gap in his awareness allowed Kailen to be inserted into his territory. It was an oversight that the Crowns correctly sought to address, and he could understand that now.

After the flame-out of the psionics program, the Crowns weren't particularly interested in weapons that couldn't be directly controlled. Countless inquiries had been made into how and why that initiative had failed so spectacularly. It was widely held that there was a flaw in their selection and grooming process, but that left those in power standing on unstable ground where Talos was concerned.

That's why it didn't come as a surprise that Operations had been feeding his research to other offsite teams. It was a prudent path toward finding a way to manipulate, if not outright control, the specimen once it was adequately weaponized. What did surprise him was when they decided to slice his operating budget in half and give it to another team before installing them on the same station.

He had left himself open, and it was only fitting for an ambitious soul like Kailen to sneak a punch past his sloppy defense. She was a genius, after all. If the circumstances were different, he would be honored to have her on his team. Her work in genetics was unparalleled, but as it stood, she was his rival. If he wasn't careful, she would become his replacement, and Eugene could not allow that.

He walked alone, finally. The buffer offered him the opportunity to breathe, relax, and focus on the work ahead. Taking time away was a brilliant call, and Lenore needed to be rewarded for an idea he would never have considered.

• • • •

Lenore wasn't sure if she believed what she was seeing. The holographic feed was locked on the sealed basin and the metallic creature inside. She'd seen it in real life for the last two years, but never like this.

The silver liquid was moving. More than that, it was moving with purpose, forming tiny needle-like tendrils that it used to poke and prod its prison. The feed had no sound, but Lenore found her mind filling in the blanks with imagined scratches and thuds for each of the specimen's experimental maneuvers. There had been scratches on the interior of the basin when she arrived that morning, and they were the topic of much conversation among the research team, but none of them would believe what she was now seeing. Even Eugene would likely lose his composure if he were with her.

Lenore tore her eyes from the floating image and cast them suspiciously around the room. Her skin hadn't stopped crawling since she'd first seen Talos 1 oozing and shifting inside its basin. She knew she was being ridiculous, but she couldn't shake the feeling that something was watching her. She hated the symptoms of irrational fear, but she was in the grip of it, regardless.

The basin hadn't been checked for punctures because it never needed to be. It occurred to Lenore that she should put someone on that immediately. If the creature found some way to breach containment or even come close to it, they needed to know.

Drawing a shaky breath, Lenore pushed herself away from her seat and marched across the darkened room toward the small door at its end. With a wave of her hand, the door slid open and bathed the servers, consoles, and security apparatus in a blinding light.

When her eyes adjusted, she stepped into the largest of the Talos project labs. Four other researchers glided through the sterile, pristine space, busying themselves with checklists and other protocols designed to return the dormant area to life. They all knew their tasks, as did she, but this new objective took priority.

Her eyes locked on the vertical isolation chamber in the center of the room, and more specifically, the basin containing the creature that floated within. She remembered the fight she'd had with her husband about whether or not they needed an isolation chamber installed in the lab, but her argument had won out, as they often did. Now she was grateful Eugene was so malleable.

Lenore wasn't sure why, but watching the evidence of the creature's autonomy and intelligence left her feeling that Talos 1 radiated pure malice. Now, looking at it, that sensation only magnified.

"Lian," she called and watched as a tall, lithe, bearded man turned at the sound of his name.

She motioned for him to come over, and after he finished rebooting the central observation console, he obliged. Lian was the least experienced hand on the research team, but he was more than a match for all of them in eagerness and excitement for the project.

He towered over her but favored her with a genuine smile, asking, "Yes?"

"I need you to inspect Talos 1's containment basin," she declared, firing a nervous glance at the silver liquid.

"Are you sure?" Lian asked with a twist of confusion on his face.

"The scratches are concerning. Give the housing a thorough inspection and then check the isolation chamber," Lenore stated, making the order clear without being overt about it.

Lian straightened, nodded, then moved toward the cylindrical cell. Lenore watched with a pang of concern and a little guilt for having tasked someone else with what she was now too afraid to do herself.

"Entry protocol enabled. Please stand clear," an automated voice called out.

Familiar alerts sounded, and the white lighting emanating from the floor and ceiling panels switched to a pale yellow before the entry door slid open. Lenore's attention locked on the well-rested project lead as he almost floated back into his natural element.

Eugene nodded his acknowledgments to those who greeted him, but his movement toward his nervously grinning wife was not arrested. She knew he would be able to read her face instantly, but the ruse wasn't meant for him. She didn't want to alarm the rest of the team before Eugene had a chance to witness her discovery.

"What's wrong?" he asked in a soft, low voice, clearly understanding the situation.

"There's something you need to see," Lenore said and led him back to the server room.

. . . .

Eugene watched as Talos 1 probed its enclosure repeatedly. It found no weakness that he could see, but he didn't expect that it would.

"This is unbelievable," he declared with a wide smile.

Lenore stood behind him, trying to hug the cold, uneasy feeling out of herself and failing.

"You always wondered if it was intelligent," she said.

"I know, but this is actual proof," Eugene said breathlessly. "This will send us down a whole new path."

Lenore cringed at his excitement. She realized he would see endless new potential for the project, but Eugene always had issues detecting the dangers of his obsessions until it was too late.

"I think we need to form new and more stringent security protocols. We didn't exactly plan for it to be smart enough to solve problems," Lenore offered a little more forcefully than she would have liked.

Eugene turned to her and tried to meet her eyes. Lenore looked away and clenched her jaw, pointedly avoiding his gaze.

"You're scared," Eugene stated, though, to him, it felt more like a question.

He'd known her for years, and in most of that time, she was a fearless confidant and a formidable scientist. Rarely did she show her fear openly, a fact that made him feel only slightly better about not recognizing it when he'd first come into the lab. The look on her face and gentle tremor in the wide eyes she'd cast upon him were clear signs that he had simply failed to interpret until now.

"Aren't you?" Lenore snapped.

Eugene didn't respond. Her reaction to this new revelation was reasonable, if uncharacteristic. She had known about the reports, just as he had. There was no doubt the creature was truly alien, but somehow this footage had pushed her to an edge he hadn't foreseen. Now, shivering in front of him, his wife and most trusted ally seemed very near to tumbling over it.

"Maybe I would be if I thought for a second even one of those reports had been written by someone rational. You saw the holo-feeds.

Every crewman they recovered was traumatically deranged," Eugene said confidently.

Lenore's face scrunched as his words hit home, but none of the anxiety she carried in her posture faded. "Maybe they had a reason to be. They were terrified and we should be too."

Eugene shook away the near panic in her voice. "If you put any living thing in a box, it will try to find a way out. This only proves intellect, not intent," he said, motioning toward the hovering image.

He watched as his words met with the part of her that already knew them to be true, and she finally began to relax. Lenore had been shaken, and that was fine. He had been shaken a few times in their relationship as well. It was their job to bring each other back to baseline when that happened, and he was grateful he had been here to do just that for her.

• • • •

Lian slipped the sensor unit over his hand until it came to rest snugly in his palm. The strap held it tight, effectively attaching the device to him. He imagined, for just a second, that it was like having a third eye in the palm of his hand, then blinked that foolishness out of his mind. He had a job to do, and the scanner was just a tool to help him do it. With a squeeze, he activated the device and felt the tiny vibrations of the sensor powering up.

The transparent metal that comprised the basin and half a dozen other things around the station was dense and sturdy, but not impenetrable. However, it took an immense amount of force to tear through it. Lian doubted Talos 1 was capable of generating that much force. It was just a semi-liquid lifeform, after all. If bones and muscles couldn't generate the power required to dent the stuff, there was no way that a few scratches would be able to do it.

Lian nodded to the two technicians watching him closely and waited for them to do the same. Nieran wore a deeply concerned look on her heart-shaped face. Jalid just smiled. It wasn't genuine, but Lian chose to ignore the distinct better-you-than-me feeling he got when he met the man's light blue eyes.

He focused his attention back on the basin and placed the scanner a little more than an inch from its surface. The vibrations in his palm strengthened as the inaudible sound reached into and through the metal. The silver creature on the other side of the container rippled in time with vibrations. It was almost hypnotic to watch the shimmering alien dance to the same rhythm that shook its way up Lian's arm. He watched as his own reflection in it seemed to grow more detailed with each passing second.

"Lian, model construction is at forty-eight percent, but we're getting some strange readings on Talos 1 itself," Nieran's voice called over the broadcast panels above him.

"I bet," Lian said as he pulled his attention away from the fascinating little alien.

He activated the onboard readout on the scanner and watched as a small holographic image blinked to life along the back of his hand. The readout showed the depth and approximate age of each blemish he scanned. To his disappointment, he couldn't get any readings on the creature from here, which was what he was most concerned about. He wanted to know everything about their guest, but that wasn't what Lenore had asked him to do.

His job was to inspect the container, not Talos 1. There were billions of credits' worth of equipment designed to do that and from safer locations than where he now stood. Putting his mind back on task, Lian worked his way down the basin. He slid his hand beneath the hovering object and froze.

The scratches he could see didn't seem all that serious. They were superficial, and as Lian now realized, entirely for show. Beneath the basin, where no feed could display and no eye had seen, there was a hole large enough to fit a man's fist.

Inside, the creature pulsed, holding every torn piece of debris it had created. Lian touched the soft cold surface of Talos 1, but before he could jerk his hand away, thin tendrils ensnared his fingers and held him in place. A thick spike of panic shredded its way through Lian's mind as the creature began to ooze from its cell on down his fingers.

"Get out of there!" Nieran's voice shouted urgently, but Lian didn't move.

An intense tingling sensation ran along his palm as the thing slinked its way around the back of his hand. It moved with purpose, slithering up past his wrist and finally into view.

The shimmering silver liquid streamed off his hand in a single thick tendril that reached back to the hole it had dripped from. Lian's eyes flicked back and forth between the advancing creature and the tear that showed in the steadily emptying basin.

"Seal the chamber!" a voice shouted, but it seemed a million miles away.

Lian heard almost nothing as the silver sent pulses of itself up the connecting tendril and onto his arm. When at last he found his voice, the lab tech screamed and flailed his arm violently, but to no avail.

The silver was undeterred. Free from its cage, the alien worked its way past his bicep. A new blade-like tendril jutted from it and sliced a hole in Lian's protective suit before slithering out of sight. In less than a second, a heavy tentacle slithered across the back of his neck, as the creature moved across his bare skin.

Lian slammed himself back against the transparent barrier as Talos 1 gathered along his spine. The sensation reminded him of a low-intensity electric shock if it could be streamed through a block of solid ice. Nothing about it was wholly unpleasant, yet it made his every hair stand on end. It was as if his cells were reminded of a truth that he'd been fortunate never to have known.

Before the pain began and the creature's invasion drove him into the endless dark, Lian's mind and lips formed a single thought.

"Predator," he said, realizing for the first and last time in his life, that he was simply prey.

• • • •

Containment alarms blared through the data processing room. The pulsing red lights worked as intended, stripping any sense of normalcy from the air.

Eugene leaped from his seat and rushed to the door with Lenore directly behind him, but it didn't slide open as usual.

Security protocols locked down all portals into and out of compromised locations in an effort to save the station. He knew this well, just like he knew his access code would override some of the less stringent parameters. But the stab of weaponized adrenaline in his brain buffered that knowledge. In a moment of pure instinct, Eugene turned to his near panic-stricken wife and pulled her into a one-armed hug. He breathed in the soft, light scent of her loyur petal shampoo and kissed her just below her hairline, as he often did.

"I need you to stay in here," he said in a gentle but firm voice.

Lenore's gaze bored into him, but she didn't speak. Her lips pursed as her mind formed a valid argument against Eugene's command, but after a second's hesitation, she simply nodded and stepped back from him.

"I'll get this under control. Then I'm coming back for you," Eugene said definitively, keeping his eyes locked on hers.

"Go," she said in a voice so soft that Eugene half thought she'd only mouthed it.

It was his turn to nod in heavy silence. Then he turned to the thick metal door and cleared his throat.

"Auxiliary entrance override," he boomed in a loud, clear voice.

The light above the door changed from its harsh red to orange as it awaited his confirmation code.

Eugene took a deep breath and put all the horrendous images his mind was conjuring to the side. He was scared, but they had robust containment strategies in place. The creature wasn't going to get out. He'd seen to that, but something had clearly gone wrong. Something big.

"Confirmation code: E. Rickten 10-18-R," he declared and watched the door's light flicker before turning a brilliant cyan.

The locks disengaged with a deep thump as bolts buried within the walls receded, allowing the door to slide open. The lab wasn't quite the picture of chaos he had expected, but it was awash in confusion and disorder. The technicians and scientists were frazzled and anxious, with many well on their way toward a total breakdown.

There were fourteen eyes in the room, not counting his own, and all but two of them were locked on the isolation chamber. The last pair roamed hungrily across every person in turn. Eugene glanced over his shoulder and gave Lenore what he hoped was a confident smile before he stepped through the door. It slid shut behind him with a thump muffled by the mechanical wail of the alarm.

A tall, lanky man stood hunched in the cylindrical chamber at the lab's center. He turned to face Eugene with slow, tentative movements. The face was empty of expression, muscles slack and almost lifeless, though the eyes were anything but.

"You leader, yes?" the man said in a voice so unnatural it curled the hair on the back of Eugene's neck.

Summoning his courage, Eugene tore his eyes away from the inhuman stare and scanned the chamber. At its core, the basin was empty. Without the creature to obscure them, the torn strips of metal now hovered just inside the gravity field. They were as plain to see as Eugene's stupidity.

He had assumed Talos 1 was, at best, just an animal. It was a careless assumption, but like usual, his arrogance and self-importance blinded him. Eugene hadn't considered the alternative. Now it stared back at him, its face cold, its eyes unblinking.

The creature was not just intelligent, it was brilliant. That brilliance had cost a man his life. While Eugene had been resting, Talos 1 was planning its escape, and it had planned well. Only a system of redundant countermeasures kept it from running free within the lab, if not the station.

Despite the horror of his oversight, Eugene couldn't help but be impressed. Though, he was distinctly less excited about Talos 1's intelligence than he had been a few moments ago.

"Talos 1?" Eugene asked.

The answer was obvious, but confirmation always cleared potential confusion. If he knew his wife at all, she would have turned the room's surveillance gear on the man in the chamber. It was precisely what he would do in her place, what any self-respecting lover of the sciences would do.

"What means Talos?" the creature in the man asked with naked curiosity.

Eugene urged himself forward against every instinct screaming for him to retreat. His focus drowned out every other person and sound in the room. The isolation chamber appeared to be completely intact, but without a proper examination that was just another dangerous assumption. So, Eugene began circling the cylinder, inspecting it as he spoke.

"Talos 1 is your designation," he said as calmly as he could manage. "Your name."

The creature laughed, and even though the sound was garbled and broken, it was immediately apparent there was no humor in it. The sound of the thing was off-putting, to say the least, but Eugene was at a loss for exactly why. At its core, the sound was very human, if much more fragmented and discordant.

"No," it said coldly. "I name me."

Eugene blinked at the statement. It was as clear a declaration of self-actualization as he'd ever heard. He was in no way prepared to admit that he addressed an equal consciousness, but it was clearly close.

"Why?" it asked next, but gave no elaboration.

Eugene stalled long enough to complete his circuit around the chamber and pull the creature's attention away from the server room door.

"That's the question, isn't it?" Eugene asked in return. "We all want that answer."

"Why I here?" it clarified.

"You're here so we can study you," Eugene said calmly. "You're here to answer some of our questions about the universe."

"To serve," it said as the muscles in the face twitched into an expression that was almost disgust. "Be tool."

Eugene wasn't sure how to respond to that. It was true, but saying so wouldn't land well. If it could hear through both the chamber and the basin, that would be impressive, but unlikely.

"Who told you that?" Eugene finally asked.

The face twitched again, and again it gave Eugene the uneasy feeling as the skin moved like little more than loose cloth. Only this time, it mimicked a smile.

"The meat... remembers," it said and watched his reaction closely.

Eugene's mind blasted through all the things Lian might have known about the project. It wasn't much compared to someone like himself, Lenore, or even Nieran, but it was enough.

Override codes were hard to come by. Only Eugene and Lenore had them, so for the moment, everything was safely locked down. The walls of the isolation chamber were four times the thickness of the basin, and the door rose out of the floor as the entire cylinder lowered and raised on command. It wouldn't be escaping from there without giving a year's worth of advance notice.

In the meantime, the team was going to have to accept what had happened and move on. Lian was a good technician and, Eugene assumed, a decent man. However, he was gone now. His loss had gained the project five days or so to gather what information they could before his body died of dehydration.

He turned to the others in the lab. They had put as much space between themselves and the cylinder as possible, each wearing a different face of abject horror. Eugene pitied them. No one had signed up for this. He had assumed human contact with the creature would be a part of the process sooner or later. But not for some time, and not in his lab. That part of the job had been offloaded to Kailen, although she rode him hard about it.

She assumed the stories were true and that the creature was a parasite of some kind. Her research moved in that direction, and as much as Eugene hated to admit it, she was right to have done so. He wasn't sure if she had made any real strides, but he was going to have to get caught up on her work, and fast.

"We're lifting the lockdown," Eugene said confidently. "The creature is still contained. Lian's situation is unfortunate. He deserved better, but he has provided us an opportunity and a rigid timeline."

The faces of his staff weren't all sympathetic, and he knew they wouldn't be. He didn't need them to like him right now. He needed them to feel something besides fear, and if anger or indignation was what it took to shake them free, so be it.

"We need to get on this quickly and efficiently," he continued. "The human body can only survive so long without food and water, and I don't intend to open that chamber for any reason.

"Run any and every test you're capable of while we have this time. I want to know everything possible.

"Find out what that thing has done to Lian and if it's reversible. We're the only people who can."

Nieran was the first to come around. She was reliable and experienced, but she was as unprepared for this as everyone else. Still, she knew how to cope with tragic surprises, or so her record had shown.

"You heard the man, get to work," she barked. "I want full biometric scans in an hour, weight and mass adjustment even sooner."

The lab crew stirred slowly but gathered speed and urgency with every step. Eugene took a deep breath and let his shoulders relax for the first time since the crisis started. It hadn't been long, and the alarms were still blaring, but the worst was over.

"You fail, you all fail," the creature wearing Lian said with a broken grin.

"We'll see about that," Eugene stated without looking back at the creature.

· · · ·

Eugene's head hurt. He'd pored over dozens of test results, and while they gave him a decent understanding of what was happening to Lian physically, they didn't tell him why.

Talos 1 was eating him alive, which was apparent just by looking at him, but it wasn't measurable by any normal means. It coated every neuron in the man's body, and it had seemingly evolved somewhat. When Eugene had first confronted the thing, it could barely form a sentence. Now it was fully capable of sharing its low opinion of him and his team with clarity and precision.

The same went for its manipulation of Lian's body. It was learning as much about what made humans work as they wished they were learning about it, but time was running out. The telltale signs of cellular shutdown were apparent in Lian's scans. His body was dying, and short of opening the chamber to slip food and water inside, there was nothing Eugene could do about it.

Watching a teammate slowly wither and die was taking its toll on everyone. Nieran was still standing strong, but Lenore was in shambles. He had removed her from duty after the second day when he found her apologizing to Lian profusely. He was aware that she had sent him inside the chamber to do the viability scan, but that didn't make what happened her fault. There was only one entity to blame for this, and it now wore Lian's his skin and bones.

None of the tests seemed to point to anything Eugene could use as a weakness. They had tested several things against the creature when it was still in liquid form, and nothing had adversely affected it. Eugene assumed that the host would be its weak point, but there was no way to test that theory without setting it loose.

"Damn it," Eugene shouted, and slashed through the holographic reports violently.

They flickered and danced before reconstituting as if mocking his frustration. If he were in a better mood, he might have found it a little funny, but he wasn't. The latest progress update had been sent to Operations, and he was expecting to have direct interference at any moment. If he could show movement, he would be more than capable of warding off such a thing, but he was drowning in failure.

"Contact Kailen Saulk," he growled.

The wall of holographic glyphs blinked away in favor of a single image that declared, "Awaiting feed."

Lenore shuffled through the shadows behind him and ran her fingers through his hair. She had become something of a transient figure in his life, and he wasn't very fond of that. He missed his headstrong wife, his confidant, and his most admired rival. What she was now was only a shell of the woman he loved, though he understood why.

Guilt was a powerful force. It motivated as many people as it left hollow and rudderless. Presently, Lenore was one of the latter, but he had hope that, in time, she would grow into the former. So, he kept his frustrations to himself and gave her the time she needed to find her own way there. It was all he could think to do.

"Kailen, huh?" she said with a croak in her voice that reminded him how long it had been since she'd last spoke to him.

Eugene eased back into her touch and let as much of his tensions bleed away as he was able.

"I need a new outlook on this," he said absently. "I'm at the end of my line, and maybe she knows something I don't."

"Maybe," Lenore said softly. "Are you going to pull her all the way in?"

"I'm thinking about it, but this is as much your project as it is mine," Eugene answered slowly, willing his eyelids to lift so he could look up at her.

She was as beautiful as ever, only now she possessed a haunting, ghost-like quality. Loose hair masked part of her face and she did nothing to clear it away. She spent most of her time in robes which now billowed around her as she swayed slightly. He could tell she was thinking over his words, but the blank expression she wore was gave nothing away. Eugene wanted her to either accept his plan or challenge it, but he couldn't tell if she would do either.

"Bring her in," Lenore said without conviction. "Show her what happened to Lian. Maybe her cloning background can provide us an advantage on the cellular breakdown you're seeing."

Eugene blinked up at her, but when he tried to share a smile, she simply walked away from him. At her absence, he felt every ounce of weight that had left him crash back down on his shoulders.

She wasn't ready to come back to him yet, but she was closer than she had been the day before. Her idea was sound. She was coming at things from a different perspective. Lenore still imagined Lian could be saved somehow, but Eugene didn't share her optimism.

He was hoping Kailen could help him find some way of hurting the damned thing so they could exert some level of control over it. If she managed to help repress cellular breakdown, that would be welcome, too. However, his top priority was putting the fear of man into the creature, not only for the project's future success but also for his own mental well-being.

• • • •

Kailen's labs were only two levels beneath his own, but given the decor, it seemed like it was on a different station.

The magnitude of superfluous items was interesting to look at but pointless to any sort of research. Artful depictions of the foamy, crimson seas of Orlessu hung on the walls. Potted plants sat near every ornately carved bench, and light music wafted over everything from the broadcast panels above.

Eugene felt like he was stepping into a therapist's office instead of a place that pursued actual scientific advancements. He assumed this was some sort of meeting room. It had that feel. The seats looked comfortable and inviting, though Eugene refrained from testing them. He wasn't here to be pampered. He was here to bury a rivalry he alone had started.

The door on the far side of the room opened and in walked Dr. Kailen Saulk. She was a tall woman with blonde hair and eyes, so blue they had to have been altered. She wore a flattering wine-colored dress that shimmered when she walked, in lieu of more traditional work attire, and favored him with a smile that seemed somehow aggressive despite its appearance.

"I was surprised when you asked for a meeting, Rickten," she said with a voice that sounded both sweet and poisonous.

Eugene cleared his throat before venturing a response.

"I would be lying if I said it was entirely my idea," he said calmly. "Lenore thinks highly of you and your work."

"And yet she isn't here," Kailen said and swept her way toward him, like one of the waves depicted in the paintings nearby.

"She's not feeling well," Eugene said, unnerved by every deliberate movement the woman made.

She stopped a reasonable distance from him and lowered herself onto one of the benches demurely. Her eye contact never broke as she settled into her seat.

Kailen was as elegant as she was intelligent. She had the grace and entrancing nature of a Grauvian winged spider and was likely twice as deadly. Everything she did was meant to make him uncomfortable, and it worked perfectly.

"Poor dear," Kailen said. "Send her my regards."

"I'd rather send her your opinion of the situation," Eugene said, brute-forcing the conversation back on track.

Kailen fixed him with an icy stare but let the sting of the comment pass.

"As I see it, the cellular degradation is irreversible. Also, given that the creature has now coated the poor man's entire brain, there's no telling how bad it's become there," she began. "The Vertoos' reports said it was capable of possessing people, but having the actual data of such a thing is..."

Kailen trailed off. Eugene couldn't tell if she had lost herself in some mental euphoria or if she was just pausing for dramatic effect, so he elected to stay silent.

The fact she had even agreed to this meeting was an unexpected kindness, especially since his data was already in her hands. He couldn't believe she was attempting to assist him now, given his treatment of both her and her team. Then again, she needed this project to stay afloat, perhaps even more than he did.

"I'd say your man is gone, and he isn't coming back," Kailen said finally. "Personally, I'd vent the air in the chamber and get Talos 1 back into its natural form as soon as possible."

"The thought crossed my mind," Eugene shared reluctantly. "But it moves autonomously. If even a millimeter of the seal is loose, we could be making a bigger problem for ourselves."

Kailen adjusted herself in her seat. Eugene watched as her manicured nails scratched lightly at her neck and realized the idea of the creature loose in the station bothered her as much as it did him.

"We? Ourselves? It sounds like you're assuming the sale a little early, Rickten," she almost growled.

"I'm assuming nothing. If Talos gets out of our control, the project is over, and we will never work in this field again," Eugene declared gruffly. "Greyvor won't be granting you a third chance."

Eugene knew the added spite wasn't necessary. If anything, it was counterproductive, but he couldn't help himself. He didn't like this woman, and he never would. He just needed her input, and even that was eating him up inside. Throwing a verbal jab here and there was to be expected.

"This is not how you ask for a woman's help. I expected Lenore to have trained you better," Kailen said with a disarming smirk.

She rose with all the veiled menace and grace of a stalking linxor before motioning for Eugene to follow her.

"I suppose that's enough small talk for now. You're here for a new perspective, and I would be remiss if I turned you away unsatisfied," Kailen said as she approached the far door.

Eugene was hesitant to follow. He remembered stories of rivals eliminating each other in the early days of the war. Projects were as valuable as pure deritrium in those days, and people did all manner of things to get and keep them.

It was a part of Sabien history that no one was particularly proud of. Many, like Eugene, thought the loss of so many brilliant minds over such trivial matters was one of the primary reasons the war hadn't ended centuries ago.

"Tell me you're not scared, doctor," Kailen called with a laugh that sounded to his ears like the gentle ringing of bells.

He forced himself to put one foot in front of the other and cross the room until he stood beside her. Eugene made sure to keep more than an arm's length between them, but the sweet smell of her perfume invaded the space he'd so carefully crafted. Everything about this woman seemed tailor-made to pull him in, to pull anyone in, but that only set his teeth on edge. It was an act. It had to be.

Kailen Saulk was known to be ruthless, efficient, and dangerous. She wasn't a physical threat, or at least she hadn't shown herself to be, yet.

However, she had destroyed the public faces of over a dozen people when the Psionics program died. It was her baby, and it was widely believed that she was supposed to take the blame for its failure.

That didn't exactly happen. She failed the Council of Crowns, and that wasn't going to go away, but she had not been banished from upper circles and stripped of her high cauling as was typical. Instead, Kailen was assigned to flagging shadow projects. In that role, she had pulled a few back from the brink. Her presence on Firaxis pointed to an attempt to do the same here.

"We began work based on the physiological specifications you so generously denied us. Luckily, I'm an acquaintance of Crown Greyvor, and he passed your transmissions on to me," Kailen said as the door slid open.

Eugene chanced a look at her and saw her wearing a warm smile that did not meet her cold blue eyes.

"I both appreciate and understand why you would be so protective of your project, but I don't forgive your foolishness," she hissed before her pleasant facade fell back into place.

"We have most of this level to ourselves," she said as she led Eugene into the type of laboratory spaces he was more comfortable with.

"What are your theories on implementation? We haven't discussed it," Eugene said, unable to tamp down his curiosity.

"Well, at first, we had nothing to go on except the survivors' reports, so we started there," she said, fixing him with a pointed glare. "We worked on possession and what we would need to facilitate and eliminate that.

"We were shooting in the dark until we started getting your reports on the creature's make-up and, most importantly, its diet."

Eugene recognized the large, rotating, mechanical pod to his left, but he almost didn't believe his eyes.

"How did you get access to a generation pod?" he asked in awe. "How did you get it into the labs without anyone knowing?"

Kailen crossed her arms and smirked.

"Plenty of people knew, just not you," she stated plainly. "We were going to have to deposit the creature into a host body eventually. I would have preferred that we give it a clone as opposed to a person, but that ship's already out of the dock, isn't it?"

Eugene ignored the jab. He had messed up and her pointing that out in her sickly-sweet way wasn't half as bad as his own sleepless nights.

"Have you produced any viable specimens?" Eugene chose to ask instead.

Kailen led him past the pod and into another section of the oversized lab. Her project was clearly better staffed and better funded than his own. Ordinarily, that would have made him jealous, but what she was doing here seemed to be more than just work for Talos.

"I have one. She's unique, however, and not for feeding to your pet monster," Kailen said without looking at him. "She's our control. I need to keep her here for study, at least until she reaches maturity."

"We don't have that kind of time," Eugene said. "If you birthed her here, she can't be more than a few months old. Talos 1 needs to be dealt with now."

"Calm yourself, Rickten. You'll have a stroke, and I don't want your drool on my floors," Kailen retorted, slowing to a stop outside of a set of segmented door panels.

Eugene fell in beside her and did his best to read her face as the doors chirped their proximity warning. There was very little there except pride and perhaps a hint of disdain.

"We are testing a few new things on this one. The urgency of your problem creates new issues for us as well, not to mention the external factors," Kailen continued. "A-274 is a special case. So far, she is working out perfectly. Even the growth accelerator we've devised is functioning well, aside from us having to repeatedly administer it."

"Growth accelerator? How?" he asked.

A wide smile broke out across Kailen's face as she basked in his dumbfounded surprise.

"Trade secret. I'm sure you understand," she said and presented her palm to the metal of the door.

It shifted and slid apart into three pieces that reminded Eugene of jagged gray teeth before they disappeared from sight.

"Shall we?" Kaitlen said and motioned for Eugene to enter ahead of her.

The room inside was dark, aside from a few weak pools of blue light cast from overhead. Eugene's eye struggled to adjust to the sharp change. What he could see in the space didn't make much sense.

The carpeted floor seemed more at home in a dormitory than a holding cell. What looked like a table for a small child rested in the room's center and against the far wall was a small bed whose white coverings glowed under the lights.

"A-2," Kailen said in a singsong voice. "We have a new visitor. Come, say hello."

A balloon of pressure expanded inside Eugene's mind with Kailen's announcement. It skipped past, disorienting and uncomfortable, jumping directly to excruciating. If he could have, Eugene would have ripped his own skull in half to relieve it, but he only managed to crumple to his knees and grunt.

"Gently now, sweetness. He's a friendly," Kailen cooed as she watched Eugene writhe helplessly beside her. "Theoretically, anyway."

To Eugene she said, "Forgive her. She's younger than she looks. We're still working with her on her abilities, and her speech."

Eugene only grunted as the pressure in his head eased, allowing him to regain control of himself. It took him a while to work his way back to his feet, and even longer to notice the little blonde girl with shadows for eyes hiding behind the bed.

Kailen smiled at the child and there was a hint of genuine warmth in the gesture this time.

"A-2, this is Doctor..."

"Euggy," the child said in a soft but definitive voice.

"Rickten, meet A-274, the future of your project," Kailen said with a haughty smirk.

• • • •

Claude rolled his seat back to the far wall. He rubbed at his forehead furiously for a moment before he launched from the chair and stormed through the holographic display of a child's bedroom.

"This can't be right," he said to himself before turning to Zhara. "Are you sure this is working like it's supposed to?"

Zhara stared back at him with sympathetic eyes and nodded slowly.

Claude heard himself hiss at the implications of what he'd seen, and what he knew would come next.

"We have to tell her," he said in a pained voice. "It's going to break her heart."

"Maybe not," Zhara said as she clutched her pillow tight. "It's not like she doesn't have a family. We love her as much as any parent would."

"More than some," Claude said softly.

Zhara didn't hear what he said, and he was grateful. It was a slip of the tongue that would have opened doors he preferred to leave closed.

"We should tell her now," Claude said, mustering his courage. "If she reads it off us, it will look like we're trying to hide it from her."

Zhara nodded again. She'd come to all these conclusions the previous night, plus one more that she wasn't ready to share with Claude just yet. As confident as she was that he would reach the same place, bringing Vision up to speed was, rightly, his priority.

"Do you want me to go with you?" she asked, fighting a sting of shame for hoping he didn't.

Claude took a moment to think before shaking the idea away.

"No. It should be me," he said with a deep, dread-filled sigh.

"Okay," was all Zhara could get through the tightening sensation in her throat as Claude stepped out of the room.

• • • •

Eavesdropping was easy when you weren't limited by the ranges of sound. For Vision, it came naturally, but there were always risks involved. Occasionally, she discovered information she wished had remained hidden. Her real name was just such a double-edged blade.

After abandoning the living room in hopes of getting some air and some space, she now sat on the balcony floor, doing her best not to cry. She'd shed too many tears, and it was time she learned how to handle herself without becoming one of the overly emotional people she so often looked down on.

Sadly, that lesson was still beyond her. Her sadness streamed down her cheeks as fast and as hot as the lightning on the horizon. Neither cared about the marks they left on what lay beneath.

"V?" Claude called from inside, but she didn't answer.

It didn't occur to her that Claude might be as affected by the revelation as she was. As deep as she was in her own despair, his desire to comfort her didn't register. Despite all the emotions and thoughts around her, only one thing echoed through her mind. She wasn't a real person.

In all the wild dreams she'd had about her lost family, Vision never imagined that it simply didn't exist. She had envisioned parents both living and dead, aunts, uncles, even grandparents and siblings, all in different orders and wildly varied configurations, but never this. Yet it explained so much. There were always questions. Where did her abilities come from? How could a child have them in the first place? Who would have a child in a place like Firaxis?

Even Zhara had puzzled over how her ocular nerves were so thoroughly destroyed at the cellular level. Now so many of those answers were laid bare, and they were as simple as they were mortifying. She was just made that way.

The gathering gloom had consumed so much of her mind that when Claude stepped onto the balcony and spotted her against the wall, she barely knew he was there.

"Found you," he said in a low, steady voice.

"I wasn't lost," Vision said, desperately trying to wipe away her tears. "Turns out I never was."

Claude eased himself to the floor beside her, making sure to press his shoulder against hers. In the past, he had discovered that physical contact seemed to help Vision in tough times. He didn't understand it nor did he get why she typically fought to keep her distance. It was just the way she was.

"Look, this doesn't mean anything," he stated, as if he were some sort of authority. "Where you come from is not important."

"The whole universe says different," Vision groaned and hugged her knees tighter. "They fought about it for centuries."

"And yet two Sabiens and a Neut are sitting here at the core of the Beita Systems," Claude said and gave Vision a nudge.

He ignored the venomous expression on her face at the gesture and continued.

"Look, I'm not the smartest man out there–"

Vision snorted. "You got that right."

Claude sighed and admitted, at least to himself, that he'd walked into that insult before returning to his statement.

"But I know a few things," he said. "People are ever-changing beings. We begin life as one thing, but we don't stay that way for long. Pretty soon, we're running everywhere trying to find out where we fit, and almost none of us ever do."

Claude felt Vision's weight as she leaned into him, but he chose not to acknowledge it just yet.

Instead, he did his best to stay still and just be there with her in the moment.

After a few seconds' hesitation, he said, "We usually find that there's no such thing as a place to belong outside of ourselves. The family we're born to or not doesn't matter as much as the family we choose to carry with us along the way. Sure, they can sometimes be the same thing, but that's not often the case.

"We are wild, unpredictable creatures in a wilder and even more unpredictable universe, and the only way I've ever been able to make any sense of anything is to focus on the people I care about. Everything else is just everything else."

Vision watched the image of him caught in her sensors, and for the first time, perhaps ever, she understood what they were.

She had always seen herself as his partner and his equal, but she wasn't either of those things. In a great many ways, she was beyond him, except she didn't really want to be. She wanted to be beside him, not in front of him, and through some happy accident, she actually was.

Firaxis had been a tomb of horror and death, but for those who had escaped it with their lives, it had also been something more. To Vision, that cold, empty place had actually provided the one thing she wanted more than anything else. If it wasn't just a crater somewhere under the swirling gases of Jaiden III, she might have thanked the monstrous station, though that was maybe a step too far.

"Look, I'm just saying, if you don't mind too much, I know a farmer turned soldier that's looking for a psionic clone turned daughter," Claude said with a cheeky grin on his face.

Vision scowled at him, but her heart wasn't in it. She wasn't ready to give up her feeling of self-loathing just yet, but she did find the offer very tempting.

"You're ridiculous, you know that?" Vision said with a smile in her voice. "I mean, that was terrible."

"Oh, I know," he said and put his arm around her. "You tell me that all the time."

Vision stiffened at his touch before she let herself melt into him. Finding out she was a clone was a shock, but already she'd been a daughter for far longer. She just wished they'd found the proper term sooner. It might have made it much easier to guilt her way onto more jobs.

"Do you think they'll come after me?" Vision asked after a moment. "When they find out..."

"I have no idea," Claude said, clipping her words off before they could be made real. "I haven't made it all the way through the drives yet."

"You think there's more?"

"There's always more, V. I'm just not used to having access to it."

Chapter 26

BERTRAND HAD KNOWN this comm would arrive from the moment Eugene took his dive in the Dead Zone. To be honest, he was surprised it hadn't come sooner. His masters were used to timely updates and prompt successes. This mission had turned out to be anything but.

The setback in the Old City and the delay in hiring DiSilva put a crimp in what appeared to be a perfectly straightforward projection. That was to say nothing about the Sabien scientist's change of heart. Everything had gone about as wrong as it could go, so Bertrand was more than a little apprehensive about the reception he'd get once the decryption resolved.

He'd gotten the heads-up on the command deck and moved as swiftly as he could back to his quarters to take the tongue-lashing he was bound to receive in peace. Those in high command had been immersed in the luxuries afforded by the state for so long they had all but forgotten how real missions actually worked. Improbable results were expected as if the billions of differing factors holding sway over each operation's fate didn't exist.

"No obstacles, only challenges," he said to himself, and let a humorless chuckle escape.

It was the mantra of the Beita Systems in many regards, and it had served them well. The "no obstacles" mindset helped people across hundreds of worlds face many of the "challenges" arrayed against them on a daily basis.

Unlike their enemy, the worlds on the Beitan side of the Neutral Territories needed to be conquered. Each one had been forged into a hospitable place for humans to live. It was a trying and often joyless process, but once accomplished, a rewarding one. Planets like Minerva Prime yielded great bounties of endless resources once mastered. The energy from this one world powered dozens more. In that way, every sacrifice made to tame it was made worthwhile in time.

Each of the Beita System worlds provided something of importance, and all were required to hold the union together. The building and maintenance of that accord made its people sturdy, self-reliant, practical and, in Bertrand's view, short-sighted. They drew harsh lines and lacked the empathy or desire to understand those who didn't clearly fit within them. It tended to make the universe colder than it needed to be.

Bertrand had fought beside former Sabiens long enough to understand that they had a different problem. There was a divide in them that threatened their very existence. Imperium worlds were softer, more accommodating. That led to a desire to secure and maintain those comforts at all costs.

That wasn't a bad thing in itself, but the upper classes had hammered their governing bodies into a rigid caste system that allowed very little mobility. Farmers were meant to give birth to farmers. Crowns gave birth to future Crowns, and in the short term, it worked. However, the odds were getting long against its continued functionality, and the war had only increased the pressure.

Bertrand didn't trust the Sabiens, and he didn't trust the truce. There were people who did, and he knew they had very valid reasons. He just couldn't unsee the threat the Imperium represented. No truce would put an end to that, not permanently. Only a Beitan victory could secure true peace, and he hoped this mission, more than any other, would put them on the path to ensuring that once and for all.

The flicker and reconfiguration of his holographic display snapped him back to the challenge at hand. He watched as a bald and bearded man he knew all too well materialized above his desk and peered down at him.

"Ah, Kerrid," the man said cheerfully.

Bertrand nodded to the holographic figure but kept his face as neutral as possible.

"Admiral Raud," he replied.

The admiral was dressed in what appeared to be civilian garb which seemed odd. Bertrand had served under Raud for the better part of his career as an officer, and in that time, he could have counted on one hand the number of times he had seen the man out of uniform.

"Drop the formalities," Raud said, waving off Bertrand's greeting. "You haven't been in the service for years, and the war is over."

Bertrand straightened at the words.

"I think we both know that's not true," he stated flatly. "If it were over, I wouldn't be here."

The admiral cracked a knowing smile that didn't quite reach his measuring eyes.

"That's what I like about you, Kerrid. You always say what everyone else is too afraid to even think."

"I take it this isn't a social call," Bertrand said, putting the conversation back on track.

Raud nodded. The movement was so slight that the hologram barely registered it.

"Echelon is in the air about your late report," he declared in a dismissive tone. "They have no patience, as always."

"I have nothing new to report, sir. My second attempt to acquire the drives is still ongoing," Bertrand said and watched as the admiral's eyes narrowed in agitation.

Raud blew out a long breath and pursed his lips, regarding Bertrand with a long, judgmental look before he spoke again.

"Look, Bertrand, none of us like being co-opted by those Ban'uta, but it's a necessary evil," he grumbled. "The prize is worth the discomfort. I know you're aware of that, but I'm calling to reaffirm it. Even the sturdiest armor has its flaws. I know yours. Don't let it get in the way."

Bertrand leaned back in his chair. The berating was softer than he had imagined, and that was a kindness Raud had likely manufactured himself. He had to know how complicated it was to operate inside the Systems without proper clearance.

No one wanted this job done faster or with better results than Bertrand. He had been stationary for too long. The hairs on the back of his neck stood on end constantly, and all he wanted to do was get back into the Black, where he felt safe and invisible.

"When my asset comes up for air, he will have the drives, and we will be in transit to Laidlaw, but I can do nothing until that time," Bertrand announced.

Raud frowned. He had clearly been hoping for some other response, but the truth was the truth. Bertrand had kept DiSilva's name out of almost every conversation he could manage, and that wasn't easy. A career man like Raud would pick up on it, but few got to be where he was by micromanaging ops.

"There's been a change in your delivery destination," Raud said, and Bertrand could see the tightening of his jaw as he chewed on the words. "Echelon wants you to deliver your package directly to Liego Minor. They have a facility there that will receive, refuel and debrief you upon arrival."

"Any reason for the change?" Bertrand asked, knowing the answer.

"I'm sure. There always is, but nothing was declared," Raud grumbled. "I was hoping you would have something that could shed some light."

He did, but again, he felt no need to share it. Undoubtedly, they didn't want prying eyes to find out exactly what Bertrand was delivering to them. Echelon was particular that way. They often did things that weren't permissible by public law, only to seek absolution later, when their projects yielded viable fruit.

What the change in delivery location really meant was that his last message from them had been kept secret from the military proper. They weren't meant to know what exactly was on the drives or about the new specimen. For Bertrand, that meant he had more wiggle room than he'd first thought. It put fewer people in the know on DiSilva, just like it left fewer people knowing of Miranda's escape.

Bertrand had only found out that last fact thanks to an old friend and former subordinate turned information broker. Details on her escape from Keetal and her ascension among the pirates had cost him a significant sum. All in all, he counted himself lucky to have the information he did. Although he had assumed others in more official channels had it as well. Clearly, he'd been mistaken.

"I have no idea, sir," Bertrand lied.

Raud grunted but said nothing else on the subject.

"Your reports are expected presently, and I want a copy of everything," the admiral said in a more official tone.

"Aye, sir," Bertrand said, rising to his feet and snapping a crisp salute.

He watched as Raud's image nodded once more, wavered, then disappeared.

Bertrand blew out a breath and eased his bones back into his seat. The stress of this mission was threatening to intensify the already miserable aging process. Hopefully, it would be done soon, and maybe then, he would finally be able to force himself into retirement.

It wouldn't happen, but it was a nice thought.

. . . .

The sun had begun its long fall behind the towers of Cascade. Deep shadows slashed their way across the busy streets of Violet, leaving them to their own celebratory lights and songs.

The district was alive with delicious smells, exotic music, and seductive movement. Truce week was a colorful event everywhere in the Beita Systems, but Yuri had never really been one to take part. For him, the war didn't really seem over. He had spent the last six years doing the exact same thing he'd done for the previous two.

Seeing people celebrating the end of the war without sparing a thought for those who had lost their lives to it was off-putting, and he was a little tired of being forced to watch it.

Growlet Pass was not the best street he'd ever been on, but it was the standard for Violet. Old buildings modified with semi-modern tech lined the thoroughfare, while dust whipped up as vehicles passed overhead.

For the first time in his career, he felt genuine gratitude for his standard-issue breather. It didn't do a great deal to keep out the smells making his stomach roar, but he could at least breathe without having to cough up mud later.

He'd taken over for Lillith ten hours ago, and he was feeling every second of that time. Soon, the storms would threaten, and he would have to move back inside, but for now, he was more than willing to stretch his legs. Staying in one place had its advantages, and early on in his new assignment, he was more than happy to view the street through the scope of a rifle, but that only lasted so long.

Everything he could gather about this mission made it seem like it could be a long-term thing. That meant a lot of sitting around and watching for anything actionable. After the botched raid, he wasn't against something less dangerous.

That mission still haunted him. He'd been on dozens of assignments as a TaskMaster, and not all of them had gone well. This was different, however. Yuri saw the wide, horrified eyes of Dr. Eugene shrinking into the distant blackness in his sleep, and he still heard his words when the world around him grew quiet.

The doctor had chosen to die rather than come back to the ship, and he just couldn't rationalize that. People killed themselves, and while it was always a waste, it rarely meant anything, at least not to him. But this was sticking with him in a way he couldn't shake. What he wanted to know was why.

Why was the ultimate question. Why was Rickten willing to die rather than share his work? Why was the research of a former Sabien so important to Echelon? Why were they willing to risk the lives of his team to get it, and why did he care so much?

He wasn't in a position to dig into it, but he wasn't able to accept his powerlessness, either. Being stuck in the city limited his options, but it did give him one decent chance to understand at least half of the story.

Silver Sights had been dormant since he'd been put on this detail. DiSilva was sent to the Old City and as far as anyone knew, he was still there. Yuri didn't doubt that he could be dead. Derelicts weren't to be underestimated, but until he got the call to fall back to the ship, his objective remained unchanged.

He had requested to move in and investigate the site, but had been denied. Apparently, Bertrand tried mending the rift between himself and the executor by putting her in charge of the ground op. So now he and his team were under new management, although it didn't change much. Until he heard different, he was still on the same leash no matter how much it chafed.

"How's the party?" a soft, gentle voice asked over his earpiece.

"I've seen better," he said and adjusted his weight against the wall.

"Maybe you should mingle. I hear it helps liven things up," the woman said in his ear.

"I'm more of the strong, silent type, Lill," he responded and locked eyes with the telltale glint of a rifle scope in a window down the street.

"Whatever you say," she said with a huff.

Lillith was a decent friend but an even better squadmate. She was as good a shot as he was and better under fire than most people he'd ever worked with. Still, she had her own quirks that made putting them together an exception to normal practices.

Strings had been pulled by his family to keep them together during their recruitment, and now they were inseparable. The Launtiks were nothing if not well connected, and Yuri's parents had interfered with his military service in the hopes of keeping their only living child safe. Yuri had resented them for that. The war was his punishment, and he deserved it, but now that it was over, he had to admit his parents had done him a favor.

As bodyguards went, Lillith was an odd choice. She wasn't particularly strong or imposing. To most, she was just a striking young woman who never quite learned how to relax. She was enigmatic and slow to share her thoughts with anyone other than him, which was to be expected considering their history. Even then, Yuri would often catch her staring at him the same way she had stared at his sister a lifetime ago. It was a little off-putting sometimes, but there was still no one he would rather take with him into a fight.

Like him, Lillith could be overly competitive, which led to a few dust-ups among their fellow soldiers, but that was a minor quibble. When situations turned south, she was all business, though it tended to take her a while to disengage. It was a trait that had saved his life when he had felt the draw to celebrate victory a hair too early.

Most people that were new to the team found her to be a bit odd, to say the least, but she was as reliable as they came. They'd fought their way out of more than a few close calls together, before, during and after their stint in the military. That built a level of trust he liked to think he wouldn't trade for anything.

"What are you doing back on?" he asked as he returned his focus to the street and the mass of people milling around in it.

"I've slept about as much as I care to," she said. "Plus, I don't need the nightmares. Keeping you out of trouble is torment enough."

Yuri ignored the last part. She took joy in making him feel like an awkward kid, and he was content to deny her that pleasure whenever possible.

Up the street, he noticed a familiar form wander into the alley beside Silver Sights. The man wasn't out of place in the crowd exactly, but Yuri had been in the business long enough to tell a soldier from a civilian, though the man he'd spotted fought for no nation.

Both he and Lillith had noticed the same man casing the street several times. He had even stopped to talk to a PlanSec officer once, which seemed odd to Yuri at the time. The dreadlocked stranger meant for his actions to seem casual, though they were anything but.

Yuri had initially dismissed him as a prospective client of the agency, but something about that assumption didn't sit well with him. There was a hitch in the man's gait that spoke to extensive time in much lighter gravity, and his clothing didn't mark him as the kind of person who could afford much time off-world.

"You see dreadlocks up the street?" Lillith asked, having seen what he had.

"Yeah, looks like he's finally making his move," Yuri grunted in concern and disapproval.

"Then you'd better stop him," Lillith said. "The last thing we need is an opportunist ruining the op."

Yuri glanced back at the window where Lillith was, and this time he saw her mischievous smirk where the rifle's glint had been.

"Fine, time to clock in," he said almost dismissively. "Keep an eye on the street and keep me informed."

"Sir, yes, sir," Lillith said, and he could almost hear the mock salute in her voice.

Yuri pushed off the wall, tapped the holstered sidearm under his jacket for reassurance, and worked his way into the crowd. He figured the street mob to be denser than it actually was, but his position against the wall made it difficult to tell for sure. Now that he was in it, Yuri found he could move more freely than he'd expected.

Getting to Silver Sights from his current location was still like moving upstream, but he made decent progress. At least three clumsy attempts were made to pick his pockets, and it made him wonder how many more skilled attempts he hadn't noticed, before he ignored the distraction.

Anything of personal value he'd left on the ship, and his data-pad was with Lillith for precisely this reason. Yuri hadn't always been a soldier, and in those days, he had been quite the hellion. He knew how places like Violet worked because he had worked them many times.

If he was honest, he was actually quite at home in the dirty, unkempt streets that wove through the lower districts of the universe. The languages were sometimes different, but the currency was always the same. Respect, boldness, and self-reliance could get you just about anything, and if they couldn't, there was always violence.

His time on the streets of the Yunari Isles had taught him to own his space, wherever he happened to be. It was a good lesson and one that had served him well.

Now he was part of a team, and while he cherished the fact that his back was always covered, he never let that wash away the lessons he'd learned in the muck of the Isles. They always came in handy when the team's full strength couldn't be brought to bear.

"Any idea what a pirate is doing so far into the Systems?" Lillith asked.

"I don't have any better ideas than I had the last five times you asked me," Yuri said and ignored the curious looks his one-sided conversation earned him from passersby.

"I wonder if the boss lady knows anything."

"What's it matter? Echelon never shares the information we need anyway," Yuri groused and shrugged off a rude, thrusting gesture aimed squarely at him.

With a final push, Yuri made his way to the opposite side of the street. Foot traffic was lighter, but the sidewalk was packed with makeshift stalls and tables filled with handmade jewelry, snacks, and other goods for sale. If he weren't in pursuit, Yuri would have considered grabbing a pastry for himself, but there wasn't time. Every second the pirate was out of sight escalated the trouble he could create.

He honestly had no idea what a pirate was doing in the city, or even the sector for that matter. What he did know was they never enriched an environment. They represented most of what was wrong with people in the universe, as far as he was concerned. They killed and robbed their way across most of the Neutral Territories, terrorizing anyone they came across. He knew that firsthand. His world was often in their crosshairs, as were many of the outer Beita Systems' planets.

Lately, things had gotten better, though. The war had tied up most of the resources now used to counter the pirate threat. Yuri suspected that might have something to do with there being pirates on a planet like Minerva Prime.

The TaskMasters dealt with their type from time to time, but never specifically to defend the people. They were usually called in if someone of importance was being targeted or threatened in a significant way. If Yuri had his way, he'd be running them out of the known universe and into the Deep Black, but the TaskMasters had other obligations.

"I'm going silent," he said and slipped fully into his operational mindset.

"Copy that," Lillith said, doing the same. "Watch your back."

His earpiece clicked and died as he reached the door with the words Silver Sights engraved on it. The building housing the detective agency was modest by every definition of the word. From the outside, it was wind-beaten and ancient enough to have been erected before the barrier that gave the district its name.

Yuri had no intel on the interior, but he wasn't expecting much given the poor state of the exterior's upkeep. It wouldn't have surprised him at all if there were massive holes in the floors, walls, and ceilings.

What he was most curious about wasn't the state of the structure, but what information it might house. He knew Bertrand had secured DiSilva's aid to close the job where his team had failed. What he didn't know was what the commander could possibly offer a civilian to guarantee that aid. If there was a record of the conversation or even just a piece of it, that might help him silence the doctor's words rattling around in his head.

There was little chance he'd be that lucky. Bertrand was more careful than that, and if DiSilva was worth his time, he would be too. Still, there was some hope, even if it was just the foolish sort.

· · · ·

Tech jobs were not the sort of thing Herill was accustomed to. He was at home shouldering his way through large, cantankerous crowds, but reflective energy systems were another matter.

His new orders were sudden and odd. Before, he'd been asked to keep an eye on one man. Now, Ashe wanted him to tap into the guy's line directly and tell her lackey what the signal frequency was. Herill didn't understand half of what that meant, but he did know it was a pain in his ass.

"Do you have the panel off?" the boyish voice of his handler asked.

Herill didn't know the kid, but it was a fair guess he was too young to be telling him what to do. There was no way whoever was on the other end of his comms had done on more than half a tour, and here he was giving commands to a veteran infiltrator.

"Yeah, panel's off, and there are four lasers," Herill said as he watched the light show with a frustrating level of ignorance as to what it meant.

"Good. What colors are they?" the handler inquired with the type of boredom in his voice that Herill could sympathize with.

The lasers cycled on and off in what seemed to him like random intervals. Each time they did so, the cables inside the panel flickered and danced with a nearly liquid flow of energy. Most of them were welded in place, but two looked suspiciously like aftermarket modifications.

"I see green, purple, and two shades of blue," Herill said once the whole cycle had been completed twice.

There was a long pause from his contact. The silence lasted long enough for Herill to recognize the deep melodic groove of the song playing in the street beyond.

"I'm going to need you to be more specific," his handler stated, ruining his enjoyment of the song. "I need to know what order the colors are in, and you have to tell me which color blue they are."

"I don't know what color blue. They're just blue," Herill growled.

"Well, are they blue like the sky or blue like an ocean?"

"Depends on the planet, Ban'uta," Herill called with a lewd three-fingered gesture that he wished the kid on the other end of the line could see.

"Fine, send an image with all of them in it, and I'll figure it out from there," the handler said with a heavy sigh.

With a huff of his own, Herill pulled out his data-pad. It took him a second to position it so that he could get the panel's interior fully within its clear frame. Then he waited. Every cell in his body told him this was a bad idea, but the job was what it was. The sooner he took care of it, the sooner he could get back to that attractive soft-belly who had been so fascinated with his hair.

It wasn't often he spent so much time on a planet and the local fare hadn't lost all their curves to the rigors of pirate life. To them, he was exotic and in a place like Violet, that went a very long way.

"So, any particular reason you're missing the party?" a confident male voice called out.

Herill froze but didn't take his eyes off his data-pad. It took a few more seconds before the lasers all cycled on at once, and he captured the image as soon as they did. His fingers worked rigorously across the face of the pad as he secured the file in a transmittable message and sent it on its way.

"I'm all partied out, stranger," he said as he turned and drew his sidearm.

He didn't register the stern, emotionless face of the stranger before a bolt of hot metal tore its way through his side. A second took him in the left thigh, and he collapsed to the ground without firing a single shot of his own.

The stranger was on him in a second. Calmly, kicking the pistol from Herill's grip and showing him the glowing barrel of his military-issue

Deadlock bolt spitter. Even with the pain in his side and leg, Herill couldn't help but laugh.

He'd always loved those guns, but on the market, they were insanely expensive. The coin required to buy one had never been within his means, but the accuracy and the silence of the weapon were clearly worth the inflated prices.

"You're wetworks, huh?" Herill coughed.

"Not so much," the stranger said. "Why are you hacking that comms array?"

Herill did his best to appear non-committal, but inside he was cursing his luck and the damned handler who had gotten him shot to pieces.

"You know how it is," Herill stated. "The orders come in, and we carry them out."

The stranger flashed a snarl at the words, but Herill didn't care. Another man would have tried his best to keep his shooter from losing his temper, but Herill had been around long enough to know how this was going to end. The only thing left was to face it the way he wanted to.

"You got any more shots in that thing or is it the piece of scrap the Sabiens say it is?" he challenged with a broader and more pained grin.

Herill figured that would get his face melted. Instead, it got the bones in his fingers stomped into a fine powder. The heat in his side and leg seemed to almost disappear, making way for the new agony slicing through his nervous system.

"There's plenty of metal left," the stranger said in a calm, flat tone. "But I'm not going to waste any more of it on a pirate."

Herill put his mind to work. There was no way he was leaving the alley alive. He was sure of that, and in his injured state, he couldn't even give the stranger a decent fight.

"The comms array," the stranger began again. "What do you want with it?"

Herill held his tongue. A long, hard death awaited him, and it would only be made longer and harder if he continued to resist. But when it came down to it, he was willing to die painfully if it meant this Ban'uta got nothing out of it.

The stranger sneered again and kicked him in the side. The fire of the wound reignited and forced a sound from his lungs that Herill had never heard himself make before. The stranger knelt beside him, and in that brief motion, the glint of a combat knife stole Herill's attention from his pain.

A wave of fresh fear washed over him. The interrogation would kick into high gear the moment that blade came free. If he had to guess, there was less than a minute until his new friend started cutting and he started screaming.

Herill wasn't an interrogator himself, but he'd sat in on his fair share. They were usually bloody, uninformative affairs, but there were places for them so long as the person in charge kept their head. The stranger seemed to have the right temperament, though whether he had the stomach for the work was another question entirely.

"Do your worst, soldier boy," Herill spat and forced another pained laugh through his teeth.

The stranger's eyes narrowed as he looked the pirate over. A cruel grin spread across his face. In a smooth motion, he turned Herill's head and plucked the earpiece free. He inspected the device with an appraising eye and nodded slightly.

"New tactic," the man said.

Herill lunged for the knife on the man's belt as best he could, but the stranger grabbed his good arm with ease and flung it away harmlessly. Surprised and truly afraid, Herill awaited the retaliatory strike that he was sure would come, but the stranger simply rose and stepped away from him. He watched his wounded subject with a guarded gaze, then slipped the pirate's earpiece into his open ear and waited.

The silence stretched on for an impossibly long moment while Herill prayed the kid wasn't stupid enough to still be on the line. He had to have heard all of this. Anyone worth their skin would have burned the signal and reported what they'd heard immediately.

Luckily, the flash of frustration that played across the stranger's face said the kid did actually have two functioning brain cells after all, and that he was going to die because of it.

"Looks like you'll have to deal with me," Herill declared with more bravado than he actually felt.

The stranger slipped the earpiece into his pocket and looked down at Herill, clearly deciding how to proceed. His face gave away nothing about his intent as he moved toward the pirate and knelt over him once more.

"Time's getting short, so I'll ask you one more time," he growled. "What were you doing?"

"Got somewhere to be?" Herill said, grinning with spite.

"Wrong answer."

The stranger's hand was a blur. Herill only caught the aftereffects of its movement. He saw the coat flare out from the man's body, then the gleam of the knife as it slashed through the air. It wasn't until the blade sank into his heart that he saw the man's arm fully again. It didn't take long for the world to blacken and freeze around him, but Herill took what solace he could in the fact he had given the soldier nothing as he embraced his end.

"Lill, are you there?" Yuri said as he slid his blade free of the pirate below him.

It took a second, and he began to consider whether the dreadlocked fool had actually been alone before she answered.

"Always," she said brightly.

"I need you to get in contact with the ship. Tell them we have pirates operating in the city. They must have a ship nearby," he stated as he wiped his blade off on the pirate's sleeve.

· · · ·

"Why would you do that?" Claude demanded.

He had been trying to keep his words from reflecting what he really felt, but in the end, he failed. Zhara's eyes widened as his question hit her with a level of intensity he couldn't control.

Vision read the typhoon coming his way before Zhara even found the words to voice it, and she chose to focus her sensors on the smoothie in front of her instead of weighing in.

"Because it needed to be done," Zhara snapped. "While you were sleeping off your day, I dug through those drives. What I found..."

Zhara's voice dropped before the words could be uttered. She had meant them as an assault on Claude's self-righteousness, but that would only do more harm. Lashing out at him might vindicate her in the moment, but all too quickly, it would pass. When it did, the desolation left in its wake would scar three people instead of wounding the pride of just one.

"... I made a decision, Claude, and now it's done."

Claude rubbed the tightening muscles in his forehead and dreaded both the argument and the headache crashing down on him.

"Didn't you think we should talk about it first?" he asked through his teeth.

Zhara crossed her arms and leaned back against the counters. He'd seen that pose more times than he liked. It meant he was in for a long night. Unfortunately for him, he had lost the ability to retreat from the situation. With his apartment under surveillance, he had no choice but to see this fight through to its, most likely, bitter end.

"I wasn't aware I had to clear my actions with you," Zhara said sharply. "I saw what needed to be done, and I did it. Isn't that what you always do?"

Claude groaned. She was right, he tended to act on instinct rather than seek approval, but that was always in service of the jobs he took.

"This is different," Claude declared. "You put yourself at risk. We could have gone together. I could have backed you up."

"So let me get this straight. You agree we should corrupt the drives, but you wanted to go with me even though PlanSec was asking about you, specifically?" Zhara asked.

"I can handle PlanSec," Claude said.

"And I can't?"

"That's not what I meant, and you know it."

"I don't know what you mean anymore, Claude. Maybe you should say it clearly, so I don't get confused."

Vision gripped the frame of her halo and winced against the onslaught bombarding her. She'd been caught in the middle of their fights before, but only the minor ones. This crossfire of thoughts and words had a different tone from the others, and it was excruciating.

Argument were always a special torment for her. Emotions had unbearable power. They sliced through her inhibitors with more frequency than other thoughts, and fights had a way of heightening them beyond anything else she had ever experienced.

If it had been a fight between strangers, Vision could have coped much better. Her own emotions would be minimal, but she actually cared about Claude and Zhara. That made everything worse.

As a couple, they had issues. Everyone did. Vision had peered deeply into both of them. She knew they were alike in ways that neither of them could fully understand. If she could only articulate that, or if she could make them see it, there would be no need for fights like this. Yet, that ability was something she did not possess.

"I didn't expect this from you of all people," Zhara said. "You're mister can-do. I figured you would at least understand."

Claude shook his head as if some invisible insect buzzed around it.

"I get it. Believe me, I get it. What doesn't make sense to me is why you would make this call all on your own."

"Are you listening to yourself? How many times have you done the same thing? How many times have you tried to protect Vision or me without us having any say in it?" Zhara asked.

"That's different, Zee...," Claude began, but the words died in his throat.

Vision sensed at least a dozen possible responses from both their minds before any words were actually chosen. Unlike Claude or Zhara, she perceived every grievances and petty dig they weeded out. During their arguments, she became a lightning rod for all their animosity, anger, hurt, and dissatisfaction with one another. The longer it went on, the harder it was for her to tell what was exaggerated emotion and what was actually real. That was assuming anything in other people's minds was ever real.

"Stop!" Vision shouted.

Her confusion and frustration rippled through the apartment like a physical force, giving form to her own feelings in a way that she didn't know was possible. Metal surfaces danced with thin arcs of static electricity as the space echoed with her thoughts. The rebounding shockwave dimmed lights, rattled dishes, and knocked utensils from their hanging places.

Vision's outburst killed Claude and Zhara's argument immediately, but not in the way she had intended. Her abilities had only affected objects around her once. But when her pulse had shaken Zhara's office her inhibitors had been removed. With her halo on a burst like this should have been impossible, yet it had happened.

It only took a second for the power to cycle back up properly and when it was done, the ringing of fallen kitchenware still lingered. All of that fell away as she found herself locked in stares of concern and confusion from the adults.

"We have more important things to deal with than this," she said into the heavy silence. "Zhara compromised the drives. That's done. The real question is, what do we do next?"

Claude was the first to break out of his shocked state but not to respond. He massaged his right arm intensely and winced audibly before collapsing to the floor with all the stiffness of a statue.

Somewhere in the back of her mind, Vision registered a shout from Zhara, but only barely. She hadn't meant to do anything other than get their attention. Whatever pulse burst out of her was as much a surprise to her as it was to everyone else.

A part of her wanted nothing more than to drop everything and rush to Claude, but she wasn't sure if that would help him or hurt him. If she wasn't in full control of her abilities, she could make things worse. Instead of moving from her seat, she did her best to calm down. The pulse had escaped her when she'd lashed out. The best thing she could think to do was to keep herself composed.

That was easier said than done. Every thought in Vision's head screamed that this was her fault. She couldn't shake the possibility that she might have just killed one of the few people who had ever really cared about her. The longer those thoughts swirled inside her, the more they threatened to tear apart the serenity she so desperately needed.

Vision could feel her heartbeat quickening and her mind racing past Claude's death and Zhara's terrified, angry reaction. It painted a picture of soldiers breaking in to take her away and the experiments they would do on her until she lost herself to pain and cruelty.

But Claude wasn't dead. He was alive, though his breathing and heart rate were erratic. The sensors gave her an idea of what was happening to his body, but something there wasn't right.

Vision could tell he was in pain, but she couldn't understand why. His body seemed fine aside from the elevated heart rate and labored breathing. There didn't seem to be a reason for it, at least not one that she could find.

"H-hurts. I-it hurts," Claude managed to say through his locked jaw.

Vision finally moved from her seat and knelt beside him.

Zhara was so busy checking his vitals she barely registered her arrival. An ocean of panic brimmed in her eyes, but somehow, she kept it at bay.

"What's wrong with him?" Vision asked as she took his hand.

Zhara shook her head but kept her eyes locked on Claude's.

"I don't know," she said, with tremors in her voice. "Is it mental?"

Vision had no idea. The last thing she wanted to do was dip into his mind. He was barely breathing. She had no idea what would happen if she tried to read him in his state.

"V," Zhara said and gave her arm a gentle squeeze. "I need you to talk to him. See if he knows something we don't, okay?"

Vision took a deep breath and held it until she was sure she could tame her raging anxiety. When she blew it out again, most of her wild thoughts went with it, allowing her to set her mind on her task.

With a determined nod, Vision focused on Claude and pushed herself past the inhibitors. It wasn't exactly easy, but what had first felt like a wall, then a fence, now felt more like a membrane. The halo held her back as long as she didn't push against it too hard. The invisible shield separating her inner world from the one outside was porous, and it had been for a while. To overcome it, she just had to push against it in an overtly conscious way.

A part of her couldn't push through, and for whatever reason, she felt comforted by that. It was as if she was still anchored and had no fear of being swept entirely away. The currents of thought around her were shallow, more like a wading pool than the boundless ocean that she felt when the halo was removed.

Only Claude and Zhara were fully opened to her as she expanded herself.

Tiny trickles of other thoughts streamed in at the edges of her perception, but she silenced them. Her focus was Claude, but Zhara's fear and shock were overpowering. The rawness of her feelings fought their way back into Vision's mind each time she tried to filter them out.

Vision briefly wondered if removing the halo would make it easier to find Claude's strands of thought and ride them back into his mind. But in the chaos, that was something she wasn't eager to attempt.

"Zhara, I need you to relax, okay?" Vision said in a flat, even voice that failed to reflect her inner concern.

The halo's sensors still recorded her the world around her, but in this state, that information was all but useless. The apartment disappeared leaving, only the white-hot mix of emotions coming from her friend as they gradually cooled into something much less distracting. Having Zhara leave the room would have been more ideal, but there was no way she would do that, and Vision would never ask her to.

She could feel a solid core of guilt running through the woman, and while she knew this wasn't her fault, Vision chose to find Claude rather than comfort Zhara. It was a cold decision, but a necessary one. Zhara was an adult. She'd cope. Plus, if they could get Claude back on his feet, her problem would resolve itself.

Vision focused her mind on the man locked inside his own body. The interference from Zhara had lessened to the point where she could all but ignore it, but there was a larger issue. Inside Claude, were two minds. One was in complete and total panic, while the other was still fighting an inner battle to remain rational but losing.

"*Claude, what can I do?*" Vision said directly into his mind.

Both Claude and his passenger shifted their focus onto her. It felt as if two spotlights had turned their blinding attention toward her at the same time. Before they fixed her in their glare, Vision could easily sense the two distinct sources, but once locked on, they seemed to merge.

"*No again. No again. Away,*" whispered the fractured thoughts of Claude's passenger.

"*I'm here to help,*" she said. "*Don't be afraid.*"

"*V, what's happening to me? I can't move.*"

Claude's thought came through the blinding haze like a cooling wind. It was reasonable and refreshing, but the tinge of panic that underlaid it was unmistakable.

"*Your body's locked up. I think I did it,*" Vision said to him.

She was glad that she could still hold back the flood of feelings threatening to break loose and consume her.

Exactly what she was and what she was capable of seemed to scare her a little more with each passing moment. Since she'd thought to question it, that fear had become a greater threat to her than any pirate or mutant had ever been. What was worse, she had no solid ideas on how to deal with it.

"*Can you undo it?*" Claude's mind inquired. "*I don't want to pressure you or anything, but I'm going to have to pee soon.*"

"Gross," Vision said and appreciated the levity, even if it was disgusting. "Zhara, I think he's fine."

Typically, juggling two conversations was simple for Vision, but this situation was anything but typical. Since Claude could barely get a word out, she was doing her best to speak into his mind, but with Zhara she was choosing the opposite. She already had to screen out Zhara's emotions. There was no way getting into her head would help the situation.

Luckily, Zhara's essence continued to cool at Vision's words, and faded even further into the periphery. Now freed from the additional strain of holding Zhara at bay, Vision was free to pour more of her focus into Claude and his passenger.

The creature was scared, and Vision's presence wasn't helping. She tried her best to calm it, but every time she shifted her focus toward it, the thing seized and so did Claude.

"His passenger is panicking," Vision stated. "Can you scan it and see exactly what it's doing to him?"

"Maybe, if I can find my old scanner," Zhara said, and her mind slipped out of Vision's perception.

"*What do you mean, it's panicking?*" Claude asked, and this time Vision was hit with all the dread woven through his response.

"*It's scared of me, I think*," Vision said. "*I'm not sure why, but it wants me to go.*"

"*You think it's doing this to me on purpose?*"

"*I want to say no, I'm not sure. I don't talk to aliens much*," she declared, and felt her emotions lurch against the bars of their confinement once again. "*Why don't you ask it?*"

"*How?*" Claude asked in earnest.

Vision thought about that for a moment. For her, perceiving the creature's thoughts was as simple a hearing a sound, but the thing had never spoken to Claude.

She wasn't sure if there was some way she could connect their minds. It wasn't the first time she'd had that idea, but given Claude's anxiety over what the creature wanted and what it could do to him, she had never felt comfortable enough to suggest it, and now wasn't the time.

"*Never mind*," she finally said. "*When Zhara gets back, I'm going to the guest room. Maybe if I'm far enough away, your friend will calm down.*"

"*Is that a good idea?*" he asked, and she could feel his desire to keep her close.

"*It's an idea. Good or bad, it's the best either of us has,*" she said as Zhara's refocused mind slid back into her perception.

"I found it, but I'm not sure it still works. I got it back in my academy days," Zhara said before a whirring sound filled the room.

With significant effort, Vision began the process of reeling her abilities back in. It was easier to force them out, but taking an action was often easier than undoing it. The strain was immense, but she was able to ignore the pins and needles in her skull long enough to retreat back into herself.

The effort caused her to fall backward with a loud groan. She just sat there for a moment, trying to shake off the lingering discomfort and disorientation before allowing the sensors to fill in her surroundings.

"Ow," she said and took the time to free her emotions from their cell once again.

Pangs of guilt, remorse, and embarrassment hit her all at the same time. The chaotic rush caused both her cheeks and eyes to burn. Vision covered her face to mask the tears threatening to boil over.

Leaving Zhara to tend to Claude, she bolted for the guest room. The apartment was spacious, and Vision cursed that luxury as she raced through it. She almost managed to slam the door before the last illusions of control slipped away from her, and the sobs began.

Chapter 27

OCTAVIAN TOOK A LONG sip from his tea, attempting to enjoy it and recenter himself when Ashe darkened his doorstep. He couldn't see her, but the proximity chime and the three sharp raps on the metal told him exactly who it was and what mood she was in.

He liked Ashe, and despite his initial desire to keep his distance emotionally, she was growing on him. She was spirited, intelligent, and inquisitive, not to mention the fact that she wasn't afraid of him. Those things were rare in combination. It didn't hurt that she looked at him like he was a canteen in the desert, either. But she was quick-tempered and lacked the subtlety he desperately needed her to have at the moment.

The ship, and by extension her crew, was not meant to sit in one place. It had only been days, but the morale and maintenance work were getting exhausting. Both were important, but Octavian's primary focus was keeping the crew in working order. One crew member in particular required more effort than others.

Miranda had barely been seen since the incident with Luudo, and while that seemed good on the surface, Octavian knew it wasn't. There was a look of shock on her face that he wasn't familiar with, and it worried him. Stewing in that moment would do nothing good for anyone. He was trying to shake it off himself, but peace of mind was still eluding him. It had taken him an hour to get the blood off him, and he still saw Luudo's wide, lifeless eyes whenever he closed his own.

The old Qutongan centering routine was a lifesaver early in his career as a soldier, but since he'd fallen out of that life, he had abandoned it. Now the ground seemed to be shifting under his feet again, and for the first time in years, he sought to rededicate himself to it.

His body was still capable of folding into the rigid poses. His legs burned, and his arms were less cooperative, but given the amount of time since he'd last formed up, he couldn't complain. It was his mind that refused to play along. It wouldn't let go, and the more he tried to quiet it, the louder his problems seemed to scream at him. He'd been at it for more than half an hour, and while the tea was helpful, Ashe's impatient banging was not.

With a huff of dissatisfaction and frustration, Octavian pushed himself off the ground and unfolded his legs to stand. His muscles protested their treatment, but he ignored the soreness and moved to the door.

Ashe glared up at him, but much of her irritability melted away when she saw him. It took her a second to recompose herself, but when she did, she hurried inside and pushed him away from the door's sensor.

"Are you out of your mind?" she asked. "Why wouldn't you get dressed before you came to the door?"

"I didn't think there was time," the room said for him. "Your knocking made it seem urgent."

"And why are you so sweaty?" Ashe continued wiping her hands on the sides of her pants.

"What do you want, Ashe?" Octavian sent to the room's broadcast system.

Ashe threw her hands into the air and finally turned away from him.

"Herill is dead," she stated with renewed heat. "He was shot trying to clone DiSilva's comms frequency."

Octavian felt the muscles in his jaw tighten at the news. He wasn't deeply connected with many of the crew members, but that didn't matter. This was the sixth death laid at Miranda's feet.

"That's five. She's gotten five of ours killed for no good reason," Ashe seethed. "She has to be stopped."

Octavian wasn't quite sure what to do. Ashe and the rest of the crew were in the dark about what had happened earlier. He was inclined to keep it that way, but it was still a battle. At this point, any additional bodies that piled up would only increase the likelihood of something stupid occurring.

"We're almost ready, but I need to know that you're on our side," Ashe said as she turned back to him.

Her eyes were unreadable, save for the solid determination he could see behind them. She searched his, but he knew all she would find there was uncertainty. He sympathized with the crew, but their plan was severely lacking. They didn't have all of the relevant information, and any action without it was dangerous. If they knew what he knew about Miranda, they wouldn't be fanning the flames of mutiny within three star systems of her.

"People aren't sold on naming you captain after it's all done, but I can convince them. I just need to know you're with us," Ashe almost pleaded.

"It's not that simple," the mechanical voice stated with none of the mixed emotions that Octavian wished he could convey through it.

"Then simplify it for me," she demanded as she broke eye contact finally. "And put something on, please."

With a smirk and a nod, Octavian opened his locker, selecting a pair of loose-fitting black pants and a sleeveless shirt. As he slid the clothes on, he thought about the best way to explain what was in his head. It wasn't always easy for him to put his thoughts into words, especially when they were this complex. He wasn't an orator at the best of times, but so much rode on what he said here.

Since the last time he'd seen her, Octavian had looked into the rumors of unrest among the crew. What he had found was that she, along with others close to the men killed in the Old City, were stirring up dissent, and it wasn't a hard thing to do.

They were right to be angry, but they didn't know what Miranda was capable of. They hadn't seen what she did to the soldiers and scientists at Keetal. They didn't see the injuries she'd shrugged off, and most importantly, they weren't aware of just how much she'd seemingly enjoyed that massacre.

Octavian had, and while he understood the emotional desire for revenge better than most, even he was appalled by the efficiency and brutality she had displayed.

"You can't take the ship," the broadcast system finally said for him. "It won't work."

"So you're not with us then," Ashe said, and there was an exasperated and definitive edge in her voice.

She sounded disappointed when he had expected her to be angry. Heat came so quickly to her that he'd assumed her first reaction would be rage. He expected her to see his reluctance as a betrayal, though it was far from it.

"That's not what I said," he responded.

"But it's what you mean."

Octavian closed his locker and met her gaze once more. There were new emotions there that made him slightly uncomfortable. They had been together for only a short time, but there was clearly something between them. He didn't put a name to it, but the fact that she came to him directly when she was hurt and now when she was frightened meant their connection was more than physical for her as well.

There hadn't been much room for relating to others in more than a cursory way in Octavian's life. The only other person he'd ever been truly close to was Miranda, but that was drastically different from this. Miranda had put her faith in him, and he had done all in his power to honor that. Together they had risen through the ranks of the Beita Systems infantry, though not as far as they could have.

When she'd accepted a firm recommendation to join the TaskMasters, she'd demanded that the same be offered to him, and in that new environment, she had looked out for him. It was only natural for him to do the same when their roles were reversed. But things were evolving rapidly, in threatening and unpredictable ways. Octavian didn't know what part he had to play, or how the situation would turn out, but he was sure he had one.

Ashe wanted him to back the crew, and more importantly, she wanted him to support her. It was written in the stern frown she wore, and while he wanted to, he wasn't sure if he could. Loyalty was important to him, but then again, so was integrity. He didn't buy into the whole right and wrong construct that so much of the universe seemed to subscribe to, but there were fundamental principles he lived by.

Many years had passed since he'd been stripped from his world, but Qutong's values died hard. Some of that culture's hold on him had been eroded over time, but he still needed to be able to look himself in the eye when this was all over. As much as he wanted to be what Ashe needed him to be, Octavian couldn't bring himself to move against his friend directly.

"I have a plan," he stated, selecting his words delicately. "A move like the one being planned will fail. There aren't enough weapons and crew aboard to take the ship from her."

Ashe fixed him with a look that told him just how ridiculous his statement sounded, but he brushed it off.

"I've seen what she can do when her hand is forced, and none of you will survive if it comes to an open fight," he declared and watched as Ashe read the intent in his face.

"So, what's your plan?" she asked with another heavy sigh.

"The captain is obsessed with revenge," the mechanical voice overhead began. "She was tortured and imprisoned by her former commander, and we have tracked him to this world."

Ashe eased herself down onto his bunk and listened intently. He could see the disdain in her face for what he was telling her, but she didn't interject. She just took in his words and did her best to understand.

"He still commands a crew of mercenaries and soldiers, but his ship has stealth tech. Her hope is to intercept him here so she can finally kill him," Octavian continued. "The upside is, if she succeeds and if we help her, there will be a ship for the taking."

Ashe's eyes lit up. The bright smile spreading across her face brought one to his as well before it abruptly faded.

"So you want to take that ship and do what with it?" she asked.

"Whatever we want," he said and sat down beside her. "It should be a more peaceful way to split the difference. Many in the crew want the captain gone, and she can't command two ships. Those unhappy with her leadership could leave in peace."

Ashe shook her head gently as she mulled over his words. They troubled her, and he knew why.

"It's doable, maybe, but I'm not sure that's going to be enough. Dogura deserves more than to be left rotting out there while his killer goes free. They all deserve more," she declared, hardening herself as she spoke.

"Ashana," he said and watched as the fire in her eyes rekindle at the name. "You are going to die if you go looking for justice."

"So. What do you care?" she spat and almost leaped to her feet.

"I do care," he said and wished more than anything that he could say it in his own voice. "I'm trying to save your life."

Ashe's face struggled to hold whatever she was feeling at bay. Octavian wasn't sure if what he said helped, but it needed saying. He wished he had more time, or at least had better timing, but it was what it was. If he could convince her to put down the sword, maybe he would get the time with her that he needed.

She looked at him for a long while and even opened her mouth to respond, but said nothing. Instead of engaging with him like he hoped she would, she simply turned and walked out of his quarters.

• • • •

Zhara watched as Claude flexed his fingers for what had to be the hundredth time, and again, like all the times before, he sighed in relief. He had been quiet since he started regaining control over his body. That, combined with Vision's disappearance into the guest room, left Zhara feeling more alone than she had in some time.

She wanted to apologize, but she didn't think she should. It felt like second nature for her to say she was sorry about her actions, even though she really wasn't. She had done what was right, and if Claude didn't see it that way, then the imperfection was his to work out. If the information on the drives got into the wrong hands, it would ruin not only his life but Vision's as well. That was if she ignored the likely outcome of the Sabien research bearing fruit.

The kill code was needed, and even now, it was doing its work. When it was finished, the trap would be set, and both Claude and Vision would be as safe as they could be. She didn't regret that, and she wouldn't allow herself to apologize for it.

"Are you and Vision okay?" Claude said in a scratchy and cracked voice.

"Are we okay?" Zhara asked with a nervous laugh. "You're the one who almost died."

"I was just frozen. You guys had to deal with it," Claude said as he tested the joints in his arms.

Zhara had managed to help him onto the couch when he first started recovering, but she'd done a poor job of it. She would have guessed he weighed anywhere between two hundred and thirty to two hundred and fifty pounds, but when he was just dead weight, she could have sworn he weighed double that. She'd managed to get his torso on the seat just high enough for his head to rest on the back cushion, but now he was using his arms to push himself into a better position.

Zhara noticed he hadn't used his legs to help, and she wondered how much longer it would take him to fully recover.

"I haven't seen Vision since she ran off to the back," Zhara said as she scanned him with her archaic device.

Claude stared at his immobile legs and willed them back under his control, but nothing happened. The alien was still actively working against him. He was reasonably sure his mind remained his own, but his body clearly wasn't.

"I have to talk to her," Claude said after a moment. "She's going through a lot right now. We can't just leave her alone."

Zhara sighed and studied the partially garbled readout from the scanner.

"You're not going anywhere. Besides, when Vision's ready, she'll come to us," Zhara said.

It was an experience statement. Only one of them had ever been a little girl, and it wasn't Claude. So, he decided to accept her take on the situation...begrudgingly.

"And you?" Claude groaned as he accepted that his positioning was as comfortable as he could make it.

Zhara forced a smile that she hoped looked more reassuring than it felt.

"I'm good. Just another day," she said and avoided meeting his eyes.

"You were right," Claude blurted out and caught her surprised glance. "I was being an idiot. You and Vision mean everything to me. I need to protect you, but I forget that you are your own people. So, new strategy. Help me keep you safe."

Zhara didn't answer immediately. She didn't really trust herself to speak on the subject just yet. It was still too raw to assume she wouldn't reflexively strike at him for bringing it up.

"It's okay. We don't have to talk this out right now if you don't want to," he said, and his change of subject flooded Zhara with relief. "How long until this code thing erases the drives?"

"It's not going to erase the drives," she said, and this time, the slight smile that crossed her lips was more anxious than anything else. "Not directly, at least."

"Then what's it do?" Claude asked.

Zhara sighed. She needed to find a way to explain what had taken years to develop and even longer to justify to the board at Artemis. Eventually, confused businessmen had killed the project despite its promise. Zhara had little hope that she could do what an entire team couldn't, but luckily her audience was more forgiving.

"The kill code compiles relevant markers and searches all connected systems for that data," she stated and winced at how technical her explanation sounded.

Claude took the information in, mulled it over, then frowned.

"How does that help us?" he asked.

"If we can get it into Echelon's network, the code will infect their system looking for those markers and kill all the data files that contain them. Ideally, it will erase everything they have on your passenger and render the drives useless," Zhara explained with an uncertain smirk.

Again, Claude took a moment to think. He trusted Zhara, but in order for her plan to work, he would have to hand the drives over to Bertrand, which still presented a problem.

"So, we have to go through with the job as usual?" he asked, just to make sure they were actually on the same page this time.

Zhara nodded, "But the code hasn't finished compiling, and I haven't set the parameters. That's going to take a while.

"I have to be precise. If I set them too narrow, it won't kill all the research, and if I set them too wide, it could erase everything Echelon has ever committed to data storage."

"That last bit doesn't sound so bad to me," Claude said, half-serious.

Zhara allowed herself to slide closer to him and run her fingers through his hair.

It was a small thing, but it made him real to her again. He had been a verbal combatant and then a patient, but now, even though he was still on the mend, he was back to just being Claude.

"You say that, but if the goal is to keep the truce alive, Echelon is a necessary evil," Zhara cooed softly. "Besides, they do good things, too."

Claude huffed humorlessly. "Name two."

Zhara frowned and sighed as nothing came to mind.

• • • •

Claude woke to the rhythm of light snoring, and arms wrapped around him. The rising sun was warm on his face, and the added pressure on his chest made him feel pleasantly weighted in the moment. He didn't have to open his eyes to tell it was Vision. She had found him on the sofa some time during the night.

She was sleeping, and since he figured she hadn't had a decent time of it, he simply laid there and enjoyed the quiet. He wasn't sure exactly when he'd fallen asleep, but he must have been nearly comatose if another person could climb onto the sofa and him not notice. Vision was in no danger of waking up on her own. Claude was tempted to just lay there for as long as it took for her to open her eyes, but his body was already protesting.

He didn't get much time to just exist with her anymore. When she was younger, she would cuddle with him most evenings, asking him questions about anything she could think of. Now she was more inclined to try and learn everything on her own.

A persistent ache crept up his legs. The throb of it was unpleasant but also welcome. It had been at least a dozen hours since he'd last felt anything in them at all, and the dull pain was a good sign.

Slowly but surely, he shifted Vision's weight and transitioned it to the oversized white cushions. Once free, he took a few tentative steps, found himself mostly stable, and began the process of finding his jacket and data-pad.

He and Zhara had come to terms, for lack of a better word, and the next steps he needed to take alone. There were parts of the plan that she would disapprove of if she knew about them. Even he disapproved of them, but they needed to be done all the same. The work ahead was going to get messy, but he'd dealt with messy before. He was as good at it as anyone could be, or so he imagined.

The rebellion of his passenger stabbed a new blade into his already wounded confidence, but in such situations, he always found it easier and more acceptable to just push on. His resolve tended to heal with each step he took, and he hoped that it would be the same this time.

His jacket was draped across one of the stools around the island that divided the living space from the kitchen. It was a ruined mess, but even in its diminished state, it was still his favorite. It still made him feel like he could take on the world when he slipped it on, and more importantly, it still covered his holster and rendered it practically invisible to the untrained eye.

He slid his data-pad off the countertop and dropped it into the interior breast pocket of the jacket, taking in the time and weather conditions before doing so.

He'd call one of the automated taxi services once he was outside the apartment. There was enough money in the account to get him most of the way to Silver Sights from Cascade, if his calculations were correct. His credits had been wearing thin for some time, but Claude tried to keep it from showing. Vision knew, and he had little doubt Zhara did as well. He half expected that was why she'd offered to move them in to begin with, but it was important to him to be able to provide Vision with a decent meal. Since he couldn't cook one, that meant a lot of Hogan's and a lot of added costs.

"Not even going to say goodbye, huh?" Zhara said from the doorway behind him.

Claude sighed. He had hoped to avoid talking for at least a few more hours, but that wasn't going to happen now.

"No need," Claude said as he turned to the beautiful scientist staring a hole through him. "I'll only be gone a few hours."

Zhara raised an eyebrow.

"You really do need a better jacket," she said as she moved into the living space.

"There's no such thing," Claude stated definitively as she closed on him.

He imagined her as a linxor stalking closer to him. She shared the predator's grace and perhaps its intent, but she far outstripped it in beauty. Her jaw was set, her eyes calculating and locked on his own. He was rooted to the spot, not through fear but rather a sense of anticipation.

"You'd be surprised," she said, and something in her voice gave him the notion that she had expected this move from him.

He knew her as well as he knew anyone these days and far better than most, but there were still times when he couldn't be sure what she wanted.

Zhara threw a glance at Vision on the couch, and something in her softened. Claude wasn't brave enough to describe it, but it was a noticeable thing. She was apparently as surprised to see her there as Claude had been.

"You think she's going to be okay?" Zhara asked, still watching the sleeping girl.

Claude found himself shrugging before he realized it.

"I have no idea," he said, taking a moment to admire the women in his life.

Zhara let a soft, fragile smile cross her lips before she turned back to him. Something new was in her eyes, and if Claude had to guess, it was in his as well. So much about their relationship was primordial, unformed. Yet these moments, when he could feel all that was left unsaid, were somehow his favorite.

It was in a moment like this when he first knew they were destined to be more than acquaintances. Another had informed him they'd be more than lovers. Now, he was adrift in a new one, though what it was trying to tell him was still unclear. If Claude had his way, he would have all the time in the universe for it to reveal itself.

"Keep your credits," she stated, breaking eye contact and slipping her data-pad from the pocket of her shimmering scarlet robe. "Take the Regent. She's fully charged, and she has priority access to travel the shipping lanes."

Claude looked at the thin metal frame of the data-pad cautiously. The sturdy transparent silicate flashed the words: "transfer pending" as Zhara flicked it at him with a hint of impatience.

"So you came out here to rush me out the door?" Claude asked with genuine curiosity.

"I came out here to find out how much time I have to get the code set up," she answered, still flicking the data-pad at him, only now she was tapping it against his arm.

The inscrutable look on her face melted into one he knew all too well. She was ten seconds away from popping him in the forehead with the data-pad if he didn't act quickly. He would have to miss out on the morning playfulness which he so enjoyed, but as was so often the case, the mission came first.

He removed his own cruder data-pad and touched its slightly warped frame to hers. They vibrated and chirped in alternating patterns before throbbing in sync and finally sending out a unified chime. Claude and Zhara caught the unspoken implications in each other's eyes before giggling like children.

"They had to know what they were doing when they made the transfer sequence," Claude said.

"I know the couple who designed it, and I can tell you, they absolutely knew what they were doing," Zhara said with a cute little snort. "They do it whenever they can."

Claude's face scrunched at the idea. "Really? At Artemis?"

Zhara nodded conspiratorially. "Yeah, avoid the bathrooms on the forty-fifth floor."

The look of disgust on Claude's face sent Zhara off into the giggles again.

"Okay, I'm going to go," he said reluctantly. "I'll be radio silent until I'm on the way back, so don't panic."

Zhara narrowed her eyes at him. "When do I panic?"

It was a rhetorical question, but Claude found himself at a loss. The closest he'd seen her come to true hysterics was the previous day, but even that had been due primarily to shock.

"I'm just–" he began, but Zhara cut him off.

"Get going," she said and flicked her wrist at him. "Just know I want my car back without so much as a scratch."

"Yes, ma'am," Claude said with a hint of mockery.

He turned to leave but hesitated when Zhara called his name.

"And Claude, I'd like you back the same way," she said, and Claude could hear the vulnerability in her words.

He didn't respond. He didn't know how to. There was a solid chance that at any moment, things could turn in a bad direction for him, and he didn't want to promise anything he wasn't sure he could deliver.

Some anonymous soul lost to time had once said, "Don't make a girl a promise if you know you can't keep it." The quote wasn't as profound as many others he'd heard in his lifetime, but it stuck with him all the same. As the door slid closed behind him and he made his way through the brightly lit halls, Claude couldn't help but wonder if it had stuck in his mind for a moment just like this.

Chapter 28

THE TRAFFIC OUT OF Cascade was rough, as always, but once Claude piloted the Regent into the shipping lanes, things smoothed out. Every other lane of the skyway had descended into a hectic spiral of manufactured urgency and natural born chaos. It was a frustrating maelstrom Claude knew well, and it would only intensify as the Truce Week festivities came to a head.

People tended to lose their minds as well as their inhibitions during long celebrations. That was an indisputable fact. The longer the party, the less composed the attendants. So, it made Claude wonder who exactly thought up the brilliant idea of devoting an entire week to the signing of what amounted to a loosely worded promissory note.

Sure, he'd enjoyed the first few, but after that, it had just become a headache. Violet always exploded into a spectacular example of civil unrest and authoritarian overreach, but even in the "tamer" districts, arrests shot through the roof. The celebration was going to be a double-edged blade, considering what he needed to do. On the one hand, there would be a sea of people to get lost in should he need to, but on the other, there would be a massive amount of collateral damage if a fight actually broke out.

Bertrand would care about the civilians, or at least the Bertrand that Claude had worked with years ago. Miranda would not share that concern. Something about her had put Claude on edge in the Old City, and if he had to guess, he would bet his last credit that she'd trample anything and anyone between her and her former commander.

He could understand that mindset. He'd actually been there himself, but he'd been denied his revenge by both time and his own morality. If he'd been as close to his old target as Miranda was to hers, he would have burned an entire planet to avenge his brother. Her vendetta was more potent than his, and he could see no way she would concern herself with right and wrong. He wasn't sure if it really mattered all that much to him. As long as Vision and Zhara were far away from the chaos, he would do whatever had to be done. If he focused on every single life in the city, he'd be unable to act at all. He couldn't allow that to happen. The stakes were too high, especially now that he knew Vision was part of the equation.

Claude's grip tightened on the steering yoke of the Regent. The padded covering cried out against the rough treatment, but he didn't register it. All he could imagine was the price the girls would have to pay if he failed to carry out the task ahead.

· · · ·

Violet was quieter than Claude had seen it in a year. The streets were filled with trash of all sorts, but the foot traffic he expected was all but absent as he piloted the Regent down and set it on the cracked street.

Silver Sights looked exactly like it had when he'd left days ago, aside from the holographic red strips cordoning off the alleyway adjacent to it. The thick buzzing of PlanSec drones spilled out from around the blind corner, trying to attract his attention, but Claude kept his focus. Crime happened. It was a very real part of life in the Violet district, though it rarely took place so close to his home.

The alley housed little of significance aside from the junctions that connected the buildings nearby to the planetary networks. A tempting target, but not for local thugs. If they were going to do anything, they'd have cut through his door and taken whatever they wanted. Instead, the building itself seemed normal, and that told him a great deal.

Of course, the alley event could have been unrelated to him, but Claude doubted it. With a reluctant huff, he opened the cab of the Regent and eased out of the impossibly comfortable seat to scan the street. Dust and trash danced lazily in the wind, making their way past him on their way to wherever such things ended up, and he payed them no mind. With suspicious eyes, he studied each window facing his office, but found nothing to hold his attention.

It was unlikely either Bertrand or Miranda would send someone sloppy to sit on his place. They had to know he would spot any weak attempts easily. As troubling as unseen spies were, it felt good to know that his former colleagues still held him in such high regard, even if they showed it in menacing ways. Still, there was something to be said about having one's skills properly respected.

As he moved up the short stairs to his door, Claude thought again about how likely it was that his place was trapped. Bertrand needed the drives, and Miranda wanted Bertrand. Neither got what they wanted by crossing him at this point, but reason wasn't always consulted in challenging situations. He slid his hand into his jacket and over his sidearm just in case.

The door read the key on his forearm and eased itself open. Cool, clean air spilled out of the building, and after a quick survey of the lobby, Claude stepped inside, letting the door seal behind him. Nothing appeared out of place, but that was to be expected. If anyone broke through the admittedly standard security systems, they wouldn't want him to know it until, of course, they did.

Claude dialed his tension down to a more manageable level and crossed into his office. The large faux wooden desk greeted him as it always did. He nodded to it as if it would somehow register his gesture, then tapped three fingers to its surface and scanned through the holo-feed he'd been viewing before leaving for the Old City. The memorial database scrolled slowly before him, just as it had days prior. Nothing was amiss, yet Claude still didn't trust it.

Pulling up the security scans, he searched through the graphs and diagrams of air pressure and temperature. Neither showed the kind of fluctuations typically caused by entering a sealed space, at least not until he had entered.

Nearly satisfied, Claude elected to check the one place any invader would had focused their attention. Embedded in the far wall of his office sat his coded safe. As with the rest of the office, nothing seemed to have been disturbed. The door was still closed and blinking its status as "secured."

"Great," he said under his breath and shook his head before exiting the office.

The safe was the best place in the building to search for the drives, yet it appeared no one had. If someone had come into his place, they had left no sign. The TaskMasters were efficient, but no one short of an Echelon ops team would have been this thorough.

The scenario made Claude's head hurt. Bertrand wasn't a trusting man. He wouldn't just wait for Claude to come to him, not with so significant a prize in the balance. The fact Silver Sights was unmolested meant Bertrand had to know he hadn't come back here. That meant he had eyes on the place, at least two pair to account for potential downtimes. Funnily enough, it was exactly what Claude would do were their positions reversed.

Claude smirked. Apparently, he'd actually missed the team watching him on the street. Perhaps he wasn't as effective a scout as he had once been. As realizations went, that one stung, though it wasn't unexpected. Skills faded when they weren't constantly being pushed.

In the TaskMasters, there'd always been a mission to test him. With his life constantly on the line, his senses were often the only things between him and an unceremonious death. They'd been sharpened to a razor's edge then, but now he lived in a city where nearly every threat was readily identified. On top of that, he had Vision, who was perhaps the best early warning system in existence. Living here had caused him to lose a step. Claude just hoped he was still capable enough to navigate the minefield he now found himself in.

Stepping into the living room of the apartment, he sighed at the disarray he'd left it in. There was a time when he would have been thoroughly admonished for such neglect. Both on the farm and in the military cleanliness and organization were regarded as virtues. In those old lives, he'd been forced to abide by strict rules, but much of that discipline faded away. It was much easier to just leave empty dishes on the table and move on.

Claude scooped up two bowls and matching glasses from the table and carried them to the kitchen, stepping over a mound of blankets on the floor and kicking aside both his and Vision's discarded socks on the way.

Hogan's wrappers lay crumpled on the counters, while the bag with the deli's checkered logo had somehow found its way onto the tiled floor. Claude ignored the bag and brushed the wrappers into the trash chute before turning to the wash counter. The cleaning basin sat full, its chem wash having stagnated while he was away. The apartment reeked of the acrid mixture of rancid food particles and decaying mineral compounds.

Rubbing his nose, Claude dropped the new dishes in with the old, and vowed to resolve the problem when he had more time. It was a vow he was sure to regret.

With a deep sigh, he made his way into Vision's room and opened the drawers under her bed. She didn't have many clothes, but he was able to dig out three outfits she might not hate and a laundry bag to stuff them in. She'd have to rough it in Zhara's skyline apartment for a while, and Claude figured a change of clothes would be appreciated by at least one of the ladies there.

He needed some extra clothes of his own, but he wasn't the priority. The call was, but it would survive him taking a few minutes to pack. Bertrand had waited this long, he could wait a while longer.

• • • •

Vision had been awake before Claude left, but she chose to pretend otherwise. He and Zhara needed the alone time, and it was both cute and a little sickening to see them acting like teenagers in love. Some point after that, she'd drifted back into the land of slumbering psionics, but now the sun demanded that she get up and do something with the day. Claude had a plan, so did Zhara, but Vision wasn't expected to do anything.

She wasn't happy with being left out, but it was understandable. From their perspective, she was a child, after all.

"But I'm a child with phenomenal powers," she thought with a troubled smile.

Discovering where she came from had been such a driving motivation for her that she had rarely focused on what she was truly capable of. Her abilities were growing in new, astonishing, and frankly terrifying ways, forcing her to learn and adapt as new dangers presented themselves. Vision could sense the power hiding just beyond out of her reach, but she was scared to push for it.

While it was exhilarating to discover and often surpass her limits, she was aware of how easily she could lose control over herself. She had paralyzed Claude and had unintentionally turned off dozens of people like so many holograms. Luckily, everyone had survived and was fine, as far as she knew, but it could have gone a different way. She was afraid that if she went too far, it would lead to an outcome that she would never be able to forgive herself for. She had been so worried she'd crippled Claude that it had been difficult for her to breathe afterward. And that had been an accident. If she pushed, if she really pushed herself, there was no telling what would happen.

The drives had referred to her as part of a weapon, and from what she had done in the last few days, she believed it completely. What troubled her most was that she knew people could be weaponized. But could a weapon ever truly make itself into a person?

"V, are you awake?" Zhara called from her room, snapping Vision out of her spiraling thoughts.

"Yeah," she answered.

The sensors in her halo could pierce most surfaces she'd come across, but thankfully not the walls of Zhara's place. It was built for privacy, and Vision was grateful. It was bad enough she was sometimes subjected to Claude and Zhara's emotional runoff. Not having to see or hear them as well was a blessing.

Zhara stepped into the living room after a moment and cast a slightly disapproving look at the girl still sprawled out on the couch.

"You're not up," Zhara said and set about prepping their first meal.

Vision sat up with an exaggerated stretch and groan.

"You didn't ask if I was up," she groused. "You asked if I was awake."

"Same thing," Zhara said dismissively. "You knew what I meant."

Zhara was dressed, though not to leave the house. Vision couldn't tell the colors, but the fabric of her loose-fitting pants and a knitted, sleeveless shirt screamed lounge clothes.

"What're you fixing?" Vision asked, smelling the first hints of sizzling protein.

"I grabbed some whikie and Eilitonian gray grass," Zhara said, withdrawing her kitchen knife with a flourish. "I figured you wouldn't mind something more exotic."

"Sounds good," Vision said, bounding from the sofa and over to the kitchen.

She could already imagine the sweet tang of the fried grass and the cheesy, buttery goodness of braised whikie.

Eiliton had the best food in the Beita Systems by her estimation. The sheer variety of edible flora and fauna on that world was unparalleled. Sure, most of it would eat you first if you weren't careful, but the flavors made it worth every risk.

Claude often had to resort to pre-processed meals when they ate at home, but Zhara didn't have that problem. She lived near enough to an open market to be able to gather the good stuff, and better than that, she could actually afford it.

Vision didn't lust after riches so much as she did food, but she had to admit Zhara's lifestyle was impressive. The apartment was exceptional compared to the one she lived in, and the idea of having enough credits to do pretty much whatever she wanted was tempting. The only downside was that Zhara was always pressed for time.

Claude had all the time in the world, but his credit situation was quite the opposite of his girlfriend's. Vision imagined a balance somewhere in the middle was the proper place for her. Although, how she'd get there one day was a complete unknown. Luckily, she had a few more years left to figure that out.

"So, Claude's gone?" Vision asked casually. "Any idea when he'll be back?"

"Nope, and I'm not going to worry about it too much. Neither should you," Zhara said, offering Vision a slice of raw whikie.

Vision took the slice, pinching its slight sponginess between her finger and thumb before munching on it enthusiastically. For a nut, its flesh was soft and tender, but in its raw form, it lacked the melty, stringy richness that she expected.

"You should be more worried about what we're going to do with that hair," Zhara said. "When was the last time you even combed it?"

Vision sighed and took a deliberately long time chewing. She hated doing her hair. It was not only a logistical nightmare, but it took forever, and it hurt to boot. She had a habit of throwing off static electricity like crazy, which was why Claude had ceded hair care to Vision, and her sensitive scalp was the reason Vision tended to cede her hair care to nature.

"Can we not?" she whined.

"Knots are what I'm concerned about," Zhara said, intentionally turning away from the pouting girl. "And quit moping. You're going to feel great when we get done."

Vision huffed loudly and made a show of parading herself out of the kitchen and onto the balcony. She wasn't looking forward to spending the day with Zhara if it meant a beauty regimen. Sure, it felt nice when it was all done, but process mattered, and to Vision, it just wasn't worth it.

She gazed out as far as her sensors allowed, which admittedly wasn't far enough, but she didn't come out here to see. She stepped out onto the balcony to feel. The morning breeze carried the first scents of the desert beyond the city. Vision let the caress of sunlight warm her both inside and out. She loved the height and how it allowed her to appreciate Minerva's winds without getting stung by the dust and particulates that swirled nearer to its surface.

As much as anywhere, Minerva Prime was her home. It was the only place she'd ever truly known, and yet there was so much she'd never experienced here. She'd only been to Divide and the Dead Zone recently. Beyond that, there was an entire world filled with things she longed to know firsthand instead of through her lessons.

Then there were all the worlds she'd never even set foot on. The universe was so vast and intriguing. All she wanted to do was experience everything it had to offer, but something about this world made it special to her. She had chosen it when Claude sought a place for them to settle, and despite many of Minerva's flaws, she hadn't regretted that decision, not really.

As the wind caught her hair and tickled across her skin, she wondered what Claude was doing. Whether he'd made it safely. What he'd found at the office and in the apartment. She found herself wishing

she could see through his eyes again. It was as strong a desire as she'd had
in a long time, so setting her jaw and closing her eyes, she quieted her
own misgivings and pushed.

. . . .

"*Why's he looking through my clothes?*" Vision asked in Claude's head.

Claude leaped to his feet, immediately spinning and reaching for his
sidearm.

"*You can hear me?*" she asked in disbelief.

"Yeah," Claude said nervously. "What are you doing in my head?"

"*I was just... you know what, never mind,*" Vision said with
exhilaration in her tone. "*I know I was doing this before, but I didn't really
have time to think about it then. This is so cool!*"

Claude forced himself to calm down and return to packing.

"Yeah, until my brain explodes," he grumbled.

"*Sorry,*" Vision thought to him. "*I'm not really sure how to turn this
off?*"

Claude sighed and shook his head. "It's fine, but if things go
sideways, I'm going to need room to think."

"*Fair enough,*" Vision replied. "*But if things get crazy, try not to die. I
have no idea what happens if I'm still connected to you.*"

"I'll try to keep that in mind," Claude said. "Now, which of these
shirts do you hate the least?"

Claude made sure to look at each for long enough for her to decide,
then when she didn't answer, he looked over them again.

"*The one on the right,*" she said finally.

"The blue one?"

"*I guess. What color blue is that?*"

"Cyan," Claude said, stuffing the shirt and pants into the bag and
moving out of the room as quickly as he could.

"*You didn't go through my–*"

"No. You and Zhara can order some new ones," Claude snapped,
completely uncomfortable.

He slung the bag over his shoulder and moved through the living room with purpose, coming to an abrupt stop at the top of the stairs.

"*Why did you–*" Vision began, but Claude cut her off.

"Ssh," was all he said as he lowered the bag to the floor slowly.

With a practiced hand, Claude drew his pistol and descended the stairs quietly. Light bounced off the floor below putting him on high alert. He knew what it looked like when the main entrance was closed, and this wasn't it. No sounds reached him, outside of his own breathing and the slight rustle of his jacket brushing against his pants, meaning whoever had entered was lying in wait for him below.

"*Wait!*" Vision shouted in his mind.

Claude winced at the intensity of her thought but stopped before his foot touched the fifth step.

"*That one creaks,*" she whispered.

Claude nodded his thanks and skipped the step, aiming his gun at the sliver of the lobby he could see from his position. Nothing seemed out of place aside from the front door being ajar. Claude waited another thirty seconds before chancing a move into the alcove at the base of the stairwell.

Everything to his left was as it should have been, and once satisfied, Claude inched forward, aiming his gun around the blind corner to his right. A hand shot out and gripped his pistol. Claude charged forward to see a wiry woman holding the barrel of his weapon. She twisted the gun and chopped him on the back of his wrist, ripping it free. It was a skillful and effective maneuver that Claude should have expected, but, again, his rust was showing.

Against pirates, he was still top tier, but this woman was trained far better.

Claude felt the silver soak through the skin on his hands, and he instinctively opened his fists into a claw-like posture. His passenger matched his act by forming two-inch serrated blades on each fingertip.

The woman's eyes went wide, and she fell backward as he lunged. Claude was inches away from her when his pistol went off.

The blast knocked him off-axis, and he crashed to the floor beside her. Quickly, he rolled back to his feet and inspected his chest. A wisp of smoke trailed from a new hole in his clothes just above his heart. The singed fabric revealed silver coating his skin for only a moment before it was reabsorbed.

"Stop!" a strong male voice called.

A man with sharp features, sleek black hair, and an obvious military bearing sauntered out of Claude's office.

"We're not here to fight," the man said as Claude glanced back and forth between him and the woman on the floor, still aiming his gun at him.

"Prove it," Claude barked and nodded toward the woman with his sidearm.

"Lill," the man called.

After a moment of hesitation, the woman removed her finger from the trigger. She got to her feet, placed both hands in the air and backed toward the man.

Claude let himself relax, but the blades at his fingertips did not retract.

"What do you want?" he asked the man, identifying him as the leader.

The man eyed the claws on Claude's hands, and the woman he called Lill did the same.

Reluctantly, Claude willed the silver to recede and felt the resistance it offered before it begrudgingly complied.

"Lill, I think we can give the man his sidearm," the leader stated and fixed the woman with a stern glance.

An entire conversation passed between them, but Claude wasn't privy to the finer details of it. They clearly knew each other well and were both soldiers or had been at some point in their recent past.

"*Who are these guys?*" Vision asked in his head.

Claude didn't answer. So far, he'd been actually talking to her, and he imagined speaking to invisible little girls would do little to put his "guests" at ease. Instead, he inspected his new visitors thoroughly. They didn't wear any insignia, nor was anything except their boots standard issue. On the man's belt was a modest combat blade for extremely close-quarters fighting. The woman didn't have one; he noticed and immediately marked her as a ranger.

He'd known a few in his time. Most rangers tended to be female, for reasons he didn't quite understand. As support fighters, they fought from greater distances than standard infantry, laying down precise fire on any target that gave their teams trouble up close.

They were assets to every squad, but none he knew were as fast or accurate in a scrap as this woman had been. It was clear the lines between infantry positions were beginning to blur in the TaskMasters, which was a good thing for the organization, and perhaps a bad thing for Claude.

The man carried himself more like a scout, but clearly wasn't one. No scout would have given away his position from across the room. That was the kind of move made by someone used to having a team around him. It reminded Claude of Miranda, though without the unsettling coldness she now possessed.

These young soldiers were Bertrand's people. Nearly everything about them screamed it. But their being here didn't make much sense. If Bertrand wanted to double-cross him for the drives, there would be time for that without forcing a confrontation on Claude's turf. The old man was smarter than this. If he took unnecessary risks, it was only because he was forced into them. That didn't appear to be the case here.

The woman slid Claude's pistol across the floor and drew her own all in one graceful motion. Claude stopped the gun with his foot but didn't move to pick it up. His eyes darted back to the man as he waited for the information he'd asked for.

"I'm Yuri, Wyvern, unit commander, and that's my second, Lillith," the man said with a gesture to the woman at his side. "We're here to ask you a few questions."

"Ask away," Claude said, before turning to inspect his front door.

The locking mechanism didn't appear broken, just hacked. The intrusion was rushed but effective, though Claude had seen better. Opening the access panel on the wall, he went to work overriding the computer and switching the door to manual control.

"What do you know about Firaxis?" Yuri asked, studying Claude's every movement carefully.

Claude sighed. Old habits died hard, apparently. These soldiers had been dropped into the grinder blindfolded, just as he had been. Firaxis was a name that few people knew, and none mentioned casually.

"Did your target in the Old City give you that name?" Claude asked, turning away from his door and locking eyes with Yuri.

Yuri said nothing, but the stillness of his gaze and the lack of any reaction on his face told Claude he had read their purpose wrong. The young soldiers standing opposite him weren't here to collect the drives. They really had come to talk.

"Bertrand knows. Why not ask him?" Claude posited coolly.

"That avenue is exhausted," the one called Lillith seethed.

Yuri glowered at her before turning back to Claude.

"You were a soldier," he began. "You've seen men die. You know it's an effort for them to even get out their final words...."

"What did the scientist ask you to do?" Claude asked, cutting to the quick.

The man called Yuri nodded his appreciation and moved to sit on one of the padded seats lining the far wall.

"He asked me to stop them," Yuri said cautiously.

Lillith leaned against the wall, keeping her pistol at the ready, and her distrustful glare locked on Claude.

Claude twisted the thin metal handle inside the panel, and the door mechanism grumbled before spurring to life. The door shut and sealed, dimming the room as the interior lights rushed to compensate for the change.

"I can only assume he meant the people I'm working for," Yuri finished.

"Echelon," Claude stated plainly. "It's their web. We're all just caught in it."

Yuri nodded. "I came here hoping you had information that could break us free."

"And what about her?" Claude asked, pointing at the woman with the sour expression.

"Lill is the person I trust most. She's here to watch my back in case you try anything stupid."

Claude half chuckled at that. She was skilled, but it was clear she couldn't stop him if he chose to attack. It wasn't something he was inclined to do, but the idea was a little amusing.

"*You're going to help them, right?*" Vision asked.

It was all he could do not to flinch at the suddenness of her question. In all the action, he had almost forgotten that she was still with him.

Claude didn't know if there was a way to answer her without actually speaking, but he tried anyway.

"*I was thinking about it,*" he thought back, in hopes she would receive it. "*Can you get a read on them?*"

"*No,*" Vision replied after a short pause. "I'm *kind of busy maintaining this thing with you right now.*"

Claude nodded, then cleared his throat, refocusing on the verbal conversation in front of him.

"I would ignore the whole thing, but I can't," Yuri shared with a confused and pained expression.

Claude understood the importance of honoring last wishes. There was something powerful about the final words spoken before a soul departed. Often, they cried for loved ones or uttered whatever phrases came into their fading minds, but when it was a wish, a task, those words weighed heavier.

"What exactly do you want to know?"

"Let's start with that," Lillith declared, pointing at his hands. "What in the hells is it?"

Claude shook his head. "Trade secret, but I can tell you it's what your people are so interested in."

"And that's what's on the drives," Yuri deduced.

Claude hesitated for a moment. He wasn't sure how much to share. Yuri's motivation for seeking him out made sense, but it could just as easily be a manipulation based on what Bertrand and Echelon knew about him. To what end he couldn't say, but to ignore the possibility was foolish.

"I have no idea. My job isn't to read files," Claude lied.

Yuri and Lillith fired pained glances at each other, but neither pressed him on it.

"Eugene believed Echelon shouldn't get those drives," Yuri said. "I need to know if he was out of his mind or if there's a reason we should listen to him."

Claude watched the woman's irksome expression as Yuri spoke. She didn't quite feel the same way he did, but she didn't interject.

Under different circumstances, Claude might have been more willing to listen to what the unit commander had to say. As it stood, he wasn't going to give them anything of value, especially knowing his second wasn't on the same page. No matter how much the kid might trust her, Claude did not.

"Echelon is shady, kid," Claude began. "They've always been shady. I think you know that. If you have any doubts about trusting them, don't."

"Why are we listening to this guy? He's hired help. What does he know?" Lillith protested with mounting annoyance.

"Why is she here?" Claude asked without trying to veil his distrust in the slightest. "She doesn't exactly seem to be helping."

"She is," Yuri stated, as if it meant everything.

Claude searched the man's features, then Lillith's, and found what he was looking for. They shared a connection that went beyond rank, though not all the way to romance. They were close, but maintained a workable distance at least up to this point, and he found himself respecting that.

"I have business to conduct while I'm here," Claude began. "So, if you're not here to bring me in, we don't have anything left to discuss."

"We are not done here," Lillith snapped.

She was still riding a combat high, and in all fairness, so was Claude. The difference was he'd spent more time fighting than she had. His past was riddled with last-minute orders to stand down, and most came after the adrenaline started pumping.

The silver had apparently not learned that lesson. It thrummed and writhed with anticipation. Claude could somehow tell it was wired to attack these strangers, and part of him definitely shared that feeling, but so far, the conversation had been civil. If what the man said was true, no further conflict was incoming.

"I want to know why Bertrand trusts you so much. Why did he come all this way to hire you?" Lillith growled at him.

"Maybe it's because I used to be a TaskMaster. Maybe it's because I have great references, or just maybe he knows that he left me for dead once, and it didn't stick," Claude said bluntly. "Only Bertrand can answer that question, but I can tell you what I do know. His position here is not as secure as he thinks it is."

Yuri nodded. "You mean the pirates."

"I do," Claude said, leaning against the wall and folding his arms over his chest.

"Are you in league with them?" Lillith demanded.

Claude laughed humorlessly.

"You see the holes in this jacket?" he asked, showcasing them. "Where do you think they came from?"

"We found one interfering with your comms array last night," Yuri informed him. "What do they want with you?"

"They don't want anything with *me*. They want the old man. Well, *she* does anyway. If I were you, I'd get as far away from him as possible," Claude warned.

A chord of guilt had been plucked deep within the moment he'd settled on his current course, and that sour note had rung through him ever since. Now, face to face with two people likely to be caught in the crossfire of his actions, it was all he could hear in his head.

"Is that a threat?" Lillith seethed.

"It's a warning," Yuri said. "Why are you warning us? What do they have planned?"

Claude lifted his hands and shrugged. He'd shared enough information. If they were smart, they could use it to stay alive when the tempest came. If not, then he'd done all he could. Vision and Zhara came first, and he would do nothing else for these soldiers for fear of jeopardizing them.

"Look, I know firsthand how things go for the grunts on the ground when the pressure gets turned up. Don't get caught without an exit strategy," Claude said, and twisted the handle once more.

The door slid open with only a slight hitch to reveal the waking street beyond. Yuri eyed the door, sighed, and stood after a long moment.

"Come on, Lill," he said, motioning for her to follow. "We have decisions to make."

The young woman glowered at Claude as she passed him, but said nothing further. Claude watched as the two exited his building and strolled into the growing procession outside.

As he watched them disappear into the mulling crowd, he acknowledged how much they reminded him of older days. He'd lost some of the rigid bearing that had once defined him.

Do you miss it? The military, I mean, Vision asked.

She'd been quiet for most of the conversation, no doubt consuming it like another Blitzer. Now he was grateful to have her company. His life on Minerva had been a good one, but there were still moments when he longed for the camaraderie of his old unit and the vibrant thrum of starship engines.

"I do," he said plainly. "Not enough to trade a second that I've had since, but yeah, I miss it."

Silence lingered for a moment as he closed and sealed his door, then walked into his office. He dropped his data-pad onto the table and waited for the broadcast connection to sync with the building's comms array. It only took a second, but while he waited, he milled over the plan, if it could be called that.

"*You're absolutely not going to do that!*" Vision practically shouted into his brain.

A stab of pain hit him behind the eyes, then faded as quickly as it had appeared.

"It's the only plan I've got," Claude groaned as he checked to make sure he hadn't been paralyzed again.

"*That's not a plan, Claude. A plan requires you to be able to predict how it will turn out,*" she informed him sharply.

"Maybe I can," Claude lied with a slight smirk.

"*I'm in your head. I can tell you're lying.*"

"Then maybe you should get out before I start thinking about the communal showers in infantry training," he bluffed.

Vision made sure to project her absolute disgust at the idea before falling silent once more.

There in the cool quiet of his office, Claude took the time to seriously consider the consequences of what he was about to set in motion.

It was a long, sobering moment before he finally said, "Establish an open channel to Kerrid."

• • • •

Bertrand wasted no time pulling up the schematics for Fauldwin's Archive. The domed building and the surrounding park blinked to holographic life in seconds, and Bertrand's sharp eyes immediately began scanning it for areas that would grant him the strategic advantage.

"And you're sure you want to meet here, instead of just at your office?" Bertrand said calmly.

A second image, this one of DiSilva, gave a wry smile. "Oh, I'm sure. The Archive is neutral ground. We'll meet there. You'll transfer the funds. I'll hand you the drives, and we go our separate ways. Assuming you don't have something else in mind?"

Bertrand waved off Claude's leading remark.

"No, not at all," Bertrand lied. "I'll work out the logistics and meet you there."

Claude's reconstructed eyes stared coldly at the older man before the image faded away, leaving only Bertrand, the Archive schematic, and Marta in the room.

The executor had been content to stay out of sensory range for the call, but now she took a seat opposite Bertrand.

"He's clever," she stated.

"Too damned clever," Bertrand barked. "And paranoid."

"After Firaxis, he has a right to be," Marta said, taking the opportunity to land a figurative jab on Bertrand.

The older man blew out a heavy breath and collapsed into his padded chair.

"I've done worse," he said with a hint of sadness in his voice. "We both have."

Marta gave Bertrand a smile that looked more like a sneer to him, then stated, "You don't know what I've done."

Bertrand huffed and waved off her statement. He didn't have the energy to play her petty game.

"I need Yuri and Lillith put on this immediately," he said.

Marta shook her head. "They're on assignment. Find someone else to do it."

Bertrand raised an eyebrow at her words. She had clearly gotten comfortable with the new arrangement. He was partially to blame, but she needed to be reminded of who's ship she was on.

"Is Echelon paying their contracts now?" Bertrand asked, silencing Marta. "If not, I need them at the Archive."

Marta didn't argue the issue further. She hadn't heard from either of them since their report about the dead pirate, and she really didn't need to. The meeting was set. All that was left was to place herself in the Archive to ensure there were no further mistakes. Yuri and Lillith could be there if it made Bertrand happy.

"Fine," she said, watching the skin on Bertrand's face redden.

Their arrangement was still extremely new, but it had already borne fruit for the both of them. Tensions on the ship had lessened to a noticeable degree, and Marta had found herself in a position of relative comfort, knowing that she had access to all data relevant to the mission.

She and Bertrand weren't friendly, and they never would be, but they had turned away from outright hostility. Despite their differing angles of approach, both had a vested interest in seeing this task completed to Echelon's desired specifications.

"You need to be ready also," Bertrand declared once his face had returned to its normal hue.

Marta eyed him intently for a moment before asking, "Why?"

"You wanted command of the troops. You have it. That means you'll be hands-on for this op," Bertrand said dryly. "Maybe your wealth of experience can help keep this from turning out like the Old City."

The daggers in his eyes were unmistakable. He meant for her to see them. While he had sought to mend in the rift between them, he'd only done it for the sake of harmony throughout the ship. In the end, they were on the same side, after all. Echelon wanted to win the war as much as he did, and Marta was here to help them reach that end. However, just because she represented an organization working toward his goal didn't mean that he had to like her. He didn't, and he took great pains to make that plain. As much as it pained him to admit it, that defiance was one more thing he and the executor had in common.

Bertrand enjoyed the idea of taking Marta into the field, although he expected things to run more smoothly than the last time his people set boots on the planet. She didn't know that, and he fully expected to see panic in her eyes at the mention of it.

Instead, he was met with a knowing, haughty stare.

"If that is all, I'll make my way back to my quarters, Captain," Marta said, lacing the words with venom.

Bertrand ignored the poison she meant for him and nodded his dismissal. Without another word and with a considerable amount of speed, the executor exited Bertrand's office and disappeared into the corridor beyond.

The old man let out a sigh that reminded him sharply of his age. Bertrand had been fighting the Sabiens since he was a teenager, and now he was fighting their shadow. The struggle had worn him thin, yet he had a sneaking suspicion his dealings with his own people had weakened his soul more than any enemy ever could.

He'd gotten word that pirates were on Minerva Prime. It was a fact, and while no one knew specifically who they were or why they were here, Bertrand believed he did. He didn't live in a universe of coincidences, at least not ones so impossibly large. It had been unbelievable finding DiSilva on this rock, but now there were pirates on the planet as well. He knew who it was, who it had to be, and he knew why she'd come.

Bertrand's conscience tortured him over having sold Miranda to the specters from Myridorn. He knew that now. The reward they'd granted him had always felt like a weight slowly crushing the life from him, but no amount of personal guilt could excuse his actions. Miranda was owed a debt, and he was the last person to deny its legitimacy, although he was not inclined to pay it just yet. The time would come. Bertrand was sure of it, but the work he had devoted his life to was still too incomplete to be left to others.

The Sabien threat still loomed over the whole of the known universe. The "peace," as the politicians liked to call it, was a temporary calm at the center of a bloody storm, and one day the winds of violence would come again. There was only one way to end it, only one way to bring clear skies and bright futures to the Beita Systems. It would require hard and, sadly, immoral choices. Choices like the one he'd made all those years ago and the one he would make tomorrow. In a perfect universe, such things wouldn't be required of good men, but in this one, good men only existed in childhood fictions.

• • • •

Ashe stood mere feet from the woman whose fall she'd spent the last year wishing for and the last days actively planning. She was flanked by Octavian, who did his best to look at her as little as possible. A courtesy, she did her very best to repay.

Octavian had requested that both women meet him on the ship's command deck, and he had done so specifically during a crew change. Why, she wasn't sure, but Ashe understood him well enough to know that the timing wasn't chosen randomly. Octavian never did anything randomly. He relied on her to bring spontaneity, and she relied on him to know what to do. So far, it was working out better than she thought it would, but the most rigorous tests were yet to come.

Miranda's face was difficult to read. A million tiny emotions contorted her features in the few moments since Ashe had delivered her news. She imagined Miranda would be elated or as close as she could get. Her quarry was going to be in the open. Not just that, but she'd been given the time and location as well. Instead of relief, joy, or even the most subtle hint of gratitude, there was a symphony playing behind her eyes, and if Ashe had to guess, it wasn't a pleasant one.

After what seemed like forever, the captain finally looked up and met Ashe's eyes. They burned into her in such a way that Ashe felt the sudden and nearly overwhelming desire to flee screaming from the command deck. She didn't, but it took an act of willpower as strong as anything she'd ever mustered to keep her feet planted on the grated flooring.

"I want full schematics of the Archive and a map of the surrounding area," Miranda said in a deeper voice than Ashe remembered her having.

Before Ashe could utter the customary, "Aye, Captain," Miranda focused her attention on Octavian. The weight of that gaze lifted instantly, and Ashe almost sighed audibly. She stole a glance at the man by her side only and saw that he was weathering the captain's stare better than she had, though just barely.

"Get me a full strike team and have every Lifter we have left prepped to move by sunrise," Miranda said with ravenous hate tearing its way through her words.

Octavian nodded, but his customary mechanical voice remained silent. He held her gaze and waited to be dismissed as Miranda's mind kept grinding on the situation to come.

"One of the bikes was still operational after the last run. Track it. We'll need a path into the city that doesn't attract too much attention," she barked before she waved for them to clear her sight.

Octavian ushered Ashe away, and in a smooth motion, handed her an earpiece. He watched as her face darkened with disapproval, but she said nothing and kept moving until they reached the lift.

The metal door slid closed, and once the lift began moving, Ashe pushed the uncomfortable piece of polymer and circuitry into her ear canal.

"Do as she says. Find the bike and find her a way into the city," Octavian stated as mechanically as the voice that relayed his words.

"Once she's off the ship, we can just take it and leave," Ashe pleaded. "There would be nothing she could do about it."

"But we'd be leaving good people behind, and I owe her more than that," he responded, and Ashe watched as the humanity returned to him.

She knew his connection to Captain Faridan ran deep, but she didn't quite understand it. She was a pirate, and to pirates there were no hang-ups about how bad situations ended so long as they did. He obviously didn't share that sentiment, and she hoped that his soldier's honor wouldn't put him on the wrong side. A growing part of her wanted to see what came next where they were concerned, and she couldn't do that if he stood in her way.

Men and women were longing to break free of Faridan's control, and she was unwilling to stand against them. If that levy broke, she would be carried away by the resulting flood, and she desperately hoped Octavian would allow himself to flow with the current as well.

"Then resolve your conscience quickly," she said in what came out more as a gruff command than she had intended. "Things are moving, and I can't stop them."

Octavian nodded severely before Ashe pulled him down for a kiss. It was deep and spoke of future desires, but it was over all too quickly. Octavian stood and looked at her with unreadable eyes. He watched her for a long moment, saying nothing before the earpiece spoke to her again.

"I can solve this," Octavian said and drew a deep breath. "I can fix this for all of us."

"You better," Ashe said, and this time her voice threatened to betray her.

Chapter 29

THE SKYWAYS OF FAULDWIN were busy, even though nearly every building in the district was closed. People flocked from Cascade to the city's undisputed heart to observe the final days of the celebration. The masses seemed to almost thrum with the excitement of another year's culmination ceremony.

Unfortunately, Claude saw every soul moving in the distant street below as a weight on his conscience. Every face in the hovercars surrounding him was another potential casualty in a conflict they had no idea even existed. And every smile he saw made him hate himself a little more for his choices.

With a heavy sigh, he did his best to put his own responsibility for what might happen to them in a tiny lockbox deep in his mind. There would be time to deal with the fallout of his actions later. Getting all of the guilt he felt into such a small and secluded space was a monumental struggle. It was one he'd been working on ever since he'd made the call yesterday, but it was only now, mere miles and minutes from his chosen location, that he managed to close the lid.

"So once I hand these things over, I can just leave, right?" Claude asked hopefully.

He was no expert on tech and certainly not coding of any sort. Claude was more than comfortable when it came to getting objects from one location to another, even through heavy resistance and unpredictable circumstances. However, dealing with things like system access points and data storage networks was beyond him.

"As long as your guy gets the drives uploaded, you should be fine," Zhara said, keeping her focus on the skyway ahead.

"And what if things go south before then?" Claude asked pointedly.

He tried to keep the obvious concern out of his voice, but failed utterly. When Zhara shot him a sidelong glance weighted with as much worry as disapproval, he realized how far off the mark he'd landed. Claude could see her jaw tighten, but she said nothing. He had been rather vague about the nature of his plan, choosing only to tell her what should happen if everything went well.

He knew she was no fool, nor was he trying to treat her like one, but there were things she would be overly concerned about. Claude knew that, and while he hadn't said much about his escape clause, Zhara was smart enough to know he had one.

The silence in the Regent's cab dragged on for what seemed like half an hour before Vision cleared her throat to shatter it.

"I still think you'll need someone watching your back like before," she chimed in from the back seat.

"Absolutely not," Claude stated flatly. "You wouldn't have been in the Old City if I didn't think you'd burn the apartment down on your own."

Vision made a point of groaning loud enough for everyone to hear before Zhara engaged the Regent's autopilot and pivoted her seat inward toward the others. She fixed them both with stern looks. Her eyes a mix of determination and worry. They took Claude by surprise, even though they shouldn't have.

"If the drives get destroyed, half of our problem is solved," she stated, shoving Vision's argument into the periphery. "If they get uploaded, all of it will be. I don't see a way that this can leave us any worse off than where we started."

Claude faked a rather convincing smile. Neither of the girls knew how likely things were to explode in his face, and he wasn't inclined to tell them. They wouldn't understand why the risks were necessary.

The code was, at best, an insurance policy. If Claude was right about Miranda, she would not miss the opportunity to take a shot at Bertrand, assuming his message was intercepted. If their positions were reversed, he could see himself being extremely tempted by such a chance, although he questioned if he would follow through with it.

Miranda had clearly become more reckless over the years, and he was banking heavily on both her recklessness and her hate. It was a risky play that, in hindsight, made him wonder if Miranda really was any worse than he was. At least she had kept her collateral damage somewhat contained, so far. If things went to plan, Claude wouldn't be able to say the same.

That was why he was sending Zhara and Vision back to the apartment as soon as possible. There was a good chance that rounds would fly at the Archive, and the last thing he needed was to have them in the line of fire. He was putting his own future on the line to secure theirs, after all. What was the point if they were killed in the process?

The Regent began its predetermined descent to street level. The towering multi-tiered buildings of Fauldwin gave way to the massive green space where the Archive was housed. Lush foliage stretched for what had to be a mile, defying the arid Minervan climate.

Center City Park was laced with smooth stone walkways that led to and around several small two-story buildings, and at the park's center rested its primary attraction. The massive dome housed hundreds of priceless relics from a world that no living soul had any memory of. Claude meant to bring Vision here as he had almost every year, and while he was technically doing that now, it wasn't the way either of them would have preferred.

Calling Bertrand down on this place had the added curse of potentially destroying it, but he needed an open public space where it would be easy to disappear. Given the timing, he couldn't think of a better location than this. It was the heart of the Truce Week celebrations in Minerva City, and there would be a decent PlanSec presence nearby. Hopefully, that meant any collateral damage would be kept to a minimum.

As horrible as it was to admit, all of that was secondary. Claude had spent much of his life believing he was a decent person, and maybe that was true on some level. Sadly, even decent people had to make hard choices when decent options were scarce.

Luckily for him, and for both Vision and Zhara, Claude knew the truth about himself. In reality, He was still just a soldier. Only now, the nation he fought for was in the hovercar with him, and the battle ahead could only be won if he shut himself off to everything else.

The Regent came to rest on the street near the park. The landing zone panels painted its white underbelly yellow as the vehicle's weight settled upon it. The car powered down its thrusters and drive engine seconds before Claude stepped out.

He looked up at immense buildings and the traffic lanes interweaving above him, marveling at the stark differences between life here and in Violet. The park provided the odd opportunity for open-air in a city where shadows were ever-present, and even on the ground, there wasn't a speck of dust to be found.

It was beautiful. This park always reminded him of the world he'd left so long ago. The heavy irrigation required to keep the plants vibrant in the middle of a desert world had the added benefit of keeping the air cool and refreshing, like the fields of Abarix in spring. He found himself wanting to run his fingers through the foliage as he had done as a child, but the mission called. Well, that and Vision.

"They're already here," she said in a voice that all but begged to come with him.

Claude reached into the Regent and took the shoulder bag containing the drives from her.

Reluctantly, she released it, but not before she fired one of her patented scowls at him. If it had been any other task, he would likely have folded and taken her along. Instead, he kissed her just below her halo and came away with a static shock so strong he half believed she'd fired it at him on purpose.

"Don't get killed," she barked at him, still wearing the same haunting scowl.

Claude turned his attention to Zhara's fragile expression. She said nothing, but she didn't need to. He leaned in and kissed her lightly, feeling her lips tremble against his.

"I'll get this done, and then we'll be free of it," he said, and he meant every word.

What he didn't say was that they would be together or that he would see them again. He didn't even say that he would live through it, and Claude had no doubt that Zhara picked up on all that he had left unspoken.

"I love you," were the only words that escaped her as she pushed him away and wiped her eyes.

For over two years, they'd been together but neither had put their feelings into those exact words. It was an archaic and rudimentary summation of what could never be accurately expressed, or so Zhara felt the need to tell him whenever he'd tried.

Now that she had said it first, Claude was so stunned he hadn't been able to say anything before she sealed the hovercar and began its preflight system check.

"*She already knows*," Vision whispered into his mind as the Regent's thrusters flared back to life and lifted the vehicle into the air.

Claude watched as the women he cared for more than anything in the universe ascended into the skyways and disappeared back into the maze of buildings. He found himself staring after them for a moment longer before drawing in a deep breath and turning to face the massive dome that held the past of his people and the future of his family.

• • • •

The sheer number of bodies packed into the Archive's atrium was impressive. Claude had seen it full before, but this was another thing entirely. A thousand conversations merged, creating a blanket of sound that laid heavy over the crowd. Beyond the first few bodies, Claude found it challenging to make out individuals at first. It took a second for him to lean into his old training, but once he did, the intimidating mass of bodies lost much of its menace.

After a moment, Claude found he could move through the sea of people, but only with the flow. His objective was the show floor two stories above, but by the time he made it to the lifts on the far side of the lobby, he had half a mind to call the whole thing off.

He had mastered the crowd, but had missed the troops no doubt stationed within it. Blending in worked both ways, and without decent sightlines, it was going to be near impossible to make out Bertrand's men before they moved on him.

The lift rose above the mob, giving Claude a proper view of the masses through its transparent structure. The four patrons inside with him paid the sight no mind, nor did they pay him any. They were all lost in their own mundane conversations.

Under normal circumstances, Claude would have gathered what information he could from them, but he was too focused on spotting the soldiers in the crowd. He found three before the second-floor alert dinged, and the lift stopped again.

The lift emptied swiftly, and a moment later, a young woman entered and favored him with a glance that immediately put him on edge. She was petite and curvy, with a caramel complexion and thick brown hair. The woman lunged at the panel and almost sealed the door on a man's hand as he tried to board.

She regarded Claude with the same uneasy suspicion he shared. There was a hardness to her stare that Claude respected instantly, though she didn't seem equally impressed.

"You must be DiSilva," she said with a slight sneer. "I don't see what the big deal is about."

Claude blew out a huff and turned to face the small woman. She was nearly two heads shorter than he was, but that didn't matter. Her bearing, expression, and presence made her status clear. Her image was well constructed, and if Claude didn't make a living by peeling away such illusions, he would have taken it at face value. Instead, he looked deeper.

A twitch assaulted the muscles at the corners of her eyes, and slightly hitched breathing gave her away. She was scared, and her fear threatened to tear down the brazen demeanor she worked so hard to project. It wasn't likely the woman would attempt anything, given how exposed as they were, but she was no pushover. That much was plain to see. What wasn't so obvious was whether the tiny tremor in her hand was because of him or not.

"Where's Bertrand?" Claude asked, choosing to skip the bravado and get straight to business.

"He's in the designated location," the woman said, staring at the thin lines of silver running down his neck and into the collar of his shirt. "I came to see the thing you carry."

Claude sighed and shook his head slowly.

"It's not a display item," he said with a low rumble in his voice. "But you're in a museum, so I'm sure you can find something else to gawk at."

The woman shrugged.

"Maybe," she said casually, sweeping her hair behind her ear. "But I'd be more interested in the white Regent that dropped you off here. That's not the kind of car just anyone could afford."

Claude fixed her with a stare that would have burned her down to ashes if such things were possible.

The woman smiled at his reaction as though it were fully expected.

"Girlfriend has expensive tastes, does she?" the woman said with a sickly-sweet voice. "A few months in Deroga can solve that."

Claude took a single step forward and watched as all of the woman's composure melted into open, wide-eyed terror. He wasn't planning on attacking her, but he did want to send a message so clearly that there was no hope of her confusing it. And with one tiny gesture, he'd done just that.

"Echelon, huh?" he said with a thin smirk. "You people have always been better wordsmiths than warriors, but if you so much as shift your weight in her direction, I will slice you into pieces so thin they'll make this lift seem opaque."

The woman took another step back and pressed herself against the far wall. She wasn't happy with her reaction, but Claude didn't think her rational mind had much to do with it. She clearly knew about the silver, and she knew at least some of what it was capable of. His threat just added weight to that. Claude was relatively sure that combined, it would keep her off the track she'd threatened to walk, but there was no real way to be sure.

What he did know was that she was Echelon, but why Bertrand would bring her here made little sense. If his former commander was having issues with them, Claude couldn't see why he would let them tag along on something so sensitive. And then it hit him.

The lift stopped, and Claude flashed a smile at the terrified woman.

"Good talk," he said and stepped out into a much thinner crowd than he'd found below.

The corridor spilled out into a massive circular room decorated with extensive display cases along its walls. Each held artifacts Claude barely recognized. One held the front end of some battered land vehicle, with a dented grille and broken polymer bubbles whose purpose he didn't know.

Another housed a large metal man stained green and half-melted to the fractured stone base beneath him.

The domed ceiling stretched up to an artificially flattened stop where the offices of the Archive workers resided. The space was huge, and the chatter inside was thick and constant. Though somehow, there was no echo. Claude assumed the abstract patterns that stretched up the walls absorbed it, keeping the massive chamber from being an elaborate torture device.

At the center of the exhibition space rested four rooms connected end to end. They formed a circle around a single thick pillar that reached through the ceiling and all the floors below. The massive column was the center point of the Archive, both in a structural sense and a metaphorical one. Claude had seen it once a year for the last six, and while he knew of the wonders it housed, he'd never actually seen any of them. The viewing rooms were almost always booked, and even if they weren't, the price to access them was too rich for his blood.

Claude took another moment to admire the construction and to wonder who exactly was responsible for making it a reality before moving on to the task at hand. The smaller crowd gave him a little more comfort, but the artifacts here were irreplaceable. That knowledge threatened to erode his resolve as he wondered if Vision would forgive him for getting the Archive destroyed.

Along the wall to his right, he noticed what looked like small reddish-brown stones adhered with an abrasive off-white substance. People were touching it and coming away with dust on their fingers while speaking in hushed, almost reverent tones. Claude shook his head. It was an ancient building material that was emulated in structures throughout the Old City, so it held no wonder for him, but to tourists and those from the inner districts, it was a marvel.

What did catch his interest was a time-wrecked image of the Flying Man. It was the first time he'd seen him look like a real flesh and blood person instead of some artistic rendering. The red cloth streaming from his back struck an oddly appealing contrast with the blue of his suit. Something about the image and the curious symbol on his chest spoke to Claude on a level he didn't quite understand.

He slowed his pace to admire it, noticing the partial transcription. He couldn't read the original lettering, as the language was long dead, but the people at the Archive had kindly translated what they could. Supposedly, it said, "You'll believe a man can..." but the ruins of time and untold tragedy robbed the message of its full meaning.

Claude eyed the chiseled features of the hero, committing the thing to memory, and moved on. The Archive would absorb all of his time and attention if he let it. While he wasn't a fan of living in the past, especially the very distant past, he couldn't deny the longing that he shared with other humans of his age.

Something extraordinary had been lost, something that was now impossible to reclaim. It didn't mean that humanity shouldn't try, though. To Claude, the struggle was the point. Perhaps it was that struggle or the loss of it that had brought on the harvest in the first place. He didn't know. No one did, but that didn't stop the speculation.

Claude shook the idea away. Now wasn't the time to wax philosophical. Work still needed to be done.

The lighter crowd made spotting Bertrand's people here a simple thing. He made out both Yuri and Lillith on opposite ends of the space as well as two others. They milled around acting like the rest of the patrons but had clearly spotted him as well. Yuri even nodded to him, which Claude found odd. Lillith took a moment to glower at him before returning to her perusal of the odds and ends on display.

Claude suppressed a smirk as he remembered an old truth from his service. His friend Jerik used to believe that a person met their replacement if they stayed in any place long enough. Claude had his doubts. The pride in him wanted to believe he had no replacement, but Lillith challenged that theory. Not for himself, but he saw shades of the old Miranda in her.

Claude had all but tuned out the soothing voice of the holographic guides, telling everyone what the various objects were thought to be used for. It didn't really matter to him if the tiny, metal, four-pronged tool was used for grooming or not. He was more interested in the room's layout, exits, potential enemy numbers, and positions. It would be difficult to escape if things went very wrong, unless he could break through the floor.

He glanced at it thoughtfully for a moment and wondered if his passenger was strong enough to rip through the thick transparent metal that separated this floor from the second.

"He's in the Cetalon viewing station," the woman from the elevator told him as she gave him a wide berth and moved further into the room.

Claude gave her a glare, then searched out his new destination. He spotted two clear exits, but both lead to lifts incapable of bearing the weight of the twenty or so civilians. Assuming the silver could tear through the floor, that would provide another exit, but that was an option he'd prefer not to endorse just yet.

Upon reaching the room marked with the multi-tentacled shape of a Cetalon, Claude waited as the door split into four panels that each rotated into their respective corners. It was a showy design when a single sliding panel door would have sufficed, but who was he to argue? The viewing station was lined with three rows of padded seats divided by a dimly lit aisle that led from the door to the large viewing window and the old man standing before it. Claude noticed the wing of some ancient craft taking up the window space.

To Claude, it looked frail and bland, but the star and bars marking on it did interest him. It was clearly a military insignia of some kind, but he didn't recognize it. Little was known about the world humanity had been stolen from or the circumstances of that theft.

To Claude's knowledge, there was nothing that spoke of a battle, but then he was no expert on the Homeworld. This was clearly part of some fighting vehicle. If he was to bet, it meant the humans of old had fought the Zephiar, and that was a good thing to know.

"You know these are new finds," the old man said as Claude made his way to him.

Bertrand didn't turn. He kept his eyes on the gray metal, searching the edges where it had apparently been sheered off by something that melted right through it.

"I wouldn't know," Claude said, taking his place beside the man but keeping a safe distance. "I haven't been able to afford a viewing like this."

Bertrand turned to him with a worn but honest smile on his face. The man's eyes were troubled, but they met Claude's and didn't waver.

"Then you picked a good spot," Bertrand said as his eyes finally made it down to Claude's tattered jacket. "Looks like you've managed to stay busy."

"Yes, but busy doesn't pay as much as it should," Claude said, stretching his neck. "How do we do this?"

Claude made a show of removing the drives from his bag but did not offer to hand them over. He watched as Bertrand's eyes both lit up with excitement and then diminished with some other emotion Claude hadn't seen on the man's face before.

Bertrand sighed and removed his data-pad from his uniform pocket, tapping it several times.

"Getting this big an amount approved was a challenge, DiSilva. I want you to know that," the older man said, focusing on his holographic screen instead of Claude.

"Then we were both able to do a little of the impossible," Claude joked, hoping that the nervousness he felt didn't ring through in his voice.

"If it were up to me, I'd just transfer this money and take the drives," Bertrand began as he slid the data-pad back into his pocket with one hand and drew an oddly bulbous short-barreled pistol with the other.

"Unfortunately for us both, it isn't up to me."

Claude took an unconscious step back. The silver in him roiled in a way that added to his unease. The pistol in Bertrand's hand was unfamiliar, and without knowing what it could do, Claude was at a loss for options.

"What are you doing?" he asked stupidly.

"You know exactly what I'm doing, DiSilva," Bertrand said with a voice that sounded hollow. "I'm winning us the war."

Claude eased the drives back into the bag slowly and continued to step back along the window.

"The war is over, Bertrand," he said, finally accepting the situation.

"No, it's just paused. Wars don't end at negotiating tables, not when they're about something real," Claude's former commander stated. "Someone always has to win, and someone always has to lose."

"So, I lose, is that it? Me, Miranda, and anyone else that has something you and your masters want have to lose so they can win. Is that how this goes, Bertrand?" Claude growled at the older man.

Bertrand absorbed his words for a moment, and it looked like he might waver. Then his face twisted with renewed determination.

"This isn't personal, DiSilva. It just has to be done," he declared, raising the gun to better his shot.

Claude barely registered the words before the pistol barked a loud, oddly melodic cry, hurling its ionic discharge into the open air. The shot was well aimed, but the projectile was slower than a typical sidearm round.

Claude could actually see it coming and had time to dodge out of the way. A part of him was genuinely curious about what the weapon was designed to do, but there wasn't time to indulge that. There was barely enough time to close the distance before Bertrand could get off a second shot.

Claude leaped toward the man. He could already see Bertrand's aim correcting and his finger depressing the trigger. With a rush of emotions that weren't all his own, Claude watched a slender tendril shoot from his palm to crush both the gun and Bertrand's trigger finger. The creature wrenched the old man's arm, forcing him to the ground. It tensed as the metal of the gun twisted, and Bertrand's hand edged toward becoming a permanent ruin.

Bertrand's howl of pain was drowned out by a thunderous boom from outside as Claude landed inches from him. Screams of panic reached Claude's ears even through the thick wall of the viewing station, but he forced himself to ignore them. He spared a moment to scan the room then turned back to his former commander.

He knew what was happening out there, and he tried not to think about it. His plan was working. Now Claude had to see it through.

Bertrand knelt in front of him, holding his wrist and giving voice to his surprise and agony. Claude forced himself to his feet as swiftly as he could while coaxing the silver to recede.

At first, it refused, instead further crushing the bones in the older man's hand until Claude was forced to shout, "That's enough!"

The room shook around him as his passenger finally relented and coiled itself back under his skin. Small arms fire resounded from beyond the sealed door, accompanied by a chorus of screams and unintelligible shouting.

Claude hazarded a glance at the door as the unmistakable roar of Lifter bikes bellowed through the walls. The weight of the drives seemed to triple as he turned back to the old commander cowering nearby.

"You called her," Bertrand said in a mix of misery and terror.

"I couldn't trust you," Claude said, pulling Bertrand to his feet and removing the bag from his shoulder. "Did you transfer the credits?"

Bertrand nodded after a long moment, unable to find the courage to look Claude in the eye. The old man's reaction was to be expected, even if it was disappointing. Claude had never seen the commander cowed in such away. He always seemed as though he was in control of every situation. Now he just seemed lost and pitiful.

"Then our business is done," Claude stated, lacing the strap of the bag over Bertrand's shoulder and under his good arm. "I'm going to forget you tried to shoot me and you are going to forget you ever saw me. Got it?"

"It's not that simple," Bertrand said, his voice strengthening again with each word. "Echelon knows you have the creature. They'll keep coming for you."

Another boom shook the floor and knocked dust from the ceiling.

"I can handle Echelon," Claude declared and meant it.

"Don't be so sure," his old commander huffed. "They have the entire nation under their thumb. What's one scout going to do?"

"Disappear, if I can," Claude said with a casual shrug. "Or tear them down world by world if I can't."

• • • •

Daylight spilled through the smoldering holes in the thick Archive walls. Smoke and ash swirled in the third-floor exhibition space stirred by the thrusters of lifter bikes. The attackers drifted down from the ruined dome to hover a mere two feet above the debris-strewn floor.

Lillith studied their slow, deliberate movements, but their engine wash made it difficult to make out the riders in any real detail. Regardless, the lack of formation and the idiotic shouts driving the civvies into a panic gave them away. They were pirates, and after her time in Violet, their appearance wasn't altogether unexpected.

Lillith fired a glance across the exhibition hall to Yuri, who had shot out a field emitter nearby and taken cover behind the broken, stone-topped counter within. Lillith followed suit, slamming her back against the warped metallic frame of an archaic wheeled vehicle and keeping her head low.

For them, the job was simple. Keep Bertrand safe. While he had been adamant about being left alone to deal with DiSilva, the pirates' arrival called the entire scenario into question.

Even before the bikes had melted holes in the walls, meeting with DiSilva without a trained ranger watching his back had been stupid on Bertrand's part. Lillith had seen what DiSilva could do. She had been all but bested by him, and it didn't sit well with her.

Yuri had said all the right things to get her to let it go, but she hadn't. Alien lifeform or not, coming so close to losing that fight was unacceptable. Lillith didn't lose fights, but now she'd been given a chance to counter that embarrassment by putting another win on the board.

She trained her sidearm on the riders nearest her position and let fly half a dozen rounds. She was excellent with a pistol, but between the distance and the atmospheric distortions caused by the bikes, landing her shots was a challenge. Lillith was sure she'd hit the lead rider at least twice, yet the woman was still seated firmly on her vehicle.

"Cease fire!" came their new boss's voice. The sound of it made the hairs on Lillith's neck stand up, but she obeyed even if it meant biting back every instinct in her.

The petite executor was crouched between Yuri and the far wall, leaving her partially exposed to the pirates. It was a mistake any soldier would have avoided, but she was anything but a soldier. The executor talked a big game, but when it came to field ops, she was as green as Beklion algae. If it was up to Lillith, she would have ignored whatever "insights" the woman thought she had, but Bertrand had left the unit under her command. Cursing under her breath, Lillith pressed tighter against the broken vehicle she'd been marveling at only a few moments earlier and waited.

Part of her wanted to take a shot at Echelon's puppet. She could always blame it on the chaos around her, and there was no doubt Yuri would back her up. But then she'd have to live with that choice and the fear that someone might discover what she'd done, assuming living was a thing she'd be doing past the next few seconds.

Grumbling to herself, Lillith stole another glance over the tortured metal, noting that she actually had hit the woman rider, but with three shots instead of just two. Ragged holes were plainly visible in her neck, bicep, and her upper torso just inches from where her heart should have been. A thin ring of silver shimmered at the outer edge of each wound, pulsing and repairing the damaged flesh before her eyes.

If the shots had caused any discomfort to the woman, it was unclear since she acknowledged only the lack of mobility in her arm. If she hadn't seen something similar the previous day, Lillith might have lost her grip on sanity. Instead, she found herself nearly obsessed with how differently this silver creature responded from the other. Where DiSilva's had seemingly deflected the rounds she'd fired at him, the pirate's let her take the rounds and regenerated rather than protect her.

There was some significance to that, but Lillith forced herself to let it go before she found herself hopelessly distracted. As the old soldier's mantra said, "If it bleeds, we can kill it," and the leader of the pirates definitely bled.

She planned to put the next round in the woman's skull just to see if she could heal her own brain but stopped short when Marta stood and stepped out of cover like a worlds-class buffoon.

Lillith watched as Yuri clawed at the executor, trying to pull her back to safety only to be ignored.

"Bertrand right?" Marta asked loudly as she negotiated chunks of broken ceiling while keeping her eyes locked on the lead pirate. "I think we both know he's the reason you're here."

The dark-skinned woman cocked her head in naked curiosity but said nothing. The move reminded Lillith of an animal more than a person, and the observation felt wrong somehow.

Marta squared herself with the lead pirate as she moved out toward the room's center. The other bikes spread out strafing her and ignoring Lillith and Yuri. Their thrusters singed the corpses of soldiers and civilians alike littering the newly warped floor, filling the air with the acrid scent of ruin and death.

"Where is he?" demanded a voice so tortured by rage that Lillith found herself wondering if it was even human.

"Believe me, I want nothing more than to hand him over to you, but he hasn't arrived yet," Marta declared with such confidence that Lillith half wanted to believe it herself. "The meet was postponed by an hour. He sent us ahead to secure the area."

Again, the pirate leader measured her response, saying nothing for a long moment and only staring at the petite caramel-skinned woman standing fearlessly before her.

Lillith found herself wishing she could do something to improve the situation, but she didn't see a way to make that happen from her position. Marta was fully exposed. Getting to her would be impossible before they were both gunned down. They would need cover.

Four stone support columns circled their side of the space with easily eight feet between them. If toppled, they might work, but each one was sturdy enough that anything less than a year's worth of concentrated small arm's fire would prove utterly useless.

Due to the nature of the mission, she hadn't elected to carry anything more potent than her sidearm, but Yuri had. He'd insisted on bringing small yield explosives like he always did. Lillith could see the telltale glint of the two detonator discs on him from where she was. She'd tried to convince him they were useless countless times, but now she was more than a little grateful his skull was so thick.

Slowly and silently, Lillith placed her sidearm on the floor, spotting the reinforcements shoving their way through the surging crowds below. It would be some time before they could help. So, she pushed them from her mind. Allies that couldn't arrive in time were allies best not considered.

With a sharp, violent wave, she grabbed Yuri's attention. There wasn't an established hand signal for "blow up the column to the right of the third enemy and bring it down on them," but she believed she got the point across quite well.

Yuri nodded and stole a glance at the column she'd indicated before flashing her a nervous smile and a thumbs up.

It would have been simpler if their personal comms hadn't crashed before the attack began. Which was in no way a coincidence. Where pirates got the tech to do such a thing was a million-credit question. As was how they managed to get military issue recon Lifter bikes.

They'd clearly come prepared, and that preparation had gotten them this far. To get the rest of the way, they would have to outfight her and Yuri. Given their numbers, elevated position, and the fact that their leader shrugged off gunshots, it seemed like they might just be able to pull it off. Then again, she and Yuri were no strangers to grim scenarios.

Yuri freed one of the palm-sized metallic discs from his belt and twisted it. Once armed, he slung the disc in a wide, horizontal arc around the room's edge and into his target. The disc's heated rim bit deep into the stonework column and stayed put.

Lillith had no idea how long a fuse he'd set on the damned thing, but she found herself wondering for the first time whether the floor would hold. It hadn't occurred to her when she'd called for the attack, but now she realized just how many souls were trapped beneath them.

The lifts were moving again, and two ferried civilians to the first floor. Hopefully, they would make it to safety, but that was an enormous hope.

"You don't look like a TaskMaster," the lead pirate stated at last.

Marta stood as still as stone while hostile eyes scanned and cataloged every inch of her with mild interest. She waited for the rest of the response, knowing it was coming.

Marta's information on Miranda Faridan said she was a focused and driven person, but she could be distracted by a significant enough challenge. That was an exploitable weakness, and Marta aimed to use it to buy time for Bertrand to complete the mission.

Lillith watched the two women face off against one another and, for a moment, wondered who was the more unyielding. Then the pirate spoke again.

"You're too well fed. Commissary rations don't build a body like that, but an Echelon stipend does," the woman's voice boomed.

Marta opened her mouth to protest, but whatever words she'd wanted to say were cut off.

"Slag her," the pirate leader said casually, and in the time it took for Marta to take half a step, a ball of plasma melted through her clothes, her skin, muscles, and finally her skeleton.

In less than three seconds, all that was left of her was a glowing puddle of plasma slowly melting its way through the floor. The executor's scream outlasted everything else she was, but the Archive's uniquely constructed dome ensured even that didn't survive for long.

Lillith was firing before she realized it. The shots seemed to startle the pirate leader, and she took another round in the side before she returned fire and pulled her bike up toward the ceiling to better protect herself. The other pirates moved to do the same, but their maneuvers put them all in the path of the marked column. The fuse ignited, and the resulting explosion rocked the building.

The disc was well placed, but Lillith expected nothing less. The force of the blast cleaved through the base of the column, like a scalpel of fire and force. The ceiling cracked under the free-hanging weight of the thing and broke away almost instantly.

Sunlight poured through the second of the Archive's wounds, catching the dance of dust and debris as the column collapsed in what seemed like slow motion. The falling column collided with one of the bikes, sending its rider on a twenty-foot fall that ended with a loud crunch, and a sickening boneless bounce before his journey ended in stillness.

The pirate leader had the sense to spin her Lifter to avoid the bulk of falling stone. The maneuver was quick and deftly executed, but it was not enough. The column clipped the bike's tail, knocking it to the floor in a hail of sparks and rent metal.

The third bike took the weight fully on the back of its rider and was forced to the ground. It slammed to the floor under the massive weight of stone and exploded, splashing the floor and much of the far wall with deep blue arcs of ionic discharge. The blinding and brilliant dance of loosed power shorted the thrusters on the remaining Lifter bike, forcing it into a dead stick landing that mostly spared both the machine and its rider.

Lillith ducked back behind her cover and counted the seconds until gunfire rained down on her position, but the shots never came. She saw Yuri doing the same, and she was about to suggest they fall back when she heard the soul shredding screams of pain and anguished determination.

The pirate leader clawed her way from under the wrecked bike, slicing her broken left leg to the bone in the process. Her screams rang off every surface in the dome before the sound-conscious construction absorbed them.

Every inch of excruciating pain moved her further from the wreckage and closer to freedom. Her eyes remained locked on the door to the viewing station ahead, and as her cries evolved into feral grunts and eventually silence, she grew closer to her aim.

Lillith peeked over the ruined antique at her side and watched the woman pull herself along the warped floor, leaving most of the flesh from her left thigh behind.

Silver, blood, and broken bone were all visible, but the former was realigning and fusing her leg before Lillith's eyes. Tiny strands of the liquid metal weaved along the exposed flesh as it grew back with a low and constant squelching sound that turned Lillith's stomach.

She came back to herself and opened fired as the woman's sickly off-white femur began to vanish under a swell of the same living silver. Four of her rounds found their mark in her upper torso, but the shot meant for the pirate's head was cut out of the air by something that moved so fast Lillith could barely see it.

When it slowed enough for her to make it out, her eyes went wide with shock and disbelief. What she saw threatened to shake her grasp on the universe and spread tiny fractures through her psyche. Three things that she registered as bladed spider legs sprouted from the injured woman's back. Two busied themselves, lifting her from the ground while a third angled itself to strike at Lillith.

In a flash of mindless instinct and embedded training, Lillith dove to the ground and rolled as the slash came down. Her momentum brought her to her feet, and she locked her attention on her own shocked face reflected in the alien appendage. The image distorted as the bladed limb turned and launched a second slash. This time it came closer to its target with swift and silent precision.

The silver streak slashed down as Lillith fell back and scrambled away. It took her a second to notice the torn fabric and shredded ballistic weave that hung open like ragged wounds. By the time she gathered herself and launched into a full sprint, the limb had retreated back to its master.

Somewhere in the distance, Yuri opened fire as Lillith rounded the circle of rooms at the exhibition's heart and lost sight of him. Her goal was to break the line of sight and hopefully regroup with him so they could find a way into Bertrand's location or out of the Archive altogether. She hoped her squadmate was doing the same thing, but since she could still hear the bark of his sidearm, he clearly wasn't.

"Damn it, Yuri, fall back!" she shouted as loudly as her laboring lungs would allow and listened for his response.

It didn't take long for the gunfire to die out. The room's sound all but disappeared save for the shallow tings of minor debris falling to the tortured floor.

She heard no words, no footsteps, and no sign that Yuri had ended the barrage of his own volition. And it was there in the newly risen silence that Lillith began to panic.

• • • •

Yuri watched as the creature that had once so clearly been a woman stalked toward him. Spindly, blade-like legs held her body aloft, dangling it like the abdomen of a giant insect while she moved slowly and purposefully in his direction.

He had fired more than a dozen rounds at the thing, and just like in DiSilva's office, standard ammunition had no apparent effect. Shots sparked off the limbs, and the rare few that found their way to the woman's body seemed to do nothing but anger her further.

There was no clear sign she felt the rounds at all, and Yuri didn't have the mind to search for subtle reactions. He was looking to kill her or at least cripple her, but neither seemed possible without destroying himself in the process.

By the time the last detonator disc came to mind, the pirate monster was already looming over him. Its legs splayed oddly as it planted itself before him. The woman at its center regarded him with curious eyes as the creature lifted one of its thin appendages and held it above him.

Yuri stared at the thing for what seemed to him like hours before the blade thinned to a stiletto's point and exploded his world into pain and delirium. The spike tore through his shoulder and lifted him from the ground as though he weighed no more than a paper doll. The woman's eyes searched out his own, and even in Yuri's state, he could see the almost vacant hunger there.

"You are a soldier," it said in a woman's voice. "I respect that, so I will give you one last chance to save your own life. Where is Kerrid Bertrand?"

Yuri entertained the idea of spitting in the woman's face, but there, in the presence of a horror he couldn't have imagined, he felt the insane futility of that action.

Without a word and with barely a thought, he released his grip on the metal spike in his shoulder and pointed to the Cetalon viewing station with his good hand.

The pirate creature turned her disturbingly human head toward the room, regarding it for a few short seconds before flinging Yuri to the ground without so much as a second glance.

"Pathetic," she huffed, and left the little man on his own to suffer in its periphery.

Yuri slammed into the frame of the display case he'd once taken cover in and bounced to the floor, losing what focus he had left on the real world. Everything blurred, swirling together with the pulsing agony that threatened to gnaw holes in his mind.

He tried to rally himself, to task his brain with assessing his injuries, and it worked. With great effort, Yuri forced the world back into focus and held his grip on consciousness. Breathing filled him with flares of searing torment that were all too familiar. He chalked this new pain up to broken ribs, though how many, he couldn't say. His right arm was unusable, and his firearm was lost. Not that it mattered. He was right-side dominant, and the rounds he had left in the weapon were just as useless as the arm.

He still had one last explosive, but he didn't want to chance using it in his state. In short, he was broken, bleeding, and useless. Disgusted with himself, Yuri could only watch the creature that had ruined him tear its way toward the VIP he was supposed to protect.

"Yuri," Lillith's voice called, breaking into his stupor.

He craned his neck to see her sprinting around the circular column in his direction. She didn't have her eyes on him. Instead, she was staring at something nearby with the same sort of slack-jawed awe and terror that he'd been struck with moments earlier.

The floor shook as something collided with the viewing station walls. Yuri didn't have the strength or the inclination to look. He already had a solid idea of what was happening, and it was anything but good.

As if the pain and confusion weren't bad enough, the shame of what he had done crashed down on him as well. The weight of all three burdens threatened to break him even further, but thin, firm fingers pulled at him, keeping him from falling too deep into his own despair.

"We have to get out of here," she said as much to herself as to him.

"I gave him up," Yuri heard himself say.

"Yeah, well, this isn't exactly something they trained us for," Lillith grumbled and dragged him into cover.

"You don't understand..." he began, but Lillith cut him off.

"I understand just fine," she said harshly. "There's nothing else you could have done. Right now, DiSilva's in there with Bertrand and he's the best chance the old man has. Now move your ass."

Yuri looked at her, and for the first time since he'd faced down the monster that had broken him, he actually saw. She was as afraid and confused as he was, but somehow, she was pushing through it. More than that, she was determined to pull him through as well.

Yuri had allowed himself to become dead weight, and he was starting to drag her down. There was more at risk here than just his own wellbeing. Others were trapped below, both soldiers and innocent civilians who had been caught in the crossfire.

Yuri forced himself to roll through the pain and almost passed out. He'd traveled through the Black for much of his life, but he'd never seen such brilliant stars as the ones dancing through his vision. It took a monstrous effort to keep his last meal in its place, but he managed, willing himself to his feet with a deep, dizzying groan.

Stumbling, he accomplished something that felt close to walking but was actually just a long fall. Lillith caught him and put his good arm over her shoulder, balancing his weight against her own.

"You focus on walking. I'll take care of the rest," Lillith promised with a short grunt of effort.

"We need to get to the transport," he said, pointing toward the lifts.

Chapter 30

THE DOOR RESISTED. It was a sturdy, multi-paneled design installed for both its appearance and security functions. The fact that it mounted so effective a defense of Miranda's long-sought target only managed to make its solid construction that much more infuriating. Dangling four feet in the air, she commanded one of her silver limbs to wail away at the unyielding metal first, then the dense stonework surrounding it. The best she had managed so far was a few dents and a multitude of scratches that were nowhere near as deep as she would have preferred.

The silver limbs had their uses, but tearing down reinforced construction wasn't one of them. They could deal significant damage to it, but they needed to be operating at maximum capacity for that. Unfortunately, they weren't. Miranda was too weak to power them to their full strength, and all other options were off the table.

The healing process was taking up too much energy, and there was no getting around that. The creature within thrived off Miranda's body, but she'd allowed it to become so damaged that the alien was prioritizing regeneration.

It wasn't a new discovery. This limitation was often used against her in the Echelon facility whenever she tried to escape. Now, just as then, she would need an outside force to break the stalemate.

Wheeling around, she noticed the two insects struggling to stay hidden and failing miserably, but they were no concern of hers. What caught her attention was the lightly damaged hoverbike on the far side of the fallen column and the battered pirate crawling back onto it.

"Bring me that," she demanded and pointed at the bike.

The pirate's face was covered by the breather, but his shock at her appearance couldn't be hidden. He recoiled instinctively as everyone did when they were exposed to her natural state. Of course, Octavian would disapprove, but then he wasn't here, and it couldn't be helped.

She would not drag her belly across the ground like some spineless worm, not when she was so much greater than that. The humans on this world were far beneath her, and it wouldn't do to have such worthless meat looking down on her, no matter what her friend might say about it later.

"Now," she growled, snapping her subordinate out of his frozen state.

She fired a glance at Bertrand's people once again and found one dancing on the edge of unconsciousness. The other was too concerned with her partner to notice Miranda's eyes on her.

She'd let them live. She'd promised one his life, and her word would be honored, despite her distaste. The other would gain the benefit of her mercy, such as it was.

The Lifter wasn't in ideal condition, but the plasma cannon seemed functional, and that was all Miranda really needed. She shoved the pirate off the bike without a word, then used her silver limbs to straddle it, lowering herself onto the seat. The terrified figure made no sound aside from the grunt of pain when he landed and promptly crab-walked his way toward the shattered debris that had once supported the dome above.

Miranda paid him little mind as she lifted the bike in the air and angled its nose toward the door. She cocked the steering yoke with a little more force than needed and allowed her anticipation to build with the whine of the weapon. As the sound pitched itself out of her hearing range, she steeled herself once more and fired.

The orb of brilliant plasma sailed toward the offending door and immediately the metal glowed under the extreme heat. It took mere seconds for the door to buckle and its moorings to melt. With a loud clang, the once impenetrable barrier finally submitted to Miranda's will.

"Bertrand!" she roared and pushed the Lifter through the arch of molten stone.

• • • •

Claude did his best to ignore the clang of metal on metal from the room below, but when he heard the pure hate bellowing Bertrand's name, he couldn't resist a glance back down to the broken display window.

Bertrand was doing his best to climb the access ladder above him, but it wasn't going well. They needed to be moving faster. The older man's crushed hand wasn't helping, and silently, Claude reprimanded the silver inside.

It had acted impulsively, and for perhaps the first time, it displayed an overt and undeniable desire apart from his own. In the end, it had accepted Claude's command, but he wondered whether it would continue to do so in the future. Claude was in control for the moment, but it seemed like things could change at any time, and it terrified him.

Being a prisoner in his own body was about as troubling a nightmare as he could imagine, and he'd been unsettlingly close to that becoming a reality already.

He had faced things that would horrify others at least a few times and came away with very little in the way of psychological damage, as far as he was aware. Nothing had shaken him quite like the hours he'd spent entombed in his own unresponsive skin. The thought of it still haunted him in a way he wasn't sure he completely understood.

"We're running out of time," Claude stated nervously as the growl of a Lifter bike echoed up the interior of the massive pillar.

The service ladder built into the side of the pristine white chamber was not the ideal way to negotiate the large open area. Mechanical arms moved up and down the hollow interior in elaborate, pre-programmed patterns. Each lifted and moved immense artifacts from their storage containers along the walls to display in the showcase windows lining the pillar. In the center there was nothing. From the roof above to the unseen termination point below, there was only empty space. It was obvious it had been left open for a massive lift of some kind, but Claude had no idea how to summon it.

Having a set of thrusters to speed them up the shaft would have been ideal. Instead, Claude was forced to coax an injured man up the ladder before death caught up to him.

Not for the first time, Claude heard Zhara's words in his head. It would be so much easier to just walk away and leave Bertrand to the fate he'd earned, but there were consequences to that decision. Miranda was dangerous, but she wasn't the primary threat facing him. For all the damage she could do, she was still one person. Claude could deal with one person, even if she had similar abilities to his own. What he couldn't deal with was a failure. The stakes were too high.

A plasma blast melted the broken display window below and heralded the arrival of Miranda. She locked eyes with Claude and sneered before angling the nose of her bike at him, Bertrand, and the drives he carried.

"Keep going. Don't stop for anything," Claude shouted up to the old man and released his grip on the ladder.

If Bertrand replied, Claude didn't hear it. The rush of air speeding past his ears drowned out the sound of everything except his pounding heart. Claude felt the silver flow into his fingers as he thought through his next move. He had less than two seconds before he impacted Miranda's bike or passed right by it.

Freefall seemed to make every detail that much clearer. The chill in the air sent goosebumps across Claude's skin as he streaked toward his pursuer. Time itself seemed to gasp, allowing Claude to witness the bloom of vibrant blue as the bike's thrusters fired.

Miranda pushed the bike to the side, steering well clear of Claude's descent. Without giving him any more thought, she cocked the plasma cannon and sent the thin mechanical escalation slicing through the wind.

Claude didn't need to track her aim. He knew she was on target, which was the problem. The plan had been to get between her and Bertrand. That would have at least bought some time. Sure, it would have probably killed him in as agonizing a way as he could imagine, but that wasn't likely to happen now.

Instinct commanded Claude to reached out toward the wall closest to his target. He felt the silver surge through his arm, extend from his fingers and dig into one of the mechanical arms mounted there.

As gravity pulled him even with the his new anchor point, the newly formed tendrils stiffened and snapped him back toward Miranda's bike. Claude felt the unmistakable rush of adrenaline before his weight and momentum slammed into the side of Miranda's bike. The impact jarred them both and spun the bike off-axis.

Miranda roared in both surprise and rage, drawing her sidearm and pumping four shots into Claude at point-blank range. The force of the first two rounds rocked his torso, but the last two were expertly aimed, hitting him in each wrist. The shots dislodged his silver claws from the bike's frame and left him weightless, just before gravity reached up to claim him once more. Miranda took a second to smirk at him, then she turned her attention back to her quarry.

Claude panicked. Again, he found himself out of reach of the bike, and he was picking up speed. The Lifter pulled away from him, and all that he could think to do was reach helplessly for its tail.

Again, he felt the silver flow from the rest of his body to reinforce his arm before launching a set of tendrils. The gleaming strands rushed through the gap, caught Miranda's bike just above its engine, and pulled him closer to it.

Claude's eyes went wide with surprise and later horror as he realized the tendrils were pulling him into the Lifter's engine wash. The heat of the burning engine dried the moisture from his eyes as his passenger retracted back into him. To his surprise, he didn't burn. Even as his shirt and jacket dissolved into ashes around him, Claude himself remained unharmed.

Miranda scowled back at him and shouted something he couldn't hear over the roar of the bike's engine. He figured it could be nothing good since the engine kicked up, intensifying its burn, and rocketed them up the pillar.

Claude lost all awareness of his surroundings. Everything blurred around him. The speed, heat, and blinding blue light all but fried his senses and left him lost to the world. It wasn't until the bike lurched and spun him out with a vicious snap that his sense of place returned. The violence of the maneuver tore his claws free once again and shot him across the empty chasm like a stone from a sling.

When the world finally crashed back into focus, Claude found himself sailing across the open center of the pillar and toward a large metal cylinder marked with the scorched letters A.S.A. The broken foil wing jutting from one side snapped off entirely as he slammed into the thing.

The massive wing flipped and twirled its way down the pillar, shattering into smaller and smaller pieces that shimmered into invisibility as they bounced off every mechanical arm on their way down.

The metal arm holding the artifact, and now Claude, compensated for the impact swiftly with both a shudder and a mild groan of complaint. Claude felt the claws on his fingers latch on to the crumpled panels of the mirrored surface beneath him. He hung there against gravity and locked his gaze on Miranda.

"Stay out of this, DiSilva!" Miranda shouted to him, and he could see the fury sparking in her eyes. "You've done your part."

Claude thought about responding, but there was no need. Miranda had already turned her attention back to Bertrand, who was scurrying up the ladder to the upper exit as fast as he could. There was a nearly bottomless abyss between Claude and the hoverbike. To clear the thirty-foot gap, he would need height, speed, and a miracle.

Miranda angled the nose of the Lifter upward once more, and this time Claude could hear the cannon finalizing its charge. There wasn't much he could do to stop her from melting his best chance to end this problem forever, at least not from where he was. And for the tenth time since crawling from Zhara's bed, he found himself weighing the cost of inaction.

With the drives destroyed, Echelon's research would stall, but it wouldn't end. They would still know both he and Miranda had the silver inside them, and they wouldn't stop coming for them. Miranda was a pirate now. She would constantly be moving, and that would make him the more tempting target. Echelon would send operatives, and they wouldn't care about collateral damage. They wouldn't care about murdering or torturing women and children to get to him, and there was only one way to make sure they didn't get that chance.

Claude scanned the pillar and found a risky path that just might give him a halfway decent jump arc. After muttering the closest thing he could to a prayer, Claude peeled one of the damaged metal plates from the artifact and forced himself into motion. Springing up and off his perch, Claude caught the mechanical arm with his empty hand and pulled himself up.

The action was faster than he expected, launching him up to land on the arm with a catlike agility provided by his passenger. He ignored the concerns forming in his mind and forced himself into a sprint. Splitting his focus between his path and his target, Claude took the time to get a better grip on the metal plate. He had only one shot at this, and if he missed, Bertrand and, more importantly, the drives were slag.

The sound of the cannon's charge rose out of his hearing range as Claude pushed himself to run faster. Again, the world blurred, but this time only at the edges of his vision as the silver assisted him. The added speed was invaluable, but he could feel the tax he was paying to tap into it, just like in the old hotel.

Still, the rush of it was intoxicating. The things the silver let him do were positively superhuman, but the cost was high. Zhara's warnings couldn't be ignored. If he kept utilizing the creature, it *would* burn him out. Unfortunately, there wasn't much he could do without it in this situation.

Step by step, the arm's bend rushed toward him, but he held his jump until the last possible second. The force of his push-off caused the metal to sing. Its protests echoed off the sterile white panels of the pillar's interior, announcing Claude's approach. The sound grabbed both Miranda's and Bertrand's attention as he sailed through the air toward the Lifter.

The jagged, broken artifact that had once been in his hand sailed through the air in a straighter, more controlled line than Claude himself. It carved through the air and struck the nose of the bike nearly two whole seconds before Claude got there.

He'd planned to land on the side of the bike and hopefully force Miranda off. Instead, his throat settled in her outstretched palm as she caught him out of the air and snarled at him, baring her teeth.

His weight and momentum still managed to jar the bike violently, but that small victory in no way made it easier to breathe under the force of her grip.

"I warned you," she seethed as she did her best to squeeze the life out of him.

Claude had a retort, but it was trapped in his collapsing windpipe. It wasn't particularly clever, but it would have done a better job at distracting her from the desperate pounding his foot was giving the nose of the bike.

By the time she noticed what he was up to, there was barely an inch of the broken panel sticking out of the plasma cannon's housing, and the blue-white heat of the gathering charge was already beginning to melt the nose of the Lifter.

"No!" Miranda said in a voice that sounded more like her old self than Claude had heard recently.

He brought his arm over hers, then down in one sharp motion. Miranda's impossibly strong grip gave way to his smooth, practiced, and forceful maneuver.

Planting one foot on the bike's seat behind Miranda, Claude jumped as high and as hard as he could, trusting his passenger to know what he needed from it.

He sailed ten feet up the pillar, banged into the smooth white paneled wall, and stuck there. Claude took a minute to blow out a thankful breath as he saw the silver claws on his fingertips once again.

Below him, the Lifter's nose was beginning to glow dangerously bright. The heat of it was already crawling its way up the wall, warping it as it went. Without looking back, Claude half climbed, half leaped his way up and around the wall in an attempt to gain distance from the coming meltdown and catch up to Bertrand.

He was amazed at the ease with which he moved. Not only was the silver augmenting his muscles and nerve impulses, but it was also thinning and flattening the edges of the claws to provide the exact amount of traction required at each given moment.

Speeding up the sheer vertical surface was almost effortless, and yet again, he felt the pull to succumb to his own temptations. Claude had almost decided to stop fighting himself over utilizing the creature when the claws disappeared and dropped him five feet instantly.

They only returned when all thoughts of abusing his newfound power had been ripped away from his mind. The serrated blades on

Claude's left hand carved through nearly a half-dozen wall panels as efficiently as a ruby laser before flattening to arrest his fall.

He dangled by one aching and likely dislocated shoulder, staring down at the massive drop below. The pounding in his ears and the dryness of his mouth gave Claude the unmistakable impression that a sizable objection had just been raised.

"Okay, fine," Claude rasped when his voice came back to him. "Point taken."

He watched as the strands of silver slowly sprouted from the fingertips of his right hand and coalesced into the familiar claws that he didn't know he could miss so much.

It took him a second to realize that the glow of the broken plasma cannon below was dying out. A proper meltdown would have cooked the power cell and detonated it. As regrettable as that would have been for the Archive, Claude and Bertrand would have been in the clear, and Miranda would be stranded, if she could survive such an explosion.

"Come on, DiSilva," the old man's voice called down to him. "I got through. Transport's meeting us in five."

Claude looked up to see Bertrand staring down from the relative safety of the roof hatch. It occurred to him for the first time that Bertrand wasn't having the same reaction to what he was seeing that everyone else did.

Certainly, Echelon had briefed him on what he'd be dealing with, but even Bertrand hadn't come face to face with an alien on this level. Yet, he wasn't filled with wide-eyed, mindless terror like Gorman had been. Even Zhara took a while to wrap her head around what she was seeing, but in the viewing room, he got the distinct feeling Bertrand feared him, not the creature.

Filing that realization away for later, Claude resumed his climb. He was almost out when the unmistakable, throaty growl of the Lifter's engines roared toward him.

He barely had time to think before something fast, hard, and heavy plowed into him and knocked him the rest of the way up and through the hatch. The course, gravel-like surface of the Archive roof greeted him eagerly and crushed the air out of his lungs on impact.

"Claude!" Miranda almost screamed. "You're getting on my bad side."

She was somewhere above him, but Claude was having trouble mustering the will to so much as roll over. He did manage to crawl once he'd forced his lungs to accept oxygen once more.

"Would have happened sooner, but you know...," he wheezed as he brought himself to one knee.

"Always liked your wit, DiSilva," Miranda said in a calmer voice. "I think I'm going to miss it."

A lance of white-hot pain fried Claude's awareness as a silver blade tore out of his abdomen and pinned him to the roof. He stared at it in disbelief as the silver in him receded from the wound as fast as it could manage.

The blade lifted and spun him to face Miranda. She hovered above him on her damaged Lifter and regarded him with cold, deep brown eyes. The Lifter's nose had been sheared off and still sputtered with wasted power and misfiring circuitry.

"Where's your alien?" she asked with legitimate curiosity. "I figured it would protect you like before."

Claude could barely register her words, let alone answer her. It felt for all the world like tiny worms were snaking out from the insect-like limb he'd been impaled with. They dug into his body, lighting his nerves on fire as they stretched further from the wound with each passing second.

"Maybe it just doesn't like you, Miranda," Claude grunted out and pointed over her shoulder.

Miranda's eyes narrowed as she searched his face carefully.

Claude struggled to smile, but all he could manage was a grimace that showed his pain more than the false confidence he was aiming for.

If he were in a better position, he might have marveled at how silent the new troop transport was, but as it stood, he couldn't hear anything over his own labored breathing.

The transport was larger than the ones he was familiar with. Its broad, flat body soared mere feet above Miranda's head, bathing them both in the warmth of its engine wash. Miranda watched with growing dread as the large troop carrier cleared the roof. It bore the TaskMasters' triple triangle insignia on the side she could see, although it was darkened to hide it from unknowing eyes. To her, it might as well have been etched in neon.

Claude was a distraction, just as he had always been. He was good for that, whether he was distracting a Sabien patrol or keeping her mind off what would come after the war. He had been a good scout, and she'd enjoyed her encounters with him, even this one, but the mission always came first.

"Bertrand!" she shouted, looking past Claude and scanning rows of boxy air cyclers droning endlessly around her.

Without another glance at the man speared on her appendage, Miranda flicked him off like dirt from under her fingernail. She pushed the bike forward, urging the silver to melt back into her as she slowly searched for her prey.

"Come out, you bastard," Miranda growled over the sound of the Lifter's engine. "Do it now, and I'll give you more dignity than you gave me."

Three rows away, Bertrand pressed his back against the nearest air cycler and waited for the sound of the Lifter to pass with practiced patience. He'd watched in disapproval as DiSilva risked his life to cripple her plasma cannon, and now he was grateful that he did. Without the ability to melt through his cover, Miranda would have to play a shell game. He could move as long as he evaded her line of sight, and that was the greatest advantage he could hope to have over her.

There was no way he'd survive a fight. She was too gifted a killer for that. Even without the creature, she was deadly with a sidearm. Given what he'd seen in the pillar, he was certain she hadn't lost any of that skill. His only chance at survival was to creep his way to the edge of the roof and pray that whoever was piloting the transport was smart enough to keep it in the air and at a decent enough angle for him to make the jump.

With one more glance, he spotted DiSilva, rolling onto his stomach. The man was bleeding profusely, but Bertrand could already see the silver sealing his wound. There wasn't time to check on him or even call to him. Miranda was hunting, and any movement or sound he made needed to be in service of his own escape. DiSilva would survive. If the last few days had taught him one thing, that was it.

He'd been an exceptional soldier before, but now he was something different, and it forced Bertrand to recognize what he had always been reluctant to admit. He was getting old, and military life took a toll. The day was fast approaching when he'd have to lay down even the TaskMasters for good, but without anyone to take the organization's reins, it would dissolve.

DiSilva had been one of his favorites for that task, but Firaxis neutralized both options he'd been establishing. Now, Faridan was obsessed with killing him, and DiSilva was as much an adversary as he had ever been an ally.

Bertrand regretted few things, but the two primary decisions that had led to him hiding on this roof were chief among them. His hand was forced in each, but the responsibility ultimately rested on him. He accepted that and assuming he got clear of Faridan and this planet, he'd have to live with it.

Pulling up his data-pad, Bertrand tapped out a short message to the transport. There was no telling if they would see it, but if they didn't and they set down on the roof, everyone aboard would be dead before he could reach them.

Their only chance of survival was to keep the canopy closed and wait for Bertrand to approach. If Miranda caught them exposed, she would take the vehicle down in seconds. It was a feat she seemed more than capable of, especially with a hoverbike at her disposal.

He ordered the pilot to keep their distance and hold their fire. The turret on the transport could likely cut Miranda down, or at least slow her down, but the firepower it generated could also punch through the rooftop. Bertrand couldn't imagine the kind of strain the Archive was already under, given the explosions and crashes he'd only heard. Carving new holes in the building seemed foolish.

With the message sent, he stole a glance above the cyclers to spot Faridan. She was between him and his destination, but the curve of the roof put him at an advantage. Summoning his courage, Bertrand moved swiftly between rows, only occasionally stopping to survey his surroundings.

If he'd been more focused, he might have noticed that Claude was missing, but his attention was on the woman who had been hunting him for the last three years. He'd spent much of that time in the Black, only occasionally setting foot on solid ground.

He half wanted this confrontation just so the ordeal would be over. He'd pictured it a thousand times on a hundred different worlds, but never here and never like this. The mixture of fear and adrenaline was intoxicating. It both exhilarated him and threatened to root him where he knelt.

Under the burnt orange sky, he could see every detail the long pursuit had etched into her. There were lines on her face he'd not seen before, and a cruelty in her movements that was once reserved for only the Sabiens. Miranda was deadly before, but there was always an edge, a line that divided the killer from the woman. Now he had a real sense that line had been erased and a new one formed. There was something inhuman about this version of her, and it came close to petrifying Bertrand.

He had faced down many enemies in his time, but every one of them was a person. They had drives and desires, wishes and dreams, but in the end, they were enemies, so he fought them, and he defeated them. Something about Miranda didn't register as a person anymore. She spoke and thought like a person, but something about her read as an "it" to him.

"Hey!" DiSilva's voice boomed, sending a shock through him as he fell back into cover.

Claude spotted Bertrand from the corner of his eye but chose to ignore him. His objective was plain, as was the next step toward achieving it.

Miranda was systematically sweeping the roof, and eventually, she would find what she was looking for. He couldn't allow that. She had a weak spot, and Claude knew it well. When they had been comrades, he helped shore it up, but now he meant to fully exploit it.

"You don't get to just poke me and run away," Claude said as he drew his sidearm. "I demand more respect than that."

He punctuated his words with gunfire. Round after round peppered his former ally, but Claude didn't take the care to aim them. Where the shots landed didn't matter, only the speed and number. He only needed to pester her to the point of fury. Any rounds that actually hit were just a bonus, even if they didn't do any significant damage.

It wasn't until his sidearm chimed in protest that he allowed it time to recharge. The cartridge was only half-blown, but there was no need to expend it needlessly. Miranda was largely immune to the weapon, but her bike and surroundings weren't. Plus, he always felt better knowing that he had a functioning weapon at his side.

Spindly silver limbs blurred through the air as they deflected all but two of Claude's shots. The remaining projectiles embedded themselves in her thigh and chest. Miranda didn't let out so much as a grunt of pain as her flesh tore apart to make way for each minute invasion. It wasn't until the second round hit home that she even noticed Claude's barrage at all.

She spun her bike to face him, and Claude saw her eyes flash pale blue. There was less of her in those eyes than he was expecting to see. He knew she hated Bertrand, but he didn't expect that hate to expose something so undeniably other.

"Enough!" she shouted, and Claude could have sworn that he heard more than one voice escape her lips. "If you are so eager to die, I will aid you."

Claude braced himself. The Lifter's engine roared as the vehicle gained speed and chewed up the distance between them. He had only a few seconds before it plowed into him, and when it got there, he needed a more complete plan. He was fast, but then so was she. The bike was the only factor that he could count in his favor.

At high speeds, the Lifter he'd ridden days earlier didn't corner exceptionally well. Miranda had the same exact model, and if he could make her miss, he had a solid shot at getting Bertrand onto the transport and away from his would-be murderer.

Claude bounced on the balls of his feet, limbering up as the bike closed in on him. His core muscles were still tight and sore where the silver had knitted them back together, but he ignored the discomfort. Lives rested on his ability to act when needed, both those he cared for and Bertrand's, such as it was. If he couldn't do that, he might as well let Miranda take his head off right then and there.

It was the move he knew she would make. Miranda was nothing if not direct with her assaults. She formed one of her extra limbs into a silver scythe as she sped into range. When the blade slashed for Claude's throat, he dropped, rolled under the slash, and sprang back to his feet, sprinting full-on past Miranda.

First hurdle successfully cleared, and now Claude poured on all the speed he could summon. The soles of his boots tore across the roof as he caught himself praying to every entity he knew of that the sloping building wouldn't cost him his footing.

Bertrand was still as adept at seizing opportunities as he had always been, Claude noticed. The old man could still move when adequately motivated, although Claude was closing on him at such a rate that he might as well have been standing still.

Claude forced himself to slow while every cell in his body screamed at him to move faster. The deep growl of the Lifter's engine shifted tones as the bike came about, aiming to run him down.

"Jump!" Claude almost screamed as Bertrand's path emptied out in front of him.

The question on Bertrand's furrowed brow didn't reach his lips. Instead, he did as he was told and jumped as high as his old bones would allow. Claude scooped him out of the air and easily adjusted to the added weight. His stride faltered only a little, but in three steps, he was back up to what he now understood was his top speed.

The slope of the dome grew more severe as he sped along it. Only seconds were left before he risked running out of roof, and he still couldn't see the transport. If it had chosen to make another pass, Claude was about to destroy both Bertrand and the drives he'd fought so hard to protect.

Miranda's bike roared louder and louder, but Claude did his best to ignore it. Looking back would only distract him, or worse, slow him down. He needed every ounce of speed he could get to make the coming jump.

The rooftop's rolling edge gave way to a vertigo-inducing view of the park below and the city beyond. Claude's stomach lurched at the sight of it before his spirits lifted. The transport hovered just beyond where the curvature of the roof led into freefall. Its sizable body had been positioned maybe a dozen feet away from the Archive's outer wall.

Bertrand looked over Claude's shoulder, and his eyes went wide. Claude caught the expression but didn't take time to imagine what Miranda was doing behind him. Instead, he poured himself into the jump.

Like before, Claude leaped into the air and didn't fully understand the force he was generating. His own near-panicked state seemed to create a feedback loop with his passenger. The farther he pushed himself, the farther it pushed itself, leading to feats that took Claude by complete surprise.

The Archive dome fell, giving way to a massive drop that Claude felt certain would consume him, but instead of falling, his trajectory kept him on the rise. A prominent part of him remembered overshooting the landing at the hotel, and a shock of fear arced through him. He had the use of his hands then. Here he didn't. If he overshot, he'd just bounce off the transport hull and paint the foliage below with his innards.

Gravity snagged him at last, and he felt her calm but incessant pull shake him out of his weightless climb. The broad body of the transport opened to catch him like a carnivorous flower, but it wasn't close enough, and Claude's fear of too much became a realization of too little. From his decaying altitude, Claude could see several soldiers struggling against their seat harnesses. He recognized his own concern mirrored on their faces as his descent gained momentum.

Eyes went wide, and curses were lost to the wind the moment the soldiers spotted Miranda. They each drew their weapons and opened fire almost simultaneously. A cacophony of miniature explosions sent projectiles sailing over Claude's head.

The rounds tore through the air, causing him to flinch instinctively, though nothing touched him. Even with the speed of his fall and the gentle movement of the transport, the TaskMasters kept their aim. It was only a slight relief that TaskMaster training requirements hadn't lapsed in the years since the war's end. He would have marveled at that fact if gravity wasn't still winning the fight against him.

"Cutting ventrals!" he heard a familiar voice shout and watched as the transport dropped like a stone.

The thrusters on the transport's belly died, dropping it into freefall along with Claude. It matched the speed of his descent and made it seem as if they were both simply hanging in mid-air. It was a cruel illusion that his body saw right through. His fall didn't change nor did its angle, but while the transport fell straight down, Claude still drifted forward slightly until, slowly, he crossed over it.

The second his shadow darkened the center of its textured flooring, Claude heard Yuri shout, "Now!"

He barely had time to roll before the vertral thrusters kicked in, and the flat body of the transport rushed up to meet him. The impact vibrated painfully through his bones. Again, the air in his lungs abandoned him as Bertrand's weight landed hard on his chest, threatening to shatter his rib cage.

The old man rolled off him with a stiff wheeze and crawled toward the cockpit.

"Close the canopy," he grunted through his short, ragged breaths.

Claude looked up at the fierce image of the screaming woman barreling down on him from above. He didn't have the energy to defend himself, and even if he did, he wasn't sure he had the will. Luckily, the armored canopy of the transport folded over him and locked into place, putting a barrier between the soldiers and the banshee careening toward them. The vehicle's running lights flickered to life as the slight weight shift of the hovercraft signaled forward movement.

Chapter 31

MIDDAY TRAFFIC WAS always monstrous to navigate in Minerva City, especially in the transition from Fauldwin back to Cascade. Even the combination of soft cushioned seats, an immersive audio system, and the dozens of harsh light filters in Zhara's Regent couldn't take the frustration out of a traffic jam.

"This is taking forever," Vision complained for what had to be the tenth time.

Zhara chewed on the inside of her lip to keep her own feelings about the situation in check. She had planned to be home and working on re-establishing her connection to the global network, but that didn't happen. Instead of having a task to keep her fingers and mind too busy for dread to seep in, she was sitting here waiting.

For the third time, Zhara sent a sensor pulse to scan the upper and lower lanes for transition points, but once again, the aggressive buzz of denial blared through the cabin. The sound crashed against something inside her that had once been sturdy but was now eroding.

The steering yoke groaned softly under her white-knuckled grip, but she didn't hear it. She didn't hear much as her resolve threatened to break down. Half of her wanted to turn the car around and go right back to the Archive, where she would force her way inside and pull Claude out of there by his ear. But that wasn't possible.

He was doing what he could to keep Vision safe, and so was she. He would likely be attacked and hunted and shot at, but it was Zhara who had to fly away and let all that happen. She knew full well he might not make it back no matter how brave a face he had presented, and it was eating her up inside.

A hand fell on Zhara's shoulder. The touch seemed to cool the rising heat that threatened to absorb her.

"Go for it," Vision said softly and gave Zhara a reassuring squeeze.

Before she even knew what she was doing, Zhara shook her head. For as much as she wanted to throw the plan out and do what felt right, she understood the sacrifice she was asked to make and the reason for it.

"No, I have to get you back. I told Claude I would," she said even though her heart wasn't in it.

Vision pulled her hand back and crossed her arms.

"You know how Claude and I met, right?" Vision asked pointedly.

Zhara sighed and let her seat envelop her. Of course, she knew the story, and she knew what Vision was implying. The problem was, Vision was a child. She didn't understand the consequences of what she was pushing for.

"What does being a kid have to do with understanding consequences?" Vision asked in reply.

Zhara didn't have an answer. There were the usual platitudes, but they all rang hollow when even she didn't completely understand them.

They were close, but Zhara didn't have the same connection Claude and Vision shared. She would do all she could to make sure Vision had a good life, but there was no way it would be a happy one if they let the person she trusted most die or disappear.

Zhara had lost her father, but she was far older than Vision when it happened. Even then, she had the solace of knowing there was nothing she could have done to save him.

"We can't go back," Zhara stated, but her voice wasn't firm.

"Yes, we can," Vision pushed. "Weren't you just yelling at Claude for making decisions for you without talking with you first?"

Zhara squeezed her eyes closed against the onslaught she felt coming. Deep breaths rushed into and out of her, and each one tasted more wrong than the last. She had words to rebut Vision's, but they were the very height of hypocrisy.

"Why does being older give you two the right to make choices for me? If this whole thing is about saving me, why can't I help save myself?" Vision finished.

The question felt more like a declaration. She had hurled Zhara's own indignation back at her. The words had been purposefully chosen to have a cataclysmic impact, and they did. They landed like seismic charges on the fault line that touched both Zhara's reason and her compassion. Before the imminent quake could shake loose Zhara's resolve to follow through with Claude's plan, she already knew what she had to do.

Vision did her best not to take pride in her work, but it was difficult. Zhara wanted to go back as much as she did, but she was getting in her own way. The nudge Vision had given her wasn't forceful or even surprising. Nothing she said was foreign to Zhara, and the fact that she had done it verbally when she now knew she had other options was, in her mind, playing fair.

Zhara sighed and dropped the car out of its lane.

Alerts blared. Their shrill beeping warned of the dozen or so moving violations Zhara was in danger of committing, but she didn't care.

She spun the steering yoke as Vision climbed into the passenger seat beside her excitedly.

"Buckle in," Zhara demanded, and Vision did as she was told, suppressing a smile the whole time.

Zhara gave Vision a sidelong glance, and for the first time, she didn't see the eleven-year-old. She recognized the woman Vision would one day become, and the sight was as impressive as it was ambiguous.

• • • •

Claude let himself just lay there for a few seconds. He'd been through a lot in a very short time, and he deserved a break. His plan had worked except for the fact that he was surrounded by Bertrand's men, on Bertrand's transport without any means of escape. The good news was he was still living, and the drives were still in play. As long as that was the case, his objectives could still be achieved.

When his strength returned, Claude pulled himself to his feet and staggered toward the cockpit.

"She's going to pursue," he said as he crossed the threshold.

Bertrand had already nestled himself into a seat at the controls opposite Lillith. Yuri looked the worst for wear, lightly bleeding from a wound in his shoulder that had been hastily plugged with a liberal amount of gray biofoam.

It took Claude a second to notice that the gunner's seat was empty and half as long to see his prediction come true on the rear holo-feed.

Bertrand took over steering from Lillith. He plugged his injured hand into the steering rig and let the soft green globe of light engulf his mangled digits. With a wince, he pulled the transport into a steep climb that forced Claude to brace himself.

"If you're so worried about her, man the guns?" the old commander barked with the grizzled confidence that Claude remembered so well.

He took the empty chair and strapped himself in. The armored transport's seat was more comfortable than he remembered, but Claude imagined many things had changed since his time.

"Get us clear of the city, and I'll open up," Claude said, slipping back into his old self easier than he was comfortable with.

"We're not leaving the city," Bertrand said without so much as a glance in his direction. "The ship's over the Admin buildings. We just need to lose her before we can board."

Claude let that sink in. He knew stealth tech existed, but when he left the TaskMasters, or when they left him, it was still too expensive and too ineffective to be put into practical use.

A series of tiny thumps danced harmlessly across the transport roof and snapped Claude back to reality.

"She's peppering us with small arms fire," Lillith said, pulling up a readout of the damage sustained.

The transport was an armored beast. A pistol couldn't do any significant damage to its hull. If this A.T. was anything like the ones Claude knew, it would take concentrated laser fire or a well-placed railgun bolt to put a hole in the thing.

As long as the top faced her, Miranda might as well have been using harsh language. The problem was, she knew that too, and her vehicle maneuvered far better. It wouldn't take her long to target the transport's thrusters. Then, gravity would do the rest.

"Get those guns up before she takes us out of the sky!" Bertrand roared.

Claude ran through what he knew of the unlocking procedure. The mechanical thunk of the turret hatch opening told him perhaps not so much had changed after all. Controlling the turret was a lot like piloting a recon drone, except it was magnetically bound to the transport, and possessed enough firepower to level a city block if used properly. It could rotate and swivel like any mounted gun, but its ability to travel anywhere along the hull made it unique.

Claude piloted the twin-barreled monstrosity around the exterior of the cockpit and locked it in place on the transport's underside. His feed gave him a clear view of the city, the lower skyways, and all eight thrusters they needed to remain airborne.

It didn't take long for Miranda to drop into view and spot his gun. She fired a few shots at it, but they bounced off harmlessly. Then, as quickly as she appeared, she left, rising out of his view.

Sitting there staring as the streets of Fauldwin raced by, Claude thought of the devastation he would unleash if he missed. Hundreds of high-impact rounds would carve through cars, walls, streets, and people with little to no repercussions. He'd put people at risk at the Archive, and he was sure some of them had died, but that was necessary. This didn't have to be.

"What difference does it make if she finds your ship?" Claude asked loudly, and he could feel the tone of the space change around him.

"She's not here alone," Yuri groaned, doing his best to stay still despite the transport's sway. "You already know that."

"But she is alone. She's alone right now. All you have to do is get your people ready and have her taken out when she follows us in," Claude rebutted. "It's the easiest thing you'll do all day."

"You don't understand the situation, DiSilva," Bertrand began. "She can't just be 'taken out.' Neither can you, if I understand correctly."

Claude flinched at the words. He knew he wasn't immortal. Was he hard to kill? Definitely, but that had been the case well before the silver.

"What are you talking about?" he asked.

"You've been out of the loop for a while. She was tested for weaknesses. The documents are... extensive. Miranda can't be killed. The best they could do was lock her in a state of constant regeneration," Bertrand said, ignoring all of the eyes that turned his way.

"Wasn't she part of your team?" Lillith asked with a tone that made it clear she already knew the truth.

Bertrand hesitated. He stole a glance at the young woman from the corner of his eye and swallowed hard.

"My hands were tied. Echelon wanted the creature. I tried to convince her to give it up, but she wouldn't, so they took her instead," he declared and did his best to keep his focus on the transport's controls.

"She couldn't just 'give it up.' It's a part of her, and you just handed her over so they could try to cut it out," Claude said as he took his hands off the controls. "Now they want you to hand me over so they can do the same exact thing to me."

Bertrand did not answer, but he didn't have to. Claude already knew the plan. He had pieced it together early on but had no choice other than to step into the trap anyway. What was worse, Claude understood Bertrand's reasons. They weren't acceptable reasons, but they made sense if you looked at the universe through a lens of fear.

Claude didn't know much about Bertrand's history, nor did he care to. What he did know was that the man hated the Sabiens the same way he once had. Claude might have made similar calls in those days, but he wasn't in those days anymore.

"When I get you to your ship, I walk," he declared in no uncertain terms. "If you get in my way, I'll hold you down while Miranda peels you apart."

The cockpit got still as the whole transport listened for Bertrand's response. He gave none, instead focusing fully on the task in front of him.

• • • •

The matte gray transport bullied its way through traffic. Sparks few as it shunted and rammed any hover cars unlucky enough to get in its way, creating chaos and confusion on the skyways.

For the first time in a while, Miranda found herself feeling small. Her bike was arguably faster and far more nimble, but without the plasma cannon, it was no match for the transport. Offensively, there wasn't much she could do to the vehicle with her sidearm, but there was a chance her silver could pry at least one of the armored plates free, provided she could get close enough.

The armor on the transport was paneled like almost every other piece of modern military tech. Industrial assembly lines had their perks, but careful craftsmanship was rarely among them. There were always tiny mistakes made, and the more parts that needed piecing together, the more numerous those mistakes became.

Miranda could already see the minuscule seams between the panels from where she was. All she had to do was focus hard enough. The silver was capable of assuming a near liquid state. If poured into the cracks and crevices of the transport's hull, it would find whatever vulnerabilities were present. She simply had to buy it the time to do so.

With a new plan in place, she wove her bike through the growing number of panicked vehicles as the operational order of the skyway dissolved into utter pandemonium. Miranda could deal with the situation for a while, but the more uncertainty the city threw her way, the more likely it was that she would make a mistake.

The Lifters weren't designed for inner-city travel, and the dust they'd inhaled since being deployed on this rock had affected their performance in ways that Miranda wasn't qualified to fully articulate. She could feel the sluggishness in the bike's responses as she cut her right thrusters, then sent the extra power to her left side. The maneuver shoved the bike out of the way of a blood-red car spinning in her direction.

It worked for the most part, although the car did clip the Lifter's tail, throwing it out of her control momentarily. The bike twirled like a Fabrian dancing girl, forcing Miranda to flatten herself to its body and wrap her silver appendages around the chassis to keep from being flung off. Every sight and sound blurred as the bike spiraled to the left and away from her target. With a swift series of adjustments, she fired the thrusters to counter the spin and settled the hoverbike on an intercept course with Bertrand's behemoth once more.

The transport pulled into the sharpest climb possible, given its size and shape. Miranda tracked its intended path up the perfectly vertical surface of a skyscraper as she brought her drive engines back to life. The transport skimmed the building's mirrored face, clearly hoping to make it into the upper passthrough.

It was a risky move. For all the lack of cornering potential the Lifters had, the sheer bulk of the transport would make it a hundred times worse. Still, it would break the line of sight if they made the inverted "L" curve, and Miranda couldn't allow that.

She fired the engines, and the bike rocketed into a matching climb, only at twice the speed. It closed the distance swiftly, but not fast enough to catch the transport. Cursing herself, Miranda adjusted her pursuit to avoid slamming headlong into some civilian's cramped little office. Gravity threatened to unseat her as Miranda flattened her angle into a sheer climb, bathing the reflective metal in the azure wash of her engine and thrusters.

Once again, she dipped into sight of the transport chassis and stared into the twin barrels of its turret. The damned thing was well placed. From its position, it could easily defend every valid target on the transport.

She was aware that taking a shot or two from the thing likely wouldn't kill her outright. It was certainly possible that between the high caliber rounds and the Lifter's inevitable explosion, there might not be enough of her body left for her alien to piece together. Miranda had her doubts about that, but she'd seen what ordnance like this could do to an entire regiment of soldiers on Diegon Minor. There was no way she'd get her hands on Bertrand if that thing opened fire on her.

But it didn't. For the second time, Miranda stared almost helplessly into those barrels, and for the second time, the turret barked but didn't bite. She stole a glance behind her and saw the city below. Countless cars stalled in a web of innocent lives, and beyond that, a busy street filled with people celebrating their relatively newfound peace.

A grin curled her lips as a realization dawned.

"Is that you?" she asked no one in particular and risked exposing herself fully to the turret.

Again, nothing happened, and her grin grew wider.

• • • •

"Take the damn shot!" Bertrand shouted at Claude, but the guns remained quiet.

It wasn't that Claude had an issue shooting Miranda. There had been a time when he would have, but that was an age long past. She was much less the person he remembered now and far more dangerous than she'd ever been. Claude wasn't concerned with what would happen if he hit her, but what would happen to the city if he missed. He'd lost allies to the type of firepower he now had at his command. There had been little left of them to commit to the Black after.

They had all stormed that occupied fort on Diegon Minor, knowing what was likely in store for them, but the people of Minerva Prime had no idea. The further he went down the path he'd chosen, the more the people of the city were forced to pay the price.

He had to draw the line somewhere, and this felt like as good a place as any.

"Fire," Bertrand commanded, but Claude simply refused.

The transport lurched once more as Bertrand forced it into a tight turn that caused the chassis to groan in protest. Claude watched as the bird's-eye view of the street curved away and left him with a view of Fauldwin's skyline.

• • • •

Miranda easily matched the transport's turn, avoiding the sparks that exploded from its armored shell as it scraped across the walls of the building's passthrough. The bulky body of her target swayed out of one lane and into another, shunting vehicles out of the way as it compensated for its mass and momentum.

Nearly every other hovercar in the passthrough cut their speed and gave the transport a wide berth, which suited Miranda just fine. As she accelerated into the gap, she found it easier to breathe without the meat of the city hemming her in. She did her best to ignore the fearful and curious eyes staring her down as she passed. It was not uncommon for her to attract eyes and snap judgments, but what she saw now was recognition.

The inner systems had a knack for building efficient networks. It was highly likely her face was already plastered on every screen in the city. Miranda hadn't spotted any drones tracking her, but that didn't mean there weren't any. She'd poured her focus into catching and killing the transport and the man inside it. Whether anyone saw her do it wasn't much of a concern.

Still, once her business was done, getting back to her ship would be a problem. If everyone knew her face, she would have an endless fight ahead. It was something she had no doubt she would survive. It would just be tiring and time-consuming.

The turret under the transport corrected its aim as she neared it once more. It still didn't fire, and she was now absolutely convinced she knew who was operating it. As tempting as it would have been to push the issue, Miranda wasn't doing all this to antagonize DiSilva. She had a particular outcome in mind, and the fact that he was still involved made it harder to achieve. Making it personal for him would only introduce more unpredictability.

She pulled the bike up and out of the turret's view once more as they passed out the far side of the passthrough. The buildings here weren't as tall, but equally impressive in their design. Many were interconnected with elevated walkways and transit routes that worked much like arteries, each feeding the beating heart of the Minervan economy.

The transport dipped its nose and dove for the cover of shorter structures. Miranda forced the Lifter's broken nose down after them and cut her engines, riding the bike through freefall. She was lighter than the transport, but it was still using its thrusters to control its descent. That was a mistake.

Minerva had a powerful gravitational pull, and while it had been a struggle for her to get used to when she'd first set foot on the planet, it was now to her benefit. Where the transport needed to arrest its momentum so it could pull up before it splattered its passengers all over its interior, Miranda had no such concerns.

The ground sped toward her, showcasing the rich detail of its decorative lights and blissfully unaware pedestrians, but Miranda wasn't gaining on the transport as swiftly as she anticipated. At this rate,

Bertrand would pull the ship out of its nosedive before she got close enough to board it. That was unacceptable.

With a low growl that was all but lost to the wind, Miranda fired the engines once more. The Lifter poured its speed into the fall, and within seconds Miranda's concerns were washed away. She'd never considered herself a conservative person, but what had to happen next seemed rash, even by her standards. There would be no coming back from it.

Luckily, the chase had given her time to regenerate, and the silver could now take on more worthwhile tasks.

· · · ·

A lump of concentrated anxiety crawled its way up Claude's throat with every millisecond of Bertrand's ill-advised dive. From where he sat, he could see only the sky. He had caught a glimpse of Miranda once more, but that had been fleeting.

Nothing but bright, open sky would allow him to fire at her with minimal concern about the city, at least until gravity caught the rounds that missed and pulled them back down at terminal velocity.

Claude had been waiting for just such an opportunity, but it wasn't likely to happen. Miranda was smart enough to know his plan and had made herself scarce rather than chance being shot out of the sky. Still, he watched and waited on the off chance she made a critical error.

Flashes of deep blue light strobed inside the cockpit, tearing his attention away from his vigil. A large thump echoed up to the cockpit from the body of the transport, followed by a series of thin metallic ticks that Claude couldn't place.

"What is that?" he asked in more of a shout than he'd intended.

"Contact alert," Yuri said with a wince. "Something's on the hull."

"Get that turret up there and cut her to pieces," Bertrand shouted with an edge of unmistakable panic.

He groaned in pain as he steered the transport out of the dive. Every piece of metal around them roared against the myriad forces that sought to shred the transport into its component parts.

Disorientation pulled at Claude's vision as his feed swirled and shifted against the movement of the transport. His stomach rolled, and against his better judgment, he looked away from the screen. The world righted, and nausea released Claude from its sudden and intense grip just in time for new torture to take him.

His passenger screamed against his nerves, but he wasn't sure why until he looked back at his holo-feed and saw Miranda. Silver poured onto the surface of her skin, forming into thick veins that concentrated around her eyes. Sparks of energy danced across them, and before his feed died, Claude saw the true face of the monster he had unleashed.

The armored body of the transport imploded with all the force of a point-blank rail shot. The soldiers harnessed within shouted against the rush of wind and an explosive boom that nearly deafened Claude.

He spotted the bright blue flash on Yuri's shocked and horrified face. He'd felt that mix of emotions before, and he didn't wish them on anyone. Claude hadn't had more than two consecutive nights of peace since his own encounter with that level of terror, and whatever the soldier was seeing through the open bulkhead would make sure he didn't either.

Claude's passenger rattled on his nerves so hard that he swore it would tear his body apart. The endless vibrations intensified until every nerve in his body registered a constant and sourceless pain. Through the agony, Claude felt something more, something that wasn't coming from him, and for the first time, he understood his passenger's fear.

A toxic mix of burnt flesh and acrid smoke wafted through the cockpit, stinging Claude's eyes and causing Yuri to wretch uncontrollably.

"Bertrand!" Miranda's voice called, and this time, Claude was sure she wasn't alone.

A thick column of electricity slashed through the open bulkhead, carving a jagged line from floor to ceiling. The brilliance of the blast ruined Claude's eyesight and killed the running lights.

"What the hell was that?" Lillith almost screamed against the rush of air and dispersing crackle of energy.

"Seal the bulkhead!" Bertrand roared at her. "Now, before she kills us all."

Lillith looked down at the flickering holo-feed in front of her. Cords of muscle tensed along her jaw as she ripped the talons of wild terror from her rational mind. There would be time to panic later. Now, she had to ensure that later actually came.

The flickering wasn't a problem. Lillith didn't need to see the readout. Her fingers blurred along pathways she knew well, yet nothing happened. The mechanism for the bulkhead door wasn't damaged; it just wasn't responding.

"Terminal's busted," she spat and gave the console a swift, strong jab.

"I got it," Claude said, ripping his harness's jammed latch into scrap metal. "Just keep this thing in the air."

Without thinking twice, Claude stepped into the doorway and felt his knees begin to buckle.

Blackened corpses lined the walls of the space beyond. They absorbed his attention so completely that, at first, Claude didn't see the creature that killed them.

Each charred body had once been a man or woman who had tried to help him. Now they were little more than twisted reminders of the path he had chosen.

"End of the line, DiSilva," Miranda's voice called through deep heaving breaths.

Amidst the smoke hung Miranda, her three spider-like limbs holding her suspended above the scarred floor. Tails of smoke streamed through a thick column of daylight pouring in from a large hole torn in the armored canopy, obscuring her features. Only the electric arcs dancing between her eyes lit the veil of pure malevolence stretched across her face.

Claude could find no response. He couldn't imagine how words would change anything. Instead, he dug his claws into the hatch and pulled with everything he had. It didn't move, but neither did Miranda. She just hung there, drawing in breath after breath, each one deeper and more bestial than those that came before. Arcs of electricity lashed across her eyes, growing wilder and singeing the nearby flesh down to the bone.

If she felt it, she showed no sign. The brightness and intensity of the arcs grew exponentially as her breathing broke into a crescendo of enraged shrieks.

As obvious as the countdown was, Claude could do little about it. If he moved for cover, the blast would carve through the cockpit once again. The last one had damaged the primary console. A second one would undoubtedly do worse.

Miranda had more than proven she could not be reasoned with. So that option wasn't even worth considering. The only thing Claude could think to do was reckless, stupid, and just as terrible as all of the other ideas he'd had lately. He released the hatch and turned to fully face his former ally. The silver in him threatened to cripple him once again, but he was getting used to that. Every time he was near Miranda, his passenger made its displeasure known. Still, that didn't change what needed to be done.

"Sometimes you just have to put it all on the line," he thought and wondered if the creature would understand.

Over his shoulder, he shouted. "Climb. Hard!"

The transport lurched as Bertrand took his command without so much as a word of protest. Claude braced himself against the shift in orientation and watched as Miranda did the same. His entire body shook as Miranda's shrieks erupted into a long, deep bellow that encompassed all the pain, frustration, and drive that had carried her this far.

Bolts of energy tore their way free of her eyes. They blasted Claude backward into the cockpit's roof but didn't carve through his body. The remaining shreds of his shirt, jacket, and much of his pants died an electrically charged death, but the silver on his skin protected him from the worst of it.

What made it through nearly scrambled Claude's brain and almost stripped him of the consciousness he desperately needed to maintain. Through willpower alone, Claude reoriented, braced himself against the power coursing through him, and took a true leap of faith.

Miranda's blast gave out just as Claude launched himself at her with everything left in him. His passenger's augmentation had always taken him by surprise, but adding its strength to Minerva's gravity sent him sailing through the bulkhead and into Miranda with enough force to tear her spider legs free of the transport's interior. Together, they crashed through the hole in the armored canopy, spiraling out into the sky beyond.

The daylight might have blinded Claude if his eyes had been open, but the heat and deep red of his eyelids told him that his plan had worked. Miranda had been stopped. Bertrand was safe. The drives would be uploaded, and the chase he had worked so hard to spare Vision and Zhara from would never begin. His job was done, and the only thing left for him to do now was fall.

Chapter 32

"YOU CAN'T BE SERIOUS," Yuri protested as he struggled to keep pace.

The hangar of the TaskMaster II radiated a frantic and inquisitive energy. Every hand not needed to keep the ship aloft had been ordered to stand guard, but that had not included Yuri. He was supposed to be in the infirmary resting and getting his wounds treated. Instead, he was doing what he did best, pursuing the objective.

In Yuri's mind, the executor's death freed them from Echelon's influence, but it had done nothing of the sort. Instead, there seemed to be no limit to the reach of Myridorn's spymasters. Armed men and women lined the concave walls of the loading dock. Some were alert and prepared for whatever came at them, but many others were simply confused. Compartmentalization was always the way of things on any military vessel, and while the TaskMaster II wasn't officially military, it definitely played the part.

When he realized no answer was coming, Yuri decided to force the issue. He grabbed his commander by the arm forcefully in a move that might have gotten him shot by another officer. Bertrand spun on him and slipped his grip with ease, but the point was made.

"I have my orders," he said, and the look on his face made his struggle plain.

"This man saved your life. He saved my life and Lillith's. We owe him more than this," Yuri pleaded.

He didn't know DiSilva particularly well in the traditional sense, but he knew the risk he had taken challenging their would-be murderer. It spoke well for the type of person DiSilva was, as did Bertrand's reliance on him to get the drives in the first place. So, it didn't square with Yuri that they were going to imprison and deliver him to what amounted to torture and bondage.

Bertrand's eyes hardened at Yuri's words.

"You think I don't know that?" he growled, keeping his voice low enough that only Yuri could hear him. "If I had my way, I'd leave him where he fell, but that's not how it works."

Yuri just watched as Bertrand spun on his heel and left the conversation behind. There was a kernel of truth to Bertrand's words. Morality never really mattered when it came to completing a mission, but that didn't mean it shouldn't.

"What in all hells is that?" a voice from behind him called in surprise.

Yuri turned to watch a man-sized silver chrysalis make its way into the cavernous gray hangar's interior. Its mirrored sheen reflected warped versions of the men and women who stared on in disbelief.

Lillith led the procession, pushing it along. Between the sour look that stained her face and the fire in her eyes, Yuri could tell she wasn't at peace with what was happening either. She locked eyes with him across the distance, and after a look of surprise at seeing him on his feet, Lillith thrust her chin in a gesture Yuri knew well. They would find each other later, but little could be done at the moment. Bertrand had settled on a course of action, and no grunt was going to shake him loose.

Yuri eyed his own twisted reflection in the bound chrysalis being dragged past him and instantly hated the warped visage he saw there. He couldn't help but think the wrongness of the image was in some way connected to the things he was being asked to allow, and suddenly later wasn't soon enough.

He let the shrill, warbling whistle that his squad used as a signal fly from his lips and watched as Lillith found him moving through the crowd to keep pace with her. He slipped free and approached the procession of armed soldiers, taking a second to glance sidelong at the chrysalis close up.

"Not now," Lillith said through a tensed jaw.

"Where are you taking him?" he whispered.

Lillith scanned for anyone that might be more interested in their conversation than they ought to be before she spoke again.

"Bertrand says he goes to the refinery vats," Lillith said, and the confusion of the order played across her features.

Yuri thought on that for a moment. Given what DiSilva could do, the brig was a poor place to house him. The grid system that stunned and burned ordinary prisoners would do little to restrain someone capable of coating their skin in metal.

"The vats?" he asked, still puzzling out the old man's logic. "Nothing living can survive in Phorano acid. It eats whole ships."

Lillith nodded and adjusted her grip on her rifle.

"I don't like this," she said, finally taking her eyes off the path ahead and focusing on Yuri. "That psycho is still out there, and we're getting ready to melt down the only person that could do anything against her."

"Maybe he won't dissolve," Yuri said. "At least not before we have a say in it."

Lillith pursed her lips, and Yuri said no more.

She was as devoted to the TaskMasters as she was to him, and Yuri knew it, but they came from the same world. They shared a very similar ethical code. There were gaps between them as there always were, but their alignments were common enough and strong enough to operate on nearly identical wavelengths. Lillith was more reasonable and much less impulsive than he was, but she did what needed doing when it mattered. Yuri believed she would do the same when he had the time and the courage to tell her about the tiny idea growing in his mind.

• • • •

The comms center was a place Bertrand rarely visited. As the commander of his own force and captain of his own ship, there was no need. It was little more than a closet crammed full of equipment he barely understood. None of that made the room or the work done there any less significant, especially not at the moment.

This trip was urgent, and at the moment Bertrand could think of no place more important to be. He had come to see a friend and deliver perhaps the most crucial package in the known universe.

The room was dimly lit and filled with the hum of equipment far down on a very long list of needed replacements. Bertrand's call for security in the hangar robbed this space of all but one of its on-duty technicians. Luckily, the person still on duty was the only one he trusted with such an important task.

"Commander," the technician said with a crisp salute.

The young Reitsiner had grown into a fine crewman in the years since the war's end. In that time, the kid who had been so nervous on the mission to Firaxis had earned a place as one of Bertrand's strongest allies aboard the ship. Few were entrusted to handle the commander's own personal business, even on his own ship, but Mattic had more than proven himself capable.

"Mattic," Bertrand said, falling into parade rest. "I need a data transmission sent to Myridorn immediately."

Mattic straightened at the commander's words. He watched eagerly as Bertrand slipped a bag from his shoulder with his good hand and handed it over.

The bag had some heft to it, and when Bertrand hesitated to release the strap, Mattic knew why the commander had delivered it personally.

"Aye, sir," the Reitsiner said, and gave a slight nod as Bertrand relinquished the drives to him.

"I want an estimate as soon as you have one," Bertrand stated, watching as Mattic placed the bag down at his workstation.

"Could be awhile yet. Big storm rolling in," the Reitsiner informed as he rubbed his scalp tattoo nervously.

It was a tick of his. Bertrand knew that, but typically Mattic had it under control. This time, the gesture had snuck out before he could step on it, and it said a great deal about his comfort level.

"Send it anyway. If we only get a partial transmission, at least some of the data will get out," Bertrand said after a moment's thought.

He couldn't take his eyes off the drives, no matter how ridiculous it was. People had died for those three small devices already, and it was likely more would meet the same fate before it was all over. In the last few hours, Bertrand had repeatedly told himself the end result was worth the cost, but doubt was beginning to creep in.

He clenched his jaw and blinked it away.

Everything that had happened was for a better future, one free from the constant threat of Sabien aggression. Securing that future was worth any price. He believed that. He had always believed it. Still, working with Echelon never felt good, but it felt right to contribute to a Beitan victory after all these years.

He had seen what the creatures were capable of, and he had a unique perspective. Bertrand's history with DiSilva and Faridan allowed him to compare what each could accomplish before and after being bonded to them. There was no way the Sabiens would be able to stand against a force armed with those things. It would be an easy win. Beita Systems forces would march through the Crown Spires of Akinos within weeks of the Echelon project's completion, and he desperately hoped to be there on that day.

The cost had to be worth that. All the lives and the erosion of Bertrand's soul would create the better place he had fought so hard for. Generations yet unborn would live easier because of the blood spilled for those drives. He just had to keep reminding himself of that.

Bertrand sighed heavily as he thought of what still needed to be done. He would face DiSilva eventually, and he would make him understand. He wouldn't hide in his quarters while the faceless hazard suits escorted DiSilva off the ship as he had done with Faridan. This time he would be man enough to look unflinchingly into the eyes of the soldier he had betrayed instead of wincing his way through a live feed of the transfer.

"Put it in three-tiered encryption. We don't want anyone picking up on it," Bertrand said before turning away toward the door.

"Sir," Mattic said, stopping Bertrand in place. "It true what they say? The executor..."

Mattic drew a sharp line across his throat with a single stubby finger and watched Bertrand for any response.

The old man nodded gravely.

Mattic let out a breath he didn't know he'd been holding in a loud, long rush. His posture eased, and the hint of a smile threatened to cross his lips before he bit it back, clearing his throat.

"Shame," he said in an almost chipper tone. "Echelon lost a true believer there, I think."

Bertrand flashed a smirk and favored the Reitsiner with an explorative glance. "They still have plenty. But if her passing bothers you, we can share a drink and talk about it."

Mattic let his smile loose at last, and it came out more relieved than he had intended.

"Aye," was the only word he could find to say as he watched his commander and captain leave the room.

• • • •

The skyway lanes that ordinarily flowed through the heart of Fauldwin's financial hub had been diverted around it instead, making for long, slow moving lines and frustrated drivers. Neither of those things was a problem for Zhara, however. Her employment status at Artemis granted her certain privileges. The company's generous donations to the Planetary Security operations budget bought quite a bit of goodwill and more than a few blind eyes.

PlanSec had its strengths but turning down credits wasn't one of them. The organization was as malleable as a child's polymer clay set. Typically, that was a big point of contention for Zhara, but now it was proving useful.

"I'm not picking up anything," Vision said, and she could hear the wince in her voice.

Vision had elected to search for Claude, and Zhara had reluctantly agreed.

She was primarily concerned that the removal of Vision's halo would lead to a loss of control. If that happened, Zhara and everyone else in an unknown radius would get turned off like low fidelity holograms, but so far, her worries proved unfounded.

"Maybe he's not here," Zhara said, hoping Claude was already on the way back to the apartment.

Vision didn't answer, and Zhara was starting to get used to that. She imagined the child was dealing with a million things at the moment. Besides, she was really trying to convince herself more than anyone else. It hadn't worked, just like the last dozen attempts, but Zhara was nothing if not persistent. Her next effort to paint the situation with an overly optimistic light died as she guided her Regent around the corner of the Van Brant high-rise hotel.

Like most of the financial area, it was built in the trendy styles of Myridorn. Everything had rounded edges as if someone had taken old buildings, shaved them down, and inserted cylinders and spheres into them to add flair. To Zhara, it was a gaudy fad, but the people who handled the credits loved spending them on pointless things.

"There's another checkpoint," Vision stated. "They don't know much more than the officers at the first one, but they are nervous."

No sooner than the words had registered in Zhara's mind, the flashing lights of PlanSec patrols came into view. She had been trying to trick herself this whole time, but the yellow and green ahead spoke to just how futile it was. PlanSec were known to flash their lights for everything from moving violations to murders to lunch breaks, but never in large enough numbers to color whole blocks.

"Is there a way around it?" Zhara asked, trying to break her attention away from the swirl of motion ahead.

"They're everywhere," Vision said, and Zhara wondered just how far the little girl's abilities could reach. "If there's a way through, I can't find it."

Zhara blew out a breath and waved her hand over the console. The cab chimed pleasantly to signal that it was listening for her command.

"Give me a radial map of my area," Zhara said in a clear and bland tone she reserved for talking to machines.

"Real-time or ideal conditions?" her car's voice asked her with eerily perfect diction.

"Real-time."

The tense expression on Vision's face eased as the conversation ended, and a small globe of light appeared to the right of the steering yoke.

Zhara found the blue arrow indicating her vehicle, then, her eyes widened as the PlanSec drones and cruisers all lit up in green. There were at least three dozen, all circling a single area at different altitudes. Vision had been right. There was no way to make it inside the perimeter without being seen by at least one, if not three, different sets of PlanSec sensors.

She pulled the Regent to a slow stop and surveyed the area ahead with her own eyes. She was still a quarter of a mile out, but the cruisers could be clearly seen making their leisurely rounds while small dots whizzed through and around them.

"I think this is as close as we can get without being stopped," Zhara said and ran her fingers through her hair to calm her frustration.

Vision didn't answer. Instead, she cocked her head to the side and scrunched her face as though she had found something odd. It was a cute reaction, and Zhara couldn't keep herself from appreciating it for that reason alone, but it definitely meant going home wasn't an option just yet.

"Did you find him?" Zhara asked, letting a little hope creep in through her anxiety.

Vision shook her head slowly.

"There are a lot of thoughts, but I can't find any coming from him. It's like his brain's turned off or..."

"... he's not here," Zhara stated firmly, stopping Vision's musings definitively. "Is there anything else?"

Vision grunted as she pushed through the currents of confusion and exasperation. The roiling waves of emotion were tinged with the same sense of dread she could sense streaming from Zhara. It was as if no one knew what was happening or what was coming next. Everyone in her perception was terrified of some unknowable transition rushing headlong toward them.

The PlanSec officers that Vision could read knew they were out of their depth. Civilians were caught in wide-eyed panic. Those touched directly by the chaos were so terrified that their thoughts barely made any sense at all. As she peered further in, Vision caught hold of an oddly calm and restrained thought strand nestled among the wild waves. It ran deep and away from the maelstrom she struggled against.

"I think I have something," Vision said, but her voice made it sound more like a question than a statement.

"Tell me it's good news," Zhara nearly pleaded, leaning back in her seat as it shifted its resistance to envelop her.

Vision hesitated, sucking her teeth for a moment before she turned to Zhara.

"That depends on your definition."

• • • •

What seemed like the whole of this world's PlanSec force was behind her, but they weren't giving chase. Odds were high that they had no idea she was even there, but Miranda couldn't rest on such assumptions, even though rest was exactly what she needed.

DiSilva's move had been stupid, reckless, and ultimately effective, as his plans tended to be. She should have expected something like it, but she hadn't, and now Bertrand was in the wind again. Worse, DiSilva's brainless divebomb attack had left her stranded at the heart of an enemy city. If she'd played the game better, half the city wouldn't be on high alert, but there would be time to beat herself up over her impulsiveness later. For now, she needed to find a way back to her ship.

Luckily, most of the district housed offices and administrative facilities, and they were closed for the holiday. Miranda had taken advantage of that fact, making her way through the ground floors of several buildings in an attempt to put distance between herself and the solidifying PlanSec perimeter, but her energy was waning. Fighting in the way that she had while in the transport and the Archive took more strength than she liked to admit, not to mention the extensive regeneration. She was drained, and still, she had nothing to show for it.

DiSilva had crashed all the way to the ground. They'd both lost consciousness, but she'd woken up to find herself dangling over a crater in the street below. Apparently, a silver limb she had not commanded carved into the side of the nearest building, sparing her the same impact.

There hadn't been time to investigate exactly what had happened, so she'd chosen to run, and she'd been running ever since. Now she finally had a chance to recover a little of the stamina she had been burning so extensively.

The building she found herself in was large, dimly lit, and, thankfully, empty. The first floor was dominated by a reception area with a small cafe off to one side. The only movement came from a fleet of cleaning drones hovering a few inches off the gray and white tiled floor.

Miranda watched them execute their tight, efficient formations and took a little time to consider how things had gone so wrong. The answer wasn't hard to find. She had gotten impatient. Attacking the Archive directly was a move that no one would have expected, and while it did give her the element of surprise, it also introduced countless unnecessary variables.

Kicking herself mentally, she made her way to the cafe and clambered over the counter to raid its stores. There wasn't anything she would prefer to eat, but she grabbed two wraps from the cooler and a few bottles of enriched water. The idea of sitting at a table in such a posh environment reeked of novelty, so she sank to the floor instead.

Sitting there, Miranda tried to picture what the lobby would be like on a business day. There would be people rushing in and out doing the mundane tasks normal people wasted their short lives on. One of them would look a lot like her, except much more miserable. That woman could sit at one of the tables surrounded by friends and coworkers, eating surprisingly good wraps and talking about how her latest project had been a complete disaster. Miranda chewed on the image and a bite of her wrap, swallowing them both down and returning to reality.

She took a deep swig of her water and sighed, letting her muscles loosen as she leaned against the cold metal counter. She could feel her body sag under its own weight, and for perhaps the first time, she truly considered giving up her crusade against the man who had caused her so much pain.

She wouldn't forgive him. She could never do that, but she might be able to walk away. So much had been lost, burned, ravaged, and destroyed in her pursuit of revenge. Realistically, the cost was beginning to outweigh the benefits. It was possible that if she stayed on her current path, there would be no benefits at all.

Octavian had spent years urging her to put down this particular sword, and she had outright ignored him. She never listened to or even attempted to process his logical arguments. She simply shut him out, but now, in the quiet stillness of her own failures, maybe it was time to reconsider.

She felt the silver in her stir for the first time in an hour, although it was weak and sluggish. The food was helping calm her nerves, and in time it would help replenish her energy, even if it was older than it should have been and cold. She finished her first wrap and immediately opened the second, which didn't taste nearly as good. The food and the quiet helped her to feel normal, or as normal as she ever felt. A part of her missed that, even though she had no idea what the word really meant anymore.

Maybe there was no normal for Miranda Faridan. Perhaps that had been taken from her, or maybe she was the one who had given it away. It didn't really matter in the end. She was what she was, and she didn't know how to turn away from it.

Lost in thought, it took her longer than it should have to recognize that the sanctity of her hiding place had been violated by the low rumble of a hover car's thrusters. The sound didn't put her on edge at first, but then the roar of it deepened and came to a stop just outside the massive translucent doors at the far end of the vestibule. The silver inside her thrummed with unease.

Like a cornered animal, Miranda's senses fed her every detail as the sound of the car cut out, doors opened, then closed and the shadows of two figures approached. Their features were masked by the opaque doors, but the height difference between them was obvious.

"She's in there," a young girl's voice stated definitively.

The taller of the two said nothing and simply tried to peer through the door.

It was pointless, and knowing that should have put Miranda at ease, but it did not. She felt as if she were exposed in a way that was entirely alien to her. She could sense eyes peering into her, and yet there was no way such a thing was possible. Still, the hairs on the back of her neck stood on end, and the silver continued its panicked dance along her nerves.

"Miranda! We're here to help," said the woman outside.

That was doubtful. Setting aside the fact this woman somehow knew her name, Miranda had no friends in the city. She didn't know many people on the entire planet, and none of them matched the shadows on the other side of those doors.

"Open up," the kid demanded with an impatient knock. "We'll take you to your ship, but we're going to need your help in return."

Against the protests of her body and the creature sheltering within it, Miranda forced herself to stand. She teetered but kept her feet before beginning the long shuffle to the entrance. It took too much time, but the further she moved from her hiding spot, the easier walking became. Eventually, she reached the doors but didn't open them. The silver rattling under her skin gave her pause. The little monster she lived with didn't react this way often. It was almost as if it was afraid.

What Miranda picked up from the thing's reactions was a nebulous, primal terror that didn't come from a place of reason or thought. It didn't make sense. The only things outside that door were a woman and a child. She was more than capable of handling both of them even without the aid of her passenger, as Claude called it. Why it would be afraid of them made no sense.

"First, I want to hear your terms," Miranda said, projecting as much strength as she could muster.

The taller shadow looked to the shorter one and shrugged before it said, "We're looking for a friend. We want your help finding him."

Miranda laughed. She couldn't help it. The fact that she hadn't put it together until this point was hilarious and more than a little sad. Her silver's reaction still didn't exactly make sense, but at least now, it was consistent. The most recent time she'd felt this cloud of dread from the creature had been in the presence of DiSilva's ward, and now it was doing it again. There was something about the little girl, but Miranda had no idea what.

"Your friend just tackled me out of a moving transport. Why should I help him or you?" Miranda growled.

The shadows hesitated and looked at each other for a moment before the short one stepped closer.

Without realizing it, Miranda took a step away from the door, then caught herself.

"That's easy. I can find the man you're looking for," the child stated with a shimmering, unsettling confidence.

Nearly everything inside Miranda screamed for her to ignore the shadows outside. She could feel something in the deep, dark places within warring with itself. Part of it begged her to walk away, but the thing that had driven her to wake up each morning since the nightmare at Firaxis calmly urged her forward.

The conflict would have lasted forever if she'd let it, but in the end, no matter how pleasant the thought of a new normal was, she needed to end her long journey.

Miranda knew herself well enough to concede that as long as her mission went unfinished, she would never be at peace. And so, she placed her own heart on the scale and ended the war within herself. Bertrand would die, and she would be the one to kill him, not time or circumstance.

The new quiet in her soul felt cold, yet comforting. It carried the soothing weight of certainty, and with her newfound resolve, Miranda Faridan opened the door.

Part III
Tempest

Chapter 33

CLAUDE WOKE WITH A panicked gasp. He could have sworn he was falling, but instead, he found himself floating. The substance around him barely qualified as a liquid. It was thick and held him in place more like soft gelatin. He could still move, albeit with great effort, but his body felt odd and detached somehow. It was similar to the way the zero-G suits felt, except there was even less sensation.

It was the smell that told him where he was. Stinging chemical odors brought urgency back to his clouded brain. Nothing on Minerva Prime smelled like the reactor room of a starship, and for six years he had been grateful for it. It was a scent every soldier knew was synonymous with disaster.

He had served on a ship where the Phorano acid had leaked from the infusion chamber. It was only a small amount, but the damage had been catastrophic. In minutes, it had eaten its way through every deck between it and the hull and into the Black. Twelve lives were lost in the decompression and the ship was crippled.

Now he found himself floundering in the pale green substance, searching for a way out as best he could with his eyesight still blurred. Details were lost to him, but what he could see was movement, lots of it. Above him, two things that could have been people made their way across a catwalk toward him.

"Hey, get me out of here!" he shouted over the roar of the industrial machinery surrounding him.

"I wanted my face to be the first one you saw when you woke up," Bertrand's familiar voice called down to him.

"I saved your life, Ban'uta!" Claude nearly screamed at the voice. "This is how you repay me?"

"I appreciate you stopping Miranda more than you know, certainly more than it appears. But as I told you before, this isn't personal. If it were, I wouldn't have approved your credits. It was the best I could do. Now your people will be taken care of," Bertrand declared.

Claude's sight cleared enough for him to determine which of the two figures was his former commander. He cast his recovering gaze around once again and lost what little hope he'd had of escaping.

He was in the center of a sealed vat as deep and wide as his apartment and filled with Phorano acid. The metal encasing him was sturdy yet still thin enough to allow both sound and light to pass through it with minimal distortion.

Over time, the acid had etched tracks in the metal, warping Claude's view of the industrial apparatus around him. The thick transparent walls of the vat still held the liquid back, which told Claude just how dismal his chances of breaking through them were.

He studied the refinery as it flooded the ore suspended in the infusion chamber with the same ooze he was trapped in. The outer surface of the mineral melted away on contact, creating a new, greenish-gray substance that drained out to fuel the ship's engines.

"Where are the drives?" Claude asked, doing everything in his power to keep from giving up.

"Safe," Bertrand stated firmly.

"So, congratulations are in order, then?" Claude snarked.

He found himself instinctively treading water, although it wasn't necessary. He did his best to keep Bertrand locked in a stare as caustic as the fumes trapped with him.

"Since you've just won a war that was already over, I guess they'll make you Grand High Lord, King of the Beitans now, huh?"

Bertrand bit back his initial response, but the soldier escorting him couldn't hide his snicker.

"I don't work for personal advancement, DiSilva. You should know that."

Claude whistled loudly.

"This new ship definitely looks like the product of altruism. What is it, two or three times the size of the old one, with an induction fuel system and backup power cell integration? A ship like this must be worth a billion credits, or the betrayal of one former TaskMaster," Claude said, making sure that the venom in his words hit its mark.

"I don't need to justify my actions to you," Bertrand spat. "The man I used to respect would have never put innocent people in the way of that monster. He would have known that his duty was to protect them."

"You left that man to die, Kerrid."

"Yet here you are," Bertrand said after a deep sigh. "If there was a better way, I'd take it, but there isn't. The thing inside you is our path to lasting peace. I wish I could make you see that."

Claude clenched his jaw. He wanted to tell Bertrand exactly what he saw, a man desperately clutching for his former relevance. And while saying it to his face would feel good, it wouldn't help the situation. Instead, Claude elected to grind it between his molars, hoping his silence would end the conversation. It wasn't going anywhere, and he needed to save his energy.

The acid bath should have eaten through him long before he even woke up. The fact that he was having such a futile debate had to be his passenger's doing. Claude wasn't sure how it could protect him from Phorano acid, but he was thankful. It was only the latest thing his passenger had guarded him against, but it was by far the most impressive.

Any quality armor could protect a man from gunfire and heat. It took a rarer material to nullify the bone-shattering force of an impact at terminal velocity, but it was possible. Far fewer substances kept their molecules bonded when exposed to Phorano acid. Vertibit glass was the only one he knew, but apparently, his knowledge was outdated.

Claude did his best to keep his mind focused. He watched through the grated catwalk above him as Bertrand spoke to the soldier at his side. The machinery drowned out the words, but Claude could guess what they were.

He was to be guarded closely but not engaged with. It was typical of a prisoner. While the location and the makeup of his cell were unique, the situation was not. Bertrand would have him collected when they reached whatever black site they were heading toward. Until then, he was stuck, waiting for his inevitable fate.

"*Claude. Claude?*" a very familiar voice called into his head.

He said nothing and did his best to act as if he hadn't "heard" it as he watched Bertrand and the soldier walk back the way they'd come.

"*I need you to respond,*" Vision informed him.

Once he was satisfied that Bertrand and the soldier were out of earshot, he whispered, "I'm here. Where are you?"

There was a pause long enough for Claude's anxiety to spike before Vision answered back, "*Your friend Miranda is helping us find you.*"

The sigh of disappointment and despair that escaped his lungs seemed like it would never end. There was only one person on the planet worse than Miranda, and that was highly debatable. Everything he'd done was to keep the girls safe, and now they had cast their lot with Faridan, or Vision had at least.

"Is Zhara with you?" he asked, trying desperately to think his way through an escape plan once again.

Another pause stretched on, but not as long as the first.

"*She's right beside me, but listen, I need to know if you're with that Bertrand guy,*" Vision thought to him in a clear, almost emotionless tone.

Claude watched as the older man stepped out of the refinery and disappeared from view. The soldier turned back his way and gave him a nervous but determined glance before breaking eye contact.

"Yeah, he's here. I'm on a ship, a big one, but I have no idea where," Claude whispered to a girl who wasn't there to hear him.

"*I can find you. Just be ready to move when everything starts.*"

"Wait, what are you planning?" Claude demanded, louder than he meant to.

"*A rescue, what else?*" Vision bragged, and this time he felt the confidence and excitement in her thoughts.

"Vision, don't. Get as far away as you can. Don't come after me! Vision!" Claude shouted, but there was no response.

She was gone, but she wouldn't have listened to him even if she weren't.

Claude did his best to douse the flames of his newfound desperation with the calm waters of rational thought. He was sealed in a vat, and while the acid was thick, it didn't give him enough resistance to launch himself into the air. He thought about trying to use a tendril of silver like he'd done before and even reached up to make it happen, but his passenger stayed attached to his skin and ignored his request. Claude assumed it was busy protecting him from the acid, and no matter how much he wanted to escape, he had to agree it was the wiser action.

The only way he could imagine freeing himself was through the tubing at the bottom of the vat. It was narrow, but there might be just enough space for him to worm his way through. Drawing a deep breath, Claude let the silver coat his head, face, and neck before submerging himself in the liquid. He was surprised that he could still see with silver coating his eyes, but that was something to parse out another time.

The acid was tiring to swim in, and it wanted nothing more than to hold him in place. Part of him knew that if he'd been thrown in when he was awake, the momentum could have helped him reach the funnel at the bottom. As it stood, both he and the silver were too exhausted to travel that distance.

Claude breached the surface once again and caught the disbelieving eyes of the soldier above. The large, armored man said nothing. He simply watched, rolled his shoulders, and adjusted his grip on his rifle as Claude roared his frustrations.

• • • •

"Is he alive? Tell me he's not hurt," Zhara blurted out once Vision had opened her eyes again.

Although the weariness was plainly visible on the girl's face, a slow smile still crept across it anyway.

"He's trapped and tired, but I think he's fine," Vision replied, then slid her halo back into place.

"'You think?'" Zhara asked indignantly.

"I can't pick up on anything except his mind, Zee. Besides, I was trying to keep quiet like you asked," Vision said.

She was seated on the room's single rigid bunk, and the hardened mattress made the tiny bed in her room seem like an excessive luxury. Everything about the bunk was thin and rough. Plus, there was only a single pillow, if it could be called that. Disappointed with the bed, Vision gave the rest of the room a once over but found nothing of interest in it.

The walls were made of the same thick and unremarkable metal as the rest of the ship, but the floors weren't grated here.

Dim light was cast into the room from the top and bottom edges of the walls, giving the space a soulless, utilitarian quality that Vision instantly hated. A large locker rested along the far wall, connected to a single slab of metal welded into the wall at waist height.

Zhara leaned against the flat plank of metal that connected the locker and what she initially assumed was a food storage unit. Tension slowly bled out of her shoulders as she allowed Vision's words to sink in. Despite everything, she was beginning to feel better, but her newfound relief was fragile. As long as she ignored how flimsy their plan was, and instead focused on what she could do at the moment, Zhara could breathe without the weight of a small planet threatening to crush her.

The covers provided were on the "desk" behind her, and while it didn't seem like they were going to stay long, the storm she could hear battering the ship didn't seem to be letting up.

"Up," she said and motioned for Vision to stand.

Vision gave her an overly dramatic sigh but did as she was asked so Zhara could dress the bed.

"You don't have to worry. I can find him again, and then I can latch on to the nearest mind that knows the exact location. I just need to relax a little first," Vision announced, answering the least of Zhara's unspoken concerns.

Tucking the covers under the first corner and moving to the second, Zhara said, "It's what comes after that worries me. We have no idea what's going to happen, V."

Vision took a moment to consider that. Her life had never been as unpredictable as it had become in the last few days. It was a little unnerving, especially since things seemed to be ratcheting up instead of down. Still, that unpredictability excited her. There was danger, certainly, but dealing with pirates who had a common enemy didn't seem anywhere near as crazy as running from Derelicts. And if she could help Claude get out of that, she could help him get out of this.

It was Zhara who concerned her. She wasn't made to deal with this level of stress. Vision could already feel the situation's weight straining her, and while she understood exactly why Zhara was so stressed, there was nothing she could do to change it.

Vision could pull on the experiences of others. She felt their confidence and even drew strength from it, but Zhara could not. She was trapped inside the confines of her own mind, never to escape. It was a different burden than the one Vision carried, but a burden all the same. A wave of pity stirred in Vision for Zhara, and everyone else who had the same restrictions, but she banished it.

"Do you trust me?" Vision asked plainly, choosing not to read the answer before it was spoken.

Zhara straightened the covers, realized the mattress wasn't a uniform rectangle, then put that irritation out of her mind to consider Vision's question.

She had never stopped to ask herself that, but her actions instinctively led her to yes. If Vision had asked the question earlier, the answer might have been different, but everything Zhara had done since dropping Claude at the Archive stemmed from trusting Vision, and in a way, that worried her.

Vision was a child, and while she wasn't a typical child, Zhara had seen her make childish decisions without understanding the consequences. Yet, she had followed the little girl's lead all the way into the belly of a ship whose inhabitants she did not know or trust.

"Yes," Zhara acknowledged and turned to face the eleven-year-old. "I do trust you. I'm just nervous about what our new friend will do and where that leaves us."

Vision plopped back down on the bed, rubbing the covers and wrinkling her nose at the coarse fabric.

"Miranda is going to go after Bertrand. She hates him and what little I've been picking up from the crew tells me they are terrified of her, so we don't have to worry too much," Vision stated as though she were talking about the weather.

"I don't see how that helps us," Zhara said and eased herself down to sit beside Vision. "Sacrificing one person's life to save another seems like a poor trade."

Vision fixed Zhara with a cold black stare as her lip curled into a frown. "So, we should leave Claude to die?"

"That's not what I said," Zhara said defensively.

"But if we didn't trade Bertrand, that's what would happen. We'd be crying at your apartment, and who knows what would be happening to him?" Vision almost snarled.

"V, I didn't..."

"Don't boil this down to the basics, Zhara. We're not talking about some random guy. This is Claude, our Claude. The one that gave up everything to keep us safe. We owe him the same," Vision said and released the covers from her clenched fists. "Besides, Miranda was always going to hunt this guy down. All we did was speed that up a little."

Zhara sighed and put her face in her hands. "I just need some time to square with all this, V. It's a lot, you know?"

Vision placed a sympathetic hand on her friend's shoulder and leaned in close to comfort her. The roiling waves of emotion radiating from her were nothing if not intense, but Vision forced them to the side and ignored the strain it required.

"I don't think time is something we're going to have," Vision said as the door to their quarters slid open.

The same scarred, grim-faced man who had met them in the cargo bay stood squarely in the doorframe, casting approving eyes at the state of the room and then at the two guests. After a moment, the room spoke for him.

"The captain requests your presence on the command deck," the broadcast system stated in a lifeless tone, but Vision read the nervous waver missing from the words.

"Showtime," she said with a smile that didn't reach her eyes.

Chapter 34

THE DUST OF MINERVA Prime vibrated and danced around the rumbling engines of the Modus Vivendi. Each particle moved to its own unique rhythm, bouncing, flipping, and tumbling over the others in what looked like a party at first, but quickly devolved into a riot. The thrusters of the ship flared, and the partygoers nearby took flight in the blinding and deafening blast.

The Modus Vivendi broke free of the planet's gravity for the first time since its arrival and shuddered from the effort. She was built for travel in the weightless vacuum of the Black. She was not supposed to fight against the claws of such persistent forces.

The Vivendi's ascent was slow at first, but she relearned her old ways quickly. In seconds, she was out of the canyon and flying skyward. A moment after that, her primary engines kicked her forward toward the bright lights of Minerva City and the end of one woman's personal war.

• • • •

Miranda stepped out of the lift corridor to the familiar sights and sounds of her command deck. Everything was as it had been when she'd left it, though the stink of death had begun its pervasive quest to overtake the otherwise stale air she had become accustomed to. She was thankful to be out of the torn, bloody rags she had arrived in, but lamented the time it had taken to get herself cleaned and presentable.

The child she'd brought back was a Sabien brain maggot. That much was undeniable. All of the pieces fit, but there was something else about her. The silver still hadn't stopped its nervous vibrations, but they had lessened now that there was a significant distance between it and the girl.

Miranda had more than a few misgivings about throwing in with something so dangerous, but she could see no other way forward. The girl had found her despite the mess she'd made of the city, so it was entirely believable that she could do what she had promised.

For the first time in a long while, she felt a genuine smile threaten to break her severe countenance. She could already see Bertrand begging for his life as she closed herself off from his pleas. It was a shame that she couldn't grant him some of the longevity that she possessed. As it stood, she could only torture him for a short while before the meat gave in and died.

As she strode onto the command dais and took her seat, Miranda endeavored to savor every moment of the coming meeting. After all, she had more than earned it.

"Give me a report on the storm," Miranda demanded as she shifted her weight and found the perching position she preferred.

The seasoned tactical officer ran his fingers through his salt and pepper hair before declaring, "It's large, captain. She's twice the size of the city."

Miranda nodded as she basked in her improving fortunes. She liked thinking of the storm tearing its way across the rocks of this world as a "she." Soon enough, the tempest outside would mask her own assault, and like sister forces, they would rip apart any obstacles that stood in their way.

"Inform me of any changes," she said as she pulled up a topographical map of the terrain between the ship and center of Minerva City.

"Aye, Captain," came the reply, but she paid it no mind.

Much of the display on the hologram was obscured by a dark swirling mass that flickered at seemingly random intervals. Miranda watched the storm as it consumed a large portion of the Violet District. There was enough space within it to circumnavigate the Dead Zone while still maintaining cover, and that was exactly what she planned to do.

The lift chimed once again, and even before the child stepped off, Miranda felt the silver begin to panic. She had gotten as used to the sensation as she could on the ride back. Now she ignored it and stood to watch the harmless-looking creature exit the corridor and step fully onto the command deck.

She was followed by the woman, Zhara, and the two were led by Octavian. He didn't look pleased with his task. Lately, that seemed to be the norm for him and yet another thing that Miranda chose to ignore.

"It's time for you to earn your keep, girl," Miranda said as she stepped down from the dais.

She motioned, and the holographic map glided across the space and settled in front of the child, orienting itself to grant her better access.

The girl's brows knitted together over her black eyes before she turned away from the map.

"I can't see it," she said, and there was no hint of concern or nervousness in her voice.

Miranda found that odd but didn't voice it. Instead, she asked, "Then how are you useful to me?"

The child smirked at her and reached up to the odd contraption on her head.

"This is going to feel... a little strange," she said in a voice that carried a hint of spite.

Vision removed her halo with something close to a flourish, and a wave of noise rolled through Miranda's skull. She dropped her to her knees immediately as the silver screamed inside her. Tears squeezed their way through her clenched eyelids as she did everything she could to calm its primal shrieking.

Vision cast her mind around the room and found that the pirates were as affected as she had thought they'd be, but Claude's former friend was taking it worse than the others. For a moment, Vision tried diving deeper into Miranda to find out why, but something in her own mind lashed out at her attempt.

The mental image it cast back at her made the hairs on Vision's arms and neck stand up.

Suddenly, she felt herself being dragged through corridors by a woman who didn't seem to care that her nails were cutting into her. People screamed, and something pursued her, something that shimmered in the dark, dead halls of *that* nightmarish place.

A warm touch on her back pulled returned Vision to reality.

"Are you okay?" Zhara asked, and Vision nodded.

Looking at herself through Zhara's eyes felt odd, as did the warm, comforting feeling she felt coming from her. It was something she'd not really felt before, and like a warm bath on a cold day, it just felt right. Vision suddenly wanted to stay there, but that wasn't what she'd come for.

"*I will be when we get this done,*" she said, only it didn't come out in actual words.

Zhara nodded and went to step away, but Vision grabbed her hand in a plea for her to stay close. Without hesitation, Zhara agreed, and Vision cast herself into the ocean of minds beyond.

Waves of shimmering confusion crashed down on her. Their rapid pace and violence caught her off-guard and it took Vision a moment to adjust to the chaos. After a moment, she could see the burnt orange of annoyance and disdain turning to blood-red hate and rage throughout the ship.

"*This may not have been the best idea,*" she thought to Zhara, and while she knew Zhara received her message, she got no response.

Turning her attention outside the ship, Vision did her best to quiet every mind except two. It didn't take her long to latch on to the dual silver threads that were Claude and his passenger. They flowed and flexed almost in unison, and they offered their own sort of comfort to her, although it was not so enveloping as Zhara's.

From him, she tried to cast herself through the minds nearby. Several relieved people had begun celebrating, but she was looking for different emotions. She found several, but only one had the right blend of determination and regret. The strand was a calm, deep green, but looking closer, Vision could tell that it was actually battling streaks of yellow and blue. She grabbed it and sunk her "fingers" in.

The feel of this mind was familiar. It was the same rational, well-structured place she'd been foolish enough to invade before, only this time Vision knew what not to do. Instead of diving deep into his memories, Vision rode the surface current of his thoughts.

She felt Bertrand's hollow satisfaction at accomplishing his mission and reunifying his crew, but she also felt his frustration with the coming storm. It was trapping him on the planet, and he desperately wanted to leave.

With more effort, Vision traded her connection with Zhara for one with Bertrand. His vision was blurred, and his mind, now that she was in it properly, was sluggish. He tipped up a glass of amber fire, and Vision recoiled at the phantom flavor that washed through her. She felt the typically firm grip Bertrand kept on his own mind loosen as he closed his eyes and allowed himself to lean back in his chair. His mind wanted to cast backward for memories of a better time, but Vision didn't have time to wade through his happy days.

"*Where are you?*" she thought sharply, and Bertrand's eyes shot open.

She felt him fight against the chemicals in his bloodstream, but he was clumsy and slow. He had forgone the ability to think straight for the desire to forget, and in so doing, he had lost the battle before it had even begun.

"*Where are you?*" Vision whispered into his mind so intently that Bertrand dropped his glass and froze in place.

Several flashes danced in front of Vision. She couldn't catch them all, but she managed to grab three and sift through them.

The first was a man with his head trapped in an orb. Wires ran down into it, and tubes pumped fluids of all colors into his arms, neck, and spine. The man screamed and screamed until, at last, his body went limp.

Vision shook that image away and focused on the second. Claude was surrounded by thick green acid while Bertrand stared down at him from a catwalk high above. They spoke, but Vision was already moving past the image before the words came into focus.

The third and final image was of the skyline near Cascade. Bertrand piloted the busted transport above the high-rise homes and rooftop rock gardens, only for a large grayish blue monster to shimmer into view and open its gaping maw. Vision ran the image back and froze it as though she were manipulating a surveillance device. The readout on the console was clear. She had their heading.

With a sly smile, Vision extracted herself from the old man's mind and returned to her own.

Zhara watched as the command crew blinked away their disorientation and went back to work, giving nervous, angry, and fearful glances at Vision. She half expected them to collapse, but something Vision had done was different than before. She had assumed the people nearby on the skyway had their cars on autopilot, but maybe she'd been wrong there too. Everyone was back to normal by the time she heard Miranda's guttural shout.

"Get that thing off my deck," she roared.

Zhara turned to see the wild creature swimming in the captain's eyes as calloused hands seized her. She fought against them, but it was fruitless. The pirate's grip was stronger than the Regent's docking clamps.

"This '*thing*' knows where Bertrand is," Vision said defiantly as the voiceless man grabbed her by the back of the neck. "Or don't you care about that anymore?"

Miranda's eyes narrowed at her words, and while the muscles in her jaw ached to spit out a retort, none came.

The silver within boiled at the assault in a mixture of rage and fear that Miranda shared. The maggot had brought her to her knees with no effort at all, and she couldn't let that stand.

"Where?" Miranda asked through her grinding teeth.

"Above the Feterrier Building in Cascade," Vision declared, staring the captain down.

Miranda fought against herself and turned her back to the child. The silver bubbled onto her hands, although she hadn't called for the action. It was acting on its own again, but why?

Anxious eyes locked on her, and silent judgments were made. The faces of her crew were twisting as their minuscule thoughts slithered between their ears. Miranda wanted only one thing more than to quiet them. So, she tugged down her sleeves and clamped down on her momentary lapse in control.

"I want these two under guard. They don't so much as breathe without my permission, understood?" Miranda barked, only for the room itself to respond swiftly.

"Wait," Zhara said in a voice that betrayed her desperation.

Miranda turned back to them, lifting an eyebrow at the plea.

"Once you get there, we'll be out of your hair. All we want is Claude. We won't be your problem after that," the woman said, and the look in her eye reminded Miranda of just how soft civilians were.

"Oh no," Miranda heard herself say. "No one leaves until I have Bertrand's head in my hands."

Chapter 35

THE CREW MEMBERS OF the TaskMaster II were anything but restful. With the mission accomplished, they wanted little more than to return to the comfort of Streamline and eventually shore leave on whatever world they found themselves on. But thanks to spiking ion levels and the coming superstorm, that wasn't going to happen for some time.

Yuri found himself sitting in the rec room with many of his peers, but he simply watched and waited while they vented their frustrations in several holographic games. Nothing about this mission set right with him, and now that he had the downtime to actually pore over it all, he finally understood why.

Every mission he'd taken part in since joining the TaskMasters had a direct and obvious path toward helping the Beitan people. Quieting an insurrection in the wilds of Eiliton had put an end to the growing power of a would-be warlord. Protecting trade routes around Urito from pirates saved the lives of citizens who were simply working to feed their families. But this job didn't have that direct link. Here, they were feeding a dying war machine the information and blood it needed to struggle on. Their actions would eventually break the peace that so many were finally becoming accustomed to and lead the universe back into a conflict that had taken countless lives.

He downed his bottle of nutrient syrup, grimaced at its sickly-sweet aftertaste, and pulled his data-pad from his back pocket. In a few short swipes, the tiny translucent square presented him with Lillith's displeased scowl.

"No," she said firmly before he could even get a word out.

"You don't even know what I'm going to ask," Yuri stated in mock offense, but nothing about his friend's scowl changed.

"Does it matter? You only ever call me like this to get me into trouble," she said with a raised eyebrow.

Yuri said nothing and waited for the silence to break her, as it always seemed to do. It only took a few seconds of exposure to such a potent weapon for the harsh, flat line of her lips to crack and her edge to fall away.

"Fine, what do you want?" she sighed, and Yuri thought he witnessed something almost playful in it.

He ignored his potential discovery and instead chose to focus on the task at hand.

"I need to talk to him," Yuri said firmly.

Her head started its usual soft, slow shake before she gave him his initial rejection, but that was par for the course.

"Absolutely not. Neither of us has the clearance, and I'm not breaking protocols again so that you can run your mouth and muddle your own brain about what we're doing here," she protested.

Yuri cast his glance around the room, fearing that someone would have taken an interest in his debate. No one had, but he started moving toward the exit just in case.

"Listen, if all this feels right to you, then, by all means, sit this out. But if you feel at all wrong about Bertrand's treatment of the man who saved our lives, and I know you do, come with me."

Lillith blew out a breath so loud and so long that he was surprised that he couldn't feel the warm rush of it through the call. At first, she said nothing and instead looked away from her screen.

Yuri knew what she was staring at. It was the same captured image Lillith always stared at when she was forced to make a choice she didn't want to make. He had the same image adhered to his bunk and, out of respect for what Lillith had shared with the woman whose eyes she was looking into, he kept quiet.

"Okay, whatever. But you follow *my* lead," Lillith growled before turning back to Yuri. "The last thing I need is a cripple landing me in the brig."

Yuri shook off the jab and nodded his assent.

It took him all of five minutes to make the lift and another three before he was knocking on Lillith's door. He'd made good time, but so had she. She was combat-ready when she met him at her door with pursed lips and a raised eyebrow.

It was the same look she always gave him when he proposed something reckless. She was studying him to see whether she could talk him out of it.

"I need you to take five minutes and think about what you're signing us up for," she said, and tightened her sidearm holster one last time.

Yuri didn't know what she expected to be fighting, but he knew better than to ask. As far as he understood, they were going to talk to the on-duty guards and maybe bribe them to take a little break while they got a chance to pick DiSilva's brain and see what they could do to help him escape.

He hadn't shared that part of the plan with Lillith yet, but when he did, he was sure she'd be on board. Lillith just needed to be a little further out on the limb with him before he let her know all the details.

"I did that on the way down here," he said, and before the words were fully out of his mouth, Lillith shook her head and stepped into the corridor. "We can handle it."

"Your whole family is crazy, you know that?" she complained. "How did I ever get mixed up with you?"

"We have my sister to thank for that," Yuri said carefully.

Lillith's gray stare danced through a dozen emotions, before it eventually landed on a weary sadness. For a brief moment, she allowed herself to imagine a universe without emerald irises like those in it, then shook away that hollow void.

Blinking back the sting, she broke eye contact with him and did her best to put the ghost haunting her in its place by busying herself with the lock code for her door.

"What could you possibly have to talk to him about this time?" Lillith asked, keeping her back to Yuri.

"I want to know about the creature," he began. "You saw what it can do. If something like that got free, what are we supposed to do against it?"

Lillith just turned to him and nodded toward the lift at the far end of the hall before taking off in that direction. Yuri had to exert a decent amount of effort to keep up with her and did his best to ignore the stabs of pain that ran through him.

"Something like that *is* free, Yuri," Lillith snorted as she stormed down the corridor.

"That makes it even more important that we talk to somebody that knows what it can do and maybe how to kill it," Yuri stated between breaths that grew shorter with every step. "They're going to send us after the other one eventually, and I need it to go better than last time."

Lillith slowed to a stop while the shallow rectangular lift cleared of passengers, then stepped inside and fixed Yuri with a suspicious look.

"You don't know that they'll send us," she said with a frown.

"You don't know that they won't," Yuri retorted, taking the space across from her. "Besides, it's not like having this information can be a bad thing."

"Oh, it can, assuming Echelon doesn't want a pair of grunts knowing how to kill their super-weapon."

Yuri shrugged off Lillith's excellent point. He couldn't argue with her, but he wasn't going to let her pragmatism punch a hole in his design. He did his best to ignore her expectant stare as the lift droned on and shifted from a vertical to a horizontal trajectory.

"Look, I know you think I'm taking a huge risk and that I've asked you to take one too, but if this is the kind of outfit that sells its own people out, is it really worth fighting for?" Yuri asked and stared Lillith down.

She squirmed under his gaze and did her best to keep her eyes from meeting his. She failed.

"You know how I feel about it, but that doesn't mean we should be willing to throw our futures away without at least taking the proper time to think it through," Lillith fired back.

"What if we don't have that kind of time?"

"Then maybe we catch the next opportunity to do the right thing instead of running after this one," she snapped.

Yuri leaned against the wall. "You wouldn't do that."

Lillith tightened her jaw before she responded to his obvious bait.

"I could."

Yuri let a smile break through. It was a weak one, but it was honest all the same.

"We both know better than that," he said with a hint of a smirk in his voice.

Lillith subconsciously straightened at his words. He'd just paid her a compliment she didn't know how to take, and her face was burning as a result. She found herself grateful that her olive skin didn't show it too much.

"So, this was never about finding a way to kill those monsters?" she asked, already knowing the answer.

"Lill," Yuri said, clearing his throat. "It's about not becoming our own kind of monsters, instead."

Lillith sighed and shook her head gently. Again, she was struck by just how alike the Launtik siblings could be. Yuri was going to try this with or without her, and as she let the last of her reservations drift away, Lillith admitted to herself that he was right.

"Fine, whatever."

· · · ·

Vision paced the floor of a room that felt more and more like a cell with each passing moment. She could feel the ship around her moving, and without having to stretch out with her abilities, she knew they had to be nearing the city.

"What happened up there?" Zhara asked, breaking the veil of silence in the room.

Vision didn't stop along her path but instead increased her speed.

"I found Claude and then Bertrand," Vision said, purposely keeping her answer short. "Just like I planned to."

"That's not what I meant, and you know it," Zhara pushed. "If something is wrong, we need to be on the same page about it."

Vision rounded another circuit on her endless journey. Her dark eyes cast downward in an involuntary admission of shame, but she pursed her lips to keep the words from spilling out.

"Pacing isn't going to help anything," Zhara said with a sigh.

"I need to do something, and this is the safest thing I can think of," Vision snapped without breaking her stride.

With minimal effort, she felt similar apprehension to her own echoed in not only Zhara but the pirate sent to stand guard outside their door. In fact, she could feel it throughout the ship. Everyone was nervous about what was to come, but not for the same reasons. There was a tension among the members of the crew. Vision had picked up on it the moment they set foot on the ship, but she was reluctant to dig any deeper and feeling the compounded unease from everyone on the ship, did nothing to help her keep calm.

"What did you do on the bridge?" Zhara asked more directly this time.

Vision turned to scowl at her, dropping out of her perpetual motion. There was some anger in her features, but mostly they revealed fear, confusion and sadness.

Zhara wanted to bring her in for a hug, but she knew the time wasn't right. Vision was working something out, and if she was unwilling to talk about it, there was no chance that she'd let anyone get close.

"She called me a thing," Vision said, more to herself than to Zhara.

"She's a pirate, V, and she was afraid. You can't take anything she says to heart," Zhara said, giving Vision a very shaky smile.

"She's not the only one. Phalen thinks I'm a thing too, and so did those scientists on Firaxis," Vision continued. "I'm starting to think maybe they're right."

"Look at the caliber of people you're talking about, V. They're some of the worst humanity has to offer. They're all either untrustworthy, corrupt, or heartless. Most are all three," Zhara said as she watched a tear escape Vision's rigid facade. "You have to consider your sources, Vision."

"Are we any better? You're a thief, Claude's a murderer, and there isn't even a word for what I am," Vision said as she turned away.

"Human," Zhara said firmly.

"What?"

"There is a word for what you are. It's human," Zhara clarified. "Just like me, and just like Claude. You struggle, and you make mistakes. Sometimes you even do bad things, but that doesn't make you any less a person."

Vision spun on her, the wetness in her eyes now brimming with heat.

"How can you say that?"

"Because it's true. Motivations matter. If you were out there ripping through the minds of innocent people for your own personal pleasure or gain, that would be one thing, but you're not," Zhara declared. "You do what you do to help people, to protect them."

"But isn't it still wrong?" Vision asked and locked Zhara in her sightless stare. "You were the one that said trading a life for a life was a bad thing."

"And you reminded me that sometimes hard choices have to be made," Zhara shared, and there was a note of distilled sadness in her voice. "Listen, in a vacuum, you might be right, but life doesn't happen in a vacuum. It gets messy and dirty, and the lines between what's wrong and what's not get blurred.

"Trying to hold on to it will drive you crazy and ruin any chance you have at being happy. The universe is too complicated for all that."

Vision pressed her back to the far wall of the space and slid down against the floor, hugging her knees.

"So, what am I supposed to do?" she asked hopelessly.

Zhara drew in a deep breath of stale, reprocessed air and let it roll out of her before she chose to answer. As she inhaled once more, she prayed that her father's words would make more sense to Vision than they had to her when she'd first heard them.

"You have to choose," Zhara said while her father's voice echoed in her mind. "The only thing a person can do is choose to be a decent human being, and when there's no way to come out of a situation whole, you try to keep as much of that decency from being sheared off by the teeth and claws of life."

Vision's face twisted as she took the words in. It wasn't the answer she hoped for, though it was impossible to say what she'd expected. Something about it felt true, though.

For all the wisdom in those words, they clearly hadn't come from Zhara, at least not originally. They felt older and out of character for someone who lived such a comfortable life.

"Who told you that?" Vision asked.

"My dad," Zhara said with a smile that rested entirely in her eyes. "He liked to say he was just a miner, but he knew a few things about life. I didn't believe him when he told me that, but I think it might not have been meant for me."

Immortality seemed like the stuff of fancy to Vision, but she liked the thought of wisdom being passed into the future in such an indirect way. It made a person's impact live on forever, even if they could not. The concept warmed her inside, melting away the cold of her uncertainty.

The advice itself was hard to quantify, but she supposed that was always the way advice seemed when you needed it. She sighed and chose to let Mr. Riggs' words comfort her, and within a few moments, she felt a little better.

"We need to get out of this room," she said, filing the conversation away for later.

Chapter 36

THE COMMOTION ON THE command deck didn't take long to die down. Octavian believed that had more to do with Miranda than the little mind worm she'd brought on board. No self-respecting pirate, or soldier for that matter, would admit they were afraid of a child, but a great many feared their captain. He'd ordered their room guarded, and once he'd gotten confirmation it was done, he returned to his post with more fire burning in him than he'd expected.

Miranda had made risky calls before and often without his knowledge or consent. Of course, she didn't need to inform him of every choice, but it seemed she always made the worst ones when he wasn't in the loop.

Bringing the girl onboard was just such a call. If she was to be believed, they now had the location of Bertrand's stealth ship, but at what cost? Psionics were dangerous. Octavian hadn't fought any himself. They had all disappeared before he joined the military, but the stories were widely known.

Miranda knew them just as well as he did. If she were in her right mind, Octavian was sure she would have put one of those silver spikes of hers through the kid's supercharged brain. Instead, she brought her here where the girl could burrow her way into everyone's minds, finding out how they thought, what they feared, and eventually using them against one another.

Now he found his captain issuing commands with more enthusiasm than he'd seen in months. It would have been a good thing, except for the foreign element in her voice that put him on edge. It sounded like an echo, but it was so faint it could have just been his imagination.

"Once we enter the city's airspace, I want all hands to battle stations. Give me full charges on the rubies, tethers, gutters, and load the dorsal launcher with a hull cracker," she barked from her perch on the command dais.

Octavian watched the tactical chief nod, but couldn't hold back any longer.

"Hold on that order," the room declared loudly and definitively.

Every eye in the space locked on him as the sound of multiple side conversations died. Only the ship's low-level vibrations and various high-pitched console pings pierced the silence as he turned his attention directly to his captain.

Miranda said nothing, but fixed him with a glare that promised murder if he didn't explain himself.

"Tethers and ruby lasers are one thing, but a hull cracker could break the ship in half if we land it properly," Octavian protested.

Nervous whispers keyed up in the space around them, but he ignored them. He was only interested in holding the attention of one person, and he hoped more than anything that he could get her to step back from the ledge she seemed determined to leap from.

"I know full well what I ordered, Officer," Miranda stated with an unmistakable spike in her voice. "I did not call for it by accident."

It wasn't the response Octavian was hoping for. It was the exact opposite, in fact. He had escalated the situation by challenging her openly, but there was only one thing he could do about that now.

"Clear the deck," he ordered through the broadcast system and waited for the message to take root.

Miranda didn't challenge his request, which was undoubtedly what the remainder of the command crew had expected. Without that, they began to file out of their positions and down to the lift. When the last of them had marched out of earshot, Octavian tapped his ear, indicating Miranda should use her earpiece.

She eyed him defiantly, slicing into him with more of her searing stare before eventually doing so.

"We need to take that ship, Captain, not destroy it. Tensions among the crew are at an all-time high, and I can only see one way to resolve that," he said into her ear.

The monotone of Octavian's words drained his plea of its emotion but not its meaning. Miranda had to struggle to understand him over the roiling intensity of the creature. The silver wanted him to pay for challenging her authority in so public a fashion, and it was right to be so offended. She shared in its anger, but she wasn't going to let it take her by surprise again, not if she could help it.

"I don't care about that ship," she said in as repressed a tone as she could manage. "It means nothing to me. It's a shell that houses the one thing I came here for, and if I have to crack it open to tear Bertrand out of it, that is what I will do."

"And what about after you destroy the ship? If the body is buried under a thousand tons of twisted metal, how will you confirm the kill? Bertrand isn't stupid, and unless you ignite their fuel system, he will have time to escape into the city," Octavian countered.

Miranda took a moment and leaned back in her chair. She'd considered this. The obvious solution was to go to the surface and hunt him down, which she was more than willing to do, but it would take time and manpower to pull off. That was, of course, the point Octavian was making. She would still need the crew, and if she blew up the ship she'd promised them, there would be an outright revolt against her.

"You're going to need the crew, at least some of them. Killing the one thing keeping them in line will only make them storm this place and tear you out of that chair," he concluded.

"They are welcome to try," she said with a predatory sneer.

"Miranda, I am trying to save you."

"No!" she shouted, lunging from her seat and stopping just inches from him. "You are trying to save *them.*"

Octavian flinched at the speed and ferocity of her movement, but stood his ground. The most primitive part of his brain demanded that he run or at least defend himself, but he held it at bay with great effort. It continued to scream into his more logical mind as her deep brown and silver eyes searched him over like those of a million carnivores on a thousand worlds. The pure menace wafting from her stripped his mind down until the only thought he could cling to was that he was not her prey.

"Do you really think a gang of lawless murderers and thieves can take that ship from experienced TaskMasters?" she asked as she began to slowly circle him.

"I believe it is better to fight for something than to die for nothing, at least for them," Octavian responded as she moved around behind him.

She could feel his fear, but also his determination. The two forces were even now, and she wondered whether the fear would eventually overtake him. It had been growing for some time, and now that she looked back on their most recent interactions, it was plain to see. How she had missed it before? She didn't know, but to a small degree, Miranda was grateful that she had. Octavian had always served her faithfully, and even through her anger, she could tell he believed he was doing so now.

She circled slowly back around in front of him before she said, "I remember what pirates did to you, Octavian. You should be the last person advocating for them. Why are you challenging me on their behalf? Is it your new hobby? Is she really that good?"

Octavian felt the fear turn to anger inside him.

"*She* has nothing to do with this," he lied, and Miranda laughed in his face.

It was an almost painful sound, an abrasive bark that left Octavian feeling even more off-kilter than the smile she wore.

"Honestly, she doesn't matter. The crew doesn't matter, and neither does that ship. I only want one man, and anything in my way dies. I don't want that to be you," Miranda growled, diminishing the bloodlust of the creature within. "Now, get off my command deck and don't come back."

Octavian bit back the cold and brutal response that bubbled up in his throat as his mind once again defeated his heart in the race for control. Instead of escalating the situation further, he simply fixed his old friend with a look that displayed his displeasure as much as any combination of words he knew and did as she commanded.

Chapter 37

OVER MILLENNIA, MINERVA City had weathered countless storms. Its people knew what they felt, sounded, and smelled like even when the charged clouds were hours away. Few storms still shocked them, and for a standard year, nothing had shaken the stone, metal, and polymer lands where they labored and played. Unfortunately, things change.

Above the city, a tapestry of light and power wove itself into existence. Each of the countless bolts of ionized particles scorched the air, leaving only an afterimage and the smell of burnt ozone in their wake. If it weren't for the forest of energy collectors dotting the rooftops, a storm cell like the one the city was now weathering would have turned it and perhaps every soul, cowering within to charred, ruined husks.

As protected as those under the white-hot canopy were, the dark mass hovering above them boasted an even greater defense. The ship had given up its invisibility in favor of energy shields that flared white with every strike of lightning, before fading out of view. Its mandate for stealth was unlikely to be broken. Nothing flew in a storm of this caliber and no eyes would wonder skyward.

• • • •

Bertrand collapsed into the captain's chair. His head was spinning, but not from the alcohol. He hadn't even been able to finish his second drink. The disorientation he fought was a product of his own panic. His breaths came short and fast, teetering him on the edge of hyperventilation despite his attempts to force his lungs back under control.

"Give me a wide-band sensor sweep," he choked out and watched as the console's crewman launched into action.

It had been decades since Bertrand last had another human being's thoughts inside his head, but he'd never forgotten the sensation. The unnatural violation had carved its way into the core of his being so deep that he would never again be without that experience. He had felt his mind worn like a glove as he was used by a Psionic and summarily discarded. This new invasion threatened to drive him back into the pure, petrifying terror that still resided deep in his memories.

Like before, he had been drinking, but this time he was not spared. Whoever had violated him wanted to know his location, and that was at least something he could work with.

Bertrand closed his eyes tight enough to see stars through his eyelids and forced the old fear back into its hole. He concentrated on what he knew, and when he looked at the map in front of him, Kerrid Bertrand felt more like himself.

All the Psionics Echelon had studied required a certain proximity to dive into a target, close proximity. That meant there must have been a ship nearby, and he needed to find it.

His newly resurrected fear had stolen too much time, but the TaskMaster II was still in the air. There had been no attack, which was curious, especially considering the storm had forced them into the open. The fact his ship wasn't destroyed or even under attack meant little. There was no escaping this world now that the TaskMaster II had been compromised.

"The storm is providing massive interference," the officer at the sensor console called.

"Keep scanning," Bertrand growled. "Someone's out there. Find them before they find us."

He didn't wait for the crewman to confirm the order and instead fingered the holographic panel at the right arm of his chair and issued a full alert throughout the ship.

The command dais raised with the soft whirring of the mechanical arm that held it aloft. Bertrand forced himself to stand, mastering his shaking legs and his wailing mind once and for all.

He pulled up a holographic readout of the clouded sky around the ship and stared into it as though he might spot what a million dedicated sensors could not.

• • • •

Claude could hear the storm through the walls. The chemicals holding him in suspension rippled with each crash of thunder. The thick ooze absorbed most of the vibrations before they could reach the lone figure at the vat's center.

Hearing anything from the storm outside told him how intense it had to be. Superstorms didn't roll through often, and while he had let most of the last one fade from his memory, he could still remember Vision's reaction. The residual charge in the air interfered with her sensors, leaving her almost completely blind. That, plus the disorienting booms of thunder, led to a night of pure panic for her. There was no reason to think this storm wasn't at least affecting her halo in the same way.

What concerned him most was whether two estimated birthdays would make a difference in how she dealt with it. A desperate need to ensure Vision's safety clawed its way through every fiber of Claude, but that wasn't possible. He just had to trust Zhara to handle whatever complications arose, no matter how much he wanted to be there himself.

Being stuck in Bertrand's trap was really wearing on him. He had no idea how long he'd been unconscious or how long he'd been floating. Luckily, the storm told him a few things. One, they were still on the planet, and two, the ship was stuck in a holding pattern until it passed.

Tech had changed a little since his time, but he doubted the basics of interstellar travel had altered that much. Returning to orbit required the shields be lowered around the engine, or the heat would be trapped inside, cooking the ship like bread in an oven. The hull of a ship like this would survive, and the internal temperatures would rise just high enough to make sweat stains a part of every crewman's uniform, but the sensor equipment would pay the ultimate price. No sensors meant no Streamline frequency readouts, and without those, the ship would be stuck crawling through the Black so slowly that everyone's great-grandchildren would be dead before they left the system.

Even if it wasn't for the storm, the amount of acid drawn from the vats was nowhere near enough to power a ship this size in motion.

Not for the first time, Claude wished he'd been awake on the journey in so he would know how to plan an escape should the unlikely opportunity present itself. As it stood, he had no knowledge of any part of the ship aside from this room, so he focused on what he could glean from it.

If ship design was like it used to be, the refinery would be among its lower decks. That meant there was tons of metal between him and the lightning. While that was a comforting thought, Claude would have gladly traded the threat of being eaten alive by acid for the risk of electrocution. That wasn't a choice he was given, however. Luckily, the telltale fatigue he associated with utilizing his passenger wasn't plaguing him just yet.

"Hey!" he shouted up to the statue of a man guarding him. "Am I supposed to just float here all the way to wherever we're going?"

The guard fired an annoyed glance at him but said nothing for the hundredth time. It wasn't unexpected, just boring. Claude hoped he might at least goad the man into interacting with him. It wouldn't be much. Even a terse exchange could potentially provide him with some usable intel.

He had just decided to give up on that plan when the doors behind the guard slipped open. Two new soldiers rolled up on the mountain of a man, and in a series of quick, well-practiced strikes, the newcomers dropped him to the grated catwalk with a bang so loud it rang off the walls of his "cell."

It took him a moment to recognize them, but when he did, he couldn't help the shocked laugh that tore its way out of him.

"How in the Homeworld did you get him in there?" Yuri asked his friend.

Lillith shrugged and scanned the area before she deigned to answer him.

"I wasn't here for that part. I was just an escort."

Yuri huffed and turned his attention to Claude.

"Can you see any way to get out?" he shouted down to Claude.

Claude shook his head before realizing they might not be able to see it, then yelled back, "The top section is sealed, and I can't swim to the bottom in this mess."

Yuri pounded his fist on the railing of the catwalk, making the metal sing until its song was consumed by the hum of machinery. He had half a mind to take Lillith's sidearm and just shoot a hole in the vat, but that wouldn't work. It took much more force than a round or two from even a standard-issue rifle to punch through Vertibit glass. Even if he could break through it, setting the acid free would kill them all. It would eat through the ship's engines and all the decks below, turning the TaskMaster II and a massive chunk of the city into little more than fire and death.

Bertrand's improvised cell was just too well thought out.

"Don't worry about me," Claude began. "You should probably..."

The rhythmic drone of the refinery shattered as alarms shouted for everyone's attention.

"... Get out of here!"

Yuri and Lillith didn't argue. They just turned and ran back the way they'd come. Yuri's eyes widened as the bulkhead door slammed into place, sealing them inside with a thud that threatened to shake the catwalk from its mooring.

Similar deep metallic clangs resounded from the other entrances as every security measure followed suit.

"You know, this might have been a bad plan after all," Yuri heard himself say.

Lillith clenched her jaw and spun to confront Claude. She marched past Yuri, ignoring him, and leaned over the catwalk, fixing Claude with a stare that might just melt his prison.

"You know what that is, don't you?" she roared.

Claude sighed and gave as much of a shrug as he could manage, given his situation.

"Yeah, that'll be my rescue."

Chapter 38

THE CALL FOR BATTLE stations rang through the ship with all the urgency of an air-raid siren. For all their discontent with their captain, the crew of the Modus Vivendi responded as they always had. Bodies moved quickly through the ship's arteries, preparing to defend her against whatever threat she had detected.

Ashe felt the familiar buzz of shields sparking to life and figured the fight was finally upon them. She didn't have an actual position during such situations, but everyone was on call to deal with boarding parties and emergency repairs.

It was unlikely enemy troops would come after the comms hub. In the heat of a battle, there were other higher priority targets to aim for. Although, killing an adversary's ability to coordinate would ultimately make them easier to take down.

As it stood, she'd been through her fair share of assaults on the Vivendi, and she'd never once had to defend the tiny space from anyone seeking to destroy it. She checked the slab in her sidearm, ensuring that there was enough of the magnetized metal to make it through a firefight or three before sliding it into its holster. The gun was bulkier than she preferred, but what it lacked in ergonomic design it made up for in stopping power.

With her weapon secured, Ashe turned her attention to the next order of business. She spotted a familiar face in the stream of bodies and grabbed the thin boy with the strips of shaved hair by the arm. Ashe ignored the indignant look in his deep brown eyes as she pulled him to the side.

"What's going on?" she asked over the cacophony of boots on metal.

Recognition dawned on the kid's all too youthful features, and he eased his defensive posture.

"Who cares? All I know is its action, and I'm all for it," the boy said, and a smirk tore across his face like a ragged gash.

"Where are they sending you?" Ashe asked, trying desperately to hold the pirate's attention long enough to get the information she needed.

"My unit's manning the tethers. Whatever the captain has us chasing must be huge," the eager pirate said with a hungry glint in his eye. "Do you mind?"

Ashe let go and raised her hands in surrender. The kid looked her up and down one more time, snorted then continued down the corridor without so much as a look back.

"I was wrong," the room behind her broadcast, startling her.

Tentative hands closed on Ashe's shoulders, and though the touch was familiar, it did little to calm her nerves. She spun to see Octavian's broken expression and instantly knew what was on his mind.

"Are you ready to do what comes next?" she asked as she pulled him into the Comms center.

She ignored the salacious glances they got from her subordinates. The soft chimes of a million messages harmlessly pinging off her search protocols filled the room, but they couldn't break the tension in the air.

Octavian didn't share her ability to disregard the other humans nearby. His eyes searched both of them carefully. Their faces were known to him, but not well. Certainly not well enough to share his conversation with them.

"Leave now," the room barked with both the suddenness and volume to produce the desired response.

It took less than a minute for Ashe's underlings to file out of the room and disappear into the bustling corridor beyond.

"Was that necessary?" she asked with a sly smile.

"If you try to take the ship by force, she'll kill everyone. There has to be another way," Octavian broadcast at a lower volume once the door was sealed.

Ashe leaned back against the console and paid no attention to the angry coded hologram buzzing around her.

"The command deck is a sealed unit. With the right cuts, we can sever its connection to the rest of the ship, but we'd be holding a sawtooth by the ears," Ashe said.

"You won't have it for long. Miranda knows the ship well. Once you shut her off, you're going to need to either find a way to kill her quickly or throw her off your trail," Octavian countered.

Ashe's brow furrowed as she studied the immense concern straining his well-worn features. She stroked her lower lip as she considered what he'd said, but kept getting stuck on his choice of words.

"We," she finally said and fixed him with her crystal blue stare. "You keep talking like you aren't part of this, and honestly, it's cute, but we're in this together.

"There are enough of us to take over every major discipline of this ship, and those that aren't willing to fight with us have chosen to sit it out and back the winner. There's only one way we can lose this fight, Octavian."

A tense and almost maniacal smirk crossed his lips at her words as he pictured all the things she hadn't considered. An image of Luudo, the infiltrator, and his half-filleted corpse rotting in the ready room floated effortlessly to the forefront.

"Promise me that you won't confront her directly," Octavian said and winced at the emotionless voice that spoke his words. "I need to hear you say it."

Ashe hesitated for a moment. The plea on his face told her everything the broadcast system could not. She read an unspoken question there. One she felt more than saw or heard, and it required a response. She simply didn't know how to give it.

"I promise," she said and meant it along with every word that she held back.

• • • •

The dim metal frame of the Modus Vivendi soared silently over the shellshocked towers at the edge of Cascade. Only the storm took notice, testing the ship's serrated edges with searing electric fingers. Each course touch caused the cruiser to shudder, but not to stop.

The augmented Sabien vessel flew sure and swift through the blinding firmament toward a target it could not see. It closed on the blocky, vaguely fish-shaped form of the TaskMaster II blindly, carving its way through the soupy atmosphere until, at long last, she found a ping on the horizon.

• • • •

"Captain, we have something on sensors," the recon tech announced in a voice that sounded both terrified and relieved.

Miranda cloned the sensor readout and stared at the growing blip. Its eerie green form hovered in front of her like a lure, and while she could easily take a bite from her current range, it was not how she wanted to announce herself.

"Is it our ship?" she inquired, squinting at the tiny dot of light.

"I don't know," came the reply, and Miranda snapped the full fire of her attention to the wire-thin man who dared speak such an undesirable truth.

"Is it a warship?" she roared, and her voice filled the nervous air of the room.

The tactical officer to her right winced and answered, "It's impossible to tell from this distance, Captain."

The deep green eyes of the officer begged her forgiveness, and reluctantly Miranda gave it. The command crew did their jobs as well as could be asked. The ship's limitations were not a weakness she could reasonably assign to them, no matter how irritating they were. So instead of launching insults and violence their way, she let her emotions cool and ran a million scenarios through her mind.

The sensors were unreliable, that could not be helped. The needed details couldn't be drawn until either the storm cleared or Miranda ordered the ship out of it. The ionic bombardment did wonders for providing cover, but it didn't only work for her.

The Vivendi's weapons systems could cut through the clouds reliably, but they needed accurate sensor data to hit their target. Neither the tethers, gutters, or flechette cannons could reach the unknown ship's distance without either falling prey to the demands of gravity or diminishing to the point of uselessness. As for the hull cracker, it wasn't worth considering unless she was guaranteed a hit.

"Find me a targeting vector on that ship and let's give her a kiss," she commanded, rechecking the coordinates the Psionic had given her. "Let's see if she's the kind of girl that kisses back."

"Aye, captain," the tactical officer called and blew out a breath of relief.

Miranda watched him speed through the gestures that would bring her the desired results and felt the thrum of her own anxiety fight with the low-level vibrations of the silver. Miranda forced her eyes closed. Chances were the ship she had targeted was just a civilian vessel stranded in the storm, but somewhere in her soul, she knew it wasn't.

Years of pursuing her prey from distances greater than her mind could fully comprehend had prepared her for this exact moment. The first salvo would be hers, and while she found herself elated by the idea of turning the man who had betrayed her into a fire of flesh and bone, Miranda couldn't help but lament the fact that she would miss seeing the life flicker and fade from him.

A great many daydreams had filled her downtime, and in all of those wistful moments, never once did she think it would come down to a battle on this scale. This was the opportunity that had come, and the ion storm set the stage perfectly. She would be a fool not to capitalize on it, especially against an adversary as formidable as Kerrid Bertrand.

The chance she had been given would not be wasted no matter how improper it felt to dispatch him so callously. Miranda's little monster demanded to be loosed on Bertrand. They both wanted the up-close kill instead of ripping him from the sky, but this was the shot they were offered.

"Calm. We almost have him," Miranda whispered so softly even she was unaware the words had crossed her lips.

"I have the target," her new favorite officer called, and she appreciated the confidence in his voice.

"Then burn them down," she said as she lightly caressed the silver pooling on her upper arm.

. . . .

Sustained lances of vivid crimson tore themselves free from the main guns of the Modus Vivendi. They carved through the deep gray, unhindered by the interference that lashed out so violently against their ship. In an instant, the beams slashed across the distance and bit into the shimmering bubble that stopped them mere feet from the armored hull of their target.

In the Black, the immense cold would have kept the thick metal of the enemy's hull cool, but in Minerva's atmosphere, the Modus Vivendi's sustained touch caused the TaskMaster's "skin" to smolder.

Ruby lasers issued no force to speak of, but that didn't make them any less dangerous. As near-instant point-to-point weapons, it was simple to splash a target with a bank of lasers and weaken their hull before penetrating it with heavier ordnance.

The armored body of the TaskMaster II didn't so much as shudder from the shots, but thousands of tiny sensors embedded in its metal skin screamed all at once. The lightning had already whipped them into a frenzy of data collection, but the heat from the lasers was impossible for them to miss.

Dozens of tiny flames lit up the sky around the ship as thrusters fired. The TaskMaster shifted, turning to face its hidden assailant more slowly than intended. Its massive weight hindered it, forcing the blockier vessel to fight against both gravity and its own momentum.

. . . .

Bertrand leaned into the turn even though he barely felt it. The dais compensated for most of the weight shift, but old habits died hard.

"Do we have the source locked?" he barked.

The holographic image in front of him mirrored the search taking place on the gunnery officer's display. Unlike its source, the captain's feed could decouple from the real-time feed and provide him a full 360-degree view of the events that had just transpired.

Bertrand gestured frenetically, forcing the image to swirl in a wide arc until he found the two red spires that had splashed across his shields.

Their convergence point was distant but still visible, and he did his best to zoom the blurry image. What he found looked like a blade pointed directly at him.

"Sending coordinates," Bertrand called. "Bring us about and light up six cannons. If Faridan wants a light show, let's give her one."

"Aye, Captain," came the reply, and the ship immediately began to shift around him.

The turn was sharper than the one he'd ordered before, but now they had something to fly toward instead of just reacting blindly. Again, he leaned into the turn, although it wasn't expressly necessary.

With a swipe, he brought his holo feed up to real-time, aligning it with the TaskMaster II's front-facing sensors. He knew who was after him. There was only one person it could be, and while the Psionic attack wasn't the type of assault he'd expected from Miranda, she was clearly capable of more than his intel suggested.

The Aumanent-class cruiser she had brought against him came into view as the ships closed on each other. It was an older Sabien ship, but a formidable one. He'd faced them before, but only in his days before founding the TaskMasters. Aumanent vessels were known to be well-armed and far more maneuverable than his ship, but that was in the Black. Minerva Prime would add to the challenge of the fight. Still, given the circumstances, he was confident he could win.

He figured Miranda would come at him hard and fast, but on foot. In his nightmares, she always leveraged her greatest advantage against him, and if she had done so here, there would have been little he could do to fend her off. As it was, she had brought the fight to him on a field he knew very well.

Bertrand's eyes locked on the gray blade as it sliced its way toward him, and for the first time in years, he felt like it was going to be a good night.

Chapter 39

CLAUDE FELT THE SHIFT in his vat before Lillith and Yuri had to brace themselves against the catwalk railings above. He didn't need a holo-feed to tell him that the ship had been engaged. A turn that sharp would have normally been negated by artificial gravity, but on a planet, there was no need to waste the power. He watched as the acid walked its way up the left side of his vat until he could place his feet against it.

A smirk curled his lip at the sensation. It had been at least a few hours since he'd felt anything even remotely as pleasant, but he couldn't focus on it. The turn was slowing, and the acid threatened to settle. Casting his eyes around his ingeniously repurposed cell, Claude found just the right place to leap, assuming the acid wouldn't severely hamper him and that his friend still had enough strength to manage it.

In preparation, the silver on his neck and chest melted back into him as the acid receded to waist height. For his part, Claude planted his feet as best he could against the straightening ship and gave the jump everything he had. It wasn't much, but his passenger was apparently as eager for freedom as he was.

The jump launched him out of the liquid and up instead of forward. Claude could feel the soft wet pop as his legs and feet came free of the acid's tenacious grip. Gravity caught up to him quickly, slowing his ascent and stalling his jump before he could reach the glass above.

He felt the fall coming and reached out. Claude was easily six feet from touching anything and even further from any hope of freedom, but he reached anyway. The cool rush of silver flowing up his torso and arm was only matched by the soothing relief Claude felt as his passenger reached with him.

The five thin, mirrored tendrils stretched across the gap. They moved through the air in a flash, but only two found purchase in the surface above. When Claude's weight snapped down, it tore one of the remaining strands loose.

He whispered another of his aimless prayers. Against all sense of decent judgment, he looked down at the sickly green substance beneath him and found himself newly grateful that he hadn't plummeted the remaining eight feet into the stuff.

His passenger was fast, but Claude wasn't sure it was quick enough to beat both gravity and the acid on its way back down to protect him. If it was late by even a few tenths of a second, there wouldn't be enough left of Claude to worry about keeping alive.

Above, the silver wove its way into a single thick rope before the individual strands merged. The mass shifted down from his fingertips into his palm, and without understanding why Claude gripped it firmly. He did his best to pull his weight up until he could grasp the silver with his free hand. Unlike before, when the creature had simply retracted and pulled him toward whatever he was attached to, this time, it reabsorbed into his body, letting him do most of the work.

Claude could feel its exhaustion as if it was his own, even though his body was much less worn out from the long soak.

"Going to make me do it all myself, huh?" he said between grunts as he pulled himself up to the glass and inspected the hold that had saved his life.

There was a puncture in the glass's surface filled with threaded silver, slowly but surely working further into it like some form of semi-solid drill. It was still an inch or more from breaking through, but Claude was too relieved to critique the speed.

His arms were his newest problem. They were already shaking from holding his full weight suspended in the air. Eventually, he would give out, but he would maintain for a while longer. The only alternative was to melt like a clump of old food in the chemical washbasin of his apartment.

"See if you can find a way out of here!" he shouted up to the stunned pair on the catwalk.

· · · ·

Yuri and Lillith bolted across the catwalk, away from the sealed bulkhead and toward the "Y" junction ahead. They moved almost in unison, except Yuri was a step and a half behind.

"How do you think that works?" he asked as he did his best to keep pace and block out the pain in his shoulder and chest.

"Shut up and keep up, Yuri. If we're stuck in here when the real shooting starts, there are a million ways we could die," Lillith shot back and frowned as she noticed that her partner was falling farther behind.

"Thanks, I was trying not to think about that," he said and instinctively took a left at the junction while Lillith took the right.

The question stayed with him as he moved, keeping his eyes open for any potential exit points. He had seen firsthand what the other one could do, but the how of it was beyond him. Nothing he'd ever seen could change from a liquid state to a solid at that speed. All the science he knew said it was impossible, especially without a significant catalyst. When its strength and flexibility were added to the equation, Yuri fully believed that the doctor had been right to want to see them destroyed. The damned things were powerful and versatile enough to have easily won the war for whichever side had them, but what then?

He had seen men lose their bearings when put in charge of other soldiers, and while a group of well-trained grunts could accomplish a lot, they weren't likely to keep you alive through a bath in Phorano acid. There was no way a weapon like that could be issued and taken away the same way a sidearm was. Soldiers would fight to keep it, leading to places Yuri would prefer not to imagine.

Letting that bleak, horrifying future fade from his mind, Yuri scanned the path ahead. The catwalk extended another twenty feet or so before hitting another "Y" junction. The split paths fed into intersection after intersection, stretching over the entire space but leading to no sure exit.

A ten-ton weight slammed down on his foolish hope that one of the doors might have malfunctioned. Apparently, the maintenance techs were good at their jobs, and Yuri cursed them for it.

The only other way out of the refinery was through the O2 system. The vents that brought breathable air into the area were located on the ceiling, but each was covered by a filtration scrubber that weighed more than Yuri cared to guess. Besides their immense size, they were secured by the same high-tension binding used to hold the hull panels together.

Even with DiSilva helping, it would be pretty much impossible to wrench them free. Even all the constant force of the Black couldn't pull those bindings apart. There was no way a few humans could manage it.

With an exasperated sigh, Yuri slowed himself to a jog and then a walk before fishing his data-pad from his pocket.

"There's nothing, Lill. We're not getting out of here," he said and winced at the hopelessness in his own voice.

There was a long silence as he looked over the honeycomb of catwalks to Lillith. She slowed herself to a stop and looked up to the vents just like he'd done moments before.

"We could try the filtration ducts. When your new friend's out, I'm sure he could get us up there," she said, with just a hint of malicious joy at her word choice.

Yuri shook his head involuntarily. "It's impossible. The binding is too strong."

Lillith gripped the catwalk railing with both hands and fixed him with a stare that he felt more than he could actually see, given the distance.

"It's the same thing we use on the flex-net of the AU-37s," she said in a tone that beckoned him to challenge her.

Yuri didn't get why she was telling him random facts about the troop transports. Of course, they used the same process. They were designed to operate both in and out of atmosphere.

Then it hit him like a rail shot at point-blank range. The pirate had cut through both the armor and the flex-net during her attack. She'd done it fast, too. No one in the transport even knew what was happening, and unfortunately, too many never got a chance to figure it out.

"Wait," he said as he finally got a grasp on what she was saying.

"Yeah," Lillith said and pushed herself off the railing. "Your definition of impossible needs adjusting."

Chapter 40

THE MODUS VIVENDI SLICED through the shrinking distance between her and the newer, better-equipped stealth ship. She swam her way both under and then around the five bolts of angry light that sped her way.

In the clouds, she was fast, but not fast enough. Three of the beams splashed her shields and lit up the tiny nerves on her skin with what the technicians on her command deck would relate to pain.

The laser cannons on the TaskMaster II ended their barrage as the Vivendi approached low and fast over the border to Cascade. The brilliant glow died immediately, leaving only the crackling light of a violent sky.

• • • •

The officers kept the best part of the ship for themselves, but that was typical. People at the top always separated themselves from the rabble, or at least that was his experience. It wasn't much of a complaint, especially at the moment. Rutza had felt his stomach lurch when the ship's artificial gravity kicked in, and that was the least of his problems. The captain tended to launch into what seemed like pointless and flashy maneuvers when a well-placed shot to the engines would suffice.

It was easy to see the problems with such a strategy from his position, but there was a high possibility that the nuances of ship-to-ship combat eluded him. Only a fool didn't allow for the certainty of not knowing everything, and while he may not have been the Modus Vivendi's greatest mind, Rutza was no fool.

Fools got sucked into duties that lead to death and disgrace. He preferred to take his percentage from the relative safety of the middle decks, and he'd volunteered for this guard post for just such a reason. Nothing on the officer's deck was essential to the ship's operation. So it would be a low priority in the coming fight.

Others had roped him into several conversations about the state of the ship, and while he wasn't pleased with it, he was no mutineer.

Captain Faridan had ascended to her position faster than anyone he'd ever heard of, and she'd dealt with one insurrection already. There was little reason for him to put his neck out in case this one went the same way.

If he were a betting man, he'd have said this attempt would end up worse than the first one, but that was an opinion best kept to himself. On the off chance he was wrong, he could always claim he backed the winning side, no matter which side that turned out to be.

The pulsing lights made the entire corridor feel like a living, breathing thing. The alert system did its job well, but it was unnerving. Sabiens had a knack for designing things that felt genuinely alien at times.

Rutza had seen images of the spire cities that existed under the waves on Akinos, and he didn't see how human hands could have built anything like them. Being from a simple planet in the Neutral Territories, he found everything about their structures unnerving.

The ship was easier for him to cope with, however. Something about its odd corners seemed innately human to him. The rough edges of the Vivendi mirrored so much of what he knew and believed about people. They weren't supposed to be smooth, ideal, flawless. But perfection was a trait the species had never achieved, and if his admittedly loose grasp on history was any indication, they never would.

The thought of a society without all the traits so many others claimed to be undesirable was horrifying to him. Humanity was an imperfection on the face of the universe and to him, it was a point of pride. Hate, greed, lust, and violence were innate in the species, and yet, they survived. They even thrived when "greater" civilizations crumbled away. Imperfection endured.

Rutza grinned to himself. He was so lost in his musings on the nature of his people he almost didn't hear the door slide open behind him.

When the gears in his head caught up to reality, he spun directly into a punch. It was a decent hit, if a little awkward, but it was nowhere near the hardest he'd ever taken. Springing back to put some distance between himself and his attacker, he found himself laughing.

The woman he was sent to guard clutched one of her hands in the other as though she didn't expect a man's cheekbone to put up any resistance. She was wholly unprepared for the push kick he launched her way, and she sprawled helplessly on the floor of her would-be cell.

Somewhere in the back of his mind, he knew he should have just sealed the doors and left it there, but where was the fun in that? She was exactly the kind of girl he liked, and he was tired of the women on the ship. With the alert running, he could indulge his own imperfections a little, and there would be no one to interrupt.

"Don't let the holo-vids fool you. It's a lot harder to knock a man out in real life," he said as he drank in the sight of the woman crawling away from him.

"Thanks for the tip," came a little girl's voice from behind him before his groin exploded in pain.

His sight blurred, and his body doubled over without him having any say in it whatsoever. The kid landed a good kick, and he was having a hard time focusing on anything but breathing when he noticed that the woman was on her feet.

She wound up to hit him again, only this time he saw that she intended to use her elbow instead of her hand. The hit crashed into his jaw so hard that his head snapped around, then whipped back. The pain elsewhere died as a sea of blackness swam up to claim him. Despite himself and all the things he would have liked to say, only one thought filled his head.

"Fast learner."

• • • •

Vision looked down at the crumpled pile of flesh and bone with disgust. It was going to take her a week to scrub off the thoughts he'd exposed her to, but the important part was they were free.

She focused through the haze of intense static that pulsed in her head. It grew to the point of pain before fading back to a bearable state, only to start the process all over again seconds later. The pirate was big, but when she compared him to Claude, he came up lacking. Somehow, he'd taken a solid hit from Zhara and kept moving, although Vision had no idea what taking a punch even felt like.

"You think someone heard that?" Vision asked, blinking rapidly as if it would clear her sensors.

"Why don't you check and see?" Zhara suggested as she shrugged and nudged the pirate with her foot.

The lump of man made no attempt to move on his own. Satisfied that he wasn't getting up, Zhara stepped around the downed pirate. She had half a mind to spit on him for all the intentions she'd seen in his eyes, but refrained. Unwilling to take her eyes off him, she found herself instinctively searching him for signs of life.

"Don't worry," Vision said in an almost giddy tone. "He'll live."

"Oh, I'm not worried," Zhara said, cradling her elbow and tearing her attention away from her attacker.

Vision squinted at her for a split second before announcing, "Yes, you were."

"Just check the hall," Zhara said and motioned toward the open door.

A nearly imperceptible frown flashed across Vision's face before she turned to do as she was told. The storm cooperated for once, and it took her a few seconds to give both directions a thorough scan. She found the narrow metallic hall as empty as it was oppressive.

Without seeing the pulsing lights of the alert, the place looked like a tomb, and she imagined it would be easy for this ship to become theirs. As unsettling as the image was, she wasn't foreign to it. The rough texture of the walls was a direct contrast to the smooth, polymer panels in Claude's dreams of Firaxis, but the lifelessness matched perfectly.

For a moment, she could have sworn it was the same place. The pulsing static of the storm must have been playing tricks on her, but if she was honest, something had been off since the command deck.

Diving into Miranda's mind had done something to her. At the time, Vision figured it was just a mental defense, but now she knew it was more significant. It felt almost like her abilities had been turned back on her somehow, but that wasn't possible. Was it? There was too much she still didn't know about herself, and now wasn't the time to try figuring it out.

Claude needed her help. There was no telling what they were doing to him on the other ship, and if she had to be a little uncomfortable to pay him back for all the times he'd kept her safe, then that was the price of being partners.

"We should go," Vision said. "Do you remember the way back to the car?"

Zhara nodded before she caught herself and said, "Yes, but there are bound to be more of them. I don't think I can do that again."

"Then we need to be fast and quiet," Vision stated, and moved into the corridor.

She read the objection Zhara wanted to raise about her taking the lead and promptly ignored it. Zhara was suffering from a case of ageism, and there wasn't time to entertain it. If the data drives had it right, Vision was the brawn in this situation, despite her age. Sure, she was a kid, but she was also the best chance any of them had to escape this situation alive. The adults would just have to accept it.

"Take a left and follow it all the way to the lift," Zhara said and followed Vision into the claustrophobic artery of the ship.

Vision moved quickly and quietly, only occasionally stopping to allow her sensors to clear enough for a decent scan before moving forward again. The lift wasn't that far, but she was trying to be as cautious as possible, considering the intense interference she had to wade through.

Rounding the corner to the lift, Vision stopped and waited for Zhara to do the same. Her sensors pinged off everything at her max range but found the tube empty. That meant a delay, and delays increased their chances of being discovered.

Vision didn't know the ship's layout aside from where she'd been, and while it seemed unlikely, they'd encounter too many pirates here, she was still wary.

"Come on, come on," Zhara chanted to herself as she tapped at the holographic panel until it changed from green to blue.

The ornately designed Sabien text took her by surprise. There were a few fields she played well in, but military technology wasn't one of them. Still, she could read Sabien, and that was what she and Vision needed.

The message was just as polite as the ones on the lift at her office and apartment building. It was every bit as hollow and mechanical here, but this one felt sorely out of place.

Still, politeness of the text aside, they were in for a wait.

"Keep those sensors dialed up," she told Vision, only to be met with a scowl and what sounded for all the world like a snort.

"Easy for you to say. You're not the one getting static pumped straight into your brain," Vision complained, but she did as she was asked.

Chapter 41

BERTRAND WATCHED AS Miranda made her first mistake. The feed floating in front of him showed her ship as clearly as he'd ever seen it. It was an Aumanent-class battlecruiser but heavily modified. Even through the interference, he could see the weapon ports carved into the otherwise smooth sensor-reflective hull. Some were clearly for additional ruby lasers, but those didn't worry him.

Along the ship's upper decks rested the familiar elongated retractable hatch that could house only one weapon. The TaskMaster II had been designed to carry such weapons from its days as a rough sketch, but the Aumanent-class was older.

Miranda must have done well for herself as a pirate to add a MAC cannon to her ship. The credits, energy, space, and crew she'd sacrificed to do it wasn't something he had any interest in calculating, but the odds she'd done so to catch him with a shot from it were astronomically high.

With that piece of kit on board, her current maneuver made more sense. The cruiser was performing a shallow dive in an attempt to pass under him.

"Give me artificial gravity and cut all thrusters!" he shouted and glared at the engineering officer, cutting off her objections before she voiced them.

The order was clear, and after only a second's hesitation, it was carried out. Bertrand's ears popped as the TaskMaster II added its own spin on the universal force. He and every other crewman onboard were familiar with the gut-wrenching sensation, having experienced dueling gravities when they first entered the atmosphere.

He almost didn't feel the ship dropping out of the sky as the second half of his command was carried out. The holo-feed gave him the lurch in his stomach that the newly engaged system threatened to deny him, though.

The cruiser seemed to be racing up to meet them when the opposite was true. Bertrand grimaced at the damage reports he foresaw, but the ship could handle it. She was built to take a hit, and a little light wrestling wouldn't do much more than leave a scar or two.

• • • •

The body of the TaskMaster II streaked downward. The bubble of its shields flared into visibility as it crashed through the charged particles of the storm toward its intended target.

The Modus Vivendi was too committed to her maneuver to break away. The planet's gravity and the mass of the other ship proved a deadly combination as the shields of both ships collided and exploded. The shimmering display of failure echoed out from both ships with a sound that no one could hear through the deep, guttural thunder rolling around them.

With their shields shattered, both ships were left exposed to Minerva Prime's full fury. Friction from her atmosphere warmed the body of the TaskMaster II as it continued its fall like a massive and impossibly expensive guillotine.

The Vivendi began her escape maneuver, but it was far too late. The reinforced hulls of both ships collided with a force that rocked the penthouse dwellers of Cascade from their beds. Tortured metal screamed through the booming thunder as the two behemoths sheared pieces from one another. The top decks of the Modus Vivendi sustained the most damage, as the hull of the vessel rolled back like the rind of some exotic fruit. The exposed decks were left open to the merciless assaults of friction fires and lightning.

The Vivendi dove and cut her own thrusters in an attempt to stave off further injury. Firing her drive engines, she propelled herself downward toward the few lights of the city that broke through the clouds.

The move gave her the separation she greatly desired, but the damage was done. The destruction of her hull rendered her incapable of travel into the Black and completely crippled her dorsal cannon.

To add insult to grievous injury, the TaskMaster II was already firing her thrusters and twisting her nose to point upward. The ship had only sustained minor damage from the collision, and given its play toward the upper atmosphere, was clearly still capable of travel in the Black.

* * * *

"Bring us about!" Miranda roared over the sirens that voiced her ship's anguish.

The scrolling text on the right side of her display carried the blood-red agony of her vessel, and while she sympathized, she could not let the bastard who had wounded them both escape.

"I want a firing solution on that ship. Give it everything we have and make sure it doesn't touch the Black," she demanded.

If the acknowledgment came, Miranda didn't hear it over her own pulse. She knew that Bertrand was a wily opponent, and she knew he had several advantages over the Modus Vivendi, but the gutters would bring them into balance.

She'd had them installed specifically for a battle like this, and while they were strictly outlawed by the truce, that agreement didn't extend to Veralles.

Miranda had lost friends to the violence of those weapons when Sabiens had gutted a ship she'd served on. Luckily for Bertrand, he was still in the atmosphere. If he wasn't, the cost in life alone would cripple his ship and kill his career, assuming he survived.

"Tethers away," called the wizened tactical officer.

Miranda watched the man give a muted celebration when the first of the superheated bolts bit into the hull of Bertrand's ship. She felt the urge to do the same, but restrained it. She looked to her side and almost expected to see Octavian there. The odds were high that Miranda could put out the fire burning that bridge after Bertrand's head was removed, but she pushed that train of thought aside, though it took more effort than she expected.

Vibrant orange arcs of energy flickered to life on her feed, and she turned her attention away from all else. The growing distance between her ship and Bertrand's slammed to a halt as she now became his anchor. It was fitting that she would be the one to drag him down now, considering he had once done the same to her. The poetic nature of the situation brought a smirk to her lips as she watched his engines flare brilliantly.

The ship lurched around her, but the distance didn't change. The tethers were pure energy and unbreakable once set, but her old commander knew that. Instead of directly fighting the streams of energy, the more advanced ship was trying to drag her into the Black with it.

"Do we have a firing solution for the gutters?" she asked the old-timer manning the tactical console.

"Seventy seconds estimated, Captain. Sooner, if the storm stops interfering with telemetry," he called back and almost winced when he did so.

"Give me full reverse thrusters. We'll make him work for it," Miranda growled and fell back into her seat.

Chapter 42

THE MACHINERY AROUND Claude roared to life with an intensity he had never experienced. In all his time aboard starships, he had never been so acutely aware of their inner workings. The acid below flushed a quarter of its previous volume into the tube feeding refinery proper. Claude pulled his attention away from the elaborate process and sent urgent thoughts to his passenger.

The silver had worked its way through to the other side of the glass, but that tiny vein of freedom was little comfort. It occurred to him that there were two other potential hosts for the creature in the same room, but he got the feeling it wouldn't abandon him, even if it was the simpler solution.

His upper body strength had all but given out after the silver cracked the glass, and now he dangled naked above a shrinking pool of acid by a sentient silver string, and that wasn't the worst of it.

The precariousness of the situation wasn't lost on him. As the glass above fractured from his passenger's steady expansion within it, Claude imagined what was happening around him. There was obviously a battle, and judging by the sharp uptick in fuel processing, he was sure that Bertrand was trying to flee. Aside from the alarms, he couldn't tell if the ship had been damaged in any significant way.

Without being closer to the action, there was no way he could know the details, but Bertrand's turning tail didn't exactly surprise him. If Miranda got close enough to send boarding parties, she would win. Given what he'd seen at the Archive, it was unlikely the soldiers aboard could stop her, at least not with the weapons they had available. She was a nightmare creature, and any real sense of the woman she'd once been was fading fast. The Miranda he had known would at least have entertained their surrender, but this new version would likely tear through the ship like a cyclone of silver and blood.

Claude tried to shake the image loose, only to be struck by the ruined corridors of Firaxis instead. He had wondered what caused the chaos there, though only in the few quiet, solitary moments he'd been able to steal. After the transport, he didn't need to guess anymore. The passengers had destroyed that place and the people inside it. If Bertrand didn't keep a significant distance between his ship and Miranda's, the same thing would happen to the TaskMaster II.

"We found a way out," Yuri's voice called, snapping Claude out of his unpleasant musings.

Lillith came to a stop on the catwalk opposite Yuri and frowned down at him. Claude got the not-so-subtle feeling that she was holding a grudge for the scuffle earlier, but he didn't have time for that. She felt what she felt. The good news was, she had at least attempted to put it aside to help him.

"Maybe it's a way out, but it could just get us frozen or diced to bits in the filtration system," she grouched.

The silver pressed Claude against the glass seconds before a web of cracks splintered out in all directions. He both saw, and oddly, felt the single strand split into five. The smaller tendrils reached out to find purchase beyond the crack before the glass imploded.

Thick shards of the stuff rained down around Claude, although only a single sliver touched him. It left a shallow slash along his shoulder blade before following its kin to the hissing, bubbling oblivion below. The cold air stung the bleeding cut, but Claude ignored it. He focused instead on helping his passenger as much as possible.

He curled himself into as tight a ball as he could manage as he rose steadily out of his former cell and descended onto what was left of the glass's slick, frigid surface. Standing for the first time in untold hours, Claude turned his attention to the most immediate inconvenience facing him.

"Hey guys," he said as a pang of modesty forced him to cover himself. "I'm going to need something to wear."

• • • •

Bertrand saw the glow on his holo-feed but was nearly helpless to do anything about it. The vibrant white of it froze him in place as it intensified under the nose of Miranda's ship.

"I'm reading a high-powered magnetic charge, Captain," rang a voice tinged with the appropriate level of fear.

"Touche," Bertrand said under his breath before shouting, "Focus all flechette turrets on those tether points and flatten us out. Get us away from the city, now!"

Every console around him exploded into a flurry of activity, and each person on the command deck flew into action. All systems had been given something to do with those few orders.

Exposing more of the TaskMaster's body was a terrible idea, but letting Miranda's shots hit his engines was worse. The ship could survive the former, but the latter would turn it into a flaming ruin, and with the city directly below, the death toll would be catastrophic.

A piece of him wanted desperately to drag DiSilva up to the bridge and rub his face in the callous disregard he'd shown for the lives of others. All of this was because of him. He had put Miranda directly on their scent, and now she had found them. Claude's carelessness meant that all those who had died during the Archive fiasco and everything since could be placed squarely on his shoulders. Worse, Bertrand knew that if he were to make that case to the man himself, it would be met with the kind of self-assured defiance that boiled his blood.

He watched and fumed as the images on his feed cycled to keep him focused on the Sabien cruiser while his ship angled toward the nearest edge of the spiral city. The growing light seemed to track his own view. For all the worlds, it seemed like Miranda was aiming directly for him personally. While that was undoubtedly true on some level, Bertrand forced himself not to entertain the thought.

"Give me an ETA on our new destination," he barked when the movement of the ships lessened.

"We'll be over open desert in twelve minutes at this speed," the lanky, raven-haired helmsman said in the same singsong voice Bertrand had once found amusing.

"Get us there faster," he growled, and the woman at the helm snapped to.

Bertrand felt the ship launch toward the city's edge despite the inertial dampening that artificial gravity provided. It was a desperate play against a desperate opponent, and it was as likely to blow up in his face as not. In the end, Bertrand had to at least try to save the lives below. Echelon may have established his priorities for the mission, but only he chose what he could live with.

He knew very well how the masters of Myridorn could lose sight of the "little" people in their grand designs. Bertrand could have fallen to such a viewpoint, and he had given himself over to it once. The consequences of that day had hunted him across the stars, but it was his conscience he could never outrun.

There were no such beings as the little people. That was a lesson he'd learned over years spent in commanding his own organization. He had lost sight of that in the face of Echelon's burning desire, and had used Miranda as a salve to soothe it. As much as he wanted to lay all the lives lost here at DiSilva's feet, and he would if given the chance, the truth still burrowed through every firing neuron in his skull. Only one choice had led to this outcome, and Bertrand was the man who had made it.

• • • •

Ashe hung suspended in the echoing shadow of the lift shaft. For all the technology that lay exposed and blinking around her, she trusted her life to a plain length of rope. One of humanity's simplest tools made it possible for her to save one of its most complex. To her mind, it was poetic, and she would have found it comforting if so much didn't weigh on her.

Below, three other technicians worked on redundancies to ensure that the protocols she set in place were foolproof. Octavian had taken the lift up to the command deck to fill the tube, providing another barrier against the fury that was undoubtedly on its way.

Ashe had let him go despite the roiling waves of dread that assaulted her even now. It had only been a short time, but she had found something in the man that surprised her. It was a comfort that he'd been there when she needed him, and this was no different.

Faridan would find out what was being done, and Octavian assumed she would tear her way through the ship until she had found those responsible. He had gone to stave that off, knowing what that meant. Ashe knew it too, and yet none of her protests were wise enough, loud enough, or angry enough to alter what he felt he had to do. In the end, she could only let him go with a kiss that held every ounce of her frustration, fear, and helplessness.

Drops of saline pattered against her gloves as she focused on the glowing cables carrying power to the command deck above. Her task was simple, and it helped to keep her mind off the fate of her newest and best living friend.

She crimped the cable in her hand and applied a tiny metal clamp, sealing and darkening the upper portions. The corresponding line above her flickered and died, adding one more column of darkness to the near-infinite space above her.

"Column 395-2 is dark," she declared, and heard the responses from the other technicians ring out around her.

"Column 395-2 rerouted," a voice called from below as a loose line of cabling flickered to electric blue life beneath them.

Ashe stared down into the abyss, and for a moment, she thought of how freeing it would be to commit herself to it. There was nothing so easy in all the worlds as falling, and she desperately wanted something easy for once. Everything had been so hard since they'd landed on this rock, but life didn't come without a struggle, at least not for her. There were still two people left to hold on for; one to make suffer and the other to save.

She tore her eyes away from the yawning chasm and placed them back on the glowing power conduits before her. With teeth clenched, she crimped another cable. As the light died, she felt one step closer to ending the woman who had caused her so much pain.

"Column 396-4 is dark," she said through her teeth, then added softly, "Just a little longer."

• • • •

Octavian stepped onto the command deck and witnessed the dimmed lights and shouts of battle. He had stood on the dais beside Miranda through countless fights, but this one felt like something historic. From the corridor, he could feel the energy of it, and he realized just how much he had missed it.

"Ease off thrusters and give us a little slack on the tethers," he heard Miranda say, and there was almost a sense of glee in her voice. "Keep us under him and away from all of the MAC gun ports."

Slowly, Octavian crept closer to the open deck. Despite feeling that he belonged there, he couldn't shake the fire still burning in his cheeks from the last encounter.

For the first time, he honestly didn't know if Miranda would greet him or kill him instantly. What he did know was that Ashe needed a distraction, and he owed it to his friend to look her in the eye as stabbed her in the back. The mutinous elements of the crew would have acted eventually, but he had given them a fighting chance at actually achieving their end goal. For his part, he owed penance. Miranda would never betray him in secret, and he would pay her the same courtesy.

Hopefully, that would be enough for her. If he fronted this rebellion, she might not rain her rage down on everyone else. It was unlikely, but there was a chance and for Ashe's sake, he had to take it.

She had no idea the full nature of his plan, but telling her would have done no good. There was a fire in that woman that he had only ever seen in one other. Ashe would come for him if she thought for one second there was no chance he'd return. He loved her for that, but it was not enough to keep her alive. Only facing his old friend could do that.

He had come unarmed as he always did, but given the task, part of him wished he had brought at least a sidearm. It was a useless gesture, but if he fired at least one shot that met its mark, it wouldn't feel as though he had just come to die.

It was possible he could talk reason into Miranda, or at least that she would see and understand what he was trying to accomplish. It was a thin hope, and like the edge of a sharpened blade, it cut through to his core and lodged itself there.

He stole a glance at his oldest friend and confidant. Miranda's eyes were locked on the hovering image of a ship he didn't recognize. It was as uglier and bulkier than the Beita Systems vessels he remembered, but it was well-armed. Even from this distance, he could see three MAC cannon ports on the thing. Bright orange tethers seized its midsection as the Modus Vivendi rode it through the sky like a carriage hitched to a stampeding warlett. But unlike the beasts of his birth world, this starship had fangs. It wouldn't be long before it turned and took a chunk out of its driver.

"Polarities locked in," Juanic called from his post on the tactical console.

Octavian watched the older man spot him but say nothing. They exchanged curt nods before he drew in a deep, shaky breath and stepped forward.

"Captain," he said through the broadcast speakers before firing her the traditional three-fingered Beitan salute. "Requesting permission to approach the dais."

The room fell silent. Miranda's stare threatened to burn a hole through his face, and yet he held his ground. The moment lasted for what seemed to him like an eternity. It was his moment of truth, and for as uncomfortable as it was, he deserved to dangle in that purgatory for his actions.

After a long internal debate that Octavian could read on her face, Miranda slid her earpiece in and said, "Permission granted."

Without another word, she turned her attention back to the hologram. She didn't acknowledge Octavian at all as he approached, but she did take a half step to the side to allow him a decent view of the feed.

"I felt I should be here for this," he said into her earpiece and got no response.

Instead, Miranda reached into the shimmering green light and drew an orange circle around a subsection of the enemy ship.

"Give me a targeting solution on this location," she said and fixed the tactical officer with a focused glare before raking it across Octavian's features.

"Aye, Captain," Juanic called and went to work, manipulating the console with fervor.

"I agree," Miranda said softly. "You should."

Chapter 43

THE LIFT DOORS OPENED onto an old chaos. Vision's sensors read mostly static, but that wasn't what her mind prioritized. Somewhere behind her ebon eyes, she was trapped in a nearly forgotten place.

What she knew of Firaxis station was limited, but somehow, she understood how wrong this was. She was too tall, too old, and yet she felt every bit like the little girl she had been in that place. She processed the memory from the inside, analyzing it and feeling it at the same time.

The sterile air of the lab stung her nose, and angry voices filled her ears, but it was the mind she touched that consumed her attention. It was wrong. The body was that of a man, but a hollow, dying one. Yet, the mind inside was desperately alive. Its thoughts flowed like fluid from one place to another, with no center, no rigidity. She felt its anger and terror, but more than that, she sensed its curiosity. It had never seen a thing like her before, and it hungered to know more about her. She returned that emotion and reached deeper into the man-like thing.

The body was sick and withering, but the creature she reached into was alive and well. It thrummed with a deep disdain for the meat encasing it, but at the same time, it needed its host.

Vision's young mind couldn't quite process all of the intricate ties the creature had to the man. Nor did she understand what it wanted from her then, but now she was wiser. It was consuming him, killing him, but the silver had no idea how to stop itself. Worse, it didn't want to.

Like Claude and his passenger, this creature was bonded to the man. They were one, even though she could only feel the alien. There was nothing of the mind that had come before. Only the thoughts of the silver remained.

"You can't do this. It isn't what I was brought onto the project for," a forceful but sweet female voice declared.

Vision found herself frustrated that her younger self hadn't turned and focused on the other people in the room, but it couldn't be helped. The memory could not be changed, and given what she'd learned on the drives, she could piece together what she needed to. They were arguing about what to do with her.

"You made that thing for this exact purpose. Now it's time to fulfill it," Rickten Eugene's voice spat back.

"She was designed as a control protocol, a way to interface with the creature and get it to follow our orders," Kailen Saulk countered. "How is that supposed to work with a child? She doesn't even understand what it is to be a person yet, let alone how to be what you want her to be."

The man shouted in frustration, then spat, "This is urgent, Saulk. A piece of Talos 1 got into Lenore, and if I don't get it out, I could lose her."

"You let your wife wander the station, knowing she was infected by that thing?"

Vision tried to shake herself out of the memory, but she couldn't. Like Claude, she was trapped in that place, only she was wide awake. She could feel herself starting to panic as every attempt she made to shove this recollection aside failed.

The child she had been was similarly ensnared by the ravenous thing before her. It needed something, something she was unwilling to part with. It did its best to warm her to it, knowing that she was in its thoughts, but the sheer otherness of its mind kept her from feeling anything other than morbid fascination.

Even Vision's younger self knew the creature was dangerous, but like all dangerous things, it was also entrancing. At the time, she didn't know it saw her merely as food. Now she understood that it would have eaten her down to nothing, but first, it would have ridden her to freedom.

It had been too weak to take the woman who had come earlier. When she'd attempted to feed its host, the creature had aimed to take her body, but it was cut off. At the time, it hoped that by leaving a shard of itself in her, it could use it to break free, but the lesser version was too immature. Now, Vision was its last chance.

For as desperate as it was, there was more than just survival driving it this time. The child was different and the oddness of her imprinted on it. Vision could feel the flood of questions mixed in with the anger, fear, and pain the creature felt. The thing had been as curious about her as she was about it. But that was something she only understood now, looking back.

Like on the command deck, Vision felt something deep inside her lurch. The sensation unseated her in a way she didn't fully understand. She felt a frightful familiarity, and something in this memory was the cause.

A manicured hand clamped down around her little arm and dragged her away. Her cries were ignored as her maker dragged her out of the lab and down the hall.

"Vision!" Zhara's voice called, breaking through the haze.

Her tone carried a hint of the growing dread Vision herself felt.

• • • •

Zhara shook Vision sharply and watched as she came back from whatever place she had fallen into. It took Zhara a second to regather her composure or as much of it as she'd been able to maintain since dropping Claude at the Archive.

"Thanks, Zee," Vision said as the environment around her streamed itself into her brain.

"What happened this time?" Zhara asked with a little more volume than she'd intended.

Vision shook her head and frowned, but didn't immediately answer. She didn't understand what was going on herself, but admitting that to Zhara would only complicate matters.

"I think I'm remembering," she said, downplaying it as much as she could.

"Remembering what?" Zhara asked.

Vision stepped past her and into the cargo hold. No pirates were present as far as she could tell, but that didn't make the area safe. Two battered hoverbikes rested in their crudely built harnesses along the wall while crates upon crates covered the floor, secured by magnets that further interfered with her sensors.

"Firaxis. Something about this ship reminds me of that place, I guess," Vision offered and hoped it would be enough to sate Zhara.

All she wanted was to get to Claude and escape. She'd had her fill of adventure, and for the first time in her life, Vision wished for the boredom of the old apartment. Between the murderous pirates, derelicts, gangsters, and now, unsettling memories, she was ready to curl up on the tattered old couch and fall asleep.

"We need to get those doors open?" Vision declared, and rushed toward the car.

Zhara followed, grabbing Vision's wrist to slow her down.

"Wait," she called as a gentle mechanical whir fell into her hearing range.

She had only just found where the noise was coming from when Vision asked, "What?"

Zhara dove and tackled the girl to the ground.

Overhead, a large turret emerged from an "I" shaped hatch in the ceiling. It spun in their direction and opened fire from all four barrels.

Both Zhara and Vision hit the ground behind a large crate just before a barrage of rounds spritzed the area where they had just been standing. Zhara waited for the whirring sound of the turret's spinning barrels to go quiet before she dared to move off Vision.

"Are you okay? Are you hurt?" Zhara asked in a hushed voice, but Vision didn't answer.

In a panic, Zhara scrambled closer to the nearest container, taking Vision with her. It took a moment, but when she realized neither of them had been hit, she allowed herself to breathe again. The rush of relief was almost dizzying to her.

"What is that thing?" Vision asked in a whisper and did her best to wiggle her way free.

"Artemis tech, but I didn't know they were selling it to pirates," Zhara said and made a little room for Vision to move easier.

With great effort and a little incredulity, Vision freed herself from Zhara's tangle of limbs and rubbed the shoulder where she'd landed. Zhara carefully eyed the crate to ensure that no part of her would stick out.

"I thought you made prosthetics for war victims," Vision said accusingly.

"Veterans, and yeah, that's what *I* do. You don't really think my work pays for that whole building, do you?" Zhara snapped with more ferocity than was warranted.

Vision ignored the spin Zhara put on the words and attributed it to the shock, relief, and concern wafting off her. Vision owed her for keeping her insides inside, and she would express her gratitude when the time came. The priority at the moment was getting past the super-gun mounted on the ceiling.

"So how do we beat this thing?" she asked, scanning the turret's housing for any imperfections.

"The good news is it's manned. So, if you're up to finding who's controlling the thing, we can get past it. Otherwise, we'll just have to wait here until they send someone to get us," Zhara said and did her best to make both options sound viable.

Vision rubbed her forehead as best she could with the halo in the way and blew out a deep breath. When she returned her focus to Zhara, she found her friend staring back at her with expectant eyes.

"I'm not sure that's a good idea. I don't really trust my own head right now," Vision said by way of protest.

"But I do," Zhara said. "Besides, I'll be here to shake you out of any mess you fall into."

Vision studied the weak smile on Zhara's face and found herself nodding before she had even fully agreed. She had asked if Zhara trusted her, and now it was time to pay her the same courtesy. Still, diving into a sea of thoughts and hoping Zhara would save her if her own resurfacing memories swam up to bite her wasn't exactly going to be a good time.

"Okay," she said, and placed her hands on her halo. "Sorry in advance."

Zhara pulled her close and waited for the pulse as the halo slid free. The psionic wave that rolled over her plunged her into a lesser version of the disorientation she'd felt back at Artemis. Her head swam, but she found it easier to focus this time.

"I'm here, V," she said and took the vacant child's hand in her own. "Do what you have to do."

. . . .

Strands of thought streamed by in every resonance and emotion Vision had ever experienced. There were countless, and each moved so wildly that she was afraid to push through them at first.

She'd never sought a person's mind she was unfamiliar with, and whoever controlled the turret was a completely unknown quantity. If she was going to find them without having to dip into every mind she came across, she needed to find something to sort by.

If she guessed correctly, the mystery man, or at least she assumed it was a man, had to be watching a holo-feed, so she began there. There were just under a hundred pirates on the ship, and to her dismay, she found the percentage using holo-tech was so high she might as well have not tried to sort them at all.

Still, there were a few that were dangling in lift tubes for unknown reasons. A few more were stealing food in the mess while no one watched, and one was just now waking up in their room. Vision shunted all of those out of her mind and started the process again.

There were roughly seventy souls, all working with holo-tech of some kind, and at least one of them was Miranda. Vision found her quickly due to the silver strand that had grown more dominant since their last meeting. She was unique on the ship but not in Vision's headspace. The other matching mind was further away but moving, and that made her smile just a little.

"*Claude's moving now,*" she thought to Zhara and immediately felt first her relief, followed by a bevy of new concerns.

Ignoring the only mind she truly wanted to visit, Vision refocused on Miranda and took special care while guiding her gently into her discard pile.

Next, she focused on the minds consuming visual information from outside the ship. It was the largest group, and in a single swipe, she instantly eliminated all but four pirates.

With that, Vision's progress slammed to a halt. Each of the remainders was so entrenched in their task that Vision could find little difference in their thoughts. If she weren't so afraid to lose herself, she would have dove further into each of them and studied their feeds through their eyes, but she wasn't desperate enough to risk that option just yet.

"How's it going, V?" Zhara's voice called, breaking into her growing frustration.

"I have another idea you aren't going to like."

• • • •

"You can't be serious," Zhara said to herself.

"It will only take a second, and, boom, our guy will light up like the Dead Zone Wall," Vision's voice echoed in her head.

Zhara stole a glance around the crate and watched as the turret pivoted in her direction before continuing its broad sweep of the area.

"It's the boom I'm worried about," she grouched and turned her attention back to the blank-faced girl talking in her mind.

"You already said you trust me. Can't take it back now."

Zhara rocked herself into as low a crouch as she could manage. Letting out a shaky breath, she summoned all the courage she could muster before facing the rain of metallic death she knew was coming her way.

With one last nervous glance back, she said, "If I survive this, we're doing that hair of yours every day."

And then she was gone.

The eruption of speed Zhara conjured surprised even her. Before she had the time to register how crazy she had to be to run out of cover in the hopes a pirate would shoot at her, she was blazing her way through the aisles of waist-high crates. She prayed the whirring sound she heard was just the wind rushing past her ears, but the hairs on the back of her neck screamed otherwise.

"Got him!"

The girl's thought blared so loud it rattled off the inside of Zhara's skull, sending a spike of pain through her strong enough to momentarily shatter her motor functions. Zhara's legs turned to gelatin, and she went down in a full-speed tumble that she saw coming but could not avoid.

Other, newer pains added to the hurt in her brain as she rolled to a stop, with her entire upper body exposed to the spinning barrels above. She winced against the oncoming assault but felt nothing except the dull ache in her head, and the sting of scrapes she'd acquired during the fall.

"*You can get up now*," Vision told her, and while snark wasn't in the words, Zhara could still feel it. "*And I never agreed to that.*"

The quad-barreled monster was still locked onto her. It even tracked her movements, but it did not fire. Cautiously, Zhara picked herself up and made her way back to Vision, staying low just in case Vision's hold slipped.

"*Stop!*"

Zhara froze, but after a moment of silence, she shook off the command and took another step before a burst of gunfire danced across the floor just in front of her.

"*Listen, Zee. You need to open the hangar door and get out of here,*" Vision declared.

"No, we go together, or I don't go at all," Zhara said and again moved toward the girl.

The turret above squeezed out three more rounds, locking Zhara in place before Vision managed to clamp down on the operator's mind once more.

"*This guy really wants to kill us, and I can't hold him much longer. He's already figuring out what we're here for. If I let him go, he'll kill the car and then us,*" she protested. "*One of us has to get to Claude. That's you.*"

Zhara fought back Vision's logic even as it hit home and began eroding her resolve. Vision was the goal. Zhara needed to save Claude, and she would, but not at any cost. There was no way she could square abandoning a little girl for a grown man, no matter how much sense it made.

"Can't you just, you know... knock him out or something?"

Zhara expected an immediate answer. What she got was nothing. The extended silence let her think about what she'd asked, and as the seconds ticked by, she found herself feeling ashamed.

"*Maybe,*" Vision finally responded. "*But I've never tried to hurt a person like that before, and I don't think I should, you know?*"

Having her request shot down by an eleven-year-old on moral grounds made her the proudest and most relieved Zhara had ever felt. The chaos of the situation was getting to her. Every sense was cranked up higher than she had ever experienced. Every detail of her surroundings was so vivid and so loud it was difficult for her to think. Every emotion was amplified as well. They played through her mind like cataclysmic explosions, rushing her thoughts and denying her the internal order she so required.

Nothing she'd ever done had taxed her conscience in such a way, and suddenly she understood the universe, its inhabitants, and its tragic history a little better. This was how good people were twisted into horrifying shadows of themselves. It was how civilized nations could begin tearing each other apart and how they'd committed to the conflict for so long.

If this tainted fog was the kind of thing Claude had to live with during the war, she could easily understand why he'd kept so much of it to himself. She had only been under this pressure for a matter of hours, and she could already feel her principles buckling under the weight of it.

"*Don't feel bad, Zee. I know you didn't really mean it,*" Vision thought to her, and for a moment, Zhara actually felt better.

"Still, there has to be something else you can do," Zhara said even as she resigned herself to this solidifying reality.

"*There is,*" Vision replied. "*The access code to the cargo doors is B-3281. Now go before he gets loose.*"

Zhara looked at the motionless girl and felt her teeth grind together. She debated just carrying her to the car, but she wasn't sure what would happen if she moved her. There was so much about Vision she didn't fully understand and probably never would.

For weeks, Zhara had been enraged at Claude for not accepting that she knew what was in her own best interest, and now she wanted to do the same to Vision. Now, she understood his position, and while there were significant differences, none of them stopped her from feeling like a massive hypocrite.

"*I'll still be here when you two get back, Zee.*" Vision echoed in her mind. "*I promise.*"

Chapter 44

CLAUDE INSPECTED THE fallen guard's sidearm and nodded his approval. Lillith took the rifle, and he didn't debate it. Obviously, she hadn't quite let go of their scuffle earlier, so he hoped it would be a peace offering, though her continued scowling made him regret it. The outfit he'd scavenged was ill-fitting and uncomfortable. The pants were too tight in the thighs, and at least three inches too long, but it beat being naked. Anything that protected him against the chill and killed any unnecessary tension counted as a net positive in his book.

"So, what's wrong with the filtration system?" he asked, tucking the sidearm into its hip holster.

Yuri cast a glance at Lillith. Once again, eye contact carried the weight of an unspoken conversation before she spoke.

"It's not designed for people. No one has been able to navigate them without a full diagram," she said and slung the rifle's strap over her shoulder.

"That shouldn't be too much of an issue. All we need to do is get outside of the doors, right?" Claude asked, turning his attention to the vents in the ceiling.

"The other problem is they're bonded same way the hull plating is, but we figured once you were up to it, you could just...," Yuri trailed off as he pointed at his eyes and then at the ceiling.

Claude's face contorted as he caught the meaning. "That's not a trick I know how to do. Is there another way? Maybe an explosive or something?"

"Sure, if you want to break the ship in half," Lillith snapped and marched away from the two men.

"We didn't exactly plan to be sealed in here," Yuri said, and leaned back against the railing.

He stared down through the grates of the catwalk and into the hole in the acid vat. The green surface had settled almost as soon as the ship was level. Now it cast a shifting reflection of the refinery's upper walkways that was as hypnotic as it was unsettling.

Claude tracked his stare, and for a moment, he found himself contemplating how difficult it would be to scoop up enough acid to melt through the doors and back to freedom. If it weren't for the battle raging outside and the threat of a sudden shift spilling it everywhere in transit, he thought it might just work, assuming he could convince his passenger.

That wasn't likely. At the moment, he was fighting a powerful urge to curl up on the grates and fall asleep beside the guard. Both he and the silver desperately needed a rest, but they weren't safe just yet.

"So, we're trapped?" Claude asked, just to be sure.

"Unless the alert gets lifted or the ship explodes... yeah," Yuri said and stretched his neck. "Are you sure you can't do the eye beams?"

Claude shrugged. If Miranda's passenger was the same as his, then it should be possible, but that was a massive assumption. Both he and Miranda were drastically different, despite being the same species. It stood to reason the silver they carried would be just as unique.

"I could try," Claude admitted with a wince. "It's not like we have any better ideas."

Yuri banged the railing before shoving himself off it. An unnatural distortion made the sound tinny and sharp. The irritating new quality stretched out, changing the constant mechanical droning into something worthy of even Lillith's full attention. Foreign vibrations merged with the distortion and forced her to turn back to the others.

"Do you hear that?" she asked, and there was a current of fear in her voice.

They all fell silent and listened. Claude caught the sound of whistling and then of glass breaking before the floor rushed up to slice the catwalk apart. A swath of the refinery carved its way through the ceiling and into the decks above with the speed and precision of a butcher's blade.

Claude grabbed Yuri and dove backward as the catwalk supports nearest to them buckled then snapped, sending the broken section on a swift and violent ascent. The ear-shattering shriek of the beam weapon drowned out all other noise. Brilliant, pure white energy sought to bleach Claude's retinas, but silver coated his eyes, protecting him.

With fingers curled between the metal of the grates, Claude held on for dear life. Above him, the attack continued to force its way deeper and deeper into the TaskMaster II. Deck after deck of the ship assaulted itself as floors met ceilings, pulverizing any and everything caught between them.

"Lill!" Yuri shouted, but his voice barely made it to Claude's ears.

Using hand signals, Claude insisted they climb their way up the ruined walkway. He met the wild, nearly unhinged look in Yuri's eyes with a more determined one and held it until he got the nod he was looking for.

Together, they struggled their way past the upward curve of the catwalk just in time for the beam to thin out and die. A cascade of debris crashed back down as gravity took back the reins of her domain. The collapse of the catwalk tore at least a dozen feet of it away. Each ruined piece sped toward a ragged gash, bouncing and spinning their way through angry clouds, and toward the piercing light of the Violet wall below.

An odd relief hit Claude. He was grateful the ships were passing out of the populated districts, but crashing into the Old City offered no better chance of survival.

He wondered if the roar of warring metal beasts was enough to scare away the monsters who lived there, though he doubted it. Already he could imagine them tracking the ships through broken streets, eager for new meat to sate their immortal hunger.

"DiSilva!" Yuri shouted through the clatter of fallen debris and the rush of wind. "You have to save Lillith."

Claude turned to see where the soldier was pointing and found her across the massive wound.

The far side of the refinery had gotten the worst of the attack. Many more of the catwalk's support struts had been shredded, leaving nothing more than a dangling wreck that threatened to rip itself apart at any moment.

Claude nodded and tested his ability to stand. Both his legs and the grates beneath him wobbled under his weight, but he managed to get himself upright. How he would cross a chasm the width of a skyway lane, he had no idea. He did know that doing so while compensating for the persistent rain of the ship's guts was unlikely to go well.

Lillith hung from the railing on the far side, doing her best to stay perfectly still. She'd managed to get to one of the junctions, which were slightly more stable, but that was as far as her luck had gotten her. If she could reach the floor of the catwalk, the grates would allow her to climb the same way Claude had, but it was impossible from her angle.

"Hold on," Claude shouted lamely as he desperately sorted through all the ways he could die attempting a rescue.

Scanning the ceiling made it clear there wasn't going to be time to react to falling debris. Below, there was still some machinery that hadn't fallen completely out of the ship yet. At least two vats of acid were still there though only one was intact, and the longer Claude waited to make a move, the more of the hull gave way.

"I hope you're rested up," Claude said to his passenger, then jogged back along the catwalk.

He'd made impressive jumps before, but even then, he'd always needed help crossing the gap. As more of the ship's innards spilled out, the wound had only grown larger.

In what felt like slow motion, Claude began his sprint. Without much thought, he reached out for a strip of ceiling, and the silver did the rest. Tendrils of malleable metal grabbed a broken piece of paneling and swung him across the gap. They released only after his momentum put him on an upswing, and just as Claude began to process how he would stick the landing, something hit him.

He didn't see what it was, but it was large, and it was solid. The breath in his lungs exploded out of him as his metal-coated chest nearly collapsed under the impact. Every thought was knocked out of his scrambled brain as consciousness slipped from him.

• • • •

"Clean hit, Captain," Juanic announced loudly to the entire command deck. His proud declaration took his eyes from his console just as the images and scrolling text dimmed, flickered, then returned, though at a significantly lower brightness.

Octavian noticed the system fault but did his best to ignore it. His attention was locked on the hovering miniature of Bertrand's ship wavering in Miranda's feed. He looked on as the best hope he had for a peaceful solution bled its fuel reserves onto the dead streets below. It felt as though his own heart had been ripped out.

He knew Miranda was going to destroy any place Bertrand found to hide. He had freed her so she could do exactly that. They had discussed and planned her revenge countless times over the years, and now that the moment was at hand, he regretted every decision he'd made that led to it.

Her face was filled with more mirth than he'd seen from her since he stormed the Echelon black site holding her years prior, and while Octavian understood her joy, he could not muster anything resembling it. Soon she would spot the troubled look on his face. He didn't have it in him to hide it. It would give away everything, and there would be no going back after that.

Miranda motioned for the feed to zoom in and laughed at what the enhanced view exposed. The elaborate mix of pumps, tubing, and machinery was known to nearly everyone who spent any significant time around starships.

The need to carry large amounts of fuel had limited travel in the Black for centuries before the Sabiens began putting functioning refineries inside the ships themselves. The mixing process was simple, but the workings required to achieve it were anything but. As the war stretched on, ships had been redesigned endlessly, cutting down their dimensions considerably.

Octavian had learned that much at the academy. The Beitans adopted similar technology into their fleets. Now, he was staring at centuries of innovation spilling into the night, and it looked for all the worlds like his hopes in flame. One spark, one flash, and every living soul aboard that ship would join them.

"Fire every forward laser we have into that breach," Miranda commanded with morbid glee, but there was no acknowledgment.

Instead of giving the traditional response, Juanic looked at his darkened console with a dumbfounded stare. The light had just flickered and died, casting the older man's sunbaked skin into shadow.

Octavian felt his stomach lurch as holographic consoles all around the dais blinked, cleared, then went dark. Mumbles and panic began to set in as confused crewmen banged on tech that wasn't meant to be touched in such aggressive ways. The pale green of the command feed fought the hardest of all the command deck lights. Soon it was the only light source in the massive room, but no one dared to gather near it.

Octavian watched the reality of his ruse dawn on Miranda. Her shoulders rose, and her posture changed into something undeniably primal. She turned toward him so slowly that he half wondered whether she would even look human when she finally faced him.

"I didn't want to believe it," Miranda said, locking her eyes on Octavian at last.

"You have changed," he said into her earpiece. "This has to end. I need you to step back from this. Everyone on this ship needs you to come to your senses."

"You need? What about what I needed, Octavian? I needed you on my side. I needed my friend, the one I haunted the stars with. The one that shed blood with me on a dozen worlds," the creature in front of him seethed, and he could see the faint flicker of disappointment in her eyes. "What happened to that man? The man that hates pirates. The man who's loyal. Their kind took your voice from you. And you chose them over me?"

Octavian considered pleading his case. He considered telling her what he saw moving behind her eyes, that even her voice was different now. He wanted to shout that she had lost control, and that she was letting that thing inside rule her. But all of that would fall on deaf ears. The woman he had sworn his loyalty to was dead, and until now he had been serving her hollow corpse.

In the end, Octavian chose to keep those words to himself. He had long ago learned that silence was a boundary. Once he had been trapped behind it; then, when he was afraid, he'd hidden behind it. Now, he wielded it like a weapon. It was his sword, and with it, he would strike the only blow he could, carving down into whatever humanity was left in the woman glaring at him.

It wouldn't be enough to save his life. He knew that. He had known that before he'd given Ashe that last kiss goodbye. He would die here, and in the end, he was resigned to it. He only hoped his blood would buy either the time Ashe needed to strip Miranda of her power and disappear into the crowded ship, or the resurrection of his only friend.

"Goodbye, old friend," With those words, Miranda turned away from him before the anguish welling in her eyes spilled over. "We will miss you."

Deek Octavian lifted his chin and closed his eyes in an act of defiance that took every ounce of his being. He saw only black as a silver blur freed him from his every burden.

Miranda stepped away as the last person she would ever trust crumpled to the deck. She could feel the tremble in her lip before she clamped it shut, hardening herself against the tidal wave of grief and doubt that threatened to sweep her away.

She would still be the victim of heartless tormenters if it hadn't been for him. The frozen corpse that still haunted her dreams would have dragged her down to be crushed and burned on the surface of Jaiden III if he hadn't carried her off Firaxis.

Now, Octavian was dead, and worse, he had died an enemy. How could she ignore that? Something he saw had brought him to side with pirates over her. Sure, there was a girl, but that couldn't have been the answer.

And just as Miranda began to peel back the layers of all she had done, the silver flowed up through her, cooling her against the heat of her emotions until she remembered what truly mattered. Bertrand was so close. They couldn't waste that, not for Octavian and definitely not for the rats plotting in the bowels of the ship.

They had come so far. To let the actions of a traitor put them off their task was foolish and wasteful. There would be no better chance than the one they had been given. This business had to be closed. Bertrand had to suffer and die.

A boundless future awaited.

Miranda caressed the silver on her palm as she put Octavian out of her mind for the last time.

"Open the shutters. We'll do this the old-fashioned way," she roared and settled herself in her seat.

• • • •

Zhara never took her hovercar out in storms. It was a rule she'd made shortly after moving to Minerva Prime. An automated cab had blacked out and forced her to kiss its roof and then its floor while its systems rebooted. That had been enough for her.

Ion storms were as beautiful and valuable as they were deadly unless the proper shielding was used. A single bolt from one could easily kill a hovercar, and assuming that didn't happen, the sudden visit to the street at terminal velocity would surely do the trick.

While the Regent was a spectacular piece of machinery, it did not account for everything. She had elected to forego ion shields when she bought the thing, mainly because of her self-imposed rule, and now she deeply regretted that decision.

The storm was finally letting up, but the winds were doing anything but. Zhara had skimmed under the pirate ship as far as she could, but now she found herself fighting the wind currents made by the two metal monsters.

Both ships looked terrible. The dorsal and ventral wounds on both trapped them in the atmosphere, and while that was good, Zhara couldn't help but wonder how long it would be until they started firing their big guns. MAC cannon rounds were designed to puncture a hull and explode. Lesser versions of that same tech were used back on the mining colony where she grew up, and they broke through rock just fine. If those rounds were used here, she wasn't sure how much damage they would do.

The upside was both ships had just passed into the Dead Zone, but that didn't mean people in Minerva City were out of danger completely. A misplaced shot could still kill hundreds, if not thousands.

Zhara never thought that following through with the plan would lead to an all-out battle over the city. If she had, she might have just gone back to her apartment. She was doubtful. As much as she wanted to think she would prioritize the safety of the masses, none of her imaginary scenarios carried the kinds of emotions she was feeling. Zhara had lost Claude, and now she had left Vision to find him. The weight of it sought to crush the air out of her, but she fought it back.

Red hot shards of metal rained through the distance between the ships, and the Regent found itself peppered with them. Zhara did her best to dodge, but the vehicle's perfect white paint job gave way to glimpses of the tortured gray metal underneath. The bright beams of orange locking the two behemoths together sliced through the night, forcing the tiny vehicle to weave around and through them. Zhara poured on more speed, the edges of her vision blurring as the car passed under the bulkier of the two fighting giants.

The flak cannon fire spared her, but greater dangers sped her way. Debris from the deep laceration in the larger ship's hull rained down, only to be caught by the wind and blown back toward the Regent. With the aid of the car's guidance system, Zhara zigged and zagged through the oncoming detritus. As the inner workings of the large ship streaked past, she thought she could see broken bodies among the wreckage.

The cost of this personal war didn't seem worth the reward, but she had risked nearly as much in her own quest. Zhara wasn't sure what the final tally would wind up being in her crusade to reunite her household, so she quieted her judgments. There was a frightening element to what people could do in the pursuit of righting wrongs, perceived or actual. She included herself in that statement. In the last few days, Zhara had surprised even herself, and something told her she hadn't reached her limits yet.

Closing on the injured monster, she witnessed the extent of the damage and couldn't help but despair. Whatever Miranda had fired had disemboweled a section of the ship that was at least five times the size of her car. There was no way for her to tell how deep the cut went, but if it had been a living thing, the ship would be operating on borrowed time.

A loud bang snapped her back to the reality of her situation. The car lurched from the impact of what appeared to be part of a catwalk. Swerving to avoid another large piece of it, Zhara piloted the Regent into the gaping hole, only to realize the damage was worse than she'd imagined.

All around her, the machinery of the starship's fuel refinery was dying. Each carefully crafted component ticked down like clockwork falling out of function. It wouldn't take long for the behemoth's beating heart to fall silent, and then the whole thing would come crashing down. Shuddering at the thought, Zhara desperately hoped she could find Claude before that happened.

There was no exit aside from the one she used as an entrance, and if the crust of the planet sealed it, that would be the end. Being entombed in the bowels of a ship was the least of Zhara's concerns, however. Several different disasters would need to be averted to pave the way to such an end. It was much more likely she would be crushed to death or blown to unrecognizable bits. Everything in the place was combustible, and if she flew too close to the wrong thing, the ship and much of the sky around it would light up in a display that would be visible from the Black.

With considerable effort, Zhara pushed forward, carefully steering her car farther inside. Further ahead, three tiny specks grew into human beings. Zhara felt some of the tension in her chest release when she recognized one of them was Claude. He hung upside down from a broken catwalk, but if he saw her, he didn't give any sign.

A woman dangled from the railing just above him, and a soldier shouted and waved his arms to get her attention. Zhara focused on Claude, piloting the Regent's hood under him, swinging its body around to avoid the rain of debris as much as possible. The woman shouted in vain, and Zhara found herself wishing she hadn't spent extra for the sound dampening cab.

Claude's feet were attached to the catwalk with a thick column of silver that gleamed in the car's running lights. The new brightness scraped across Claude's face, and a sound that Zhara couldn't have named if she tried escaped her lips when his eyes fluttered open. He smiled when he saw her, and it was every bit as bright as the light reflecting off his passenger.

The silver retracted into his bare feet, and he dropped. It was a short fall, but Claude twisted in the air to stick the landing with a heavy thud.

He motioned up toward the woman and waited for Zhara to nod her understanding before leaping the twelve feet back up to the catwalk.

Zhara was surprised by how much the car shifted as he launched off it. She hadn't seen exactly what the creature could do with her own eyes before, and the researcher in her was fascinated. The way it augmented him in real time was impressive, however, it couldn't erase her irritation at the new dent left in her hood. She didn't think of herself as a car person, but the Regent was as good a vehicle as she could ask for. It was handsome, and it handled like a dream, but until this moment, she would have said it was just a thing that could be replaced. Yet, Zhara couldn't deny her aggravation with the new contours Claude had given it.

As if he was trying to add insult to the Regent's injury, Claude landed in almost the exact same spot and made the manageable dent so much worse. He did wince at the landing, but it couldn't be helped. The woman he carried in his arms didn't seem to be all that excited, and he couldn't let go of her fast enough. Zhara watched as the woman said something to him that left Claude shrugging before he jumped away again.

One of the rear doors opened, and the female soldier dropped in and regarded her with wary eyes. Zhara nodded to the raven-haired woman with the cold gray eyes, then studied the aggressive-looking rifle she carried.

"Hi," Zhara said, trying to mask anxiety with etiquette. "I'm Zhara."

The woman inspected the car before turning her attention back to its driver and letting her hardened expression soften just a hair.

"Lillith," she said as she ran her fingers over the hand-stitched upholstery, then gave an approving nod. "So, you're the one DiSilva answers to."

Zhara stiffened and cleared her throat, "Actually, the person with that honor is waiting back on the other ship."

The woman called Lillith raised a quizzical eyebrow.

"Tell me it's not that pirate thing," she said, and her disdain soured her whole face.

Zhara shook her head but didn't volunteer any more information. There was no time to explain in sufficient detail. Besides, the idea of telling this stranger that she'd left a child on a ship full of lawless opportunists didn't feel like something worth doing.

Another thud rang out as Claude landed on the back of the car, giving it a matching blemish.

"Oh, he is definitely paying to buff that out," Zhara said, then noticed the smug, knowing look on Lillith's face.

The doors on the passenger side of the car opened, and both men climbed inside. Claude eased himself into the front seat while the newcomer settled in beside Lillith.

"That's Yuri and Lillith. They tried to..." Claude's sentence died as he scanned the cab. "Zhara..."

"We're going back for her now," she said before he could even ask the question.

"You left her behind?" he asked as confusion and anger raced for the honor of tainting his words.

"There was a turret. So, she stopped the operator, and then I didn't know if I should move her or not," Zhara said, feeling the rush of emotions getting the better of her. "She told me to get you and come back. So that's what we're doing."

Claude took a long, slow, and deep breath. His fingers worked vigorously to grind the tension from the muscles in his forehead.

"Is she safe?" he asked once he was sure it wouldn't come out as a shout.

"She will be when we get back to her," Zhara said and met the fire in Claude's eyes with the blaze burning in her own.

Claude bit back his response and gave a barely perceptible nod before turning to their guests in the back seat. "Buckle in and check your weapons," he told them with the forcefulness of a commanding officer. "We're going into enemy territory."

Yuri and Lillith put up no argument, although Claude could see their apprehension. There would be a time to discuss the chain of command between them, but where Vision was concerned, they were just going to have to follow his lead. That was beyond debate.

Zhara watched as Claude followed his own advice before spinning the car around and piloting it back through the jagged rift below.

Chapter 45

IT WAS TOO MUCH. WITHOUT her halo, Vision received every ounce of raw emotion around her. The anticipation, anxiety, guilt, loss, and soul-shredding terror of both pirates and soldiers tore through her like meteors through the atmosphere.

She desperately wanted to close herself off from it, but the constant stream left her in so much pain she could barely move. At first, she tried to pick through the noise, but that quickly became impossible. Something had happened in the battle outside, and a tidal wave of ragged thoughts knocked her from her stable place. It buried her farther beneath the sea of minds than she ever imagined she would go.

In those depths, there were no individual threads, just the pounding, unrelenting pressure of invasive emotions. They pressed in on her from all sides, and she couldn't understand any of them. At least when she had been in the mind of the Derelict, she had known where he ended and she began, but the brutal blackness that trapped her now was corrosive. It threatened to devour everything as it ate its way deep into her core.

Vision didn't know which way to swim to escape it. Every possible direction felt equally hopeless, so she fought to hold her position. She remembered what Claude had told her when she was still just a kid. He'd said that if she ever got lost, she should find a safe place and stay there. He promised he would always find her, and she believed it. So that's what she did. She stayed put and waited for him to honor his word.

With the darkness seeping in through every tiny crack in her own mind, Vision pulled back. She focused on reinforcing herself against the savage onslaught and prayed the waters stilled. She hoped this would lead to some peace, but no such thing awaited her. The conflict, fear, and hate that threatened to break her down from outside were mirrored within, and with no better options, Vision embraced it.

The oppression around her bled away, leaving the memorized scent of Firaxis's sterilized air. She found herself alone amidst blaring alarms and stampeding adults. She held her space in the center of the corridor as the blur of bodies sped around her. Like panicked beasts, they each bleated and brayed in their base voices. Terrified, they ran toward what they hoped would be safety.

None of them knew what they were running from, not exactly, but she did. She could feel the alien presence as it closed on her with all its slow, enticing menace. She had broken away from Kailen to explore it, and now a part of the creature came for her.

It was weaker, lesser somehow, but no less alluring. It was a piece of a whole, just as Vision was, but perhaps even more so. It lacked the presence of the creature in the lab, and it flowed through a different body. Like a ghost, it haunted the halls of the residential strut in the form of a lost woman.

Unlike the hollow man in the lab, Vision could feel the woman still. She was there, but greatly diminished. The thing coursing through her mind wasn't strong enough to consume her completely; however, for reasons Vision could only barely sense, she had given herself up. She had pushed herself down until the only things that Vision could read from her were a ceaseless, wailing despair and the names "Liam" and "Eugene."

The stronger of the two minds was much easier for her to understand. She could feel the frigid, howling emptiness in it and the ravenous desire to have that gap filled by something powerful and freeing. She was that thing, and while she was not inclined to become one with the creature, she did want to touch it one more time. Of all the minds she had sampled, this creature was by far the most exciting. It needed a guiding hand, an architect, to give it proper form and purpose. Vision thought she could be what it needed if only she could reach into it without the interference of people who believed they knew better.

She moved from the depths of wild bodies into a place where only those who could see opportunity through the haze of chaos dwelled. Greed ruled here, and the few people roaming the market were filled with it. They were no less bestial in their pursuit of useless things than the others were in their stampede toward a false security.

Vision could feel the compulsive need to acquire more. It drove them, fueled their every action, but to her the compulsion had been alien. At the time, she couldn't understand it, but she didn't judge them too harshly. A sense of finality gripped every mind firmly enough to strangle more complex thoughts. It clawed at her as well, though she was able to fight it back. Their fear was contagious, poisoning everything they had made of themselves and bringing about the end they so dreaded.

The collective certainty within the market was almost a tangible thing to Vision. It increased her own panic as it wove increasingly vivid illusions of inbound death. Like everyone she had met since tearing herself free of her creator, Vision believed them, however, she didn't know why. There were worse ways to meet the end than being surrounded by the things people had tried and failed to attain in better times. A part of her sympathized with that sentiment. She was doing the same, after all.

Freedom was something that had long eluded her, and now, amidst dying gasps of order and reason, she'd found a way to claim it, if only for a short while. Most of the adults ignored her outright, but a few did take the time to warn her away. In those few, she felt the warmth of genuine compassion, although it didn't overpower the darker need gripping them. For all the words they gave her, none abandoned their spoils to see her to safety.

In the end, she wasn't looking for their kindness. She hadn't come here seeking safety or compassion. She'd come here to face the thing that moved in her shadow. Even now, it traced her steps. It grew closer with every corner that clipped her. Feeling her way along the walls and railings of the multi-tiered space, she struggled to keep her shrinking lead.

For all her curiosity, there was an undeniable dread tingling along her spine, and she hated it. The animal part of her needed to run. It didn't know how to do anything else, and she didn't know how to fight it.

Despite all the things Vision could do, she could not master herself. There was a growing sensation of hopelessness creeping along every nerve of her body as she felt the alien thing close in. Everything else faded away as her perception narrowed until there was only the creature in pursuit. Like the soulless dolls in her tiny room, it moved without thought. She could feel it, but only its intent, its drive.

She grasped the frame of a door and hurried inside. The sound of her steps echoed off far walls and high ceilings, but the reverberation was no help. Flailing in the dark void, she reached out for anything to steady herself, to bind her in the real, but found nothing.

The creature entered behind her. It was as silently as a spirit and stalked toward her with the confidence of a well-practiced predator. It reached out for her, and Vision fought against its cold, thin fingers.

She reached into the mind of the woman stuffed down deep inside and found a cowering form crying endlessly. Vision tried to prod the woman into action, but she did not stir. With effort, Vision dug herself into the woman's broken mind and pulled a name from her as the creature tackled her to the floor.

The name was all she had, and she hoped using it would spur the woman to remember herself and take control back from the creature driving her. As the hot stink of breath splashed across Vision's face, she lost control of that terrified animal part of herself and screamed the last word to enter her panicked mind.

"Lenore!"

• • • •

The ship shuddered under a ripple of unseen energy. Ashe was rocked by a pressure so intense that it threatened to tear her skull open. She clutched at her scalp and screamed out for the ghost of a person she had never known.

Before tears and darkness stole her senses from her, she watched as every lit tube around her blinked out. Against the failing systems and cables, she saw that she wasn't alone in her torment. As she faded, Ashe heard every one of the technicians scream the same name.

• • • •

The pale green of Miranda's feed frayed out of focus as she heard the tortured shouts erupt around her. The combined sound of them reverberated inside her skull, pounding until she had no choice but to echo them.

The faintest hint of memory played against her splintering mind. She saw a faceless woman through glass and watched her crumple. She felt herself pour into that woman until pain shattered the image. It felt like she had lost an arm, but when she reached over, she found it where it had always been. Regardless of what her senses told her, she knew she wasn't whole, and for some reason, she thought of DiSilva.

The confusion of it merged with the roiling waves of intense pain until she couldn't think anymore. Black spots danced in her eyes, and at last, she gave in.

• • • •

Bertrand collapsed on the floor of the command dais and fought the growing urge to vomit. He knew this was another psionic attack, but the screams of "Lenore" that filled the air around him made no sense.

It sounded like every person on the command deck was screaming that name, if not the entire ship. The echo of it played both inside his mind and all around him. It drove him nearly insane.

His faltering eyes caught the flickers and failures throughout his ship before he lost himself, and his own voice joined the unnatural chorus. Bertrand lost focus on the world, the ship, and himself as he screamed his throat raw.

• • • •

The Regent didn't escape the assault. Claude and Zhara fought against the immense wave of psionic force as it bored its way into every fiber of their being. The two soldiers in the back hadn't been as lucky. They had broken into an earsplitting shriek almost instantly and then blacked out.

"It's her!" Zhara shouted over the noise in her brain.

Claude only nodded with unfocused eyes. He couldn't speak. He could barely move as the silver inside him panicked once again. This time it didn't freeze, but it did resist his commands, which scared him even more. When his passenger made its autonomy known, it always shoved a series of terrifying questions into the forefront of his mind. Just how much control did it have over him? When and why would it exert it, and could he resist?

"Eugene. Liam," he heard himself say.

The names had come from his lips, but not from his mind. He felt his passenger pushing itself against his consciousness, and he bristled at the sensation. If it wanted control of his body, it was going to have to wait until he died. When he was a corpse, it could have its run of the universe, but not until.

"Vision," he said as forcefully as he could manage.

"Female, child, Vision?" it answered in his voice.

Zhara cut Claude a sidelong glance that boiled over with unspoken terror. Claude's eyes met hers, but he couldn't offer her any comfort. He was every bit as afraid as she was.

"Yes," he thought, hoping that if he could keep the conversation internal, it might somehow help Zhara.

"Save, stop, protect," it replied, and Claude sighed.

He had only half-believed Vision when she said the silver had spoken to her, but now he knew better. There was little doubt it was alive and that it had a will of its own, but now that knowledge meant so much more than it ever had before.

"I will," Claude thought and winced at the tiny spike of pain that came as part of the creature's reply.

"No! Hurt, pain, death!" it shouted into his mind, and the massive amount of fear pouring through him made the message as clear as any he'd ever received.

He shared that fear, but unlike his newly vocal passenger, he was unwilling to let it stop him.

Vision was in danger, and he had to save her. If he could do so without turning into a living statue, that would be ideal, but regardless, he would drag Vision out of that ship even he took his final breath in the process.

"Female, adult, Zhara," the silver chanted at him, and at first, he didn't understand.

He locked eyes with the woman beside him, then registered the clenched jaw and swimming eyes she focused through. In his near stupor, he hadn't noticed how well she was functioning.

"Zhara," he said aloud and realized how odd and limiting it felt to only communicate with sound instead of the near-complete transmission of context, experience, and emotion that he'd been sharing with the thing inside him.

Her wide dancing eyes glanced at him for a brief second before she focused them back on the dark and vicious clouds beyond.

"Is it talking?" she asked, and Claude could hear all of the uncertain vibrations in her voice.

"Yes," he said as plainly as he could manage. "It says I can't..."

"You can't what?" Zhara said, and her voice solidified with both curiosity and a little annoyance.

"I can't go in there, not while this is going on," Claude said.

The words tasted foul in his mouth, and all he wanted to do was spit them out. Nothing was as demeaning as being powerless. There hadn't been many times in his life when he'd felt that way, but each one had cost him greatly.

The irony wasn't lost on him. The creature swimming along his nervous system made him stronger and faster than he had ever been. It made his reflexes sharper. He was even made more durable than any normal man, but he couldn't wake a little girl from her nightmare.

Vision must have been terrified. She was broadcasting to every soul around her, and it wasn't the first time. The halls of Firaxis came rushing into his mind, and he didn't like the implication. Claude had stepped over bodies with no injuries, no apparent signs of trauma, and all had been long dead. A part of him knew there would soon be two ships with identical halls if something wasn't done.

"What are we supposed to do?" Zhara said slowly as she jabbed at the flickering readouts on the dashboard.

"You have to get her," he said severely. "You're the only other person she trusts."

"If you can't go near her, what makes you think I can?" Zhara snapped as a gust of wind scrapped the car against the hull of the pirate ship.

Claude blinked away the spots in his vision as the sparks danced into the distance behind them. He glanced behind him to see the limp bodies in the backseat.

"Zhara, I need you to do this. Vision needs you to do this. I'll freeze up before I can get to her," he said as clearly and honestly as he could.

"What if I can't? What if..." Zhara asked, and Claude understood the mix of emotions coursing through her.

"Then you won't have to wait long for all of us to join you," he said and did his best to struggle a smile.

It felt more like a crack splitting his face apart than anything reassuring, but the look she gave told him she didn't see it that way.

"When you put it like that, how can a girl refuse?" Zhara said and breathed a heavy sigh.

Claude felt the weight of the world in that breath and wanted nothing more than to take that weight onto himself. So much of what he had done was to avoid putting the people he cared for most in danger. He had almost walked away from Zhara for that reason. He had stepped into Bertrand's trap and put himself in Miranda's crosshairs, and here he was, sending Zhara into the most dangerous scenario he could imagine.

He clenched his fists so tight he could feel the silver rise to his palms to protect him against his own fingernails. The cool sensation enraged him, and he wished the creature had never come to him. If he could have ripped the thing out of his body and cast it into the electrified night, he would have done so in seconds. But that wasn't a choice left to him.

Chapter 46

OMINOUS CLOUDS SHREDDED their way toward clearer skies as two metal monstrosities passed over the ruins of Minerva Prime's first free settlement. The last bark of thunder pealed across the more modest skyline, announcing that the planet's rage had passed. Each ship bore the scars of her aimless fury, yet they had survived. Through blind luck, the electric tongues of Minerva's ire missed their fragile engines. Every gun was now silent as the human beings who controlled them screamed inside their massive metal crypts. Darkness and the howls of hungry winds eagerly filled the void.

The Regent moved with blistering speed and focus as it sped across the once smooth skin of the Sabien leviathan. Staying close, it avoided most of the turbulence as it passed in the opposite direction.

Like an insect buzzing the carcass of a mammoth, the tiny vehicle zipped this way and that, avoiding the vibrant, orange arcs that still connected the Sabien cruiser to the stealth carrier.

The Modus Vivendi's cargo hold was located near the ship's tail and served as its primary entry point. In ideal conditions, it allowed for boarding crews to depart the vessel en masse in their efforts to cripple and consume anything of value from other vessels.

This time, it would serve the exact opposite purpose. The only thing of value was already nestled in that space, and the struggling hovercar had come to steal it away.

• • • •

Zhara did her best to prepare herself for what she was about to walk into, but truthfully, she had no idea. It had only been a short time since she had left Vision, but there was no mental onslaught then. For all she knew, her head might pop like an overripe melon once she stepped inside the ship.

The only comfort she had was that in all of her research on Psionics, she had found no cases of exploded skulls. Still, she couldn't shake the image. In the days since removing Vision's halo in her office, she had become somewhat accustomed to the rushing waves of Vision's power. She wondered whether that had more to do with the girl's desire not to hurt her than any growing immunity, but there was no way to tell.

Zhara stole a glance at Claude and immediately spotted the beads of sweat streaming along his bare skin. He trembled with mounting intensity as they drew closer, and she wished there was a way to do this without having him endure so much pain. If she had it to do all over again, Zhara would have spent more time studying the creature under his skin. She'd wanted to, but there never seemed to be enough hours in the day. Instead, she'd done as he had asked and put that time into Vision, only to find herself staring into the barren landscape of all she didn't know.

"I think I can get you inside," Claude said through ragged, labored breaths. "You'll have to be quick."

Zhara only nodded and slowed the car to match the Vivendi's speed less than a hundred feet from the cargo doors. Turning her seat to face him, she gave as confident a smile as she could muster.

"If I don't see you again, I need you to know that I never stopped wanting to be with you," she said, and the words came out more shallow than she'd meant them.

"I know," Claude said, shivering as he massaged his hands. "Things should have never been rocky between us. I just wanted to protect you from... well, this."

Zhara freed herself from her harness and stood to kiss him on the forehead.

"Let me do this before I lose my nerve," she said and slid the steering yoke across the dashboard to him.

Zhara watched his brow furrow as he focused on bringing the control readout to life on his side of the car. When his fingers slowly wrapped around the steering yoke, she thought she almost heard the whine of stressed metal.

"I hate this," he grumbled as he pushed the hovercar toward the open door.

The Regent moved shakily, and Zhara wondered how much of that was because of Claude's worsening condition. The wind streaming off the pirates' ship buffeted them and couldn't have been helping him avoid the walls of the open portal.

The pressure in her head grew in intensity with every inch they progressed. Even if she hadn't just left her, Zhara imagined she could have found Vision by the growth and shrinkage of that sensation alone.

Claude shouted, and the pained sound of it startled her back to herself. Several thin spikes pierced his hands from the inside, pinning him to the steering yoke.

The agony and mindless fear on his face nearly broke her as the nose of the Regent cleared the lowered gangplank. Without thinking or considering how dangerous it was, Zhara threw open the door and leaped toward the cargo hold. For a split second, she could see the broken, toppled buildings and stagnant pools of the Dead Zone waiting far below. Her jump had put her at the mercy of the planet itself, and for the first time, she wondered if it would betray her.

The thousands of feet to the surface had a dizzying effect, and while it lasted less than a second, she seemed to dangle in the open air for an eternity before cool, sturdy metal cut her off from the horror show beneath.

Wind and psionic force buckled her instantly, but she managed to wave Claude away. A part of her had been a little dubious of his claims that he couldn't go himself. She didn't fully trust the thing eating him alive, but seeing the metal tear its way through him reminded her of his description of Firaxis. He hadn't exactly been open about his experience there, but she knew a corpse had stabbed him and the idea of him becoming something similar forced her into action.

Claude's worried eyes met hers as the Regent scraped across the end of the gangplank. Instead of flying away to wait for her, he chose to pull the car around sideways to block as much of the wind as he could.

He smiled at her again before a new spike exploded from his shoulder and through the back of his seat.

Zhara turned away instantly and forced herself to move forward. Her traitorous mind replayed the snapshot of pain on his face, and it was more than she could stand. Banishing the image, she made deliberate strides into the cargo hold, praying she reached Vision before the silver had time to puncture something vital.

• • • •

Even the blackness of her nearly broken mind didn't provide rest for Miranda Faridan. Although much of the pain had stopped, blinding fury still remained. She couldn't let go of it even as she found herself in the most terrifying place she'd ever known.

It was familiar with its sterile passageways and transparent walls. Each clear surface showcased laboratories, but unlike the dead quiet and emptiness of her time, the halls of Firaxis Station now teemed with frantic screaming life.

Faces Miranda had seen, both frozen in death and alive aboard her own ship, flooded past her with blind silver eyes. They flowed around and through her, creating a powerful current of bodies that she could not touch. It was odd, but not unexpected. Somewhere deep at her core, she knew this wasn't real. She'd been snared in a figment, or maybe a memory, just not one of hers.

The lab she knew loomed ahead, complete with the corpse she still saw in her nightmares. This time it tried desperately to crawl through the hole it had spent much of its remaining life force to make. Its movements were slow and labored as the white fog of unrelenting cold poured around it and into the corridor.

It wasn't dying exactly, but it was losing its fight against the chemical chill. Miranda caught herself hoping that this time it would fail to escape and die, but there was no point. She knew how this memory would end. It didn't matter if it was hers or not. She had seen and felt the outcome a million times before.

The freezing man turned to her, and she froze. Its blind, ruptured eyes didn't focus on her, but she knew it saw her perfectly, regardless. In another time, she might have run, might have opened fire, but in this place, she kept her eyes locked on the reanimated corpse.

Its mouth opened, stripping flesh from its bottom lip only to have it cling to the upper one as it spoke with voices she felt more than heard.

"There you are, creature. You cruel, pitiless, soulless thing," it chanted before its ruined, cracked face twisted into a distorted grin. "Our time is ending, and your debt will soon be paid."

"I don't owe anyone anything," Miranda said, but she couldn't find the confidence to make her words believable.

"Oh, you do, and I think you know it," the dead man said.

Miranda reached for her sidearm, only to find it missing. The holster she always wore was gone, as was every stitch of clothing she knew she was still wearing. Yet, she stood naked before the corpse of her nightmares and felt the surreality of her situation.

"You have used me for your own ends, creature. Together we have robbed and killed our way across a sea of stars, and in all that time, you only ever sought one end," it recounted with a fair amount of glee. "But my services are not free, not even when I am not myself."

"To hell with you," Miranda said and gave the command to her body to turn, but nothing happened.

"Mmm, petulance, the truest ally of frightened children. And here I thought you better than that," the freezing man said as he pulled himself free of the door.

Miranda felt the icy fangs of her dread bite deep into her. The corpse never made it into the corridor. It attacked her in the lab. Out here, she should have been safe, and somehow, she wasn't.

"I'm not afraid of you," she stammered, shivering with the cold of the approaching man and her own sweat.

"But you are. You may hide it well from others, but I know your mind. Fear drives you. It rattles your bones in quiet isolation, and it boils your blood when you are defied. Everything you are is formed by fear, but you are stronger for it.

"Your rage, your desire for power, and above all, your need for vengeance are gifts granted to you by years of terror and pain. Lesser things shatter under such weight, but you have not. Do not let it break you now," the dying man said as he stalked toward her on legs that cracked and broke apart like shards of bloody ice.

The words were as sweet in her mind as they were poisonous. Flattery did nothing for her when spoken by those without power, and this thing was anything but powerless. It held her firmly in its grip, and it still lavished its version of praise upon her when it had no need to.

In her quest to find and kill the man who had broken her, she had leaned into that power. She had reveled in the strength, speed, and resilience it provided, but she never considered the cost.

Miranda had felt the fatigue and the strain. She had glimpsed the mind slumbering beneath her own, but somehow, she had ignored it. Now it breached the surface and was pulling her down into the depths to drown her.

As the flesh of the frozen man's cheeks split and fell away, she realized exactly where she was. Miranda had spent these last years of her life in a prison without walls, trapped by the expectations and demands of others. She fought, and she bled to break free of it, only to discover that she had been building a more efficient and effective cage all on her own.

"You're going to kill me," she declared, knowing it was true.

"In a way," the shattering monster said, stalking ever closer. "Your knowledge and experiences will live on, the rest will disappear, but I would not have you go unfulfilled. No child should fade from the universe without a last wish. I will grant you yours."

Her vision dimmed as the monster moved within arm's reach of her. Miranda sent her last requests to her body. She demanded that it run, that it fight, that it try to hide, and when it defied her yet again, she was left with only one last thought.

"Bertrand," she said through her chattering teeth.

"We will watch him die together. You will live to see it with unclouded eyes. This I vow," it said as its teeth cracked and broke apart in a cruel rictus.

"Why?" Miranda asked and hated herself for shaking uncontrollably.

The dead thing ignored her tremors as if they weren't an uncommon sight. Its head quirked to the side as it considered the question. Miranda thought it was an oddly animalistic gesture, but that brought her no comfort. Its dead, sightless eyes stared off, but soon it turned its full attention back to her. It stretched its grin wider than humanly possible and lost even more frigid flesh as a result.

"Because of all the creatures I have taken, you have impressed me the most," it said with a sense of wonder in its voices. "All you have done has been in pursuit of but one goal. You live when you should be long dead. You slough off everything that would hold you back, and even now, you barter with the bringer of your end to see your task completed."

Miranda watched with petrified eyes as the dead man circled around her. It inspected her like a farmer might examine a new warlett, or a discerning driver might scrutinize a new hovercar. It made her skin crawl, but for the first time, she chose to stare right back at the monster.

"Yours is a species of children lost in the Black. Abandoned slaves fumbling forward, seeking purpose where there is none. Unlike the others, you are not driven by pointless sentiment and idealism. Of all that I have claimed, you are the most like me."

As the broken, dead grin of the monster became all that she could see, Miranda felt the truth in every word the creature spoke. The dread that shook her to her bones abated, and the compliment she had been paid took root.

In the end, what she sought most in the whole of the universe would still be hers. She would still watch her betrayer suffer and die. That was worth every cost she had paid. It had been her fuel through indignity and loss. Now it would be her sustenance in death; against the protests of her basest animal nature, she agreed to the corpse's terms.

Chapter 47

THE CARGO HOLD WAS not how Zhara remembered it. The neat rows of magnetically locked crates no longer kept their uniform distances. Instead, they looked as though they had been disturbed with all the subtlety of a planetary collision. What had been linear aisles now rippled outward in concentric circles.

She cast a watering eye at the turret that had threatened her life before, only to find it crumpled by the same unseen force. If she had the time, she would have either congratulated Vision on finding a more permanent solution or lost herself questioning how the sturdy metal had been flattened and smeared into a paste on the ceiling. Rather than wasting more time, she set her sights on the ragged voice screaming in the distance. With great effort, she pushed against the pressure in her head, each step turning intangible energy into something that felt more and more like a physical barrier.

The name Lenore transformed from an itch in the back of her mind to a scream pulsing through Zhara's every neuron. She remembered what had happened to the soldiers when they had uttered it and bit down on her lip before it could escape and send her into unconsciousness as well. All she wanted to do was reach the girl at the epicenter of this new tempest and bring her back to herself. Yet her muscles threatened to betray her at every turn. Tears washed away much of her sight, and the new weight nearly locked her feet to the grated floor.

"Vision!" Zhara shouted, uncertain if the pulsing waves of force and noise were physical or just in her head.

A new blast of the eternal shriek slammed into her and almost knocked her to her knees. Zhara clutched her head as if to hold its contents in against what felt like an imminent explosion. She willed herself forward, past the crates and toward the humble image of a crying child.

Vision was lost. She hadn't moved from the spot Zhara had left her in, and yet everything else had changed so drastically. In her white-knuckled grip, she held the one thing that might bring her back from the void she'd cast herself into.

Looking at the halo, Zhara feared what would happen if she were to slide the inhibitors into place while the girl's mind was actively engaged elsewhere. It was yet another in an embarrassingly long list of things she didn't know. What she did understand, at least partially, was that if she did nothing, people would die. Maybe Vision would eventually come back from whatever nightmare she had gotten lost in, but Claude would be no more.

She touched the girl's shoulder, and the blinding flash of static electricity singed her palm. Zhara recoiled, wincing from the sudden shock, then reached out for the halo. New arcs of power attached themselves to her as she touched Vision's hands, but the pain from these was so much less. Slowly, Zhara prised Vision's fingers away from the flexible frame until it was free.

The device felt lighter than it ever had before, and Zhara hesitated. She hadn't built it to contend with this kind of power, and she doubted it would do more than disintegrate when she placed it on the girl's head.

Once more, she tried to rouse Vision by touch, and once more, she was attacked by the residual energy radiating from her. She fought against the pain to shake her, but nothing happened. The banshee's cry that assaulted Zhara continued unabated. With no other choice, she held the halo above wisps of blonde hair floating on psionic winds.

Despite the urgency and the pain, Zhara lowered it slowly and evenly onto the child's head. She crowned Vision with the limitations and boundaries she so desperately needed. The idea of shackling a child was sickeningly offensive. Even now, having followed all the clues to their likely outcome, Zhara still hated that she was constraining Vision.

There would be a time when the girl could control the power she possessed, and on that day, Zhara would gladly smash the cage she had built for her. Vision, like all children, deserved the freedom to make decisions about their own lives, when they could do so responsibly.

The flexible mesh of metal, wires, and sensors kissed the skin of Vision's paling forehead, and unlike last time, Zhara heard the pop. It was a low-frequency, rolling echo that shoved every structured thought out of her conscious mind.

As the wave that ended Vision's unknowing assault rolled through the room, the ship and then the sky around it, every light, motor, and engine that wasn't built into the halo flickered and failed.

Zhara crumpled to the floor but kept her unfocusing eyes on the girl. The blurry shape stirred, gasping and turning to her. Cold hands checked over her clumsily as Vision panicked.

"I thought you were going to get Claude," she said, but Zhara's hearing was already fading. "I told you to get him."

A final thought danced to the fore of Zhara's mind before unbidden slumber pulled her away.

"She doesn't know."

• • • •

The flare of the Modus Vivendi's engines coughed and died as the ship went dark. Every vivid orange tether that once bound her to her prey vanished as the two ships gave in to the longing embrace of the planet below.

The broad face of the TaskMaster II was the first to kiss the most primitive structures built by free hands. Bertrand's ship broke through the furthest district of the Old City like a bludgeon against old bones. Shattered debris exploded into the night sky, only to rain down upon the battered hull of its offender.

The dead metal beast carved a broad, deep line across the long-abandoned streets, markets, and residences unlucky enough to be in its path. The gash in its belly caught on the rough world's surface and tore wide before the ship broke in half. Bisected momentum drove the ship's head away from its tail, sending the two along different trajectories until the friction fires that boiled beneath the engines caught up to the slug trail of green fluids. The broken beast exploded, sending heavy armored hull plates, rocks, and the occasional Derelict flying for miles.

The clap of the explosion rocked the Modus Vivendi, who had fared better without power, however, only marginally so. She was built with better aerodynamics, and thus she glided better in the cool night air.

Her weight still pulled her down, and while she had remained aloft longer than Bertrand's ship, gravity still claimed her. The sleek hunter sliced her way through tenements and open courtyards, burying her nose deep into the rock below and raising her tail helplessly into the sky. If she still had use of her thrusters, it might have been possible to prevent the brutal flip that came next as the tip of the thinly designed "blade" snapped.

• • • •

Claude woke to the grinning maw of impending death. He didn't have time to blink away the dreamless sleep he'd been jerked out of. All he had time to do was react.

He was falling. Everyone in the Regent was, and that was to say nothing of the ship outside. He had meant to pull the hovercar back, but didn't get far enough to avoid getting battered by the body of the ship.

The reinforced viewports were cracked; they whistled as wind leaked through. The Regent was dead, and despite Claude's fight with the controls, nothing happened. The pirate ship had fallen from the sky, and at the moment, it sat upright like a dagger thrown into the dirt. It was teetering on a broken tip, and the fall was coming.

Claude looked on, helpless to affect the outcome in any way. A groan cut through the film of near silence behind him. It was followed immediately by a gasp that was so loud and long Claude thought the woman's lungs might burst. He expected a scream to follow, but that didn't happen. Lillith just clawed her way up to the seat beside him and hastily strapped herself in. She didn't speak to him but instead went to work stripping apart the vehicle's dashboard and tinkering with the mechanisms inside.

"What are you doing?" Claude asked, but she didn't respond.

Lillith tugged a cable loose, licked the connection on its end, and set it aside. Claude chose to watch her work instead of watching the world rush toward them, and with confusion, he studied her disassembly of the rifle she carried.

Practiced hands tucked every discarded part of the gun under one leg or another to keep them from bouncing around the cab. It took Lillith less than four seconds to strip the weapon down to its charge box and plug it into the Regent's cable she'd set aside.

"Drive!" she shouted, and Claude pulled up on the steering yoke.

At first, nothing happened. The scream of speed keyed up in his ears, prepping for its eventual crescendo. He did his best to ignore it and revved the car's engine repeatedly. On the third cycle, the Regent sprang to life.

"We don't have much charge," Lillith said and pressed herself back in her seat.

Claude didn't need to be told any more than that. He pulled the nose of the hovercar up and raced toward the body of the Modus Vivendi.

The ship was no longer teetering; now it was careening toward its final resting place. The Regent's speed was decent but not enough to match or beat Minerva's gravity. Claude wasn't going to get there in time. He would arrive late, and while that didn't stop him from trying, the facts were what they were.

"Thank you," he said, and out of the corner of his eye, he saw Lillith nod.

• • • •

Vision had barely been able to lift Zhara into the empty container by the time the ship went vertical. Luckily, the code was the same as the cargo door, and she was grateful for either the laziness or the efficiency of pirate security procedures. What she wasn't grateful for was the crash. It had left her hanging from the edge of the opened container and her grip was failing her. Vision did her best to summon what strength she had, but the muscles in her arm threatened one last cataclysmic revolt.

Zhara was still unconscious, and Vision envied her. If she could have slept through the world turning upside down like this, then snoring her way through Claude's nightmares would have been the easiest thing in the world.

With a determined grunt, Vision poured every ounce of herself into the impossible one-armed pull-up that she desperately needed to do. The fibers of her muscles strained and cried their painful wail, but she managed to get some height before the gravity of the situation shifted again.

The cargo hold slid from its new vertical axis to one that turned her surroundings on their head. A pull-up was something Vision could at least imagine herself doing, but pulling herself backward and diagonally into a container while punching in the code before she fell out was utterly impossible.

A warm hand clamped down on hers and pulled her halfway up. Vision looked up, and when she saw the red strain on Zhara's face, her heart leaped. Aiding her rescuer, Vision half crawled and half fell into the container. Zhara braced herself against its walls, and Vision did the same, although it was a simpler task for longer limbs.

"You have to close it," Vision said. "Be quick, the lid slides on fast."

Zhara nodded and clung to the edge of the container. She leaned outside and felt Vision grip her ankle in a symbolic show of steadying her.

The keypad interface was hilariously old, but so was the container. Holo-panels could be hacked, but keys would always need a hand to press them.

"Code?"

"B-3281!" Vision shouted back and immediately heard the tones of the keys being typed.

Zhara ducked into the container just before the lid slid into place, and the seal gave a long, low hiss. Sealed in the darkness, she felt the ship roll over and did her best to shield Vision from crashing into the metal walls, ceiling, and floor of their new environment.

The ship rolled around them, but the magnetic grip of the container didn't fail. Even as they flipped upside down and Zhara felt Vision's weight crush the air out of her, the crate held its position.

Zhara's newly black world exploded in pain as the tangle of limbs and angles that was Vision came to rest squarely on top of her.

"Do you think it's over now?" Vision's voice echoed in the pure darkness.

Zhara grunted as bony joints carved their way across her but bit the discomfort back.

"Maybe," Zhara answered through gritted teeth. "Tell Claude we're here."

She felt the short vibration of Vision nodding and wondered if the sparks that shot through the dark of her closed eyelids could be interpreted as her ribs being broken or just bruised.

Chapter 48

DIM LIGHT CUT ACROSS the void that had once been the Modus Vivendi's command deck. The ship's cries of pain still echoed through the space, but there were no voices. The smell of fresh blood filled Miranda's nostrils, telling her what her eyes could not. A part of her knew that death surrounded her, but the abundance of that metallic scent painted a clearer picture. The impact had been devastating. Starlight filtered through falling dust and debris, providing her with a single destination.

In her mind, Miranda could feel the silver stirring her from her sluggish state in an attempt to get her moving. It wasn't exactly impatient, but it was driven. Since it didn't have the same limitations, the creature within her wasn't disoriented by the crash and the preceding assault. They both knew the cause of the crash was somewhere below decks, and neither believed the child to be dead. Miranda wasn't sure how, but that was a mystery only she was concerned with.

"*Bertrand*," the silver reminded her, and she nodded as if the thing were able to see the gesture.

"I didn't forget," she said, but only corpses heard.

Without her consent, the silver grew from her to form the bladed limbs she had so often believed were her own constructs. They lifted her from the broken floor effortlessly and carried her across the newly ruined seat of her power. She could only watch as the crack that split the sealed deck in half grew wider with each step. Moving on her own was an impossibility, at least for now. With shrinking reluctance, Miranda realized she was simply along for the ride. The creature spurred her forward, and she was grateful to be alert enough to understand what was happening.

Flames licked at the night behind marred buildings and overgrown monuments lost to history. Her personal war had turned an abandoned city into what looked like an active war zone. No gunshots reached her ears, but that didn't matter. The battle was over.

Miranda dangled above the rubble, and shattered streets as her ally and killer carried her to the one thing she had left in the universe. She was so lost in the coming moment that she only barely recognized the low rumble of a battered hovercar as it half flew, half fell, toward the wreckage.

"Claude," she said, and the name felt cooler on her lips than she had expected.

He had played his part, and now her need for him was over. The questions she once wanted to ask him no longer mattered. What he had done or was trying to do was inconsequential to her now. The husk of Bertrand's ship held the only light left in her dimming perception, and there would be no further distractions.

She reached for the reins of her own motor functions and found the monster inside more than willing to allow her to copilot them to their vengeance.

· · · ·

Yuri shook away the last remnants of grogginess as he leaned between the two front seats. Lillith braced herself against the disassembled dashboard as Claude forced the nose of the hovercar toward the wreck of the enemy ship.

"What did this?" Yuri asked as he stared at the destruction in disbelief.

"Not what, who," Claude replied almost by instinct, and he pulled up from the dive to skim rubble below.

The Modus Vivendi lay bent, broken, and partially burning with her belly exposed to the sky. The engines were dark, but not all of her was as lifeless as it had been moments before. Tiny specks of movement streamed across her surface as those who had survived the disaster now tried their best to flee.

Claude found himself relieved. He had thought survivors were outside of the range of possibility. But pirates scurried into the dead streets in droves. He had little doubt that what had happened here had been the same thing that killed Firaxis all those years ago, but the end result was clearly different. He had Zhara to thank, and he would spend the rest of his life doing just that, providing they managed to get out of the Old City before the Derelicts summoned enough courage or curiosity to investigate.

"There," Lillith said and pointed to the bent rectangular opening that had once been the ship's cargo hold.

Claude forced the Regent closer and cut the speed, drifting inside. It was dim and still aside from the rumble of thrusters.

"I'm setting her down," Claude said and ignored the concerned looks from his passengers. "See if there's anything that can help us get back into the city."

The struts of the Regent had barely begun to spark against the ceiling of the cargo hold when Claude leaped from the vehicle.

"Vision! Zhara!" he shouted and heard his voice echo off warped metal all around him.

The echo faded into relative silence as he waited for a response. For what seemed like an eternity, he searched for any sign of life but found none. Claude clambered over felled hoverbikes and toppled shelving as he made his way farther inside. The ship didn't seem unstable, at least not where he was. There was no way she would ever fly again, but one day soon, she would be a lovely home for a very different kind of unsavory dweller.

"Claude, are you there?" Vision said, breaking into his rambling thoughts.

"Yeah, I'm here in the cargo hold. Where are you?" Claude asked after he tucked away the wave of emotions that threatened to bowl him over.

"I don't know exactly. We're stuffed in one of the containers on the floor," Vision answered.

Claude scanned the area but saw no such container before it dawned on him what "floor" she was talking about. Craning his head up to the metal boxes above him, he swore under his breath.

"All right, give me a second," he responded, then turned back to the hovercar.

It only took him a few seconds to jog back across the area he'd already covered. When he did, he found Yuri and Lillith moving toward the exit.

"Where are you two going?"

The two TaskMasters turned to him almost in unison, but only Yuri chose to answer.

"We have people on the other ship. We have to get them out before the Derelicts come," he stated in a tone that left no room for debate or delay.

Claude wanted to ask them for help, but he refrained. There wasn't much they could do that he couldn't accomplish on his own. The Regent had enough juice to hover for the minute or two needed to rescue Zhara and Vision. Even if it didn't, he was reasonably confident he could find a way to work around it. He nodded to them, but they didn't need his permission. A brief smile cracked Lillith's stern face as she turned and continued into the wasteland ahead of Yuri.

"I'll be out there to help as soon as I get the girls," Claude finally declared, and Yuri returned his words with a nod of his own.

Claude watched them for a few seconds longer, then turned his attention back to the task at hand.

The Regent had seen better days, although it would likely never see them again. Smoke rolled out of the engine compartment, and the once pristine white enamel finish was dented, scraped and pockmarked, nearly out of recognition. Some of the wounds still had pieces of jagged metal embedded in them, and Claude marveled at how well-made the vehicle was.

His car might have survived the night, providing it hadn't been melted to slag and blown all across the Dead Zone, but the luxury sedan had more guts than he'd expected.

"One last ride," he said to her, and patted the car like a beloved pet before slipping inside.

The Regent stuttered and stammered, but eventually, she did come to life. Claude could have sworn the thrusters had lost much of their kick, but he disregarded his suspicion. She still had enough to fly, and in less than a minute, he was floating just a few feet below the rings of armored containers.

It didn't take much for him to figure out they had to be near the center, but that still left the possibility of them being in any of the five boxes there.

"Tell me where you are. Can you scan outside the container, V?"

"*Let me check*," she said, then after a moment responded, "*I can hear the car.*"

"Well, let me know when it gets the loudest," Claude said and slowly piloted the Regent around the circle.

He wanted to move faster, but there was no telling how much life the rifle's charge box had left. It was designed to fuel the mini rail system. Rarely did they fire sustained barrages, and even then, the pull was nothing like the thruster system of a hovercar.

"*There,*" Vision shouted into his mind, and Claude felt the quiver of the creature inside him send pinpricks through his entire body.

He stopped the car and swung the door open. There were easily eighteen feet between him and the mound of toppled gear on the ceiling below. Putting the distance out of his mind, Claude jumped, swung himself over the door and onto the Regent's hood. He settled in the dents he'd created earlier and reached up to the lid of the container directly above him. It was sturdily constructed and locked in place with a mostly airtight seal.

The silver on his hands streamed off and flowed like mercury through the tiny cracks. It took a moment for the seal to give and a few more for the lid to drop away entirely. Claude grunted and nearly crumpled under the unexpected weight of it, but his passenger reinforced his arms, chest, spine, and legs once it had fully returned to him. Zhara and Vision both rested on the lid, but only Vision peeked over it to give him a weak but warm grin.

"So," she began, "still alive, huh?"

"Looks that way," Claude stated as he shifted their weight.

"You're both welcome," Zhara wheezed as Claude sat them down on the roof of the car.

"If you two will have a seat, I'll get us down from here," Claude said as the girls stepped onto the Regent's hood so he could hurl the container's lid into the distance.

Vision surveyed the area with her sensors and gave a long, impressed whistle. "You two don't play around, do you? How did you flip the whole starship over?"

Claude fired a confused glance at Zhara, but she just shrugged. Significant implications were there, but instead of digging into them, he reversed his earlier maneuver to land back in the driver's seat. The thrusters protested once more but did as they were told, easing the car and its passengers back down. Zhara and Vision laid back against the viewport, taking a moment to stretch and fill their lungs with all the air they could manage.

Claude set his mind to a different task. It bothered him that Vision seemed not to remember what had happened. She'd lost control, and the results were clear. Her not knowing she was responsible for crashing the ship didn't sit well with him. It put him in an impossible scenario. If Claude chose to keep it from her, that would seem like a betrayal. The trust they'd built could be destroyed, but if he told her what she had done, both here and on Firaxis, the weight of the lives lost might break her. Zhara peered at him through the viewport and frowned at the expression on his face. She was likely running the same calculations through her mind, and Claude wondered if she'd found an acceptable solution.

The Regent moaned and whined as the landing struts touched down once more. The console lights flickered and dimmed, but they stayed on even though this was likely her as far as she would go.

"We need to get moving if we want to catch one of the transports back into the city," he said as he slid out of the bucket seat and onto the uneven surface that passed for the floor.

"What about my car?" Zhara asked and looked lovingly at the ruins of her favorite vehicle.

"I'll buy you a new one," Claude stated with a nonchalant shrug.

"Wait. They paid us?" Vision asked.

She was already digging out the answer, and her face lit up when she found it.

"We're rich!" she said and began a dance that Claude didn't think the human body could produce without having a seizure.

"Come on, dancing queen. All the money in the worlds won't buy us safe passage if the Derelicts come back," he said and motioned for them to walk ahead of him.

"I'm going to miss that car," Zhara huffed before turning away from it and falling into step with the others. "But this time, I want one with ion shielding and four drink holders."

"And seat massagers," Vision added excitedly. "What about you Claude? What do you want?"

He took a second, then pulled them close. The blue-black sky was starting to melt away as the orange sun rose to claim its rightful place.

Claude took a deep breath and let the light warm him both inside and out before he said, "I'm fine with whatever."

Epilogues

Miranda

THE STORM STILL GRUMBLED in the distance, but Miranda paid it no mind. Like so much of the world around her, it was just side chatter. She had reclaimed control over her body, and now she chose to walk on her own legs instead of relying entirely on the silver.

Fires in the distance danced and sputtered, their orange and red heat blending with the coming morning. The sight filled Miranda with both a sense of urgency and gratitude. She stumbled crossing a downed building, and the silver extended its leg to steady her. The thing was nothing if not helpful in the moment, although in a way it always had been.

She had always leaned on it, and it had always supported her. It had sometimes even carried her forward when her own resolve had been shaken. There was a fear in that. A fear that she was being controlled. But what did that matter if the controlling hand brought you to the one place you wanted to be?

A wasteland was a fitting backdrop to witness at the end. It was a landscape Miranda had cultivated for herself and for those around her. For that, she was not sorry. Octavian had chosen to die in defiance. The pirates were nothing more than vermin that fed from her table, then turned to bite her. Each of them had sown similar chaos in countless lives. In fact, they had done so for far longer than Miranda had. The Modus Vivendi was not a ship commissioned by her, nor was her crew recruited from noble green worlds. She was not responsible for their fates any more than they were responsible for hers. They had used each other, and now that arrangement had been terminated.

She crested the last mound of detritus and let her eyes fall on the sum of her efforts. The severed head of the TaskMaster II reminded her of an axe. It lay half-buried in the stony crust of the planet as if it had been cast down by an angry god.

Not far away, the rest of the ship was nothing but a pillar of fire reaching up high enough for the civilian districts to see it. Soldiers were filing out of the wreckage and putting distance between them and it. The procedure was standard. She had been through countless drills designed to teach how best to save your life and the lives of your comrades should your ship fail in any of a million ways.

None of them seemed to notice her as she slid down into the gully with them. If any did, no reaction reached her ears. Once her feet landed on firmer and more leveled ground, Miranda continued her long walk toward the ship. She aimed for a broken gap in the ship's armor and pressed herself through it.

Ragged talons of metal each took their tax of blood and flesh as she broke through to the shattered halls of Bertrand's ship. The silver tingled with anticipation as she moved through the corridors, largely by memory. It wasn't the same as the vessel she had served on, but the layouts of Beitan ships didn't vary immensely. The command decks were often in the same places as were the captain's quarters.

She walked confidently, ignoring the small fires and forcing her way through broken doors until she reached the sealed orb of the command deck. The silver vibrated as she pressed her hand to the crack in it. Nothing felt out of the ordinary, but the silver streamed from her fingers, filling the thin gap between the doors. It took more effort than she suspected, but she was able to force the mechanism open just enough to fit her tall, slender frame through.

Like the command deck on her own ship, this one also smelled of blood and death, but it had not been spared from the fires that burned throughout the rest of the vessel. The domed space was lit by them, causing shadows to dance across the walls and smoke to pool above.

The cries of those trapped and dying echoed off dead metal, and she ignored them. Saving the lives of the innocent was a task for fools who believed themselves heroes. Miranda was much more pragmatic. The fates of others were theirs to sort out.

Moving through the burning tomb, a writhing form caught her attention. As if prepared for her arrival, an old man clawed at the panels of the floor. His bloody fingers lacked their nails and now left only trails of red as he struggled fruitlessly to free himself from the wonders of new and failed technology. The command dais had all but cut him in two. He would have been long dead if it had, but instead, it had simply crushed his lower body and pinned it beneath more weight than Miranda could estimate.

A cruel smile curled her lips as she noticed the captain's chair resting alone on the dais.

"I guess the captain really does get to go down with his ship," she said and almost laughed out loud.

"Help... me..." Bertrand wheezed as she circled around him to stop where he could see her.

The old man's eyes went wide at first, but swiftly returned to something close to normal. Pain and fear spiraled in his gaze and twisted his features. But the man she had come to hate was still there.

"Do it," he commanded.

Miranda's grin widened, and this time she did laugh. There was no humor in the cold cackle, only hard-won satisfaction.

Silver streamed from her back and shoulders, creating a simple framework seat that she lowered herself into.

"You don't give me orders anymore, Bertrand," she said, locking her hate-filled eyes on his. "I came here to torture you to death, but the ship you traded my life for is doing a fine job."

"Miranda... please," he begged, and reached out to touch her boot with torn fingers.

She eyed the streaks of dark blood he left on the black leathery surface, then slid her foot just out of reach.

"Don't," she spat. "You don't get to beg me for your life. You get to take it like the man you claim to be."

Bertrand's face stiffened at the words. Miranda doubted it was the insult that steeled him, but the situation itself. He had lost, and what was worse, he had lost to a ghost. She was an apparition of his own making. If he had been the commander and captain he should have been, the entirety of the last three years wouldn't have gone the way that they had, not for either of them.

"Now that we're here at the end of all this," Miranda said with a flourish. "I want to know why."

Bertrand coughed and spat blood onto the brushed metal floor. His eyes craned up to hers once more with a question that didn't cross his red-stained lips.

"Why do all this? Why betray me and yourself this way? You could have retired. You could be anywhere else in the Systems. Why?" Miranda asked with a genuine curiosity that surprised even her.

Bertrand laughed. It sounded as much like a wheeze as it did an expression of humor, but Miranda didn't judge.

"To win the war," he croaked.

"The war is over, Kerrid. It's been over for years."

A sad smile crept across the old man's dying face before he spoke again.

"Wars aren't won by negotiation, Faridan. They're won by breaking the enemy. As long as both Akinos and Myridorn stand, the war still rages. You just can't see it yet," he rasped.

Miranda had to struggle to hear his words, but they did ring true in some way. There was a cold sense to his view, and if she still cared about the Beita Systems and its wellbeing, she might have agreed with him.

"Well, I have good news for you, old man," she said after mulling over his statement for a moment. "Neither of us will live to find out if you're right."

Thin shallow breaths blew across the deck as Kerrid Bertrand's strength gave out. He wanted to die looking her in the eye, but in the end, his body betrayed him, just as his ship had done. The crew had left him to his fate, and only his truest enemy sat with him before his passing. For some, that would have been an insulting way to die, but for the commander of the TaskMasters, it was well earned.

Miranda watched the life fade from her great enemy and felt an odd lack of emotions at the sight. Bertrand had burned in the forefront of her brain for so long, yet finally seeing him laid low filled her with nothing.

She had expected satisfaction. She had hoped for joy or elation. Many times, she had daydreamed about dancing on his grave or desecrating his still-warm corpse, but now that the moment had arrived, there was only a void and the creature that rushed to fill it.

A cold like none she had ever experienced crept its way up her spine and blossomed inside her skull like the blooming of an ice flower. The edges of each razor-sharp petal cut away a piece of her until there was nothing left but a phantom inclination of who she once was. And soon, even that was carved away.

Silver eyes opened to regard the fallen ship with a cool, immutable glare. The creature that wore Miranda stood and reabsorbed its matter back into itself before politely stepping over the dead man on the floor.

It said nothing as it surveyed the monument of waste and loss around it, then stepped out into a universe of endless possibilities.

Ashe

THE WRECK OF THE MODUS Vivendi called to her, but Ashe couldn't bear to look at it anymore. She had given years of her life to that ship and her heart to members of its crew.

Minerva Prime didn't hold any real place of value for her, but it did have the one thing she wanted more than anything else. There were few places in the universe where a person could truly disappear. It was rare to be marooned on a world that didn't care where you came from, and she had been more than lucky to be on such a one.

There were worse places, and she had been to more than a few of them. Minerva could be beautiful in the right light, though it was hard to see from her perch in the Old City.

Ashe cranked the Lifter bike and listened to its low growl. She had helped more than a few people get clear, but this bike she'd claimed for herself. It was in decent shape but wasn't without its own scars. Like her, it had seen better days and worse ones too. What mattered most was that they still had miles left to travel.

Again, arid winds rolled off the dead ship and reminded her of the few people she would truly miss. When she got to safety, she would take the time to mourn and pay her respects, but first came the long ride.

She kicked off the ground and felt thrusters roar to life. The bike bore her weight as if it were born to.

Violet's wall was somewhere ahead, and while she couldn't see it, she could feel it somehow. There would be a place for her in Minerva City. It had a place for everyone, and if fortune sided with her, she wouldn't have to sacrifice too much of herself to find it.

Revving the handles on the Lifter, she roared off. The hot wind of the planet snatched at the streams of blue hair she'd finally let loose. Ashe pulled up as the buildings grew larger, and the wreck of her old life shrank into the distance.

It would never disappear entirely, nothing ever did, but eventually, it would hurt less. She would put it away and only take it out on special occasions. It would not define her, that much she had already decided.

The open roar of the bike echoed out into the distance as she pushed it to its maximum speed. Tiny particles crashed into her, bringing just the slightest hints of pain. The last tears she would shed for pirates and soldiers streamed across her face as the desert winds blew away all that was left of Ashe.

A chuckle found its way to her, as she was forced to admit that Dogura was right. He always had been.

Ashana was still there.

Silver Sights

CLAUDE LEANED BACK in his chair and reveled in the mixture of pain and pleasure accompanying the loud pop of his spine. It had been another long day. They all had. He'd spent the better part of a week trying to get Silver Sights back up and running.

There weren't any new clients, and the repairman he called to retool his comms array had come and gone. All the signs were there, but he still didn't want to admit the truth. It was time to move on. Minerva City had been good to him. She'd been good to Vision and even better to Zhara, but those good times were coming to a close. The anonymity he and Vision had enjoyed for years was shattered by the Bertrand job, and now it just didn't feel the same. It didn't feel safe.

An investigation had been called into the pirate attack over the Dead Zone, or so the military called it. Zhara had tried to convince him that nothing could lead back to them, but he couldn't really trust it.

She was often right. Claude knew that, and he'd run through the scenario in his head a million times. His clothes, his data-pad, even his gun had all been melted down as far as he knew. Vision came back with everything she had left with, but they had abandoned the Regent. Any investigator worth two credits would track that to Zhara and then Artemis and then them. Any way he sliced it, they couldn't stay.

The office was already mostly packed, as was the apartment upstairs. Zhara and Vision were up there putting the finishing touches on her room while he was supposed to be doing the same down here. He just wasn't ready to let all of his hard work go. It felt like a monumental failure to lose everything, but he did his best to remember what truly mattered.

Vision and Zhara were safe. They were all together, and no matter where they went next, they still would be. That was worth the loss. It was worth everything, and he was smart enough to realize that.

Groaning to himself, he eased out of the comfortable faux leather chair and ambled around the desk toward the frosted glass door that bore his name. With more love than he thought he possessed for it, Claude ran his fingers along the heat etched letters and felt a smile pull at the corner of his lips.

"It was a good run," he said in a low, reverent voice.

"Who knows, they might need a Silver Sights where we're going," Vision said as she entered the lobby and sat a large, mostly empty polymer container on one of the chairs. "Where are we going, anyway?"

Zhara cleared the stairway with a container of her own and shot him a disapproving glance when she saw that he carried nothing.

"First, we're going to see my mother before she makes me pull my hair out, but after that, who knows," Zhara said as she crossed the room and shoved her tote into Claude's empty arms.

He opened his mouth to protest, but decided against it. She had already turned her back to him and was ushering Vision to the door. Claude followed, taking in the sights and smells of his place for what seemed like the last time.

The door opened with its familiar hiss. Zhara and Vision stopped in their tracks as two individuals stepped inside. Claude didn't recognize them until they removed their breathers and turned to him.

"Are you leaving?" Yuri asked before he offered to take the tote from Vision.

She gladly dumped it into his arms and shot a beaming grin at him, then at Zhara. Something passed between them that Claude didn't quite catch, but given the laugh that Lillith suppressed, she clearly did.

Zhara turned to Claude with a questioning look before he said, "I'll meet you at Hogan's."

"Yes!" Vision almost shouted and dragged Zhara out the door. "I've got to have one more Blitzer before we go."

Claude moved past the newcomers and into the blazing sun. The dust was acceptable, given the light winds. The sky was almost white with the sun overhead, but Claude ignored the glare and stuffed his tote into the rental car.

Yuri followed suit before stopping to lean on the vehicle.

"We need to talk," he said gravely. "Lill and I are trying to find the best place to start looking for Echelon's project, but we have no leads. We were hoping you could give us something to go on."

Claude sighed and moved back into the building. He motioned at the two chairs in the lobby and waited as Yuri and Lillith took them.

"You shouldn't do this," he said once the door sealed itself.

"So you've said," Lillith replied, throwing a pointed glare at Yuri.

Yuri shook his head and inched himself up until he was only technically sitting in the chair.

"I have to. You know what would happen if they actually managed to succeed," he said, and Claude thought he could hear a hint of excitement in his voice.

Claude's fingers found their way to his forehead instinctively.

"Did Bertrand upload the drives?" he asked without looking at either of them.

"We don't know," Lillith answered. "The TaskMaster was a big ship, and grunts don't really interface with techs and officers that much."

Yuri nodded. "In the chaos, I don't even know if anyone that worked comms survived the crash."

Claude leaned back against the wall and let out a deep breath.

"The first thing I would do is work that angle. If someone in comms did walk away. They might know, and if they don't, they might know the frequency used to transmit data. All comms buoys hold records of frequencies and times," Claude explained.

"And if it's not there?" Lillith asked and fixed him with the same storm gray stare that Yuri so deftly ignored.

"Then I guess you have to get creative," Claude replied, crossing his arms. "I still say you should leave this alone. Echelon won't take a loss lightly."

"You didn't see the look on his face, DiSilva," Yuri said defiantly. "After everything that I've seen... that you've seen. Someone has to stop them from getting their hands on that kind of power."

Claude shook his head. He didn't know Yuri well, but there was a spark in him that was all too familiar. A younger version of himself had thrown away a promising career for the sake of nameless innocents, and now Yuri was making the same choice. Who was he to stop him? And given how things had turned out for him, this might actually be the right course of action.

"We should go," Lillith said, nodding to Claude and standing.

She made it halfway to the door before Yuri left his seat. The look on her face was half annoyance and half understanding. Claude wondered how she managed to pull off such nuance while still scowling.

"Once I know something, I'll shoot you a message to let you know if you're clear," Yuri said, clearly not satisfied with the advice he'd been given.

"Don't. The whole point of this move is to start clean," Claude said and walked them to the door. "Be careful."

Yuri let the sour look vanish from his face before he said, "I'm always careful."

Claude watched as they walked back up the street from wherever they'd come. He wondered how far Yuri would take this last request and why Lillith didn't just cut him loose. There was a good chance they were committing suicide in slow motion, but he'd just done the same thing, and here he was.

Turning away, Claude left the two former TaskMasters to their fates. Firaxis was now as firmly behind him as it had ever been. Soon Silver Sights, the Violet District, and all of Minerva Prime would be too. That left just a few things for him to take care of.

The searing sun lit thin swirls of dust around his feet as Claude made his way down the street toward the mouthwatering aromas he already missed. A genuine and unrestrained smile stretched across his face as he spotted Zhara and Vision through Hogan's window.

They didn't notice him and continued their animated conversation. Vision's face was practically glowing, and the red stain on her lips was obvious even at a distance. Claude took a moment longer to admire them both, then moved toward the door. He could have watched them all day, but he was dying to know what they were talking about. Besides, there was a Julo wrap and a glass of Winterine calling his name.

The girls noticed him as he made his way to their table, and Vision made room for him to sit beside her.

"So, ladies, what do we do now?"

Don't miss out!

Visit the website below and you can sign up to receive emails whenever W J Long III publishes a new book. There's no charge and no obligation.

https://books2read.com/r/B-A-DEDW-NPQDC

BOOKS 2 READ

Connecting independent readers to independent writers.

About the Author

Husband, Father, Writer, Geek. These are just a few words that describe lifelong storyteller W J Long III.

These days he resides in rural North Carolina with his family, dreaming up new tales to share with the wider world when he's not experimenting with new ways to make the people around him laugh.